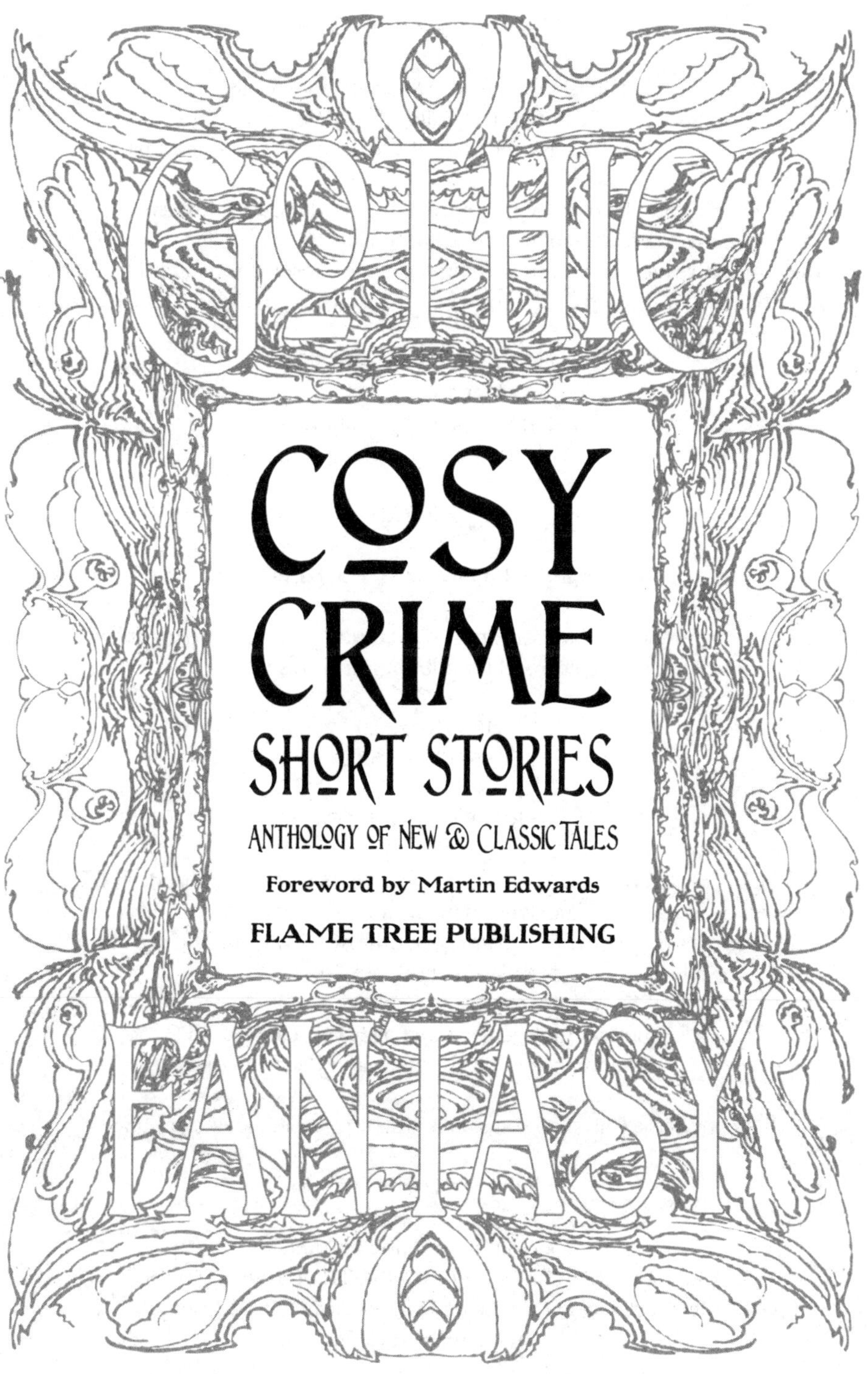

COSY CRIME

SHORT STORIES

ANTHOLOGY OF NEW & CLASSIC TALES

Foreword by Martin Edwards

FLAME TREE PUBLISHING

This is a FLAME TREE Book

Publisher & Creative Director: Nick Wells
Senior Project Editor: Josie Mitchell

Publisher's Note: Due to the historical nature of the classic text, we're aware that there may be some language used which has the potential to cause offence to the modern reader. However, wishing overall to preserve the integrity of the text, rather than imposing contemporary sensibilities, we have left it unaltered.

FLAME TREE PUBLISHING
6 Melbray Mews, Fulham,
London SW6 3NS, United Kingdom
www.flametreepublishing.com

First published 2019

19 21 23 22 20
1 3 5 7 9 10 8 6 4 2

ISBN: 978-1-78755-267-8

The cover image is created by Flame Tree Studio based on artwork by Slava Gerj and Gabor Ruszkai.

A copy of the CIP data for this book is available from the British Library.

Printed and bound in China

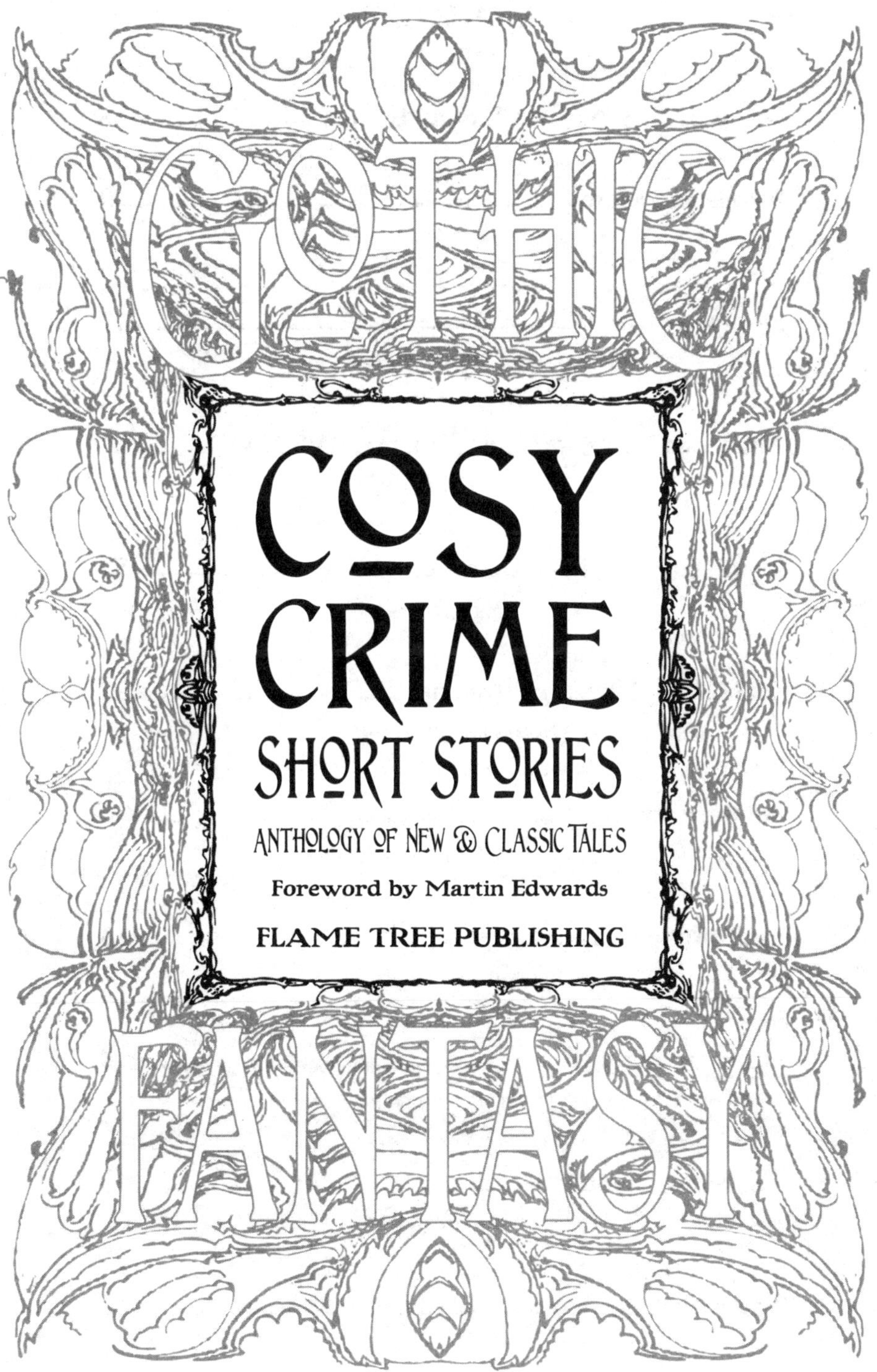

COSY CRIME
SHORT STORIES

ANTHOLOGY OF NEW & CLASSIC TALES

Foreword by Martin Edwards

FLAME TREE PUBLISHING

Contents

Foreword: Cosy Crime Short Stories

THIS BOOK GATHERS cosy crime stories, ancient and modern. As with other anthologies in the series, readers have the chance to enjoy – and also to compare – the work of renowned authors of the past with their successors in the present day.

In the real world, of course, crime is usually anything but cosy. Yet generations of readers have enjoyed fiction dealing with crime, and there are plenty of theories as to why this might be. Is it to do with the satisfaction of seeing life disrupted by crime, only for order to be restored, usually thanks to the intervention of a gifted detective? Does it help us to understand why people commit crimes, especially from rational motives, such as desire to benefit from an inheritance? Is reading about crime simply an effective means of confronting our darkest fears? Or is the label 'cosy' itself a red herring? The debate seems likely to run and run.

The style and content of many crime stories have also encouraged people to label them as 'cosy'. Agatha Christie's mysteries, perhaps especially those featuring Miss Jane Marple, are typical: highly successful examples of fiction that avoids graphic descriptions of sex and violence or detailed exploration of morbid psychology. The emphasis is on the puzzle, although today Christie's stories also have a good deal of interest and value as social documents, casting light on the period in which she wrote.

The vintage mysteries in this book were mostly written before the 'Golden Age of Murder' between the two world wars, when Christie came to the fore. The authors represented here include two who earned enduring fame, Arthur Conan Doyle and G.K. Chesterton. Doyle wrote a diverse range of stories, but there is no doubt that he owes his reputation to the creation of Sherlock Holmes. 'The Man with the Watches,' the story included in this book, is not a Holmes case (it was published after Holmes supposedly met his end at the Reichenbach Falls, and before his celebrated resurrection) but it's highly enjoyable, and some commentators have suggested that the unnamed investigator in the story is, in fact, the great man himself.

Chesterton's story, 'The Secret Garden', is one of the most notable to feature the little priest-detective, Father Brown, who after Holmes was perhaps the most famous sleuth in fiction in the first quarter of the twentieth century. In contrast, Violet Strange, created by Anna Katherine Green, is little remembered today, yet she remains of historical interest as an early example of the young female detective. 'The Fordwych Castle Mystery' features another woman sleuth, this time a representative of the official police, Lady Molly of Scotland Yard.

The Big Bow Mystery, by the celebrated Jewish author Israel Zangwill, is one of the finest locked room mysteries of the nineteenth century, while Arnold Bennett, a renowned bestseller in his day, is represented by a substantial extract from *The Grand Babylon Hotel*. Together with freshly commissioned mysteries from contemporary writers, these stories will afford readers much entertainment by the fireside. What could be cosier?

Martin Edwards
www.martinedwardsbooks.com

Publisher's Note

The challenge of figuring out a puzzle or mystery has always held a charm and an intrigue, and crime fiction is usually able to give us the most satisfying conclusions, which is often not the case in the real world. Early writers of the nineteenth century such as Catherine Louisa Pirkis and Anna Katherine Green began our interests in detective characters who would use their intelligence and deductive skills to come up with the solution to a crime. These stories paved the way for later writers in 'The Golden Age of Murder' such as Agatha Christie and her famous Hercule Poirot and Miss Marple, as well as G.K. Chesterton and his Father Brown. We hope this collection gives you a sense of where this subgenre of crime started, including some old favourites as well as stories and writers you may not have come across before.

We had a fantastic number of contemporary submissions, and have thoroughly enjoyed delving into authors' stories featuring many different kinds of cosy crime. From hushed, fire lit conversations to locked-room mysteries, each story helps us to explore the mysterious side of crime, allowing us to ponder over what really happened from the comfort of our armchairs. Making the final selection is always a tough decision, but ultimately we chose a collection of stories we hope sit alongside each other and with the classic fiction, to provide a fantastic *Cosy Crime Short Stories* book for all to enjoy.

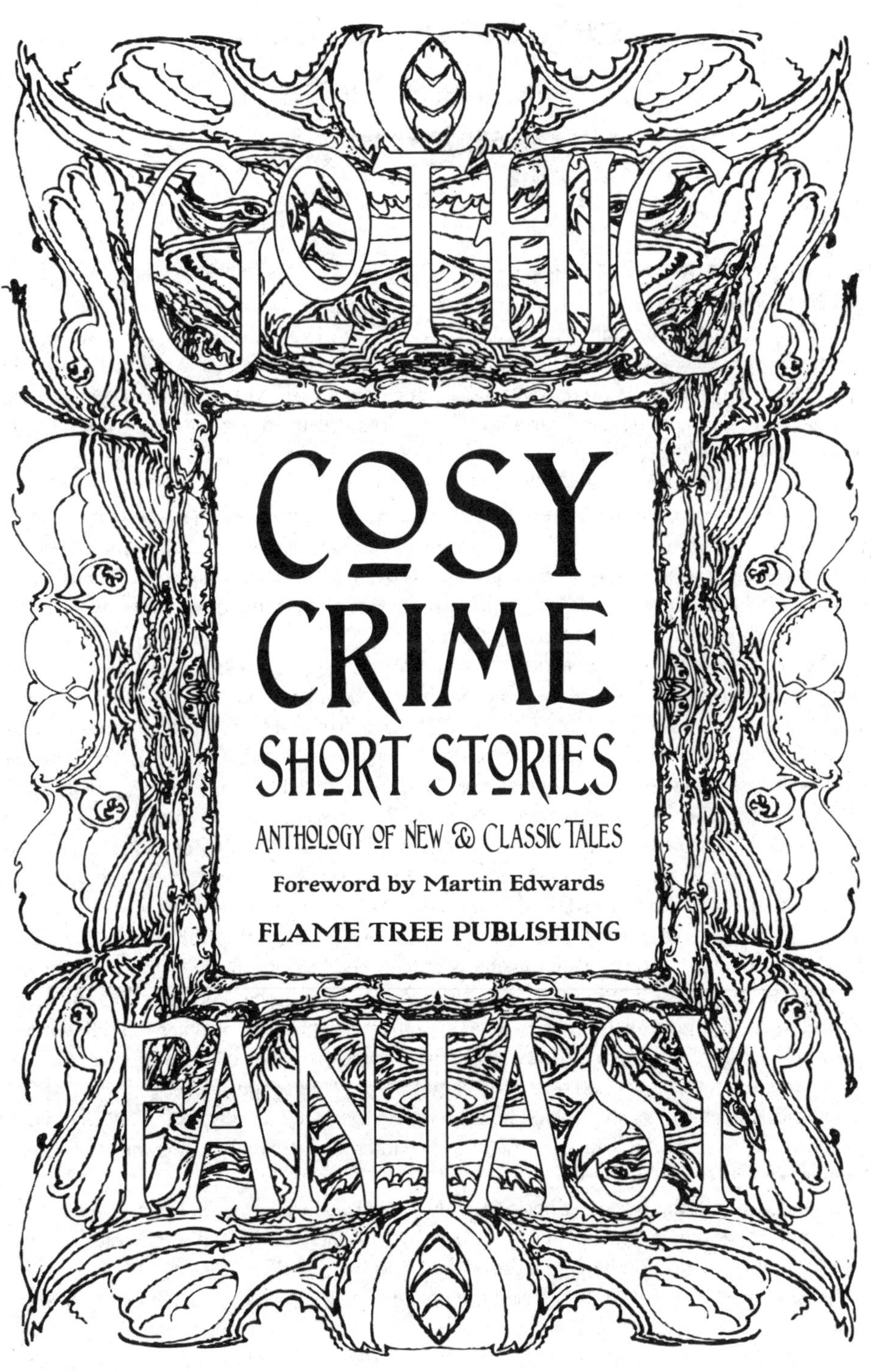
GOTHIC
COSY CRIME
SHORT STORIES
ANTHOLOGY OF NEW & CLASSIC TALES
Foreword by Martin Edwards
FLAME TREE PUBLISHING
FANTASY

Honey of a Jam

Stephanie Bedwell-Grime

THE LAST THING Liv Chandler wanted to do on New Year's Day was to investigate a mischief complaint.

She'd been up late the night before at a local New Year's Eve bash and the party had gone on into the early hours of the morning. As a volunteer cop, it wasn't even supposed to be her shift. Carter was supposed to be on duty, but he'd come down with a virulent case of the flu, or so he'd said. He'd been at the same party, so she was doubtful. In any case, it didn't sound like he was fit for duty, so the job was hers.

Early New Year's Day, the Mitchells had reported the theft of a couple of their bee hives. Bee hives, she thought, seriously? As she climbed into her car she was certain it was a prank staged by a couple of kids who'd imbibed a little too heartily. It seemed like the kind of mischief that could go horribly wrong on the perpetrator. Surely by midday cooler heads – or perhaps aching heads – would prevail and the bees would turn up. Hopefully none the worse for wear. In the meantime, she was honor-bound to investigate.

The Mitchells lived on the outskirts of town. Everyone knew they kept bees. They sold their honey at the farmer's market. She turned off the main road and onto the lane that led to the Mitchells' place. It wasn't much of a driveway, just some well worn ruts through the brush. She winced at the sound of last season's weeds brushing the underside of her car. The Mitchells were waiting for her in front of the house, wearing only light jackets in the unseasonably warm weather. The town had seen its first green Christmas in many years and the forecast hadn't called for snow any time soon. Her stomach growled at their offer of coffee and leftover Christmas cake and she politely declined. What she really needed was sleep and she wouldn't be getting that until she'd investigated the crime and filed her report.

The pleasantries over, the Mitchells led the way out to where their hives were kept. Sure enough a couple of the hives were missing. A trail of muddy footprints led to a clearing where a truck had been parked. When the Mitchells had discovered the crime, they'd inadvertently covered those footprints with their own, making the perpetrator's prints hard to differentiate. Tire tracks ran through the brush back to the main road where they blended with the tracks of every other truck that had been by overnight and became indistinguishable.

Liv shook her head as she walked back to where the Mitchells were waiting. What would someone want with two bee hives in the dead of winter? She decided the answer to that didn't matter so much as getting the Mitchells' hives back.

Liv reached into the pocket of her coat, only to realize she'd forgotten her notebook. In an attempt to cover that gaffe, she pulled out her smartphone. She'd make some notes in it and transfer them to her report when she got to the station.

"It looks like whoever did this carried the hives to a truck parked off in the brush. Any idea how much those hives weighed?"

"About 75 pounds," Mr. Mitchell said. "They aren't the kind of thing you can carry very far."

"And did you hear anything suspicious last night?"

Mr. Mitchell glanced at his wife. "The Walkers had a party. We were there quite late and went straight to bed when we got home. We didn't notice anything missing until this morning."

Had everyone been at the Walkers' party? Liv didn't remember seeing the Mitchells there, but that didn't necessarily mean anything. Most of the town had been there. The party had spilled out of the house into the Walkers' party space in a converted barn. The Walkers rented the space in the spring and summer, making it a great pre-made party venue.

"This is terrible," Mrs. Mitchell said. "Bees shouldn't be moved in the winter. The bees cluster around the queen to keep her warm. If the cluster is shaken apart, the bees could freeze."

Liv made a note of that in her phone. "Do you have any idea why someone would want to steal a couple of your hives?"

Mr. Mitchell shook his head. "We assumed it was kids. They're out of school for the holidays and looking for something to do. We figured they probably thought it was a cool hoax, not knowing the damage they could be doing."

That had been Liv's initial assessment too. Now she wasn't so sure. There were other questions she had to ask.

"Do you know of anyone who would want to deliberately damage your hives or your business?"

A look of horror crossed the Mitchells' faces. "No," Mr. Mitchell said. "Everyone loves our honey."

That much was true. The Mitchells did a booming business at the farmers market in the summer months.

"No business rivals, no enemies?"

The Mitchells traded another appalled glance. "We're the only honey producers in the area," Mrs. Mitchell said.

"We have no business rivals," Mr. Mitchell added.

"Just have to ask the questions." Liv tucked her phone back into her pocket. She nodded to the Mitchells. "We'll do our best to locate your hives and get them back to you. Happy New Year. Try to have a nice holiday anyway."

"Happy New Year," the Mitchells echoed hollowly.

Bees, Liv thought again and climbed back into her car.

The station was quiet and dark when Liv arrived. The only light came from the dispatcher's window where Wanda was busily playing solitaire on her phone. She looked up as Liv entered. "Happy New Year."

"Would have been happier if I could have stayed in bed a while longer."

"Oh, poor baby." Wanda was only about five years older than Liv, but she ruled the station like a mother hen. "Go have some coffee and suck it up."

"Well, thanks for the sympathy."

Wanda grinned. "You got it. Any idea who took the bees?"

Liv shook her head. "There were some footprints in the mud and some tire tracks. Got some photos of those. But once the truck got to the main road, the tracks got mixed up with all those coming out of the Walkers' party. Can't tell which way they went after that."

"Still, bees would be hard to hide."

"You'd think. I did a quick drive by on my way down here, but I didn't spot anything. Since it happened overnight, the bees could be anywhere by now. Tomorrow I'll drop in on Mark and see if he recognizes any of the tire tracks." Mark ran an auto shop in the next town over.

"Sounds like a plan," Wanda said and returned to her game. She looked up a moment later. "Oh, I left you and Carter a little something for the holidays. It's in the bottom drawer of the desk."

"Thanks!" Liv wandered by the break room. Break closet was more like it. Since there were rarely more than two people on duty and no one actually took breaks, it was comprised only of a table and two chairs. An ancient coffee maker sat on a shelf beside what had to be the world's smallest microwave oven. Liv lifted the pot and glanced dubiously at the contents. Wanda had clearly made the coffee when she'd come on shift hours ago and the contents were in the process of turning into brown sludge. Liv shrugged and poured herself a cup anyway. She needed the caffeine and she felt too tired to make another pot. Predictably, it tasted awful. Almost awful enough to jolt her awake.

She left the break room and took a seat at one of the two desks in the small station. Moving a half-full cup of coffee that had to have been there for at least a week to the side, she sat down and booted up the computer.

Liv was halfway through her report and thinking fondly of going home and getting back in bed, when she heard the phone ring at Wanda's desk. A few seconds later, Wanda appeared at her desk. Liv's heart sank. No bed for her. Not yet.

"Sorry, Liv."

Something in the tone of Wanda's voice brought her to immediate awareness. "What? What's happened now?"

"The Robinsons were out walking their dog this morning and they stumbled upon a body out by the main road."

"A body." Liv felt her heart plummet to the vicinity of her boots. She was equipped to deal with a couple of stolen beehives, but a murder was way out of her area of expertise. "Could they tell if it was anyone we know?"

Wanda shook her head. "They say it's a real mess."

"Call Carter and tell him that unless he's actually dying he needs to be back on duty. Tell him to meet me out there."

Liv took a big swig of the foul coffee for fortification. Shutting down the computer, she pocketed her phone and headed for her car.

She arrived at the scene to find Carter throwing up in a ditch behind his car.

Someone had thrown a blanket over the body. It lay in a misshapen mound on the shoulder of the main road.

Carter raised his head as she approached. He wiped his mouth on the sleeve of his jacket and studied her with red rimmed eyes. His blond hair was disheveled and he looked a shade paler than usual.

"I was doing okay until I looked at that." He motioned in the direction of the body.

"The Robinsons said it was bad."

"You could say that."

Liv knew she had to go over there and take a look. She glanced around but saw no signs of the Robinsons. "Did you get a chance to talk to the Robinsons? Before you..." She motioned toward the ditch.

Carter straightened. "Yeah. They were taking their morning walk along the main road. Their dog was running a little ahead of them, when it suddenly starts barking like crazy. When they caught up to the dog, they discovered the body."

"Could you tell who it was?"

Carter gave a sharp shake of his head, bent over and vomited again into the ditch. Liv took a step back.

He wiped his mouth on the cuff of his jacket again and straightened. "No. The face is a mess. You'll see."

"Okay. I'll have a look." She knew she had to. Still, her feet refused to move in that direction. Carter was bent over the ditch again. She had no choice. Liv walked toward the body.

Crouching by the side of the road, she lifted the blanket. The first glimpse made her swallow hard. She could not, *would* not join Carter puking in the ditch. She swallowed again and lowered her gaze.

The face was red and swollen beyond all recognition. It seemed to have been punctured in hundreds of places. Almost…as if it had been stung.

First stolen bees and now a dead body. At first the two had seemed like completely separate occurrences. Now they were starting to paint a disturbing picture.

Was this the bee thief? If so, where had he come from?

After snapping off a few shots on her phone, Liv stood and looked around. Brush and scrub lined the roadway before the taller trees began. If someone had been stung countless times, they might try running toward the road for help. She'd need to take a closer look for footprints. But there was something that bothered her even more.

If this was the bee thief, then where were the bees?

She remembered from a long ago science class that stinging killed honey bees. On someone who'd been stung that many times, she'd expect to find a dead bee or two nearby. Liv bent close to the road and studied the gravel. No bees.

Carter was back on his feet again. He walked unsteadily toward her, keeping his gaze averted from the body even though she'd covered it up again. "What are you looking for?"

"Bees."

He gave her a long look. "Okaay. I'm going to go sit in my car. Let me know when you're done, so I can call the morgue.

She nodded and bent to study the gravel once more. Not a bee in sight. Yet the body had clearly been stung multiple times. She couldn't find any tracks leading in or out of the brush, nor was the gravel disturbed.

Liv was starting to see a more sinister picture. The body under the blanket had to have been stung somewhere else and later dumped by the side of the road.

Add in a couple of missing beehives and it led to a much darker series of events. A practical joke gone terribly wrong? Or a much more disturbing scenario?

She walked back to Carter's car and found him with his head back and his eyes closed. He sat up as she approached.

"Ready to call the morgue?" he asked as she climbed into the passenger seat.

Liv shook her head. "Not yet. We need to think about this for a moment. I think we might be dealing with something more complicated. We might be dealing with a murder."

Carter took one long look at her before opening his door and puking onto the roadway. He wiped his mouth on his jacket again and turned to look at her. "How do you figure?"

She pointed to the covered body. "We've got a guy who's clearly been stung. Like not once or twice or even ten times. It's like he was stung by an entire hive of bees."

"We're not doctors. We have no way of knowing what stung him."

"True enough. And if we didn't have a couple of missing bee hives, I'd agree with you."

Carter nodded gingerly, apparently trying not to move his head very much. "You have a point, but that doesn't make it a murder. We don't even know for sure if getting stung was what killed him."

"No, but there aren't any signs of whatever did sting him. No dead bees or other insects on the body or on the road. So I'm thinking that means his body was moved. And if that's what happened then why? If it does have anything to do with our missing hives – if it was something like a drunken prank gone awry – then why not just call 911? Why dump the body by the side of the road?"

Carter ran a hand over his face. "Maybe whoever did it got scared. And I agree, it's weird, but not necessarily a murder."

"At the very least we might be looking at criminal negligence. We need to investigate further."

Carter held up his hands. Oh, no, no. I say we call the morgue, go back to the station and write this up and then we wait until the Chief gets back from holiday in a couple of days and let him decide what he wants to do about it."

Liv gave him a hard look. "That's a tempting thought, but you know we can't do that."

Carter leaned his head back against the seat and uttered a deep sigh. "No, I don't suppose we can. Monty will be at least expecting something of an investigation when he returns."

Two days, Liv thought. Monty would be back in a couple of days. All they had to do was not botch it up before then. When Monty returned he'd probably want to take over the investigation himself.

Liv pulled out her phone. "We'll call the morgue to come get our John Doe here. And then you and I better get back to the station, file the paperwork and get on the case."

Carter groaned. "I'm going to need an antacid and a coffee. In that order."

* * *

Turned out Monty had a stash of antacids in his desk as well as a cache of flavored coffee in neat individual packs. Carter figured it was the least he could do for them and commandeered both.

Liv gratefully accepted a cup of Monty's hazelnut flavored coffee. It was as close as she was going to get to a holiday meal. Carter was looking a little less green after a handful of Monty's antacids and a little more awake after another dose of caffeine as they sat across the desk from each other and tried to decide how to proceed next.

"I'm still going with weird coincidence," Carter said.

Liv sat back in her chair. "We've got a couple of missing bee hives and a dead guy with no identification who's apparently been stung to death. How can that possibly be a coincidence?"

"But think of the alternative. What you're suggesting is that someone intentionally set out to kill someone…with bees." He paused to take a cautious sip of his coffee. "Do you know how crazy that sounds? I mean, what possible motive would they have?"

What motive indeed, Liv thought. Carter was right. It did sound crazy. But she couldn't shake the feeling that there was more to the crime than a ridiculous hoax and a bizarre accident.

She finished her coffee and set down her cup. "We need to find those bee hives."

A couple of hours later they'd searched every field and backyard in town. No one reported seeing a couple of errant bee hives. Liv's stomach was growling and Carter looked like he might fall over.

Liv climbed back into her car and let go a long sigh. "How about we drive over to Milly's and get the all day breakfast? It's probably the only place that's open today." Milly's was in the next town over. The place was run by Milly herself as well as a couple of staff. It was right on the main highway and rarely closed.

Carter's eyelids snapped open. "I could probably stomach some toast." He leaned back against the headrest and shut his eyes again.

"Milly's it is then." Liv started the car and turned off the road onto the main highway.

This time of year the highway was usually down to two narrow lanes banked high with snow. It felt odd to see green grass and bare trees instead. Even the evergreens should have been laden down with snow. It was a strange New Year's Day and growing stranger with every minute.

Pondering that thought, she nearly missed the glint of light off something metal hidden in the brush.

"What's that?" Liv hit the brakes.

Carter sat up, blinking. "What?"

After a quick glance behind her to make sure the road was clear, Liv backed her car up onto the shoulder. Together they got out of the car and began walking toward the brush.

"Looks like a vehicle hidden in the brush." Carter circled around to the far side of the object.

Liv looked back toward the highway. "I didn't see any skid marks on the road." She studied the foliage around them. "But the brush is crushed here."

"Almost like someone drove deliberately into the bush."

Liv cupped her hands around her mouth. "Hello? Anyone need help in there?"

Only a light wind through the trees answered them. They crept closer.

Sure enough a silver pickup sat nestled between two pine trees, almost as if it had driven off the road and become wedged there. Stray leaves and bits of branches covered the front window. Liv brushed them aside. Peering in the window, they found the vehicle empty.

Carter circled the trees, looking at the car from all sides. "No signs of an accident. It doesn't look like it hit another vehicle before running off the road." He walked a little further. "Also, there are no plates."

"Which means that whoever put it here did it deliberately."

"And tried to disguise the identity of the vehicle."

"We can try tracking the VIN number," Liv suggested.

"That's probably our quickest way of finding out who this thing belongs to." Carter reached for his phone. "You call the VIN in to Wanda and get her working on that. I'll arrange for a tow."

An hour later the truck was on its way to the pound and they still hadn't had breakfast. Carter looked around the woods, his gaze stopping where the truck had been hidden. "This is the weirdest New Year's Day ever. Monty's not even going to believe this stuff."

"You never know he just might." Their small town didn't see a lot of action, but Monty had been on the force a long time. Liv held up her phone. "Should we head for Milly's? I can tell Wanda to phone us if she finds anything."

Carter paled only slightly at the mention of food. "Sure, I could probably use that toast now."

Milly's was surprisingly busy being the only place open on the holiday. Liv and Carter managed to find a booth with a little more privacy than the others near the back of the diner. Liv ordered the all day breakfast while Carter nibbled gingerly on some toast. She was halfway through her eggs when her phone rang.

"Hey, I have a name for you," Wanda said without preamble as soon as she answered. "That car you asked me to trace is owned by a guy by the name of Michael Sheer."

"Michael Sheer." Liv scribbled the name on a napkin. "Got anything else on him?"

"A picture from his driver's license." Wanda sounded anxious to get back to her game of solitaire. "Sending it to you now."

Carter tilted his head to read what Liv had written and was already typing the name into the browser on his phone.

As soon as Liv disconnected her phone pinged with a message from Wanda. She opened it and stared at the photo on the screen.

The last time she'd seen that face it had been nearly unrecognizable. Hundreds of stings had obscured the features. Still, the resemblance was unmistakable. She turned the phone toward Carter. "You think this is our guy?"

Carter squinted at the photo on her phone. "I think so." He glanced down at his own phone. "And according to this, he's a high-power executive at some big agricultural company that also produces…honey."

He met her eyes across the table. "I think we need to talk to the Mitchells."

As one they got to their feet. Liv put down enough money to cover their bill.

"Hey," Milly called as they almost raced through the door. "You want that wrapped up to go?"

Liv turned long enough to hold up her phone so Milly would understand they couldn't wait before running toward the parking lot. Carter reached his car first. She heard his motor start as she climbed into her own vehicle.

They formed an odd convoy heading back on the highway. The main road was almost deserted. One car passed them as they turned off the road. They headed down the Mitchells' overgrown driveway, only to find the Mitchells' truck coming down the driveway toward them.

Liv worried the truck might leave the path and go around them. It was certainly heavy and high enough to attempt it. For a moment the Mitchells stared at the two cars clogging their driveway. Liv knew they were close enough to recognize both her and Carter. Would they try to make a run from law enforcement? Then again, she reasoned, the Mitchells didn't know why they were there. Finally, Mr. Mitchell turned off the ignition.

Carter got out of his car. Liv followed.

In the truck's cab, Mr. Mitchell said something curt to his wife. Liv imagined it was something like, "Stay here, I'll do all the talking."

They walked to meet him.

"Have you found our hives?" Mr. Mitchell asked hopefully.

Walking up beside Carter, Liv shook her head. "Actually, we have a few more questions."

Mr. Mitchell shifted on the spot. "We were just on our way somewhere. We're in a bit of a hurry."

"On New Year's Day?" Carter began walking toward the back of the truck where something in the bed was covered with a large tarp.

"We've been invited to a dinner." Mr. Mitchell turned to watch his progress.

Suddenly Carter began vigorously swatting the air.

"What is it?" Liv called.

Carter turned toward her. "A bee."

Before Mr. Mitchell could protest, Carter seized a corner of the tarp and lifted it. Freed by the sudden movement a couple of bees flew toward him moving sluggishly in the cool air. Carter swore.

Liv dashed toward the truck, coming to a quick stop when she saw what lay beneath the tarp.

"The missing bee hives?" She could tell by the look on Mr. Mitchell's face that was exactly what they were.

"I think we need to have a talk," Carter said.

Mr. Mitchell stared at the hives in the back of his truck as if he'd never seen them before. "This isn't what it looks like."

Mrs. Mitchell climbed out of the truck and came to stand by her husband.

"To be honest, it doesn't look good," Liv said. "You're driving around with the hives you just reported stolen in the back of your truck."

Mr. Mitchell drew himself up. "Never said they were the same hives."

"And we've got a dead man out on the highway who's clearly been stung multiple times."

By their stunned expressions, Liv guessed this was news to the Mitchells.

Mrs. Mitchell gasped. "He's dead?"

Mr. Mitchell shot his wife a dark glance. "Now Buttercup, don't say another word until we get ourselves a lawyer."

Mrs. Mitchell glanced from the hives back to Liv and Carter. Her mouth moved, but no sound came out. For a moment she seemed to be considering whether to say something or not. Finally, she turned to her husband. "No, hon, I never signed on for – for *this!*"

"Is there something you want to tell us, Mrs. Mitchell?" Carter prompted.

"He was threatening us. We just wanted to teach him a lesson." Her legs seemed to give out and she crumpled toward the ground before her husband caught her.

Mr. Mitchell uttered a long sigh. "You might as well come up to the house. We'll tell you it all."

Once again Liv found herself sitting at the Mitchells' table. This time Carter was with her and no one offered Christmas cake or coffee.

"Michael Sheer *was* threatening us," Mr. Mitchell began. "We weren't entirely truthful with you before. Our business was in trouble and his conglomerate offered to buy us out."

"We definitely needed a buyer," Mrs. Mitchell agreed, "but they offered us so little money we were going to lose either way. And this," she waved a hand at the land beyond their small kitchen, "this is our only investment."

Mr. Mitchell cleared his throat. "We thought we'd...well, make a point. Show them that beekeeping wasn't something to be trifled with, not something to be just sucked up into the corporate machine with no thought given to the bees or the people who make it work."

"It's an art." Mrs. Mitchell sounded indignant. "Bees are important for the environment. Did you know—"

Mr. Mitchell put his hand on her knee, silencing her.

"So you what?" Carter asked. "Set some bees loose on him?"

Mr. Mitchell's shoulders sagged. "Pretty much."

"Actually," Mrs. Mitchell sounded inordinately proud. "We trained the bees."

"Now Buttercup—" her husband warned.

But Mrs. Mitchell, once she started talking, didn't seem inclined to stop. "We read on the internet that this university had trained bees to recognize faces. It seemed simple enough. You just reward them with sugar. So we tried it ourselves. Who knew it would work?"

Mr. Mitchell had his head in his hands.

"And once you'd trained the bees to recognize Michael Sheer, you what?"

"Sicced the bees on him, as you said." Mr. Mitchell sounded tired. He looked up at his wife. "Buttercup, we really shouldn't—"

"It would have all been fine, if he hadn't started waving his arms like a city boy. The bees got agitated and he...well, he got stung. We didn't know he had the bee allergy."

Mr. Mitchell took up the story. "We tried to help him. We said we'd call for help, but he panicked and went running off into the trees. We couldn't find him."

Mrs. Mitchell held her coffee cup in her hands. "It sounds so terrible to say it now, but we didn't know what else to do. We hid the hives with the trained bees, parked his truck in the woods and went to the party."

"So everyone in town would see you there?" Liv asked. Mrs. Mitchell was right. Put that way, it did sound awful. Far more cold-blooded than she would ever have suspected the Mitchells of being capable of. Then again, desperate people did desperate things.

"And the hives?" Carter prompted. "Why did you report the hives stolen?"

Mr. Mitchell stared at the table top. "By the next morning, we kind of suspected the whole thing had gone about as wrong as it could. We reported them stolen to throw you off the trail."

It almost had thrown them off the trail. Everyone had taken the missing hives for a New Year's Eve prank. If Michael Sheer hadn't made it to the main road before he collapsed, if he'd perished in the woods, they might not have known what had happened to him.

She offered the Mitchells a level stare. "You know we're going to have to take you in."

Mrs. Mitchell stood up and offered Liv her hands. "Yes, I imagine you are."

* * *

"This has to be the strangest New Year's Day ever." Liv finished the last of her report and filed it. The Mitchells were in separate holding cells down the hall. Thankfully, they weren't causing any trouble. The station seemed strangely quiet once Wanda had left for the day.

Carter glanced up from his own paperwork. "If there's a stranger one, I don't want to know about it. This time next year I plan to be sitting on a beach like Monty."

"Monty's not going to believe this one."

"No, he's not." Carter stood and picked up his car keys. "But since you were the first one on the scene, I'm going to leave it to you to tell him." Pocketing his keys, he began to head toward the door.

"Thanks a bunch," Liv called after him. "But you're wrong. Next year it's going to be me on the beach. You and Monty can deal with the weird stuff." Suddenly remembering Wanda's presents, she added, "Don't forget your gift."

Carter turned back. "What gift?"

"Wanda said she left us both a little something for the holidays. She put them in the bottom drawer."

Carter sat down and pulled out the drawer. Liv came around the side of the desk. Nestled between the flotsam of forgotten files and old lunch bags were two brightly-wrapped gifts. One bore her name, the other Carter's.

Carter picked his up and hefted it in his hand. By the way he held it, Liv could tell it was heavy. He reached into the drawer and handed her the other. "Should we open them together?"

Liv took the small package and set it down on her desk. "One, two, three…"

Together they ripped off the wrapping. The contents of two identical jars of amber liquid gleamed in the overhead lights.

Liv groaned. "It's honey."

Carter looked a little green. "Does Monty have any more any more antacids in his drawer?"

The Grand Babylon Hotel

Chapters VI–XXII

Arnold Bennett

[Publisher's Note: American millionaire, Theodore Racksole and his daughter Nella notice that odd things are happening in the very exclusive Grand Babylon Hotel that Racksole is the new owner of. Miss Spencer, a loyal hotel clerk, disappears and Prince Eugen doesn't turn up for his stay despite his appointment to meet his uncle Prince Aribert. And then Dimmock, an equerry to the princes, is found poisoned and soon afterwards his body disappears. This extract starts on the same evening, with a ball in the Gold Room.]

Chapter VI
In the Gold Room

AT THE GRAND BABYLON a great ball was given that night in the Gold Room, a huge saloon attached to the hotel, though scarcely part of it, and certainly less exclusive than the hotel itself. Theodore Racksole knew nothing of the affair, except that it was an entertainment offered by a Mr. and Mrs. Sampson Levi to their friends. Who Mr. and Mrs. Sampson Levi were he did not know, nor could anyone tell him anything about them except that Mr. Sampson Levi was a prominent member of that part of the Stock Exchange familiarly called the Kaffir Circus, and that his wife was a stout lady with an aquiline nose and many diamonds, and that they were very rich and very hospitable. Theodore Racksole did not want a ball in his hotel that evening, and just before dinner he had almost a mind to issue a decree that the Gold Room was to be closed and the ball forbidden, and Mr. and Mrs. Sampson Levi might name the amount of damages suffered by them. His reasons for such a course were threefold – first, he felt depressed and uneasy; second, he didn't like the name of Sampson Levi; and, third, he had a desire to show these so-called plutocrats that their wealth was nothing to him, that they could not do what they chose with Theodore Racksole, and that for two pins Theodore Racksole would buy them up, and the whole Kaffir Circus to boot. But something warned him that though such a high-handed proceeding might be tolerated in America, that land of freedom, it would never be tolerated in England. He felt instinctively that in England there are things you can't do, and that this particular thing was one of them. So the ball went forward, and neither Mr. nor Mrs. Sampson Levi had ever the least suspicion what a narrow escape they had had of looking very foolish in the eyes of the thousand or so guests invited by them to the Gold Room of the Grand Babylon that evening.

The Gold Room of the Grand Babylon was built for a ballroom. A balcony, supported by arches faced with gilt and lapis-lazulo, ran around it, and from this vantage men and maidens and chaperons who could not or would not dance might survey the scene. Everyone knew this, and most people took advantage of it. What everyone did not know – what no one knew – was that higher up than the balcony there was a little barred window in the end wall from which the hotel authorities might keep a watchful eye, not only on the dancers, but on the occupants of the balcony itself.

It may seem incredible to the uninitiated that the guests at any social gathering held in so gorgeous and renowned an apartment as the Gold Room of the Grand Babylon should need the observation of a watchful eye. Yet so it was. Strange matters and unexpected faces had been descried from the little window, and more than one European detective had kept vigil there with the most eminently satisfactory results.

At eleven o'clock Theodore Racksole, afflicted by vexation of spirit, found himself gazing idly through the little barred window. Nella was with him.

Together they had been wandering about the corridors of the hotel, still strange to them both, and it was quite by accident that they had lighted upon the small room which had a surreptitious view of Mr. and Mrs. Sampson Levi's ball. Except for the light of the chandelier of the ball-room the little cubicle was in darkness. Nella was looking through the window; her father stood behind.

"I wonder which is Mrs. Sampson Levi?" Nella said, "and whether she matches her name. Wouldn't you love to have a name like that, Father – something that people could take hold of – instead of Racksole?"

The sound of violins and a confused murmur of voices rose gently up to them.

"Umph," said Theodore. "Curse those evening papers!" he added, inconsequently but with sincerity.

"Father, you're very horrid tonight. What have the evening papers been doing?"

"Well, my young madame, they've got me in for one, and you for another; and they're manufacturing mysteries like fun. It's young Dimmock's death that has started 'em."

"Well, Father, you surely didn't expect to keep yourself out of the papers. Besides, as regards newspapers, you ought to be glad you aren't in New York. Just fancy what the dear old Herald would have made out of a little transaction like yours of last night."

"That's true," assented Racksole. "But it'll be all over New York tomorrow morning, all the same. The worst of it is that Babylon has gone off to Switzerland."

"Why?"

"Don't know. Sudden fancy, I guess, for his native heath."

"What difference does it make to you?"

"None. Only I feel sort of lonesome. I feel I want someone to lean up against in running this hotel."

"Father, if you have that feeling you must be getting ill."

"Yes," he sighed, "I admit it's unusual with me. But perhaps you haven't grasped the fact, Nella, that we're in the middle of a rather queer business."

"You mean about poor Mr. Dimmock?"

"Partly Dimmock and partly other things. First of all, that Miss Spencer, or whatever her wretched name is, mysteriously disappears. Then there was the stone thrown into your bedroom. Then I caught that rascal Jules conspiring with Dimmock at three o'clock in the morning. Then your precious Prince Aribert arrives without any suite – which I believe is a most peculiar and wicked thing for a Prince to do – and moreover I find my daughter on very intimate terms with the said Prince. Then young Dimmock goes and dies, and there is to be an inquest; then Prince Eugen and his suite, who were expected here for dinner, fail to turn up at all—"

"Prince Eugen has not come?"

"He has not; and Uncle Aribert is in a deuce of a stew about him, and telegraphing all over Europe. Altogether, things are working up pretty lively."

"Do you really think, Dad, there was anything between Jules and poor Mr. Dimmock?"

"Think! I know! I tell you I saw that scamp give Dimmock a wink last night at dinner that might have meant – well!"

"So you caught that wink, did you, Dad?"

"Why, did you?"

"Of course, Dad. I was going to tell you about it."

The millionaire grunted.

"Look here, Father," Nella whispered suddenly, and pointed to the balcony immediately below them. "Who's that?" She indicated a man with a bald patch on the back of his head, who was propping himself up against the railing of the balcony and gazing immovable into the ball-room.

"Well, who is it?"

"Isn't it Jules?"

"Gemini! By the beard of the prophet, it is!"

"Perhaps Mr. Jules is a guest of Mrs. Sampson Levi."

"Guest or no guest, he goes out of this hotel, even if I have to throw him out myself."

Theodore Racksole disappeared without another word, and Nella followed him.

But when the millionaire arrived on the balcony floor he could see nothing of Jules, neither there nor in the ball-room itself. Saying no word aloud, but quietly whispering wicked expletives, he searched everywhere in vain, and then, at last, by tortuous stairways and corridors returned to his original post of observation, that he might survey the place anew from the vantage ground. To his surprise he found a man in the dark little room, watching the scene of the ball as intently as he himself had been doing a few minutes before. Hearing footsteps, the man turned with a start.

It was Jules.

The two exchanged glances in the half light for a second.

"Good evening, Mr. Racksole," said Jules calmly. "I must apologize for being here."

"Force of habit, I suppose," said Theodore Racksole drily.

"Just so, sir."

"I fancied I had forbidden you to re-enter this hotel?"

"I thought your order applied only to my professional capacity. I am here tonight as the guest of Mr. and Mrs. Sampson Levi."

"In your new role of man-about-town, eh?"

"Exactly."

"But I don't allow men-about-town up here, my friend."

"For being up here I have already apologized."

"Then, having apologized, you had better depart; that is my disinterested advice to you."

"Good night, sir."

"And, I say, Mr. Jules, if Mr. and Mrs. Sampson Levi, or any other Hebrews or Christians, should again invite you to my hotel you will oblige me by declining the invitation. You'll find that will be the safest course for you."

"Good night, sir."

Before midnight struck Theodore Racksole had ascertained that the invitation-list of Mr. and Mrs. Sampson Levi, though a somewhat lengthy one, contained no reference to any such person as Jules.

He sat up very late. To be precise, he sat up all night. He was a man who, by dint of training, could comfortably dispense with sleep when he felt so inclined, or when circumstances made such a course advisable. He walked to and fro in his room, and cogitated as few people beside Theodore Racksole could cogitate. At six a.m. he took a stroll round the business part of his premises, and watched the supplies come in from Covent Garden, from Smithfield, from Billingsgate, and from other strange places. He found the proceedings of the kitchen department quite interesting, and made mental notes of things that he would have altered, of men whose wages he would increase and men whose wages he would reduce. At seven a.m. he happened to be standing near the luggage lift, and witnessed the descent of vast quantities of luggage, and its disappearance into a Carter Paterson van.

"Whose luggage is that?" he inquired peremptorily.

The luggage clerk, with an aggrieved expression, explained to him that it was the luggage of nobody in particular, that it belonged to various guests, and was bound for various destinations; that it was, in fact, 'expressed' luggage despatched in advance, and that a similar quantity of it left the hotel every morning about that hour.

Theodore Racksole walked away, and breakfasted upon one cup of tea and half a slice of toast.

At ten o'clock he was informed that the inspector of police desired to see him. The inspector had come, he said, to superintend the removal of the body of Reginald Dimmock to the mortuary adjoining the place of inquest, and a suitable vehicle waited at the back entrance of the hotel.

The inspector had also brought subpoenas for himself and Prince Aribert of Posen and the commissionaire to attend the inquest.

"I thought Mr. Dimmock's remains were removed last night," said Racksole wearily.

"No, sir. The fact is the van was engaged on another job."

The inspector gave the least hint of a professional smile, and Racksole, disgusted, told him curtly to go and perform his duties.

In a few minutes a message came from the inspector requesting Mr. Racksole to be good enough to come to him on the first floor. Racksole went. In the ante-room, where the body of Reginald Dimmock had originally been placed, were the inspector and Prince Aribert, and two policemen.

"Well?" said Racksole, after he and the Prince had exchanged bows. Then he saw a coffin laid across two chairs. "I see a coffin has been obtained," he remarked. He approached it. "It's empty," he observed unthinkingly.

"Just so," said the inspector. "The body of the deceased has disappeared. And his Serene Highness Prince Aribert informs me that though he has occupied a room immediately opposite, on the other side of the corridor, he can throw no light on the affair."

"Indeed, I cannot!" said the Prince, and though he spoke with sufficient calmness and dignity, you could see that he was deeply pained, even distressed.

"Well, I'm—" murmured Racksole, and stopped.

Chapter VII
Nella and the Prince

IT APPEARED impossible to Theodore Racksole that so cumbrous an article as a corpse could be removed out of his hotel, with no trace, no hint, no clue as to the time or the manner of the performance of the deed. After the first feeling of surprise, Racksole grew coldly and severely angry. He had a mind to dismiss the entire staff of the hotel. He personally examined the night-watchman, the chambermaids and all other persons who by chance might or ought to know something of the affair; but without avail. The corpse of Reginald Dimmock had vanished utterly – disappeared like a fleshless spirit.

Of course there were the police. But Theodore Racksole held the police in sorry esteem. He acquainted them with the facts, answered their queries with a patient weariness, and expected nothing whatever from that quarter. He also had several interviews with Prince Aribert of Posen, but though the Prince was suavity itself and beyond doubt genuinely concerned about the fate of his dead attendant, yet it seemed to Racksole that he was keeping something back, that he hesitated to say all he knew. Racksole, with characteristic insight, decided that the death of Reginald Dimmock was only a minor event, which had occurred, as it were, on the fringe of some far more profound mystery. And, therefore, he decided to wait, with his eyes very wide open, until something else happened that would throw light on the business. At the moment he took only one measure – he arranged that the theft of Dimmock's body should not appear in the newspapers. It is astonishing how well a secret can be kept, when the possessors of the secret are handled with the proper mixture of firmness and persuasion. Racksole managed this very neatly. It was a complicated job, and his success in it rather pleased him.

At the same time he was conscious of being temporarily worsted by an unknown group of schemers, in which he felt convinced that Jules was an important item. He could scarcely look Nella in the eyes. The girl had evidently expected him to unmask this conspiracy at once, with a single stroke of the millionaire's magic wand. She was thoroughly accustomed, in the land of her birth, to seeing him achieve impossible feats. Over there he was a 'boss'; men trembled before his name; when he wished a thing to happen – well, it happened; if he desired to know a thing, he just knew it. But here, in London, Theodore Racksole was not quite the same Theodore Racksole. He dominated New York; but London, for the most part, seemed not to take much interest in him; and there were certainly various persons in London who were capable of snapping their fingers at him – at Theodore Racksole. Neither he nor his daughter could get used to that fact.

As for Nella, she concerned herself for a little with the ordinary business of the bureau, and watched the incomings and outgoings of Prince Aribert with a kindly interest. She perceived, what her father had failed to perceive, that His Highness had assumed an attitude of reserve merely to hide the secret distraction and dismay which consumed him. She saw that the poor fellow had no settled plan in his head, and that he was troubled by something which, so far, he had confided to nobody. It came to her knowledge that each morning he walked to and fro on the Victoria Embankment, alone, and apparently with no object. On the third morning she decided that driving exercise on the Embankment would be good for her health, and thereupon ordered a carriage and issued forth, arrayed in a miraculous putty-coloured gown. Near Blackfriars Bridge she met the Prince, and the carriage was drawn up by the pavement.

"Good morning, Prince," she greeted him. "Are you mistaking this for Hyde Park?"

He bowed and smiled.

"I usually walk here in the mornings," he said.

"You surprise me," she returned. "I thought I was the only person in London who preferred the Embankment, with this view of the river, to the dustiness of Hyde Park. I can't imagine how it is that London will never take exercise anywhere except in that ridiculous Park. Now, if they had Central Park—"

"I think the Embankment is the finest spot in all London," he said.

She leaned a little out of the landau, bringing her face nearer to his.

"I do believe we are kindred spirits, you and I," she murmured; and then, "Au revoir, Prince!"

"One moment, Miss Racksole." His quick tones had a note of entreaty.

"I am in a hurry," she fibbed; "I am not merely taking exercise this morning. You have no idea how busy we are."

"Ah! Then I will not trouble you. But I leave the Grand Babylon tonight."

"Do you?" she said. "Then will your Highness do me the honour of lunching with me today in Father's room? Father will be out – he is having a day in the City with some stockbroking persons."

"I shall be charmed," said the Prince, and his face showed that he meant it.

Nella drove off.

If the lunch was a success that result was due partly to Rocco, and partly to Nella. The Prince said little beyond what the ordinary rules of the conversational game demanded. His hostess talked much and talked well, but she failed to rouse her guest. When they had had coffee he took a rather formal leave of her.

"Goodbye, Prince," she said, "but I thought – that is, no I didn't. Goodbye."

"You thought I wished to discuss something with you. I did; but I have decided that I have no right to burden your mind with my affairs."

"But suppose – suppose I wish to be burdened?"

"That is your good nature."

"Sit down," she said abruptly, "and tell me everything; mind, everything. I adore secrets."

Almost before he knew it he was talking to her, rapidly, eagerly.

"Why should I weary you with my confidences?" he said. "I don't know, I cannot tell; but I feel that I must. I feel that you will understand me better than anyone else in the world. And yet why should you understand me? Again, I don't know. Miss Racksole, I will disclose to you the whole trouble in a word. Prince Eugen, the hereditary Grand Duke of Posen, has disappeared. Four days ago I was to have met him at Ostend. He had affairs in London. He wished me to come with him. I sent Dimmock on in front, and waited for Eugen. He did not arrive. I telegraphed back to Cologne, his last stopping-place, and I learned that he had left there in accordance with his programme; I learned also that he had passed through Brussels. It must have been between Brussels and the railway station at Ostend Quay that he disappeared. He was travelling with a single equerry, and the equerry, too, has vanished. I need not explain to you, Miss Racksole, that when a person of the importance of my nephew contrives to get lost one must proceed cautiously. One cannot advertise for him in the London Times. Such a disappearance must be kept secret. The people at Posen and at Berlin believe that Eugen is in London, here, at this hotel; or, rather, they did so believe. But this morning I received a cypher telegram from – from His Majesty the Emperor, a very peculiar telegram, asking when Eugen might be expected to return to Posen, and requesting that he should go first to Berlin. That telegram was addressed to myself. Now, if the Emperor thought that Eugen was here, why should he have caused the telegram to be addressed to me? I have hesitated for three days, but I can hesitate no longer. I must myself go to the Emperor and acquaint him with the facts."

"I suppose you've just got to keep straight with him?" Nella was on the point of saying, but she checked herself and substituted, "The Emperor is your chief, is he not? 'First among equals,' you call him."

"His Majesty is our over-lord," said Aribert quietly.

"Why do you not take immediate steps to inquire as to the whereabouts of your Royal nephew?" she asked simply. The affair seemed to her just then so plain and straightforward.

"Because one of two things may have happened. Either Eugen may have been, in plain language, abducted, or he may have had his own reasons for changing his programme and keeping in the background – out of reach of telegraph and post and railways."

"What sort of reasons?"

"Do not ask me. In the history of every family there are passages—" He stopped.

"And what was Prince Eugen's object in coming to London?"

Aribert hesitated.

"Money," he said at length. "As a family we are very poor – poorer than anyone in Berlin suspects."

"Prince Aribert," Nella said, "shall I tell you what I think?" She leaned back in her chair, and looked at him out of half-closed eyes. His pale, thin, distinguished face held her gaze as if by some fascination. There could be no mistaking this man for anything else but a Prince.

"If you will," he said.

"Prince Eugen is the victim of a plot."

"You think so?"

"I am perfectly convinced of it."

"But why? What can be the object of a plot against him?"

"That is a point of which you should know more than me," she remarked drily.

"Ah! Perhaps, perhaps," he said. "But, dear Miss Racksole, why are you so sure?"

"There are several reasons, and they are connected with Mr. Dimmock. Did you ever suspect, your Highness, that that poor young man was not entirely loyal to you?"

"He was absolutely loyal," said the Prince, with all the earnestness of conviction.

"A thousand pardons, but he was not."

"Miss Racksole, if any other than yourself made that assertion, I would – I would—"

"Consign them to the deepest dungeon in Posen?" she laughed, lightly.

"Listen." And she told him of the incidents which had occurred in the night preceding his arrival in the hotel.

"Do you mean, Miss Racksole, that there was an understanding between poor Dimmock and this fellow Jules?"

"There was an understanding."

"Impossible!"

"Your Highness, the man who wishes to probe a mystery to its root never uses the word 'impossible.' But I will say this for young Mr. Dimmock. I think he repented, and I think that it was because he repented that he – er – died so suddenly, and that his body was spirited away."

"Why has no one told me these things before?" Aribert exclaimed.

"Princes seldom hear the truth," she said.

He was astonished at her coolness, her firmness of assertion, her air of complete acquaintance with the world.

"Miss Racksole," he said, "if you will permit me to say it, I have never in my life met a woman like you. May I rely on your sympathy – your support?"

"My support, Prince? But how?"

"I do not know," he replied. "But you could help me if you would. A woman, when she has brain, always has more brain than a man."

"Ah!" she said ruefully, "I have no brains, but I do believe I could help you."

What prompted her to make that assertion she could not have explained, even to herself. But she made it, and she had a suspicion – a prescience – that it would be justified, though by what means, through what good fortune, was still a mystery to her.

"Go to Berlin," she said. "I see that you must do that; you have no alternative. As for the rest we shall see. Something will occur. I shall be here. My father will be here. You must count us as your friends."

He kissed her hand when he left, and afterwards, when she was alone, she kissed the spo his lips had touched again and again. Now, thinking the matter out in the calmness of solitude all seemed strange, unreal, uncertain to her. Were conspiracies actually possible nowadays? Did queer things actually happen in Europe? And did they actually happen in London hotels? She dined with her father that night.

"I hear Prince Aribert has left," said Theodore Racksole.

"Yes," she assented. She said not a word about their interview.

Chapter VIII
Arrival and Departure of the Baroness

ON THE FOLLOWING morning, just before lunch, a lady, accompanied by a maid and a considerable quantity of luggage, came to the Grand Babylon Hotel. She was a plump, little old lady, with white hair and an old-fashioned bonnet, and she had a quaint, simple smile of surprise at everything in general.

Nevertheless, she gave the impression of belonging to some aristocracy, though not the English aristocracy. Her tone to her maid, whom she addressed in broken English – the girl being apparently English – was distinctly insolent, with the calm, unconscious insolence peculiar to a certain type of Continental nobility. The name on the lady's card ran thus: 'Baroness Zerlinski'. She desired rooms on the third floor. It happened that Nella was in the bureau.

"On the third floor, madam?" questioned Nella, in her best clerkly manner.

"I did say on de tird floor," said the plump little old lady.

"We have accommodation on the second floor."

"I wish to be high up, out of de dust and in de light," explained the Baroness.

"We have no suites on the third floor, madam."

"Never mind, no mattaire! Have you not two rooms that communicate?"

Nella consulted her books, rather awkwardly.

"Numbers 122 and 123 communicate."

"Or is it 121 and 122?" the little old lady remarked quickly, and then bit her lip.

"I beg your pardon. I should have said 121 and 122."

At the moment Nella regarded the Baroness's correction of her figures as a curious chance but afterwards, when the Baroness had ascended in the lift, the thing struck her as somewhat strange. Perhaps the Baroness Zerlinski had stayed at the hotel before. For the sake of convenience an index of visitors to the hotel was kept and the index extended back for thirty years. Nella examined it, but it did not contain the name of Zerlinski. Then it was that Nella began to imagine, what had swiftly crossed her mind when first the Baroness presented herself at the bureau, that the features of the Baroness were remotely familiar to her. She thought, not that she had seen the old lady's face before, but that she had seen somewhere, some time, a face of a similar cast. It occurred to Nella to look at the 'Almanach de Gotha' – that record of all the mazes of Continental blue blood; but the 'Almanach de Gotha' made no reference to any barony of Zerlinski. Nella inquired where the Baroness meant to take lunch, and was informed that a table had been reserved for her in the dining-room, and she at once decided to lunch in the dining-room herself. Seated in a corner, half-hidden by a pillar, she could survey all the guests, and watch each group as it entered or left. Presently the Baroness appeared, dressed in black, with a tiny lace shawl, despite the June warmth; very stately, very quaint, and gently smiling. Nella observed her intently. The lady ate heartily, working without haste and without delay through the elaborate menu of the luncheon. Nella noticed that she had beautiful white teeth. Then a remarkable thing happened. A cream puff was served to the Baroness by way of sweets, and Nella was astonished to see the little lady remove the top, and with a spoon quietly take something from the interior which looked like a piece of folded paper. No one who had not been watching with the eye of a lynx would have noticed anything extraordinary in the action; indeed, the chances were nine hundred and ninety-nine to one that it would pass unheeded. But, unfortunately for the Baroness, it was the thousandth chance that happened. Nella jumped up, and walking over to the Baroness, said to her:

"I'm afraid that the tart is not quite nice, your ladyship."

"Thanks, it is delightful," said the Baroness coldly; her smile had vanished. "Who are you? I thought you were de bureau clerk."

"My father is the owner of this hotel. I thought there was something in the tart which ought not to have been there."

Nella looked the Baroness full in the face. The piece of folded paper, to which a little cream had attached itself, lay under the edge of a plate.

"No, thanks." The Baroness smiled her simple smile.

Nella departed. She had noticed one trifling thing besides the paper – namely, that the Baroness could pronounce the English 'th' sound if she chose.

That afternoon, in her own room, Nella sat meditating at the window for long time, and then she suddenly sprang up, her eyes brightening.

"I know," she exclaimed, clapping her hands. "It's Miss Spencer, disguised! Why didn't I think of that before?" Her thoughts ran instantly to Prince Aribert. "Perhaps I can help him," she said to herself, and gave a little sigh. She went down to the office and inquired whether the Baroness had given any instructions about dinner. She felt that some plan must be formulated. She wanted to get hold of Rocco, and put him in the rack. She knew now that Rocco, the unequalled, was also concerned in this mysterious affair.

"The Baroness Zerlinski has left, about a quarter of an hour ago," said the attendant.

"But she only arrived this morning."

"The Baroness's maid said that her mistress had received a telegram and must leave at once. The Baroness paid the bill, and went away in a four-wheeler."

"Where to?"

"The trunks were labelled for Ostend."

Perhaps it was instinct, perhaps it was the mere spirit of adventure; but that evening Nella was to be seen of all men on the steamer for Ostend which leaves Dover at eleven p.m. She told no one of her intentions – not even her father, who was not in the hotel when she left. She had scribbled a brief note to him to expect her back in a day or two, and had posted this at Dover. The steamer was the Marie Henriette, a large and luxurious boat, whose state-rooms on deck vie with the glories of the Cunard and White Star liners. One of these state-rooms, the best, was evidently occupied, for every curtain of its windows was carefully drawn. Nella did not hope that the Baroness was on board; it was quite possible for the Baroness to have caught the eight o'clock steamer, and it was also possible for the Baroness not to have gone to Ostend at all, but to some other place in an entirely different direction. Nevertheless, Nella had a faint hope that the lady who called herself Zerlinski might be in that curtained stateroom, and throughout the smooth moonlit voyage she never once relaxed her observation of its doors and its windows.

The Maria Henriette arrived in Ostend Harbour punctually at two a.m. in the morning. There was the usual heterogeneous, gesticulating crowd on the quay.

Nella kept her post near the door of the state-room, and at length she was rewarded by seeing it open. Four middle-aged Englishmen issued from it. From a glimpse of the interior Nella saw that they had spent the voyage in card-playing.

It would not be too much to say that she was distinctly annoyed. She pretended to be annoyed with circumstances, but really she was annoyed with Nella Racksole. At two in the morning, without luggage, without any companionship, and without a plan of campaign, she found herself in a strange foreign port – a port of evil repute, possessing some of the worst-managed hotels in Europe. She strolled on the quay for a few minutes, and then she saw the smoke of another steamer in the offing. She inquired from an official what that steamer might be, and was told that it was the eight o'clock from Dover, which had broken down, put into Calais for some slight necessary repairs, and was arriving at its destination nearly four hours late. Her mercurial spirits rose again. A minute ago she was regarding herself as no better than a ninny engaged in a wild-goose chase. Now she felt that after all she had been very sagacious and cunning. She was morally sure that she would find the Zerlinski woman on this second steamer, and she took all the credit to herself in advance. Such is human nature.

The steamer seemed interminably slow in coming into harbour. Nella walked on the Digue for a few minutes to watch it the better. The town was silent and almost deserted. It had a false and sinister aspect. She remembered tales which she had heard of this glittering resort, which in the season holds more scoundrels than any place in Europe, save only Monte Carlo. She remembered that the gilded adventurers of every nation under the sun forgathered there either for business or pleasure, and that some of the most wonderful crimes of the latter half of the century had been schemed and matured in that haunt of cosmopolitan iniquity.

When the second steamer arrived Nella stood at the end of the gangway, close to the ticket-collector. The first person to step on shore was – not the Baroness Zerlinski, but Miss Spencer herself! Nella turned aside instantly, hiding her face, and Miss Spencer, carrying a small bag, hurried with assured footsteps to the Custom House. It seemed as if she knew the port of Ostend fairly well. The moon shone like day, and Nella had full opportunity to observe her quarry. She could see now quite plainly that the Baroness Zerlinski had been only Miss Spencer in disguise. There was the same gait, the same movement of the head and of the hips; the white hair was easily to be accounted for by a wig, and the wrinkles by a paint brush and some grease paints. Miss Spencer, whose hair was now its old accustomed yellow, got through the Custom House without difficulty, and Nella saw her call a closed carriage and say something to the driver. The vehicle drove off. Nella jumped into the next carriage – an open one – that came up.

"Follow that carriage," she said succinctly to the driver in French.

"Bien, madame!" The driver whipped up his horse, and the animal shot forward with a terrific clatter over the cobbles. It appeared that this driver was quite accustomed to following other carriages.

"Now I am fairly in for it!" said Nella to herself. She laughed unsteadily, but her heart was beating with an extraordinary thump.

For some time the pursued vehicle kept well in front. It crossed the town nearly from end to end, and plunged into a maze of small streets far on the south side of the Kursaal. Then gradually Nella's equipage began to overtake it. The first carriage stopped with a jerk before a tall dark house, and Miss Spencer emerged. Nella called to her driver to stop, but he, determined to be in at the death, was engaged in whipping his horse, and he completely ignored her commands. He drew up triumphantly at the tall dark house just at the moment when Miss Spencer disappeared into it. The other carriage drove away. Nella, uncertain what to do, stepped down from her carriage and gave the driver some money. At the same moment a man reopened the door of the house, which had closed on Miss Spencer.

"I want to see Miss Spencer," said Nella impulsively. She couldn't think of anything else to say.

"Miss Spencer?"

"Yes; she's just arrived."

"It's OK, I suppose," said the man.

"I guess so," said Nella, and she walked past him into the house. She was astonished at her own audacity.

Miss Spencer was just going into a room off the narrow hall. Nella followed her into the apartment, which was shabbily furnished in the Belgian lodging-house style.

"Well, Miss Spencer," she greeted the former Baroness Zerlinski, "I guess you didn't expect to see me. You left our hotel very suddenly this afternoon, and you left it very suddenly a few days ago; and so I've just called to make a few inquiries."

To do the lady justice, Miss Spencer bore the surprising ordeal very well.

She did not flinch; she betrayed no emotion. The sole sign of perturbation was in her hurried breathing.

"You have ceased to be the Baroness Zerlinski," Nella continued. "May I sit down?"

"Certainly, sit down," said Miss Spencer, copying the girl's tone. "You are a fairly smart young woman, that I will say. What do you want? Weren't my books all straight?"

"Your books were all straight. I haven't come about your books. I have come about the murder of Reginald Dimmock, the disappearance of his corpse, and the disappearance of Prince Eugen of Posen. I thought you might be able to help me in some investigations which I am making."

Miss Spencer's eyes gleamed, and she stood up and moved swiftly to the mantelpiece.

"You may be a Yankee, but you're a fool," she said.

She took hold of the bell-rope.

"Don't ring that bell if you value your life," said Nella.

"If what?" Miss Spencer remarked.

"If you value your life," said Nella calmly, and with the words she pulled from her pocket a very neat and dainty little revolver.

Chapter IX
Two Women and the Revolver

"YOU – YOU'RE only doing that to frighten me," stammered Miss Spencer, in a low, quavering voice.

"Am I?" Nella replied, as firmly as she could, though her hand shook violently with excitement, could Miss Spencer but have observed it. "Am I? You said just now that I might be a Yankee girl, but I was a fool. Well, I am a Yankee girl, as you call it; and in my country, if they don't teach revolver-shooting in boarding-schools, there are at least a lot of girls who can handle a revolver. I happen to be one of them. I tell you that if you ring that bell you will suffer."

Most of this was simple bluff on Nella's part, and she trembled lest Miss Spencer should perceive that it was simple bluff. Happily for her, Miss Spencer belonged to that order of women who have every sort of courage except physical courage. Miss Spencer could have withstood successfully any moral trial, but persuade her that her skin was in danger, and she would succumb. Nella at once divined this useful fact, and proceeded accordingly, hiding the strangeness of her own sensations as well as she could.

"You had better sit down now," said Nella, "and I will ask you a few questions."

And Miss Spencer obediently sat down, rather white, and trying to screw her lips into a formal smile.

"Why did you leave the Grand Babylon that night?" Nella began her examination, putting on a stern, barrister-like expression.

"I had orders to, Miss Racksole."

"Whose orders?"

"Well, I'm – I'm – the fact is, I'm a married woman, and it was my husband's orders."

"Who is your husband?"

"Tom Jackson – Jules, you know, head waiter at the Grand Babylon."

"So Jules's real name is Tom Jackson? Why did he want you to leave without giving notice?"

"I'm sure I don't know, Miss Racksole. I swear I don't know. He's my husband, and, of course, I do what he tells me, as you will some day do what your husband tells you. Please heaven you'll get a better husband than mine!"

Miss Spencer showed a sign of tears.

Nella fingered the revolver, and put it at full cock. "Well," she repeated, "why did he want you to leave?" She was tremendously surprised at her own coolness, and somewhat pleased with it, too.

"I can't tell you, I can't tell you."

"You've just got to," Nella said, in a terrible, remorseless tone.

"He – he wished me to come over here to Ostend. Something had gone wrong. Oh! he's a fearful man, is Tom. If I told you, he'd—"

"Had something gone wrong in the hotel, or over here?"

"Both."

"Was it about Prince Eugen of Posen?"

"I don't know – that is, yes, I think so."

"What has your husband to do with Prince Eugen?"

"I believe he has some – some sort of business with him, some money business."

"And was Mr. Dimmock in this business?"

"I fancy so, Miss Racksole. I'm telling you all I know, that I swear."

"Did your husband and Mr. Dimmock have a quarrel that night in Room 111?"

"They had some difficulty."

"And the result of that was that you came to Ostend instantly?"

"Yes; I suppose so."

"And what were you to do in Ostend? What were your instructions from this husband of yours?"

Miss Spencer's head dropped on her arms on the table which separated her from Nella, and she appeared to sob violently.

"Have pity on me," she murmured, "I can't tell you any more."

"Why?"

"He'd kill me if he knew."

"You're wandering from the subject," observed Nella coldly. "This is the last time I shall warn you. Let me tell you plainly I've got the best reasons for being desperate, and if anything happens to you I shall say I did it in self-defence. Now, what were you to do in Ostend?"

"I shall die for this anyhow," whined Miss Spencer, and then, with a sort of fierce despair, "I had to keep watch on Prince Eugen."

"Where? In this house?"

Miss Spencer nodded, and, looking up, Nella could see the traces of tears in her face.

"Then Prince Eugen was a prisoner? Some one had captured him at the instigation of Jules?"

"Yes, if you must have it."

"Why was it necessary for you specially to come to Ostend?"

"Oh! Tom trusts me. You see, I know Ostend. Before I took that place at the Grand Babylon I had travelled over Europe, and Tom knew that I knew a thing or two."

"Why did you take the place at the Grand Babylon?"

"Because Tom told me to. He said I should be useful to him there."

"Is your husband an Anarchist, or something of that kind, Miss Spencer?"

"I don't know. I'd tell you in a minute if I knew. But he's one of those that keep themselves to themselves."

"Do you know if he has ever committed a murder?"

"Never!" said Miss Spencer, with righteous repudiation of the mere idea.

"But Mr. Dimmock was murdered. He was poisoned. If he had not been poisoned why was his body stolen? It must have been stolen to prevent inquiry, to hide traces. Tell me about that."

"I take my dying oath," said Miss Spencer, standing up a little way from the table, "I take my dying oath I didn't know Mr. Dimmock was dead till I saw it in the newspaper."

"You swear you had no suspicion of it?"

"I swear I hadn't."

Nella was inclined to believe the statement. The woman and the girl looked at each other in the tawdry, frowsy, lamp-lit room. Miss Spencer nervously patted her yellow hair into shape, as if gradually recovering her composure and equanimity. The whole affair seemed like a dream to Nella, a disturbing, sinister nightmare. She was a little uncertain what to say. She felt that she had not yet got hold of any very definite information. "Where is Prince Eugen now?" she asked at length.

"I don't know, miss."

"He isn't in this house?"

"No, miss."

"Ah! We will see presently."

"They took him away, Miss Racksole."

"Who took him away? Some of your husband's friends?"

"Some of his – acquaintances."

"Then there is a gang of you?"

"A gang of us – a gang! I don't know what you mean," Miss Spencer quavered.

"Oh, but you must know," smiled Nella calmly. "You can't possibly be so innocent as all that, Mrs. Tom Jackson. You can't play games with me. You've just got to remember that I'm what you call a Yankee girl. There's one thing that I mean to find out, within the next five minutes, and that is – how your charming husband kidnapped Prince Eugen, and why he kidnapped him. Let us begin with the second question. You have evaded it once."

Miss Spencer looked into Nella's face, and then her eyes dropped, and her fingers worked nervously with the tablecloth.

"How can I tell you," she said, "when I don't know? You've got the whip-hand of me, and you're tormenting me for your own pleasure." She wore an expression of persecuted innocence.

"Did Mr. Tom Jackson want to get some money out of Prince Eugen?"

"Money! Not he! Tom's never short of money."

"But I mean a lot of money – tens of thousands, hundreds of thousands?"

"Tom never wanted money from anyone," said Miss Spencer doggedly.

"Then had he some reason for wishing to prevent Prince Eugen from coming to London?"

"Perhaps he had. I don't know. If you kill me, I don't know." Nella stopped to reflect. Then she raised the revolver. It was a mechanical, unintentional sort of action, and certainly she had no intention of using the weapon, but, strange to say, Miss Spencer again cowered before it. Even at that moment Nella wondered that a woman like Miss Spencer could be so simple as to think the revolver would actually be used. Having absolutely no physical cowardice herself, Nella had the greatest difficulty in imagining that other people could be at the mercy of a bodily fear. Still, she saw her advantage, and used it relentlessly, and with as much theatrical gesture as she could command. She raised the revolver till it was level with Miss Spencer's face, and suddenly a new, queer feeling took hold of her. She knew that she would indeed use that revolver now, if the miserable woman before her drove her too far. She felt afraid – afraid of herself; she was in the grasp of a savage, primeval instinct. In a flash she saw Miss Spencer dead at her feet – the police – a court of justice – the scaffold. It was horrible.

"Speak," she said hoarsely, and Miss Spencer's face went whiter.

"Tom did say," the woman whispered rapidly, awesomely, "that if Prince Eugen got to London it would upset his scheme."

"What scheme? What scheme? Answer me."

"Heaven help me, I don't know." Miss Spencer sank into a chair. "He said Mr. Dimmock had turned tail, and he should have to settle him and then Rocco—"

"Rocco! What about Rocco?" Nella could scarcely hear herself. Her grip of the revolver tightened.

Miss Spencer's eyes opened wider; she gazed at Nella with a glassy stare.

"Don't ask me. It's death!" Her eyes were fixed as if in horror.

"It is," said Nella, and the sound of her voice seemed to her to issue from the lips of some third person.

"It's death," repeated Miss Spencer, and gradually her head and shoulders sank back, and hung loosely over the chair. Nella was conscious of a sudden revulsion. The woman had surely fainted. Dropping the revolver she ran round the table. She was herself again – feminine, sympathetic, the old Nella. She felt immensely relieved that this had happened. But at the same instant Miss Spencer sprang up from the chair like a cat, seized the revolver, and with a wild movement of the arm flung it against the window. It crashed through the glass, exploding as it went, and there was a tense silence.

"I told you that you were a fool," remarked Miss Spencer slowly, "coming here like a sort of female Jack Sheppard, and trying to get the best of me. We are on equal terms now. You frightened me, but I knew I was a cleverer woman than you, and that in the end, if I kept on long enough, I should win. Now it will be my turn."

Dumbfounded, and overcome with a miserable sense of the truth of Miss Spencer's words, Nella stood still. The idea of her colossal foolishness swept through her like a flood. She felt almost ashamed. But even at this juncture she had no fear. She faced the woman bravely, her mind leaping about in search of some plan. She could think of nothing but a bribe – an enormous bribe.

"I admit you've won," she said, "but I've not finished yet. Just listen."

Miss Spencer folded her arms, and glanced at the door, smiling bitterly.

"You know my father is a millionaire; perhaps you know that he is one of the richest men in the world. If I give you my word of honour not to reveal anything that you've told me, what will you take to let me go free?"

"What sum do you suggest?" asked Miss Spencer carelessly.

"Twenty thousand pounds," said Nella promptly. She had begun to regard the affair as a business operation.

Miss Spencer's lip curled.

"A hundred thousand."

Again Miss Spencer's lip curled.

"Well, say a million. I can rely on my father, and so may you."

"You think you are worth a million to him?"

"I do," said Nella.

"And you think we could trust you to see that it was paid?"

"Of course you could."

"And we should not suffer afterwards in any way?"

"I would give you my word, and my father's word."

"Bah!" exclaimed Miss Spencer: "how do you know I wouldn't let you go free for nothing? You are only a rash, silly girl."

"I know you wouldn't. I can read your face too well."

"You are right," Miss Spencer replied slowly. "I wouldn't. I wouldn't let you go for all the dollars in America."

Nella felt cold down the spine, and sat down again in her chair. A draught of air from the broken window blew on her cheek. Steps sounded in the passage; the door opened, but Nella did not turn round. She could not move her eyes from Miss Spencer's. There was a noise of rushing water in her ears. She lost consciousness, and slipped limply to the ground.

Chapter X
At Sea

IT SEEMED to Nella that she was being rocked gently in a vast cradle, which swayed to and fro with a motion at once slow and incredibly gentle. This sensation continued for some time, and there was added to it the sound of a quick, quiet, muffled beat. Soft, exhilarating breezes wafted her forward in spite of herself, and yet she remained in a delicious calm. She wondered if her mother was kneeling by her side, whispering some lullaby in her childish ears. Then strange colours swam before her eyes, her eyelids wavered, and at last she awoke. For a few moments her gaze travelled to and fro in a vain search for some clue to her surroundings, was aware of nothing except sense of repose and a feeling of relief that some mighty and fatal struggle was over; she cared not whether she had conquered or suffered defeat in the struggle of her soul with some other soul; it was finished, done with, and the consciousness of its conclusion satisfied and contented her. Gradually her brain, recovering from its obsession, began to grasp the phenomena of her surroundings, and she saw that she was on a yacht, and that the yacht was moving. The motion of the cradle was the smooth rolling of the vessel; the beat was the beat of its screw; the strange colours were the cloud tints thrown by the sun as it rose over a distant and receding shore in the wake of the yacht; her mother's lullaby was the crooned song of the man at the wheel. Nella all through her life had had many experiences of yachting. From the waters of the River Hudson to those bluer tides of the Mediterranean Sea, she had yachted in all seasons and all weathers. She loved the water, and now it seemed deliciously right and proper that she should be on the water again. She raised her head to look round, and then let it sink back: she was fatigued, enervated; she desired only solitude and calm; she had no care, no anxiety, no responsibility: a hundred years might have passed since her meeting with Miss Spencer, and the memory of that meeting appeared to have faded into the remotest background of her mind.

It was a small yacht, and her practised eye at once told that it belonged to the highest aristocracy of pleasure craft. As she reclined in the deck-chair (it did not occur to her at that moment to speculate as to the identity of the person who had led her therein) she examined all visible details of the vessel. The deck was as white and smooth as her own hand, and the seams ran along its length like blue veins. All the brass-work, from the band round the slender funnel to the concave surface of the binnacle, shone like gold.

The tapered masts stretched upwards at a rakish angle, and the rigging seemed like spun silk. No sails were set; the yacht was under steam, and doing about seven or eight knots. She judged that it was a boat of a hundred tons or so, probably Clyde-built, and not more than two or three years old.

No one was to be seen on deck except the man at the wheel: this man wore a blue jersey; but there was neither name nor initial on the jersey, nor was there a name on the white life-buoys lashed to the main rigging, nor on the polished dinghy which hung on the starboard davits. She called to the man, and called again, in a feeble voice, but the steerer took no notice of her, and continued his quiet song as though nothing else existed in the universe save the yacht, the sea, the sun, and himself.

Then her eyes swept the outline of the land from which they were hastening, and she could just distinguish a lighthouse and a great white irregular dome, which she recognized as the Kursaal at Ostend, that gorgeous rival of the gaming palace at Monte Carlo. So she was leaving Ostend. The rays of the sun fell on her caressingly, like a restorative. All around the water was changing from wonderful greys and dark blues to still more wonderful pinks and translucent unearthly greens; the magic kaleidoscope of dawn was going forward in its accustomed way, regardless of the vicissitudes of mortals.

Here and there in the distance she descried a sail – the brown sail of some Ostend fishing-boat returning home after a night's trawling. Then the beat of paddles caught her ear, and a steamer blundered past, wallowing clumsily among the waves like a tortoise. It was the Swallow from London. She could see some of its passengers leaning curiously over the aft-rail. A girl in a mackintosh signalled to her, and mechanically she answered the salute with her arm. The officer of the bridge of the Swallow hailed the yacht, but the man at the wheel offered no reply. In another minute the Swallow was nothing but a blot in the distance.

Nella tried to sit straight in the deck-chair, but she found herself unable to do so. Throwing off the rug which covered her, she discovered that she had been tied to the chair by means of a piece of broad webbing. Instantly she was alert, awake, angry; she knew that her perils were not over; she felt that possibly they had scarcely yet begun. Her lazy contentment, her dreamy sense of peace and repose, vanished utterly, and she steeled herself to meet the dangers of a grave and difficult situation.

Just at that moment a man came up from below. He was a man of forty or so, clad in irreproachable blue, with a peaked yachting cap. He raised the cap politely.

"Good morning," he said. "Beautiful sunrise, isn't it?" The clever and calculated insolence of his tone cut her like a lash as she lay bound in the chair. Like all people who have lived easy and joyous lives in those fair regions where gold smoothes every crease and law keeps a tight hand on disorder, she found it hard to realize that there were other regions where gold was useless and law without power. Twenty-four hours ago she would have declared it impossible that such an experience as she had suffered could happen to anyone; she would have talked airily about civilization and the nineteenth century, and progress and the police. But her experience was teaching her that human nature remains always the same, and that beneath the thin crust of security on which we good citizens exist the dark and secret forces of crime continue to move, just as they did in the days when you couldn't go from Cheapside to Chelsea without being set upon by thieves. Her experience was in a fair way to teach her this lesson better than she could have learnt it even in the bureaux of the detective police of Paris, London, and St Petersburg.

"Good morning," the man repeated, and she glanced at him with a sullen, angry gaze.

"You!" she exclaimed, "You, Mr. Thomas Jackson, if that is your name! Loose me from this chair, and I will talk to you." Her eyes flashed as she spoke, and the contempt in them added mightily to her beauty. Mr. Thomas Jackson, otherwise Jules, erstwhile head waiter at the Grand Babylon, considered himself a connoisseur in feminine loveliness, and the vision of Nella Racksole smote him like an exquisite blow.

"With pleasure," he replied. "I had forgotten that to prevent you from falling I had secured you to the chair"; and with a quick movement he unfastened the band. Nella stood up, quivering with fiery annoyance and scorn.

"Now," she said, fronting him, "what is the meaning of this?"

"You fainted," he replied imperturbably. "Perhaps you don't remember."

The man offered her a deck-chair with a characteristic gesture. Nella was obliged to acknowledge, in spite of herself, that the fellow had distinction, an air of breeding. No one would have guessed that for twenty years he had been an hotel waiter. His long, lithe figure, and easy, careless carriage seemed to be the figure and carriage of an aristocrat, and his voice was quiet, restrained, and authoritative.

"That has nothing to do with my being carried off in this yacht of yours."

"It is not my yacht," he said, "but that is a minor detail. As to the more important matter, forgive me that I remind you that only a few hours ago you were threatening a lady in my house with a revolver."

"Then it was your house?"

"Why not? May I not possess a house?" He smiled.

"I must request you to put the yacht about at once, instantly, and take me back." She tried to speak firmly.

"Ah!" he said, "I am afraid that's impossible. I didn't put out to sea with the intention of returning at once, instantly." In the last words he gave a faint imitation of her tone.

"When I do get back," she said, "when my father gets to know of this affair, it will be an exceedingly bad day for you, Mr. Jackson."

"But supposing your father doesn't hear of it—"

"What?"

"Supposing you never get back?"

"Do you mean, then, to have my murder on your conscience?"

"Talking of murder," he said, "you came very near to murdering my friend, Miss Spencer. At least, so she tells me."

"Is Miss Spencer on board?" Nella asked, seeing perhaps a faint ray of hope in the possible presence of a woman.

"Miss Spencer is not on board. There is no one on board except you and myself and a small crew – a very discreet crew, I may add."

"I will have nothing more to say to you. You must take your own course."

"Thanks for the permission," he said. "I will send you up some breakfast."

He went to the saloon stairs and whistled, and a Negro boy appeared with a tray of chocolate. Nella took it, and, without the slightest hesitation, threw it overboard. Mr. Jackson walked away a few steps and then returned.

"You have spirit," he said, "and I admire spirit. It is a rare quality."

She made no reply. "Why did you mix yourself up in my affairs at all?" he went on. Again she made no reply, but the question set her thinking: why had she mixed herself up in this mysterious business? It was quite at variance with the usual methods of her gay and butterfly existence to meddle at all with serious things. Had she acted merely from a desire to see justice done and wickedness punished? Or was it the desire of adventure? Or was it, perhaps, the desire to be of service to His Serene Highness Prince Aribert? "It is no fault of mine that you are in this fix," Jules continued. "I didn't bring you into it. You brought yourself into it. You and your father – you have been moving along at a pace which is rather too rapid."

"That remains to be seen," she put in coldly.

"It does," he admitted. "And I repeat that I can't help admiring you – that is, when you aren't interfering with my private affairs. That is a proceeding which I have never tolerated from anyone – not even from a millionaire, nor even from a beautiful woman." He bowed. "I will tell you what I propose to do. I propose to escort you to a place of safety, and to keep you there till my operations are concluded, and the possibility of interference entirely removed. You spoke just now of murder. What a crude notion that was of yours! It is only the amateur who practises murder—"

"What about Reginald Dimmock?" she interjected quickly.

He paused gravely.

"Reginald Dimmock," he repeated. "I had imagined his was a case of heart disease. Let me send you up some more chocolate. I'm sure you're hungry."

"I will starve before I touch your food," she said.

"Gallant creature!" he murmured, and his eyes roved over her face. Her superb, supercilious beauty overcame him. "Ah!" he said, "what a wife you would make!" He approached nearer to her. "You and I, Miss Racksole, your beauty and wealth and my brains – we could conquer the world. Few men are worthy of you, but I am one of the few. Listen! You might do worse. Marry me. I am a great man; I shall be greater. I adore you. Marry me, and I will save your life. All shall be well. I will begin again. The past shall be as though there had been no past."

"This is somewhat sudden – Jules," she said with biting contempt.

"Did you expect me to be conventional?" he retorted. "I love you."

"Granted," she said, for the sake of the argument. "Then what will occur to your present wife?"

"My present wife?"

"Yes, Miss Spencer, as she is called."

"She told you I was her husband?"

"Incidentally she did."

"She isn't."

"Perhaps she isn't. But, nevertheless, I think I won't marry you." Nella stood like a statue of scorn before him.

He went still nearer to her. "Give me a kiss, then; one kiss – I won't ask for more; one kiss from those lips, and you shall go free. Men have ruined themselves for a kiss. I will."

"Coward!" she ejaculated.

"Coward!" he repeated. "Coward, am I? Then I'll be a coward, and you shall kiss me whether you will or not."

He put a hand on her shoulder. As she shrank back from his lustrous eyes, with an involuntary scream, a figure sprang out of the dinghy a few feet away. With a single blow, neatly directed to Mr. Jackson's ear, Mr. Jackson was stretched senseless on the deck. Prince Aribert of Posen stood over him with a revolver. It was probably the greatest surprise of Mr. Jackson's whole life.

"Don't be alarmed," said the Prince to Nella, "my being here is the simplest thing in the world, and I will explain it as soon as I have finished with this fellow."

Nella could think of nothing to say, but she noticed the revolver in the Prince's hand.

"Why," she remarked, "that's my revolver."

"It is," he said, "and I will explain that, too."

The man at the wheel gave no heed whatever to the scene.

Chapter XI
The Court Pawnbroker

"MR. SAMPSON LEVI wishes to see you, sir."

These words, spoken by a servant to Theodore Racksole, aroused the millionaire from a reverie which had been the reverse of pleasant. The fact was, and it is necessary to insist on it, that Mr. Racksole, owner of the Grand Babylon Hotel, was by no means in a state of self-satisfaction. A mystery had attached itself to his hotel, and with all his acumen and knowledge of things in general he was unable to solve that mystery. He laughed at the fruitless efforts of the police, but he could not honestly say that his own efforts had been less barren. The public was talking, for, after all, the disappearance of poor Dimmock's body had got noised abroad in an indirect sort of way, and Theodore Racksole did not like the idea of his impeccable hotel being the subject of sinister rumours. He wondered, grimly, what the public and the Sunday newspapers would say if they were aware of all the other phenomena, not yet common property: of Miss Spencer's disappearance, of Jules' strange visits, and of the non-arrival of Prince Eugen of Posen. Theodore Racksole had worried his brain without result. He had conducted an elaborate private investigation without result, and he had spent a certain amount of money without result. The police said that they had a clue; but Racksole remarked that it was always the business of the police to have a clue, that they seldom had more than a clue, and that a clue without some sequel to it was a pretty stupid business. The only sure thing in the whole affair was that a cloud rested over his hotel, his beautiful new toy, the finest of its kind. The cloud was not interfering with business, but, nevertheless, it was a cloud, and he fiercely resented its presence; perhaps it would be more correct to say that he fiercely resented his inability to dissipate it.

"Mr. Sampson Levi wishes to see you, sir," the servant repeated, having received no sign that his master had heard him.

"So I hear," said Racksole. "Does he want to see me, personally?"

"He asked for you, sir."

"Perhaps it is Rocco he wants to see, about a menu or something of that kind?"

"I will inquire, sir," and the servant made a move to withdraw.

"Stop," Racksole commanded suddenly. "Desire Mr. Sampson Levi to step this way."

The great stockbroker of the 'Kaffir Circus' entered with a simple unassuming air. He was a rather short, florid man, dressed like a typical Hebraic financier, with too much watch-chain and too little waistcoat. In his fat hand he held a gold-headed cane, and an absolutely new silk hat – for it was Friday, and Mr. Levi purchased a new hat every Friday of his life, holiday times only excepted. He breathed heavily and sniffed through his nose a good deal, as though he had just performed some Herculean physical labour. He glanced at the American millionaire with an expression in which a slight embarrassment might have been detected, but at the same time his round, red face disclosed a certain frank admiration and good nature.

"Mr. Racksole, I believe – Mr. Theodore Racksole. Proud to meet you, sir."

Such were the first words of Mr. Sampson Levi. In form they were the greeting of a third-rate chimney-sweep, but, strangely enough, Theodore Racksole liked their tone. He said to himself that here, precisely where no one would have expected to find one, was an honest man.

"Good day," said Racksole briefly. "To what do I owe the pleasure—"

"I expect your time is limited," answered Sampson Levi. "Anyhow, mine is, and so I'll come straight to the point, Mr. Racksole. I'm a plain man. I don't pretend to be a gentleman or any nonsense of that kind. I'm a stockbroker, that's what I am, and I don't care who knows it. The other night I had a ball in this hotel. It cost me a couple of thousand and odd pounds, and, by the way, I wrote out a cheque for your bill this morning. I don't like balls, but they're useful to me, and my little wife likes 'em, and so we give 'em. Now, I've nothing to say against the hotel management as regards that ball: it was very decently done, very decently, but what I want to know is this – Why did you have a private detective among my guests?"

"A private detective?" exclaimed Racksole, somewhat surprised at this charge.

"Yes," Mr. Sampson Levi said firmly, fanning himself in his chair, and gazing at Theodore Racksole with the direct earnest expression of a man having a grievance. "Yes; a private detective. It's a small matter, I know, and I dare say you think you've got a right, as proprietor of the show, to do what you like in that line; but I've just called to tell you that I object. I've called as a matter of principle. I'm not angry; it's the principle of the thing."

"My dear Mr. Levi," said Racksole, "I assure you that, having let the Gold Room to a private individual for a private entertainment, I should never dream of doing what you suggest."

"Straight?" asked Mr. Sampson Levi, using his own picturesque language.

"Straight," said Racksole smiling.

"There was a gent present at my ball that I didn't ask. I've got a wonderful memory for faces, and I know. Several fellows asked me afterwards what he was doing there. I was told by someone that he was one of your waiters, but I didn't believe that. I know nothing of the Grand Babylon; it's not quite my style of tavern, but I don't think you'd send one of your own waiters to watch my guests – unless, of course, you sent him as a waiter; and this chap didn't do any waiting, though he did his share of drinking."

"Perhaps I can throw some light on this mystery," said Racksole. "I may tell you that I was already aware that man had attended your ball uninvited."

"How did you get to know?"

"By pure chance, Mr. Levi, and not by inquiry. That man was a former waiter at this hotel – the head waiter, in fact – Jules. No doubt you have heard of him."

"Not I," said Mr. Levi positively.

"Ah!" said Racksole, "I was informed that everyone knew Jules, but it appears not. Well, be that as it may, previously to the night of your ball, I had dismissed Jules. I had ordered him never to enter the Babylon again. But on that evening I encountered him here – not in the Gold Room, but in the hotel itself. I asked him to explain his presence, and he stated he was your guest. That is all I know of the matter, Mr. Levi, and I am extremely sorry that you should have thought me capable of the enormity of placing a private detective among your guests."

"This is perfectly satisfactory to me," Mr. Sampson Levi said, after a pause.

"I only wanted an explanation, and I've got it. I was told by some pals of mine in the City I might rely on Mr. Theodore Racksole going straight to the point, and I'm glad they were right. Now as to that feller Jules, I shall make my own inquiries as to him. Might I ask you why you dismissed him?"

"I don't know why I dismissed him."

"You don't know? Oh! Come now! I'm only asking because I thought you might be able to give me a hint why he turned up uninvited at my ball. Sorry if I'm too inquisitive."

"Not at all, Mr. Levi; but I really don't know. I only sort of felt that he was a suspicious character. I dismissed him on instinct, as it were. See?"

Without answering this question Mr. Levi asked another. "If this Jules is such a well-known person," he said, "how could the feller hope to come to my ball without being recognized?"

"Give it up," said Racksole promptly.

"Well, I'll be moving on," was Mr. Sampson Levi's next remark. "Good day, and thank ye. I suppose you aren't doing anything in Kaffirs?"

Mr. Racksole smiled a negative.

"I thought not," said Levi. "Well, I never touch American rails myself, and so I reckon we sha'n't come across each other. Good day."

"Good day," said Racksole politely, following Mr. Sampson Levi to the door.

With his hand on the handle of the door, Mr. Levi stopped, and, gazing at Theodore Racksole with a shrewd, quizzical expression, remarked:

"Strange things been going on here lately, eh?"

The two men looked very hard at each other for several seconds.

"Yes," Racksole assented. "Know anything about them?"

"Well – no, not exactly," said Mr. Levi. "But I had a fancy you and I might be useful to each other; I had a kind of fancy to that effect."

"Come back and sit down again, Mr. Levi," Racksole said, attracted by the evident straightforwardness of the man's tone. "Now, how can we be of service to each other? I flatter myself I'm something of a judge of character, especially financial character, and I tell you – if you'll put your cards on the table, I'll do ditto with mine."

"Agreed," said Mr. Sampson Levi. "I'll begin by explaining my interest in your hotel. I have been expecting to receive a summons from a certain Prince Eugen of Posen to attend him here, and that summons hasn't arrived. It appears that Prince Eugen hasn't come to London at all. Now, I could have taken my dying davy that he would have been here yesterday at the latest."

"Why were you so sure?"

"Question for question," said Levi. "Let's clear the ground first, Mr. Racksole. Why did you buy this hotel? That's a conundrum that's been puzzling a lot of our fellows in the City for some days past. Why did you buy the Grand Babylon? And what is the next move to be?"

"There is no next move," answered Racksole candidly, "and I will tell you why I bought the hotel; there need be no secret about it. I bought it because of a whim." And then Theodore Racksole gave this little Jew, whom he had begun to respect, a faithful account of the transaction with Mr. Felix Babylon. "I suppose," he added, "you find a difficulty in appreciating my state of mind when I did the deal."

"Not a bit," said Mr. Levi. "I once bought an electric launch on the Thames in a very similar way, and it turned out to be one of the most satisfactory purchases I ever made. Then it's a simple accident that you own this hotel at the present moment?"

"A simple accident – all because of a beefsteak and a bottle of Bass."

"Um!" grunted Mr. Sampson Levi, stroking his triple chin.

"To return to Prince Eugen," Racksole resumed. "I was expecting His Highness here. The State apartments had been prepared for him. He was due on the very afternoon that young Dimmock died. But he never came, and I have not heard why he has failed to arrive; nor have I seen his name in the papers. What his business was in London, I don't know."

"I will tell you," said Mr. Sampson Levi, "he was coming to arrange a loan."

"A State loan?"

"No – a private loan."

"Whom from?"

"From me, Sampson Levi. You look surprised. If you'd lived in London a little longer, you'd know that I was just the person the Prince would come to. Perhaps you aren't aware that down Throgmorton Street way I'm called 'The Court Pawnbroker,' because I arrange loans for the minor, second-class Princes of Europe. I'm a stockbroker, but my real business is financing some of the little Courts of Europe. Now, I may tell you that the Hereditary Prince of Posen particularly wanted a million, and he wanted it by a certain date, and he knew that if the affair wasn't fixed up by a certain time here he wouldn't be able to get it by that certain date. That's why I'm surprised he isn't in London."

"What did he need a million for?"

"Debts," answered Sampson Levi laconically.

"His own?"

"Certainly."

"But he isn't thirty years of age?"

"What of that? He isn't the only European Prince who has run up a million of debts in a dozen years. To a Prince the thing is as easy as eating a sandwich."

"And why has he taken this sudden resolution to liquidate them?"

"Because the Emperor and the lady's parents won't let him marry till he has done so! And quite right, too! He's got to show a clean sheet, or the Princess Anna of Eckstein-Schwartzburg will never be Princess of Posen. Even now the Emperor has no idea how much Prince Eugen's debts amount to. If he had – !"

"But would not the Emperor know of this proposed loan?"

"Not necessarily at once. It could be so managed. Twig?" Mr. Sampson Levi laughed. "I've carried these little affairs through before. After marriage it might be allowed to leak out. And you know the Princess Anna's fortune is pretty big! Now, Mr. Racksole," he added, abruptly changing his tone, "where do you suppose Prince Eugen has disappeared to? Because if he doesn't turn up today he can't have that million. Today is the last day. Tomorrow the money will be appropriated, elsewhere. Of course, I'm not alone in this business, and my friends have something to say."

"You ask me where I think Prince Eugen has disappeared to?"

"I do."

"Then you think it's a disappearance?"

Sampson Levi nodded. "Putting two and two together," he said, "I do. The Dimmock business is very peculiar – very peculiar, indeed. Dimmock was a left-handed relation of the Posen family. Twig? Scarcely anyone knows that. He was made secretary and companion to Prince Aribert, just to keep him in the domestic circle. His mother was an Irishwoman, whose misfortune was that she was too beautiful. Twig?" (Mr. Sampson Levi always used this extraordinary word when he was in a communicative mood.) "My belief is that Dimmock's death has something to do with the disappearance of Prince Eugen. The only thing that passes me is this: Why should anyone want to make Prince Eugen disappear? The poor little Prince hasn't an enemy in the world. If he's been 'copped,' as they say, why has he been 'copped'? It won't do anyone any good."

"Won't it?" repeated Racksole, with a sudden flash.

"What do you mean?" asked Mr. Levi.

"I mean this: Suppose some other European pauper Prince was anxious to marry Princess Anna and her fortune, wouldn't that Prince have an interest in stopping this loan of yours to Prince Eugen? Wouldn't he have an interest in causing Prince Eugen to disappear – at any rate, for a time?"

Sampson Levi thought hard for a few moments.

"Mr. Theodore Racksole," he said at length, "I do believe you have hit on something."

Chapter XII
Rocco and Room No. 111

ON THE AFTERNOON of the same day – the interview just described had occurred in the morning – Racksole was visited by another idea, and he said to himself that he ought to have thought of it before. The conversation with Mr. Sampson Levi had continued for a considerable time, and the two men had exchanged various notions, and agreed to meet again, but the theory that Reginald Dimmock had probably been a traitor to his family – a traitor whose repentance had caused his death – had not been thoroughly discussed; the talk had tended rather to Continental politics, with a view to discovering what princely family might have an interest in the temporary disappearance of Prince Eugen. Now, as Racksole considered in detail the particular affair of Reginald Dimmock, deceased, he was struck by one point especially, to wit: Why had Dimmock and Jules manoeuvred to turn Nella Racksole out of Room No. 111 on that first night? That they had so manoeuvred, that the broken window-pane was not a mere accident, Racksole felt perfectly sure. He had felt perfectly sure all along; but the significance of the facts had not struck him. It was plain to him now that there must be something of extraordinary and peculiar importance about Room No. 111. After lunch he wandered quietly upstairs and looked at Room No. 111; that is to say, he looked at the outside of it; it happened to be occupied, but the guest was leaving that evening. The thought crossed his mind that there could be no object in gazing blankly at the outside of a room; yet he gazed; then he wandered quickly down again to the next floor, and in passing along the corridor of that floor he stopped, and with an involuntary gesture stamped his foot.

"Great Scott!" he said, "I've got hold of something – No. 111 is exactly over the State apartments."

He went to the bureau, and issued instructions that No. 111 was not to be re-let to anyone until further orders. At the bureau they gave him Nella's note, which ran thus:

> *Dearest Papa, – I am going away for a day or two on the trail of a clue.*
> *If I'm not back in three days, begin to inquire for me at Ostend. Till then leave me alone. – Your sagacious daughter, NELL.*

These few words, in Nella's large scrawling hand, filled one side of the paper. At the bottom was a P.T.O. He turned over, and read the sentence, underlined, 'P.S. – Keep an eye on Rocco.'

"I wonder what the little creature is up to?" he murmured, as he tore the letter into small fragments, and threw them into the waste-paper basket.

Then, without any delay, he took the lift down to the basement, with the object of making a preliminary inspection of Rocco in his lair. He could scarcely bring himself to believe that this suave and stately gentleman, this enthusiast of gastronomy, was concerned in the machinations of Jules and other rascals unknown. Nevertheless, from habit, he obeyed his daughter, giving her credit for a certain amount of perspicuity and cleverness.

The kitchens of the Grand Babylon Hotel are one of the wonders of Europe.

Only three years before the events now under narration Felix Babylon had had them newly installed with every device and patent that the ingenuity of two continents could supply. They covered nearly an acre of superficial space.

They were walled and floored from end to end with tiles and marble, which enabled them to be washed down every morning like the deck of a man-of-war.

Visitors were sometimes taken to see the potato-paring machine, the patent plate-dryer, the Babylon-spit (a contrivance of Felix Babylon's own), the silver-grill, the system of connected stock-pots, and other amazing phenomena of the department. Sometimes, if they were fortunate, they might also see the artist who sculptured ice into forms of men and beasts for table ornaments, or the first napkin-folder in London, or the man who daily invented fresh designs for pastry and blancmanges. Twelve chefs pursued their labours in those kitchens, helped by ninety assistant chefs, and a further army of unconsidered menials. Over all these was Rocco, supreme and unapproachable. Half-way along the suite of kitchens, Rocco had an apartment of his own, wherein he thought out those magnificent combinations, those marvellous feats of succulence and originality, which had given him his fame. Visitors never caught a glimpse of Rocco in the kitchens, though sometimes, on a special night, he would stroll nonchalantly through the dining-room, like the great man he was, to receive the compliments of the hotel habituals – people of insight who recognized his uniqueness.

Theodore Racksole's sudden and unusual appearance in the kitchen caused a little stir. He nodded to some of the chefs, but said nothing to anyone, merely wandering about amid the maze of copper utensils, and white-capped workers. At length he saw Rocco, surrounded by several admiring chefs. Rocco was bending over a freshly-roasted partridge which lay on a blue dish. He plunged a long fork into the back of the bird, and raised it in the air with his left hand. In his right he held a long glittering carving-knife. He was giving one of his world-famous exhibitions of carving. In four swift, unerring, delicate, perfect strokes he cleanly severed the limbs of the partridge. It was a wonderful achievement – how wondrous none but the really skilful carver can properly appreciate. The chefs emitted a hum of applause, and Rocco, long, lean, and graceful, retired to his own apartment. Racksole followed him. Rocco sat in a chair, one hand over his eyes; he had not noticed Theodore Racksole.

"What are you doing, M. Rocco?" the millionaire asked smiling. "Ah!" exclaimed Rocco, starting up with an apology. "Pardon! I was inventing a new mayonnaise, which I shall need for a certain menu next week."

"Do you invent these things without materials, then?" questioned Racksole.

"Certainly. I do dem in my mind. I tink dem. Why should I want materials? I know all flavours. I tink, and tink, and tink, and it is done. I write down. I give the recipe to my best chef – dere you are. I need not even taste, I know how it will taste. It is like composing music. De great composers do not compose at de piano."

"I see," said Racksole.

"It is because I work like dat dat you pay me three thousand a year," Rocco added gravely.

"Heard about Jules?" said Racksole abruptly.

"Jules?"

"Yes. He's been arrested in Ostend," the millionaire continued, lying cleverly at a venture. "They say that he and several others are implicated in a murder case – the murder of Reginald Dimmock."

"Truly?" drawled Rocco, scarcely hiding a yawn. His indifference was so superb, so gorgeous, that Racksole instantly divined that it was assumed for the occasion.

"It seems that, after all, the police are good for something. But this is the first time I ever knew them to be worth their salt. There is to be a thorough and systematic search of the hotel tomorrow," Racksole went on. "I have mentioned it to you to warn you that so far as you are concerned the search is of course merely a matter of form. You will not object to the detectives looking through your rooms?"

"Certainly not," and Rocco shrugged his shoulders.

"I shall ask you to say nothing about this to anyone," said Racksole. "The news of Jules' arrest is quite private to myself. The papers know nothing of it. You comprehend?"

Rocco smiled in his grand manner, and Rocco's master thereupon went away.

Racksole was very well satisfied with the little conversation. It was perhaps dangerous to tell a series of mere lies to a clever fellow like Rocco, and Racksole wondered how he should ultimately explain them to this great master-chef if his and Nella's suspicions should be unfounded, and nothing came of them. Nevertheless, Rocco's manner, a strange elusive something in the man's eyes, had nearly convinced Racksole that he was somehow implicated in Jules' schemes – and probably in the death of Reginald Dimmock and the disappearance of Prince Eugen of Posen.

That night, or rather about half-past one the next morning, when the last noises of the hotel's life had died down, Racksole made his way to Room 111 on the second floor. He locked the door on the inside, and proceeded to examine the place, square foot by square foot. Every now and then some creak or other sound startled him, and he listened intently for a few seconds. The bedroom was furnished in the ordinary splendid style of bedrooms at the Grand Babylon Hotel, and in that respect called for no remark. What most interested Racksole was the flooring. He pulled up the thick Oriental carpet, and peered along every plank, but could discover nothing unusual.

Then he went to the dressing-room, and finally to the bathroom, both of which opened out of the main room. But in neither of these smaller chambers was he any more successful than in the bedroom itself. Finally he came to the bath, which was enclosed in a panelled casing of polished wood, after the manner of baths. Some baths have a cupboard beneath the taps, with a door at the side, but this one appeared to have none. He tapped the panels, but not a single one of them gave forth that 'curious hollow sound' which usually betokens a secret place. Idly he turned the cold-tap of the bath, and the water began to rush in. He turned off the cold-tap and turned on the waste-tap, and as he did so his knee, which was pressing against the panelling, slipped forward. The panelling had given way, and he saw that one large panel was hinged from the inside, and caught with a hasp, also on the inside. A large space within the casing of the end of the bath was thus revealed. Before doing anything else, Racksole tried to repeat the trick with the waste-tap, but he failed; it would not work again, nor could he in any way perceive that there was any connection between the rod of the waste-tap and the hasp of the panel. Racksole could not see into the cavity within the casing, and the electric light was fixed, and could not be moved about like a candle. He felt in his pockets, and fortunately discovered a box of matches. Aided by these, he looked into the cavity, and saw nothing; nothing except a rather large hole at the far end – some three feet from the casing. With some difficulty he squeezed himself through the open panel, and took a half-kneeling, half-sitting posture within. There he struck a match, and it was a most unfortunate thing that in striking, the box being half open, he set fire to all the matches, and was half smothered in the atrocious stink of phosphorus which resulted. One match burned clear on the floor of the cavity, and, rubbing his eyes, Racksole picked it up, and looked down the hole which he had previously descried. It was a hole apparently bottomless, and about eighteen inches square. The curious part about the hole was that a rope-ladder hung down it. When he saw that rope-ladder Racksole smiled the smile of a happy man.

The match went out.

Should he make a long journey, perhaps to some distant corner of the hotel, for a fresh box of matches, or should he attempt to descend that rope-ladder in the dark? He decided on the latter course, and he was the more strongly moved thereto as he could now distinguish a faint, a very faint tinge of light at the bottom of the hole.

With infinite care he compressed himself into the well-like hole, and descended the latter. At length he arrived on firm ground, perspiring, but quite safe and quite excited. He saw now that the tinge of light came through a small hole in the wood. He put his eye to the wood, and found that he had a fine view of the State bathroom, and through the door of the State bathroom into the State bedroom. At the massive marble-topped washstand in the State bedroom a man was visible, bending over some object which lay thereon.

The man was Rocco!

Chapter XIII
In The State Bedroom

IT WAS OF COURSE plain to Racksole that the peculiar passageway which he had, at great personal inconvenience, discovered between the bathroom of No. 111 and the State bathroom on the floor below must have been specially designed by some person or persons for the purpose of keeping a nefarious watch upon the occupants of the State suite of apartments. It was a means of communication at once simple and ingenious. At that moment he could not be sure of the precise method employed for it, but he surmised that the casing of the waterpipes had been used as a 'well', while space for the pipes themselves had been found in the thickness of the ample brick walls of the Grand Babylon. The eye-hole, through which he now had a view of the bedroom, was a very minute one, and probably would scarcely be noticed from the exterior. One thing he observed concerning it, namely, that it had been made for a man somewhat taller than himself; he was obliged to stand on tiptoe in order to get his eye in the correct position. He remembered that both Jules and Rocco were distinctly above the average height; also that they were both thin men, and could have descended the well with comparative ease. Theodore Racksole, though not stout, was a well-set man with large bones.

These things flashed through his mind as he gazed, spellbound, at the mysterious movements of Rocco. The door between the bathroom and the bedroom was wide open, and his own situation was such that his view embraced a considerable portion of the bedroom, including the whole of the immense and gorgeously-upholstered bedstead, but not including the whole of the marble washstand. He could see only half of the washstand, and at intervals Rocco passed out of sight as his lithe hands moved over the object which lay on the marble. At first Theodore Racksole could not decide what this object was, but after a time, as his eyes grew accustomed to the position and the light, he made it out.

It was the body of a man. Or, rather, to be more exact, Racksole could discern the legs of a man on that half of the table which was visible to him. Involuntarily he shuddered, as the conviction forced itself upon him that Rocco had some unconscious human being helpless on that cold marble surface. The legs never moved. Therefore, the hapless creature was either asleep or under the influence of an anaesthetic – or (horrible thought!) dead.

Racksole wanted to call out, to stop by some means or other the dreadful midnight activity which was proceeding before his astonished eyes; but fortunately he restrained himself.

On the washstand he could see certain strangely-shaped utensils and instruments which Rocco used from time to time. The work seemed to Racksole to continue for interminable hours, and then at last Rocco ceased, gave a sign of satisfaction, whistled several bars from 'Cavalleria Rusticana', and came into the bath-room, where he took off his coat, and very quietly washed his hands. As he stood calmly and leisurely wiping those long fingers of his, he was less than four feet from Racksole, and the cooped-up millionaire trembled, holding his breath, lest Rocco should detect his presence behind the woodwork. But nothing happened, and Rocco returned unsuspectingly to the bedroom. Racksole saw him place some sort of white flannel garment over the prone form on the table, and then lift it bodily on to the great bed, where it lay awfully still. The hidden watcher was sure now that it was a corpse upon which Rocco had been exercising his mysterious and sinister functions.

But whose corpse? And what functions? Could this be a West End hotel, Racksole's own hotel, in the very heart of London, the best-policed city in the world? It seemed incredible, impossible; yet so it was. Once more he remembered what Felix Babylon had said to him and realized the truth of the saying anew. The proprietor of a vast and complicated establishment like the Grand Babylon could never know a tithe of the extraordinary and queer occurrences which happened daily under his very nose; the atmosphere of such a caravanserai must necessarily be an atmosphere of mystery and problems apparently inexplicable. Nevertheless, Racksole thought that Fate was carrying things with rather a high hand when she permitted his chef to spend the night hours over a man's corpse in his State bedroom, this sacred apartment which was supposed to be occupied only by individuals of Royal Blood. Racksole would not have objected to a certain amount of mystery, but he decidedly thought that there was a little too much mystery here for his taste. He thought that even Felix Babylon would have been surprised at this.

The electric chandelier in the centre of the ceiling was not lighted; only the two lights on either side of the washstand were switched on, and these did not sufficiently illuminate the features of the man on the bed to enable Racksole to see them clearly. In vain the millionaire strained his eyes; he could only make out that the corpse was probably that of a young man. Just as he was wondering what would be the best course of action to pursue, he saw Rocco with a square-shaped black box in his hand. Then the chef switched off the two electric lights, and the State bedroom was in darkness. In that swift darkness Racksole heard Rocco spring on to the bed. Another half-dozen moments of suspense, and there was a blinding flash of white, which endured for several seconds, and showed Rocco standing like an evil spirit over the corpse, the black box in one hand and a burning piece of aluminium wire in the other. The aluminium wire burnt out, and darkness followed blacker than before.

Rocco had photographed the corpse by flashlight.

But the dazzling flare which had disclosed the features of the dead man to the insensible lens of the camera had disclosed them also to Theodore Racksole. The dead man was Reginald Dimmock!

Stung into action by this discovery, Racksole tried to find the exit from his place of concealment. He felt sure that there existed some way out into the State bathroom, but he sought for it fruitlessly, groping with both hands and feet. Then he decided that he must ascend the rope-ladder, make haste for the first-floor corridor, and intercept Rocco when he left the State apartments. It was a painful and difficult business to ascend that thin and yielding ladder in such a confined space, but Racksole was managing it very nicely, and had nearly reached the top, when, by some untoward freak of chance, the ladder broke above his weight, and he slipped ignominiously down to the bottom of the wooden tube. Smothering an excusable curse, Racksole crouched, baffled. Then he saw that the force of his fall had somehow opened a trap-door at his feet. He squeezed through, pushed open another tiny door, and in another second stood in the State bathroom. He was dishevelled, perspiring, rather bewildered; but he was there. In the next second he had resumed absolute command of all his faculties.

Strange to say, he had moved so quietly that Rocco had apparently not heard him. He stepped noiselessly to the door between the bathroom and the bedroom, and stood there in silence. Rocco had switched on again the lights over the washstand and was busy with his utensils.

Racksole deliberately coughed.

Chapter XIV
Rocco Answers Some Questions

ROCCO TURNED round with the swiftness of a startled tiger, and gave Theodore Racksole one long piercing glance.

"D—n!" said Rocco, with as pure an Anglo-Saxon accent and intonation as Racksole himself could have accomplished.

The most extraordinary thing about the situation was that at this juncture Theodore Racksole did not know what to say. He was so dumbfounded by the affair, and especially by Rocco's absolute and sublime calm, that both speech and thought failed him.

"I give in," said Rocco. "From the moment you entered this cursed hotel I was afraid of you. I told Jules I was afraid of you. I knew there would be trouble with a man of your kidney, and I was right; confound it! I tell you I give in. I know when I'm beaten. I've got no revolver and no weapons of any kind. I surrender. Do what you like."

And with that Rocco sat down on a chair. It was magnificently done. Only a truly great man could have done it. Rocco actually kept his dignity.

For answer, Racksole walked slowly into the vast apartment, seized a chair, and, dragging it up to Rocco's chair, sat down opposite to him. Thus they faced each other, their knees almost touching, both in evening dress. On Rocco's right hand was the bed, with the corpse of Reginald Dimmock. On Racksole's right hand, and a little behind him, was the marble washstand, still littered with Rocco's implements. The electric light shone on Rocco's left cheek, leaving the other side of his face in shadow. Racksole tapped him on the knee twice.

"So you're another Englishman masquerading as a foreigner in my hotel," Racksole remarked, by way of commencing the interrogation.

"I'm not," answered Rocco quietly. "I'm a citizen of the United States."

"The deuce you are!" Racksole exclaimed.

"Yes, I was born at West Orange, New Jersey, New York State. I call myself an Italian because it was in Italy that I first made a name as a chef – at Rome. It is better for a great chef like me to be a foreigner. Imagine a great chef named Elihu P. Rucker. You can't imagine it. I changed my nationality for the same reason that my friend and colleague, Jules, otherwise Mr. Jackson, changed his."

"So Jules is your friend and colleague, is he?"

"He was, but from this moment he is no longer. I began to disapprove of his methods no less than a week ago, and my disapproval will now take active form."

"Will it?" said Racksole. "I calculate it just won't, Mr. Elihu P. Rucker, citizen of the United States. Before you are very much older you'll be in the kind hands of the police, and your activities, in no matter what direction, will come to an abrupt conclusion."

"It is possible," sighed Rocco.

"In the meantime, I'll ask you one or two questions for my own private satisfaction. You've acknowledged that the game is up, and you may as well answer them with as much candour as you feel yourself capable of. See?"

"I see," replied Rocco calmly, "but I guess I can't answer all questions. I'll do what I can."

"Well," said Racksole, clearing his throat, "what's the scheme all about? Tell me in a word."

"Not in a thousand words. It isn't my secret, you know."

"Why was poor little Dimmock poisoned?" The millionaire's voice softened as he looked for an instant at the corpse of the unfortunate young man.

"I don't know," said Rocco. "I don't mind informing you that I objected to that part of the business. I wasn't made aware of it till after it was done, and then I tell you it got my dander up considerable."

"You mean to say you don't know why Dimmock was done to death?"

"I mean to say I couldn't see the sense of it. Of course he – er – died, because he sort of cried off the scheme, having previously taken a share of it. I don't mind saying that much, because you probably guessed it for yourself. But I solemnly state that I have a conscientious objection to murder."

"Then it was murder?"

"It was a kind of murder," Rocco admitted. "Who did it?"

"Unfair question," said Rocco.

"Who else is in this precious scheme besides Jules and yourself?"

"Don't know, on my honour."

"Well, then, tell me this. What have you been doing to Dimmock's body?"

"How long were you in that bathroom?" Rocco parried with sublime impudence.

"Don't question me, Mr. Rucker," said Theodore Racksole. "I feel very much inclined to break your back across my knee. Therefore I advise you not to irritate me. What have you been doing to Dimmock's body?"

"I've been embalming it."

"Em – balming it."

"Certainly; Richardson's system of arterial fluid injection, as improved by myself. You weren't aware that I included the art of embalming among my accomplishments. Nevertheless, it is so."

"But why?" asked Racksole, more mystified than ever. "Why should you trouble to embalm the poor chap's corpse?"

"Can't you see? Doesn't it strike you? That corpse has to be taken care of. It contains, or rather, it did contain, very serious evidence against some person or persons unknown to the police. It may be necessary to move it about from place to place. A corpse can't be hidden for long; a corpse betrays itself. One couldn't throw it in the Thames, for it would have been found inside twelve hours. One couldn't bury it – it wasn't safe. The only thing was to keep it handy and movable, ready for emergencies. I needn't inform you that, without embalming, you can't keep a corpse handy and movable for more than four or five days. It's the kind of thing that won't keep. And so it was suggested that I should embalm it, and I did. Mind you, I still objected to the murder, but I couldn't go back on a colleague, you understand. You do understand that, don't you? Well, here you are, and here it is, and that's all."

Rocco leaned back in his chair as though he had said everything that ought to be said. He closed his eyes to indicate that so far as he was concerned the conversation was also closed. Theodore Racksole stood up.

"I hope," said Rocco, suddenly opening his eyes, "I hope you'll call in the police without any delay. It's getting late, and I don't like going without my night's rest."

"Where do you suppose you'll get a night's rest?" Racksole asked.

"In the cells, of course. Haven't I told you I know when I'm beaten. I'm not so blind as not to be able to see that there's at any rate a prima facie case against me. I expect I shall get off with a year or two's imprisonment as accessory after the fact – I think that's what they call it. Anyhow, I shall be in a position to prove that I am not implicated in the murder of this unfortunate nincompoop." He pointed, with a strange, scornful gesture of his elbow, to the bed. "And now, shall we go? Everyone is asleep, but there will be a policeman within call of the watchman in the portico. I am at your service. Let us go down together, Mr. Racksole. I give you my word to go quietly."

"Stay a moment," said Theodore Racksole curtly; "there is no hurry. It won't do you any harm to forego another hour's sleep, especially as you will have no work to do tomorrow. I have one or two more questions to put to you."

"Well?" Rocco murmured, with an air of tired resignation, as if to say, "What must be must be."

"Where has Dimmock's corpse been during the last three or four days, since he – died?"

"Oh!" answered Rocco, apparently surprised at the simplicity of the question. "It's been in my room, and one night it was on the roof; once it went out of the hotel as luggage, but it came back the next day as a case of Demerara sugar. I forget where else it has been, but it's been kept perfectly safe and treated with every consideration."

"And who contrived all these manoeuvres?" asked Racksole as calmly as he could.

"I did. That is to say, I invented them and I saw that they were carried out. You see, the suspicions of your police obliged me to be particularly spry."

"And who carried them out?"

"Ah! that would be telling tales. But I don't mind assuring you that my accomplices were innocent accomplices. It is absurdly easy for a man like me to impose on underlings – absurdly easy."

"What did you intend to do with the corpse ultimately?" Racksole pursued his inquiry with immovable countenance.

"Who knows?" said Rocco, twisting his beautiful moustache. "That would have depended on several things – on your police, for instance. But probably in the end we should have restored this mortal clay" – again he jerked his elbow – "to the man's sorrowing relatives."

"Do you know who the relatives are?"

"Certainly. Don't you? If you don't I need only hint that Dimmock had a Prince for his father."

"It seems to me," said Racksole, with cold sarcasm, "that you behaved rather clumsily in choosing this bedroom as the scene of your operations."

"Not at all," said Rocco. "There was no other apartment so suitable in the whole hotel. Who would have guessed that anything was going on here? It was the very place for me."

"I guessed," said Racksole succinctly.

"Yes, you guessed, Mr. Racksole. But I had not counted on you. You are the only smart man in the business. You are an American citizen, and I hadn't reckoned to have to deal with that class of person."

"Apparently I frightened you this afternoon?"

"Not in the least."

"You were not afraid of a search?"

"I knew that no search was intended. I knew that you were trying to frighten me. You must really credit me with a little sagacity and insight, Mr. Racksole. Immediately you began to talk to me in the kitchen this afternoon I felt you were on the track. But I was not frightened. I merely decided that there was no time to be lost – that I must act quickly. I did act quickly, but, it seems, not quickly enough. I grant that your rapidity exceeded mine. Let us go downstairs, I beg."

Rocco rose and moved towards the door. With an instinctive action Racksole rushed forward and seized him by the shoulder.

"No tricks!" said Racksole. "You're in my custody and don't forget it."

Rocco turned on his employer a look of gentle, dignified scorn. "Have I not informed you," he said, "that I have the intention of going quietly?"

Racksole felt almost ashamed for the moment. It flashed across him that a man can be great, even in crime.

"What an ineffable fool you were," said Racksole, stopping him at the threshold, "with your talents, your unique talents, to get yourself mixed up in an affair of this kind. You are ruined. And, by Jove! you were a great man in your own line."

"Mr. Racksole," said Rocco very quickly, "that is the truest word you have spoken this night. I was a great man in my own line. And I am an ineffable fool. Alas!" He brought his long arms to his sides with a thud.

"Why did you do it?"

"I was fascinated – fascinated by Jules. He, too, is a great man. We had great opportunities, here in the Grand Babylon. It was a great game. It was worth the candle. The prizes were enormous. You would admit these things if you knew the facts. Perhaps some day you will know them, for you are a fairly clever person at getting to the root of a matter. Yes, I was blinded, hypnotized."

"And now you are ruined."

"Not ruined, not ruined. Afterwards, in a few years, I shall come up again. A man of genius like me is never ruined till he is dead. Genius is always forgiven. I shall be forgiven. Suppose I am sent to prison. When I emerge I shall be no gaol-bird. I shall be Rocco – the great Rocco. And half the hotels in Europe will invite me to join them."

"Let me tell you, as man to man, that you have achieved your own degradation. There is no excuse."

"I know it," said Rocco. "Let us go."

Racksole was distinctly and notably impressed by this man – by this master spirit to whom he was to have paid a salary at the rate of three thousand pounds a year. He even felt sorry for him. And so, side by side, the captor and the captured, they passed into the vast deserted corridor of the hotel.

Rocco stopped at the grating of the first lift.

"It will be locked," said Racksole. "We must use the stairs tonight."

"But I have a key. I always carry one," said Rocco, and he pulled one out of his pocket, and, unfastening the iron screen, pushed it open. Racksole smiled at his readiness and aplomb.

"After you," said Rocco, bowing in his finest manner, and Racksole stepped into the lift.

With the swiftness of lighting Rocco pushed forward the iron screen, which locked itself automatically. Theodore Racksole was hopelessly a prisoner within the lift, while Rocco stood free in the corridor.

"Goodbye, Mr. Racksole," he remarked suavely, bowing again, lower than before. "Goodbye: I hate to take a mean advantage of you in this fashion, but really you must allow that you have been very simple. You are a clever man, as I have already said, up to a certain point. It is past that point that my own cleverness comes in. Again, goodbye. After all, I shall have no rest tonight, but perhaps even that will be better that sleeping in a police cell. If you make a great noise you may wake someone and ultimately get released from this lift. But I advise you to compose yourself, and wait till morning. It will be more dignified. For the third time, goodbye."

And with that Rocco, without hastening, walked down the corridor and so out of sight.

Racksole said never a word. He was too disgusted with himself to speak. He clenched his fists, and put his teeth together, and held his breath. In the silence he could hear the dwindling sound of Rocco's footsteps on the thick carpet.

It was the greatest blow of Racksole's life.

The next morning the high-born guests of the Grand Babylon were aroused by a rumour that by some accident the millionaire proprietor of the hotel had remained all night locked up in the lift. It was also stated that Rocco had quarrelled with his new master and incontinently left the place. A duchess said that Rocco's departure would mean the ruin of the hotel, whereupon her husband advised her not to talk nonsense.

As for Racksole, he sent a message for the detective in charge of the Dimmock affair, and bravely told him the happenings of the previous night.

The narration was a decided ordeal to a man of Racksole's temperament.

"A strange story!" commented Detective Marshall, and he could not avoid a smile. "The climax was unfortunate, but you have certainly got some valuable facts."

Racksole said nothing.

"I myself have a clue," added the detective. "When your message arrived I was just coming up to see you. I want you to accompany me to a certain spot not far from here. Will you come, now, at once?"

"With pleasure," said Racksole.

At that moment a page entered with a telegram. Racksole opened it read:

"Please come instantly. Nella. Hotel Wellington, Ostend."

He looked at his watch.

"I can't come,' he said to the detective. I'm going to Ostend."

"To Ostend?"

"Yes, now."

"But really, Mr. Racksole," protested the detective. "My business is urgent."

"So's mine," said Racksole.

In ten minutes he was on his way to Victoria Station.

Chapter XV
End of the Yacht Adventure

WE MUST NOW return to Nella Racksole and Prince Aribert of Posen on board the yacht without a name. The Prince's first business was to make Jules, otherwise Mr. Tom Jackson, perfectly secure by means of several pieces of rope. Although Mr. Jackson had been stunned into a complete unconsciousness, and there was a contused wound under his ear, no one could say how soon he might not come to himself and get very violent. So the Prince, having tied his arms and legs, made him fast to a stanchion.

"I hope he won't die," said Nella. "He looks very white."

"The Mr. Jacksons of this world," said Prince Aribert sententiously, "never die till they are hung. By the way, I wonder how it is that no one has interfered with us. Perhaps they are discreetly afraid of my revolver – of your revolver, I mean."

Both he and Nella glanced up at the imperturbable steersman, who kept the yacht's head straight out to sea. By this time they were about a couple of miles from the Belgian shore.

Addressing him in French, the Prince ordered the sailor to put the yacht about, and make again for Ostend Harbour, but the fellow took no notice whatever of the summons. The Prince raised the revolver, with the idea of frightening the steersman, and then the man began to talk rapidly in a mixture of French and Flemish. He said that he had received Jules' strict orders not to interfere in any way, no matter what might happen on the deck of the yacht. He was the captain of the yacht, and he had to make for a certain English port, the name of which he could not divulge: he was to keep the vessel at full steam ahead under any and all circumstances. He seemed to be a very big, a very strong, and a very determined man, and the Prince was at a loss what course of action to pursue. He asked several more questions, but the only effect of them was to render the man taciturn and ill-humoured.

In vain Prince Aribert explained that Miss Nella Racksole, daughter of millionaire Racksole, had been abducted by Mr. Tom Jackson; in vain he flourished the revolver threateningly; the surly but courageous captain said merely that that had nothing to do with him; he had instructions, and he should carry them out. He sarcastically begged to remind his interlocutor that he was the captain of the yacht.

"It won't do to shoot him, I suppose," said the Prince to Nella. "I might bore a hole into his leg, or something of that kind."

"It's rather risky, and rather hard on the poor captain, with his extraordinary sense of duty," said Nella. "And, besides, the whole crew might turn on us. No, we must think of something else."

"I wonder where the crew is," said the Prince.

Just then Mr. Jackson, prone and bound on the deck, showed signs of recovering from his swoon. His eyes opened, and he gazed vacantly around. At length he caught sight of the Prince, who approached him with the revolver well in view.

"It's you, is it?" he murmured faintly. "What are you doing on board? Who's tied me up like this?"

"See here!" replied the Prince, "I don't want to have any arguments, but this yacht must return to Ostend at once, where you will be given up to the authorities."

"Really!" snarled Mr. Tom Jackson. "Shall I!" Then he called out in French to the man at the wheel, "Hi Andrea! let these two be put off in the dinghy."

It was a peculiar situation. Certain of nothing but the possession of Nella's revolver, the Prince scarcely knew whether to carry the argument further, and with stronger measures, or to accept the situation with as much dignity as the circumstances would permit.

"Let us take the dinghy," said Nella; "we can row ashore in an hour."

He felt that she was right. To leave the yacht in such a manner seemed somewhat ignominious, and it certainly involved the escape of that profound villain, Mr. Thomas Jackson. But what else could be done? The Prince and Nella constituted one party on the vessel; they knew their own strength, but they did not know the strength of their opponents. They held the hostile ringleader bound and captive, but this man had proved himself capable of giving orders, and even to gag him would not help them if the captain of the yacht persisted in his obstinate course. Moreover, there was a distinct objection to promiscuous shooting. The Prince felt that there was no knowing how promiscuous shooting might end.

"We will take the dinghy," said the Prince quickly, to the captain.

A bell rang below, and a sailor and the Negro boy appeared on deck. The pulsations of the screw grew less rapid. The yacht stopped. The dinghy was lowered. As the Prince and Nella prepared to descend into the little cock-boat Mr. Tom Jackson addressed Nella, all bound as he lay.

"Goodbye," he said, "I shall see you again, never fear."

In another moment they were in the dinghy, and the dinghy was adrift. The yacht's screw churned the water, and the beautiful vessel slipped away from them. As it receded a figure appeared at the stem. It was Mr. Thomas Jackson.

He had been released by his minions. He held a white handkerchief to his ear, and offered a calm, enigmatic smile to the two forlorn but victorious occupants of the dinghy. Jules had been defeated for once in his life; or perhaps it would be more just to say that he had been out-manoeuvred. Men like Jules are incapable of being defeated. It was characteristic of his luck that now, in the very hour when he had been caught red-handed in a serious crime against society, he should be effecting a leisurely escape – an escape which left no clue behind.

The sea was utterly calm and blue in the morning sun. The dinghy rocked itself lazily in the swell of the yacht's departure. As the mist cleared away the outline of the shore became more distinct, and it appeared as if Ostend was distant scarcely a cable's length. The white dome of the great Kursaal glittered in the pale turquoise sky, and the smoke of steamers in the harbour could be plainly distinguished. On the offing was a crowd of brown-sailed fishing luggers returning with the night's catch. The many-hued bathing-vans could be counted on the distant beach. Everything seemed perfectly normal. It was difficult for either Nella or her companion to realize that anything extraordinary had happened within the last hour. Yet there was the yacht, not a mile off, to prove to them that something very extraordinary had, in fact, happened. The yacht was no vision, nor was that sinister watching figure at its stern a vision, either.

"I suppose Jules was too surprised and too feeble to inquire how I came to be on board his yacht," said the Prince, taking the oars.

"Oh! How did you?" asked Nella, her face lighting up. "Really, I had almost forgotten that part of the affair."

"I must begin at the beginning and it will take some time," answered the Prince. "Had we not better postpone the recital till we get ashore?"

"I will row and you shall talk," said Nella. "I want to know now."

He smiled happily at her, but gently declined to yield up the oars.

"Is it not sufficient that I am here?" he said.

"It is sufficient, yes," she replied, "but I want to know."

With a long, easy stroke he was pulling the dinghy shorewards. She sat in the stern-sheets.

"There is no rudder," he remarked, "so you must direct me. Keep the boat's head on the lighthouse. The tide seems to be running in strongly; that will help us. The people on shore will think that we have only been for a little early morning excursion."

"Will you kindly tell me how it came about that you were able to save my life, Prince?" she said.

"Save your life, Miss Racksole? I didn't save your life; I merely knocked a man down."

"You saved my life," she repeated. "That villain would have stopped at nothing. I saw it in his eye."

"Then you were a brave woman, for you showed no fear of death." His admiring gaze rested full on her. For a moment the oars ceased to move.

She gave a gesture of impatience.

"It happened that I saw you last night in your carriage," he said. "The fact is, I had not had the audacity to go to Berlin with my story. I stopped in Ostend to see whether I could do a little detective work on my own account.

It was a piece of good luck that I saw you. I followed the carriage as quickly as I could, and I just caught a glimpse of you as you entered that awful house. I knew that Jules had something to do with that house. I guessed what you were doing. I was afraid for you. Fortunately I had surveyed the house pretty thoroughly. There is an entrance to it at the back, from a narrow lane. I made my way there. I got into the yard at the back, and I stood under the window of the room where you had the interview with Miss Spencer. I heard everything that was said. It was a courageous enterprise on your part to follow Miss Spencer from the Grand Babylon to Ostend. Well, I dared not force an entrance, lest I might precipitate matters too suddenly, and involve both of us in a difficulty. I merely kept watch. Ah, Miss Racksole! you were magnificent with Miss Spencer; as I say, I could hear every word, for the window was slightly open. I felt that you needed no assistance from me. And then she cheated you with a trick, and the revolver came flying through the window. I picked it up, I thought it would probably be useful. There was a silence. I did not guess at first that you had fainted. I thought that you had escaped. When I found out the truth it was too late for me to intervene. There were two men, both desperate, besides Miss Spencer—"

"Who was the other man?" asked Nella.

"I do not know. It was dark. They drove away with you to the harbour. Again I followed. I saw them carry you on board. Before the yacht weighed anchor I managed to climb unobserved into the dinghy. I lay down full length in it, and no one suspected that I was there. I think you know the rest."

"Was the yacht all ready for sea?"

"The yacht was all ready for sea. The captain fellow was on the bridge, and steam was up."

"Then they expected me! How could that be?"

"They expected some one. I do not think they expected you."

"Did the second man go on board?"

"He helped to carry you along the gangway, but he came back again to the carriage. He was the driver."

"And no one else saw the business?"

"The quay was deserted. You see, the last steamer had arrived for the night."

There was a brief silence, and then Nella ejaculated, under her breath.

"Truly, it is a wonderful world!"

And it was a wonderful world for them, though scarcely perhaps, in the sense which Nella Racksole had intended. They had just emerged from a highly disconcerting experience. Among other minor inconveniences, they had had no breakfast. They were out in the sea in a tiny boat. Neither of them knew what the day might bring forth. The man, at least, had the most serious anxieties for the safety of his Royal nephew. And yet – and yet – neither of them wished that that voyage of the little boat on the summer tide should come to an end. Each, perhaps unconsciously, had a vague desire that it might last for ever, he lazily pulling, she directing his course at intervals by a movement of her distractingly pretty head. How was this condition of affairs to be explained? Well, they were both young; they both had superb health, and all the ardour of youth; and – they were together.

The boat was very small indeed; her face was scarcely a yard from his. She, in his eyes, surrounded by the glamour of beauty and vast wealth; he, in her eyes, surrounded by the glamour of masculine intrepidity and the brilliance of a throne.

But all voyages come to an end, either at the shore or at the bottom of the sea, and at length the dinghy passed between the stone jetties of the harbour. The Prince rowed to the nearest steps, tied up the boat, and they landed. It was six o'clock in the morning, and a day of gorgeous sunlight had opened. Few people were about at that early hour.

"And now, what next?" said the Prince. "I must take you to an hotel."

"I am in your hands," she acquiesced, with a smile which sent the blood racing through his veins. He perceived now that she was tired and overcome, suffering from a sudden and natural reaction.

At the Hotel Wellington the Prince told the sleepy door-keeper that they had come by the early train from Bruges, and wanted breakfast at once. It was absurdly early, but a common English sovereign will work wonders in any Belgian hotel, and in a very brief time Nella and the Prince were breakfasting on the verandah of the hotel upon chocolate that had been specially and hastily brewed for them.

"I never tasted such excellent chocolate," claimed the Prince.

The statement was wildly untrue, for the Hotel Wellington is not celebrated for its chocolate. Nevertheless Nella replied enthusiastically, "Nor I."

Then there was a silence, and Nella, feeling possibly that she had been too ecstatic, remarked in a very matter-of-fact tone: "I must telegraph to Papa instantly."

Thus it was that Theodore Racksole received the telegram which drew him away from Detective Marshall.

Chapter XVI
The Woman with the Red Hat

"THERE IS ONE THING, Prince, that we have just got to settle straight off," said Theodore Racksole.

They were all three seated – Racksole, his daughter, and Prince Aribert – round a dinner table in a private room at the Hotel Wellington. Racksole had duly arrived by the afternoon boat, and had been met on the quay by the other two. They had dined early, and Racksole had heard the full story of the adventures by sea and land of Nella and the Prince. As to his own adventure of the previous night he said very little, merely explaining, with as little detail as possible, that Dimmock's body had come to light.

"What is that?" asked the Prince, in answer to Racksole's remark.

"We have got to settle whether we shall tell the police at once all that has occurred, or whether we shall proceed on our own responsibility. There can be no doubt as to which course we ought to pursue. Every consideration of prudence points to the advisability of taking the police into our confidence, and leaving the matter entirely in their hands."

"Oh, Papa!" Nella burst out in her pouting, impulsive way. "You surely can't think of such a thing. Why, the fun has only just begun."

"Do you call last night fun?" questioned Racksole, gazing at her solemnly.

"Yes, I do," she said promptly. "Now."

"Well, I don't," was the millionaire's laconic response; but perhaps he was thinking of his own situation in the lift.

"Do you not think we might investigate a little further," said the Prince judiciously, as he cracked a walnut, "just a little further – and then, if we fail to accomplish anything, there would still be ample opportunity to consult the police?"

"How do you suggest we should begin?" asked Racksole.

"Well, there is the house which Miss Racksole so intrepidly entered last evening" – he gave her the homage of an admiring glance; "you and I, Mr. Racksole, might examine that abode in detail."

"Tonight?"

"Certainly. We might do something."

"We might do too much."

"For example?"

"We might shoot someone, or get ourselves mistaken for burglars. If we outstepped the law, it would be no excuse for us that we had been acting in a good cause."

"True," said the Prince. "Nevertheless—" He stopped.

"Nevertheless you have a distaste for bringing the police into the business. You want the hunt all to yourself. You are on fire with the ardour of the chase. Is not that it? Accept the advice of an older man, Prince, and sleep on this affair. I have little fancy for nocturnal escapades two nights together. As for you, Nella, off with you to bed. The Prince and I will have a yarn over such fluids as can be obtained in this hole."

"Papa," she said, "you are perfectly horrid tonight."

"Perhaps I am," he said. "Decidedly I am very cross with you for coming over here all alone. It was monstrous. If I didn't happen to be the most foolish of parents – There! Goodnight. It's nine o'clock. The Prince, I am sure, will excuse you."

If Nella had not really been very tired Prince Aribert might have been the witness of a good-natured but stubborn conflict between the millionaire and his spirited offspring. As it was, Nella departed with surprising docility, and the two men were left alone.

"Now," said Racksole suddenly, changing his tone, "I fancy that after all I'm your man for a little amateur investigation tonight. And, if I must speak the exact truth, I think that to sleep on this affair would be about the very worst thing we could do. But I was anxious to keep Nella out of harm's way at any rate till tomorrow. She is a very difficult creature to manage, Prince, and I may warn you," he laughed grimly, "that if we do succeed in doing anything tonight we shall catch it from her ladyship in the morning. Are you ready to take that risk?"

"I am," the Prince smiled. "But Miss Racksole is a young lady of quite remarkable nerve."

"She is," said Racksole drily. "I wish sometimes she had less."

"I have the highest admiration for Miss Racksole," said the Prince, and he looked Miss Racksole's father full in the face.

"You honour us, Prince," Racksole observed. "Let us come to business. Am I right in assuming that you have a reason for keeping the police out of this business, if it can possibly be done?"

"Yes," said the Prince, and his brow clouded. "I am very much afraid that my poor nephew has involved himself in some scrape that he would wish not to be divulged."

"Then you do not believe that he is the victim of foul play?"

"I do not."

"And the reason, if I may ask it?"

"Mr. Racksole, we speak in confidence – is it not so? Some years ago my foolish nephew had an affair – an affair with a feminine star of the Berlin stage. For anything I know, the lady may have been the very pattern of her sex, but where a reigning Prince is concerned scandal cannot be avoided in such a matter. I had thought that the affair was quite at an end, since my nephew's betrothal to Princess Anna of Eckstein-Schwartzburg is shortly to be announced. But yesterday I saw the lady to whom I have referred driving on the Digue. The coincidence of her presence here with my nephew's disappearance is too extraordinary to be disregarded."

"But how does this theory square with the murder of Reginald Dimmock?"

"It does not square with it. My idea is that the murder of poor Dimmock and the disappearance of my nephew are entirely unconnected – unless, indeed, this Berlin actress is playing into the hands of the murderers. I had not thought of that."

"Then what do you propose to do tonight?"

"I propose to enter the house which Miss Racksole entered last night and to find out something definite."

"I concur," said Racksole. "I shall heartily enjoy it. But let me tell you, Prince, and pardon me for speaking bluntly, your surmise is incorrect. I would wager a hundred thousand dollars that Prince Eugen has been kidnapped."

"What grounds have you for being so sure?"

"Ah!" said Racksole, "that is a long story. Let me begin by asking you this. Are you aware that your nephew, Prince Eugen, owes a million of money?"

"A million of money!" cried Prince Aribert astonished. "It is impossible!"

"Nevertheless, he does," said Racksole calmly. Then he told him all he had learnt from Mr. Sampson Levi.

"What have you to say to that?" Racksole ended. Prince Aribert made no reply.

"What have you to say to that?" Racksole insisted.

"Merely that Eugen is ruined, even if he is alive."

"Not at all," Racksole returned with cheerfulness. "Not at all. We shall see about that. The special thing that I want to know just now from you is this: Has any previous application ever been made for the hand of the Princess Anna?"

"Yes. Last year. The King of Bosnia sued for it, but his proposal was declined."

"Why?"

"Because my nephew was considered to be a more suitable match for her."

"Not because the personal character of his Majesty of Bosnia is scarcely of the brightest?"

"No. Unfortunately it is usually impossible to consider questions of personal character when a royal match is concerned."

"Then, if for any reason the marriage of Princess Anna with your nephew was frustrated, the King of Bosnia would have a fair chance in that quarter?"

"He would. The political aspect of things would be perfectly satisfactory."

"Thanks!" said Racksole. "I will wager another hundred thousand dollars that someone in Bosnia – I don't accuse the King himself – is at the bottom of this business. The methods of Balkan politicians have always been half-Oriental. Let us go."

"Where?"

"To this precious house of Nella's adventure."

"But surely it is too early?"

"So it is," said Racksole, "and we shall want a few things, too. For instance, a dark lantern. I think I will go out and forage for a lantern."

"And a revolver?" suggested Prince Aribert.

"Does it mean revolvers?" The millionaire laughed. "It may come to that."

"Here you are, then, my friend," said Racksole, and he pulled one out of his hip pocket. "And yours?"

"I," said the Prince, "I have your daughter's."

"The deuce you have!" murmured Racksole to himself.

It was then half past nine. They decided that it would be impolitic to begin their operations till after midnight. There were three hours to spare.

"Let us go and see the gambling," Racksole suggested. "We might encounter the Berlin lady."

The suggestion, in the first instance, was not made seriously, but it appeared to both men that they might do worse than spend the intervening time in the gorgeous saloon of the Kursaal, where, in the season, as much money is won and lost as at Monte Carlo. It was striking ten o'clock as they entered the rooms. There was a large company present – a company which included some of the most notorious persons in Europe. In that multifarious assemblage all were equal. The electric light shone coldly and impartially on the just and on the unjust, on the fool and the knave, on the European and the Asiatic. As usual, women monopolized the best places at the tables.

The scene was familiar enough to Prince Aribert, who had witnessed it frequently at Monaco, but Theodore Racksole had never before entered any European gaming palace; he had only the haziest idea of the rules of play, and he was at once interested. For some time they watched the play at the table which happened to be nearest to them. Racksole never moved his lips.

With his eyes glued on the table, and ears open for every remark, of the players and the croupier, he took his first lesson in roulette. He saw a mere youth win fifteen thousand francs, which were stolen in the most barefaced manner by a rouged girl scarcely older than the youth; he saw two old gamesters stake their coins, and lose, and walk quietly out of the place; he saw the bank win fifty thousand francs at a single turn.

"This is rather good fun," he said at length, "but the stakes are too small to make it really exciting. I'll try my luck, just for the experience. I'm bound to win."

"Why?" asked the Prince.

"Because I always do, in games of chance," Racksole answered with gay confidence. "It is my fate. Then tonight, you must remember, I shall be a beginner, and you know the tyro's luck."

In ten minutes the croupier of that table was obliged to suspend operations pending the arrival of a further supply of coin.

"What did I tell you?" said Racksole, leading the way to another table further up the room. A hundred curious glances went after him. One old woman, whose gay attire suggested a false youthfulness, begged him in French to stake a five-franc piece for her. She offered him the coin. He took it, and gave her a hundred-franc note in exchange. She clutched the crisp rustling paper, and with hysterical haste scuttled back to her own table.

At the second table there was a considerable air of excitement. In the forefront of the players was a woman in a low-cut evening dress of black silk and a large red picture hat. Her age appeared to be about twenty-eight; she had dark eyes, full lips, and a distinctly Jewish nose. She was handsome, but her beauty was of that forbidding, sinister order which is often called Junoesque. This woman was the centre of attraction. People said to each other that she had won a hundred and sixty thousand francs that day at the table.

"You were right," Prince Aribert whispered to Theodore Racksole; "that is the Berlin lady."

"The deuce she is! Has she seen you? Will she know you?"

"She would probably know me, but she hasn't looked up yet."

"Keep behind her, then. I propose to find her a little occupation." By dint of a carefully-exercised diplomacy, Racksole manoeuvred himself into a seat opposite to the lady in the red hat. The fame of his success at the other table had followed him, and people regarded him as a serious and formidable player. In the first turn the lady put a thousand francs on double zero; Racksole put a hundred on number nineteen and a thousand on the odd numbers.

Nineteen won. Racksole received four thousand four hundred francs. Nine times in succession Racksole backed number nineteen and the odd numbers; nine times the lady backed double zero. Nine times Racksole won and the lady lost. The other players, perceiving that the affair had resolved itself into a duel, stood back for the most part and watched those two. Prince Aribert never stirred from his position behind the great red hat. The game continued. Racksole lost trifles from time to time, but ninety-nine hundredths of the luck was with him. As an English spectator at the table remarked, "he couldn't do wrong." When midnight struck the lady in the red hat was reduced to a thousand francs. Then she fell into a winning vein for half an hour, but at one o'clock her resources were exhausted. Of the hundred and sixty thousand francs which she was reputed to have had early in the evening, Racksole held about ninety thousand, and the bank had the rest.

It was a calamity for the Juno of the red hat. She jumped up, stamped her foot, and hurried from the room. At a discreet distance Racksole and the Prince pursued her.

"It might be well to ascertain her movements," said Racksole.

Outside, in the glare of the great arc lights, and within sound of the surf which beats always at the very foot of the Kursaal, the Juno of the red hat summoned a fiacre and drove rapidly away. Racksole and the Prince took an open carriage and started in pursuit. They had not, however, travelled more than half a mile when Prince Aribert stopped the carriage, and, bidding Racksole get out, paid the driver and dismissed him.

"I feel sure I know where she is going," he explained, "and it will be better for us to follow on foot."

"You mean she is making for the scene of last night's affair?" said Racksole.

"Exactly. We shall – what you call, kill two birds with one stone."

Prince Aribert's guess was correct. The lady's carriage stopped in front of the house where Nella Racksole and Miss Spencer had had their interview on the previous evening, and the lady vanished into the building just as the two men appeared at the end of the street. Instead of proceeding along that street, the Prince led Racksole to the lane which gave on to the backs of the houses, and he counted the houses as they went up the lane. In a few minutes they had burglariously climbed over a wall, and crept, with infinite caution, up a long, narrow piece of ground – half garden, half paved yard, till they crouched under a window – a window which was shielded by curtains, but which had been left open a little.

"Listen," said the Prince in his lightest whisper, "they are talking."

"Who?"

"The Berlin lady and Miss Spencer. I'm sure it's Miss Spencer's voice."

Racksole boldly pushed the french window a little wider open, and put his ear to the aperture, through which came a beam of yellow light.

"Take my place," he whispered to the Prince, "they're talking German. You'll understand better."

Silently they exchanged places under the window, and the Prince listened intently.

"Then you refuse?" Miss Spencer's visitor was saying.

There was no answer from Miss Spencer.

"Not even a thousand francs? I tell you I've lost the whole twenty-five thousand."

Again no answer.

"Then I'll tell the whole story," the lady went on, in an angry rush of words. "I did what I promised to do. I enticed him here, and you've got him safe in your vile cellar, poor little man, and you won't give me a paltry thousand francs."

"You have already had your price." The words were Miss Spencer's. They fell cold and calm on the night air.

"I want another thousand."

"I haven't it."

"Then we'll see."

Prince Aribert heard a rustle of flying skirts; then another movement – a door banged, and the beam of light through the aperture of the window suddenly disappeared. He pushed the window wide open. The room was in darkness, and apparently empty.

"Now for that lantern of yours," he said eagerly to Theodore Racksole, after he had translated to him the conversation of the two women, Racksole produced the dark lantern from the capacious pocket of his dust coat, and lighted it. The ray flashed about the ground.

"What is it?" exclaimed Prince Aribert with a swift cry, pointing to the ground. The lantern threw its light on a perpendicular grating at their feet, through which could be discerned a cellar.

They both knelt down, and peered into the subterranean chamber. On a broken chair a young man sat listlessly with closed eyes, his head leaning heavily forward on his chest.

In the feeble light of the lantern he had the livid and ghastly appearance of a corpse.

"Who can it be?" said Racksole.

"It is Eugen," was the Prince's low answer.

Chapter XVII
The Release of Prince Eugen

"EUGEN," Prince Aribert called softly. At the sound of his own name the young man in the cellar feebly raised his head and stared up at the grating which separated him from his two rescuers. But his features showed no recognition. He gazed in an aimless, vague, silly manner for a few seconds, his eyes blinking under the glare of the lantern, and then his head slowly drooped again on to his chest. He was dressed in a dark tweed travelling suit, and Racksole observed that one sleeve – the left – was torn across the upper part of the cuff, and that there were stains of dirt on the left shoulder. A soiled linen collar, which had lost all its starch and was half unbuttoned, partially encircled the captive's neck; his brown boots were unlaced; a cap, a handkerchief, a portion of a watch-chain, and a few gold coins lay on the floor. Racksole flashed the lantern into the corners of the cellar, but he could discover no other furniture except the chair on which the Hereditary Prince of Posen sat and a small deal table on which were a plate and a cup.

"Eugen," cried Prince Aribert once more, but this time his forlorn nephew made no response whatever, and then Aribert added in a low voice to Racksole: "Perhaps he cannot see us clearly."

"But he must surely recognize your voice," said Racksole, in a hard, gloomy tone. There was a pause, and the two men above ground looked at each other hesitatingly. Each knew that they must enter that cellar and get Prince Eugen out of it, and each was somehow afraid to take the next step.

"Thank God he is not dead!" said Aribert.

"He may be worse than dead!" Racksole replied.

"Worse than— What do you mean?"

"I mean – he may be mad."

"Come," Aribert almost shouted, with a sudden access of energy – a wild impulse for action. And, snatching the lantern from Racksole, he rushed into the dark room where they had heard the conversation of Miss Spencer and the lady in the red hat. For a moment Racksole did not stir from the threshold of the window. "Come," Prince Aribert repeated, and there was an imperious command in his utterance. "What are you afraid of?"

"I don't know," said Racksole, feeling stupid and queer; "I don't know."

Then he marched heavily after Prince Aribert into the room. On the mantelpiece were a couple of candles which had been blown out, and in a mechanical, unthinking way, Racksole lighted them, and the two men glanced round the room. It presented no peculiar features: it was just an ordinary room, rather small, rather mean, rather shabby, with an ugly wallpaper and ugly pictures in ugly frames. Thrown over a chair was a man's evening-dress jacket. The door was closed. Prince Aribert turned the knob, but he could not open it.

"It's locked," he said. "Evidently they know we're here."

"Nonsense," said Racksole brusquely; "how can they know?" And, taking hold of the knob, he violently shook the door, and it opened. "I told you it wasn't locked," he added, and this small success of opening the door seemed to steady the man. It was a curious psychological effect, this terrorizing (for it amounted to that) of two courageous full-grown men by the mere apparition of a helpless creature in a cellar. Gradually they both recovered from it. The next moment they were out in the passage which led to the front door of the house. The front door stood open. They looked into the street, up and down, but there was not a soul in sight. The street, lighted by three gas-lamps only, seemed strangely sinister and mysterious.

"She has gone, that's clear," said Racksole, meaning the woman with the red hat.

"And Miss Spencer after her, do you think?" questioned Aribert.

"No. She would stay. She would never dare to leave. Let us find the cellar steps."

The cellar steps were happily not difficult to discover, for in moving a pace backwards Prince Aribert had a narrow escape of precipitating himself to the bottom of them. The lantern showed that they were built on a curve.

Silently Racksole resumed possession of the lantern and went first, the Prince close behind him. At the foot was a short passage, and in this passage crouched the figure of a woman. Her eyes threw back the rays of the lantern, shining like a cat's at midnight. Then, as the men went nearer, they saw that it was Miss Spencer who barred their way. She seemed half to kneel on the stone floor, and in one hand she held what at first appeared to be a dagger, but which proved to be nothing more romantic than a rather long bread-knife.

"I heard you, I heard you," she exclaimed. "Get back; you mustn't come here."

There was a desperate and dangerous look on her face, and her form shook with scarcely controlled passionate energy.

"Now see here, Miss Spencer," Racksole said calmly, "I guess we've had enough of this fandango. You'd better get up and clear out, or we'll just have to drag you off."

He went calmly up to her, the lantern in his hand. Without another word she struck the knife into his arm, and the lantern fell extinguished. Racksole gave a cry, rather of angry surprise than of pain, and retreated a few steps. In the darkness they could still perceive the glint of her eyes.

"I told you you mustn't come here," the woman said. "Now get back."

Racksole positively laughed. It was a queer laugh, but he laughed, and he could not help it. The idea of this woman, this bureau clerk, stopping his progress and that of Prince Aribert by means of a bread-knife aroused his sense of humour. He struck a match, relighted the candle, and faced Miss Spencer once more.

"I'll do it again," she said, with a note of hard resolve.

"Oh, no, you won't, my girl," said Racksole; and he pulled out his revolver, cocked it, raised his hand.

"Put down that plaything of yours," he said firmly.

"No," she answered.

"I shall shoot."

She pressed her lips together.

"I shall shoot," he repeated. "One – two – three."

Bang, bang! He had fired twice, purposely missing her. Miss Spencer never blenched. Racksole was tremendously surprised – and he would have been a thousandfold more surprised could he have contrasted her behaviour now with her abject terror on the previous evening when Nella had threatened her.

"You've got a bit of pluck," he said, "but it won't help you. Why won't you let us pass?"

As a matter of fact, pluck was just what she had not, really; she had merely subordinated one terror to another. She was desperately afraid of Racksole's revolver, but she was much more afraid of something else.

"Why won't you let us pass?"

"I daren't," she said, with a plaintive tremor; "Tom put me in charge."

That was all. The men could see tears running down her poor wrinkled face.

Theodore Racksole began to take off his light overcoat.

"I see I must take my coat off to you," he said, and he almost smiled. Then, with a quick movement, he threw the coat over Miss Spencer's head and flew at her, seizing both her arms, while Prince Aribert assisted.

Her struggles ceased – she was beaten.

"That's all right," said Racksole: "I could never have used that revolver – to mean business with it, of course."

They carried her, unresisting, upstairs and on to the upper floor, where they locked her in a bedroom. She lay in the bed as if exhausted.

"Now for my poor Eugen," said Prince Aribert.

"Don't you think we'd better search the house first?" Racksole suggested; "it will be safer to know just how we stand. We can't afford any ambushes or things of that kind, you know."

The Prince agreed, and they searched the house from top to bottom, but found no one. Then, having locked the front door and the french window of the sitting-room, they proceeded again to the cellar.

Here a new obstacle confronted them. The cellar door was, of course, locked; there was no sign of a key, and it appeared to be a heavy door. They were compelled to return to the bedroom where Miss Spencer was incarcerated, in order to demand the key of the cellar from her. She still lay without movement on the bed.

"Tom's got it," she replied, faintly, to their question: "Tom's got it, I swear to you. He took it for safety."

"Then how do you feed your prisoner?" Racksole asked sharply.

"Through the grating," she answered.

Both men shuddered. They felt she was speaking the truth. For the third time they went to the cellar door. In vain Racksole thrust himself against it; he could do no more than shake it.

"Let's try both together," said Prince Aribert. "Now!" There was a crack.

"Again," said Prince Aribert. There was another crack, and then the upper hinge gave way. The rest was easy. Over the wreck of the door they entered Prince Eugen's prison.

The captive still sat on his chair. The terrific noise and bustle of breaking down the door seemed not to have aroused him from his lethargy, but when Prince Aribert spoke to him in German he looked at his uncle.

"Will you not come with us, Eugen?" said Prince Aribert; "you needn't stay here any longer, you know."

"Leave me alone," was the strange reply; "leave me alone. What do you want?"

"We are here to get you out of this scrape," said Aribert gently. Racksole stood aside.

"Who is that fellow?" said Eugen sharply.

"That is my friend Mr. Racksole, an Englishman – or rather, I should say, an American – to whom we owe a great deal. Come and have supper, Eugen."

"I won't," answered Eugen doggedly. "I'm waiting here for her. You didn't think anyone had kept me here, did you, against my will? I tell you I'm waiting for her. She said she'd come."

"Who is she?" Aribert asked, humouring him.

"She! Why, you know! I forgot, of course, you don't know. You mustn't ask. Don't pry, Uncle Aribert. She was wearing a red hat."

"I'll take you to her, my dear Eugen." Prince Aribert put his hands on the other's shoulder, but Eugen shook him off violently, stood up, and then sat down again.

Aribert looked at Racksole, and they both looked at Prince Eugen. The latter's face was flushed, and Racksole observed that the left pupil was more dilated than the right. The man started, muttered odd, fragmentary scraps of sentences, now grumbling, now whining.

"His mind is unhinged," Racksole whispered in English.

"Hush!" said Prince Aribert. "He understands English." But Prince Eugen took no notice of the brief colloquy.

"We had better get him upstairs, somehow," said Racksole.

"Yes," Aribert assented. "Eugen, the lady with the red hat, the lady you are waiting for, is upstairs. She has sent us down to ask you to come up. Won't you come?"

"Himmel!" the poor fellow exclaimed, with a kind of weak anger. "Why did you not say this before?"

He rose, staggered towards Aribert, and fell headlong on the floor. He had swooned. The two men raised him, carried him up the stone steps, and laid him with infinite care on a sofa. He lay, breathing queerly through the nostrils, his eyes closed, his fingers contracted; every now and then a convulsion ran through his frame.

"One of us must fetch a doctor," said Prince Aribert.

"I will," said Racksole. At that moment there was a quick, curt rap on the french window, and both Racksole and the Prince glanced round startled. A girl's face was pressed against the large window-pane. It was Nella's.

Racksole unfastened the catch, and she entered.

"I have found you," she said lightly; "you might have told me. I couldn't sleep. I inquired from the hotel-folks if you had retired, and they said no; so I slipped out. I guessed where you were." Racksole interrupted her with a question as to what she meant by this escapade, but she stopped him with a careless gesture. "What's this?" She pointed to the form on the sofa.

"That is my nephew, Prince Eugen," said Aribert.

"Hurt?" she inquired coldly. "I hope not."

"He is ill," said Racksole, "his brain is turned."

Nella began to examine the unconscious Prince with the expert movements of a girl who had passed through the best hospital course to be obtained in New York.

"He has got brain fever," she said. "That is all, but it will be enough. Do you know if there is a bed anywhere in this remarkable house?"

Chapter XVIII
In the Night Time

"HE MUST on no account be moved," said the dark little Belgian doctor, whose eyes seemed to peer so quizzically through his spectacles; and he said it with much positiveness.

That pronouncement rather settled their plans for them. It was certainly a professional triumph for Nella, who, previous to the doctor's arrival, had told them the very same thing. Considerable argument had passed before the doctor was sent for. Prince Aribert was for keeping the whole affair a deep secret among their three selves. Theodore Racksole agreed so far, but he suggested further that at no matter what risk they should transport the patient over to England at once. Racksole had an idea that he should feel safer in that hotel of his, and better able to deal with any situation that might arise. Nella scorned the idea. In her quality of an amateur nurse, she assured them that Prince Eugen was much more seriously ill than either of them suspected, and she urged that they should take absolute possession of the house, and keep possession till Prince Eugen was convalescent.

"But what about the Spencer female?" Racksole had said.

"Keep her where she is. Keep her a prisoner. And hold the house against all comers. If Jules should come back, simply defy him to enter – that is all.

There are two of you, so you must keep an eye on the former occupiers, if they return, and on Miss Spencer, while I nurse the patient. But first, you must send for a doctor."

"Doctor!" Prince Aribert had said, alarmed. "Will it not be necessary to make some awkward explanation to the doctor?"

"Not at all!" she replied. "Why should it be? In a place like Ostend doctors are far too discreet to ask questions; they see too much to retain their curiosity. Besides, do you want your nephew to die?"

Both the men were somewhat taken aback by the girl's sagacious grasp of the situation, and it came about that they began to obey her like subordinates.

She told her father to sally forth in search of a doctor, and he went. She gave Prince Aribert certain other orders, and he promptly executed them.

By the evening of the following day, everything was going smoothly. The doctor came and departed several times, and sent medicine, and seemed fairly optimistic as to the issue of the illness. An old woman had been induced to come in and cook and clean. Miss Spencer was kept out of sight on the attic floor, pending some decision as to what to do with her. And no one outside the house had asked any questions. The inhabitants of that particular street must have been accustomed to strange behaviour on the part of their neighbours, unaccountable appearances and disappearances, strange flittings and arrivals. This strong-minded and active trio – Racksole, Nella, and Prince Aribert – might have been the lawful and accustomed tenants of the house, for any outward evidence to the contrary.

On the afternoon of the third day Prince Eugen was distinctly and seriously worse. Nella had sat up with him the previous night and throughout the day.

Her father had spent the morning at the hotel, and Prince Aribert had kept watch. The two men were never absent from the house at the same time, and one of them always did duty as sentinel at night. On this afternoon Prince Aribert and Nella sat together in the patient's bedroom. The doctor had just left. Theodore Racksole was downstairs reading the New York Herald. The Prince and Nella were near the window, which looked on to the back-garden.

It was a queer shabby little bedroom to shelter the august body of a European personage like Prince Eugen of Posen. Curiously enough, both Nella and her father, ardent democrats though they were, had been somehow impressed by the royalty and importance of the fever-stricken Prince – impressed as they had never been by Aribert. They had both felt that here, under their care, was a species of individuality quite new to them, and different from anything they had previously encountered. Even the gestures and tones of his delirium had an air of abrupt yet condescending command – an imposing mixture of suavity and haughtiness. As for Nella, she had been first struck by the beautiful 'E' over a crown on the sleeves of his linen, and by the signet ring on his pale, emaciated hand. After all, these trifling outward signs are at least as effective as others of deeper but less obtrusive significance. The Racksoles, too, duly marked the attitude of Prince Aribert to his nephew: it was at once paternal and reverential; it disclosed clearly that Prince Aribert continued, in spite of everything, to regard his nephew as his sovereign lord and master, as a being surrounded by a natural and inevitable pomp and awe. This attitude, at the beginning, seemed false and unreal to the Americans; it seemed to them to be assumed; but gradually they came to perceive that they were mistaken, and that though America might have cast out 'the monarchial superstition', nevertheless that 'superstition' had vigorously survived in another part of the world.

"You and Mr. Racksole have been extraordinarily kind to me," said Prince Aribert very quietly, after the two had sat some time in silence.

"Why? How?" she asked unaffectedly. "We are interested in this affair ourselves, you know. It began at our hotel – you mustn't forget that, Prince."

"I don't," he said. "I forget nothing. But I cannot help feeling that I have led you into a strange entanglement. Why should you and Mr. Racksole be here – you who are supposed to be on a holiday! – hiding in a strange house in a foreign country, subject to all sorts of annoyances and all sorts of risks, simply because I am anxious to avoid scandal, to avoid any sort of talk, in connection with my misguided nephew? It is nothing to you that the Hereditary Prince of Posen should be liable to a public disgrace. What will it matter to you if the throne of Posen becomes the laughing-stock of Europe?"

"I really don't know, Prince," Nella smiled roguishly. "But we Americans have, a habit of going right through with anything we have begun."

"Ah!" he said, "who knows how this thing will end? All our trouble, our anxieties, our watchfulness, may come to nothing. I tell you that when I see Eugen lying there, and think that we cannot learn his story until he recovers, I am ready to go mad. We might be arranging things, making matters smooth, preparing for the future, if only we knew – knew what he can tell us. I tell you that I am ready to go mad. If anything should happen to you, Miss Racksole, I would kill myself."

"But why?" she questioned. "Supposing, that is, that anything could happen to me – which it can't."

"Because I have dragged you into this," he replied, gazing at her. "It is nothing to you. You are only being kind."

"How do you know it is nothing to me, Prince?" she asked him quickly.

Just then the sick man made a convulsive movement, and Nella flew to the bed and soothed him. From the head of the bed she looked over at Prince Aribert, and he returned her bright, excited glance. She was in her travelling-frock, with a large white Belgian apron tied over it. Large dark circles of fatigue and sleeplessness surrounded her eyes, and to the Prince her cheek seemed hollow and thin; her hair lay thick over the temples, half covering the ears. Aribert gave no answer to her query – merely gazed at her with melancholy intensity.

"I think I will go and rest," she said at last. "You will know all about the medicine."

"Sleep well," he said, as he softly opened the door for her. And then he was alone with Eugen. It was his turn that night to watch, for they still half-expected some strange, sudden visit, or onslaught, or move of one kind or another from Jules. Racksole slept in the parlour on the ground floor.

Nella had the front bedroom on the first floor; Miss Spencer was immured in the attic; the last-named lady had been singularly quiet and incurious, taking her food from Nella and asking no questions, the old woman went at nights to her own abode in the purlieus of the harbour. Hour after hour Aribert sat silent by his nephew's bed-side, attending mechanically to his wants, and every now and then gazing hard into the vacant, anguished face, as if trying to extort from that mask the secrets which it held. Aribert was tortured by the idea that if he could have only half an hour's, only a quarter of an hour's, rational speech with Prince Eugen, all might be cleared up and put right, and by the fact that that rational talk was absolutely impossible on Eugen's part until the fever had run its course. As the minutes crept on to midnight the watcher, made nervous by the intense, electrical atmosphere which seems always to surround a person who is dangerously ill, grew more and more a prey to vague and terrible apprehensions. His mind dwelt hysterically on the most fatal possibilities.

He wondered what would occur if by any ill-chance Eugen should die in that bed – how he would explain the affair to Posen and to the Emperor, how he would justify himself. He saw himself being tried for murder, sentenced (him – a Prince of the blood!), led to the scaffold... a scene unparalleled in Europe for over a century! ... Then he gazed anew at the sick man, and thought he saw death in every drawn feature of that agonized face. He could have screamed aloud. His ears heard a peculiar resonant boom. He started – it was nothing but the city clock striking twelve. But there was another sound – a mysterious shuffle at the door. He listened; then jumped from his chair. Nothing now! Nothing! But still he felt drawn to the door, and after what seemed an interminable interval he went and opened it, his heart beating furiously. Nella lay in a heap on the door mat. She was fully dressed, but had apparently lost consciousness. He clutched at her slender body, picked her up, carried her to the chair by the fire-place, and laid her in it. He had forgotten all about Eugen.

"What is it, my angel?" he whispered, and then he kissed her – kissed her twice. He could only look at her; he did not know what to do to succour her.

At last she opened her eyes and sighed.

"Where am I?" she asked vaguely, in a tremulous tone as she recognized him. "Is it you? Did I do anything silly? Did I faint?"

"What has happened? Were you ill?" he questioned anxiously. He was kneeling at her feet, holding her hand tight.

"I saw Jules by the side of my bed," she murmured; "I'm sure I saw him; he laughed at me. I had not undressed. I sprang up, frightened, but he had gone, and then I ran downstairs – to you."

"You were dreaming," he soothed her.

"Was I?"

"You must have been. I have not heard a sound. No one could have entered.

But if you like I will wake Mr. Racksole."

"Perhaps I was dreaming," she admitted. "How foolish!"

"You were over-tired," he said, still unconsciously holding her hand. They gazed at each other. She smiled at him.

"You kissed me," she said suddenly, and he blushed red and stood up before her. "Why did you kiss me?"

"Ah! Miss Racksole," he murmured, hurrying the words out. "Forgive me. It is unforgivable, but forgive me. I was overpowered by my feelings. I did not know what I was doing."

"Why did you kiss me?" she repeated.

"Because – Nella! I love you. I have no right to say it."

"Why have you no right to say it?"

"If Eugen dies, I shall owe a duty to Posen – I shall be its ruler."

"Well!" she said calmly, with an adorable confidence. "Papa is worth forty millions. Would you not abdicate?"

"Ah!" he gave a low cry. "Will you force me to say these things? I could not shirk my duty to Posen, and the reigning Prince of Posen can only marry a Princess."

"But Prince Eugen will live," she said positively, "and if he lives—"

"Then I shall be free. I would renounce all my rights to make you mine, if – if—"

"If what, Prince?"

"If you would deign to accept my hand."

"Am I, then, rich enough?"

"Nella!" He bent down to her.

Then there was a crash of breaking glass. Aribert went to the window and opened it. In the starlit gloom he could see that a ladder had been raised against the back of the house. He thought he heard footsteps at the end of the garden.

"It was Jules," he exclaimed to Nella, and without another word rushed upstairs to the attic. The attic was empty. Miss Spencer had mysteriously vanished.

Chapter XIX
Royalty at the Grand Babylon

THE ROYAL APARTMENTS at the Grand Babylon are famous in the world of hotels, and indeed elsewhere, as being, in their own way, unsurpassed. Some of the palaces of Germany, and in particular those of the mad Ludwig of Bavaria, may possess rooms and saloons which outshine them in gorgeous luxury and the mere wild fairy-like extravagance of wealth; but there is nothing, anywhere, even on Eighth Avenue, New York, which can fairly be called more complete, more perfect, more enticing, or – not least important – more comfortable.

The suite consists of six chambers – the ante-room, the saloon or audience chamber, the dining-room, the yellow drawing-room (where Royalty receives its friends), the library, and the State bedroom – to the last of which we have already been introduced. The most important and most impressive of these is, of course, the audience chamber, an apartment fifty feet long by forty feet broad, with a superb outlook over the Thames, the Shot Tower, and the higher signals of the South-Western Railway. The decoration of this room is mainly in the German taste, since four out of every six of its Royal occupants are of Teutonic blood; but its chief glory is its French ceiling, a masterpiece by Fragonard, taken bodily from a certain famous palace on the Loire. The walls are of panelled oak, with an eight-foot dado of Arras cloth imitated from unique Continental examples. The carpet, woven in one piece, is an antique specimen of the finest Turkish work, and it was obtained, a bargain, by Felix Babylon, from an impecunious Roumanian Prince. The silver candelabra, now fitted with electric light, came from the Rhine, and each had a separate history. The Royal chair – it is not etiquette to call it a throne, though it amounts to a throne – was looted by Napoleon from an Austrian city, and bought by Felix Babylon at the sale of a French collector. At each corner of the room stands a gigantic grotesque vase of German faÃ¯ence of the sixteenth century. These were presented to Felix Babylon by William the First of Germany, upon the conclusion of his first incognito visit to London in connection with the French trouble of 1875.

There is only one picture in the audience chamber. It is a portrait of the luckless but noble Dom Pedro, Emperor of the Brazils. Given to Felix Babylon by Dom Pedro himself, it hangs there solitary and sublime as a reminder to Kings and Princes that Empires may pass away and greatness fall. A certain Prince who was occupying the suite during the Jubilee of 1887 – when the Grand Babylon had seven persons of Royal blood under its roof – sent a curt message to Felix that the portrait must be removed. Felix respectfully declined to remove it, and the Prince left for another hotel, where he was robbed of two thousand pounds' worth of jewellery. The Royal audience chamber of the Grand Babylon, if people only knew it, is one of the sights of London, but it is never shown, and if you ask the hotel servants about its wonders they will tell you only foolish facts concerning it, as that the Turkey carpet costs fifty pounds to clean, and that one of the great vases is cracked across the pedestal, owing to the rough treatment accorded to it during a riotous game of Blind Man's Buff, played one night by four young Princesses, a Balkan King, and his aides-de-camp.

In one of the window recesses of this magnificent apartment, on a certain afternoon in late July, stood Prince Aribert of Posen. He was faultlessly dressed in the conventional frock-coat of

English civilization, with a gardenia in his button-hole, and the indispensable crease down the front of the trousers. He seemed to be fairly amused, and also to expect someone, for at frequent intervals he looked rapidly over his shoulder in the direction of the door behind the Royal chair. At last a little wizened, stooping old man, with a distinctly German cast of countenance, appeared through the door, and laid some papers on a small table by the side of the chair.

"Ah, Hans, my old friend!" said Aribert, approaching the old man. "I must have a little talk with you about one or two matters. How do you find His Royal Highness?"

The old man saluted, military fashion. "Not very well, your Highness," he answered. "I've been valet to your Highness's nephew since his majority, and I was valet to his Royal father before him, but I never saw—" He stopped, and threw up his wrinkled hands deprecatingly.

"You never saw what?" Aribert smiled affectionately on the old fellow. You could perceive that these two, so sharply differentiated in rank, had been intimate in the past, and would be intimate again.

"Do you know, my Prince," said the old man, "that we are to receive the financier, Sampson Levi – is that his name? – in the audience chamber? Surely, if I may humbly suggest, the library would have been good enough for a financier?"

"One would have thought so," agreed Prince Aribert, "but perhaps your master has a special reason. Tell me," he went on, changing the subject quickly, "how came it that you left the Prince, my nephew, at Ostend, and returned to Posen?"

"His orders, Prince," and old Hans, who had had a wide experience of Royal whims and knew half the secrets of the Courts of Europe, gave Aribert a look which might have meant anything. "He sent me back on an – an errand, your Highness."

"And you were to rejoin him here?"

"Just so, Highness. And I did rejoin him here, although, to tell the truth, I had begun to fear that I might never see my master again."

"The Prince has been very ill in Ostend, Hans."

"So I have gathered," Hans responded drily, slowly rubbing his hands together. "And his Highness is not yet perfectly recovered."

"Not yet. We despaired of his life, Hans, at one time, but thanks to an excellent constitution, he came safely through the ordeal."

"We must take care of him, your Highness."

"Yes, indeed," said Aribert solemnly, "his life is very precious to Posen."

At that moment, Eugen, Hereditary Prince of Posen, entered the audience chamber. He was pale and languid, and his uniform seemed to be a trouble to him. His hair had been slightly ruffled, and there was a look of uneasiness, almost of alarmed unrest, in his fine dark eyes. He was like a man who is afraid to look behind him lest he should see something there which ought not to be there. But at the same time, here beyond doubt was Royalty. Nothing could have been more striking than the contrast between Eugen, a sick man in the shabby house at Ostend, and this Prince Eugen in the Royal apartments of the Grand Babylon Hotel, surrounded by the luxury and pomp which modern civilization can offer to those born in high places. All the desperate episode of Ostend was now hidden, passed over. It was supposed never to have occurred. It existed only like a secret shame in the hearts of those who had witnessed it. Prince Eugen had recovered; at any rate, he was convalescent, and he had been removed to London, where he took up again the dropped thread of his princely life. The lady with the red hat, the incorruptible and savage Miss Spencer, the unscrupulous and brilliant Jules, the dark, damp cellar, the horrible little bedroom – these things were over.

Thanks to Prince Aribert and the Racksoles, he had emerged from them in safety. He was able to resume his public and official career. The Emperor had been informed of his safe arrival in London, after an unavoidable delay in Ostend; his name once more figured in the Court chronicle of the newspapers. In short, everything was smothered over. Only – only Jules, Rocco, and Miss Spencer were still at large; and the body of Reginald Dimmock lay buried in the domestic mausoleum of the palace at Posen; and Prince Eugen had still to interview Mr. Sampson Levi.

That various matters lay heavy on the mind of Prince Eugen was beyond question. He seemed to have withdrawn within himself. Despite the extraordinary experiences through which he had recently passed, events which called aloud for explanations and confidence between the nephew and the uncle, he would say scarcely a word to Prince Aribert. Any allusion, however direct, to the days at Ostend, was ignored by him with more or less ingenuity, and Prince Aribert was really no nearer a full solution of the mystery of Jules' plot than he had been on the night when he and Racksole visited the gaming tables at Ostend. Eugen was well aware that he had been kidnapped through the agency of the woman in the red hat, but, doubtless ashamed at having been her dupe, he would not proceed in any way with the clearing-up of the matter.

"You will receive in this room, Eugen?" Aribert questioned him.

"Yes," was the answer, given pettishly. "Why not? Even if I have no proper retinue here, surely that is no reason why I should not hold audience in a proper manner?... Hans, you can go." The old valet promptly disappeared.

"Aribert," the Hereditary Prince continued, when they were alone in the chamber, "you think I am mad."

"My dear Eugen," said Prince Aribert, startled in spite of himself. "Don't be absurd."

"I say you think I am mad. You think that that attack of brain fever has left its permanent mark on me. Well, perhaps I am mad. Who can tell? God knows that I have been through enough lately to drive me mad."

Aribert made no reply. As a matter of strict fact, the thought had crossed his mind that Eugen's brain had not yet recovered its normal tone and activity. This speech of his nephew's, however, had the effect of immediately restoring his belief in the latter's entire sanity. He felt convinced that if only he could regain his nephew's confidence, the old brotherly confidence which had existed between them since the years when they played together as boys, all might yet be well. But at present there appeared to be no sign that Eugen meant to give his confidence to anyone.

The young Prince had come up out of the valley of the shadow of death, but some of the valley's shadow had clung to him, and it seemed he was unable to dissipate it.

"By the way," said Eugen suddenly, "I must reward these Racksoles, I suppose. I am indeed grateful to them. If I gave the girl a bracelet, and the father a thousand guineas – how would that meet the case?"

"My dear Eugen!" exclaimed Aribert aghast. "A thousand guineas! Do you know that Theodore Racksole could buy up all Posen from end to end without making himself a pauper. A thousand guineas! You might as well offer him sixpence."

"Then what must I offer?"

"Nothing, except your thanks. Anything else would be an insult. These are no ordinary hotel people."

"Can't I give the little girl a bracelet?" Prince Eugen gave a sinister laugh.

Aribert looked at him steadily. "No," he said.

"Why did you kiss her – that night?" asked Prince Eugen carelessly.

"Kiss whom?" said Aribert, blushing and angry, despite his most determined efforts to keep calm and unconcerned.

"The Racksole girl."

"When do you mean?"

"I mean," said Prince Eugen, "that night in Ostend when I was ill. You thought I was in a delirium. Perhaps I was. But somehow I remember that with extraordinary distinctness. I remember raising my head for a fraction of an instant, and just in that fraction of an instant you kissed her. Oh, Uncle Aribert!"

"Listen, Eugen, for God's sake. I love Nella Racksole. I shall marry her."

"You!" There was a long pause, and then Eugen laughed. "Ah!" he said. "They all talk like that to start with. I have talked like that myself, dear uncle; it sounds nice, and it means nothing."

"In this case it means everything, Eugen," said Aribert quietly. Some accent of determination in the latter's tone made Eugen rather more serious.

"You can't marry her," he said. "The Emperor won't permit a morganatic marriage."

"The Emperor has nothing to do with the affair. I shall renounce my rights.

I shall become a plain citizen."

"In which case you will have no fortune to speak of."

"But my wife will have a fortune. Knowing the sacrifices which I shall have made in order to marry her, she will not hesitate to place that fortune in my hands for our mutual use," said Aribert stiffly.

"You will decidedly be rich," mused Eugen, as his ideas dwelt on Theodore Racksole's reputed wealth. "But have you thought of this," he asked, and his mild eyes glowed again in a sort of madness. "Have you thought that I am unmarried, and might die at any moment, and then the throne will descend to you – to you, Aribert?"

"The throne will never descend to me, Eugen," said Aribert softly, "for you will live. You are thoroughly convalescent. You have nothing to fear."

"It is the next seven days that I fear," said Eugen.

"The next seven days! Why?"

"I do not know. But I fear them. If I can survive them—"

"Mr. Sampson Levi, sire," Hans announced in a loud tone.

Chapter XX
Mr. Sampson Levi Bids Prince Eugen Good Morning

PRINCE EUGEN started. "I will see him," he said, with a gesture to Hans as if to indicate that Mr. Sampson Levi might enter at once.

"I beg one moment first," said Aribert, laying a hand gently on his nephew's arm, and giving old Hans a glance which had the effect of precipitating that admirably trained servant through the doorway.

"What is it?" asked Prince Eugen crossly. "Why this sudden seriousness? Don't forget that I have an appointment with Mr. Sampson Levi, and must not keep him waiting. Someone said that punctuality is the politeness of princes."

"Eugen," said Aribert, "I wish you to be as serious as I am. Why cannot we have faith in each other? I want to help you. I have helped you. You are my titular Sovereign; but on the other hand I have the honour to be your uncle:

I have the honour to be the same age as you, and to have been your companion from youth up. Give me your confidence. I thought you had given it me years ago, but I have lately discovered that you had your secrets, even then. And now, since your illness, you are still more secretive."

"What do you mean, Aribert?" said Eugen, in a tone which might have been either inimical or friendly. "What do you want to say?"

"Well, in the first place, I want to say that you will not succeed with the estimable Mr. Sampson Levi."

"Shall I not?" said Eugen lightly. "How do you know what my business is with him?"

"Suffice it to say that I know. You will never get that million pounds out of him."

Prince Eugen gasped, and then swallowed his excitement. "Who has been talking? What million?" His eyes wandered uneasily round the room. "Ah!" he said, pretending to laugh. "I see how it is. I have been chattering in my delirium. You mustn't take any notice of that, Aribert. When one has a fever one's ideas become grotesque and fanciful."

"You never talked in your delirium," Aribert replied; "at least not about yourself. I knew about this projected loan before I saw you in Ostend."

"Who told you?" demanded Eugen fiercely.

"Then you admit that you are trying to raise a loan?"

"I admit nothing. Who told you?"

"Theodore Racksole, the millionaire. These rich men have no secrets from each other. They form a coterie, closer than any coterie of ours. Eugen, and far more powerful. They talk, and in talking they rule the world, these millionaires. They are the real monarchs."

"Curse them!" said Eugen.

"Yes, perhaps so. But let me return to your case. Imagine my shame, my disgust, when I found that Racksole could tell me more about your affairs than I knew myself. Happily, he is a good fellow; one can trust him; otherwise I should have been tempted to do something desperate when I discovered that all your private history was in his hands. Eugen, let us come to the point; why do you want that million? Is it actually true that you are so deeply in debt? I have no desire to improve the occasion. I merely ask."

"And what if I do owe a million?" said Prince Eugen with assumed valour.

"Oh, nothing, my dear Eugen, nothing. Only it is rather a large sum to have scattered in ten years, is it not? How did you manage it?"

"Don't ask me, Aribert. I've been a fool. But I swear to you that the woman whom you call "the lady in the red hat" is the last of my follies. I am about to take a wife, and become a respectable Prince."

"Then the engagement with Princess Anna is an accomplished fact?"

"Practically so. As soon as I have settled with Levi, all will be smooth.

Aribert, I wouldn't lose Anna for the Imperial throne. She is a good and pure woman, and I love her as a man might love an angel."

"And yet you would deceive her as to your debts, Eugen?"

"Not her, but her absurd parents, and perhaps the Emperor. They have heard rumours, and I must set those rumours at rest by presenting to them a clean sheet."

"I am glad you have been frank with me, Eugen," said Prince Aribert, "but I will be plain with you. You will never marry the Princess Anna."

"And why?" said Eugen, supercilious again.

"Because her parents will not permit it. Because you will not be able to present a clean sheet to them. Because this Sampson Levi will never lend you a million."

"Explain yourself."

"I propose to do so. You were kidnapped – it is a horrid word, but we must use it – in Ostend."

"True."

"Do you know why?"

"I suppose because that vile old red-hatted woman and her accomplices wanted to get some money out of me. Fortunately, thanks to you, they didn't."

"Not at all," said Aribert. "They wanted no money from you. They knew well enough that you had no money. They knew you were the naughty schoolboy among European Princes, with no sense of responsibility or of duty towards your kingdom. Shall I tell you why they kidnapped you?"

"When you have done abusing me, my dear uncle."

"They kidnapped you merely to keep you out of England for a few days, merely to compel you to fail in your appointment with Sampson Levi. And it appears to me that they succeeded. Assuming that you don't obtain the money from Levi, is there another financier in all Europe from whom you can get it – on such strange security as you have to offer?"

"Possibly there is not," said Prince Eugen calmly. "But, you see, I shall get it from Sampson Levi. Levi promised it, and I know from other sources that he is a man of his word. He said that the money, subject to certain formalities, would be available till—"

"Till?"

"Till the end of June."

"And it is now the end of July."

"Well, what is a month? He is only too glad to lend the money. He will get excellent interest. How on earth have you got into your sage old head this notion of a plot against me? The idea is ridiculous. A plot against me? What for?"

"Have you ever thought of Bosnia?" asked Aribert coldly.

"What of Bosnia?"

"I need not tell you that the King of Bosnia is naturally under obligations to Austria, to whom he owes his crown. Austria is anxious for him to make a good influential marriage."

"Well, let him."

"He is going to. He is going to marry the Princess Anna."

"Not while I live. He made overtures there a year ago, and was rebuffed."

"Yes; but he will make overtures again, and this time he will not be rebuffed. Oh, Eugen! can't you see that this plot against you is being engineered by some persons who know all about your affairs, and whose desire is to prevent your marriage with Princess Anna? Only one man in Europe can have any motive for wishing to prevent your marriage with Princess Anna, and that is the man who means to marry her himself." Eugen went very pale.

"Then, Aribert, do you mean to convey to me that my detention in Ostend was contrived by the agents of the King of Bosnia?"

"I do."

"With a view to stopping my negotiations with Sampson Levi, and so putting an end to the possibility of my marriage with Anna?"

Aribert nodded.

"You are a good friend to me, Aribert. You mean well. But you are mistaken.

You have been worrying about nothing."

"Have you forgotten about Reginald Dimmock?"

"I remember you said that he had died."

"I said nothing of the sort. I said that he had been assassinated. That was part of it, my poor Eugen."

"Pooh!" said Eugen. "I don't believe he was assassinated. And as for Sampson Levi, I will bet you a thousand marks that he and I come to terms this morning, and that the million is in my hands before I leave London." Aribert shook his head.

"You seem to be pretty sure of Mr. Levi's character. Have you had much to do with him before?"

"Well," Eugen hesitated a second, "a little. What young man in my position hasn't had something to do with Mr. Sampson Levi at one time or another?"

"I haven't," said Aribert.

"You! You are a fossil." He rang a silver bell. "Hans! I will receive Mr. Sampson Levi."

Whereupon Aribert discreetly departed, and Prince Eugen sat down in the great velvet chair, and began to look at the papers which Hans had previously placed upon the table.

"Good morning, your Royal Highness," said Sampson Levi, bowing as he entered. "I trust your Royal Highness is well."

"Moderately, thanks," returned the Prince.

In spite of the fact that he had had as much to do with people of Royal blood as any plain man in Europe, Sampson Levi had never yet learned how to be at ease with these exalted individuals during the first few minutes of an interview. Afterwards, he resumed command of himself and his faculties, but at the beginning he was invariably flustered, scarlet of face, and inclined to perspiration.

"We will proceed to business at once," said Prince Eugen. "Will you take a seat, Mr. Levi?"

"I thank your Royal Highness."

"Now as to that loan which we had already practically arranged – a million, I think it was," said the Prince airily.

"A million," Levi acquiesced, toying with his enormous watch chain.

"Everything is now in order. Here are the papers and I should like to finish the matter up at once."

"Exactly, your Highness, but—"

"But what? You months ago expressed the warmest satisfaction at the security, though I am quite prepared to admit that the security, is of rather an unusual nature. You also agreed to the rate of interest. It is not everyone, Mr. Levi, who can lend out a million at 5-1/2 per cent. And in ten years the whole amount will be paid back. I – er – I believe I informed you that the fortune of Princess Anna, who is about to accept my hand, will ultimately amount to something like fifty millions of marks, which is over two million pounds in your English money." Prince Eugen stopped. He had no fancy for talking in this confidential manner to financiers, but he felt that circumstances demanded it.

"You see, it's like this, your Royal Highness," began Mr. Sampson Levi, in his homely English idiom. "It's like this. I said I could keep that bit of money available till the end of June, and you were to give me an interview here before that date. Not having heard from your Highness, and not knowing your Highness's address, though my German agents made every inquiry, I concluded, that you had made other arrangements, money being so cheap this last few months."

"I was unfortunately detained at Ostend," said Prince Eugen, with as much haughtiness as he could assume, "by – by important business. I have made no other arrangements, and I shall have need of the million. If you will be so good as to pay it to my London bankers—"

"I'm very sorry," said Mr. Sampson Levi, with a tremendous and dazzling air of politeness, which surprised even himself, "but my syndicate has now lent the money elsewhere. It's in South America – I don't mind telling your Highness that we've lent it to the Chilean Government."

"Hang the Chilean Government, Mr. Levi," exclaimed the Prince, and he went white. "I must have that million. It was an arrangement."

"It was an arrangement, I admit," said Mr. Sampson Levi, "but your Highness broke the arrangement."

There was a long silence.

"Do you mean to say," began the Prince with tense calmness, "that you are not in a position to let me have that million?"

"I could let your Highness have a million in a couple of years' time."

The Prince made a gesture of annoyance. "Mr. Levi," he said, "if you do not place the money in my hands tomorrow you will ruin one of the oldest of reigning families, and, incidentally, you will alter the map of Europe. You are not keeping faith, and I had relied on you."

"Pardon me, your Highness," said little Levi, rising in resentment, "it is not I who have not kept faith. I beg to repeat that the money is no longer at my disposal, and to bid your Highness good morning."

And Mr. Sampson Levi left the audience chamber with an awkward, aggrieved bow. It was a scene characteristic of the end of the nineteenth century – an overfed, commonplace, pursy little man who had been born in a Brixton semi-detached villa, and whose highest idea of pleasure was a Sunday up the river in an expensive electric launch, confronting and utterly routing, in a hotel belonging to an American millionaire, the representative of a race of men who had fingered every page of European history for centuries, and who still, in their native castles, were surrounded with every outward circumstance of pomp and power.

"Aribert," said Prince Eugen, a little later, "you were right. It is all over. I have only one refuge—"

"You don't mean—" Aribert stopped, dumbfounded.

"Yes, I do," he said quickly. "I can manage it so that it will look like an accident."

Chapter XXI
The Return of Felix Babylon

ON THE EVENING of Prince Eugen's fateful interview with Mr. Sampson Levi, Theodore Racksole was wandering somewhat aimlessly and uneasily about the entrance hall and adjacent corridors of the Grand Babylon. He had returned from Ostend only a day or two previously, and had endeavoured with all his might to forget the affair which had carried him there – to regard it, in fact, as done with. But he found himself unable to do so. In vain he remarked, under his breath, that there were some things which were best left alone: if his experience as a manipulator of markets, a contriver of gigantic schemes in New York, had taught him anything at all, it should surely have taught him that. Yet he could not feel reconciled to such a position. The mere presence of the princes in his hotel roused the fighting instincts of this man, who had never in his whole career been beaten. He had, as it were, taken up arms on their side, and if the princes of Posen would not continue their own battle, nevertheless he, Theodore Racksole, wanted to continue it for them. To a certain extent, of course, the battle had been won, for Prince Eugen had been rescued from an extremely difficult and dangerous position, and the enemy – consisting of Jules, Rocco, Miss Spencer, and perhaps others – had been put to flight. But that, he conceived, was not enough; it was very far from being enough. That the criminals, for criminals they decidedly were, should still be at large, he regarded as an absurd anomaly. And there was another point: he had said nothing to the police of all that had occurred. He disdained the police, but he could scarcely fail to perceive that if the police should by accident gain a clue to the real state of the case he might be placed rather awkwardly, for the simple reason that in the eyes of the law it amounted to a misdemeanour to conceal as much as he had concealed. He asked himself, for the thousandth time, why he had adopted a policy of concealment from the police, why he had become in any way interested in the Posen matter, and why, at this present moment, he should be so anxious to prosecute it further? To the first two questions he replied, rather lamely, that he had been influenced by Nella, and also by a natural spirit of adventure; to the third he replied that he had always been in the habit of carrying things through, and was now actuated by a mere childish, obstinate desire to carry this one through. Moreover, he was splendidly conscious of his perfect ability to carry it through. One additional impulse he had, though he did not admit it to himself, being by nature adverse to big words, and that was an abstract love of justice, the Anglo-Saxon's deep-found instinct for helping the right side to conquer, even when grave risks must thereby be run, with no corresponding advantage.

He was turning these things over in his mind as he walked about the vast hotel on that evening of the last day in July. The Society papers had been stating for a week past that London was empty, but, in spite of the Society papers, London persisted in seeming to be just as full as ever. The Grand Babylon was certainly not as crowded as it had been a month earlier, but it was doing a very passable business. At the close of the season the gay butterflies of the social community have a habit of hovering for a day or two in the big hotels before they flutter away to castle and country-house, meadow and moor, lake and stream. The great basket-chairs in the portico were well filled by old and middle-aged gentlemen engaged in enjoying the varied delights of liqueurs, cigars, and the full moon which floated so serenely above the Thames. Here and there a pretty woman on the arm of a cavalier in immaculate attire swept her train as she turned to and fro in the promenade of the terrace. Waiters and uniformed commissionaires and gold-braided doorkeepers moved noiselessly about; at short intervals the chief of the doorkeepers blew his shrill whistle and hansoms drove up with tinkling bell to take away a pair of butterflies to some place of amusement or boredom; occasionally a private carriage drawn by expensive and self-conscious horses put the hansoms to shame by its mere outward glory. It was a hot night, a night for the summer woods, and save for the vehicles there was no rapid movement of any kind. It seemed as though the world – the world, that is to say, of the Grand Babylon – was fully engaged in the solemn processes of digestion and small-talk. Even the long row of the Embankment gas-lamps, stretching right and left, scarcely trembled in the still, warm, caressing air. The stars overhead looked down with many blinkings upon the enormous pile of the Grand Babylon, and the moon regarded it with bland and changeless face; what they thought of it and its inhabitants cannot, unfortunately, be recorded. What Theodore Racksole thought of the moon can be recorded: he thought it was a nuisance. It somehow fascinated his gaze with its silly stare, and so interfered with his complex meditations. He glanced round at the well-dressed and satisfied people – his guests, his customers. They appeared to ignore him absolutely.

Probably only a very small percentage of them had the least idea that this tall spare man, with the iron-grey hair and the thin, firm, resolute face, who wore his American-cut evening clothes with such careless ease, was the sole proprietor of the Grand Babylon, and possibly the richest man in Europe. As has already been stated, Racksole was not a celebrity in England.

The guests of the Grand Babylon saw merely a restless male person, whose restlessness was rather a disturber of their quietude, but with whom, to judge by his countenance, it would be inadvisable to remonstrate. Therefore Theodore Racksole continued his perambulations unchallenged, and kept saying to himself, "I must do something." But what? He could think of no course to pursue.

At last he walked straight through the hotel and out at the other entrance, and so up the little unassuming side street into the roaring torrent of the narrow and crowded Strand. He jumped on a Putney bus, and paid his fair to Putney, fivepence, and then, finding that the humble occupants of the vehicle stared at the spectacle of a man in evening dress but without a dustcoat, he jumped off again, oblivious of the fact that the conductor jerked a thumb towards him and winked at the passengers as who should say, "There goes a lunatic." He went into a tobacconist's shop and asked for a cigar. The shopman mildly inquired what price.

"What are the best you've got?" asked Theodore Racksole.

"Five shillings each, sir," said the man promptly.

"Give me a penny one," was Theodore Racksole's laconic request, and he walked out of the shop smoking the penny cigar. It was a new sensation for him.

He was inhaling the aromatic odours of Eugene Rimmel's establishment for the sale of scents when a gentleman, walking slowly in the opposite direction, accosted him with a quiet, "Good evening, Mr. Racksole." The millionaire did not at first recognize his interlocutor, who wore a travelling overcoat, and was carrying a handbag. Then a slight, pleased smile passed over his features, and he held out his hand.

"Well, Mr. Babylon," he greeted the other, "of all persons in the wide world you are the man I would most have wished to meet."

"You flatter me," said the little Anglicized Swiss.

"No, I don't," answered Racksole; "it isn't my custom, any more than it's yours. I wanted to have a real good long yarn with you, and lo! here you are! Where have you sprung from?"

"From Lausanne," said Felix Babylon. "I had finished my duties there, I had nothing else to do, and I felt homesick. I felt the nostalgia of London, and so I came over, just as you see," and he raised the handbag for Racksole's notice. "One toothbrush, one razor, two slippers, eh?" He laughed. "I was wondering as I walked along where I should stay – me, Felix Babylon, homeless in London."

"I should advise you to stay at the Grand Babylon," Racksole laughed back.

"It is a good hotel, and I know the proprietor personally."

"Rather expensive, is it not?" said Babylon.

"To you, sir," answered Racksole, "the inclusive terms will be exactly half a crown a week. Do you accept?"

"I accept," said Babylon, and added, "You are very good, Mr. Racksole."

They strolled together back to the hotel, saying nothing in particular, but feeling very content with each other's company.

"Many customers?" asked Felix Babylon.

"Very tolerable," said Racksole, assuming as much of the air of the professional hotel proprietor as he could. "I think I may say in the storekeeper's phrase, that if there is any business about I am doing it. Tonight the people are all on the terrace in the portico – it's so confoundedly hot – and the consumption of ice is simply enormous – nearly as large as it would be in New York."

"In that case," said Babylon politely, "let me offer you another cigar."

"But I have not finished this one."

"That is just why I wish to offer you another one. A cigar such as yours, my good friend, ought never to be smoked within the precincts of the Grand Babylon, not even by the proprietor of the Grand Babylon, and especially when all the guests are assembled in the portico. The fumes of it would ruin any hotel."

Theodore Racksole laughingly lighted the Rothschild Havana which Babylon gave him, and they entered the hotel arm in arm. But no sooner had they mounted the steps than little Felix became the object of numberless greetings. It appeared that he had been highly popular among his quondam guests. At last they reached the managerial room, where Babylon was regaled on a chicken, and Racksole assisted him in the consumption of a bottle of Heidsieck Monopole, Carte d'Or.

"This chicken is almost perfectly grilled," said Babylon at length. "It is a credit to the house. But why, my dear Racksole, why in the name of Heaven did you quarrel with Rocco?"

"Then you have heard?"

"Heard! My dear friend, it was in every newspaper on the Continent. Some journals prophesied that the Grand Babylon would have to close its doors within half a year now that Rocco had deserted it. But of course I knew better. I knew that you must have a good reason for allowing Rocco to depart, and that you must have made arrangements in advance for a substitute."

"As a matter of fact, I had not made arrangements in advance," said Theodore Racksole, a little ruefully; "but happily we have found in our second sous-chef an artist inferior only to Rocco himself. That, however, was mere good fortune."

"Surely," said Babylon, "it was indiscreet to trust to mere good fortune in such a serious matter?"

"I didn't trust to mere good fortune. I didn't trust to anything except Rocco, and he deceived me."

"But why did you quarrel with him?"

"I didn't quarrel with him. I found him embalming a corpse in the State bedroom one night—"

"You what?" Babylon almost screamed.

"I found him embalming a corpse in the State bedroom," repeated Racksole in his quietest tones.

The two men gazed at each other, and then Racksole replenished Babylon's glass.

"Tell me," said Babylon, settling himself deep in an easy chair and lighting a cigar.

And Racksole thereupon recounted to him the whole of the Posen episode, with every circumstantial detail so far as he knew it. It was a long and complicated recital, and occupied about an hour. During that time little Felix never spoke a word, scarcely moved a muscle; only his small eyes gazed through the bluish haze of smoke. The clock on the mantelpiece tinkled midnight.

"Time for whisky and soda," said Racksole, and got up as if to ring the bell; but Babylon waved him back.

"You have told me that this Sampson Levi had an audience of Prince Eugen today, but you have not told me the result of that audience," said Babylon.

"Because I do not yet know it. But I shall doubtless know tomorrow. In the meantime, I feel fairly sure that Levi declined to produce Prince Eugen's required million. I have reason to believe that the money was lent elsewhere."

"H'm!" mused Babylon; and then, carelessly, "I am not at all surprised at that arrangement for spying through the bathroom of the State apartments."

"Why are you not surprised?"

"Oh!" said Babylon, "it is such an obvious dodge – so easy to carry out. As for me, I took special care never to involve myself in these affairs. I knew they existed; I somehow felt that they existed. But I also felt that they lay outside my sphere. My business was to provide board and lodging of the most sumptuous kind to those who didn't mind paying for it; and I did my business. If anything else went on in the hotel, under the rose, I long determined to ignore it unless it should happen to be brought before my notice; and it never was brought before my notice. However, I admit that there is a certain pleasurable excitement in this kind of affair and doubtless you have experienced that."

"I have," said Racksole simply, "though I believe you are laughing at me."

"By no means," Babylon replied. "Now what, if I may ask the question, is going to be your next step?"

"That is just what I desire to know myself," said Theodore Racksole.

"Well," said Babylon, after a pause, "let us begin. In the first place, it is possible you may be interested to hear that I happened to see Jules today."

"You did!" Racksole remarked with much calmness. "Where?"

"Well, it was early this morning, in Paris, just before I left there. The meeting was quite accidental, and Jules seemed rather surprised at meeting me. He respectfully inquired where I was going, and I said that I was going to Switzerland. At that moment I thought I was going to Switzerland. It had occurred to me that after all I should be happier there, and that I had better turn back and not see London any more. However, I changed my mind once again, and decided to come on to London, and accept the risks of being miserable there without my hotel. Then I asked Jules whither he was bound, and he told me that he was off to Constantinople, being interested in a new French hotel there. I wished him good luck, and we parted."

"Constantinople, eh!" said Racksole. "A highly suitable place for him, I should say."

"But," Babylon resumed, "I caught sight of him again."

"Where?"

"At Charing Cross, a few minutes before I had the pleasure of meeting you. Mr. Jules had not gone to Constantinople after all. He did not see me, or I should have suggested to him that in going from Paris to Constantinople it is not usual to travel via London."

"The cheek of the fellow!" exclaimed Theodore Racksole. "The gorgeous and colossal cheek of the fellow!"

Chapter XXII
In the Wine Cellars of the Grand Babylon

"DO YOU KNOW anything of the antecedents of this Jules," asked Theodore Racksole, helping himself to whisky.

"Nothing whatever," said Babylon. "Until you told me, I don't think I was aware that his true name was Thomas Jackson, though of course I knew that it was not Jules. I certainly was not aware that Miss Spencer was his wife, but I had long suspected that their relations were somewhat more intimate than the nature of their respective duties in the hotel absolutely demanded. All that I do know of Jules – he will always be called Jules – is that he gradually, by some mysterious personal force, acquired a prominent position in the hotel. Decidedly he was the cleverest and most intellectual waiter I have ever known, and he was specially skilled in the difficult task of retaining his own dignity while not interfering with that of other people.

I'm afraid this information is a little too vague to be of any practical assistance in the present difficulty."

"What is the present difficulty?" Racksole queried, with a simple air.

"I should imagine that the present difficulty is to account for the man's presence in London."

"That is easily accounted for," said Racksole.

"How? Do you suppose he is anxious to give himself up to justice, or that the chains of habit bind him to the hotel?"

"Neither," said Racksole. "Jules is going to have another try – that's all."

"Another try at what?"

"At Prince Eugen. Either at his life or his liberty. Most probably the former this time; almost certainly the former. He has guessed that we are somewhat handicapped by our anxiety to keep Prince Eugen's predicament quite quiet, and he is taking advantage, of that fact. As he already is fairly rich, on his own admission, the reward which has been offered to him must be enormous, and he is absolutely determined to get it. He has several times recently proved himself to be a daring fellow; unless I am mistaken he will shortly prove himself to be still more daring."

"But what can he do? Surely you don't suggest that he will attempt the life of Prince Eugen in this hotel?"

"Why not? If Reginald Dimmock fell on mere suspicion that he would turn out unfaithful to the conspiracy, why not Prince Eugen?"

"But it would be an unspeakable crime, and do infinite harm to the hotel!"

"True!" Racksole admitted, smiling. Little Felix Babylon seemed to brace himself for the grasping of his monstrous idea.

"How could it possibly be done?" he asked at length.

"Dimmock was poisoned."

"Yes, but you had Rocco here then, and Rocco was in the plot. It is conceivable that Rocco could have managed it – barely conceivable. But without Rocco I cannot think it possible. I cannot even think that Jules would attempt it. You see, in a place like the Grand Babylon, as probably I needn't point out to you, food has to pass through so many hands that to poison one person without killing perhaps fifty would be a most delicate operation. Moreover, Prince Eugen, unless he has changed his habits, is always served by his own attendant, old Hans, and therefore any attempt to tamper with a cooked dish immediately before serving would be hazardous in the extreme."

"Granted," said Racksole. "The wine, however, might be more easily got at. Had you thought of that?"

"I had not," Babylon admitted. "You are an ingenious theorist, but I happen to know that Prince Eugen always has his wine opened in his own presence. No doubt it would be opened by Hans. Therefore the wine theory is not tenable, my friend."

"I do not see why," said Racksole. "I know nothing of wine as an expert, and I very seldom drink it, but it seems to me that a bottle of wine might be tampered with while it was still in the cellar, especially if there was an accomplice in the hotel."

"You think, then, that you are not yet rid of all your conspirators?"

"I think that Jules might still have an accomplice within the building."

"And that a bottle of wine could be opened and recorked without leaving any trace of the operation?" Babylon was a trifle sarcastic.

"I don't see the necessity of opening the bottle in order to poison the wine," said Racksole. "I have never tried to poison anybody by means of a bottle of wine, and I don't lay claim to any natural talent as a poisoner, but I think I could devise several ways of managing the trick. Of course, I admit I may be entirely mistaken as to Jules' intentions."

"Ah!" said Felix Babylon. "The wine cellars beneath us are one of the wonders of London. I hope you are aware, Mr. Racksole, that when you bought the Grand Babylon you bought what is probably the finest stock of wines in England, if not in Europe. In the valuation I reckoned them at sixty thousand pounds. And I may say that I always took care that the cellars were properly guarded. Even Jules would experience a serious difficulty in breaking into the cellars without the connivance of the wine-clerk, and the wine-clerk is, or was, incorruptible."

"I am ashamed to say that I have not yet inspected my wines," smiled Racksole; "I have never given them a thought. Once or twice I have taken the trouble to make a tour of the hotel, but I omitted the cellars in my excursions."

"Impossible, my dear fellow!" said Babylon, amused at such a confession, to him – a great connoisseur and lover of fine wines – almost incredible. "But really you must see them tomorrow. If I may, I will accompany you."

"Why not tonight?" Racksole suggested, calmly.

"To-night! It is very late: Hubbard will have gone to bed."

"And may I ask who is Hubbard? I remember the name but dimly."

"Hubbard is the wine-clerk of the Grand Babylon," said Felix, with a certain emphasis. "A sedate man of forty. He has the keys of the cellars. He knows every bottle of every bin, its date, its qualities, its value. And he's a teetotaler. Hubbard is a curiosity. No wine can leave the cellars without his knowledge, and no person can enter the cellars without his knowledge. At least, that is how it was in my time," Babylon added.

"We will wake him," said Racksole.

"But it is one o'clock in the morning," Babylon protested.

"Never mind – that is, if you consent to accompany me. A cellar is the same by night as by day. Therefore, why not now?"

Babylon shrugged his shoulders. "As you wish," he agreed, with his indestructible politeness.

"And now to find this Mr. Hubbard, with his key of the cupboard," said Racksole, as they walked out of the room together. Although the hour was so late, the hotel was not, of course, closed for the night. A few guests still remained about in the public rooms, and a few fatigued waiters were still in attendance. One of these latter was despatched in search of the singular Mr. Hubbard, and it fortunately turned out that this gentleman had not actually retired, though he was on the point of doing so. He brought the keys to Mr. Racksole in person, and after he had had a little chat with his former master, the proprietor and the ex-proprietor of the Grand Babylon Hotel proceeded on their way to the cellars.

These cellars extend over, or rather under, quite half the superficial areas of the whole hotel – the longitudinal half which lies next to the Strand.

Owing to the fact that the ground slopes sharply from the Strand to the river, the Grand Babylon is, so to speak, deeper near the Strand than it is near the Thames. Towards the Thames there is, below the entrance level, a basement and a sub-basement. Towards the Strand there is basement, sub-basement, and the huge wine cellars beneath all. After descending the four flights of the service stairs, and traversing a long passage running parallel with the kitchen, the two found themselves opposite a door, which, on being unlocked, gave access to another flight of stairs. At the foot of this was the main entrance to the cellars. Outside the entrance was the wine-lift, for the ascension of delicious fluids to the upper floors, and, opposite, Mr. Hubbard's little office. There was electric light everywhere.

Babylon, who, as being most accustomed to them, held the bunch of keys, opened the great door, and then they were in the first cellar – the first of a suite of five. Racksole was struck not only by the icy coolness of the place, but also by its vastness. Babylon had seized a portable electric handlight, attached to a long wire, which lay handy, and, waving it about, disclosed the dimensions of the place. By that flashing illumination the subterranean chamber looked unutterably weird and mysterious, with its rows of numbered bins, stretching away into the distance till the radiance was reduced to the occasional far gleam of the light on the shoulder of a bottle. Then Babylon switched on the fixed electric lights, and Theodore Racksole entered upon a personally-conducted tour of what was quite the most interesting part of his own property.

To see the innocent enthusiasm of Felix Babylon for these stores of exhilarating liquid was what is called in the North 'a sight for sair een'.

He displayed to Racksole's bewildered gaze, in their due order, all the wines of three continents – nay, of four, for the superb and luscious Constantia wine of Cape Colony was not wanting in that most catholic collection of vintages. Beginning with the unsurpassed products of Burgundy, he continued with the clarets of Medoc, Bordeaux, and Sauterne; then to the champagnes of Ay, Hautvilliers, and Pierry; then to the hocks and moselles of Germany, and the brilliant imitation champagnes of Main, Neckar, and Naumburg; then to the famous and adorable Tokay of Hungary, and all the Austrian varieties of French wines, including Carlowitz and Somlauer; then to the dry sherries of Spain, including purest Manzanilla, and Amontillado, and Vino de Pasto; then to the wines of Malaga, both sweet and dry, and all the 'Spanish reds' from Catalonia, including the dark

'Tent' so often used sacramentally; then to the renowned port of Oporto. Then he proceeded to the Italian cellar, and descanted upon the excellence of Barolo from Piedmont, of Chianti from Tuscany, of Orvieto from the Roman States, of the 'Tears of Christ' from Naples, and the commoner Marsala from Sicily. And so on, to an extent and with a fullness of detail which cannot be rendered here.

At the end of the suite of cellars there was a glazed door, which, as could be seen, gave access to a supplemental and smaller cellar, an apartment about fifteen or sixteen feet square.

"Anything special in there?" asked Racksole curiously, as they stood before the door, and looked within at the seined ends of bottles.

"Ah!" exclaimed Babylon, almost smacking his lips, "therein lies the cream of all."

"The best champagne, I suppose?" said Racksole.

"Yes," said Babylon, "the best champagne is there – a very special Sillery, as exquisite as you will find anywhere. But I see, my friend, that you fall into the common error of putting champagne first among wines. That distinction belongs to Burgundy. You have old Burgundy in that cellar, Mr. Racksole, which cost me – how much do you think? – eighty pounds a bottle. Probably it will never be drunk," he added with a sigh. "It is too expensive even for princes and plutocrats."

"Yes, it will," said Racksole quickly. "You and I will have a bottle up tomorrow."

"Then," continued Babylon, still riding his hobby-horse, "there is a sample of the Rhine wine dated 1706 which caused such a sensation at the Vienna Exhibition of 1873. There is also a singularly glorious Persian wine from Shiraz, the like of which I have never seen elsewhere. Also there is an unrivalled vintage of Romanée-Conti, greatest of all modern Burgundies. If I remember right Prince Eugen invariably has a bottle when he comes to stay here. It is not on the hotel wine list, of course, and only a few customers know of it. We do not precisely hawk it about the dining-room."

"Indeed!" said Racksole. "Let us go inside."

They entered the stone apartment, rendered almost sacred by the preciousness of its contents, and Racksole looked round with a strangely intent and curious air. At the far side was a grating, through which came a feeble light.

"What is that?" asked the millionaire sharply.

"That is merely a ventilation grating. Good ventilation is absolutely essential."

"Looks broken, doesn't it?" Racksole suggested and then, putting a finger quickly on Babylon's shoulder, "there's someone in the cellar. Can't you hear breathing, down there, behind that bin?"

The two men stood tense and silent for a while, listening, under the ray of the single electric light in the ceiling. Half the cellar was involved in gloom. At length Racksole walked firmly down the central passage-way between the bins and turned to the corner at the right.

"Come out, you villain!" he said in a low, well-nigh vicious tone, and dragged up a cowering figure.

He had expected to find a man, but it was his own daughter, Nella Racksole, upon whom he had laid angry hands.

The complete and unabridged text is available online, from *flametreepublishing.com/extras*

Longfellow's Private Detection Service

Joshua Boyce

SHE WALKED with a deliberate, determined pace. All about her, the people in the streets carried about their business: exchanging money for goods and services; bits of gossip and rumour for rapt attention and social standing. Some traded in both, she noted, as she passed a newsstand. She paused briefly to look at the most recent copy of *The Illustrated London News*: Prince Albert had married Lady Elizabeth less than a week ago. She smiled and walked on, just a little taller. After all, she herself was royalty, of a sort.

Albeit, the macabre sort.

The brass plaque greeted her as she walked up the steps to her destination: *Longfellow's Private Detection Service*. Her uncle was Sir Lawrence Longfellow. Yes, *the* Longfellow. The man who had consulted on, and de facto solved, scores of cases over the past two decades. The man who had walked into Toronto's City Hall and provided critical assistance in solving a string of cat burglaries simply by pointing to overlooked information he had read in the papers. It was commonly said that if he had begun sleuthing a few decades earlier that the Whitechapel murders would not be unsolved. Put simply, if Conan Doyle's famous detective had been based in Toronto, he would be her uncle.

She had arrived early. It was quintessential to detective work to always be on one's game. A *Longfellow's* detective was therefore required always to be early. And this applied most especially for her, not only for practical reasons – she was a woman, after all – but because of the name she bore.

She went up to the offices. The door being slightly ajar, she knocked politely to make her presence known before entering. By the state of him, she could tell her uncle hadn't slept. Wadsworth had just served tea. A single cup, she noted. She had been summoned, but wasn't expected to take tea. Could this mean that—

"Yes," Sir Lawrence said, after the briefest appraisal of her expression, "you are going on a case on your own. That case, in point of fact." He motioned to the file on the table by the door.

"Does this mean—"

"You're still an Inspector's Apprentice. Consider this your final examination."

She managed to suppress a look of glee. The product of many years' practise.

"The case is in the country; I've hired a motorcar for you." He took out his pocket watch. It was new; not the usual one he carried. It clashed with his attire. He looked up from the watch and gave her a mock look of reproach and a wry smile. "A gift from an old friend." He returned it to his pocket.

"Mr. Wickham helped with a case a few years ago. I was contacted this morning when they discovered his body. Everything I have is there, including the complicating factor. The motorcar should be just arriving. On you go now, Etty."

* * *

The ride was an opportunity to familiarise herself with the case, only there was precious little there. Just the notes he had jotted from his telephone conversation: the victim was a Mr. Reginald Wickham; he had been found dead in a walk-in freezer, probably killed by the bullet in his chest; the bullet was likely a small calibre. The complicating factor was the walk-in freezer. It was going to be dreadfully difficult to determine the time of the murder, and that meant that reasonable doubt would be more readily available for any prospective suspects to appeal to.

The rest of the information would be available from a Constable York when she arrived. Of course, at their present speed that would take two hours. She looked out the window to take in the view.

* * *

The recent Mr. Wickham had owned quite the estate. It was any wonder that he needed his own freezer if he hosted social gatherings. She noted that she ought to invest in whatever it was he had done in life.

The motorcar slowed to a halt in front of the steps as a constable made his way down. He opened the door for her. She took in his appearance: tall, though not excessively so, lean, right-handed, and a relative newcomer to policing. He also seemed quite surprised to see her.

"Er…hello, miss?"

"Loretta Longfellow," she answered as she showed her credentials. She swept the yard with her gaze.

"Inspector's Apprentice?" he asked.

"Yes. Sir Lawrence is my uncle. He sent me to aid in the case."

"I was under the impression that it was Sir Lawrence himself who would be attending." He looked more than a little crestfallen. She tried not to take it personally. Her uncle was a famous detective, and many people wanted to meet him. The desire was greater amongst policemen.

"Not today, I'm afraid. Now, I should like to the see the crime scene and the body – pray, tell me they're still in the same place?"

Her straight-to-business approach woke him to the task at hand. "Oh, of course. The only thing that's changed is that there's a sheet covering the body. The scene itself is roped off."

He turned and led her down the side of the manor to a servant's entrance. It led into the kitchen, and from there into the walk-in freezer. It was no wonder that no one heard any shots. It was tucked away from any rooms in which anyone actually slept.

"Apologies, Miss Longfellow, I haven't switched off the freezer, so it's quite cold in there."

"I'm sure I'll manage. It was right not to alter the crime scene." He brightened slightly at the praise. She realised that she had been quite brusque with him, to the point that she hadn't even asked the poor man's name. In pursuing his duties, her uncle had warned her, a detective may come off as aloof, or even rude. It was a side effect of a detective's first duty: paying attention to everything. In paying attention to everything, one split one's awareness in an unacceptable way when one was engaged in social niceties. She turned back before entering.

"I'm sorry, that's quite rude of me; what was your name?"

"Harry, err, that is, Constable York, Ma'am." He smiled and removed his helmet as he answered. She offered her hand and he took it. She had a man's handshake; he didn't seem to mind.

Social mores acknowledged, it was time to get back to it. She opened the door and walked in. First she saw her breath, then the covered shape on the floor. Constable York pulled back the sheet and she saw the blankly staring eyes of the dead man. It was difficult to tell through his clothes, but the bullet seemed to have either struck the heart directly, or close enough to it.

Her uncovered hands were beginning to shake.

"We should wait for the coroner to arrive to do anything else," she said, rubbing her hands together. "We don't want to do anything that might disturb the evidence. In the meantime, we can search for the gun, and interview anyone who was in the house at the time."

"Right. I've seen to it that the staff are waiting in the parlour. He has a wife and two sons: they're away, but returning sometime today. They were notified when the body was found."

"Good work, Constable. When was the last time Mr. Wickham was seen alive?"

He consulted his notes. "About midnight he finished a brandy in his study. His butler thought that he was going to turn in for the night. The chef found him in the freezer this morning. Apparently they were preparing for some high society to-do this evening."

"We'll have to use that as our working time of death, then. The freezer is going to make it difficult for the coroner to determine. It was a good choice, if our killer wanted to obscure the time of the murder."

* * *

Three servants had gathered in the parlour, seated on the chesterfield facing two chairs that Constable York had arranged. Mr. Smithers, Miss Foster and Monsieur Anatole. The butler, maid and chef, respectively. They struck quite the tableau: the butler was stoic, the maid was crying into a handkerchief, and the newly hired chef was utterly bewildered.

"To begin," Loretta said, pencil poised over her handheld notepad, "where were each of you at midnight?" She turned to the butler first.

He cleared his throat and answered. "I had just set out Mr. Wickham's night attire in his bedroom. When I saw him emerging from his study, he dismissed me for the night." He looked off into space. "That's the last I saw of him."

Loretta jotted down her notes while taking in all the particulars of the man's expressions. She turned to the maid once she was finished.

"Well, I had finished my cleaning early, so I was in bed," she said, through quiet sobs. "I didn't find out about..." she stifled another round of sobs "...poor Mr. Wickham until after I set out his place settings for breakfast."

Loretta saw that she would be of no further use in questioning. She avoided showing her contempt for such displays. She turned to Monsieur Anatole.

"I 'ave never met the man. I only just found 'is body when I went to check the freezer."

None of them gave any obvious signs that they were being untruthful. But then, she had just met them and had no baseline from which to judge. Better to try a different approach.

"May I see your hands, please?" she asked.

All three assented. She smelled every hand in the room, excluding her own and York's, of course. None smelled like gunpowder.

"All right," she said, as she returned her notes to her purse, "that's all for now, but I'll need everyone to remain on the premises. But do stay away from the freezer and Mr. Wickham's bedroom and study."

York followed her from the room. "Shall we check around some more for the gun?" he asked.

"Yes, that's about all we can do, now. I'd be shocked if any of them were guilty. I suppose one can wash off the smell of gunpowder, but it's difficult."

"Indeed," York agreed.

They had only searched a few rooms when Mr. Smithers notified them that the recent Wickham's wife and eldest son had returned. The coroner arrived at almost the same time. York led the coroner to the crime scene while Loretta returned to the parlour to question the mother and son. She was greeted by a rather curious sight. She had only just introduced herself when she noticed that the man and woman awaiting them could have been husband and wife themselves. She was only, possibly, five years older than he?

"Oh, I do apologise. I was given to understand that Mr. Wickham's *wife* and son had returned," she said.

The man barely stifled a laugh. The woman stiffened. Clearly, she was used to this mistake.

"I am his second wife. Elizabeth Wickham," she said. Loretta reddened slightly.

"I must apologise again, then, and offer my deepest condolences for your loss."

The room went silent for a long moment.

"There's no gentle way to broach this subject," Loretta began, "but I want to make it clear that these questions are routine, and I accuse no one of anything. Yet." She sat in the chair facing them. "I must ask your whereabouts at midnight last night."

"Well, that's easy enough for me," the man answered. "I'm Arthur Wickham, by the way. We were both staying with family friends – the MacKenzie family – in Etobicoke. I was in my room at the time. Though I can't vouch for *Mrs.* Wickham." He looked at her with an amusement that failed to hide his contempt.

Mrs. Wickham straightened, obviously practiced in avoiding the bait.

"I was also in my room," she said.

"Do either of you own a gun?" Loretta asked.

"No," Mrs. Wickham answered.

"I do," Arthur said, "but I left it at the MacKenzie residence in Etobicoke. I went hunting with Jim MacKenzie while I was there."

Loretta was unsurprised to find that Arthur's hands smelled faintly of gunpowder residue.

"I will need you to remain here Mr. Wickham. I must go to the coroner. I'm sure Mr. Smithers will bring you food and drink."

Loretta went directly to the crime scene. *What a lovely little nest of vipers*, she thought as she went.

Dr. Shaftesbury, the coroner, had removed the body from the freezer.

"It would have been difficult to estimate the time of death with the accuracy you're likely to require," Dr. Shaftesbury said. "Rigor has begun, but the cold will play bloody havoc with the temperature."

"I'm sorry," Loretta replied, "but did you say that it *would have been* difficult?"

York grinned. "We found his watch. Broken."

"Stuck at what time?" she asked, urgently.

"Half past six," he replied. "Just about half an hour before he was discovered."

* * *

Loretta and York spent the next hour searching the grounds and repeating the questions to everyone involved. The revelation of the watch had complicated things intolerably. The result was that everyone with motive had no means of committing the crime, because they had been too far from the scene to have acted. They had confirmed the alibi for both Arthur and Mrs. Wickham. The other son was also ruled out: he had been reached at his hotel in Kingston after the body was discovered, and was on his way by train. The hotel manager had confirmed.

If that wasn't enough, all those close enough to have committed the crime were completely lacking in any real motive. None of them had any sort of grudge against Wickham, and none had any financial stake in his life or death.

"We have either means with no discernable motive, or motive, but with no possible means," Loretta said as they searched the bushes of the grounds. "Even should we accuse someone, the Crown would be foolish to follow through with charges."

"Well, we'll just have to keep looking, then," York answered. "I'm sure there's no rush, murder cases aren't usually solved in a day, as far as I understand. We'll find that gun eventually."

York was right. She shouldn't get ahead of herself. It was just because her uncle had called this her 'final examination'. She was trying too hard to impress him. Besides, what were the odds that her uncle would select for her final examination a case that could be solved in the space of a day? Quite long, surely.

She took a deep breath. "It's possible that this was assassination. That the culprit came here for this purpose and then fled. We'll have to search for traces all along the grounds, and look at the financial information for his wife and sons. They may have alibis for their persons, but not for any contractual alliances they may have made."

"Yes, that would fit the evidence. Of course, there's been no sign of a broken window, or a door pried open, but we may be dealing with a professional."

"Yes, we may indeed. I'm going to walk the house again."

"Really? Haven't you looked at everything?"

"Yes, but not closely enough. You are an admirer of my uncle, yes?"

He blushed slightly. "Well, um, that is…I suppose so, yes."

"Come with me and I'll show you his most important lesson."

* * *

"There has been a great deal of misinformation regarding my uncle's methods in both the popular press and fictional accounts of his exploits. The accuracy comes in reporting the outcome of cases – well, mostly – but the methods are poorly understood. I've read in one source, for instance, that my uncle has twelve rules of detection; in another that he has thirty-seven. Neither are true. My uncle applies a rigorous understanding of the different systems of logic in discerning the guilty from the innocent, but he has only one rule peculiar to the art of detection."

"I'm sorry, there's more than one system of logic?"

"Of course," she answered, incredulous. She sometimes forgot that these lessons constituted a considerable portion of her education. "Deductive, inductive and abductive. Possibly there are as many distinct systems of logic as there are distinct avenues of inquiry. Detectives rarely deduce the guilty party – in the logical sense, that is. We take the data and come up with an explanation that suits them. Then we test that explanation against new data. Any datum may undermine the explanation. That is closer to abductive logic than pure deduction. Detection is essentially a creative art."

"All right, I think I follow. But, what's this rule, then?"

"The rule is to pay attention."

"To what?"

"To everything. He calls it *cataloguing*: building a catalogue of data about everything that may be germane to a case. It's how one derives the material with which to construct one's explanation."

"It's a bit complicated. But at the same time it's wonderfully simple."

"Well, yes. The difficulty comes when trying to force the human mind to engage in this approach. It's woefully ill-adapted to it."

They continued to walk through the house. Her expression carefully neutral as she looked scanned every object without focussing too heavily on any one in particular.

"Is there anywhere specific we should start?" York asked.

She stopped and considered the question.

"Whenever one comes upon a difficult spot, my uncle says that it is best to review the evidence one already has."

And then she almost smacked herself on the forehead for starting in the house.

"In this case, I think we should have another look at the body," she said. "There is something that I haven't seen."

* * *

They walked up to the body just as the coroner's assistants were preparing to load it into a wagon to go for the autopsy.

"Excuse me," Loretta said, "I'd like to see the personal effects, if it's not too much trouble."

"As you like," answered one of the assistants. He handed her a bag.

"Thank you very much." She rummaged through the contents of his pockets until she came across the broken watch. She looked it over carefully for a moment before realising that she would fail this test. She suddenly felt unsteady, as though the ground had fallen from under her feet. She supposed it had, in a way.

"What is it?" asked York. "Is something wrong?"

"I'm not sure," she answered. "I'll have to take this watch to consult with my uncle. Is that all right?"

Neither York nor Dr. Shaftesbury had any objection.

* * *

The ride back was a blur. She had no idea what would happen. The future had always been so certain, and now she was left with nothing but doubt. She found the door to her uncle's office open once again. This time, there were two glasses; but with scotch, not tea. Her uncle stood, looking out the window.

"I won't be passing this examination," she said, dispensing with all formalities. "Perhaps you could give me another case?"

Sir Lawrence held the outside world in his gaze for some time before he turned.

"Would you like to know why?"

"No," she whispered, a single tear escaping her stoic mask.

"I'm sorry," he said. "I take it you recognised the watch?"

"You had an exact copy made, and you broke it at a time that would make it impossible for you or anyone with any real motive to have means. Those that remained had means, but no motive. When I saw you this morning, you looked dishevelled, like you hadn't slept. Which isn't uncharacteristic, but under the circumstances, fits with the explanation that you killed him sometime between midnight and one o'clock, then travelled back to your Toronto office." She exhaled, then sat down and drank the scotch. "All true," he nodded.

She sat staring ahead for several minutes before he spoke.

"I need to tell you my reasons," he said. "I would like to say that I have always wanted to commit the perfect crime, but, although true on some level, it is rather trite. Wickham was a bad man. I know that he was, but he had managed to destroy the evidence I needed to prove it. He did not *help* me with a case years ago, he was the *object* of my investigation years ago." His expression darkened. "Before he was *Wickham*."

He looked out the window. "My only unsolved case..."

"Anyhow, that is not the only reason," he continued. "The other reason is *you*." She looked up suddenly. "I have wanted nothing more than for you to inherit my business, to have what you always wanted. But you are a woman and we are constrained by the attitudes of our time – ill-supported though they may be. The only way for anyone to take you seriously as my replacement, I reasoned, was for you to foil my own attempt at the perfect crime.

"Which you did, I might add, in an impressively short time." He sat and sipped his scotch, looking at her with unrestrained pride.

"No, this..." she shook her head adamantly. "This...this doesn't *help* me. Can't you see the horrible problem you've created for me?"

"That no one will trust the family name once I'm a convicted murderer?"

"Well, that too, I suppose. But no, I am referring to the epistemic problem."

He tilted his head. "Oh?"

"Your lessons have guided me in solving this case, and several others alongside you. But do those lessons come from my uncle the detective, or my uncle the murderer?"

He downed the rest of his scotch. "Well, I would say that you should trust in your training to help you decide, but we mustn't beg the question."

She laughed, in spite of herself.

"I would hope that you know how deeply I care about you, Etty. And that I'm truly sorry to leave you in your present position, but this was the only apparent solution to an interminable problem. Wickham had to be dealt with."

He poured another measure of scotch for each of them.

"Now, the gun is in my coat pocket, which you'll find on the hanger there. You'd best alert the police."

* * *

The police had come and gone, their faces white with disbelief and horror at what the famed detective had done. He had worked tirelessly to unmask the guilty, all the while wearing a mask of his own. None of them could quite believe it. She thought the papers would wax rhapsodic in some such way about the vagaries of fate. But she knew with absolute certainty that she had just lost her uncle.

She looked around the office. She had also gained the family business, for what it was worth. And she would certainly soon learn what worth remained.

She sipped on her third glass of scotch as the phone rang.

She let it ring as she closed her eyes, trying to decide whether she could ever find the strength to continue on in this damned profession.

She opened her eyes, decided.

"Longfellow's Private Detection Service, Inspector Longfellow speaking," she answered.

The Clever Mrs. Straithwaite

Ernest Bramah

Chapter I

MR. CARLYLE HAD ARRIVED at The Turrets in the very best possible spirits. Everything about him, from his immaculate white spats to the choice gardenia in his buttonhole, from the brisk decision with which he took the front-door steps to the bustling importance with which he had positively brushed Parkinson aside at the door of the library, proclaimed consequence and the extremely good terms on which he stood with himself.

"Prepare yourself, Max," he exclaimed. "If I hinted at a case of exceptional delicacy that will certainly interest you by its romantic possibilities—?"

"I should have the liveliest misgivings. Ten to one it would be a jewel mystery," hazarded Carrados, as his friend paused with the point of his communication withheld, after the manner of a quizzical youngster with a promised bon-bon held behind his back. "If you made any more of it I should reluctantly be forced to the conclusion that the case involved a society scandal connected with a priceless pearl necklace."

Mr. Carlyle's face fell.

"Then it *is* in the papers, after all?" he said, with an air of disappointment.

"What is in the papers, Louis?"

"Some hint of the fraudulent insurance of the Hon. Mrs. Straithwaite's pearl necklace," replied Carlyle.

"Possibly," admitted Carrados. "But so far I have not come across it."

Mr. Carlyle stared at his friend, and marching up to the table brought his hand down on it with an arresting slap.

"Then what in the name of goodness are you talking about, may I ask?" he demanded caustically. "If you know nothing of the Straithwaite affair, Max, what other pearl necklace case are you referring to?"

Carrados assumed the air of mild deprecation with which he frequently apologized for a blind man venturing to make a discovery.

"A philosopher once made the remark—"

"Had it anything to do with Mrs. Straithwaite's – the Hon. Mrs. Straithwaite's – pearl necklace? And let me warn you, Max, that I have read a good deal both of Mill and Spencer at odd times."

"It was neither Mill nor Spencer. He had a German name, so I will not mention it. He made the observation, which, of course, we recognize as an obvious commonplace when once it has been expressed, that in order to have an accurate knowledge of what a man will do on any occasion it is only necessary to study a single characteristic action of his."

"Utterly impracticable," declared Mr. Carlyle.

"I therefore knew that when you spoke of a case of exceptional interest to *me*, what you really meant, Louis, was a case of exceptional interest to *you*."

Mr. Carlyle's sudden thoughtful silence seemed to admit that possibly there might be something in the point.

"By applying, almost unconsciously, the same useful rule, I became aware that a mystery connected with a valuable pearl necklace and a beautiful young society belle would appeal the most strongly to your romantic imagination."

"Romantic! I, romantic? Thirty-five and a private inquiry agent! You are positively feverish, Max."

"Incurably romantic – or you would have got over it by now: the worst kind."

"Max, this may prove a most important and interesting case. Will you be serious and discuss it?"

"Jewel cases are rarely either important or interesting. Pearl necklace mysteries, in nine cases out of ten, spring from the miasma of social pretence and vapid competition and only concern people who do not matter in the least. The only attractive thing about them is the name. They are so barren of originality that a criminological Linnæus could classify them with absolute nicety. I'll tell you what, we'll draw up a set of tables giving the solution to every possible pearl necklace case for the next twenty-one years."

"We will do any mortal thing you like, Max, if you will allow Parkinson to administer a bromo-seltzer and then enable me to meet the officials of the Direct Insurance without a blush."

For three minutes Carrados picked his unerring way among the furniture as he paced the room silently but with irresolution in his face. Twice his hand went to a paper-covered book lying on his desk, and twice he left it untouched.

"Have you ever been in the lion-house at feeding-time, Louis?" he demanded abruptly.

"In the very remote past, possibly," admitted Mr. Carlyle guardedly.

"As the hour approaches it is impossible to interest the creatures with any other suggestion than that of raw meat. You came a day too late, Louis." He picked up the book and skimmed it adroitly into Mr. Carlyle's hands. "I have already scented the gore, and tasted in imagination the joy of tearing choice morsels from other similarly obsessed animals."

"'Catalogue des monnaies grecques et romaines,'" read the gentleman. "'To be sold by auction at the Hotel Drouet, Paris, salle 8, April the 24th, 25th, etc.' H'm." He turned to the plates of photogravure illustration which gave an air to the volume. "This is an event, I suppose?"

"It is the sort of dispersal we get about once in three years," replied Carrados. "I seldom attend the little sales, but I save up and then have a week's orgy."

"And when do you go?"

"Today. By the afternoon boat – Folkestone. I have already taken rooms at Mascot's. I'm sorry it has fallen so inopportunely, Louis."

Mr. Carlyle rose to the occasion with a display of extremely gentlemanly feeling – which had the added merit of being quite genuine.

"My dear chap, your regrets only serve to remind me how much I owe to you already. *Bon voyage*, and the most desirable of Eu—Eu—well, perhaps it would be safer to say, of Kimons, for your collection."

"I suppose," pondered Carrados, "this insurance business might have led to other profitable connexions?"

"That is quite true," admitted his friend. "I have been trying for some time – but do not think any more of it, Max."

"What time is it?" demanded Carrados suddenly.

"Eleven-twenty-five."

"Good. Has any officious idiot had anyone arrested?"

"No, it is only—"

"Never mind. Do you know much of the case?"

"Practically nothing as yet, unfortunately. I came—"

"Excellent. Everything is on our side. Louis, I won't go this afternoon – I will put off till the night boat from Dover. That will give us nine hours."

"Nine hours?" repeated the mystified Carlyle, scarcely daring to put into thought the scandalous inference that Carrados's words conveyed.

"Nine full hours. A pearl necklace case that cannot at least be left straight after nine hours' work will require a column to itself in our chart. Now, Louis, where does this Direct Insurance live?"

Carlyle had allowed his blind friend to persuade him into – as they had seemed at the beginning – many mad enterprises. But none had ever, in the light of his own experience, seemed so foredoomed to failure as when, at eleven-thirty, Carrados ordered his luggage to be on the platform of Charing Cross Station at eight-fifty and then turned light-heartedly to the task of elucidating the mystery of Mrs. Straithwaite's pearl necklace in the interval.

The head office of the Direct and Intermediate Insurance Company proved to be in Victoria Street. Thanks to Carrados's speediest car, they entered the building as the clocks of Westminster were striking twelve, but for the next twenty minutes they were consigned to the general office while Mr. Carlyle fumed and displayed his watch ostentatiously. At last a clerk slid off his stool by the speaking-tube and approached them.

"Mr. Carlyle?" he said. "The General Manager will see you now, but as he has another appointment in ten minutes he will be glad if you will make your business as short as possible. This way, please."

Mr. Carlyle bit his lip at the pompous formality of the message but he was too experienced to waste any words about it and with a mere nod he followed, guiding his friend until they reached the Manager's room. But, though subservient to circumstance, he was far from being negligible when he wished to create an impression.

"Mr. Carrados has been good enough to give us a consultation over this small affair," he said, with just the necessary touches of deference and condescension that it was impossible either to miss or to resent. "Unfortunately he can do little more as he has to leave almost at once to direct an important case in Paris."

The General Manager conveyed little, either in his person or his manner, of the brisk precision that his message seemed to promise. The name of Carrados struck him as being somewhat familiar – something a little removed from the routine of his business and a matter therefore that he could unbend over. He continued to stand comfortably before his office fire, making up by a tolerant benignity of his hard and bulbous eye for the physical deprivation that his attitude entailed on his visitors.

"Paris, egad?" he grunted. "Something in your line that France can take from us since the days of – what's-his-name – Vidocq, eh? Clever fellow, that, what? Wasn't it about him and the Purloined Letter?"

Carrados smiled discreetly.

"Capital, wasn't it?" he replied. "But there is something else that Paris can learn from London, more in your way, sir. Often when I drop in to see the principal of one of their chief houses or the head of a Government department, we fall into an entertaining discussion of this or that subject that may be on the tapis. 'Ah, monsieur,' I say, after perhaps half-an-hour's conversation, 'it is very amiable of you and sometimes I regret our insular methods, but it is not thus that great businesses are formed. At home, if I call upon one of our princes of industry – a railway director, a merchant, or the head of one of our leading insurance companies – nothing will tempt him for a moment from the stern outline of the business in hand. You are too complaisant; the merest gossip takes advantage of you.'"

"That's quite true," admitted the General Manager, occupying the revolving chair at his desk and assuming a serious and very determined expression. "Slackers, I call them. Now, Mr. Carlyle, where are we in this business?"

"I have your letter of yesterday. We should naturally like all the particulars you can give us."

The Manager threw open a formidable-looking volume with an immense display of energy, sharply flattened some typewritten pages that had ventured to raise their heads, and lifted an impressive finger.

"We start here, the 27th of January. On that day Karsfeld, the Princess Street jeweller, y'know, who acted as our jewellery assessor, forwards a proposal of the Hon. Mrs. Straithwaite to insure a pearl necklace against theft. Says that he has had an opportunity of examining it and passes it at five thousand pounds. That business goes through in the ordinary way; the premium is paid and the policy taken out.

"A couple of months later Karsfeld has a little unpleasantness with us and resigns. Resignation accepted. We have nothing against him, you understand. At the same time there is an impression among the directors that he has been perhaps a little too easy in his ways, a little too – let us say, expansive, in some of his valuations and too accommodating to his own clients in recommending to us business of a – well – speculative basis; business that we do not care about and which we now feel is foreign to our traditions as a firm. However" – the General Manager threw apart his stubby hands as though he would shatter any fabric of criminal intention that he might be supposed to be insidiously constructing – "that is the extent of our animadversion against Karsfeld. There are no irregularities and you may take it from me that the man is all right."

"You would propose accepting the fact that a five-thousand-pound necklace was submitted to him?" suggested Mr. Carlyle.

"I should," acquiesced the Manager, with a weighty nod. "Still – this brings us to April the third – this break, so to speak, occurring in our routine, it seemed a good opportunity for us to assure ourselves on one or two points. Mr. Bellitzer – you know Bellitzer, of course; know *of* him, I should say – was appointed *vice* Karsfeld and we wrote to certain of our clients, asking them – as our policies entitled us to do – as a matter of form to allow Mr. Bellitzer to confirm the assessment of his predecessor. Wrapped it up in silver paper, of course; said it would certify the present value and be a guarantee that would save them some formalities in case of ensuing claim, and so on. Among others, wrote to the Hon. Mrs. Straithwaite to that effect – April fourth. Here is her reply of three days later. Sorry to disappoint us, but the necklace has just been sent to her bank for custody as she is on the point of leaving town. Also scarcely sees that it is necessary in her case as the insurance was only taken so recently."

"That is dated April the seventh?" inquired Mr. Carlyle, busy with pencil and pocket-book.

"April seventh," repeated the Manager, noting this conscientiousness with an approving glance and then turning to regard questioningly the indifferent attitude of his other visitor. "That put us on our guard – naturally. Wrote by return regretting the necessity and suggesting that a line to her bankers, authorizing them to show us the necklace, would meet the case and save her any personal trouble. Interval of a week. Her reply, April sixteenth. Thursday last. Circumstances have altered her plans and she has returned to London sooner than she expected. Her jewel-case has been returned from the bank, and will we send our man round – 'our man,' Mr. Carlyle! – on Saturday morning not later than twelve, please."

The Manager closed the record book, with a sweep of his hand cleared his desk for revelations, and leaning forward in his chair fixed Mr. Carlyle with a pragmatic eye.

"On Saturday Mr. Bellitzer goes to Luneburg Mansions and the Hon. Mrs. Straithwaite shows him the necklace. He examines it carefully, assesses its insurable value up to five thousand, two hundred and fifty pounds, and reports us to that effect. But he reports something else, Mr. Carlyle. It is not the necklace that the lady had insured."

"Not the necklace?" echoed Mr. Carlyle.

"No. In spite of the number of pearls and a general similarity there are certain technical differences, well known to experts, that made the fact indisputable. The Hon. Mrs. Straithwaite has been guilty of misrepresentation. Possibly she has no fraudulent intention. We are willing to pay to find out. That's your business."

Mr. Carlyle made a final note and put away his book with an air of decision that could not fail to inspire confidence.

"Tomorrow," he said, "we shall perhaps be able to report something."

"Hope so," vouchsafed the Manager. "'Morning."

From his position near the window, Carrados appeared to wake up to the fact that the interview was over.

"But so far," he remarked blandly, with his eyes towards the great man in the chair, "you have told us nothing of the theft."

The Manager regarded the speaker dumbly for a moment and then turned to Mr. Carlyle.

"What does he mean?" he demanded pungently.

But for once Mr. Carlyle's self-possession had forsaken him. He recognized that somehow Carrados had been guilty of an appalling lapse, by which his reputation for prescience was wrecked in that quarter forever, and at the catastrophe his very ears began to exude embarrassment.

In the awkward silence Carrados himself seemed to recognize that something was amiss.

"We appear to be at cross-purposes," he observed. "I inferred that the disappearance of the necklace would be the essence of our investigation."

"Have I said a word about it disappearing?" demanded the Manager, with a contempt-laden raucity that he made no pretence of softening. "You don't seem to have grasped the simple facts about the case, Mr. Carrados. Really, I hardly think— Oh, come in!"

There had been a knock at the door, then another. A clerk now entered with an open telegram.

"Mr. Longworth wished you to see this at once, sir."

"We may as well go," whispered Mr. Carlyle with polite depression to his colleague.

"Here, wait a minute," said the Manager, who had been biting his thumb-nail over the telegram. "No, not you" – to the lingering clerk – "you clear." Much of the embarrassment that had troubled Mr. Carlyle a minute before seemed to have got into the Manager's system. "I don't understand this," he confessed awkwardly. "It's from Bellitzer. He wires: '*Have just heard alleged robbery Straithwaite pearls. Advise strictest investigation.*'"

Mr. Carlyle suddenly found it necessary to turn to the wall and consult a highly coloured lithographic inducement to insure. Mr. Carrados alone remained to meet the Manager's constrained glance.

"Still, *he* tells us really nothing about the theft," he remarked sociably.

"No," admitted the Manager, experiencing some little difficulty with his breathing, "he does not."

"Well, we still hope to be able to report something tomorrow. Goodbye."

It was with an effort that Mr. Carlyle straightened himself sufficiently to take leave of the Manager. Several times in the corridor he stopped to wipe his eyes.

"Max, you unholy fraud," he said, when they were outside, "you knew all the time."

"No; I told you that I knew nothing of it," replied Carrados frankly. "I am absolutely sincere."

"Then all I can say is, that I see a good many things happen that I don't believe in."

Carrados's reply was to hold out a coin to a passing newsboy and to hand the purchase to his friend who was already in the car.

"There is a slang injunction to 'keep your eyes skinned.' That being out of my power, I habitually 'keep my ears skinned.' You would be surprised to know how very little you hear, Louis, and how much you miss. In the last five minutes up there I have had three different newsboys' account of this development."

"By Jupiter, she hasn't waited long!" exclaimed Mr. Carlyle, referring eagerly to the headlines. "'PEARL NECKLACE SENSATION. SOCIETY LADY'S £5000 TRINKET DISAPPEARS.' Things are moving. Where next, Max?"

"It is now a quarter to one," replied Carrados, touching the fingers of his watch. "We may as well lunch on the strength of this new turn. Parkinson will have finished packing; I can telephone him to come to us at Merrick's in case I require him. Buy all the papers, Louis, and we will collate the points."

The undoubted facts that survived a comparison were few and meagre, for in each case a conscientious journalist had touched up a few vague or doubtful details according to his own ideas of probability. All agreed that on Tuesday evening – it was now Thursday – Mrs. Straithwaite had formed one of a party that had occupied a box at the new Metropolitan Opera House to witness the performance of *La Pucella*, and that she had been robbed of a set of pearls valued in round figures at five thousand pounds. There agreement ended. One version represented the theft as taking place at the theatre. Another asserted that at the last moment the lady had decided not to wear the necklace that evening and that its abstraction had been cleverly effected from the flat during her absence. Into a third account came an ambiguous reference to Markhams, the well-known jewellers, and a conjecture that their loss would certainly be covered by insurance.

Mr. Carlyle, who had been picking out the salient points of the narratives, threw down the last paper with an impatient shrug.

"Why in heaven's name have we Markhams coming into it now?" he demanded. "What have they to lose by it, Max? What do you make of the thing?"

"There is the second genuine string – the one Bellitzer saw. That belongs to someone."

"By gad, that's true – only five days ago, too. But what does our lady stand to make by that being stolen?"

Carrados was staring into obscurity between an occasional moment of attention to his cigarette or coffee.

"By this time the lady probably stands to wish she was well out of it," he replied thoughtfully. "Once you have set this sort of stone rolling and it has got beyond you—" He shook his head.

"It has become more intricate than you expected?" suggested Carlyle, in order to afford his friend an opportunity of withdrawing.

Carrados pierced the intention and smiled affectionately.

"My dear Louis," he said, "one-fifth of the mystery is already solved."

"One-fifth? How do you arrive at that?"

"Because it is one-twenty-five and we started at eleven-thirty."

He nodded to their waiter, who was standing three tables away, and paid the bill. Then with perfect gravity he permitted Mr. Carlyle to lead him by the arm into the street, where their car was waiting, Parkinson already there in attendance.

"Sure I can be of no further use?" asked Carlyle. Carrados had previously indicated that after lunch he would go on alone, but, because he was largely sceptical of the outcome, the professional man felt guiltily that he was deserting. "Say the word?"

Carrados smiled and shook his head. Then he leaned across.

"I am going to the opera house now; then, possibly, to talk to Markham a little. If I have time I must find a man who knows the Straithwaites, and after that I may look up Inspector Beedel if he is at the Yard. That is as far as I can see yet, until I call at Luneburg Mansions. Come round on the third anyway."

"Dear old chap," murmured Mr. Carlyle, as the car edged its way ahead among the traffic. "Marvellous shots he makes!"

In the meanwhile, at Luneburg Mansions, Mrs. Straithwaite had been passing anything but a pleasant day. She had awakened with a headache and an overnight feeling that there was some unpleasantness to be gone on with. That it did not amount to actual fear was due to the enormous self-importance and the incredible ignorance which ruled the butterfly brain of the young society beauty – for in spite of three years' experience of married life Stephanie Straithwaite was as yet on the enviable side of two and twenty.

Anticipating an early visit from a particularly obnoxious sister-in-law, she had remained in bed until after lunch in order to be able to deny herself with the more conviction. Three journalists who would have afforded her the mild excitement of being interviewed had called and been in turn put off with polite regrets by her husband. The objectionable sister-in-law postponed her visit until the afternoon and for more than an hour Stephanie 'suffered agonies.' When the visitor had left and the martyred hostess announced her intention of flying immediately to the consoling society of her own bridge circle, Straithwaite had advised her, with some significance, to wait for a lead. The unhappy lady cast herself bodily down upon a couch and asked whether she was to become a nun. Straithwaite merely shrugged his shoulders and remembered a club engagement. Evidently there was no need for him to become a monk: Stephanie followed him down the hall, arguing and protesting. That was how they came jointly to encounter Carrados at the door.

"I have come from the Direct Insurance in the hope of being able to see Mrs. Straithwaite," he explained, when the door opened rather suddenly before he had knocked. "My name is Carrados – Max Carrados."

There was a moment of hesitation all round. Then Stephanie read difficulties in the straightening lines of her husband's face and rose joyfully to the occasion.

"Oh yes; come in, Mr. Carrados," she exclaimed graciously. "We are not quite strangers, you know. You found out something for Aunt Pigs; I forget what, but she was most frantically impressed."

"Lady Poges," enlarged Straithwaite, who had stepped aside and was watching the development with slow, calculating eyes. "But, I say, you are blind, aren't you?"

Carrados's smiling admission turned the edge of Mrs. Straithwaite's impulsive, "Teddy!"

"But I get along all right," he added. "I left my man down in the car and I found your door first shot, you see."

The references reminded the velvet-eyed little mercenary that the man before her had the reputation of being quite desirably rich, his queer taste merely an eccentric hobby. The consideration made her resolve to be quite her nicest possible, as she led the way to the drawing-room. Then Teddy, too, had been horrid beyond words and must be made to suffer in the readiest way that offered.

"Teddy is just going out and I was to be left in solitary bereavement if you had not appeared," she explained airily. "It wasn't very compy only to come to see me on business by the way, Mr. Carrados, but if those are your only terms I must agree.

Straithwaite, however, did not seem to have the least intention of going. He had left his hat and stick in the hall and he now threw his yellow gloves down on a table and took up a negligent position on the arm of an easy-chair.

"The thing is, where do we stand?" he remarked tentatively.

"That is the attitude of the insurance company, I imagine," replied Carrados.

"I don't see that the company has any standing in the matter. We haven't reported any loss to them and we are not making any claim, so far. That ought to be enough."

"I assume that they act on general inference," explained Carrados. "A limited liability company is not subtle, Mrs. Straithwaite. This one knows that you have insured a five-thousand-pound pearl necklace with it, and when it becomes a matter of common knowledge that you have had one answering to that description stolen, it jumps to the conclusion that they are one and the same."

"But they aren't – worse luck," explained the hostess. "This was a string that I let Markhams send me to see if I would keep."

"The one that Bellitzer saw last Saturday?"

"Yes," admitted Mrs. Straithwaite quite simply.

Straithwaite glanced sharply at Carrados and then turned his eyes with lazy indifference to his wife.

"My dear Stephanie, what are you thinking of?" he drawled. "Of course those could not have been Markhams' pearls. Not knowing that you are much too clever to do such a foolish thing, Mr. Carrados will begin to think that you have had fraudulent designs upon his company."

Whether the tone was designed to exasperate or merely fell upon a fertile soil, Stephanie threw a hateful little glance in his direction.

"I don't care," she exclaimed recklessly; "I haven't the least little objection in the world to Mr. Carrados knowing exactly how it happened."

Carrados put in an instinctive word of warning, even raised an arresting hand, but the lady was much too excited, too voluble, to be denied.

"It doesn't really matter in the least, Mr. Carrados, because nothing came of it," she explained. "There never were any real pearls to be insured. It would have made no difference to the company, because I did not regard this as an ordinary insurance from the first. It was to be a loan."

"A loan?" repeated Carrados.

"Yes. I shall come into heaps and heaps of money in a few years' time under Prin-Prin's will. Then I should pay back whatever had been advanced."

"But would it not have been better – simpler – to have borrowed purely on the anticipation?"

"We have," explained the lady eagerly. "We have borrowed from all sorts of people, and both Teddy and I have signed heaps and heaps of papers, until now no one will lend any more."

The thing was too tragically grotesque to be laughed at. Carrados turned his face from one to the other and by ear, and by even finer perceptions, he focussed them in his mind – the delicate, feather-headed beauty, with the heart of a cat and the irresponsibility of a kitten, eye and mouth already hardening under the stress of her frantic life, and, across the room, her debonair consort, whose lank pose and nonchalant attitude towards the situation Carrados had not yet categorized.

Straithwaite's dry voice, with its habitual drawl, broke into his reflection.

"I don't suppose for a moment that you either know or care what this means, my dear girl, but I will proceed to enlighten you. It means the extreme probability that unless you can persuade Mr. Carrados to hold his tongue, you, and – without prejudice – I also, will get two years' hard. And yet, with unconscious but consummate artistry, it seems to me that you have perhaps done the trick; for, unless I am mistaken, Mr Carrados will find himself unable to take advantage of your guileless confidence, whereas he would otherwise have quite easily found out all he wanted."

"That is the most utter nonsense, Teddy," cried Stephanie, with petulant indignation. She turned to Carrados with the assurance of meeting understanding. "We know Mr. Justice Enderleigh very well indeed, and if there was any bother I should not have the least difficulty in getting him to take the case privately and in explaining everything to him. But why should there be? Why indeed?" A brilliant little new idea possessed her. "Do you know any of these insurance people at all intimately, Mr. Carrados?"

"The General Manager and I are on terms that almost justify us in addressing each other as 'silly ass,'" admitted Carrados.

"There you see, Teddy, you needn't have been in a funk. Mr. Carrados would put everything right. Let me tell you exactly how I had arranged it. I dare say you know that insurances are only too pleased to pay for losses: it gives them an advertisement. Freddy Tantroy told me so, and his father is a director of hundreds of companies. Only, of course, it must be done quite regularly. Well, for months and months we had both been most frightfully hard up, and, unfortunately, everyone else – at least all our friends – seemed just as stony. I had been absolutely racking my poor brain for an idea when I remembered papa's wedding present. It was a string of pearls that he sent me from Vienna, only a month before he died; not real, of course, because poor papa was always quite utterly on the verge himself, but very good imitation and in perfect taste. Otherwise I am sure papa would rather have sent a silver penwiper, for although he had to live abroad because of what people said, his taste was simply exquisite and he was most romantic in his ideas. What do you say, Teddy?"

"Nothing, dear; it was only my throat ticking."

"I wore the pearls often and millions of people had seen them. Of course our own people knew about them, but others took it for granted that they were genuine for me to be wearing them. Teddy will tell you that I was almost babbling in delirium, things were becoming so ghastly, when an idea occurred. Tweety – she's a cousin of Teddy's, but quite an aged person – has a whole coffer full of jewels that she never wears and I knew that there was a necklace very like mine among them. She was going almost immediately to Africa for some shooting, so I literally flew into the wilds of Surrey and begged her on my knees to lend me her pearls for the Lycester House dance. When I got back with them I stamped on the clasp and took it at once to Karsfeld in Princess Street. I told him they were only paste but I thought they were rather good and I wanted them by the next day. And of course he looked at them, and then looked again, and then asked me if I was certain they were imitation, and I said, 'Well, we had never thought twice about it, because poor papa was always rather chronic, only certainly he did occasionally have fabulous streaks at the tables,' and finally, like a great owl, Karsfeld said:

"'I am happy to be able to congratulate you, madam. They are undoubtedly Bombay pearls of very fine orient. They are certainly worth five thousand pounds.'"

From this point Mrs. Straithwaite's narrative ran its slangy, obvious course. The insurance effected – on the strict understanding of the lady with herself that it was merely a novel form of loan, and after satisfying her mind on Freddy Tantroy's authority that the Direct and Intermediate could stand a temporary loss of five thousand pounds – the genuine pearls were returned to the cousin in the wilds of Surrey and Stephanie continued to wear the counterfeit. A decent interval was allowed to intervene and the plot was on the point of maturity when the company's request for a scrutiny fell like a thunderbolt. With many touching appeals to Mr. Carrados to picture her frantic distraction, with appropriate little gestures of agony and despair, Stephanie described her absolute prostration, her subsequent wild scramble through the jewel stocks of London to find a substitute. The danger over, it became increasingly necessary to act without delay, not only to anticipate possible further curiosity on the part of the insurance, but in order to secure the means with which to meet an impending obligation held over them by an inflexibly obdurate Hebrew.

The evening of the previous Tuesday was to be the time; the opera house, during the performance of *La Pucella*, the place. Straithwaite, who was not interested in that precise form of drama, would not be expected to be present, but with a false moustache and a few other touches which his experience as an amateur placed within his easy reach, he was to occupy a stall, an end stall somewhere beneath his wife's box. At an agreed signal Stephanie would jerk open the catch of the necklace, and as she leaned forward the ornament would trickle off her neck and disappear into the arena beneath. Straithwaite, the only one prepared for anything happening, would have no difficulty in securing it. He would look up quickly as if to identify the box, and with the jewels in his hand walk deliberately out into the passage. Before anyone had quite realized what was happening he would have left the house.

Carrados turned his face from the woman to the man.

"This scheme commended itself to you, Mr. Straithwaite?"

"Well, you see, Stephanie is so awfully clever that I took it for granted that the thing would go all right."

"And three days before, Bellitzer had already reported misrepresentation and that two necklaces had been used!"

"Yes," admitted Straithwaite, with an air of reluctant candour, "I had a suspicion that Stephanie's native ingenuity rather fizzled there. You know, Stephanie dear, there *is* a difference, it seems, between Bombay and Californian pearls."

"The wretch!" exclaimed the girl, grinding her little teeth vengefully. "And we gave him champagne!"

"But nothing came of it; so it doesn't matter?" prompted Straithwaite.

"Except that now Markhams' pearls have gone and they are hinting at all manner of diabolical things," she wrathfully reminded him.

"True," he confessed. "That is by way of a sequel, Mr. Carrados. I will endeavour to explain that part of the incident, for even yet Stephanie seems unable to do me justice."

He detached himself from the arm of the chair and lounged across the room to another chair, where he took up exactly the same position.

"On the fatal evening I duly made my way to the theatre – a little late, so as to take my seat unobserved. After I had got the general hang I glanced up occasionally until I caught Stephanie's eye, by which I knew that she was there all right and concluded that everything was going along quite jollily. According to arrangement, I was to cross the theatre immediately the first curtain fell and standing opposite Stephanie's box twist my watch chain until it was certain that she had seen me. Then Stephanie was to fan herself three times with her programme. Both, you will see, perfectly innocent operations, and yet conveying to each other the intimation that all was well. Stephanie's idea, of course. After that, I would return to my seat and Stephanie would do her part at the first opportunity in Act II.

"However, we never reached that. Towards the end of the first act something white and noiseless slipped down and fell at my feet. For the moment I thought they were the pearls gone wrong. Then I saw that it was a glove – a lady's glove. Intuition whispered that it was Stephanie's before I touched it. I picked it up and quietly got out. Down among the fingers was a scrap of paper – the corner torn off a programme. On it were pencilled words to this effect:

Something quite unexpected. Can do nothing tonight. Go back at once and wait. May return early. Frightfully worried.—S.

"You kept the paper, of course?"

"Yes. It is in my desk in the next room. Do you care to see it?"

"Please."

Straithwaite left the room and Stephanie flung herself into a charming attitude of entreaty.

"Mr. Carrados, you will get them back for us, won't you? It would not really matter, only I seem to have signed something and now Markhams threaten to bring an action against us for culpable negligence in leaving them in an empty flat."

"You see," explained Straithwaite, coming back in time to catch the drift of his wife's words, "except to a personal friend like yourself, it is quite impossible to submit these clues. The first one alone would raise embarrassing inquiries; the other is beyond explanation. Consequently I have been obliged to concoct an imaginary burglary in our absence and to drop the necklace case among the rhododendrons in the garden at the back, for the police to find."

"Deeper and deeper," commented Carrados.

"Why, yes. Stephanie and I are finding that out, aren't we, dear? However, here is the first note; also the glove. Of course I returned immediately. It was Stephanie's strategy and I was under her orders. In something less than half-an-hour I heard a motor car stop outside. Then the bell here rang.

"I think I have said that I was alone. I went to the door and found a man who might have been anything standing there. He merely said: 'Mr. Straithwaite?' and on my nodding handed me a letter. I tore it open in the hall and read it. Then I went into my room and read it again. This is it:

Dear T.,—Absolutely ghastly. We simply must put off tonight. Will explain that later. Now what do you think? Bellitzer is here in the stalls and young K. D. has asked him to join us at supper at the Savoy. It appears that the creature is Something and I suppose the D.'s want to borrow off him. I can't get out of it and I am literally quaking. Don't you see, he will spot something? Send me the M. string at once and I will change somehow before supper. I am scribbling this in the dark. I have got the Willoughby's man to take it. Don't, don't fail.—S.

"It is ridiculous, preposterous," snapped Stephanie. "I never wrote a word of it – or the other. There was I, sitting the whole evening. And Teddy – oh, it is maddening!"

"I took it into my room and looked at it closely," continued the unruffled Straithwaite. "Even if I had any reason to doubt, the internal evidence was convincing, but how could I doubt? It read like a continuation of the previous message. The writing was reasonably like Stephanie's under the circumstances, the envelope had obviously been obtained from the box-office of the theatre and the paper itself was a sheet of the programme. A corner was torn off; I put against it the previous scrap and they exactly fitted." The gentleman shrugged his shoulders, stretched his legs with deliberation and walked across the room to look out of the window. "I made them up into a neat little parcel and handed it over," he concluded.

Carrados put down the two pieces of paper which he had been minutely examining with his finger-tips and still holding the glove addressed his small audience collectively.

"The first and most obvious point is that whoever carried out the scheme had more than a vague knowledge of your affairs, not only in general but also relating to this – well, loan, Mrs. Straithwaite."

"Just what I have insisted," agreed Straithwaite. "You hear that, Stephanie?"

"But who is there?" pleaded Stephanie, with weary intonation. "Absolutely no one in the wide world. Not a soul."

"So one is liable to think offhand. Let us go further, however, merely accounting for those who are in a position to have information. There are the officials of the insurance company who suspect something; there is Bellitzer, who perhaps knows a little more. There is the lady in Surrey from whom the pearls were borrowed, a Mr. Tantroy who seems to have been consulted, and, finally, your own servants. All these people have friends, or underlings, or observers. Suppose Mr. Bellitzer's confidential clerk happens to be the sweetheart of your maid?"

"They would still know very little."

"The arc of a circle may be very little, but, given that, it is possible to construct the entire figure. Now your servants, Mrs. Straithwaite? We are accusing no one, of course."

"There is the cook, Mullins. She displayed alarming influenza on Tuesday morning, and although it was most frightfully inconvenient I packed her off home without a moment's delay. I have a horror of the influ. Then Fraser, the parlourmaid. She does my hair – I haven't really got a maid, you know."

"Peter," prompted Straithwaite.

"Oh yes, Beta. She's a daily girl and helps in the kitchen. I have no doubt she is capable of any villainy."

"And all were out on Tuesday evening?"

"Yes. Mullins gone home. Beta left early as there was no dinner, and I told Fraser to take the evening after she had dressed me so that Teddy could make up and get out without being seen."

Carrados turned to his other witness.

"The papers and the glove have been with you ever since?"

"Yes, in my desk."

"Locked?"

"Yes."

"And this glove, Mrs. Straithwaite? There is no doubt that it is yours?"

"I suppose not," she replied. "I never thought. I know that when I came to leave the theatre one had vanished and Teddy had it here."

"That was the first time you missed it?"

"Yes."

"But it might have gone earlier in the evening – mislaid or lost or stolen?"

"I remember taking them off in the box. I sat in the corner farthest from the stage – the front row, of course – and I placed them on the support."

"Where anyone in the next box could abstract one without much difficulty at a favourable moment."

"That is quite likely. But we didn't see anyone in the next box."

"I have half an idea that I caught sight of someone hanging back," volunteered Straithwaite.

"Thank you," said Carrados, turning towards him almost gratefully. "That is most important – that you think you saw someone hanging back. Now the other glove, Mrs. Straithwaite; what became of that?"

"An odd glove is not very much good, is it?" said Stephanie. "Certainly I wore it coming back. I think I threw it down somewhere in here. Probably it is still about. We are in a frantic muddle and nothing is being done."

The second glove was found on the floor in a corner. Carrados received it and laid it with the other.

"You use a very faint and characteristic scent, I notice, Mrs. Straithwaite," he observed.

"Yes; it is rather sweet, isn't it? I don't know the name because it is in Russian. A friend in the Embassy sent me some bottles from Petersburg."

"But on Tuesday you supplemented it with something stronger," he continued, raising the gloves delicately one after the other to his face.

"Oh, eucalyptus; rather," she admitted. "I simply drenched my handkerchief with it."

"You have other gloves of the same pattern?"

"Have I? Now let me think! Did you give them to me, Teddy?"

"No," replied Straithwaite from the other end of the room. He had lounged across to the window and his attitude detached him from the discussion. "Didn't Whitstable?" he added shortly.

"Of course. Then there are three pairs, Mr. Carrados, because I never let Bimbi lose more than that to me at once, poor boy."

"I think you are rather tiring yourself out, Stephanie," warned her husband.

Carrados's attention seemed to leap to the voice; then he turned courteously to his hostess.

"I appreciate that you have had a trying time lately, Mrs. Straithwaite," he said. 'Every moment I have been hoping to let you out of the witness-box—"

"Perhaps tomorrow—" began Straithwaite, recrossing the room.

"Impossible; I leave town tonight," replied Carrados firmly. "You have three pairs of these gloves, Mrs. Straithwaite. Here is one. The other two—?"

"One pair I have not worn yet. The other – good gracious, I haven't been out since Tuesday! I suppose it is in my glove-box."

"I must see it, please."

Straithwaite opened his mouth, but as his wife obediently rose to her feet to comply he turned sharply away with the word unspoken.

"These are they," she said, returning.

"Mr. Carrados and I will finish our investigation in my room," interposed Straithwaite, with quiet assertiveness. "I should advise you to lie down for half-an-hour, Stephanie, if you don't want to be a nervous wreck tomorrow."

"You must allow the culprit to endorse that good advice, Mrs. Straithwaite," added Carrados. He had been examining the second pair of gloves as they spoke and he now handed them back again. "They are undoubtedly of the same set," he admitted, with extinguished interest, "and so our clue runs out."

"I hope you don't mind," apologized Straithwaite, as he led his guest to his own smoking-room. "Stephanie," he confided, becoming more cordial as two doors separated them from the lady, "is a creature of nerves and indiscretions. She forgets. Tonight she will not sleep. Tomorrow she will suffer." Carrados divined the grin. "So shall I!"

"On the contrary, pray accept my regrets," said the visitor. "Besides," he continued, "there is nothing more for me to do here, I suppose..."

"It is a mystery," admitted Straithwaite, with polite agreement. "Will you try a cigarette?"

"Thanks. Can you see if my car is below?" They exchanged cigarettes and stood at the window lighting them.

"There is one point, by the way, that may have some significance." Carrados had begun to recross the room and stopped to pick up the two fictitious messages. "You will have noticed that this is the outside sheet of a programme. It is not the most suitable for the purpose; the first inner sheet is more convenient to write on, but there the date appears. You see the inference? The programme was obtained before—"

"Perhaps. Well—?" for Carrados had broken off abruptly and was listening.

"You hear someone coming up the steps?"

"It is the general stairway."

"Mr. Straithwaite, I don't know how far this has gone in other quarters. We may only have a few seconds before we are interrupted."

"What do you mean?"

"I mean that the man who is now on the stairs is a policeman or has worn the uniform. If he stops at your door—"

The heavy tread ceased. Then came the authoritative knock.

"Wait," muttered Carrados, laying his hand impressively on Straithwaite's tremulous arm. "I may recognize the voice."

They heard the servant pass along the hall and the door unlatched; then caught the jumble of a gruff inquiry.

"Inspector Beedel of Scotland Yard!" The servant repassed their door on her way to the drawing-room. "It is no good disguising the fact from you, Mr. Straithwaite, that you may no longer be at liberty. But I am. *Is there anything you wish done?*"

There was no time for deliberation. Straithwaite was indeed between the unenviable alternatives of the familiar proverb, but, to do him justice, his voice had lost scarcely a ripple of its usual sang-froid.

"Thanks," he replied, taking a small stamped and addressed parcel from his pocket, "you might drop this into some obscure pillar-box, if you will."

"The Markham necklace?"

"Exactly. I was going out to post it when you came."

"I am sure you were."

"And if you could spare five minutes later – if I am here—"

Carrados slid his cigarette-case under some papers on the desk.

"I will call for that," he assented. "Let us say about half-past eight."

* * *

"I am still at large, you see, Mr. Carrados; though after reflecting on the studied formality of the inspector's business here, I imagine that you will scarcely be surprised."

"I have made it a habit," admitted Carrados, "never to be surprised."

"However, I still want to cut a rather different figure in your eyes. You regard me, Mr. Carrados, either as a detected rogue or a repentant ass?"

"Another excellent rule is never to form deductions from uncertainties."

Straithwaite made a gesture of mild impatience.

"You only give me ten minutes. If I am to put my case before you, Mr. Carrados, we cannot fence with phrases.... Today you have had an exceptional opportunity of penetrating into our mode of life. You will, I do not doubt, have summed up our perpetual indebtedness and the easy credit that our connexion procures; Stephanie's social ambitions and expensive popularity; her utterly extravagant incapacity to see any other possible existence; and my tacit acquiescence. You will, I know, have correctly gauged her irresponsible, neurotic temperament, and judged the result of it in conflict with my own. What possibly has escaped you, for in society one has to disguise these things, is that I still love my wife.

"When you dare not trust the soundness of your reins you do not try to pull up a bolting horse. For three years I have endeavoured to guide Stephanie round awkward comers with as little visible restraint as possible. When we differ over any project upon which she has set her heart Stephanie has one strong argument."

"That you no longer love her?"

"Well, perhaps; but more forcibly expressed. She rushes to the top of the building – there are six floors, Mr. Carrados, and we are on the second – and climbing on to the banister she announces her intention of throwing herself down into the basement. In the meanwhile I have followed her and drag her back again. One day I shall stay where I am and let her do as she intends."

"I hope not," said Carrados gravely.

"Oh, don't be concerned. She will then climb back herself. But it will mark an epoch. It was by that threat that she obtained my acquiescence to this scheme – that and the certainty that she would otherwise go on without me. But I had no intention of allowing her to land herself – to say nothing of us both – behind the bars of a prison if I could help it. And, above all, I wished to cure her of her fatuous delusion that she is clever, in the hope that she may then give up being foolish.

"To fail her on the occasion was merely to postpone the attempt. I conceived the idea of seeming to cooperate and at the same time involving us in what appeared to be a clever counter-fraud. The thought of the real loss will perhaps have a good effect; the publicity will certainly prevent her from daring a second 'theft.' A sordid story, Mr. Carrados," he concluded. "Do not forget your cigarette-case in reality."

The paternal shake of Carrados's head over the recital was neutralized by his benevolent smile.

"Yes, yes," he said. "I think we can classify you, Mr. Straithwaite. One point – the glove?"

"That was an afterthought. I had arranged the whole story and the first note was to be brought to me by an attendant. Then, on my way, in my overcoat pocket I discovered a pair of Stephanie's gloves which she had asked me to carry the day before. The suggestion flashed – how much more convincing if I could arrange for her to seem to drop the writing in that way. As she said, the next box *was* empty; I merely took possession of it for a few minutes and quietly drew across one of her gloves. And that reminds me – of course there was nothing in it, but your interest in them made me rather nervous."

Carrados laughed outright. Then he stood up and held out his hand.

"Goodnight, Mr. Straithwaite," he said, with real friendliness. "Let me give you the quaker's advice: Don't attempt another conspiracy – but if you do, don't produce a 'pair' of gloves of which one is still suggestive of scent, and the other identifiable with eucalyptus!"

"Oh—!" said Straithwaite.

"Quite so. But at all hazard suppress a second pair that has the same peculiarity. Think over what it must mean. Goodbye."

Twelve minutes later Mr. Carlyle was called to the telephone.

"It is eight-fifty-five and I am at Charing Cross," said a voice he knew. "If you want local colour contrive an excuse to be with Markham when the first post arrives tomorrow." A few more words followed, and an affectionate valediction.

"One moment, my dear Max, one moment. Do I understand you to say that you will post me on the report of the case from Dover?"

"No, Louis," replied Carrados, with cryptic discrimination. "I only said that I will post you on *a* report of the case from Dover."

Peppermint Tea

Sarah Holly Bryant

WHAT SOUNDED like a two-stroke chainsaw purred by day and what sounded like an alien invasion, probably coyotes, screamed by night. There was nobody left to blame. Janine was in the woods in a permanent state of both danger and the ultimate safety. She spent long days alone in the cabin, wondering how this disaster could have been avoided. Perhaps the tougher part to wrap her head around, was determining if her situation was in fact a disaster at all. She got what she ultimately wanted, just in a completely round about borderline catastrophic way, that left her stranded here. Wherever here was.

People told the guttural, real, hard truth to strangers, often just as easily or easier than they shared it with loved ones. But Janine couldn't tell her husband anything real. What she wanted was something primal. It wasn't as though she were the first to crave it. The very continuance of the planet relied on people wanting what she wanted. And it didn't even necessarily have to be from the beginning. Janine had ample time to tell John her dream at any point during their four-year marriage or the five years they dated before that. Janine spent nearly a decade unable to talk to her husband. How ironic, that she was still unable to communicate, stuck inside an isolated cabin. Her cellphone glared blankly back up at her, as if it were as perplexed as she was.

Before Janine and John fell in love and learned to keep secrets from one another, they had each been in a relationship with someone named Charlie. Janine dated a tall blond guy named Charlie with a beard that looked like straw and smelled like cigarettes. John dated a short brunette with ears that looked like they belonged to a baby and the shiniest tongue ring ever. It was as if female Charlie were balancing a gleaming gum drop on her tongue all day long. She rolled it around and rested it against her front teeth when thinking (which was rare). While they were dating, John thought he'd never tire of that little silver gem.

John loved to listen to the occasional metal on tooth clank that Charlie's mouth made. He wished she would do it more often, but of course never asked her to. That would have been too intimate. Eventually, he did tire of the tongue ring. He was sick of kissing it and looking at it and listening to it swirl around inside Charlie's mouth. He began to think of Charlie's mouth like a cave within her head, where the piercing lived. He tired of the body and the soul of female Charlie too, that is once he discovered something shinier. Janine. But that was before the cabin.

If you want to get technical about it, Janine and John were still married. She had only been in this place for a few weeks now, or was it months? Was she to blame or was John? Or was it one or both of the Charlies? Nothing ever happened here except the constant internal mania of thinking and regretting. Think. Regret. Think more. Regret different things. Think you can change the past. Regret the choices you made. Repeat.

Janine did daily calf raises and went to the bathroom in the bucket she was provided. It seemed like she was using the bucket more and more lately. She went outside when permitted and always saw the same lonely crow studying her. She listened to the sounds of logging trucks and the work those who drove them did. She ate and she slept of course, even though it felt like neither happened nearly enough. This was her existence in the cabin, with the occasional tearful breakdown in between. Oh and of course dinners with her captor.

In life BC (before the cabin), Janine loved to sleep in on weekends and listen to her husband move around below their second-floor bedroom. She welcomed the sounds of him cooking, fixing things, watching TV and doing whatever it was he did on those mornings when he wasn't working at the pharmacy. There is no sleep more comforting than the sleep of a wife knowing her husband is busy in their home; it meant he cared deeply. Of course, they never told one another that they cared deeply. Too intimate.

Maybe John was working on something in their home right now Janine thought. She imagined him printing out 'MISSING' signs, with her photo on them. Wouldn't it be funny if they were hung on the trees alongside the two-lane blacktop road that led to the forest? Which picture had he chosen? She imagined him marinating a brisket for a BBQ in preparation for her miraculous return. Yes, that's what he must be doing now she thought. Janine wondered if he still wore his wedding ring. Janine wondered if he knew she was in the long-lost cabin above the lumpy hills. She wondered if he cared. Perhaps he had stopped looking for her, or never even started searching to begin with. It had been her choice never to tell him what she wanted.

Her current cabin predicament was rooted in the pregnancies of women Janine envied. They were the ones to blame. Celebrities all seemed to be pregnant. Everywhere she looked someone was having one or sometimes two or even more babies! It was the most precious news on earth, to say the words, we are expecting. She watched as the impregnated universe waddled around to and fro. She had wanted so badly to join them on their walk. And now she could.

Janine's belly was growing week to week, though the cabin seemed to shrink. This had been the path she chose, wasn't it? Even if the circumstances weren't ideal, this was what she craved so desperately, wasn't it? Janine ate her daily morning oatmeal and picked at her cuticles and wondered if Crow was a good name for a boy. She tracked time by the awkward evenings she and her captor shared. As time went on, she began to look forward to these demented dinners.

Before Janine and John got together, the foursome often talked about what they liked or loathed to eat and drink. Food was a very safe topic. They reviewed what types of sushi they positively would not eat. Eel! And their favorite pizza toppings. Mushrooms! BC, Male Charlie and Janine adored peppermint tea. While John thought it tasted like someone put gum in hot water. Female Charlie used to say that the flavor she liked the most was red. She liked red drinks and red candy and red desserts. There was a time when John thought this was the cutest thing he'd ever heard. But as anyone who has been in love knows, the things that were once the most endearing often become those that are the most irritating.

Janine also had quite an adorable habit. She'd refer to things as little this and little that. She'd say, my little pants are still in the dryer. Do you want to bring your little gym bag with you on our trip? John thought this was cute and Janine believed she was super cute when she said such things. Now thinking back, it was stupid. Harmless but still stupid and Janine regretted ever speaking in such a way. That was baby talk after all and she and John never talked about babies.

The four of them, John and Charlie, Janine and Charlie lived in a suburb that looked and smelled like a suburb. Weekends were alive with children playing in yards where family pets guarded them and parents filled their trunks with food and sporting goods. Their lives were as full as their trunks...in some cases. And that's exactly what Janine wanted. People waved to each other when they took out their garbage and smiled knowingly when they saw one another struggling with a car seat or a dog pulling too strongly on a leash. If Janine had just told John what she needed they could have been one of those families.

BC, the two couples went on double dates around their suburban hometown trying things like dim sum, which the Charlies hated, and curries which Janine and John loved. Janine and male Charlie drank vodka and ginger ales while female Charlie and John ordered tequila sunrises. John would joke that he'd added a little something special to their drinks, rubbing his thumb and pointer finger together as if grinding a little sedative or stimulant into them. He'd say things like, what's your pleasure? Tell the friendly pharmacist. Who is going home with whom? Life went on like that for a while. Talk about food. Go on double dates. Fantasize about your best friend's girlfriend. Repeat.

Janine and John eventually betrayed their Charlies. With hearts racing and eyes smiling they made out behind the house Janine and the female Charlie shared with a third girl. Janine couldn't remember the third girl's name anymore. How could she forget the person's name she cohabitated with? Janine cried on the floor of the cabin when she thought about things like this.

To snap herself out of dark moments, Janine recalled her and John's first kiss. Long ago, John returned Janine's little jacket, which she left at his place during one of his famous BBQs. They lingered outside making excuses why they each had to leave, until there weren't any left. Once their words stopped getting in the way they kissed. John enjoyed their tongue ring-less kiss and Janine slept in her little jacket that night.

John was totally not the one for her anyway. That's what female Charlie said when John dumped her. Charlie told her mother that she thought he was like a tuna sandwich. Reliable. Consistent. Forgettable. When he confessed to her that he had feelings for their friend Janine, she thought it was kind of funny. Janine and John, wow talk about lame. Charlie liked to say things like, dating is just a numbers game. Dating is about weeding out the wrongs ones. She also liked to have rebound sex and share her stories with friends and the third roommate over red drinks mixed with booze.

Male Charlie did not feel as ambivalent as female Charlie did about getting passed over. When Janine broke it off with him, he was shattered. He literally felt like his insides were in pieces and as though his extremities had gone electric with fear and anger. His appetite flew out the window like the Cabin's lonely crow. Charlie slept with the light on in his room for a month after Janine said it was over. He drank peppermint tea and cried until he puked up hot green bile. He called her every day. Sometimes hanging up immediately and other times screaming at her for being such a bitch. Slut. Demon. He wrote her letters professing his undying love for her and telling her she was such a doll. Beauty. Angel.

But like all things, time does seem to appease situations of great stress. That or the total opposite. After the Charlies were dumped it appeared that the J and J were happy. They were often spotted at the Indian place for their lunch buffet and they moved in together across town. It appeared that female Charlie was dating a tattoo shop owner and that it was really getting serious. He's the one! It appeared that male Charlie was getting his life back together. Made his bed. Found a new roommate. Combed his beard. Got an El Dorado.

Male Charlie had never met anyone like Janine before. She liked music from the 1960s and laughed like a revving motorcycle. She didn't bash their suburban oasis, instead she'd refer adoringly to its downtown as, the village. When he thought of Janine he thought of phrases like, warm heart, good egg, salt of the earth. She was like a banana bread or chicken pot pie. She wore slippers and perfume that smelled like vanilla. She had the ability to make you feel cozy just by sitting beside her on a couch. When she cheated on him with his best friend, male Charlie felt like he'd been duped. But that was BC.

The word cabin conjures up feelings of comfort and privacy and nostalgia. But not this cabin. The bed was plopped in the center of the living space, a lone island. Wasn't this place meant to be a bunkhouse? So where are the bunks? There was just one bed, some primitive appliances that added up to something like a kitchen and the little bathroom bucket. Ugh, using the word little again. And to describe something so disgusting. Not even Janine could make this cabin cozy. Her cell phone looked so out of place in the rustic landscape. Like an alien from another time or another planet. Then again sometimes Janine felt that way too.

The cabin's only full-time resident would gaze out at the forest above her and wonder if there were other people like her. Those who got just what they wanted. She felt her belly jut out above her hips like some sort of offering. It was the very gift she'd laid in bed wishing for all those years with John. Shhhh, don't tell him what you want, he'll leave you. Janine thought she saw the lonely crow glaring at her through one of the few windows in the cabin. Was it judging her selfishness or pitying her? She felt like telling the crow that she wasn't the only one who had kept an important secret.

A long time BC, John's doctor said having a vasectomy was a minor procedure with major implications. It wasn't that John thought he'd be a terrible father or that he resented his own parents or anything, he just didn't want to add to the population personally. John didn't feel the pull of fatherhood and thought there were too many unwanted things in the world already; be it furniture, cats or kids.

John was a pharmacist. He worked hard so that one vacation at a time he could see the world. He worked hard so that he could donate to charities that he cared about and even to some he didn't. John came from a family of five and had nieces and nephews for days. He defined his success by the lab coat he proudly wore to work each day. Making the decision to never be a father was one less in a slew of decisions that always needed making. Dinner. Girlfriends. Breakups.

Female Charlie was in no way involved in John's decision to undergo reproductive snipping. When he told her that he had the minor procedure with major implications, she clanked her tongue ring, squinted at him and shrugged her small shoulders towards her even smaller ears. John figured that girls talk and so Janine must in turn know what he'd done. They were roommates for crying out loud. All those years they dated and all those years they were married, he figured Janine knew. But she didn't.

A figurine of a dark-haired man with warm brown eyes stood atop their wedding cake. He wore a lab coat and tuxedo pants with shiny black shoes. Beside him stood the quintessential bride ready to follow his lead. When there were two different ways to go in life, she would trust his decision. Until she couldn't any longer. Janine spent night after night resenting the husband who lay beside her for never talking about having children, in between vividly fantasizing about decorating a nursery. Circus. Safari. Flowers. The irony was magical fairy forest had been her favorite theme. Babies were on her mind all the time back then. Now that she was pregnant, she rarely thought about babies. Janine often wondered if she would begin to fall in love with her captor, like she'd heard sometimes happens. That might make the situation more tolerable. She had once loved him after all.

Janine and John never discussed growing their family. Janine assumed John didn't want children and John assumed Janine didn't either. Only one assumption was correct. Janine took birth control pills and John knew it. Janine pondered all of this as she rubbed her aching puffy legs together. She wondered if most assumptions were right fifty percent of the time.

Her thighs felt like they were tied up by ropes, which was just silly because it was only her hands that were occasionally tied up by ropes. Her legs were like the tree trunks she could make out in the distant forest above the cabin. She had to remind herself that this is what she wanted.

BC, Janine had a small timeframe in which to make a choice that would last a lifetime. There were two directions her future could go. She carry on, letting the impatience of her ticking clock deafen her marriage. Or she could take matters into her own hands and if it happened, it was meant to be. She stopped taking her birth control pills one morning after she'd marveled at her co-worker's striped sundress, tenting from her enormous stomach. Her plan was to have an accidental surprise.

Janine enjoyed the game of trashing her pills in different places. Garbage disposal. Drains. The park. Flower pots. Little pills she thought. Big impact! One by one and day by day she increased her chances of getting what she wanted. Too bad she couldn't literally double her chances she thought. And that's when her plan blasted through like a high-speed train. Her plan involved the only person who she knew would do what needed to be done. Charlie. Male Charlie that is.

He didn't look much like John, but he would have to do. Janine had a cousin with the brightest blue eyes born to her aunt and uncle who had soft brown ones. Janine lived ten miles across town from Charlie as the crow flies. His 1973 Cadillac El Dorado was well known even if he wasn't. That's how she found him. It was as if he had been waiting for her all these years. Nearly a decade later, male Charlie still found the sweetness in Janine irresistible.

Male Charlie was certainly willing to have a little local tryst with Janine. Sure, why not! That's what she referred to it as. Little local tryst. Which meant sex at his place, which was John's old place, a few times a week. He lied to Janine that he was fine with it being casual. She found herself face to face with his smoky straw beard over and over again. One affair. Lots of sex. Always unprotected. Three months. Two potential fathers. One her husband. One her captor.

Janine's period was late, she felt exhausted and she vomited three mornings in a row. It was a textbook pregnancy. By day she felt guilty and nervous and like she'd made a horrible mistake and by night she gripped her belly and tears of joy fell from her eyes as she pretended to sleep. She'd hold her stomach and the lump in her throat. John snored while she cooed at their fetus. But was it theirs really? Each night she told herself that she would tell John the very next morning. Not about the affair, but about their baby! They'd buy a pregnancy test, he'd wait outside the bathroom door and she'd act surprised at the positive result. Janine continued to believe fifty percent odds were good ones.

During their little local tryst Janine found out that male Charlie's parents died in a car crash soon after she'd broken up with him. This complicated things. He had fallen into a depression, gotten into some trouble with the law, never gotten over her, that sort of thing. He told her the only things going for him were the remote cabin in the forest and the classic Cadillac they'd left him. When he described them during their affair, Janine never imagined that she would ever be inside either of them.

Charlie and Charlie were in touch throughout the years. When male Charlie's parents died, female Charlie drank red drinks with him. She made him laugh and encouraged him to keep on keepin' on. He was never quite right after all the trauma he'd experienced and he felt sure that he could never love again. Unless of course it was love with Janine. Female Charlie talked to him about seeing a therapist. She mentioned to him he might want to take some time off of work. Move out of John and his old place. And knowing he always liked a bit of gossip, she told him about John's secret surgery.

As quickly as the little local tryst had started, it ended. But no tears from Charlie this time. Janine said she'd needed to stop their affair because she was pregnant. She was pregnant all along she'd said. Of course, it was her husband John's she'd said. Male Charlie knew the truth and wasn't going to let precious Janine go this time. He'd take her to the coziest safest place he knew. The cabin above the lumpy hills where the lone crow watched over things. Their baby would never know what heartbreak or cell service were.

BC, Janine eventually told John she was pretty sure she was pregnant. Initially he thought rationally about it. There was a fifty percent chance that either his surgery hadn't worked or that the baby wasn't his. He didn't like those odds. He felt like his wife in a lot of ways. So full but yet so drained. Without showing any emotion other than joy, he hugged her and told her the news was just wonderful. She'd told him she wanted to buy the pregnancy test herself and would be right back to pee on the stick. Except she never returned.

En route to the pregnancy test section of the drug store, Janine saw female Charlie standing in the toothpaste isle. Her big belly jutting over and past the rows of choices. Janine thought it was the baby, if you wanted to get technical about it, not Charlie who was lingering above the mouthwashes. I have one too Janine thought. Before she could turn around unnoticed, Charlie spotted her.

Waving like a big happy flappy bird about to take flight, female Charlie, only feet away from Janine, squealed with delight at having seen her old roommate next to boxes of denture cream. The two former friends caught up as former friends do. Charlie still lived in town and now had cravings for white things. Even white toothpaste she said. She hated anything with colors and thought it was just the funniest turn of events.

Charlie's belly was filled with babies as it turned out. She gets to have two Janine thought. Janine didn't want to cut Charlie's babies out from their womb or anything crazy like that. But jealousy of pregnant women had become her routine way of thinking. Eventually under the fluorescent lights, Janine confided in Charlie that she too was expecting. Me too! When? What is it? Wow! Charlie's voice seemed different without the tongue ring. Or maybe it was just the shock in her tone when she giggled and remarked how John's surgery must have been reversible.

Janine never bought the test that day. She didn't need to. She could feel the tall blond baby growing inside of her. Female Charlie had revealed a certain truth that she couldn't unhear. As she walked back to her car in the drug store parking lot, empty handed and hearted, she sensed someone or something following her. It was male Charlie in the El Dorado. It happened so fast. He grabbed her, put her in the passenger seat, took her cell phone and told her what she already knew. This was his baby dammit! The little family drove and drove into the forest.

Male Charlie made Janine peppermint tea each evening in the cabin because he'd never stopped loving her. Their daily dinners kept her alive because she needed the food he brought. But they were also killing her. There were nights when he would drink too much whiskey and peppermint tea and leave his portable phone charger on the floor or hanging out of his pants pocket like puppy on a leash. In those moments, Janine would link her cell phone to suck what it could for a few seconds at a time like a nursing baby to a breast.

Janine pictured male Charlie with a checklist each time he visited. Toileted, check. Didn't run away, check. Still pregnant with my baby, check. Poor John, check. Janine had a lot of time to think now that she was in her dull world of panic and boredom. She'd focus on the minutia of her relationship with John by day and what she wished she'd said. Then at night, her mind would be ravaged with thoughts of the things she should have told her husband. And the one critical thing he should have told her.

While Janine pondered in the cabin, female Charlie would go on to have twins. Her husband tattooed the names of their two girls inside an infinity symbol on her ankle. She never thought about John again. She never thought about Janine again. And she certainly never thought that she had been the one to reveal a secret so big, that it would destroy a family before it could even begin. And then John called her.

Charlie was a cute girl with spunk and that shiny tongue ring, who John would remember as being good in bed, easy to break up with and someone he periodically looked up online, using his private computer at the pharmacy. You know, just to see how life had turned out for her. But this time he needed more from her. He needed to find out if she knew where his wife was. Nearly six weeks had gone by and the police had turned up nothing.

Female Charlie congratulated John and told him it was nice to hear from him. John felt like the last to know the big news. How could Janine have told his ex-girlfriend before she was even sure? Female Charlie cracked her gum and told John she had no clue where his wife was. She slipped in that she was surprised he could have children and that Janine looked pretty surprised too when she mentioned it in the toothpaste isle. Isn't life funny! So, Janine knew the truth. Which meant she was ashamed. Which meant she turned to the biological father. Which had to be someone she knew. Janine wasn't the type to sleep with just anyone. John knew who she was with and guessed where. His former roommate used to talk about a very special place that only crows knew about. John asked female Charlie if she could do him one favor and keep it a permanent secret this time.

Female Charlie and John found the cabin with instincts neither of them knew they had. They made an important stop at the pharmacy first and then she dropped him off with a wink and a knowing look at the base of the cabin. He arrived to find his wife on the floor looking at her cell phone's empty face. She told him she had a little battery but no service. She made a little mistake but could fix it. She was a little sorry but wasn't he too? Male Charlie would be back soon with no time to waste. John sprinkled the lethal drugs from the pharmacy into a mug and brewed a pot of peppermint tea. Now they just needed to wait for the El Dorado to arrive while John hid outside in the trees. Charlie drank and soon went down with a thud that shook the cabin to its dark core, cracking his skull on the base of the bed and then landing him beard first into the makeshift toilet.

Janine and John found Charlie's car keys and drove off towards the lumpy hills without saying a word. They linked hands. Their secrets forever safe. The baby forever theirs. They passed a carnival on their way back to town. Bright lights, games, children and smells of spun sugar surrounded them. They didn't let themselves watch too long; just until the joy of the playful place wore off. Meanwhile back at the cabin, the not-so-deadly deadly cocktail began to wear off too.

Eykiltimac Stump Acres

Jeffrey B. Burton

"HE'S SAYING it again."

"What?"

"At breakfast today he kept on about Eykiltimac Stump Acres. Said it two or three times and nodded at his companions."

"Doesn't ring a bell." I looked at Jane, the nurse's assistant. What a saint she is, providing the elbow grease necessary to take care of all the lost souls in this the final wing of the assisted care nursing home…the Alzheimer's wing.

"Eykiltimac wasn't a resort you two used to visit? Or perhaps someplace his parents took him when he was a child?"

"There was a Stump Acres south of Fairmont. But it was just several miles of wooded area outside of town. Not much to see."

"Often, at this stage, I've noticed the memories get reshuffled. You know, the earlier ones get placed in front."

"Yes, but I can't recall him ever talking about any 'Eykiltimac.' Hmm?"

I walked into the day room and there he sat. Dwight. My Dwighty. Easy to spot with that distinguished mane of silver hair. Even now I get a little giddy. I watch him from behind for a bit, just pretending he's at home in his worn, old recliner, loafing after a long day's work, reading the paper and telling me how delicious the smells are coming from the kitchen. Even when I threw something together on the fly or cooked the roast too long till it tasted like shoe leather. He always said something positive.

I love my Dwight. I visit him every day since the harsh reality finally broke through my stubborn collection of little denials and I realized that I just couldn't manage, at seventy-eight, to care for him at home anymore. It was, without any doubt, the most painful decision I'd ever made. But you see Dwight started to wander outside whenever I took a bath or got on the phone in a different room. Dwight and I have always loved our walks together. Alone, he'd get disoriented, confused, and frightened. Thank God the neighbors knew, and cared, and helped.

Dwight and I have been married fifty-eight years. We celebrated our fifty-eighth wedding anniversary right here in this sitting room. The kids and grandkids were all here for our special day. And it had been a good day for Dwight – with brief recognitions and half conversations.

He's deteriorated noticeably since then.

But whenever I approach him from behind, like this, I can pause a second or two and let the fantasy bring me back to the sixties, or seventies, or eighties. He still knows me. My name may escape him, but he knows.

Dwight and I are both Fairmont kids. Small town born and bred. Spent our first year of marriage there, too. Although the John Deere sales job took us to the big city, we never changed. Married Dwight the week of my twentieth birthday. He was twenty-two, back from a stint in the army, and raring for life, but still hayseed enough to take little old me out for a cherry coke, and a walk around the lake. I knew it was real that very first night Dwight kissed me and told me he could see his future swirling about in the deep blue wells of my eyes. I reckon I saw mine, too.

Wouldn't have missed it for the entire world.

"Why hello Honey." I came around and took hold of his hand. Always the gentleman, Dwight stood and gave me a peck on the cheek. We sat for awhile, held hands, gave inseparable warmth to each other. I didn't try to force conversation. It wasn't needed and would only verify how far my husband had fallen. But Jane's questions had piqued my curiosity.

"Dwighty," I said and he looked my way. "They say you've been talking about Eykiltimac Stump Acres." Dwight stared at my face and I gave it one more try. "Eykiltimac Stump Acres."

"Ah yes…yes." There was a momentary gleam in his eyes as though I'd whispered his mother's name, a fleeting focus, a kernel of togetherness. "*Eykiltimac Stump Acres.*"

"What Hon?" I thought I'd heard something else…something confusing. "What did you say?"

But it was gone. Lost in the past. Like all our other days. Dwight continued to nod his head like a guilty schoolboy listening to the headmaster. A habit I'd long recognized as meaning nothing except, perhaps, a fragment of remaining knowledge regarding human interaction.

I sat by my love all day.

* * *

I woke with a cold start. Nights were hardest with Dwight no longer around to comfort me after a bad dream. Only this wasn't a dream. It had come to me, slowly, like mist over a lake. I knew it sounded ridiculous. But it was past two in the morning, a time when your mind starts to wander toward places it shouldn't. Places where you think the unthinkable. Thoughts to be laughed at in the light of day. Nevertheless I found myself wide awake, frightened, and wandering into one such shadowy spot. I realized what Dwight had mumbled this afternoon. It buzzed inside my head like bees about a hive.

I-kilt-im-at Stump Acres...

* * *

I still drive. Did most of it these past years, when we both knew it wouldn't be safe for Dwight to get behind the wheel of the big green Buick anymore. I got in the car without a second thought this morning and decided to put some fresh cut flowers on the graves of my parents, look around, perhaps dig up a memory or two. Getting to Fairmont was a lot easier than it had been in years gone by, ever since they put in the interstate. Cut the time in half.

By two o'clock I found myself at the Fairmont library. The librarian – she was a new face, but then I'd been away for so many years they were all new to me – showed me where the microfiche from the Fairmont Tribunes were kept. I'd worked at Fairmont's library myself over half a century ago. Much different back then, back before they'd moved to the new building, which by now was far from new itself. You could see how the wood was cracked, dry rotting around the windows. There was a light smell of mold.

All things age.

Stump Acres was densely wooded, an area used mostly by hunters during deer season. It had, in fact, been at Stump Acres where an old childhood chum of mine, Craig Muntean, had been accidentally shot and killed by one of his hunting mates years and years ago. That was in the days before the hunters started wearing those big orange parkas for all the others to see.

Truth be known, Craig had been my first boyfriend from way back in elementary school. The Muntean family had been shattered at the loss of their only son. It had been a tragedy all around. I know we hadn't been five years out of high school when I'd heard about Craig's unfortunate death. Dwight and I were only in our first years of marriage. My little Joey had just been born when I'd heard the news. With that timeframe in mind I began my search.

It didn't take as long as I'd thought. The Tribune only came out twice weekly back then, perhaps it still does. There it was, above the fold.

Fairmont Man Dies in Hunting Accident.

Good grief. Poor Craig. Never given a chance to live, to flourish…to love. I read the detailed article and wiped at moist eyes with my sleeve.

It turned out that the authorities never found out which other hunter had shot Craig. It was most likely a stray bullet that had traveled some distance before finding a new home in Craig's lung. Or perhaps the hunter knew what he'd done, had seen it up close, panicked, and was too afraid to step forward. Fairmont is a small community, and something like that would've been hard to live with.

Very hard.

* * *

A few minutes out of Fairmont, I pulled the green Buick over to the side of Interstate 90, closed my eyes and rubbed at my temples. It was ludicrous for me to even think such nonsense. I should be ashamed of myself. Dwight had simply muttered something incoherent after I'd mentioned what the nurse's aide had said. Dwight just parroted back some disjointed syllables. That's all it had been.

And nothing more.

A moment later I turned the Buick around and headed back to town. Took a room at the Holiday Inn. When Dwight and I first met, I had been lightly dating a gentleman by the name of Pete Henderson. Pete had been the summer lifeguard at Lake Sisseton. He had been a young man who'd just completed his first year of studies at the University, but he spent his summers in Fairmont giving swimming lessons and watching over the crowd of people frolicking at the local beach.

Pete's brother Harlan had married my high school girlfriend's sister, Gwen Wharton. It had given us a basis to strike up a conversation. Pete was certainly a bronzed Adonis, tall and sharply muscular, a great swimmer, like Johnny Weissmuller, which is why everyone called him Tarzan. Unfortunately, Pete was as dull as yesterday's dishwater. He loved swimming, had won numerous championships in high school, and didn't really talk about anything else. We were never more than casual friends who caught a handful of movies together.

Pete had fallen by the wayside as soon as I'd met Dwight.

There was only one Wharton phone number in the Fairmont phonebook, the slim phone directory sitting on the table in my suite. I didn't know quite what to say. I knew Loretta had moved to California eons ago, right after her marriage. After a decade of Christmas cards, we'd eventually lost touch. I felt awkward, like a fool, but I dialed the number.

"Hello." It was a woman's voice, she sounded middle-age.

"Uh hi." I almost hung up. "My name is Ann-Marie Warner. I grew up with a Loretta Wharton and I was wondering if—"

"Oh yes, Aunt Loretta."

"Excellent," I said, "I was afraid I didn't have the correct number."

"We're the only Whartons left in Fairmont. Would you like Loretta's number? She lives in California."

"Loretta's still there, huh? I'm kind of embarrassed but the last time I saw Loretta was at her wedding."

"Oh boy, I guess you haven't been in touch with her in quite a while then?"

"We kind of lost touch over the years. I've been trying to look up some old Fairmont girlfriends of mine."

"Let me get you her phone number."

"That would be great," I said, then took the plunge. "Say, how are Gwen and Harlan?"

"You knew them, too?"

"I sure did. Gwen was so pretty. We all wanted to look just like her. Loretta and I were a few years younger, but Gwen would let us play with her makeup."

"Goodness sakes. Well now, Harlan passed away awhile back. Lung cancer. Gwen lives in the Cities near her kids."

"I'm sorry to hear about Harlan. Come to think of it, I also knew Harlan's brother Pete." I squeezed the phone tightly. "Would you happen to know how he's doing?"

"Oh girl," she said, "you have been away a long while. Pete died before I was born. He drowned in Lake Sisseton."

According to Loretta's niece, lifeguard Pete Henderson had drowned in Lake Sisseton one summer night. Some kids, out later than their parents would have liked, found Pete's lifeless body bobbing and floating near one of the docks. My swimming Adonis, the local Tarzan and championship lifeguard, had drowned in less than four feet of water.

* * *

This morning I'd traveled from Fairmont to Mankato. For you see there was only one other man who'd ever been in my life, however insignificantly. I remember that warm June night on the picnic blanket in the park when Dwight and I had confided our past romances to one another. Almost sixty years ago, but now clear as yesterday. It was the sort of talk that lovers have as they share past secrets and other such silliness with one another. I'd confessed to having had a secret crush on my freshman English teacher at Mankato State University. Professor Applegate – with his bushel of strawberry blond curls and horn-rimmed glasses – had been so young, so poetic, barely out of college himself. It was a silly school girl's crush that had amounted to nothing beyond signing up for all his courses.

But I'd laughingly shared that with Dwight.

At the Mankato State Alumni Office, I dug through shelves of musty yearbooks as they forged ever onward after my years there, half a century ago. Every year held another picture of a slightly more worn, more ruffled Professor Applegate. About fifteen yearbooks passed before I tripped across the dedication. It was on the very last page.

The dedication was to Mankato State's Professor Applegate who had died earlier that semester. At the bottom of this full page picture of the professor read a brief passage from Hamlet: *Good night, sweet Prince, And flights of angels sing thee to thy rest.* Beneath that quotation, in smaller font, were the dates of his birth and untimely death. Unfortunately, nothing in the yearbook alluded as to how the late Professor had passed away.

Of late I'd become an unlikely expert at culling through old newspapers. The reason it took longer than expected was the feeling of dread, of me putting off the inevitable, of not wanting to confront the unthinkable. I delayed for hours over coffee before going to the local library. But by the early afternoon I had it all laid out in front of me. The police would have tossed it up to a simple hit and run, possibly some damn fool driving drunk, except for one small fact. The evidence at the scene pointed out how the car that ran down Professor Applegate on that dark, deserted street had then stopped, backed up, and run over him again.

And again.

And again.

In those days John Deere had Dwight doing all that tri-state traveling he'd hated so much. Kept him away from me, he'd always say. And I remember one particularly dark night when he came home after midnight. The kids were asleep. Dwight apologized endlessly for being late, and for causing me any undue worry, which was the last thing he'd ever want, but, he told me, he'd hit an enormous deer that had jumped onto the road from out of nowhere. The Chrysler, Dwight had informed me, was one hellish mess, and to just leave it for him to clean up. He spent most of the next two days alone in the garage, scrubbing gristle off the grill, pounding out the dents, replacing a headlamp and both front tires, adding a touch of paint here and there.

* * *

I sit here next to Dwight and hold his hand.

How many millions of times have I held this hand? I find it all quite impossible to believe. Delusions of a silly old woman approaching senility herself. Craig was simply killed in a horrible hunting accident. A drunken, failing student had most likely ran over Professor Applegate. Pete Henderson lived to swim and, unfortunately, drowned as a result of his lifelong passion.

In the course of my many, many years, I don't know why any of these events should have seemed sinister or connected. I've seen too many strange things unfold daily on TV and in the newspaper. I'm ashamed of myself for taking it to such a ridiculous extreme. The whole thing is more a reflection of me than of Dwight. But, even now, in the cool light of day, the doubts linger and dance.

Insistently. In the back of my mind.

And I find myself transfixed by Dwight's profile.

"Dwight, dear," I whisper and softly kiss my husband's cheek. "Do you remember Pete Henderson? You know, the lifeguard from Fairmont? The one I dated, briefly, before we met?"

Dwight stares at me. His eyes are glazed and dull as they search my face. It was as though he could sense something important but couldn't quite connect, couldn't quite understand.

"Pete Henderson? You remember? That big lifeguard at Sisseton?" The questioning became too painful, too wrenching to continue. I leaned over and gave Dwight a hug, wanting to pull his warmth into me, wanting so desperately to squeeze back the past.

"*I-killed-im-at the lake...*"

"What Dwighty?" I looked up. "What did you just say?"

But Dwight's eyes were now unfocused, dim. He began to nod his head, meaninglessly, like a leaf in a warm breeze.

Oh dear Dwighty. Dear sweet Dwighty. You know you've always been my knight in shining armor. I've always thought of you in that mythical manner. Right from the very first. I love you so much, Dwight. Always have. Always will. And I've always known that you've loved me too. It's been so obvious throughout our many, many years together.

But until now, until this very moment...I just never knew how much.

Death in Lively

C.B. Channell

LIKE EVERY MORNING in Lively, Wisconsin, the local business owners gathered in the town square. Unlike every other morning we weren't sipping coffee and trading gossip. We were staring at a dead body. Priscilla Markey's dead body, to be precise; our now former owner of the local gourmet ice cream/candy/popcorn store. Someone had put a lot of knife wounds into Priscilla's midsection.

There was one notable absence, but that was quickly remedied. Heavy footsteps and gutteral muttering preceded Mack Stendahl, diner owner and publican, as he pushed through the small crowd. When he saw Priscilla's mangled body he let out a cry that scared the birds right out of the square.

"No! It can't be!" He fell to his knees, clutching his head. Priscilla was – had been – his fiance. "Who would do such a thing?"

Officer Dick Lee, our occasionally reliable local constable, showed up just then, in time for Mack to leap to his feet and grab the policeman by the throat. It took two men, Jerry Cone, the deli/cheese shop owner, and police Chief Joe Huxtable (my husband), who had arrived a moment later to pull Mack off him.

"Don't make me arrest you," Huxtable cautioned Mack. Mack looked like he might be about to attack the Chief, but the words penetrated and he calmed a bit, though his massive body continued to tremble. Jerry and his sister Eleanor, the town seamstress, closed around him, offering murmuring comfort.

I stood slightly aside. I owned the town bookstore. I'd been one of the few to befriend Priscilla a few years before when she'd moved to Lively from Chicago. Small-town Cheeseheads were often ambivalent about the neighbors to the south but Priscilla had worked hard to earn peoples' trust and create a business that was integral to the town. The fact that she'd moved here of her own accord and met Mack afterward endeared her a bit; she hadn't been dragged from the city by a handsome face and sturdy build. Still, she would always be, at some level, an outsider.

Dick looked at Priscilla and shook his head. "Probably a drifter, drug addict looking for cash. Priscilla was in the wrong place at the wrong time."

I liked Dick, but his theory didn't make sense to me. There were extensive wounds but as far as I could tell, they weren't deep. In another life I'd been a nurse and it was clear that most of the wounds weren't fatal. But one had gone under the ribcage and probably punctured the lung; another looked like it had been dragged across her inner thigh. Rough cut or no, slashing through the femoral artery likely accounted for the pool of blood beneath Priscilla. I'd like to think she hadn't suffered, but from the myriad of shallow stab wounds in her abdomen it didn't look that way. The killing took several minutes at least. Why would a drifter stay so long, risk getting caught?

I glanced back up and saw Angela Martin from the mayor's office stepping out of the courthouse. We were in the section of the town square furthest from the government building, so she couldn't immediately see what the gathering was about. As people in Lively often randomly gathered, it probably didn't appear to be much at first sight.

"Leslie?"

I turned to Officer Lee. "Did you see Priscilla leave her store yesterday?" he asked.

I thought about it then shook my head. "I passed the store after I closed, about seven last night, and there was a light on in the back." As I spoke, I noticed Eleanor looking around, start, then stare nervously at her feet. I turned to see Mack glowering at her. Wedding plan troubles? I wondered.

"I didn't see Priscilla specifically," I added. "But then, I didn't look, either." My eyes were drawn again to the body; ants and other little things were crawling on her. "Angela came by the store shortly before I closed; maybe she saw Priscilla." I turned to ask Angela, assuming she'd crossed the green by now, but she wasn't there. She wasn't on the steps, but the mayor was, and he didn't look happy as he hurried toward us.

Soon the coroner arrived. More townspeople had gathered and watched her work from outside the crime scene tape. I listened as she read notes into her phone. There wasn't much beyond what I'd already observed. I was about to return to my shop when I caught part of Eleanor's questioning.

"So you didn't actually see her?" Dick was saying.

"N—no. I was supposed to; she wanted another fitting, I had the dress, and I wanted to go in through the back, always afraid of someone spilling chocolate sauce or something..."

"I thought this was after she'd closed," said Joe, stepping into the conversation.

"Well...no, not exactly. See, I went to the back and..." she faded off and looked toward Mack again. This time he wasn't looking at her; he was staring where Angela had been moments before, a stricken look on his face. I suddenly wanted to go over and comfort him, and even took a step in his direction. But then he turned to me and the expression on his face hardened into a twisted rage. It passed like a summer storm, and a low moan seemed to deflate him.

"Eleanor? And what?" asked Joe. He was clearly exasperated with her.

"Nothing," she whispered.

Not nothing, I thought and from the looks on the faces of our police force, they didn't think so either. However, I recognized the closed expressions on the faces of my neighbors. If anyone knew anything, they weren't saying so.

* * *

Mack closed the diner that day but kept the pub open. Eleanor returned home, where she kept shop. Jerry went back to the deli, though clearly they wouldn't be doing much business. Everyone gathered at either the pub or the bookstore, where I had seating and served coffee. There was no chance I was going to miss what was said today.

The first to arrive was my husband. He barely acknowledged me as he poured himself a cup of black coffee and sat in the food and drink area. I was about to approach him when the phone rang; it was Betsy from the bakery telling me she was on her way with my daily order of pastries, and so sorry she didn't get it here in the morning like she usually did what with all...

I assured her everything was fine and tried to hurry her off the phone so I could talk to Joe, but Betsy was remarkable in her chatty-staying-power ability, even for a small towner. Joe finished his coffee just as I was signing off.

"Wait a few for pastries, Joe?" I encouraged, but he only shook his head, thanked me, paid and headed toward the door, only to be nearly run over by Angela from the courthouse.

"Whoa, there, Angie! Where's the fire?"

Angela (only a few people dared call her Angie) flushed bright red, mumbled something, then hurried past him. He stopped in the door to watch her for a moment, then thought better of it.

As the door swung shut, she hustled over to the counter.

"Leslie," she whispered, even though we were alone, "you have to help me!"

I paused. Angela was a self-sufficient entity; I'd never known her to ask for help from anyone except when she broke her leg and couldn't tend her garden the way she liked. Even then she supervised. Luckily, her leg healed before every friendly neighbor quit.

"It's about Priscilla. And…and Mack."

So something *was* up. That look from Mack hadn't been accidental.

"He didn't do it! We were nowhere near the square!" she blurted.

I pride myself on being bright and observant but sometimes even I'm slow.

"You and Mack?" I asked, whispering to match her voice now.

She nodded miserably. "We didn't mean to. I mean…well, we have a history, you know that."

"Yes." History. They dated in high school. They went to prom. Then Angela went to Madison for her degree in city planning and Mack continued to run his father's diner until the old man died, then took over the neighboring pub when the owners decided to leave Lively and go to Florida.

"Priscilla was all wrong for him. You know that. *Everyone* knows that. I mean, really, a Chicago girl? Leslie, I don't trust Joe. I need you to find out who did this."

I held my tongue. In fact, I *didn't* know that. Quite the contrary. I thought Priscilla was about the best thing to happen to Mack. He'd been devastated when Angela left, and frankly, she came back a snob.

She stared at me, wide-eyed and agitated, while I struggled to figure out what to say when Betsy, bless her heart, tromped through the door with a giant tray full of donuts and Kringle slices.

"Sooooo sorry I'm late!" she launched and there was no chance for anyone else to speak for at least ten minutes. I could have kissed her.

So Angela left without a promise from me, but my curiosity was piqued. It couldn't hurt to ask a few questions, keep my eyes open, right?

* * *

The next morning, I picked up my pastry tray on the way to work. Betsy wasn't the greatest listener, but she might have heard something and I wanted to get it fresh and early if I could. I also didn't want her barging in again later, disturbing my customers, and possibly suspects.

Betsy rewarded me with a fresh cream horn, hot and rich. I gratefully devoured it, waistline be damned, while she chattered on. I nodded as I wiped sweet cheese from my chin, when her chatter went to Priscilla.

"Couldn't happen to a nicer gal," she said with uncharacteristic bitterness.

I started. "What do you mean? Priscilla was nice enough."

She snorted. "Maybe for you. She was a bookworm, right? But when it came to sweets…oh no! She was Princess Priscilla from Chicago, where they know all about gourmet sweet things! Do you know she mixed sea salt in with her caramel ice cream topping? Salt!" Betsy shook her head. I nodded sympathetically, though the salted caramel sundae was one of my favorites.

"She always criticized my baking. Thought it was too simple, no complex flavors. I mean, really! How complicated do you want a cupcake to be?"

Again, I declined to speak.

"At least she won't get her hands on this place now," she added darkly.

"She tried to buy you out?"

"Tried to have me shut down! Called the health inspector and everything! I mean, every shop has a *few* violations, right? It's not like my place is filthy or anything. I wanted to call them on her back, but you can just bet she made sure her place was pristine! Anyway, I managed to talk my way out of a shutdown, but not before I had to fork over a fine and pay for an industrial cleaning." She shook her head, still angry even though her tormentor was dead.

Murdered.

Suddenly, the cream horn wasn't sitting well in my stomach, and it wasn't just the revelation that Betsy was less than fastidious in her cleaning habits. I took my tray and hurried back to my store. I didn't believe that Betsy had killed Priscilla. Not that I didn't think she was capable, it was just that I didn't think she could do it and not announce it to everyone. But if Priscilla had gone after Betsy, maybe she'd offended some of our other Lively residents.

I packed up a few pastries and a thermos of my special coffee blend and left the store in my assistant's capable hands, and headed across the square to the police station, next to the courthouse. I waved to Eleanor, who was wandering about the square examining the ground near where Priscilla's body had been. She started when she saw me, then walked in the other direction. She looked awkward, but then she usually did. And given the current circumstances in Lively, it wasn't all that strange for people to be acting strange.

I pushed open the door beneath the sign 'Lively Police Headquarters.'

Although I didn't normally deliver pastries, it wasn't completely without precedent. Last summer when we'd had a spate of hubcap robberies, mine included, I'd made a point of bringing treats and poking my nose into police business.

"Wow! Thanks, Leslie!" said Dick.

"We don't know who did it yet," said Joe at the same time. I smiled and let them pick out their Kringles.

"I know that," I said. "You haven't arrested anyone. Know anything at all?"

Joe had a grim look, the one that screamed 'I AM A SERIOUS POLICEMAN' but Dick jumped in exuberantly. "We've got the murder weapon!"

Joe glared at him, then looked at me. "It'll be out soon enough. The mayor's wife was already here."

The mayor's wife owned the town newspaper. She prided herself on not sucking up to her husband.

"You told her?" I asked, incredulous.

"Noooo," said Joe.

"She walked in and overheard us discussing it," said Dick around a mouthful of raspberry filling and sugary icing.

Joe gave me look that indicated she overheard Dick being indiscrete. Not that figuring that out would take any real detective work.

"Cheese knife!" cried Dick happily.

"Dick, what if Leslie's the killer and you just told her what we know?" said Joe in exasperation.

Dick looked so chagrined that I couldn't stifle a giggle and even Joe relented a little. "Sorry, buddy, but let's keep it close to the vest from here on out."

Dick nodded enthusiastically and gave a thumbs-up.

Uninvited, I followed Joe into his office.

"Leslie…" he began.

"A cheese knife?" I interrupted, incredulous.

He hesitated, then pulled an evidence bag from his desk drawer. There was a blade in it without a handle.

"You can see right here where it broke off just above the hilt," he said, pointing. "The coroner pulled it out of her abdomen."

I peered at the bloody blade and winced. It was dull and small. It had to have been painful. "So no fingerprints," I said.

He shook his head and spread his arms. "Sorry, Trixie Belden."

"Well, thanks, anyway. Enjoy the Kringle." I kissed him then hurried out.

Disregarding the law, I crossed the quad directly to save time. Suddenly, my foot struck something hard not far from where Priscilla had been found. I bent to see it, then pulled a paper napkin from the bag before I picked up what looked like a bloody rock. On closer examination I realized it was a knife handle. Small. Like from a cheese knife. There was a dark brown smudge that could have been a fingerprint. But what made my stomach jump was the stamp near the bottom: an oval with 'CFM&C' in the middle of it. Cone's Fine Meats and Cheeses. I wrapped it carefully and pocketed it.

I knew I should take it immediately back to Joe, but Angela's pleading voice and my own curiosity convinced me to look into this myself. I went straight to the deli. Jerry was wiping down the obviously spotless counter. He seemed distracted. I forced away uncharitable thoughts.

"Terrible thing," he said in greeting. Jerry wasn't one for small talk.

"Jerry, do you sell those cheese…platers and knives that you use for your platters?" I asked. I hoped he didn't notice the sudden catch.

He eyed me closely. "Nope. Never have. Though they do go out, like you said, with my catered platters. Best catered lunch in town," he added proudly.

"Absolutely," I agreed. They weren't fancy, any more than Betsy's pastries were, but they were true Wisconsin platters, loaded with heavy cheddars and greasy meats. I loved them.

"Have you catered anything recently?" I asked, and pretended to look through the deli case. I felt, rather than saw, him scowl.

"Are you trying to suggest something to me?" he asked.

I sighed. It really was impossible to be subtle in a small town, but I didn't want to give away what the police knew. "It's just, when I saw…Priscilla…I noticed the knife wounds didn't seem very deep. I was trying to think what would make shallow wounds last night looking at my knife block, and it occurred to me a paring knife or cheese knife might do it I just thought if one of your knives had gone missing…"

He perked up a little at that. "Well, you know, that may well be. They do go missing fron time to time. I suppose anyone in town could have one."

Jerry was a known skinflint, and the few times I'd had him 'cater' an event at my store h was fastidious about making sure he left with everything that was his, including his chea cheese knives. I was processing this when he said, "Heck, if it was one of my knives it wa likely one Priscilla herself took."

I perked up then.

He nodded, grew a little lost in thought. "We had a meeting about the appetizers for the wedding. She wanted some shar-koo-ter-ee board, so I set up a platter. Apparently, my platters weren't what she wanted. She wanted cutting boards." He sniffed. "Cutting boards! For serving." He shook his head. "Boy, they do things strange in 'Illinoize.'"

"So she stole the knife?" I pressed.

He nodded. "Pretty sure. Couldn't find it after she left. Took that, and a pair of serving tongs. Huh. What do I get for her wasting my time?" He refocused on me, then looked down again at the knife handle. "Well, I suppose I ought to thank you for returning this," he said, reaching for it.

I snatched it up quickly, my face burning. He looked shocked, then angry.

"Sorry, Jerry," I said, "But I have to give this to Joe."

"Now wait a minute..." he began, but I hurried out the door, nearly running over Eleanor in the process.

"Nell!" I heard Jerry shout, "get in here!"

I walked fast. I didn't want to run; around here that would attract attention and get me stopped every two feet, totally negating the purpose of hurrying. I burst back into the police station, ignored Dick's startled cry and barged into Joe's office.

"I think I have the other half of your murder weapon." I pulled my find from my pocket, carefully unwrapped it and placed it on Joe's desk.

Joe once again pulled out the blade. The two pieces fit perfectly right where the blade had snapped only slightly above the hilt. He sighed, a deep, sad sound. "Dick, take prints off this, see if we have a match in our database. And I guess it's time for me to visit Jerry and get a print. I hope it doesn't match."

But it probably does, I thought. The stolen knives tale sounded like so much smoke. It's not like everyone didn't know what the stamp on the handles of those knives meant.

I stood in front of the police station and watched him enter the deli when Angela tapped my shoulder.

"Well?" she whispered.

I turned suddenly very irritated with her. "If you know something..." I paused. Something that had been niggling at me began to take shape.

Angela started to reply when I rudely took off running. There was one business owner who didn't have her shop on the square, wasn't usually in our daily morning group of gossips.

And who would have easy access to, would likely have owned, a few of Jerry's knives.

I knew I should get Joe first, but my intuition was screaming that every second lost could cost us our culprit, so I ran despite the stitch forming in my side. I reached the old Victorian painted lady just as Eleanor was loading a suitcase into the backseat of her old Toyota.

"Nell!" I cried breathlessly. She turned, went white, then yanked on the door handle. She'd neglected to unlock it, however, and she stumbled backwards. I reached her just before she could try again, then fell to my knees.

"Nell," I choked.

"Stop," she said, and looking up I realized she was pointing a pistol at me.

"Why?" I gasped, now truly terrified.

"It wasn't planned," she said, her eyes darting behind me. Looking for Joe, no doubt.

I reached across my midsection.

"Stop!" she repeated, her voice more shrill, the gun beginning to quake.

"It's…it's a stitch," I wheezed. "Just…holding…" Which was true. What was also true was my phone was in my left pocket which I slipped my right hand into now. On the screen was an emergency call 'button' that would ring my Chief of Police husband (rather than 911). I thumbed it, hoping I was being discrete, hoping I would hit it. It wouldn't make a sound and I would only know it worked if I lived. I didn't think Eleanor wanted to kill me, but she was desperate.

"She hated the dress! I changed it so many times, paid for the lace and silk out of my own pocket!" She sobbed, the gun wavered. I thought she was going to drop it, but then she got a grip again. "She went to a chain store in Milwaukee! Wouldn't pay me! My business is suffering; this wedding was going to get me back in the black!"

"And instead it sent you closer to bankruptcy," I said having regained my breath and my wits. Please, Joe, get my call! I thought.

"No offense to your husband, but if Angela hadn't interfered and got you looking around the police would never have figured it out! But I've lost everything now, I have to go! I don't want to hurt you, so stay put for half an hour after I'm gone." She opened the car door, had the car started and was pulling out almost before the door closed again. I rolled out of the way just in time.

Then: "Stop!" A familiar voice. Tires squealed.

Terrified, I opened my eyes. Joe stood in front of the Toyota on the street. Eleanor had tried to back away, only to encounter Dick in the town's only patrol car behind her. I sobbed with relief.

* * *

Joe had offered to grill Dick the biggest steak he'd ever seen along with a good bottle of wine, but Dick, bless his Dairyland soul, wanted bratwurst wrapped in cheese and bacon with a six-pack of Pabst Blue Ribbon. Turned out my phone gambit hadn't worked quite the way I'd expected. The Lively police force knew to come to Eleanor's because of Dick. He'd taken the print and matched it against a file of business owner's prints that the town had compiled some years back, for reasons none of us could now remember. The bloody print on the knife was Eleanor's; no one else's was on it. And instead of calling Joe, when I'd fiddled with my phone I'd recorded her confession.

We sat on our deck and Joe turned to me with a grin. "Well, 'Trixie,' looks like you'll both make detective grade!"

The Safety Match

Anton Chekhov

Chapter I

ON THE MORNING of October 6, 1885, in the office of the Inspector of Police of the second division of S— District, there appeared a respectably dressed young man, who announced that his master, Marcus Ivanovitch Klausoff, a retired officer of the Horse Guards, separated from his wife, had been murdered. While making this announcement the young man was white and terribly agitated. His hands trembled and his eyes were full of terror.

"Whom have I the honour of addressing?" asked the inspector.

"Psyekoff, Lieutenant Klausoff's agent; agriculturist and mechanician!"

The inspector and his deputy, on visiting the scene of the occurrence in company with Psyekoff, found the following: Near the wing in which Klausoff had lived was gathered a dense crowd. The news of the murder had sped swift as lightning through the neighbourhood, and the peasantry, thanks to the fact that the day was a holiday, had hurried together from all the neighbouring villages. There was much commotion and talk. Here and there, pale, tear-stained faces were seen. The door of Klausoff's bedroom was found locked. The key was inside.

"It is quite clear that the scoundrels got in by the window!" said Psyekoff as they examined the door.

They went to the garden, into which the bedroom window opened. The window looked dark and ominous. It was covered by a faded green curtain. One corner of the curtain was slightly turned up, which made it possible to look into the bedroom.

"Did any of you look into the window?" asked the inspector.

"Certainly not, your worship!" answered Ephraim, the gardener, a little gray-haired old man, who looked like a retired sergeant. "Who's going to look in, if all their bones are shaking?"

"Ah, Marcus Ivanovitch, Marcus Ivanovitch!" sighed the inspector, looking at the window, "I told you you would come to a bad end! I told the dear man, but he wouldn't listen! Dissipation doesn't bring any good!"

"Thanks to Ephraim," said Psyekoff; "but for him, we would never have guessed. He was the first to guess that something was wrong. He comes to me this morning, and says: 'Why is the master so long getting up? He hasn't left his bedroom for a whole week!' The moment he said that, it was just as if someone had hit me with an axe. The thought flashed through my mind, 'We haven't had a sight of him since last Saturday, and today is Sunday'! Seven whole days – not a doubt of it!"

"Ay, poor fellow!" again sighed the inspector. "He was a clever fellow, finely educated, and kind-hearted at that! And in society, nobody could touch him! But he was a waster,

God rest his soul! I was prepared for anything since he refused to live with Olga Petrovna. Poor thing, a good wife, but a sharp tongue! Stephen!" the inspector called to one of his deputies, "go over to my house this minute, and send Andrew to the captain to lodge an information with him! Tell him that Marcus Ivanovitch has been murdered. And run over to the orderly; why should he sit there, kicking his heels? Let him come here! And go as fast as you can to the examining magistrate, Nicholas Yermolaïyevitch. Tell him to come over here! Wait; I'll write him a note!"

The inspector posted sentinels around the wing, wrote a letter to the examining magistrate, and then went over to the director's for a glass of tea. Ten minutes later he was sitting on a stool, carefully nibbling a lump of sugar, and swallowing the scalding tea.

"There you are!" he was saying to Psyekoff; "there you are! A noble by birth! A rich man – a favourite of the gods, you may say, as Pushkin has it, and what did he come to? He drank and dissipated and – there you are – he's murdered."

After a couple of hours the examining magistrate drove up. Nicholas Yermolaïyevitch Chubikoff – for that was the magistrate's name – was a tall, fleshy old man of sixty, who had been wrestling with the duties of his office for a quarter of a century. Everybody in the district knew him as an honest man, wise, energetic, and in love with his work. He was accompanied to the scene of the murder by his inveterate companion, fellow worker, and secretary, Dukovski, a tall young fellow of twenty-six.

"Is it possible, gentlemen?" cried Chubikoff, entering Psyekoff's room, and quickly shaking hands with everyone. "Is it possible? Marcus Ivanovitch? Murdered? No! It is impossible! Im-poss-i-ble!"

"Go in there!" sighed the inspector.

"Lord, have mercy on us! Only last Friday I saw him at the fair in Farabankoff. I had a drink of vodka with him, save the mark!"

"Go in there!" again sighed the inspector.

They sighed, uttered exclamations of horror, drank a glass of tea each, and went to the wing.

"Get back!" the orderly cried to the peasants.

Going to the wing, the examining magistrate began his work by examining the bedroom door. The door proved to be of pine, painted yellow, and was uninjured. Nothing was found which could serve as a clue. They had to break in the door.

"Everyone not here on business is requested to keep away!" said the magistrate, when, after much hammering and shaking, the door yielded to axe and chisel. "I request this, in the interest of the investigation. Orderly, don't let anyone in!"

Chubikoff, his assistant, and the inspector opened the door, and hesitatingly, one after the other, entered the room. Their eyes met the following sight: Beside the single window stood the big wooden bed with a huge feather mattress. On the crumpled feather bed lay a tumbled, crumpled quilt. The pillow, in a cotton pillow-case, also much crumpled, was dragging on the floor. On the table beside the bed lay a silver watch and a silver twenty-kopeck piece. Beside them lay some sulphur matches. Beside the bed, the little table, and the single chair, there was no furniture in the room. Looking under the bed, the inspector saw a couple of dozen empty bottles, an old straw hat, and a quart of vodka. Under the table lay one top boot, covered with dust. Casting a glance around the room, the magistrate frowned and grew red in the face.

"Scoundrels!" he muttered, clenching his fists.

"And where is Marcus Ivanovitch?" asked Dukovski in a low voice.

"Mind your own business!" Chubikoff answered roughly. "Be good enough to examine the floor! This is not the first case of the kind I have had to deal with! Eugraph Kuzmitch," he said turning to the inspector, and lowering his voice, "in 1870 I had another case like this. But you must remember it – the murder of the merchant Portraitoff. It was just the same there. The scoundrels murdered him, and dragged the corpse out through the window—"

Chubikoff went up to the window, pulled the curtain to one side, and carefully pushed the window. The window opened.

"It opens, you see! It wasn't fastened. Hm! There are tracks under the window. Look! There is the track of a knee! Somebody got in there. We must examine the window thoroughly."

"There is nothing special to be found on the floor," said Dukovski. "No stains or scratches. The only thing I found was a struck safety match. Here it is! So far as I remember, Marcus Ivanovitch did not smoke. And he always used sulphur matches, never safety matches. Perhaps this safety match may serve as a clue!"

"Oh, do shut up!" cried the magistrate deprecatingly. "You go on about your match! I can't abide these dreamers! Instead of chasing matches, you had better examine the bed!"

After a thorough examination of the bed, Dukovski reported:

"There are no spots, either of blood or of anything else. There are likewise no new torn places. On the pillow there are signs of teeth. The quilt is stained with something which looks like beer and smells like beer. The general aspect of the bed gives grounds for thinking that a struggle took place on it."

"I know there was a struggle, without your telling me! You are not being asked about a struggle. Instead of looking for struggles, you had better—"

"Here is one top boot, but there is no sign of the other."

"Well, and what of that?"

"It proves that they strangled him, while he was taking his boots off. He hadn't time to take the second boot off when—"

"There you go! – and how do you know they strangled him?"

"There are marks of teeth on the pillow. The pillow itself is badly crumpled, and thrown a couple of yards from the bed."

"Listen to his foolishness! Better come into the garden. You would be better employed examining the garden than digging around here. I can do that without you!"

When they reached the garden they began by examining the grass. The grass under the window was crushed and trampled. A bushy burdock growing under the window close to the wall was also trampled. Dukovski succeeded in finding on it some broken twigs and a piece of cotton wool. On the upper branches were found some fine hairs of dark blue wool.

"What colour was his last suit?" Dukovski asked Psyekoff.

"Yellow crash."

"Excellent! You see they wore blue!"

A few twigs of the burdock were cut off, and carefully wrapped in paper by the investigators. At this point Police Captain Artsuybasheff Svistakovski and Dr. Tyutyeff arrived. The captain bade them "Good day!" and immediately began to satisfy his curiosity. The doctor, a tall, very lean man, with dull eyes, a long nose, and a pointed chin, without greeting anyone or asking about anything, sat down on a log, sighed, and began:

"The Servians are at war again! What in heaven's name can they want now? Austria, it's all your doing!"

The examination of the window from the outside did not supply any conclusive data. The examination of the grass and the bushes nearest to the window yielded a series of useful clues. For example, Dukovski succeeded in discovering a long, dark streak, made up of spots, on the grass, which led some distance into the centre of the garden. The streak ended under one of the lilac bushes in a dark brown stain. Under this same lilac bush was found a top boot, which turned out to be the fellow of the boot already found in the bedroom.

"That is a blood stain made some time ago," said Dukovski, examining the spot.

At the word "blood" the doctor rose, and going over lazily, looked at the spot.

"Yes, it is blood!" he muttered.

"That shows he wasn't strangled, if there was blood," said Chubikoff, looking sarcastically at Dukovski.

"They strangled him in the bedroom; and here, fearing he might come round again, they struck him a blow with some sharp-pointed instrument. The stain under the bush proves that he lay there a considerable time, while they were looking about for some way of carrying him out of the garden."

"Well, and how about the boot?"

"The boot confirms completely my idea that they murdered him while he was taking his boots off before going to bed. He had already taken off one boot, and the other, this one here, he had only had time to take half off. The half-off boot came off of itself, while the body was dragged over, and fell—"

"There's a lively imagination for you!" laughed Chubikoff. "He goes on and on like that! When will you learn enough to drop your deductions? Instead of arguing and deducing, it would be much better if you took some of the blood-stained grass for analysis!"

When they had finished their examination, and drawn a plan of the locality, the investigators went to the director's office to write their report and have breakfast. While they were breakfasting they went on talking:

"The watch, the money, and so on – all untouched—" Chubikoff began, leading off the talk, "show as clearly as that two and two are four that the murder was not committed for the purpose of robbery."

"The murder was committed by an educated man!" insisted Dukovski.

"What evidence have you of that?"

"The safety match proves that to me, for the peasants hereabouts are not ye acquainted with safety matches. Only the landowners use them, and by no means al of them. And it is evident that there was not one murderer, but at least three. Two hel him, while one killed him. Klausoff was strong, and the murderers must have known it!

"What good would his strength be, supposing he was asleep?"

"The murderers came on him while he was taking off his boots. If he was taking of his boots, that proves that he wasn't asleep!"

"Stop inventing your deductions! Better eat!"

"In my opinion, your worship," said the gardener Ephraim, setting the samovar o the table, "it was nobody but Nicholas who did this dirty trick!"

"Quite possible," said Psyekoff.

"And who is Nicholas?"

"The master's valet, your worship," answered Ephraim. "Who else could it be? He a rascal, your worship! He's a drunkard and a blackguard, the like of which Heave should not permit! He always took the master his vodka and put the master to be Who else could it be? And I also venture to point out to your worship, he once boaste at the public house that he would kill the master! It happened on account of Aquilin the woman, you know. He was making up to a soldier's widow. She pleased the maste he master made friends with her himself, and Nicholas – naturally, he was mad! He is olling about drunk in the kitchen now. He is crying, and telling lies, saying he is sorry or the master—"

The examining magistrate ordered Nicholas to be brought. Nicholas, a lanky young ellow, with a long, freckled nose, narrow-chested, and wearing an old jacket of his naster's, entered Psyekoff's room, and bowed low before the magistrate. His face was leepy and tear-stained. He was tipsy and could hardly keep his feet.

"Where is your master?" Chubikoff asked him.

"Murdered! Your worship!"

As he said this, Nicholas blinked and began to weep.

"We know he was murdered. But where is he now? Where is his body?"

"They say he was dragged out of the window and buried in the garden!"

"Hum! The results of the investigation are known in the kitchen already! – That's bad! Vhere were you, my good fellow, the night the master was murdered? Saturday night, hat is."

Nicholas raised his head, stretched his neck, and began to think.

"I don't know, your worship," he said. "I was drunk and don't remember."

"An alibi!" whispered Dukovski, smiling, and rubbing his hands.

"So-o! And why is there blood under the master's window?"

Nicholas jerked his head up and considered.

"Hurry up!" said the Captain of Police.

"Right away! That blood doesn't amount to anything, your worship! I was cutting a hicken's throat. I was doing it quite simply, in the usual way, when all of a sudden it broke way and started to run. That is where the blood came from."

Ephraim declared that Nicholas did kill a chicken every evening, and always in some ew place, but that nobody ever heard of a half-killed chicken running about the garden, hough of course it wasn't impossible.

"An alibi," sneered Dukovski; "and what an asinine alibi!"

"Did you know Aquilina?"

"Yes, your worship, I know her."

"And the master cut you out with her?"

"Not at all. *He* cut me out – Mr. Psyekoff there, Ivan Mikhailovitch; and the master cut van Mikhailovitch out. That is how it was."

Psyekoff grew confused and began to scratch his left eye. Dukovski looked at him ttentively, noted his confusion, and started. He noticed that the director had dark blue rousers, which he had not observed before. The trousers reminded him of the dark blue hreads found on the burdock. Chubikoff in his turn glanced suspiciously at Psyekoff.

"Go!" he said to Nicholas. "And now permit me to put a question to you, Mr. Psyekoff.)f course you were here last Saturday evening?"

"Yes! I had supper with Marcus Ivanovitch about ten o'clock."

"And afterward?"

"Afterward – afterward. Really, I do not remember," stammered Psyekoff. "I had a good eal to drink at supper. I don't remember when or where I went to sleep. Why are you all ooking at me like that, as if I was the murderer?"

"Where were you when you woke up?"

"I was in the servants' kitchen, lying behind the stove! They can all confirm it. How got behind the stove I don't know—"

"Do not get agitated. Did you know Aquilina?"

"There's nothing extraordinary about that—"

"She first liked you and then preferred Klausoff?"

"Yes. Ephraim, give us some more mushrooms! Do you want some more tea Eugraph Kuzmitch?"

A heavy, oppressive silence began and lasted fully five minutes. Dukovski silentl kept his piercing eyes fixed on Psyekoff's pale face. The silence was finally broken b the examining magistrate:

"We must go to the house and talk with Maria Ivanovna, the sister of the deceased Perhaps she may be able to supply some clues."

Chubikoff and his assistant expressed their thanks for the breakfast, and wen toward the house. They found Klausoff's sister, Maria Ivanovna, an old maid of forty five, at prayer before the big case of family icons. When she saw the portfolios in he guests' hands, and their official caps, she grew pale.

"Let me begin by apologizing for disturbing, so to speak, your devotions," began th gallant Chubikoff, bowing and scraping. "We have come to you with a request. Of course you have heard already. There is a suspicion that your dear brother, in some way o other, has been murdered. The will of God, you know. No one can escape death, neithe czar nor ploughman. Could you not help us with some clue, some explanation—?"

"Oh, don't ask me!" said Maria Ivanovna, growing still paler, and covering her fac with her hands. "I can tell you nothing. Nothing! I beg you! I know nothing – What ca I do? Oh, no! no! – not a word about my brother! If I die, I won't say anything!"

Maria Ivanovna began to weep, and left the room. The investigators looked at eac other, shrugged their shoulders, and beat a retreat.

"Confound the woman!" scolded Dukovski, going out of the house. "It is clear sh knows something, and is concealing it! And the chambermaid has a queer expressio too! Wait, you wretches! We'll ferret it all out!"

In the evening Chubikoff and his deputy, lit on their road by the pale moon, wende their way homeward. They sat in their carriage and thought over the results of the da Both were tired and kept silent. Chubikoff was always unwilling to talk while travellin and the talkative Dukovski remained silent, to fall in with the elder man's humour. Bu at the end of their journey the deputy could hold in no longer, and said:

"It is quite certain," he said, "that Nicholas had something to do with the matter. *No dubitandum est!* You can see by his face what sort of a case he is! His alibi betrays hir body and bones. But it is also certain that he did not set the thing going. He was onl the stupid hired tool. You agree? And the humble Psyekoff was not without some sligh share in the matter. His dark blue breeches, his agitation, his lying behind the stove i terror after the murder, his alibi and – Aquilina—"

"'Grind away, Emilian; it's your week!' So, according to you, whoever knew Aquilina i the murderer! Hothead! You ought to be sucking a bottle, and not handling affairs! Yo were one of Aquilina's admirers yourself – does it follow that you are implicated too?"

"Aquilina was cook in your house for a month. I am saying nothing about that! Th night before that Saturday I was playing cards with you, and saw you, otherwise I shoul be after you too! It isn't the woman that matters, old chap! It is the mean, nasty, lo spirit of jealousy that matters. The retiring young man was not pleased when they go the better of him, you see! His vanity, don't you see? He wanted revenge. Then, thos thick lips of his suggest passion. So there you have it: wounded self-love and passio

That is quite enough motive for a murder. We have two of them in our hands; but who is the third? Nicholas and Psyekoff held him, but who smothered him? Psyekoff is shy, timid, an all-round coward. And Nicholas would not know how to smother with a pillow. His sort use an axe or a club. Some third person did the smothering; but who was it?"

Dukovski crammed his hat down over his eyes and pondered. He remained silent until the carriage rolled up to the magistrate's door.

"Eureka!" he said, entering the little house and throwing off his overcoat. "Eureka, Nicholas Yermolaïyevitch! The only thing I can't understand is, how it did not occur to me sooner! Do you know who the third person was?"

"Oh, for goodness sake, shut up! There is supper! Sit down to your evening meal!"

The magistrate and Dukovski sat down to supper. Dukovski poured himself out a glass of vodka, rose, drew himself up, and said, with sparkling eyes:

"Well, learn that the third person, who acted in concert with that scoundrel Psyekoff, and did the smothering, was a woman! Yes-s! I mean – the murdered man's sister, Maria Ivanovna!"

Chubikoff choked over his vodka, and fixed his eyes on Dukovski.

"You aren't – what's-its-name? Your head isn't what-do-you-call-it? You haven't a pain in it?"

"I am perfectly well! Very well, let us say that I am crazy; but how do you explain her confusion when we appeared? How do you explain her unwillingness to give us any information? Let us admit that these are trifles. Very well! All right! But remember their relations. She detested her brother. She never forgave him for living apart from his wife. She of the Old Faith, while in her eyes he is a godless profligate. There is where the germ of her hate was hatched. They say he succeeded in making her believe that he was an angel of Satan. He even went in for spiritualism in her presence!"

"Well, what of that?"

"You don't understand? She, as a member of the Old Faith, murdered him through fanaticism. It was not only that she was putting to death a weed, a profligate – she was freeing the world of an anti-christ! – and there, in her opinion, was her service, her religious achievement! Oh, you don't know those old maids of the Old Faith. Read Dostoyevsky! And what does Lyeskoff say about them, or Petcherski? It was she, and nobody else, even if you cut me open. She smothered him! O treacherous woman! wasn't that the reason why she was kneeling before the icons, when we came in, just to take our attention away? 'Let me kneel down and pray,' she said to herself, 'and they will think I am tranquil and did not expect them!' That is the plan of all novices in crime, Nicholas Yermolaïyevitch, old pal! My dear old man, won't you intrust this business to me? Let me personally bring it through! Friend, I began it and I will finish it!"

Chubikoff shook his head and frowned.

"We know how to manage difficult matters ourselves," he said; "and your business is not to push yourself in where you don't belong. Write from dictation when you are dictated to; that is your job!"

Dukovski flared up, banged the door, and disappeared.

"Clever rascal!" muttered Chubikoff, glancing after him. "Awfully clever! But too much of a hothead. I must buy him a cigar case at the fair as a present."

The next day, early in the morning, a young man with a big head and a pursed-up mouth, who came from Klausoff's place, was introduced to the magistrate's office. He said he was the shepherd Daniel, and brought a very interesting piece of information.

"I was a bit drunk," he said. "I was with my pal till midnight. On my way home, as I was drunk, I went into the river for a bath. I was taking a bath, when I looked up. Two men were walking along the dam, carrying something black. 'Shoo!' I cried at them. They got scared, and went off like the wind toward Makareff's cabbage garden. Strike me dead, if they weren't carrying away the master!"

That same day, toward evening, Psyekoff and Nicholas were arrested and brought under guard to the district town. In the town they were committed to the cells of the prison.

Chapter II

A FORTNIGHT PASSED.

It was morning. The magistrate Nicholas Yermolaïyevitch was sitting in his office before a green table, turning over the papers of the 'Klausoff case'; Dukovski was striding restlessly up and down like a wolf in a cage.

"You are convinced of the guilt of Nicholas and Psyekoff," he said, nervously plucking at his young beard. "Why will you not believe in the guilt of Maria Ivanovna? Are there not proofs enough for you?"

"I don't say I am not convinced. I am convinced, but somehow I don't believe it! There are no real proofs, but just a kind of philosophizing – fanaticism, this and that—"

"You can't do without an axe and bloodstained sheets. Those jurists! Very well, I'll prove it to you! You will stop sneering at the psychological side of the affair! To Siberia with your Maria Ivanovna! I will prove it! If philosophy is not enough for you, I have something substantial for you. It will show you how correct my philosophy is. Just give me permission—"

"What are you going on about?"

"About the safety match! Have you forgotten it? I haven't! I am going to find out who struck it in the murdered man's room. It was not Nicholas that struck it; it was not Psyekoff, for neither of them had any matches when they were examined; it was the third person, Maria Ivanovna. I will prove it to you. Just give me permission to go through the district to find out."

"That's enough! Sit down. Let us go on with the examination."

Dukovski sat down at a little table, and plunged his long nose in a bundle of papers.

"Bring in Nicholas Tetekhoff!" cried the examining magistrate.

They brought Nicholas in. Nicholas was pale and thin as a rail. He was trembling.

"Tetekhoff!" began Chubikoff. "In 1879 you were tried in the Court of the First Division, convicted of theft, and sentenced to imprisonment. In 1882 you were tried a second time for theft, and were again imprisoned. We know all—"

Astonishment was depicted on Nicholas's face. The examining magistrate's omniscience startled him. But soon his expression of astonishment changed to extreme indignation. He began to cry and requested permission to go and wash his face and quiet down. They led him away.

"Bring in Psyekoff!" ordered the examining magistrate.

They brought in Psyekoff. The young man had changed greatly during the last few days. He had grown thin and pale, and looked haggard. His eyes had an apathetic expression.

"Sit down, Psyekoff," said Chubikoff. "I hope that today you are going to be reasonable, and will not tell lies, as you did before. All these days you have denied that you had anything to do with the murder of Klausoff, in spite of all the proofs that testify against you. That is foolish. Confession will lighten your guilt. This is the last time I am going to talk to you. If you do not confess today tomorrow it will be too late. Come, tell me all—"

"I know nothing about it. I know nothing about your proofs," answered Psyekoff almost inaudibly.

"It's no use! Well, let me relate to you how the matter took place. On Saturday evening you were sitting in Klausoff's sleeping room, and drinking vodka and beer with him." (Dukovski fixed his eyes on Psyekoff's face, and kept them there all through the examination.) "Nicholas was waiting on you. At one o'clock, Marcus Ivanovitch announced his intention of going to bed. He always went to bed at one o'clock. When he was taking off his boots, and was giving you directions about details of management, you and Nicholas, at a given signal, seized your drunken master and threw him on the bed. One of you sat on his legs, the other on his head. Then a third person came in from the passage – a woman in a black dress, whom you know well, and who had previously arranged with you as to her share in your criminal deed. She seized a pillow and began to smother him. While the struggle was going on the candle went out. The woman took a box of safety matches from her pocket, and lit the candle. Was it not so? I see by your face that I am speaking the truth. But to go on. After you had smothered him, and saw that he had ceased breathing, you and Nicholas pulled him out through the window and laid him down near the burdock. Fearing that he might come round again, you struck him with something sharp. Then you carried him away, and laid him down under a lilac bush for a short time. After resting awhile and considering, you carried him across the fence. Then you entered the road. After that comes the dam. Near the dam, a peasant frightened you. Well, what is the matter with you?"

"I am suffocating!" replied Psyekoff. "Very well – have it so. Only let me go out, please!"

They led Psyekoff away.

"At last! He has confessed!" cried Chubikoff, stretching himself luxuriously. "He has betrayed himself! And didn't I get round him cleverly! Regularly caught him napping—"

"And he doesn't deny the woman in the black dress!" exulted Dukovski. "But all the same, that safety match is tormenting me frightfully. I can't stand it any longer. Goodbye! I am off!"

Dukovski put on his cap and drove off. Chubikoff began to examine Aquilina. Aquilina declared that she knew nothing whatever about it.

At six that evening Dukovski returned. He was more agitated than he had ever been before. His hands trembled so that he could not even unbutton his greatcoat. His cheeks glowed. It was clear that he did not come empty-handed.

"*Veni, vidi, vici!*" he cried, rushing into Chubikoff's room, and falling into an armchair. "I swear to you on my honour, I begin to believe that I am a genius! Listen, devil take us all! It is funny, and it is sad. We have caught three already – isn't that so? Well, I have found the fourth, and a woman at that. You will never believe who it is! But listen. I went to Klausoff's village, and began to make a spiral round it. I visited all the little shops, public houses, dram shops on the road, everywhere asking for safety matches. Everywhere they said they hadn't any. I made a wide round. Twenty times I lost faith, and twenty times I got it back again. I knocked about the whole day, and only an hour ago I got on the track. Three versts from here. They gave me a packet of ten boxes. One box was missing. Immediately: 'Who bought the other box?' 'Such-a-one! She was pleased with them!' Old man! Nicholas Yermolaïyevitch! See what a fellow who was expelled from the seminary and who has read Gaboriau can do! From today on I begin to respect myself! Oof! Well, come!"

"Come where?"

"To her, to number four! We must hurry, otherwise – otherwise I'll burst with impatience! Do you know who she is? You'll never guess! Olga Petrovna, Marcus Ivanovitch's wife – his own wife – that's who it is! She is the person who bought the matchbox!"

"You – you – you are out of your mind!"

"It's quite simple! To begin with, she smokes. Secondly, she was head and ears in love with Klausoff, even after he refused to live in the same house with her, because she was always scolding his head off. Why, they say she used to beat him because she loved him so much. And then he positively refused to stay in the same house. Love turned sour. 'Hell hath no fury like a woman scorned.' But come along! Quick, or it will be dark. Come!"

"I am not yet sufficiently crazy to go and disturb a respectable honourable woman in the middle of the night for a crazy boy!"

"Respectable, honourable! Do honourable women murder their husbands? After that you are a rag, and not an examining magistrate! I never ventured to call you names before, but now you compel me to. Rag! Dressing-gown! – Dear Nicholas Yermolaïyevitch, do come, I beg of you—!"

The magistrate made a deprecating motion with his hand.

"I beg of you! I ask, not for myself, but in the interests of justice. I beg you! I implore you! Do what I ask you to, just this once!"

Dukovski went down on his knees.

"Nicholas Yermolaïyevitch! Be kind! Call me a blackguard, a ne'er-do-weel, if I am mistaken about this woman. You see what an affair it is. What a case it is. A romance! A woman murdering her own husband for love! The fame of it will go all over Russia. They will make you investigator in all important cases. Understand, O foolish old man!"

The magistrate frowned, and undecidedly stretched his hand toward his cap.

"Oh, the devil take you!" he said. "Let us go!"

It was dark when the magistrate's carriage rolled up to the porch of the old country house in which Olga Petrovna had taken refuge with her brother.

"What pigs we are," said Chubikoff, taking hold of the bell, "to disturb a poor woman like this!"

"It's all right! It's all right! Don't get frightened! We can say that we have broken a spring."

Chubikoff and Dukovski were met at the threshold by a tall buxom woman of three and twenty, with pitch-black brows and juicy red lips. It was Olga Petrovna herself, apparently not the least distressed by the recent tragedy.

"Oh, what a pleasant surprise!" she said, smiling broadly. "You are just in time for supper. Kuzma Petrovitch is not at home. He is visiting the priest, and has stayed late. But we'll get on without him! Be seated. You have come from the examination?"

"Yes. We broke a spring, you know," began Chubikoff, entering the sitting room and sinking into an armchair.

"Take her unawares – at once!" whispered Dukovski; "take her unawares!"

"A spring – hum – yes – so we came in."

"Take her unawares, I tell you! She will guess what the matter is if you drag things out like that."

"Well, do it yourself as you want. But let me get out of it," muttered Chubikoff, rising and going to the window.

"Yes, a spring," began Dukovski, going close to Olga Petrovna and wrinkling his long nose. "We did not drive over here – to take supper with you or – to see Kuzma Petrovitch. We came here to ask you, respected madam, where Marcus Ivanovitch is, whom you murdered!"

"What? Marcus Ivanovitch murdered?" stammered Olga Petrovna, and her broad face suddenly and instantaneously flushed bright scarlet. "I don't – understand!"

"I ask you in the name of the law! Where is Klausoff? We know all!"

"Who told you?" Olga Petrovna asked in a low voice, unable to endure Dukovski's glance.

"Be so good as to show us where he is!"

"But how did you find out? Who told you?"

"We know all! I demand it in the name of the law!"

The examining magistrate, emboldened by her confusion, came forward and said:

"Show us, and we will go away. Otherwise, we—"

"What do you want with him?"

"Madam, what is the use of these questions? We ask you to show us! You tremble, you are agitated. Yes, he has been murdered, and, if you must have it, murdered by you! Your accomplices have betrayed you!"

Olga Petrovna grew pale.

"Come!" she said in a low voice, wringing her hands.

"I have him – hid – in the bath house! Only for heaven's sake, do not tell Kuzma Petrovitch. I beg and implore you! He will never forgive me!"

Olga Petrovna took down a big key from the wall, and led her guests through the kitchen and passage to the courtyard. The courtyard was in darkness. Fine rain was falling. Olga Petrovna walked in advance of them. Chubikoff and Dukovski strode behind her through the long grass, as the odour of wild hemp and dishwater splashing under their feet reached them. The courtyard was wide. Soon the dishwater ceased, and they felt freshly broken earth under their feet. In the darkness appeared the shadowy outlines of trees, and among the trees a little house with a crooked chimney.

"That is the bath house," said Olga Petrovna. "But I implore you, do not tell my brother! If you do, I'll never hear the end of it!"

Going up to the bath house, Chubikoff and Dukovski saw a huge padlock on the door.

"Get your candle and matches ready," whispered the examining magistrate to his deputy.

Olga Petrovna unfastened the padlock, and let her guests into the bath house. Dukovski struck a match and lit up the anteroom. In the middle of the anteroom stood a table. On the table, beside a sturdy little samovar, stood a soup tureen with cold cabbage soup and a plate with the remnants of some sauce.

"Forward!"

They went into the next room, where the bath was. There was a table there also. On the table was a dish with some ham, a bottle of vodka, plates, knives, forks.

"But where is it – where is the murdered man?" asked the examining magistrate.

"On the top tier," whispered Olga Petrovna, still pale and trembling.

Dukovski took the candle in his hand and climbed up to the top tier of the sweating frame. There he saw a long human body lying motionless on a large feather bed. A slight snore came from the body.

"You are making fun of us, devil take it!" cried Dukovski. "That is not the murdered man! Some live fool is lying here. Here, whoever you are, the devil take you!"

The body drew in a quick breath and stirred. Dukovski stuck his elbow into it. It raised a hand, stretched itself, and lifted its head.

"Who is sneaking in here?" asked a hoarse, heavy bass. "What do you want?"

Dukovski raised the candle to the face of the unknown, and cried out. In the red nose, dishevelled, unkempt hair, the pitch-black moustache, one of which was jauntily twisted and pointed insolently toward the ceiling, he recognized the gallant cavalryman Klausoff.

"You – Marcus – Ivanovitch? Is it possible?"

The examining magistrate glanced sharply up at him, and stood spellbound.

"Yes, it is I. That's you, Dukovski? What the devil do you want here? And who's that other mug down there? Great snakes! It is the examining magistrate! What fate has brought him here?"

Klausoff rushed down and threw his arms round Chubikoff in a cordial embrace. Olga Petrovna slipped through the door.

"How did you come here? Let's have a drink, devil take it! Tra-ta-ti-to-tum – let us drink! But who brought you here? How did you find out that I was here? But it doesn't matter! Let's have a drink!"

Klausoff lit the lamp and poured out three glasses of vodka.

"That is – I don't understand you," said the examining magistrate, running his hands over him. "Is this you or not you!"

"Oh, shut up! You want to preach me a sermon? Don't trouble yourself! Young Dukovski, empty your glass! Friends, let us bring this – What are you looking at? Drink!"

"All the same, I do not understand!" said the examining magistrate, mechanically drinking off the vodka. "What are you here for?"

"Why shouldn't I be here, if I am all right here?"

Klausoff drained his glass and took a bite of ham.

"I am in captivity here, as you see. In solitude, in a cavern, like a ghost or a bogey. Drink! She carried me off and locked me up, and – well, I am living here, in the deserted bath house, like a hermit. I am fed. Next week I think I'll try to get out. I'm tired of it here!"

"Incomprehensible!" said Dukovski.

"What is incomprehensible about it?"

"Incomprehensible! For Heaven's sake, how did your boot get into the garden?"

"What boot?"

"We found one boot in the sleeping room and the other in the garden."

"And what do you want to know that for? It's none of your business! Why don't you drink, devil take you? If you wakened me, then drink with me! It is an interesting tale, brother, that of the boot! I didn't want to go with Olga. I don't like to be bossed. She came under the window and began to abuse me. She always was a termagant. You know what women are like, all of them. I was a bit drunk, so I took a boot and heaved it at her. Ha-ha-ha! Teach her not to scold another time! But it didn't! Not a bit of it! She climbed in at the window, lit the lamp, and began to hammer poor tipsy me. She thrashed me, dragged me over here, and locked me in. She feeds me now – on love, vodka, and ham! But where are you off to, Chubikoff? Where are you going?"

The examining magistrate swore, and left the bath house. Dukovski followed him, crestfallen. They silently took their seats in the carriage and drove off. The road never seemed to them so long and disagreeable as it did that time. Both remained silent. Chubikoff trembled with rage all the way. Dukovski hid his nose in the collar of his overcoat, as if he was afraid that the darkness and the drizzling rain might read the shame in his face.

When they reached home, the examining magistrate found Dr. Tyutyeff awaiting him. The doctor was sitting at the table, and, sighing deeply, was turning over the pages of the *Neva*.

"Such goings on there are in the world!" he said, meeting the examining magistrate with a sad smile. "Austria is at it again! And Gladstone also to some extent—"

Chubikoff threw his cap under the table, and shook himself.

"Devils' skeletons! Don't plague me! A thousand times I have told you not to bother me with your politics! This is no question of politics! And you," said Chubikoff, turning to Dukovski and shaking his fist, "I won't forget this in a thousand years!"

"But the safety match? How could I know?"

"Choke yourself with your safety match! Get out of my way! Don't make me mad, or the devil only knows what I'll do to you! Don't let me see a trace of you!"

Dukovski sighed, took his hat, and went out.

"I'll go and get drunk," he decided, going through the door, and gloomily wending his way to the public house.

The Secret Garden

G.K. Chesterton

ARISTIDE VALENTIN, Chief of the Paris Police, was late for his dinner, and some of his guests began to arrive before him. These were, however, reassured by his confidential servant, Ivan, the old man with a scar, and a face almost as grey as his moustaches, who always sat at a table in the entrance hall – a hall hung with weapons. Valentin's house was perhaps as peculiar and celebrated as its master. It was an old house, with high walls and tall poplars almost overhanging the Seine; but the oddity – and perhaps the police value – of its architecture was this: that there was no ultimate exit at all except through this front door, which was guarded by Ivan and the armoury. The garden was large and elaborate, and there were many exits from the house into the garden. But there was no exit from the garden into the world outside; all round it ran a tall, smooth, unscalable wall with special spikes at the top; no bad garden, perhaps, for a man to reflect in whom some hundred criminals had sworn to kill.

As Ivan explained to the guests, their host had telephoned that he was detained for ten minutes. He was, in truth, making some last arrangements about executions and such ugly things; and though these duties were rootedly repulsive to him, he always performed them with precision. Ruthless in the pursuit of criminals, he was very mild about their punishment. Since he had been supreme over French – and largely over European – policial methods, his great influence had been honourably used for the mitigation of sentences and the purification of prisons. He was one of the great humanitarian French freethinkers; and the only thing wrong with them is that they make mercy even colder than justice.

When Valentin arrived he was already dressed in black clothes and the red rosette – an elegant figure, his dark beard already streaked with grey. He went straight through his house to his study, which opened on the grounds behind. The garden door of it was open, and after he had carefully locked his box in its official place, he stood for a few seconds at the open door looking out upon the garden. A sharp moon was fighting with the flying rags and tatters of a storm, and Valentin regarded it with a wistfulness unusual in such scientific natures as his. Perhaps such scientific natures have some psychic prevision of the most tremendous problem of their lives. From any such occult mood, at least, he quickly recovered, for he knew he was late, and that his guests had already begun to arrive. A glance at his drawing-room when he entered it was enough to make certain that his principal guest was not there, at any rate. He saw all the other pillars of the little party; he saw Lord Galloway, the English Ambassador – a choleric old man with a russet face like an apple, wearing the blue ribbon of the Garter. He saw Lady Galloway, slim and threadlike, with silver hair and a face sensitive and superior. He saw her daughter, Lady Margaret Graham, a pale and pretty girl with an elfish face and copper-coloured hair. He saw the Duchess of Mont St. Michel, black-eyed and opulent, and with her her two daughters, black-eyed and opulent also. He saw Dr. Simon, a typical French scientist, with glasses, a pointed brown beard, and a forehead barred with those parallel wrinkles which are the penalty of superciliousness, since they come through constantly elevating the eyebrows. He saw Father Brown, of Cobhole, in Essex, whom he had recently met in England. He saw – perhaps with more interest than any of these – a tall man in uniform, who had bowed to the Galloways without receiving any very hearty acknowledgment, and who now advanced alone to pay his respects to his host. This was Commandant O'Brien, of the French Foreign Legion. He was a slim yet somewhat swaggering figure, clean-shaven, dark-haired, and blue-eyed, and, as seemed natural in an officer of that famous regiment of victorious failures and successful suicides, he had an air at once dashing and melancholy. He was by birth an Irish gentleman, and in boyhood had known the Galloways – especially Margaret Graham. He had left his country after some crash of debts, and now expressed his complete freedom from British etiquette by swinging about in uniform, sabre and spurs. When he bowed to the Ambassador's family, Lord and Lady Galloway bent stiffly, and Lady Margaret looked away.

But for whatever old causes such people might be interested in each other, their distinguished host was not specially interested in them. No one of them at least was in his eyes the guest of the evening. Valentin was expecting, for special reasons, a man of world-wide fame, whose friendship he had secured during some of his great detective tours and triumphs in the United States. He was expecting Julius K. Brayne, that multi-millionaire whose colossal and even crushing endowments of small religions have occasioned so much easy sport and easier solemnity for the American and English papers. Nobody could quite make out whether Mr. Brayne was an atheist or a Mormon or a Christian Scientist; but he was ready to pour money into any intellectual vessel, so long as it was an untried vessel. One of his hobbies was to wait for the American Shakespeare – a hobby more patient than angling. He admired Walt Whitman, but thought that Luke P. Tanner, of Paris, Pa., was more 'progressive' than Whitman any day. He liked anything that he thought 'progressive.' He thought Valentin 'progressive,' thereby doing him a grave injustice.

The solid appearance of Julius K. Brayne in the room was as decisive as a dinner bell. He had this great quality, which very few of us can claim, that his presence was as big as his absence. He was a huge fellow, as fat as he was tall, clad in complete evening black, without so much relief as a watch-chain or a ring. His hair was white and well brushed back like a German's; his face was red, fierce and cherubic, with one dark tuft under the lower lip that threw up that otherwise infantile visage with an effect theatrical and even Mephistophelean. Not long, however, did that salon merely stare at the celebrated American; his lateness had already become a domestic problem, and he was sent with all speed into the dining-room with Lady Galloway on his arm.

Except on one point the Galloways were genial and casual enough. So long as Lady Margaret did not take the arm of that adventurer O'Brien, her father was quite satisfied; and she had not done so, she had decorously gone in with Dr. Simon. Nevertheless, old Lord Galloway was restless and almost rude. He was diplomatic enough during dinner, but when, over the cigars, three of the younger men – Simon the doctor, Brown the priest, and the detrimental O'Brien, the exile in a foreign uniform – all melted away to mix with the ladies or smoke in the conservatory, then the English diplomatist grew very undiplomatic indeed. He was stung every sixty seconds with the thought that the scamp O'Brien might be signalling to Margaret somehow; he did not attempt to imagine how. He was left over the coffee with Brayne, the hoary Yankee who believed in all religions, and Valentin, the grizzled Frenchman who believed in none. They could argue with each other, but neither could appeal to him. After a time this 'progressive' logomachy had reached a crisis of tedium; Lord Galloway got up also and sought the drawing-room. He lost his way in long passages for some six or eight minutes: till he heard the high-pitched, didactic voice of the doctor, and then the dull voice of the priest, followed by general laughter. They also, he thought with a curse, were probably arguing about 'science and religion.' But the instant he opened the salon door he saw only one thing – he saw what was not there. He saw that Commandant O'Brien was absent, and that Lady Margaret was absent too.

Rising impatiently from the drawing-room, as he had from the dining-room, he stamped along the passage once more. His notion of protecting his daughter from the Irish-Algerian n'er-do-well had become something central and even mad in his mind. As he went towards the back of the house, where was Valentin's study, he was surprised to meet his daughter, who swept past with a white, scornful face, which was a second enigma. If she had been with O'Brien, where was O'Brien! If she had not been with O'Brien, where had she been? With a sort of senile and passionate suspicion he groped his way to the dark back parts of the mansion, and eventually found a servants' entrance that opened on to the garden. The moon with her scimitar had now ripped up and rolled away all the storm-wrack. The argent light lit up all four corners of the garden. A tall figure in blue was striding across the lawn towards the study door; a glint of moonlit silver on his facings picked him out as Commandant O'Brien.

He vanished through the French windows into the house, leaving Lord Galloway in an indescribable temper, at once virulent and vague. The blue-and-silver garden, like a scene in a theatre, seemed to taunt him with all that tyrannic tenderness against which his worldly authority was at war. The length and grace of the Irishman's stride enraged him as if he were a rival instead of a father; the moonlight maddened him. He was trapped as if by magic into a garden of troubadours, a Watteau fairyland; and, willing to shake off such amorous imbecilities by speech, he stepped briskly after his enemy. As he did so he tripped over some tree or stone in the grass; looked down at it first with irritation and then a second time with curiosity. The next instant the moon and the tall poplars looked at an unusual sight – an elderly English diplomatist running hard and crying or bellowing as he ran.

His hoarse shouts brought a pale face to the study door, the beaming glasses and worried brow of Dr. Simon, who heard the nobleman's first clear words. Lord Galloway was crying: "A corpse in the grass – a blood-stained corpse." O'Brien at last had gone utterly out of his mind.

"We must tell Valentin at once," said the doctor, when the other had brokenly described all that he had dared to examine. "It is fortunate that he is here;" and even as he spoke the great detective entered the study, attracted by the cry. It was almost amusing to note his typical transformation; he had come with the common concern of a host and a gentleman, fearing that some guest or servant was ill. When he was told the gory fact, he turned with all his gravity instantly bright and businesslike; for this, however abrupt and awful, was his business.

"Strange, gentlemen," he said as they hurried out into the garden, "that I should have hunted mysteries all over the earth, and now one comes and settles in my own back-yard. But where is the place?" They crossed the lawn less easily, as a slight mist had begun to rise from the river; but under the guidance of the shaken Galloway they found the body sunken in deep grass – the body of a very tall and broad-shouldered man. He lay face downwards, so they could only see that his big shoulders were clad in black cloth, and that his big head was bald, except for a wisp or two of brown hair that clung to his skull like wet seaweed. A scarlet serpent of blood crawled from under his fallen face.

"At least," said Simon, with a deep and singular intonation, "he is none of our party."

"Examine him, doctor," cried Valentin rather sharply. "He may not be dead."

The doctor bent down. "He is not quite cold, but I am afraid he is dead enough," he answered. "Just help me to lift him up."

They lifted him carefully an inch from the ground, and all doubts as to his being really dead were settled at once and frightfully. The head fell away. It had been entirely sundered from the body; whoever had cut his throat had managed to sever the neck as well. Even Valentin was slightly shocked. "He must have been as strong as a gorilla," he muttered.

Not without a shiver, though he was used to anatomical abortions, Dr. Simon lifted the head. It was slightly slashed about the neck and jaw, but the face was substantially unhurt. It was a ponderous, yellow face, at once sunken and swollen, with a hawk-like nose and heavy lids – a face of a wicked Roman emperor, with, perhaps, a distant touch of a Chinese emperor. All present seemed to look at it with the coldest eye of ignorance. Nothing else could be noted about the man except that, as they had lifted his body, they had seen underneath it the white gleam of a shirt-front defaced with a red gleam of blood. As Dr. Simon said, the man had never been of their party. But he might very well have been trying to join it, for he had come dressed for such an occasion.

Valentin went down on his hands and knees and examined with his closest professional attention the grass and ground for some twenty yards round the body, in which he was assisted less skillfully by the doctor, and quite vaguely by the English lord. Nothing rewarded their grovellings except a few twigs, snapped or chopped into very small lengths, which Valentin lifted for an instant's examination and then tossed away.

"Twigs," he said gravely; "twigs, and a total stranger with his head cut off; that is all there is on this lawn."

There was an almost creepy stillness, and then the unnerved Galloway called out sharply:

"Who's that! Who's that over there by the garden wall!"

A small figure with a foolishly large head drew waveringly near them in the moonlit haze; looked for an instant like a goblin, but turned out to be the harmless little priest whom they had left in the drawing-room.

"I say," he said meekly, "there are no gates to this garden, do you know."

Valentin's black brows had come together somewhat crossly, as they did on principle at the sight of the cassock. But he was far too just a man to deny the relevance of the remark. "You are right," he said. "Before we find out how he came to be killed, we may have to find out how he came to be here. Now listen to me, gentlemen. If it can be done without prejudice to my position and duty, we shall all agree that certain distinguished names might well be kept out of this. There are ladies, gentlemen, and there is a foreign ambassador. If we must mark it down as a crime, then it must be followed up as a crime. But till then I can use my own discretion. I am the head of the police; I am so public that I can afford to be private. Please Heaven, I will clear everyone of my own guests before I call in my men to look for anybody else. Gentlemen, upon your honour, you will none of you leave the house till tomorrow at noon; there are bedrooms for all. Simon, I think you know where to find my man, Ivan, in the front hall; he is a confidential man. Tell him to leave another servant on guard and come to me at once. Lord Galloway, you are certainly the best person to tell the ladies what has happened, and prevent a panic. They also must stay. Father Brown and I will remain with the body."

When this spirit of the captain spoke in Valentin he was obeyed like a bugle. Dr. Simon went through to the armoury and routed out Ivan, the public detective's private detective. Galloway went to the drawing-room and told the terrible news tactfully enough, so that by the time the company assembled there the ladies were already startled and already soothed. Meanwhile the good priest and the good atheist stood at the head and foot of the dead man motionless in the moonlight, like symbolic statues of their two philosophies of death.

Ivan, the confidential man with the scar and the moustaches, came out of the house like a cannon ball, and came racing across the lawn to Valentin like a dog to his master. His livid face was quite lively with the glow of this domestic detective story, and it was with almost unpleasant eagerness that he asked his master's permission to examine the remains.

"Yes; look, if you like, Ivan," said Valentin, "but don't be long. We must go in and thrash this out in the house."

Ivan lifted the head, and then almost let it drop.

"Why," he gasped, "it's – no, it isn't; it can't be. Do you know this man, sir?"

"No," said Valentin indifferently; "we had better go inside."

Between them they carried the corpse to a sofa in the study, and then all made their way to the drawing-room.

The detective sat down at a desk quietly, and even without hesitation; but his eye was the iron eye of a judge at assize. He made a few rapid notes upon paper in front of him, and then said shortly: "Is everybody here?"

"Not Mr. Brayne," said the Duchess of Mont St. Michel, looking round.

"No," said Lord Galloway in a hoarse, harsh voice. "And not Mr. Neil O'Brien, I fancy. I saw that gentleman walking in the garden when the corpse was still warm."

"Ivan," said the detective, "go and fetch Commandant O'Brien and Mr. Brayne. Mr. Brayne, I know, is finishing a cigar in the dining-room; Commandant O'Brien, I think, is walking up and down the conservatory. I am not sure."

The faithful attendant flashed from the room, and before anyone could stir or speak Valentin went on with the same soldierly swiftness of exposition.

"Everyone here knows that a dead man has been found in the garden, his head cut clean from his body. Dr. Simon, you have examined it. Do you think that to cut a man's throat like that would need great force? Or, perhaps, only a very sharp knife?"

"I should say that it could not be done with a knife at all," said the pale doctor.

"Have you any thought," resumed Valentin, "of a tool with which it could be done?"

"Speaking within modern probabilities, I really haven't," said the doctor, arching his painful brows. "It's not easy to hack a neck through even clumsily, and this was a very clean cut. It could be done with a battle-axe or an old headsman's axe, or an old two-handed sword."

"But, good heavens!" cried the Duchess, almost in hysterics, "there aren't any two-handed swords and battle-axes round here."

Valentin was still busy with the paper in front of him. "Tell me," he said, still writing rapidly, "could it have been done with a long French cavalry sabre?"

A low knocking came at the door, which, for some unreasonable reason, curdled everyone's blood like the knocking in Macbeth. Amid that frozen silence Dr. Simon managed to say: "A sabre – yes, I suppose it could."

"Thank you," said Valentin. "Come in, Ivan."

The confidential Ivan opened the door and ushered in Commandant Neil O'Brien, whom he had found at last pacing the garden again.

The Irish officer stood up disordered and defiant on the threshold. "What do you want with me?" he cried.

"Please sit down," said Valentin in pleasant, level tones. "Why, you aren't wearing your sword. Where is it?"

"I left it on the library table," said O'Brien, his brogue deepening in his disturbed mood. "It was a nuisance, it was getting—"

"Ivan," said Valentin, "please go and get the Commandant's sword from the library." Then, as the servant vanished, "Lord Galloway says he saw you leaving the garden just before he found the corpse. What were you doing in the garden?"

The Commandant flung himself recklessly into a chair. "Oh," he cried in pure Irish, "admirin' the moon. Communing with Nature, me bhoy."

A heavy silence sank and endured, and at the end of it came again that trivial and terrible knocking. Ivan reappeared, carrying an empty steel scabbard. "This is all I can find," he said.

"Put it on the table," said Valentin, without looking up.

There was an inhuman silence in the room, like that sea of inhuman silence round the dock of the condemned murderer. The Duchess's weak exclamations had long ago died away. Lord Galloway's swollen hatred was satisfied and even sobered. The voice that came was quite unexpected.

"I think I can tell you," cried Lady Margaret, in that clear, quivering voice with which a courageous woman speaks publicly. "I can tell you what Mr. O'Brien was doing in the garden, since he is bound to silence. He was asking me to marry him. I refused; I said in my family circumstances I could give him nothing but my respect. He was a little angry at that; he did not seem to think much of my respect. I wonder," she added, with rather a wan smile, "if he will care at all for it now. For I offer it him now. I will swear anywhere that he never did a thing like this."

Lord Galloway had edged up to his daughter, and was intimidating her in what he imagined to be an undertone. "Hold your tongue, Maggie," he said in a thunderous whisper. "Why should you shield the fellow? Where's his sword? Where's his confounded cavalry—"

He stopped because of the singular stare with which his daughter was regarding him, a look that was indeed a lurid magnet for the whole group.

"You old fool!" she said in a low voice without pretence of piety, "what do you suppose you are trying to prove? I tell you this man was innocent while with me. But if he wasn't innocent, he was still with me. If he murdered a man in the garden, who was it who must have seen – who must at least have known? Do you hate Neil so much as to put your own daughter—"

Lady Galloway screamed. Everyone else sat tingling at the touch of those satanic tragedies that have been between lovers before now. They saw the proud, white face of the Scotch aristocrat and her lover, the Irish adventurer, like old portraits in a dark house. The long silence was full of formless historical memories of murdered husbands and poisonous paramours.

In the centre of this morbid silence an innocent voice said: "Was it a very long cigar?"

The change of thought was so sharp that they had to look round to see who had spoken.

"I mean," said little Father Brown, from the corner of the room, "I mean that cigar Mr. Brayne is finishing. It seems nearly as long as a walking-stick."

Despite the irrelevance there was assent as well as irritation in Valentin's face as he lifted his head.

"Quite right," he remarked sharply. "Ivan, go and see about Mr. Brayne again, and bring him here at once."

The instant the factotum had closed the door, Valentin addressed the girl with an entirely new earnestness.

"Lady Margaret," he said, "we all feel, I am sure, both gratitude and admiration for your act in rising above your lower dignity and explaining the Commandant's conduct. But there is a hiatus still. Lord Galloway, I understand, met you passing from the study to the drawing-room, and it was only some minutes afterwards that he found the garden and the Commandant still walking there."

"You have to remember," replied Margaret, with a faint irony in her voice, "that I had just refused him, so we should scarcely have come back arm in arm. He is a gentleman, anyhow; and he loitered behind – and so got charged with murder."

"In those few moments," said Valentin gravely, "he might really—"

The knock came again, and Ivan put in his scarred face.

"Beg pardon, sir," he said, "but Mr. Brayne has left the house."

"Left!" cried Valentin, and rose for the first time to his feet.

"Gone. Scooted. Evaporated," replied Ivan in humorous French. "His hat and coat are gone, too, and I'll tell you something to cap it all. I ran outside the house to find any traces of him, and I found one, and a big trace, too."

"What do you mean?" asked Valentin.

"I'll show you," said his servant, and reappeared with a flashing naked cavalry sabre, streaked with blood about the point and edge. Everyone in the room eyed it as if it were a thunderbolt; but the experienced Ivan went on quite quietly:

"I found this," he said, "flung among the bushes fifty yards up the road to Paris. In other words, I found it just where your respectable Mr. Brayne threw it when he ran away."

There was again a silence, but of a new sort. Valentin took the sabre, examined it, reflected with unaffected concentration of thought, and then turned a respectful face to O'Brien. "Commandant," he said, "we trust you will always produce this weapon if it is wanted for police examination. Meanwhile," he added, slapping the steel back in the ringing scabbard, "let me return you your sword."

At the military symbolism of the action the audience could hardly refrain from applause.

For Neil O'Brien, indeed, that gesture was the turning-point of existence. By the time he was wandering in the mysterious garden again in the colours of the morning the tragic futility of his ordinary mien had fallen from him; he was a man with many reasons for happiness. Lord Galloway was a gentleman, and had offered him an apology. Lady Margaret was something better than a lady, a woman at least, and had perhaps given him something better than an apology, as they drifted among the old flowerbeds before breakfast. The whole company was more lighthearted and humane, for though the riddle of the death remained, the load of suspicion was lifted off them all, and sent flying off to Paris with the strange millionaire – a man they hardly knew. The devil was cast out of the house – he had cast himself out.

Still, the riddle remained; and when O'Brien threw himself on a garden seat beside Dr. Simon, that keenly scientific person at once resumed it. He did not get much talk out of O'Brien, whose thoughts were on pleasanter things.

"I can't say it interests me much," said the Irishman frankly, "especially as it seems pretty plain now. Apparently Brayne hated this stranger for some reason; lured him into the garden, and killed him with my sword. Then he fled to the city, tossing the sword away as he went. By the way, Ivan tells me the dead man had a Yankee dollar in his pocket. So he was a countryman of Brayne's, and that seems to clinch it. I don't see any difficulties about the business."

"There are five colossal difficulties," said the doctor quietly; "like high walls within walls. Don't mistake me. I don't doubt that Brayne did it; his flight, I fancy, proves that. But as to how he did it. First difficulty: Why should a man kill another man with a great hulking sabre, when he can almost kill him with a pocket knife and put it back in his pocket? Second difficulty: Why was there no noise or outcry? Does a man commonly see another come up waving a scimitar and offer no remarks? Third difficulty: A servant watched the front door all the evening; and a rat cannot get into Valentin's garden anywhere. How did the dead man get into the garden? Fourth difficulty: Given the same conditions, how did Brayne get out of the garden?"

"And the fifth," said Neil, with eyes fixed on the English priest who was coming slowly up the path.

"Is a trifle, I suppose," said the doctor, "but I think an odd one. When I first saw how the head had been slashed, I supposed the assassin had struck more than once. But on examination I found many cuts across the truncated section; in other words, they were struck after the head was off. Did Brayne hate his foe so fiendishly that he stood sabring his body in the moonlight?"

"Horrible!" said O'Brien, and shuddered.

The little priest, Brown, had arrived while they were talking, and had waited, with characteristic shyness, till they had finished. Then he said awkwardly:

"I say, I'm sorry to interrupt. But I was sent to tell you the news!"

"News?" repeated Simon, and stared at him rather painfully through his glasses.

"Yes, I'm sorry," said Father Brown mildly. "There's been another murder, you know."

Both men on the seat sprang up, leaving it rocking.

"And, what's stranger still," continued the priest, with his dull eye on the rhododendrons, "it's the same disgusting sort; it's another beheading. They found the second head actually bleeding into the river, a few yards along Brayne's road to Paris; so they suppose that he—"

"Great Heaven!" cried O'Brien. "Is Brayne a monomaniac?"

"There are American vendettas," said the priest impassively. Then he added: "They want you to come to the library and see it."

Commandant O'Brien followed the others towards the inquest, feeling decidedly sick. As a soldier, he loathed all this secretive carnage; where were these extravagant amputations going to stop? First one head was hacked off, and then another; in this case (he told himself bitterly) it was not true that two heads were better than one. As he crossed the study he almost staggered at a shocking coincidence. Upon Valentin's table lay the coloured picture of yet a third bleeding head; and it was the head of Valentin himself. A second glance showed him it was only a Nationalist paper, called The Guillotine, which every week showed one of its political opponents with rolling eyes and writhing features just after execution; for Valentin was an anti-clerical of some note. But O'Brien was an Irishman, with a kind of chastity even in his sins; and his gorge rose against that great brutality of the intellect which belongs only to France. He felt Paris as a whole, from the grotesques on the Gothic churches to the gross caricatures in the newspapers. He remembered the gigantic jests of the Revolution. He saw the whole city as one ugly energy, from the sanguinary sketch lying on Valentin's table up to where, above a mountain and forest of gargoyles, the great devil grins on Notre Dame.

The library was long, low, and dark; what light entered it shot from under low blinds and had still some of the ruddy tinge of morning. Valentin and his servant Ivan were waiting for them at the upper end of a long, slightly-sloping desk, on which lay the mortal remains, looking enormous in the twilight. The big black figure and yellow face of the man found in the garden confronted them essentially unchanged. The second head, which had been fished from among the river reeds that morning, lay streaming and dripping beside it; Valentin's men were still seeking to recover the rest of this second corpse, which was supposed to be afloat. Father Brown, who did not seem to share O'Brien's sensibilities in the least, went up to the second head and examined it with his blinking care. It was little more than a mop of wet white hair, fringed with silver fire in the red and level morning light; the face, which seemed of an ugly, empurpled and perhaps criminal type, had been much battered against trees or stones as it tossed in the water.

"Good morning, Commandant O'Brien," said Valentin, with quiet cordiality. "You have heard of Brayne's last experiment in butchery, I suppose?"

Father Brown was still bending over the head with white hair, and he said, without looking up:

"I suppose it is quite certain that Brayne cut off this head, too."

"Well, it seems common sense," said Valentin, with his hands in his pockets. "Killed in the same way as the other. Found within a few yards of the other. And sliced by the same weapon which we know he carried away."

"Yes, yes; I know," replied Father Brown submissively. "Yet, you know, I doubt whether Brayne could have cut off this head."

"Why not?" inquired Dr. Simon, with a rational stare.

"Well, doctor," said the priest, looking up blinking, "can a man cut off his own head? I don't know."

O'Brien felt an insane universe crashing about his ears; but the doctor sprang forward with impetuous practicality and pushed back the wet white hair.

"Oh, there's no doubt it's Brayne," said the priest quietly. "He had exactly that chip in the left ear."

The detective, who had been regarding the priest with steady and glittering eyes, opened his clenched mouth and said sharply: "You seem to know a lot about him, Father Brown."

"I do," said the little man simply. "I've been about with him for some weeks. He was thinking of joining our church."

The star of the fanatic sprang into Valentin's eyes; he strode towards the priest with clenched hands. "And, perhaps," he cried, with a blasting sneer, "perhaps he was also thinking of leaving all his money to your church."

"Perhaps he was," said Brown stolidly; "it is possible."

"In that case," cried Valentin, with a dreadful smile, "you may indeed know a great deal about him. About his life and about his—"

Commandant O'Brien laid a hand on Valentin's arm. "Drop that slanderous rubbish, Valentin," he said, "or there may be more swords yet."

But Valentin (under the steady, humble gaze of the priest) had already recovered himself. "Well," he said shortly, "people's private opinions can wait. You gentlemen are still bound by your promise to stay; you must enforce it on yourselves – and on each other. Ivan here will tell you anything more you want to know; I must get to business and write to the authorities. We can't keep this quiet any longer. I shall be writing in my study if there is any more news."

"Is there any more news, Ivan?" asked Dr. Simon, as the chief of police strode out of the room.

"Only one more thing, I think, sir," said Ivan, wrinkling up his grey old face, "but that's important, too, in its way. There's that old buffer you found on the lawn," and he pointed without pretence of reverence at the big black body with the yellow head. "We've found out who he is, anyhow."

"Indeed!" cried the astonished doctor, "and who is he?"

"His name was Arnold Becker," said the under-detective, "though he went by many aliases. He was a wandering sort of scamp, and is known to have been in America; so that was where Brayne got his knife into him. We didn't have much to do with him ourselves, for he worked mostly in Germany. We've communicated, of course, with the German police. But, oddly enough, there was a twin brother of his, named Louis Becker, whom we had a great deal to do with. In fact, we found it necessary to guillotine him only yesterday. Well, it's a rum thing, gentlemen, but when I saw that fellow flat on the lawn I had the greatest jump of my life. If I hadn't seen Louis Becker guillotined with my own eyes, I'd have sworn it was Louis Becker lying there in the grass. Then, of course, I remembered his twin brother in Germany, and following up the clue—"

The explanatory Ivan stopped, for the excellent reason that nobody was listening to him. The Commandant and the doctor were both staring at Father Brown, who had sprung stiffly to his feet, and was holding his temples tight like a man in sudden and violent pain.

"Stop, stop, stop!" he cried; "stop talking a minute, for I see half. Will God give me strength? Will my brain make the one jump and see all? Heaven help me! I used to be fairly good at thinking. I could paraphrase any page in Aquinas once. Will my head split – or will it see? I see half – I only see half."

He buried his head in his hands, and stood in a sort of rigid torture of thought or prayer, while the other three could only go on staring at this last prodigy of their wild twelve hours.

When Father Brown's hands fell they showed a face quite fresh and serious, like a child's. He heaved a huge sigh, and said: "Let us get this said and done with as quickly as possible. Look here, this will be the quickest way to convince you all of the truth." He turned to the doctor. "Dr. Simon," he said, "you have a strong head-piece, and I heard you this morning asking the five hardest questions about this business. Well, if you will ask them again, I will answer them."

Simon's pince-nez dropped from his nose in his doubt and wonder, but he answered at once. "Well, the first question, you know, is why a man should kill another with a clumsy sabre at all when a man can kill with a bodkin?"

"A man cannot behead with a bodkin," said Brown calmly, "and for this murder beheading was absolutely necessary."

"Why?" asked O'Brien, with interest.

"And the next question?" asked Father Brown.

"Well, why didn't the man cry out or anything?" asked the doctor; "sabres in gardens are certainly unusual."

"Twigs," said the priest gloomily, and turned to the window which looked on the scene of death. "No one saw the point of the twigs. Why should they lie on that lawn (look at it) so far from any tree? They were not snapped off; they were chopped off. The murderer occupied his enemy with some tricks with the sabre, showing how he could cut a branch in mid-air, or what-not. Then, while his enemy bent down to see the result, a silent slash, and the head fell."

"Well," said the doctor slowly, "that seems plausible enough. But my next two questions will stump anyone."

The priest still stood looking critically out of the window and waited.

"You know how all the garden was sealed up like an air-tight chamber," went on the doctor. "Well, how did the strange man get into the garden?"

Without turning round, the little priest answered: "There never was any strange man in he garden."

There was a silence, and then a sudden cackle of almost childish laughter relieved the strain. The absurdity of Brown's remark moved Ivan to open taunts.

"Oh!" he cried; "then we didn't lug a great fat corpse on to a sofa last night? He hadn't got nto the garden, I suppose?"

"Got into the garden?" repeated Brown reflectively. "No, not entirely."

"Hang it all," cried Simon, "a man gets into a garden, or he doesn't."

"Not necessarily," said the priest, with a faint smile. "What is the nest question, doctor?"

"I fancy you're ill," exclaimed Dr. Simon sharply; "but I'll ask the next question if you like. How did Brayne get out of the garden?"

"He didn't get out of the garden," said the priest, still looking out of the window.

"Didn't get out of the garden?" exploded Simon.

"Not completely," said Father Brown.

Simon shook his fists in a frenzy of French logic. "A man gets out of a garden, or he doesn't," he cried.

"Not always," said Father Brown.

Dr. Simon sprang to his feet impatiently. "I have no time to spare on such senseless talk," he cried angrily. "If you can't understand a man being on one side of a wall or the other, I won't rouble you further."

"Doctor," said the cleric very gently, "we have always got on very pleasantly together. If only for the sake of old friendship, stop and tell me your fifth question."

The impatient Simon sank into a chair by the door and said briefly: "The head and shoulders were cut about in a queer way. It seemed to be done after death."

"Yes," said the motionless priest, "it was done so as to make you assume exactly the one simple falsehood that you did assume. It was done to make you take for granted that the head belonged to the body."

The borderland of the brain, where all the monsters are made, moved horribly in the Gaelic O'Brien. He felt the chaotic presence of all the horse-men and fish-women that man's unnatural fancy has begotten. A voice older than his first fathers seemed saying in his ear: "Keep out of he monstrous garden where grows the tree with double fruit. Avoid the evil garden where died he man with two heads." Yet, while these shameful symbolic shapes passed across the ancient mirror of his Irish soul, his Frenchified intellect was quite alert, and was watching the odd priest as closely and incredulously as all the rest.

Father Brown had turned round at last, and stood against the window, with his face in dense shadow; but even in that shadow they could see it was pale as ashes. Nevertheless, he spoke quite sensibly, as if there were no Gaelic souls on earth.

"Gentlemen," he said, "you did not find the strange body of Becker in the garden. You did not find any strange body in the garden. In face of Dr. Simon's rationalism, I still affirm that Becker was only partly present. Look here!" (pointing to the black bulk of the mysterious corpse) "you never saw that man in your lives. Did you ever see this man?"

He rapidly rolled away the bald, yellow head of the unknown, and put in its place the white-maned head beside it. And there, complete, unified, unmistakable, lay Julius K. Brayne.

"The murderer," went on Brown quietly, "hacked off his enemy's head and flung the sword far over the wall. But he was too clever to fling the sword only. He flung the head over the wall also. Then he had only to clap on another head to the corpse, and (as he insisted on a private inquest) you all imagined a totally new man."

"Clap on another head!" said O'Brien staring. "What other head? Heads don't grow on garden bushes, do they?"

"No," said Father Brown huskily, and looking at his boots; "there is only one place where they grow. They grow in the basket of the guillotine, beside which the chief of police, Aristide Valentin, was standing not an hour before the murder. Oh, my friends, hear me a minute more before you tear me in pieces. Valentin is an honest man, if being mad for an arguable cause is honesty. But did you never see in that cold, grey eye of his that he is mad! He would do anything, anything, to break what he calls the superstition of the Cross. He has fought for it and starved for it, and now he has murdered for it. Brayne's crazy millions had hitherto been scattered among so many sects that they did little to alter the balance of things. But Valentin heard a whisper that Brayne, like so many scatter-brained sceptics, was drifting to us; and that was quite a different thing. Brayne would pour supplies into the impoverished and pugnacious Church of France; he would support six Nationalist newspapers like The Guillotine. The battle was already balanced on a point, and the fanatic took flame at the risk. He resolved to destroy the millionaire, and he did it as one would expect the greatest of detectives to commit his only crime. He abstracted the severed head of Becker on some criminological excuse, and took it home in his official box. He had that last argument with Brayne, that Lord Galloway did not hear the end of; that failing, he led him out into the sealed garden, talked about swordsmanship, used twigs and a sabre for illustration, and—"

Ivan of the Scar sprang up. "You lunatic," he yelled; "you'll go to my master now, if I take you by—"

"Why, I was going there," said Brown heavily; "I must ask him to confess, and all that."

Driving the unhappy Brown before them like a hostage or sacrifice, they rushed together into the sudden stillness of Valentin's study.

The great detective sat at his desk apparently too occupied to hear their turbulent entrance. They paused a moment, and then something in the look of that upright and elegant back made the doctor run forward suddenly. A touch and a glance showed him that there was a small box of pills at Valentin's elbow, and that Valentin was dead in his chair; and on the blind face of the suicide was more than the pride of Cato.

The Body in Beaver Woods
A Mrs. Kominski Mystery

Gregory Von Dare

IT WAS MID-DECEMBER when handyman Joe Burton pulled into Mrs. Kominski's suburban driveway. The sky looked like steel wool and the gusting wind had a warning edge to it. Voices on Joe's car radio chattered about another big snow coming to Chicago and a body found in Beaver Woods that morning. Those who called-in blamed that corpse on everything from drug lords to flying saucers. Joe hoped it wasn't spacemen. They scared him.

Mrs. Kominski hobbled down her wooden front steps as Joe drove up. She had dressed for a trip to Siberia and clutched a large faux alligator handbag. Ada Kominski was in her late 1980s and had buried two husbands. Their names? She couldn't remember. The small, spry widow had silver hair, dark eyes, high cheek bones and a pointed nose that she stuck into everyone's business.

"We're going to Beaver Woods. And to store after," she said to Joe.

Joe was fifty-eight; tall, stocky, bug-eyed and barrel-chested. He was not the sharpest tool on the bench but had a big, open heart. He provided a one-man taxi service for Mrs. Kominski after she gave up her driver's license two years ago, to the great relief of Cook County.

"Beaver Woods this time a' year? Why?"

"They arrested him for murder!"

"Who?"

"Daniel Shoes, my second cousin."

"No kiddin? He killed the guy in Beaver Woods?"

Mrs. Kominski raised her sharp chin, which always meant trouble. "They said Daniel's fingerprints were all over the gun, the murder weapon. I'm sure it's a lie."

"Gonna snow bad today."

"Then let's got a move on," said the old widow, struggling to fasten her seat belt.

"Yes, ma'am." Joe backed out carefully and headed for the woods. It was only a ten minute drive.

* * *

A thick frosting of fresh snow lay on the ground at Beaver Woods. All winter, the woods was a somber, deserted place of bare trees and icy black ponds, shunned by most of the locals. The only time you saw people at Beaver Woods in December was when they came out to run their dogs; or teens who were up to no good. It was a perfect place to dump a body.

Mrs. Kominski pointed toward the back of the parking lot. "Lookit, a police car. Park over here, Joe. I hope it's Sergeant Polanski. His father died young, poor man. And his mother had to remarry to stay out of the poorhouse."

As they climbed out of Joe's car and braced themselves against the Arctic winds, a lone figure moved about within a ring of police tape, about a hundred yards into the woods. It was a uniformed officer with graying, curly hair and a bushy mustache. The man was thin and wiry with olive skin, sad eyes and a prominent nose. He shuffled around the crime scene like a busy beetle, kicking leaves and tamping down clumps of snow.

He had collected several small red flags on short metal rods that marked various points of evidence. Joe stepped on a dry twig, and as it snapped the policeman's head turned. Mrs. Kominski was about to speak when he held a hand out to them, palm forward, in a gesture that said, 'stop'.

"Mrs. Kominski, I can't let you come any closer. I got orders, *strict* orders from Lieutenant O'Malley about that."

Mrs. Kominski paused and so did Joe. "Sergeant Polanski, I was just saying I hoped it was you here. Didn't I Joe?"

Joe nodded like a big bobble-head figure.

"Well, that's nice ma'am, but I still can't let ya get any closer. The Lieutenant is worried about evidence, see? And he told me that when you showed up here, I was to keep you far away from the crime scene."

Mrs. Kominski took a pair of bifocals from her purse – a big, imitation alligator-skin item she picked up at Walmart five years ago. It had been repaired here and there with silver duct tape, the clasp was history and one handle was hanging on by a thread but that was no reason to discard a perfectly good bag.

"We just want to have a look. Is that so bad?"

"No. But I got my orders, you know?"

"Who was it?"

"Who was who?"

"The body, the dead body!" said Mrs. Kominski, peevish and snappy.

"It was Town Councilman Stuart Nagy," replied the sergeant. "We're still trying to figure out what he was doin' here last night."

"Parsifal!" said Mrs Kominski. "I don't see what that has to do with my Daniel."

"Well, ya know," said Polanski, "Your cousin got into a brannigan with Nagy a few years back. We was short-handed and Daniel was all alone in a radio car. He had the stones to give Nagy a parking ticket outside Town Hall. And the Councilman didn't like it. They started swingin' at each other and it took three other cops to pull 'em apart. Everybody on the force knew about it. They say that's why Daniel never got promoted, 'cause of Mr. Nagy."

Mrs. Kominski wasn't listening. She focused on the ground where the body had lain. There was a muddy man-sized spot, bare of snow. Leaves had been pressed down into the damp earth and stained dark red with blood. Small, hard flakes of snow were falling from the sky now. One of them landed on Joe's long nose and he crossed his popped eyes to stare at it.

Mrs. Kominski pointed to the center of the crime scene. "Looks like he fell on his a-s-s. Must have been shot from the front, otherwise he'd have gone down face-first. Where was the gun?"

Before he could stop himself, the Sergeant gestured to a red flag only a few feet from where the body had been.

"Oh," said Mrs. Kominski, peering at the spot. "Then he dropped it after. Didn't pocket it, didn' throw it into the woods or the lake. Almost like he wanted you to find it. Isn't that so, Sergeant?"

"Now look," Polansky said, pointing toward the parking lot, "you gotta leave and right now O'Malley will have my stripes if I let you stay."

Mrs. Kominski raised her pointed chin. "Aren't those evidence markers you're holding?"

"Ah, come on, Mrs. K. I'm just removing the clutter. Easier to make sense of the scene late Anyway, it's what the Lieutenant told me to do."

Mrs. Kominski noticed a slight flicker in the distance. Good thing she had her glasses on. It was that raggedy homeless veteran she had heard gossip about. Some people said he ate live squirrels. He moved silently and hid behind a big beech tree. Sergeant Polansky didn't see him.

"Come on, Joe. I can tell we're not welcome here. Let's go to store and then back home. My rheumatiz won't stand much more of this cold."

Joe nodded. "I'm right behind ya, Ada."

When they were in Joe's car and the heater had finally started circulating some warm air, Joe turned to Mrs. Kominski. "That Sergeant Polanski?"

"What about him?"

"He sure don't look Polish."

"Well, you can't judge a book by it's cover, can you?"

"What kinda book?"

"How about some nice hot chocolate with marshmallows at my house?"

"I thought we was going to store?"

"Later Joe – we have a murder to solve."

* * *

Joe drank hot chocolate at Mrs. Kominski's kitchen table while she flipped through her three address books. One was the old address book that was falling apart. The second was a new address book that she got at the dollar store and the third was the one she wrote names and addresses in when she couldn't find the other two.

"Parsifal!" said Mrs. Kominski. "I know he's in here.... Ha!"

She carefully dialed a number on the pink kitchen phone.

"Y'ello...Stuben's."

"Frank, it's Ada Kominski."

"Long time, Ada. Wait, let me put you on speakerphone. Right in the middle of an embalming job here. Let me get the gloves off.... Hang on a second..."

Frank Albright was a free-lance undertaker. Ever since his dad got dementia and ran their family mortuary into bankruptcy, he picked up work wherever he could. He moved from one funeral home to the next, saving his money against the day he could open a place of his own and bring the Albright name back to prominence.

He had thick, muscular arms, dark, oily hair and a broad Slavic face that could smile or scowl with equal speed. Frank wore big, aviator glasses that went out of style in the Carter administration.

"There we go," he said. "Got the gloves off and I can talk for a minute. What's up?"

"How are you liking it?"

"At Stuben's? Ahhhh.... Well, it's a clean place. No rats to speak of. But Otto junior is a cheapskate and it gets on your nerves. Now, what can I do you for? We gotta keep it short because Mr. Abe Malinowsky is on the table here, ready for the juice and I can't keep him waiting."

"Abe Malinowsky passed? God rest his soul," said Mrs. Kominski. "Stuart Nagy, the town councilman was killed yesterday and I wondered if you knew, from the grapevine, who was going to lay him out."

"Funny you should ask. I got him in a drawer here at Stuben's. And catch this! Lieutenant O'Malley brings the wife in to identify him, right? She looks at the body, says *'yeah that's him,'* turns on her heel and walks out. Never shed a tear for the guy. All's he got wrong with him is the one bullet hole in the middle of his forehead. Which is a real pain for me 'cause they want to have an open-casket viewing. He was shot from close range, I think. Got powder burns on his face and chin. I'd say he was on his knees too since the bullet came in on a steep angle. What they call 'execution style.'"

"Is that so?" said Mrs. Kominski.

"By the way, Nagy's wife and O'Malley was mighty friendly with each other, if you know what I'm sayin'."

Mrs. Kominski's head was buzzing with the news. But she crossed herself and said, "Well, God have mercy on his soul."

"Why the interest in Nagy? You know him from the old neighborhood? From St. Margaret's parish?"

"You won't believe this but they arrested my second-cousin Daniel Shoes for the murder! Maybe you remember Daniel was a Vietnam vet and a former policeman himself."

"No kiddin'? You think he did it?"

Ada Kominski loved asking questions but she almost never answered one. "I was just wondering, Frank, didn't your family's old funeral parlor border on Beaver Woods?"

"Yeah. We was at the north end of the forest preserve. Had a huge parking lot."

"Ever see a homeless man living in the woods there?"

"Oh yeah, sure. There was a crazy Gulf War vet who hung around there. Name of Terry Hillman. He'd come to the back door of the parlor sometimes for a handout. If I wasn't working on a client, I'd give him half a ham sandwich, a bag of chips or whatever. He was crazy for French fries. He would tell me all kinds of stories about goin's on in the woods. The guy missed nothing. I think he was some kinda spotter in the Marines. You tellin' me he passed?"

"No, no, just curious."

"That's your reputation, Ada. Well, gotta go. Up to my elbows in formaldehyde. Take care, now." Frank hung up the phone and tugged his thick rubber gloves back on.

"All right, Malinowsky, ya' old socialist. Here it comes." He took a long, sharp needle, thick as a pencil, and jammed it into Mr. Malinowsky's torso. Frank stepped back and opened a valve, a thoughtful frown on his face. The embalming fluid gurgled through a blonde surgical rubber hose as it flooded into the body.

Frank heard footsteps behind him and turned.

"Hey, Lieutenant, what can I do you for?"

* * *

"Hello, Dolores, it's Ada. Call me when you get home. It's very important. Thanks."

"Wait, Ada. I'm here. I'm talking to you." Dolores Kovaks was one of Mrs. Kominski's best chums from Pilsen, their old neighborhood south of the Chicago Loop.

"Oh, I thought you was that question machine you got hooked up to your phone."

"You mean the answering machine?"

"Yeah, that."

"What do you need, Ada, 'cause I'm in the middle of doing dishes."

"Well, I won't bother you if you're so busy."

Dolores sighed. "No, it's all right."

"What do you know about Stuart Nagy, the town councilman?"

"Ha! That crook. He's got money coming in from all sides, they say. Maybe even some from the mob."

"A floor mop?"

Dolores raised her voice. "No, honey, the *MOB*. Gangsters. He was in a racket where the city takes over peoples' property and pays them a pittance, supposed to be for public works or some such. But then they sell it to a crooked contractor for big bucks and the original owner is left high and dry. And Nagy pockets the difference."

"Stuart Nagy was the body they found in Beaver Woods this morning. Somebody shot him right between the eyes."

"Well I'll be damned. I saw some of his shady deals go through when I worked at the town hall years ago. Nagy had to quit that racket eventually. There was a big scandal about a family pizza place the city took over, the owner committed suicide. I can't think of the name."

While she spoke to Dolores, Mrs. Kominski peered out her front window at the car her neighbors had just brought home, "Oh lookit Charlie, it's a big car. Have you ever seen such a big car? I wonder how much they paid for it."

"What about the car," said Dolores. "Is it an SUV? A lot of people are buying them these days. My uncle Jerry—"

"I know what that is. The high ones. I have to rest my a-s-s on the seat and swing my legs way up to get in."

"Ada, my dishwater's getting cold. You aren't nosing into this murder, are you?"

"I am not nosy. I may be curious and ask questions. I been called a *buttinski* by some. I may be a lot of things, but I ain't nosy! You get back to your cleaning and I'll call you later."

"Don't call till tonight, Ada. I got laundry to do after."

"All right, Dory. You be careful now. I heard from my neighbor a woman got her arm caught in the dryer and it spun her around so hard she never stood up straight again." Mrs. Kominski hung up and called Joe Burton. "Joe, get your car out, we're going back to Beaver Woods."

"It's awful cold out there," he said, pouting. "And it makes my nose run."

"Dress warm, Joe, 'cause it's awful cold out there. We'll stop at Burger Queen for hamburgers."

"OK, Ada. I'll be over in a half hour."

* * *

Light, powdery snow fell at Beaver Woods. The chilly silence pressed down like a block of granite. Joe parked his car at the edge of the forest.

"Should we have our hamburgers now?" he said. "I don't like 'em cold."

"You can eat yours now, Joe. I'm saving mine for bait to catch a big fish."

Joe laughed and snorted. "There ain't no big fish in Beaver Lake, Ada. You oughtta know that."

"Oh, lookit how deep the snow is."

As they hiked into the frozen woods, Mrs. Kominski gathered a knitted scarf tight around her stringy neck. She clutched her big purse close to her body, hoping the hamburger and fries wouldn't get cold right away. Great Beaver Lake was still and dark, barely a ripple on the gloss of its surface. Drifting light fog reduced visibility and made the bare woods into a gloomy scene from Grimm's fairy tales.

In the distance, there was a flicker of dark against light. Mrs. Kominski grabbed Joe's arm. "Do you see him, Joe? Over there?"

"I saw sumthin' move."

"Joe tell him we got a hamburger for him. A fresh burger and fries. And call him Mister."

"HEY, MISTER!" Joe yelled. "We got a hamburger for ya'. Come and get it. A nice hot 'burger and French fries."

Like a wary animal, a forgotten feral cat, a skinny, bearded, poorly dressed man peaked from around a tree. He wore a threadbare hoodie under a shredded overcoat. His eyes had a crazed, haunted look.

Joe waved to him. "Come on over," he said. "I got food for you. Good food and warm."

As the man hesitantly walked up to them, Mrs. Kominski said softly, "You know what happened here, don't you. A man got shot and you saw who did it, yes?"

The raggedy man nodded, his eyes fixed on the white paper bag Joe held out to him.

"You eat," said Mrs. Kominski, "and then tell me all about it."

"It was a copper that done it," said the raggedy man, reaching for the bag.

* * *

"Hello, Ada, it's Dory."

"Sorry for what?"

"No, honey, DORY, your friend Dolores."

"Don't tell me your dryer grabbed you and spun you around!"

"No, but I got a gem for you. I called up Stuart Nagy's secretary to tell her condolences. And while we was talking, she tells me that the councilman was worried that someone was following him, stalking him. He was gonna meet with Lieutenant O'Malley to talk about it."

"Jesus, Mary and Joseph!"

"And I got another one for you. She remembered that man who owned the pizza parlor, the one who committed suicide? His name was DiLuca, Bobby DiLuca. After he died his widow remarried. But I don't know who."

"I do."

* * *

"Hey O'Malley!"

At the sound of his name, Lieutenant Lawrence O'Malley turned his head with a start. The abrasive O'Malley had a ruddy complexion and bushy white hair, penetrating brown eyes and a curving nose like a hawk's beak. His lips were a thin pink gash in a deeply lined face. Reflexively, his hand reached for his gun.

"Whoa, Lucky. Take it easy. Captain Ovitz wants to see you in his office. Somethin' about overtime?"

"You gotta be kiddin' me," said O'Malley.

Sergeant Miller shrugged and raised his eyebrows. "Hey, don't shoot the messenger. That's all they told me, so..."

"Yeah, all right," said O'Malley, rising. He turned and scanned the office. "Hey, Polanski come along will ya'? I may need some moral support."

Sergeant Polansky nodded and fell in step behind the frowning Lieutenant.

O'Malley knocked on the glass panel of Captain Ovitz' door and heard a voice tell him to come in. With a grim smile the Lieutenant pushed the door open and stepped into the room. Polansky followed right after him. Polanski saw Captain Ovitz sitting at the desk, tilted back in his chair, his feet up on the blotter, just as two pairs of strong arms seized him from behind.

"What da hell is this?" Polanski roared.

"Sit 'im down, boys," said Lieutenant O'Malley, moving next to the desk. "Let's see if we can get a nice, clean confession."

"I didn't do a goddamned thing, and you know it," growled Polansky.

"We got a witness that sez otherwise. We know you shot Nagy in cold blood. You spit on his face and we lifted your DNA from that. No question it was you. Then you had the stones to frame Danny Shoes, ya' bastard. Now spill it!" O'Malley banged his fist on the desk so hard Polanski flinched.

"It was for my dad. My real dad, Bobby DiLuca," said Polanski. "The best man you'd ever want to meet. That shitheel Nagy drove him to the grave." Tears spilled down his hardened face like warm summer rain rolls down a polished gravestone.

* * *

Mrs. Kominski gave Daniel Shoes a big hug when he came over to visit her after his release from county jail. He eased himself into one of the armchairs in the pristine living room and put his sore leg up on a footstool. The tall, husky Vietnam vet and former cop had bad joints from his rough and tumble life and a beer belly that was worthy of the name. His soft voice and mild expression didn't quite cover a deep anger that went back to the bloody jungles of 'Nam.

"They told me you was responsible for gettin' me out, Ada. I won't forget it."

Charlie woofed and wagged his tail. He was an old beagle with long droopy ears and short legs. Charlie was spoiled, fat as a sausage and paid no attention to Mrs. Kominski's commands.

Ada Kominski shook her finger at Charlie. "You come here now and leave Daniel alone. He's been through enough. Come here by me and sit nice." Charlie sagged down where he was and drooled like an overflowing bathtub. "Lieutenant O'Malley couldn't figure out how your old gun got there. And Polanski wouldn't say."

Daniel pulled a grimace. "I got a pretty good idea. T'ree years ago I was in pursuit of a couple a skinhead car jackers and I got lucky when a train blocks 'em on East Avenue. So I gets out with my piece drawn and goes up to da car and tells 'em to get out and flatten. Well, they both come at me at once and jump me. Now I already got one metal hip and a bum knee. Against two young guys, I got no chance. We roll around and I get off one shot and hit one of da guys in his ass, I kid you not."

"Oh, Daniel!"

"Upshot is both of 'em got away and I'm layin' there with a busted hip, elbow's sprained real bad and a concussion. I start looking around for my piece, and it ain't there. Polansky was my backup that day and he was first on da scene. It musta been him. He snags my gun and stashes it in an evidence bag so the prints stay on it. Me and everyone else thinks them car-jackers got it."

Mrs. Kominski nodded. "Polansky waited so long to get his revenge – and he did."

"Yeah," said Daniel, shaking his head, "Ya know, he found his dad hangin' in da back room when he was just sixteen. I think it kinda made him...well, off in da head. I owe ya' one, Ada, big time."

"We're glad it all worked out. Aren't we, Charlie? Now we can all have a happy Christmas." Mrs. Kominski reached down to pet Charlie's sleek head and he licked her shiny, wrinkled hand. Charlie wagged his tail furiously. He knew a treat was coming his way. Holiday or not.

The Glorious Pudge

Amanda C. Davis

THERE WAS some kind of nature program going on down the beach, but I had better things to do. I had cold cash in my purse from my last case, a brand new bikini that I was spilling out of like some lush statue losing her toga, and a smorgasbord of hot ladies stretched on every other beach blanket from here to the boardwalk. Ladyhorse Cove was heaven. High school, and in fact anything resembling school, was welcome to jump into the sea.

Pudge Padrelli. Girl detective. Officially on vacation.

Someone faceplanted beside me, and I exercised my brilliant deductive mind to I.D. that someone as my eternal BFF. I handed over my bottle of water. "Swear to god, Yeoung. I've never seen anyone drown on dry land."

He gave me a dirty look. "Screw you."

I made kissyfaces at him. We are in platonic love.

"This water tastes like sand," said Yeoung. "This blows. We should be out looking for lost jewels and missing persons and, like, dead bodies."

I rolled over onto my stomach, enjoying the gentle slosh of the junk in my trunk. Feast your eyes, folks. "Here's my plan," I said, my cheek and nose smooshed against the plastic canvas of the lounge chair. "I am going to tan until I have soft-boiled every egg in my ovaries. I am going to have strawberry daiquiris for dinner and do literally anything it takes to get the waitress to put rum in them. I am going to go to the luau, pretend to be eighteen, shake what my mama gave me, mack on anyone who looks like she might enjoy it, and spend as much of the evening making out as I possibly can. That is my day. Dead bodies do not even rate."

Yeoung muttered something about Nancy Drew not being this lazy. I begged to differ. In a murmur. With my eyes closed.

Of course, that's when people started screaming.

Yeoung was on his feet before I was on my elbows. I raised my sunglasses in the direction o the screams. The nature program must have just gotten exciting.

"Bring the backpack," I muttered. I grabbed my phone and we Baywatch'd it down the beach toward the screams.

There were fifteen or twenty people crowded around a park ranger holding a clam rake, anc a river of rubberneckers filling in around them. I shouldered through to the front. And stopped

Catch of the day: severed hand.

* * *

Yeoung got to work on crowd control while I crouched for a better look.

"Get away from that," the park ranger yelped. "Wait for the police."

"I'm the police," I said, because there wasn't anyone there to contradict me, and starte taking pictures. "Yeoung?" He tossed me the backpack. I gloved up and got out an evidence ba

(Ziploc brand, because we are professionals) and a pair of Tweezers, which I used to roll the former body part onto its knuckles.

"Hey Watson," I said. "What's wrong with this picture?"

He bent down beside me. "No longer attached to the arm, Holmes."

"Try again, smartass." I took a few pictures from this angle. There was a palm-reader down the boardwalk and I thought it might be funny to see what she'd say.

"Couple of tan lines on the fingers but no rings," he said. "Extra little bit of wrist stub, which is gross, hooray, but also doesn't seem to indicate that it detached naturally. Speaking of which." He waggled his fingers. "I've gotten wrinklier washing the dog than this guy is after however long in the wet sand."

I looked up at the ranger. "Where'd this thing come from?"

"We were raking for clams," he said helplessly.

"I don't think a clam did this," said Yeoung. "What else lives in this sand? Anything that might have gotten nibbly?"

"Half a dozen types of crab," said the park ranger. "Nibbly? I'm gonna puke."

Yeoung stood abruptly. "I smell peaches." Which of course is our code word for the Actual Police. Fuzz, get it? We're very clever. Yeoung threw everything into the backpack and performed his world-class magic trick of melting into the crowd.

I dropped the hand like a hot potato and stood up. "Who dug this up?" I said. "You?"

The park ranger didn't answer right away, but his eyes went to the crowd. One of the girls in the front had sand on her knees and the meaty parts of her hand were red. If anyone here had been raking clams, this was the one. "Her?" I said. The ranger nodded.

"Good luck," I told him. Before he could reply, I went to the girl and whisked her lovely ass out of there.

She was a little taller than me, with straight blonde hair I was sure would be brunette by winter, and she didn't resist when I looped her elbow and guided her out of the crowd. I steered us toward the water. Maybe looking like a couple would buy us a little cop-free time together.

I said, "I've got to hand it to you."

She turned slowly to look at me, like she only just realized I was there. Which stung a little. "For what?"

"It was a joke," I said. "Never mind. I'm Pudge."

"Abra," she said.

"Weird name," I said.

It got a rise out of her, which was what I'd hoped for. "This from a girl named Pudge?"

"If the shoe fits," I said, with a shrug. "You dug that thing up?"

"Yeah."

"Pretty gross."

"Yeah."

"How far down was it?"

Her eyes flickered away. "I don't know, like, not sticking out? I was raking for clams and felt the tines catch on something. When I dug it up, it turned out to be a hand."

I gave her arm a friendly pat. "That must have freaked you out. Come all the way out here on vacation just to run into that."

"Oh," she said, "I live around here." Then she clammed up again. (Get it? So clever.)

We gazed out over the ocean together. So she was a local teenager who'd signed up for a tourist activity. Nothing about that was normal. "Did it come out palm up or down?"

She hesitated. "Up."

"Like...this?" I guided her hand up from her side, then gently rotated her wrist until her palm pointed to the sky. "Or like this?" I put my hand palm-down on top of hers, very lightly. Because I don't care what Yeoung says, it is totes okay to mix business with pleasure.

"Um." She was flustered. Win. "It was...up. Like mine." And she didn't move her hand.

From the corner of my eye I saw one of the Ladyhorse Cove cops leave the nature-program group and start toward us. Time to wrap up both enterprises. "Listen," I said. "There's a luau tonight at eight. Do you want to go with me?"

"Tonight?" she said. "Um. I'm busy."

"I'm not hearing no," I said, letting go of her hand. "It'll be fun. I bust a hella move." I demonstrated my single-lady hands-up maneuver.

She wavered. "I – can't. I've got to stay home tonight."

The cop reached us. I pretended to be surprised.

"Sorry to interrupt," she said. To the girl she said, "Can I have a minute of your time?"

The girl's eyes went to me, almost desperately, but I raised my hands. "Do what the nice lady says. Luau tonight?" And then I double-finger-gunned her. And then I regretted it. And then I retreated to the lounge chair, where Yeoung was waiting for me wearing his Spock face.

"Pudge," he said patiently, "I have told you one million times not to hit on the witnesses."

I sniffed. "You're just jealous I got there first."

He looked back toward her. "All right, she's hot."

"Smokin'," I said. "Which is inevitable, I guess, what with her *pants on fire*."

He raised his brows further, as if that was possible. "You think..."

"Our star witness is mad lying."

"Huh," he said, brow furrowed. "No wrinkles, no scrapes...no way that hand was in the sand for more than, like, a second. She didn't find it there. She planted it." He looked at me. "I don't know which is more important – where the hand really came from or why she lied about it."

I turned to the circle of cops. Another couple of cars were pulling up near the boardwalk, including a dune buggy coming over the sand. This was going to be the local crime of the century.

"'Why,'" I said. "The important question is always 'why'. Tends to answer everything else, and you know I love me some investigative shortcuts. Come on – we can't let that girl out of our sight. She's our best clue walking." I pulled on some jeans. "Also I think I have a chance with her. So don't screw that up."

"Screw *you*," he said.

Best friends forever.

* * *

Yeoung and I have our doctorates in Following People, and we bought each other Internet degrees to prove it, but the girl from the beach was so bad at not being followed that elephants could have done it. After the police let her go, she made a beeline into town. We followed in our usual sleuthy way. We even had time to walk through a Starbucks for some macchiatos. Finally the touristy main streets gave way to more sparse ones, peppered with small run-down houses near marshy woodlands far from the shore. She went into one of them.

"Through the front door and everything," I said, as we paused a block away. "This girl is not a career criminal."

"Either that, or she won't last long enough to become one," said Yeoung.

I said, "I'm breaking up with you."

He made a face. "Shut up. It wasn't *that* mean."

"It was a joke, doofus," I said. "I was telling you that we should split up. Detective-style."

"Detectives don't talk like that," he said, but he handed me my phone before shouldering the equipment backpack. What are best friends for, if not knowing when and when not to put up with your crap?

"I'll take the left side," he said. "No heroics."

"Heroes die, cowards live," I agreed. We shook on it.

Yeoung disappeared around the back of the house, and I slunk around on the right.

It was a two-story-plus-attic, big for the area, with a cellar – rare on the coast. I hushed my slush along the filthy siding, edging toward a window on the first floor. It was closed and the curtains were pulled. *In this heat?* I thought. *That's not suspicious at all.*

"Hey!" someone said. "What are you doing?"

I turned. The speaker was a gym-built redhead wearing a beater and saggy jeans, with a sunburn and a scowl. I ran through my mental file of cover stories and came up with one that seemed to fit the locale.

"I'm looking to party tonight. I heard you could fix me up."

He barely blinked. "Who told you that?"

"Some blonde." I strolled around to the front porch where he stood with the door hanging open. I craned my neck to see past him into the house, but to be honest, I don't have that much neck. "Amber or somebody."

His face clouded. "I don't know what you're talking about. Get out of here."

"Hey," I said, angling closer for a better view, "what about my – *what the hell is that?*"

Pudge Padrelli. Girl detective. All-American blabbermouth.

Then again – it's not every day you peek into someone's living room and find a full-size taxidermied horse.

The redhead heaved me inside and slammed the door. Painting the air blue with f-bombs, he grabbed me and clasped a hand over my mouth. I bit him. He loosed another airstrike. He hauled me through the house, past the dead horse, to a door in the dining room, which he opened and then – without so much as a "Geronimo!" – threw me down a set of stairs.

Thank God I am bouncy. I picked up a bruise on every step, but I landed unbroken on my side. The floor was clammy; everything was dark. I found my breath somewhere above me. "SON OF A BITCH," I roared up the stairs. The door remained shut.

A voice behind me said, "Maybe don't do that."

Yeoung.

I slumped. "We are not good at sneaking, are we?"

"No," he said, "we are not." He came and sat beside me on the bottom stair. "He took the backpack. Do you still have your phone?"

I racked my pockets. "No. I suck." I leaned into his shoulder. "You okay?"

"Sure," he said. "I mean, I'm a prisoner in a basement, but whatever. You?"

"Super."

"Oh yeah," he said. "Uh, don't look in that corner."

Sucker-bait if I ever heard it, but then, I've always been a sucker.

The darkness dimmed into a murky grayscale as my eyes got used to the dark. Slowly, shapes emerged. Tools against the walls. Debris and old equipment on the concrete floor. And in the corner...everything that used to be attached to our McGuffin, the severed hand.

I groaned. "Oh, please let him be dead."

"He's dead," Yeoung said.

I shouldn't have been surprised. Rare the severed hand that belongs to a living victim. "Did you examine it?"

His voice took on disgust. "Did I perform a forensic analysis on a corpse in a basement in the dark?"

"Well?" I said.

His shoulders dropped. "...yes."

I laughed. "And?"

"I couldn't go nuts, obviously, in the freakin' dark, but – there's not really any blood. Not even around his wrist stump."

"You're gross and I love you," I said. "That rules out all kinds of crap. Did you notice that stuffed horse?"

He raised his head. "Shh."

There was shouting from above, in more than one voice – then a thud, a short scream, more thuds, and the basement door opened and the girl from the beach came flying into our arms. She extracted herself from us as the door closed again. "SON OF A BITCH," she roared up the stairs. I slightly misplaced my heart.

"Are you okay?" I said.

She turned at the sound of my voice, recoiling slightly. "*You*?" she said. "I thought he said he caught some junkie. What are *you* doing here?"

I put on my winningest smile. "Uh—"

"You know there's a dead body down here," said Yeoung.

Abra turned to him. "Are you the police?"

"Sort of," said Yeoung, while I said, "Hell no." We glared at each other.

"I'll be honest," I said. "Dead bodies I've seen before. But stuffed horses is new to me."

She put her face in her hands. "You saw the horse?"

"It's hard to miss," said Yeoung. "Care to explain?"

She hesitated. "Eddie would kill us both."

Not a good sign. "Hit us with the truth," I said. "You can trust us."

She sniffed. "Did you...recognize the horse?"

Yeoung said, with predictable smart-assery, "I can't say we've been introduced."

"It's a local thing," she said. "It's a really famous – there was a book – it's a long story."

"Ladyhorse Cove," I said. "And that's the ladyhorse."

She nodded. "The horse is valuable. But it's been in storage for years. Nobody was paying attention to it."

Fishy. "So how'd it end up in your dining room?"

She hesitated again. "Well – Eddie's got a friend – he stole it out of storage and brought it here—"

Here's the part with the murder, I thought.

"—and the guy dropped dead of a heart attack in the kitchen."

I am often wrong.

Now that she'd started talking, it was as if she couldn't stop. "What were we gonn do? We had the stolen horse in a trailer in the yard and a dead guy in the bathroom. S

Eddie put the dead guy down here. We have to get rid of the evidence, he says. But the horse is worth like two million dollars to the right people. We have to keep the horse."

"Aha," said Yeoung. "So the hand came off after he was dead. Yeah, that makes sense."

"He made me take it down to the shore and pretend to find it," she said. "There's maybe three cops on this island. He figured if they were all busy with the hand, he'd have time to move the horse inside and get rid of the trailer it came in. After we sell it, we're getting out of town."

I said, "You do realize that plan is terrible."

Abra looked hurt.

"Hey boss," said Yeoung. "I hate to remind you, but we could use a terrible plan of our own right now. Something escapey." He turned to Abra. "Unless you think your brother's just going to let us go?"

"Not a chance," she said. "Not until tomorrow morning, anyway."

"How's that?" said Yeoung.

"The buyer's coming in tonight," said Abra. "Once he makes the sale, the evidence will be gone, and he'll have the cash in hand. We can get out of this stupid tourist town. He'll let us out tomorrow morning. We just have to wait until the deal's done."

I looked at the corpse in the corner. Even if he'd died naturally, which seemed too convenient, it was a grim reminder. "I don't think so, Abra."

"N—no," she said. "Trust me."

Oh geez, how to break it to her? Luckily, Yeoung came to my rescue.

"We've seen the body," he said. "We've seen the horse. He's not just trying to keep us out of the way. He's keeping us alive because he can't risk three extra bodies stinking up the place before the final sale. Sorry. Either we get out of here, or we get iced."

"'Iced'?" I said. "You nerd."

"Listen, at least it's an established slang term!" he snapped. "'I'm breaking up with you' has never meant 'let's split up' in the history of anything."

"No," said Abra. Her voice shook. "No, that isn't true. He wouldn't kill somebody on purpose. He wouldn't kill...me."

But I recognized the way she said it. She was lying to herself, and she knew it.

"Two million bucks does bad things to people," said Yeoung.

She looked so lost that I knew I had to do a little lying myself. "Listen," I said, "that's a worst-case scenario. Maybe your brother's going to do exactly what he says – let us go, take you along when he leaves. But what about the buyer? What if *he* hears something, or gets nervous? Abra – we are trapped. That's never a good place to be. Help us get away from here. We'll figure out the rest."

She put her fingers on her forehead. "Eddie's gonna be pissed."

"He'll understand," I said. "Think. Is there any way out of here?"

"Uh," she said. "I guess – I think there's a vent down here. But it's covered up."

Yeoung leapt into action, pacing the room, staring at the lines where the ceiling met the walls. I contributed by patting Abra's shoulder in a soothing manner. At last he called out, "Daylight!" He made some basketball-leaps, fingers outstretched, and after four or five tries, a piece of canvas tore away and a beautiful ray of light fell across the dirt floor.

We crowded around the vent.

"I can squeeze through," said Yeoung.

"Me too," said Abra.

They looked at me.

I sighed. "Hips don't lie," I said. "I'm not getting out through that." I drew a breath. "You two get out, get the police, and come back for me."

"BALONEY," said Yeoung. "No heroics!"

"It's not heroics, it's physics," I snapped. "My gas is not compressible, if you get my drift. Take Abra and send in the hot fuzz. Trust me, it's the best thing you can do for me."

"Screw YOU," he said.

"BITE ME," I said. I turned before I could cry. "Help me find a ladder."

He did it without saying a word. Which didn't help.

"Here," said Abra. She pulled out a stepladder from under the stairs. She shoved it at Yeoung. "You go. I'm staying."

"The hell!" said Yeoung, now sounding genuinely distressed. "I'm not leaving two girls alone in a killer horse thief's basement. No offense," he added to Abra.

"You need to go," I told Abra. "Don't worry about me."

"I don't want to."

I took her by the shoulders and rotated her toward the ladder that Yeoung was setting up. "Tough nuts. I'll see you on the outside."

She hesitated at the foot of the ladder – but Yeoung grabbed her and hoisted her up, and gave her enough of a boost to help her get her arms through the vent opening and wriggle out onto the grass.

"Beat feet, Watson," I said.

He glared at me. "You better be alive when I get back."

"Elementary."

He slugged me and didn't look back as he left. That's how I know he loves me.

I went back to the stairs and sat down. "It's just me and you, kid," I said to the one-handed corpse.

The door behind me creaked open.

Usain Bolt could not have moved as fast as I moved then. I was off the staircase and crouched under the stairs before my breath caught up with me. The top step creaked. Eddie's delightful twang echoed on the concrete bricks. "Abra!"

I tried to force my heart to stop pounding so loud.

Eddie shifted. "Dammit."

The situation became suddenly, terribly clear to me. Yeoung and Abra had barely left. They might not be out of sight yet. If Eddie realized they were gone – if he went looking for them – he might just catch up.

"We're here," I squeaked.

He took another step. "Abe?"

"Don't – don't hurt us."

"Abra, come on up," said Eddie. He sounded impatient. "I don't know what got into me. Nerves, I guess. Get out here. We're gonna do this just like we said."

Oh, crapping crap. "Go away. Don't hurt us."

"Just get on up here."

I didn't say anything.

"Son a'...." He shifted back to the top step.

I had to hold him here. "No!" I said. I crept out from under the staircase – just enough that we could see each other through the railing. "Don't leave us down here Let us go."

"You shut up," he sneered. "See what lookin' to party gets you?" He turned a little, and I saw for the first time that he had a rifle in his hand. *This is getting real, Pudge*, I thought. *Real like the Velveteen Rabbit.* I heard Yeoung's voice in my head: *Detectives don't talk like that.*

Screw him. If I was going to risk my life for his, I was going to talk any way I wanted.

I moved a little farther into view. "Hey," I said. "You like to party?"

He eyed me over. "What are you, fifteen?"

"I'm legal," I said. "Just looking for some fun. You look fun."

He snorted. "You look like tons of fun."

"All curves, no angles," I said. "You probably don't even know how fun it can be."

He came down another step.

Every gross moment was another moment they could use to escape; every foot closer he came to me was a yard further from them. Still. We held each other at bay. Maybe we could come to an agreement about whether or not he ought to shoot me.

"Come over here," he said.

I walked to the bottom of the stairs, i.e. the gallows. "Come and get me."

He raised his chin. And took another step.

The door swung open behind him, and light from the dining room blazed down, giving him the glow of an angel. He whipped around, rifle in hand. I didn't waste a living moment. I charged. I hit the back of his knees, and he tumbled backward over me, down the stairs, and hit the dirt hard. He twitched and lay still.

I scooted after him just far enough to snatch the rifle; then I was off again, bounding up stairs like a deer. I didn't even have to close the door behind me. When I fell out into the dining room, Yeoung's skinny arms caught me; the door slammed, and I heard a key turn in the lock. Abra came to help us both up.

I stared at them. "No heroics?" I said.

Yeoung shrugged. "Maybe you're a bad influence."

I hugged him like he was a teddy bear with no bones to break. Wise man that he is, he didn't even complain.

* * *

By the time we got sorted out at the police station, it was nearly dark. I found Abra in a chair near some policeman's desk. She looked both desperately unhappy to be there and determined to stay as long as she had to. When I sat across from her, she snuck a glance over at me.

"Sorry I can't make the luau," she said. "I kind of wanted to see you bust that move."

"Oh," I said. "Ha ha...I'd show you now, but they might arrest me for arson."

She squinted. "For...arson?"

"For – setting a police station on fire? Because I'm so hot? I'm so sorry I just put you through that. Bad habit."

She took my hand. "It's fine."

Ee hee hee. I composed myself. "I think you're going to be all right," I said. "Just tell the truth. You were coerced. Nobody's going to make you pay for your brother's crimes."

She looked down. "Here's hoping."

I gave her hand a squeeze. "Hey. I'll testify for you. Juries love my breezy style. I can't promise what they'll think of Yeoung, but—"

She kissed me.

Anything could have been responsible for the heat that rose in my face: her soft hand, her sunburnt lips, her scent, her nearness, the fact that we were surrounded by active-duty cops. Anything.

She ended it first. I was left with my lips extended and my eyes closed. I opened them to see her inches away, smiling. "Thanks," she said.

A policewoman came over. "Your lawyer is here," she said to Abra.

Abra drew a breath. "Wish me luck."

"You'll be fine," I said.

She looked over her shoulder at me before disappearing into one of the interrogation rooms.

I dropped my head into my arms and only looked up when I felt someone tugging my hair. Yeoung. I made my best internet sad-face. "Forever alone."

"Goddammit, Casanova," he said, "that's one hot chick more than *I* got to make out with today. Let's go hit up the luau and even the score before I get really cranky."

I looped my arm around his elbow. "You got it. And hey, I guess I'll see her again at the trial."

"Shameless," he said.

"Glorious," I said. "Ready to shake your money-maker?"

He said, "Until my ass rains quarters."

Butt jokes, heartbreak, mortal peril, sun, kisses, dead body parts, and a stuffed horse.

I've had worse vacations.

The Man with the Watches

Arthur Conan Doyle

THERE ARE MANY who will still bear in mind the singular circumstances which, under the heading of the Rugby Mystery, filled many columns of the daily Press in the spring of the year 1892. Coming as it did at a period of exceptional dullness, it attracted perhaps rather more attention than it deserved, but it offered to the public that mixture of the whimsical and the tragic which is most stimulating to the popular imagination. Interest drooped, however, when, after weeks of fruitless investigation, it was found that no final explanation of the facts was forthcoming, and the tragedy seemed from that time to the present to have finally taken its place in the dark catalogue of inexplicable and unexpiated crimes. A recent communication (the authenticity of which appears to be above question) has, however, thrown some new and clear light upon the matter. Before laying it before the public it would be as well, perhaps, that I should refresh their memories as to the singular facts upon which this commentary is founded. These facts were briefly as follows:

At five o'clock on the evening of the 18th of March in the year already mentioned a train left Euston Station for Manchester. It was a rainy, squally day, which grew wilder as it progressed, so it was by no means the weather in which any one would travel who was not driven to do so by necessity. The train, however, is a favourite one among Manchester business men who are returning from town, for it does the journey in four hours and twenty minutes, with only three stoppages upon the way. In spite of the inclement evening it was, therefore, fairly well filled upon the occasion of which I speak. The guard of the train was a tried servant of the company – a man who had worked for twenty-two years without blemish or complaint. His name was John Palmer.

The station clock was upon the stroke of five, and the guard was about to give the customary signal to the engine-driver when he observed two belated passengers hurrying down the platform. The one was an exceptionally tall man, dressed in a long black overcoat with Astrakhan collar and cuffs. I have already said that the evening was an inclement one, and the tall traveller had the high, warm collar turned up to protect his throat against the bitter March wind. He appeared, as far as the guard could judge by so hurried an inspection, to be a man between fifty and sixty years of age, who had retained a good deal of the vigour and activity of his youth. In one hand he carried a brown leather Gladstone bag. His companion was a lady, tall and erect, walking with a vigorous step which outpaced the gentleman beside her. She wore a long, fawn-coloured dust-cloak, a black, close-fitting toque, and a dark veil which concealed the greater part of her face. The two might very well have passed as father and daughter. They walked swiftly down the line of carriages, glancing in at the windows, until the guard, John Palmer, overtook them.

"Now, then, sir, look sharp, the train is going," said he.

"First-class," the man answered.

The guard turned the handle of the nearest door. In the carriage, which he had opened, there sat a small man with a cigar in his mouth. His appearance seems to have impressed itself upon the guard's memory, for he was prepared, afterwards, to describe or to identify him. He was a man of thirty-four or thirty-five years of age, dressed in some grey material, sharp-nosed, alert, with a ruddy, weather-beaten face, and a small, closely cropped black beard. He glanced up as the door was opened. The tall man paused with his foot upon the step.

"This is a smoking compartment. The lady dislikes smoke," said he, looking round at the guard.

"All right! Here you are, sir!" said John Palmer. He slammed the door of the smoking carriage, opened that of the next one, which was empty, and thrust the two travellers in. At the same moment he sounded his whistle and the wheels of the train began to move. The man with the cigar was at the window of his carriage, and said something to the guard as he rolled past him, but the words were lost in the bustle of the departure. Palmer stepped into the guard's van, as it came up to him, and thought no more of the incident.

Twelve minutes after its departure the train reached Willesden Junction, where it stopped for a very short interval. An examination of the tickets has made it certain that no one either joined or left it at this time, and no passenger was seen to alight upon the platform. At 5.14 the journey to Manchester was resumed, and Rugby was reached at 6.50, the express being five minutes late.

At Rugby the attention of the station officials was drawn to the fact that the door of one of the first-class carriages was open. An examination of that compartment, and of its neighbour, disclosed a remarkable state of affairs.

The smoking carriage in which the short, red-faced man with the black beard had been seen was now empty. Save for a half-smoked cigar, there was no trace whatever of its recent occupant. The door of this carriage was fastened. In the next compartment, to which attention had been originally drawn, there was no sign either of the gentleman with the Astrakhan collar or of the young lady who accompanied him. All three passengers had disappeared. On the other hand, there was found upon the floor of this carriage – the one in which the tall traveller and the lady had been – a young man, fashionably dressed and of elegant appearance. He lay with his knees drawn up, and his head resting against the further door, an elbow upon either seat. A bullet had penetrated his heart and his death must have been instantaneous. No one had seen such a man enter the train, and no railway ticket was found in his pocket, neither were there any markings upon his linen, nor papers nor personal property which might help to identify him. Who he was, whence he had come, and how he had met his end were each as great a mystery as what had occurred to the three people who had started an hour and a half before from Willesden in those two compartments.

I have said that there was no personal property which might help to identify him, but it is true that there was one peculiarity about this unknown young man which was much commented upon at the time. In his pockets were found no fewer than six valuable gold watches, three in the various pockets of his waistcoat, one in his ticket-pocket, one in his breast-pocket, and one small one set in a leather strap and fastened round his left wrist. The obvious explanation that the man was a pickpocket, and that this was his plunder, was discounted by the fact that all six were of American make, and of a type which is rare in England. Three of them bore the mark of the Rochester Watchmaking Company; one was by Mason, of Elmira; one was unmarked; and the small one, which was highly jewelled and ornamented, was from Tiffany, of New York. The other contents of his pocket consisted of an ivory knife with a corkscrew by Rodgers, of Sheffield; a small circular mirror, one inch in diameter; a re-admission slip to the Lyceum theatre; a silver box full of vesta matches, and a brown leather cigar-case containing two cheroots – also two pounds fourteen shillings in money. It was clear, then, that whatever motives may have led to his death, robbery was not among them. As already mentioned, there were no markings upon the man's linen, which appeared to be new, and no tailor's name upon his coat. In appearance he was young, short, smooth-cheeked, and delicately featured. One of his front teeth was conspicuously stopped with gold.

On the discovery of the tragedy an examination was instantly made of the tickets of all passengers, and the number of the passengers themselves was counted. It was found that only three tickets were unaccounted for, corresponding to the three travellers who were missing. The express was then allowed to proceed, but a new guard was sent with it, and John Palmer was detained as a witness at Rugby. The carriage which included the two compartments in question was uncoupled and side-tracked. Then, on the arrival of Inspector Vane, of Scotland Yard, and of Mr. Henderson, a detective in the service of the railway company, an exhaustive inquiry was made into all the circumstances.

That crime had been committed was certain. The bullet, which appeared to have come from a small pistol or revolver, had been fired from some little distance, as there was no scorching of the clothes. No weapon was found in the compartment (which finally disposed of the theory of suicide), nor was there any sign of the brown leather bag which the guard had seen in the hand of the tall gentleman. A lady's parasol was found upon the rack, but no other trace was to be seen of the travellers in either of the sections. Apart from the crime, the question of how or why three passengers (one of them a lady) could get out of the train, and one other get in during the unbroken run between Willesden and Rugby, was one which excited the utmost curiosity among the general public, and gave rise to much speculation in the London Press.

John Palmer, the guard, was able at the inquest to give some evidence which threw a little light upon the matter. There was a spot between Tring and Cheddington, according to his statement, where, on account of some repairs to the line, the train had for a few minutes slowed down to a pace not exceeding eight or ten miles an hour. At that place it might be possible for a man, or even for an exceptionally active woman, to have left the train without serious injury. It was true that a gang of platelayers was there, and that they had seen nothing, but it was their custom to stand in the middle between the metals, and the open carriage door was upon the far side, so that it was conceivable that someone might have alighted unseen, as the darkness would by that time be drawing in. A steep embankment would instantly screen anyone who sprang out from the observation of the navvies.

The guard also deposed that there was a good deal of movement upon the platform at Willesden Junction, and that though it was certain that no one had either joined or left the train there, it was still quite possible that some of the passengers might have changed unseen from one compartment to another. It was by no means uncommon for a gentleman to finish his cigar in a smoking carriage and then to change to a clearer atmosphere. Supposing that the man with the black beard had done so at Willesden (and the half-smoked cigar upon the floor seemed to favour the supposition), he would naturally go into the nearest section, which would bring him into the company of the two other actors in this drama. Thus the first stage of the affair might be surmised without any great breach of probability. But what the second stage had been, or how the final one had been arrived at, neither the guard nor the experienced detective officers could suggest.

A careful examination of the line between Willesden and Rugby resulted in one discovery which might or might not have a bearing upon the tragedy. Near Tring, at the very place where the train slowed down, there was found at the bottom of the embankment a small pocket Testament, very shabby and worn. It was printed by the Bible Society of London, and bore an inscription: 'From John to Alice. Jan. 13th, 1856,' upon the fly-leaf. Underneath was written: 'James, July 4th, 1859,' and beneath that again: 'Edward. Nov. 1st, 1869,' all the entries being in the same handwriting. This was the only clue, if it could be called a clue, which the police obtained, and the coroner's verdict of 'Murder by a person or persons unknown' was thc unsatisfactory cnding of a singular case. Advertisement, rewards, and inquiries proved equally fruitless, and nothing could be found which was solid enough to form the basis for a profitable investigation.

It would be a mistake, however, to suppose that no theories were formed to account for the facts. On the contrary, the Press, both in England and in America, teemed with suggestions and suppositions, most of which were obviously absurd. The fact that the watches were of American make, and some peculiarities in connection with the gold stopping of his front tooth, appeared to indicate that the deceased was a citizen of the United States, though his linen, clothes, and boots were undoubtedly of British manufacture. It was surmised, by some, that he was concealed under the seat, and that, being discovered, he was for some reason, possibly because he had overheard their guilty secrets, put to death by his fellow-passengers. When coupled with generalities as to the ferocity and cunning of anarchical and other secret societies, this theory sounded as plausible as any.

The fact that he should be without a ticket would be consistent with the idea of concealment, and it was well known that women played a prominent part in the Nihilistic propaganda. On the other hand, it was clear, from the guard's statement, that the man must have been hidden there *before* the others arrived, and how unlikely the coincidence that conspirators should stray exactly into the very compartment in which a spy was already concealed! Besides, this explanation ignored the man in the smoking carriage, and gave no reason at all for his simultaneous disappearance. The police had little difficulty in showing that such a theory would not cover the facts, but they were unprepared in the absence of evidence to advance any alternative explanation.

There was a letter in the *Daily Gazette*, over the signature of a well-known criminal investigator, which gave rise to considerable discussion at the time. He had formed a hypothesis which had at least ingenuity to recommend it, and I cannot do better than append it in his own words.

"Whatever may be the truth," said he, "it must depend upon some bizarre and rare combination of events, so we need have no hesitation in postulating such events in our explanation. In the absence of data we must abandon the analytic or scientific method of investigation, and must approach it in the synthetic fashion. In a word, instead of taking known events and deducing from them what has occurred, we must build up a fanciful explanation if it will only be consistent with known events. We can then test this explanation by any fresh facts which may arise. If they all fit into their places, the probability is that we are upon the right track, and with each fresh fact this probability increases in a geometrical progression until the evidence becomes final and convincing.

"Now, there is one most remarkable and suggestive fact which has not met with the attention which it deserves. There is a local train running through Harrow and King's Langley, which is timed in such a way that the express must have overtaken it at or about the period when it eased down its speed to eight miles an hour on account of the repairs of the line. The two trains would at that time be travelling in the same direction at a similar rate of speed and upon parallel lines. It is within everyone's experience how, under such circumstances, the occupant of each carriage can see very plainly the passengers in the other carriages opposite to him. The lamps of the express had been lit at Willesden, so that each compartment was brightly illuminated, and most visible to an observer from outside.

"Now, the sequence of events as I reconstruct them would be after this fashion. This young man with the abnormal number of watches was alone in the carriage of the slow train. His ticket, with his papers and gloves and other things, was, we will suppose, on the seat beside him. He was probably an American, and also probably a man of weak intellect. The excessive wearing of jewellery is an early symptom in some forms of mania.

"As he sat watching the carriages of the express which were (on account of the state of the line) going at the same pace as himself, he suddenly saw some people in it whom he knew. We will suppose for the sake of our theory that these people were a woman whom he loved and a man whom he hated – and who in return hated him. The young man was excitable and impulsive. He opened the door of his carriage, stepped from the footboard of the local train to the footboard of the express, opened the other door, and made his way into the presence of these two people. The feat (on the supposition that the trains were going at the same pace) is by no means so perilous as it might appear.

"Having now got our young man without his ticket into the carriage in which the elder man and the young woman are travelling, it is not difficult to imagine that a violent scene ensued. It is possible that the pair were also Americans, which is the more probable as the man carried a weapon – an unusual thing in England. If our supposition of incipient mania is correct, the young man is likely to have assaulted the other. As the upshot of the quarrel the elder man shot the intruder, and then made his escape from the carriage, taking the young lady with him. We will suppose that all this happened very rapidly, and that the train was still going at so slow a pace that it was not difficult for them to leave it. A woman might leave a train going at eight miles an hour. As a matter of fact, we know that this woman *did* do so.

"And now we have to fit in the man in the smoking carriage. Presuming that we have, up to this point, reconstructed the tragedy correctly, we shall find nothing in this other man to cause us to reconsider our conclusions. According to my theory, this man saw the young fellow cross from one train to the other, saw him open the door, heard the pistol-shot, saw the two fugitives spring out on to the line, realized that murder had been done, and sprang out himself in pursuit. Why he has never been heard of since – whether he met his own death in the pursuit, or whether, as is more likely, he was made to realize that it was not a case for his interference – is a detail which we have at present no means of explaining. I acknowledge that there are some difficulties in the way. At first sight, it might seem improbable that at such a moment a murderer would burden himself in his flight with a brown leather bag. My answer is that he was well aware that if the bag were found his identity would be established. It was absolutely necessary for him to take it with him. My theory stands or falls upon one point, and I call upon the railway company to make strict inquiry as to whether a ticket was found unclaimed in the local train through Harrow and King's Langley upon the 18th of March. If such a ticket were found my case is proved. If not, my theory may still be the correct one, for it is conceivable either that he travelled without a ticket or that his ticket was lost."

To this elaborate and plausible hypothesis the answer of the police and of the company was, first, that no such ticket was found; secondly, that the slow train would never run parallel to the express; and, thirdly, that the local train had been stationary in King's Langley Station when the express, going at fifty miles an hour, had flashed past it. So perished the only satisfying explanation, and five years have elapsed without supplying a new one. Now, at last, there comes a statement which covers all the facts, and which must be regarded as authentic. It took the shape of a letter dated from New York, and addressed to the same criminal investigator whose theory I have quoted. It is given here in extenso, with the exception of the two opening paragraphs, which are personal in their nature:

"You'll excuse me if I'm not very free with names. There's less reason now than there was five years ago when mother was still living. But for all that, I had rather cover up our tracks all I can. But I owe you an explanation, for if your idea of it was wrong, it was a mighty ingenious one all the same. I'll have to go back a little so as you may understand all about it.

"My people came from Bucks, England, and emigrated to the States in the early fifties. They settled in Rochester, in the State of New York, where my father ran a large dry goods store. There were only two sons: myself, James, and my brother, Edward. I was ten years older than my brother, and after my father died I sort of took the place of a father to him, as an elder brother would. He was a bright, spirited boy, and just one of the most beautiful creatures that ever lived. But there was always a soft spot in him, and it was like mould in cheese, for it spread and spread, and nothing that you could do would stop it. Mother saw it just as clearly as I did, but she went on spoiling him all the same, for he had such a way with him that you could refuse him nothing. I did all I could to hold him in, and he hated me for my pains.

"At last he fairly got his head, and nothing that we could do would stop him. He got off into New York, and went rapidly from bad to worse. At first he was only fast, and then he was criminal; and then, at the end of a year or two, he was one of the most notorious young crooks in the city. He had formed a friendship with Sparrow MacCoy, who was at the head of his profession as a bunco-steerer, green goods-man, and general rascal. They took to card-sharping, and frequented some of the best hotels in New York. My brother was an excellent actor (he might have made an honest name for himself if he had chosen), and he would take the parts of a young Englishman of title, of a simple lad from the West, or of a college undergraduate, whichever suited Sparrow MacCoy's purpose. And then one day he dressed himself as a girl, and he carried it off so well, and made himself such a valuable decoy, that it was their favourite game afterwards. They had made it right with Tammany and with the police, so it seemed as if nothing could ever stop them, for those were in the days before the Lexow Commission, and if you only had a pull, you could do pretty nearly everything you wanted.

"And nothing would have stopped them if they had only stuck to cards and New York, but they must needs come up Rochester way, and forge a name upon a check. It was my brother that did it, though everyone knew that it was under the influence of Sparrow MacCoy. I bought up that check, and a pretty sum it cost me. Then I went to my brother, laid it before him on the table, and swore to him that I would prosecute if he did not clear out of the country. At first he simply laughed. I could not prosecute, he said, without breaking our mother's heart, and he knew that I would not do that. I made him understand, however, that our mother's heart was being broken in any case, and that I had set firm on the point that I would rather see him in a Rochester gaol than in a New York hotel. So at last he gave in, and he made me a solemn promise that he would see Sparrow MacCoy no more, that he would go to Europe, and that he would turn his hand to any honest trade that I helped him to get. I took him down right away to an old family friend, Joe Willson, who is an exporter of American watches and clocks, and I got him to give Edward an agency in London, with a small salary and a 15 per cent. commission on all business. His manner and appearance were so good that he won the old man over at once, and within a week he was sent off to London with a case full of samples.

"It seemed to me that this business of the check had really given my brother a fright, and that there was some chance of his settling down into an honest line of life. My mother had spoken with him, and what she said had touched him, for she had always been the best of mothers to him, and he had been the great sorrow of her life. But I knew that this man Sparrow MacCoy had a great influence over Edward, and my chance of keeping the lad straight lay in breaking the connection between them. I had a friend in the New York detective force, and through him I kept a watch upon MacCoy. When within a fortnight of my brother's sailing I heard that MacCoy had taken a berth in the *Etruria*, I was as certain as if he had told me that he was going over to England for the purpose of coaxing Edward back again into the ways that he had left. In an instant I had resolved to go also, and to put my influence against MacCoy's. I knew it was a losing fight, but I thought, and my mother thought, that it was my duty. We passed the last night together in prayer for my success, and she gave me her own Testament that my father had given her on the day of their marriage in the Old Country, so that I might always wear it next my heart.

"I was a fellow-traveller, on the steamship, with Sparrow MacCoy, and at least I had the satisfaction of spoiling his little game for the voyage. The very first night I went into the smoking-room, and found him at the head of a card table, with half-a-dozen young fellows who were carrying their full purses and their empty skulls over to Europe. He was settling down for his harvest, and a rich one it would have been. But I soon changed all that.

"'Gentlemen,' said I, 'are you aware whom you are playing with?'

"'What's that to you? You mind your own business!' said he, with an oath.

"'Who is it, anyway?' asked one of the dudes.

"'He's Sparrow MacCoy, the most notorious cardsharper in the States.'

"Up he jumped with a bottle in his hand, but he remembered that he was under the flag of the effete Old Country, where law and order run, and Tammany has no pull. Gaol and the gallows wait for violence and murder, and there's no slipping out by the back door on board an ocean liner.

"'Prove your words, you—!' said he.

"'I will!' said I. 'If you will turn up your right shirt-sleeve to the shoulder, I will either prove my words or I will eat them.'

"He turned white and said not a word. You see, I knew something of his ways, and I was aware that part of the mechanism which he and all such sharpers use consists of an elastic down the arm with a clip just above the wrist. It is by means of this clip that they withdraw from their hands the cards which they do not want, while they substitute other cards from another hiding-place. I reckoned on it being there, and it was. He cursed me, slunk out of the saloon, and was hardly seen again during the voyage. For once, at any rate, I got level with Mister Sparrow MacCoy.

"But he soon had his revenge upon me, for when it came to influencing my brother he outweighed me every time. Edward had kept himself straight in London for the first few weeks, and had done some business with his American watches, until this villain came across his path once more. I did my best, but the best was little enough. The next thing I heard there had been a scandal at one of the Northumberland Avenue hotels: a traveller had been fleeced of a large sum by two confederate card-sharpers, and the matter was in the hands of Scotland Yard. The first I learned of it was in the evening paper, and I was at once certain that my brother and MacCoy were back at their old games. I hurried at once to Edward's lodgings. They told me that he and a tall gentleman (whom I recognized as

MacCoy) had gone off together, and that he had left the lodgings and taken his things with him. The landlady had heard them give several directions to the cabman, ending with Euston Station, and she had accidentally overheard the tall gentleman saying something about Manchester. She believed that that was their destination.

"A glance at the time-table showed me that the most likely train was at five, though there was another at 4.35 which they might have caught. I had only time to get the later one, but found no sign of them either at the depôt or in the train. They must have gone on by the earlier one, so I determined to follow them to Manchester and search for them in the hotels there. One last appeal to my brother by all that he owed to my mother might even now be the salvation of him. My nerves were overstrung, and I lit a cigar to steady them. At that moment, just as the train was moving off, the door of my compartment was flung open, and there were MacCoy and my brother on the platform.

"They were both disguised, and with good reason, for they knew that the London police were after them. MacCoy had a great Astrakhan collar drawn up, so that only his eyes and nose were showing. My brother was dressed like a woman, with a black veil half down his face, but of course it did not deceive me for an instant, nor would it have done so even if I had not known that he had often used such a dress before. I started up, and as I did so MacCoy recognized me. He said something, the conductor slammed the door, and they were shown into the next compartment. I tried to stop the train so as to follow them, but the wheels were already moving, and it was too late.

"When we stopped at Willesden, I instantly changed my carriage. It appears that I was not seen to do so, which is not surprising, as the station was crowded with people. MacCoy, of course, was expecting me, and he had spent the time between Euston and Willesden in saying all he could to harden my brother's heart and set him against me. That is what I fancy, for I had never found him so impossible to soften or to move. I tried this way and I tried that; I pictured his future in an English gaol; I described the sorrow of his mother when I came back with the news; I said everything to touch his heart, but all to no purpose. He sat there with a fixed sneer upon his handsome face, while every now and then Sparrow MacCoy would throw in a taunt at me, or some word of encouragement to hold my brother to his resolutions.

"'Why don't you run a Sunday-school?' he would say to me, and then, in the same breath: 'He thinks you have no will of your own. He thinks you are just the baby brother and that he can lead you where he likes. He's only just finding out that you are a man as well as he.'

"It was those words of his which set me talking bitterly. We had left Willesden, you understand, for all this took some time. My temper got the better of me, and for the first time in my life I let my brother see the rough side of me. Perhaps it would have been better had I done so earlier and more often.

"'A man!' said I. 'Well, I'm glad to have your friend's assurance of it, for no one would suspect it to see you like a boarding-school missy. I don't suppose in all this country there is a more contemptible-looking creature than you are as you sit there with that Dolly pinafore upon you.' He coloured up at that, for he was a vain man, and he winced from ridicule.

"'It's only a dust-cloak,' said he, and he slipped it off. 'One has to throw the coppers off one's scent, and I had no other way to do it.' He took his toque off with the veil attached, and he put both it and the cloak into his brown bag. 'Anyway, I don't need to wear it until the conductor comes round,' said he.

"'Nor then, either,' said I, and taking the bag I slung it with all my force out of the window. 'Now,' said I, 'you'll never make a Mary Jane of yourself while I can help it. If nothing but that disguise stands between you and a gaol, then to gaol you shall go.'

"That was the way to manage him. I felt my advantage at once. His supple nature was one which yielded to roughness far more readily than to entreaty. He flushed with shame, and his eyes filled with tears. But MacCoy saw my advantage also, and was determined that I should not pursue it.

"'He's my pard, and you shall not bully him,' he cried.

"'He's my brother, and you shall not ruin him,' said I. 'I believe a spell of prison is the very best way of keeping you apart, and you shall have it, or it will be no fault of mine.'

"'Oh, you would squeal, would you?' he cried, and in an instant he whipped out his revolver. I sprang for his hand, but saw that I was too late, and jumped aside. At the same instant he fired, and the bullet which would have struck me passed through the heart of my unfortunate brother.

"He dropped without a groan upon the floor of the compartment, and MacCoy and I, equally horrified, knelt at each side of him, trying to bring back some signs of life. MacCoy still held the loaded revolver in his hand, but his anger against me and my resentment towards him had both for the moment been swallowed up in this sudden tragedy. It was he who first realized the situation. The train was for some reason going very slowly at the moment, and he saw his opportunity for escape. In an instant he had the door open, but I was as quick as he, and jumping upon him the two of us fell off the footboard and rolled in each other's arms down a steep embankment. At the bottom I struck my head against a stone, and I remembered nothing more. When I came to myself I was lying among some low bushes, not far from the railroad track, and somebody was bathing my head with a wet handkerchief. It was Sparrow MacCoy.

"'I guess I couldn't leave you,' said he. 'I didn't want to have the blood of two of you on my hands in one day. You loved your brother, I've no doubt; but you didn't love him a cent more than I loved him, though you'll say that I took a queer way to show it. Anyhow, it seems a mighty empty world now that he is gone, and I don't care a continental whether you give me over to the hangman or not.'

"He had turned his ankle in the fall, and there we sat, he with his useless foot, and I with my throbbing head, and we talked and talked until gradually my bitterness began to soften and to turn into something like sympathy. What was the use of revenging his death upon a man who was as much stricken by that death as I was? And then, as my wits gradually returned, I began to realize also that I could do nothing against MacCoy which would not recoil upon my mother and myself. How could we convict him without a full account of my brother's career being made public – the very thing which of all others we wished to avoid? It was really as much our interest as his to cover the matter up, and from being an avenger of crime I found myself changed to a conspirator against Justice. The place in which we found ourselves was one of those pheasant preserves which are so common in the Old Country, and as we groped our way through it I found myself consulting the slayer of my brother as to how far it would be possible to hush it up.

"I soon realized from what he said that unless there were some papers of which we knew nothing in my brother's pockets, there was really no possible means by which the police could identify him or learn how he had got there. His ticket was in MacCoy's pocket, and so was the ticket for some baggage which they had left at the depôt. Like most Americans, he had found it cheaper and easier to buy an outfit in London than to bring one from New York, so that all his linen and clothes were new and unmarked. The bag, containing the dust cloak, which I had thrown out of the window, may have fallen among some bramble patch where it is still concealed, or may have been carried off by some tramp, or may have come into the possession of the police, who kept the incident to themselves. Anyhow, I have seen nothing about it in the London papers. As to the watches, they were a selection from those which had been intrusted to him for business purposes. It may have been for the same business purposes that he was taking them to Manchester, but – well, it's too late to enter into that.

"I don't blame the police for being at fault. I don't see how it could have been otherwise. There was just one little clew that they might have followed up, but it was a small one. I mean that small circular mirror which was found in my brother's pocket. It isn't a very common thing for a young man to carry about with him, is it? But a gambler might have told you what such a mirror may mean to a cardsharper. If you sit back a little from the table, and lay the mirror, face upwards, upon your lap, you can see, as you deal, every card that you give to your adversary. It is not hard to say whether you see a man or raise him when you know his cards as well as your own. It was as much a part of a sharper's outfit as the elastic clip upon Sparrow MacCoy's arm. Taking that, in connection with the recent frauds at the hotels, the police might have got hold of one end of the string.

"I don't think there is much more for me to explain. We got to a village called Amersham that night in the character of two gentlemen upon a walking tour, and afterwards we made our way quietly to London, whence MacCoy went on to Cairo and I returned to New York. My mother died six months afterwards, and I am glad to say that to the day of her death she never knew what happened. She was always under the delusion that Edward was earning an honest living in London, and I never had the heart to tell her the truth. He never wrote; but, then, he never did write at any time, so that made no difference. His name was the last upon her lips.

"There's just one other thing that I have to ask you, sir, and I should take it as a kind return for all this explanation, if you could do it for me. You remember that Testament that was picked up. I always carried it in my inside pocket, and it must have come out in my fall. I value it very highly, for it was the family book with my birth and my brother's marked by my father in the beginning of it. I wish you would apply at the proper place and have it sent to me. It can be of no possible value to any one else. If you address it to X, Bassano's Library, Broadway, New York, it is sure to come to hand."

Tenant for Life

Andrew Forrester

IT OFTEN HAPPENS to us detectives – and when I say us detectives, of course, I mean both men and women operatives – that we are the first movers in matters of great ultimate importance to individuals in particular, and the public at large.

For instance, a case in point only came under my notice a few weeks since.

A lady of somewhat solitary and reserved life, residing alone, but for a housekeeper, died suddenly. Strangely enough, her son arrived at the house two hours before the lady breathed her last. The house in which the death took place being far from a town, and it being necessary that the son should almost immediately return to London, the house was left for some time in the care, or it were more consistent to say under the control, of the housekeeper already mentioned – a woman who bore a far from spotless character in the neighbourhood of her late mistress's dwelling.

To curtail that portion of this instance of the but poorly comprehended efficacy of the detective police, which does not immediately bear upon the argument under consideration, it may be said in a few words that in the time which elapsed between the departure and arrival of the son, the house was very effectively stripped.

The son, of course, was put almost immediately in possession of the suspicions of several neighbours as to the felony which they felt sure had been committed, and this gentleman was very quickly in a position to convince himself that a robbery had been effected.

The housekeeper was spoken to, told of her crime, which insolently she denied, and was at once dismissed, she foolishly threatening law proceedings, on the score of defamation of character.

The son of the deceased lady refused to take any action in the matter of the robbery, urging that he could not have his mother's name and death mixed up with police court proceedings, and he allowed the affair, as he supposed, to blow over, though it should be here observed that he suffered very considerable inconvenience by the absence of certain papers which were associated with the death of his mother.

Four months pass, and now the police appear upon the scene, and with an efficiency which is an instance of the value of the detective force. The police had, of course, in the ordinary way of business, heard of the robbery referred to, but could not move in it while no prosecutor gave them the word to move. But if the police had not moved in the case, they had not forgotten it.

A robbery takes place in the neighbourhood, and a search-warrant is granted. A search is prosecuted, and in a shed beyond a small house, belonging to a couple whom the housekeeper already mentioned knew, and who had been up at the house while the house-keeper was left in solo charge of it, was found a japanned cash-box.

The detective who made this discovery almost immediately identified the box with the robbery at the house of the late lady, and upon finding, after a close examination, the initial of her surname scratched upon the lid, he became so convinced his conjecture was right, that, upon his own responsibility, he took the tenant of the house in question into custody.

The case went clear against the unhappy man. The police, by a wonderful series of fortunate guesses and industrious inquiries, found out the son, and this latter was enabled to produce a key, one of a household bunch belonging to his late mother, that opened the cash-box in question, which had been forced in such a manner that the cash-box had not been broken.

This gentleman, however, refused to prosecute, and the prisoner got off with the fright of his arrest and an examination.

Which of the two, the gentleman or the detective, did his duty to society is a question I leave to be answered by my readers. My aim in quoting this instance of the operation of the detective system is to show how valuable it may become, even where should-be prosecutors make the mistake of supposing that leniency and patience form a much better course of conduct than one of justice and fair retribution.

The detective police frequently start cases and discover prosecutors in people who have had no idea of filling any such position.

Many cases of this character, several of them really important, have come under my own direction. Perhaps the most important is that which I am about to relate, and to which I have given the title of 'Tenant for Life.'

This case, as it frequently happens, came upon me when I was least expecting business, and when, indeed, I had 'put the shutters up for the day,' as an old detective companion of mine – a fellow long since dead (he was killed by a most gentlemanly banker who had left town for good, and who, after flooring John Hemmings, left England for good also) – would say.

It was on a Sunday when I got the first inkling of one of the most extraordinary cases which has come under my observation. It is on Sundays that I always put the shutters up. Even when I am not engaged in a case, I relax on a Sunday. I will not work if I can help it on a Sunday. I swim through the week, so to speak, for Sunday, and then I have twenty-four hours' rest before I plunge into my sea of detections once more.

I am what is called a talking companion, and I am bound to admit that women are in the habit of talking scandal, with me for a hearer, within three hours of my making their acquaintance.

Amongst others that I knew some years ago was a Mrs., Flemps. I think I first made her acquaintance because her name struck me as out of the common – it was out of the common, for I had not known her twenty-four hours before I learnt that she was married to a cabman, who on his father's side was a Dutchman who had been in the eel tirade at Billingsgate market.

It was this acquaintance, it was the mere notice of the name of Flemps, which led to the extraordinary chain of events which I shall now place before the reader exactly as I linked them together – premising only that I shall sink my part in the narrative, as fully as I shall be able.

As I have said above, I make Sunday a holiday, and coming to know the Flempses, and ascertaining that the cabman – perhaps with some knowledge of that cheerful way of spending the Sunday which I have heard distinguishes foreigners – was in the habit of using his cab as a private vehicle on a Sunday, and driving his wife out, I found my seventh days even more cheerful than I had yet discovered them to be. In plain English, during the summer through which I knew the Flempses, I frequently drove out of London with them a few miles into the country.

Flemps used to drive, of course, and I and his wife were inside, with all the windows down, in order that we might get as much of the country air as possible.

I find, by reference to the diary I have kept since I entered the service, and at which I work equally for pleasure, and to relieve my mind of particulars which would overweight it, for I may add that in this diary, which would be intolerable printed, I fix down every word of a case I hear, as closely as I can remember it, and every particular as near as I can shape it – I say I find, by reference to my diary, that it was the fourth Sunday I rode out with the Flempses, and the sixth week of my acquaintance with those people, whom upon the whole I found very respectable, that I got the first inkling of one of the best, even if one of the most dissatisfactory, cases in which I was ever engaged.

The conversation which called up my curiosity I am enabled to reproduce almost as it was spoken, for by the time the ride was over I had got so good a thread of the case in my head, that I thought it necessary to book what I had already learnt.

Mrs. Flemps was a worthy woman, who loved to hear herself talk, a failing it is said with her sex. From the hour in which I made her familiar with me, I ceased to talk much to the good woman; I listened only, and rarely opened my mouth except to ask a question.

By the way, I should add here that I in no way sponged upon the Flempses; I always contributed more than one-third to the eatables and drinkables we took with us in the cab, and thereby I think I paid my share of the cab, which would have taken them whether I had been in London or Jericho.

The first words used by the couple in reference to the case attracted my attention.

We had got into the cab, she and I, and he was looking ill at the window as he smoothed his old hat round and round.

"Jemmy," he said, her name being Jemima, "where shall us drive today?"

"Well, Jan," said she – he had been christened after his Dutch father – "we aint been Little Fourpenny Number Two way this blessed summer."

"*That's* it," said Jan, with a triumphant, crowing tone. "Little Fourpenny Number Two."

And mounting his box, he drove out of the yard so briskly that for a moment, as we went over the kerbstone, I thought the only road we were about to take was that of destruction.

The extraordinary highway we were about to take naturally led me to make some inquiries; for it can readily be understood by the public that if there is one thing a detective – whether female or male – is less able to endure than another, it is a mystery.

"That's a queer road we're going, Mrs. Flemps," said I; and speaking after the manner of her class – for I may say that half the success of a detective depends upon his or her sympathy with the people from whom either is endeavouring to pick up information.

"Yes," said Mrs. Flemps; and as she sighed I knew that there was more in the remark than would have appeared to an ordinary listener. I do not use the words 'ordinary listener' at all in a vain sense, but simply with a business meaning.

"Is it a secret?"

"What, Little Fourpenny?" she called out, as we bumped over the London stones.

"Number Two," I added, with a smile.

She shook her head.

"There was no number two," she replied, "though there ought to have been."

Now this answer was puzzling. Both husband and wife felt mutual sympathy in the affair of 'Little Fourpenny Number Two' and yet it appeared no Little Fourpenny Number Two had ever existed.

"Tell me all about it, Mrs. Flemps," said I, "if it's no secret."

She answered in these words – "Which I will, my dear, when we reach the gardings, but can't a jolting over the stones."

We drove six miles out of London, and got on the level country road. There is no need to say whither we went, because *places* are of no value in this narrative.

It is enough to say it was six miles out of London, and on a level country.

As we made a turn in the road Mrs. Flemps became somewhat excited; and almost immediately afterwards the cabman turned round, – and looking at his wife, he said –

"We're a coming to the werry spot."

The cab was drawn about two hundred yards further on, and then Jan Flemps pulled rein, and got off his box.

"There's the werry milestone," he said, pointing to one at the side of the road; "and the werry identical where I lost Little Fourpenny Number Two."

And it was at this point that Mrs, F. remarked –

"Cuss the thutty pound."

"Never mind, old woman, we wanted it bad enough then, Lord knows; and but for it this cab might never ha' been druv by me, so put an han'some mug on it, old woman."

The reader will concede that this conversation was sufficiently appetising to attract any one – to a detective it spoke volumes.

I said nothing till the cab was once more in motion, and I could tell how heartily the cabman appreciated the spot by the slow pace at which we left it behind us, and by the several times he looked back lingeringly at the milestone.

Meanwhile Mrs. Flemps, within the cab, was shaking her head dolefully; and I could see, by the wistful, far-away appearance of her eyes, that in thought she was a long way beyond me and the cab.

When she woke up, which she did in a short time with an exclamation, and such a rough, cutting sentence as I have noticed the rougher sort of folk are in the habit of making the termination of any show of sentiment, I reminded her that she had promised to tell me the history of Little Fourpenny.

"Wait, my dear, till we get to the gardings, and Jan himself will oblige. He tells the tale better nor I do."

Therefore I said no more till we had ended our plain dinner at the tea-gardens which were our destination. The meal done, and Jan at his pipe, I reminded Mrs. F. once more of her promise; and she mentioning the matter to the cabman, it appeared to me that he was not at all disinclined to refresh himself with a recital of the history.

It is necessary that I should give it, in order that the reader may appreciate how a detective can work out a case.

"I were a going home in my cab one night, more nor a little time ago."

"It were in 'forty-eight, when the French were a fighting Lony Philippe," said the cabman's wife.

"I was a goin' home, not in the best o' humours, when a comin' across 'amstead 'eath I overtook a woman a staggerin' under what I thought were a bundle."

"It were a child," said Mrs. Flemps.

"Yes, it were," the cabman continued; "and it had on'y been in this precious world a fortnight. I pulled up, seein' her staggerin'; and to cut it short here-abouts, I told her she might come up on the box along o' me, for it were not likely I could let a tramp in on the cushions. She were werry weak, and the infant were the poorest lookin' kid I ever seed – yet purty to look at as I sor by the gass."

"As he sord by the gass!" responded Jemima.

"Well, after some conversation with that young woman, I pulled up at a public, and treated her and your obedient; and which whether it were the rum put me up to it, or it were in me before and I knowed it not, no sooner had I swallowed that rum than the idea was plain and wisible afore me. 'What are you a goin' to do with it?' I said, pointing to the young un. 'I don't know,' says she a lookin' out towards London. 'Father?' says I. 'No,' says she. I then looks out, and points towards London, which she thereupon shook her head; but she didn't turn on the water, being, I think, too far gone for that. 'Which,' said I, 'if you can do nothin' for her (knowin' as she'd told me it was a girl) somebody else may – my old woman and me, you see, never havin' had no family.'"

"Never having had no family – more's the pity," responded Mrs. Flemps.

"'Why,' says she, continued the cabman, 'who'd be troubled with another woman's child? – women have enough trouble with their own.' 'I would,' says I, 'my old woman never having had any, and not likely to mend matters.' 'Will you?' says she, and such a hawful light came upon that young woman's face as I never wish to see on another. 'Yes,' says I, 'and it shall be all fair and above board, and I'll give you my old woman's address, and what money I've got for her' – which it came about she got called Little Fourpenny, being that sum I had in my pocket after payin' for the rum, after a whole day out and only a shillin' fare. Well, the longs and the shorts of it are that that there wretched young woman gave me up the baby, and I gived her the fourpence, and she got down off the cab and went down a turning, and blest if ever she looked back once, and blest if ever she called at our place once – p'r'aps she lost the address though, and if she did, why she were not so bad after all, and p'r'aps she died – anyhow, that's how we came by Little Fourpenny."

"That's how we came by Little Fourpenny," responded Mrs. F., adding, as a kind of Amen, "blesser little 'art."

"Yes," said I, "but what of Little Fourpenny Number Two?"

"Ha, that's on'y five year ago. My Jemmy – meanin' Jemima, wasn't best pleased when I brought that poor Little Fourpenny home, and I think she thought I knew'd more of it than I did till she growed so uncommon unlike me – but let my wife have thought as she might, I'm sure no mother was ev'er sorrier than her were when Little Fourpenny was took and changed for the better."

"Much for the better!" said Mrs. F., with two or three tears in her eyes, as I detected.

"Lord, I see her now a cornin' with my dinner, bein' not so much nor ten year old, and all the rank with a word for Little Fourpenny. All the fellers o' the rank wanted to stand when Little Fourpenny went off the road, which it was but nat'ral. Yes, we missed her when she died at nine."

"At nine," responded Mrs, F., adding, "five years ago."

"And it was but nat'ral we should think as our Fourpenny was a good one, and as we was alone and might find another, which was the reason, as p'r'aps I began lookin' after Little Fourpenny Number Two, and bless you, my dear, cabmen, and I dersay policemen, don't have to look far any night o' the week without finding a wand'rin' woman as 'as got a little un she don't know what on earth to do with."

"Little Fourpenny hadn't been off the rank three months afore, sittin' on that very milestone as I pointed out, and one evenin' in this very month o' July, there I saw her. My 'art was in my mouth, for it was as though all them years had never been, and jest as though Little Fourpenny's mother was jest afore my boss's head agin. It was another on 'em. She was a woman with a little un as she didn't know what on earth to do with. Which I spoke to her, and havin' that experience of our gal, I soon made 'er understand me, though I do assure yer my 'art was in my mouth as I thought o' the other. She didn't understand me a' fust, but she did at last, and I thought she were arf 'er 'ed abit by the way she went on, sayin' as Providence 'ad interfered, when it were on'y me.

And she took the address greedy-like, but when I offered her the five shillins, doin' it pleasant like and callin' her mate, she shrinks back she does, and calls out to Heaven if she can sell her child. Which then promisin' to call and see my old woman, and kissin' the child till it got into my throat agin', she run orf with her arms wide out, and goin' from side to side like a jibber – which she never come to see the old woman!"

"Which she never come!" responded Mrs. F.; adding, "which if she had what could I 'a said, and which if she'd tore my eyes out I could not ha' complained."

"For you see," continued the cabman, "that there child and that there old woman o' mine never met."

"Never met!" responded Mrs. Flemps.

"For you must know," continued the cabman, "I sold that there child o' that there woman afore I'd left that there milestone a mile behind."

"A mile behind!" adds Mrs. Flemps, shaking her head.

"Lord lead us not into temptation, but I could not resist that there thutty poun', bein' at that identkle time worry hard up, owin' to havin' to pay damages for runnin' down a hold man which was more frightened nor hurt, but the obstinest old party ever a man druv, and had to pay 'im that identkle sum o' thutty poun's, which it seemed to me a kind o' providence when the woman offered that identkle sum, since it seemed to me as I was taken pity on acos of runnin' down that obstnit old gent while hard a thinkin' o' lost Little Fourpenny."

Now by this time my curiosity had been thoroughly roused. It was impossible to avoid comprehending that the child that the wretched mother had given up to the cabman had been literally sold by him within twenty minutes of the time when he came into the possession of her.

And perhaps it is necessary that I should remark that I was not struck with the idea that it was at all unlikely that this cabman should have met a second woman in his life ready to part with her child. I am, detective as I live, almost as much ashamed as pained to admit that there is not a night passes in this large city of London during which you are unable to find wretched mothers ready to part with their children. Perhaps I should add that my experience leads me to believe that these poor women are mothers for the first time – mothers of but a very short duration, and that therefore, while they have not been with their, little ones long enough to be unable to separate from them, they are still under the influence of that horror of their position, and consequent fear or dread of the child, which is the result of their memory of a time when they were free and respected. These young women are mostly seduced servant and work girls. Poor things! – we detectives, especially us women detectives, know quite enough of such matters.

Said I to the cabman –

"Who was the woman who took the child?"

"Why, 'ow should *I* know? I was a joggin' on, with the little un on the floor o' the cab, atween the two cushions to prevent collisions, when she calls 'Cab!' to me. ''Gaged,' says I. 'I'll pay you anythink,' says she. 'Well,' thinks I, 'anyhow you're a queer customer.' She were about thirty – a wild looking party as ever I saw by the gas-lamp, under which she was standin', but she were a real lady, and had dark eyes. 'Can't do it,' says I. Then she says, 'Have you come fa down the road?' 'About three miles,' says I. 'Ha,' says she, ''ave you seen a woman with a child? which, continued the cabman, you might ha' knocked me orf my box when she made that there remark – 'a poor woman,' says she, 'with a very young child?' And then as luck would have it – or *ill* luck – which sometimes I think it were one, and at other times I'm sure it were the other; as some luck would 'ave it, at this identkle moment, the child sets up a howlin' fine 'What's that? – oh, what's that?' she asks, a fly in' at the cab-windy, and I can tell you I wa nearly a tumblin' orf my box, I was so took aback. 'Heaven 'ave sent it!' says she, lookin' in the cab, and I s'pose seein' on'y the child there at the bottom o' the cab, 'which,' says I, 'it's that identkle young woman's you was speakin' of!' Then she screals out she does; an' if there'd been a p'leaceman about *I* should ha' been in Queer Street, savin' your presence, my dear, a talkin' about the p'leace on a Sunday. Then I ups and tells her that me and my missus have lost our Little Fourpenny, and how I've got the kid; and then she calls out again that Heaven is at the bottom of it, and she says – 'My good man,' says she, 'here's thutty poun's,' which there was, all in gold, 'and take it, and give me the child,' and then she says, 'how that I can have no love for the child – not havin' ever seen it afore and 'ow by doin' as she wished, I might do great good, and, to cut it short – after a time – I gived 'er the child, and I took the thutty poun's; and that's how it was my old woman never, never saw the little un, and how it was, as I hoped that there poor mother would never call at our house. She never did; so p'r'aps them poor mothers are all alike, and don't care to look them in the face as they once deserted, and can't reasonubly ask back again, and that's how it was that my old woman never saw Little Fourpenny Number Two."

"Never saw Little Fourpenny Number Two!" responded Mrs. Flemps.

Now I may say at once that this tale, told in common English, by an ordinary man, smoking his common clay pipe in a plain tea-gardens in the suburbs of London – this tale called forth all the acumen and wits with which nature has endowed me. The detective was all alive as that extraordinary recital, told with no intention for effect, was slowly unfolded to me, with many stops and waves of the pipe, and repetitions with which I have not favoured the reader.

It was a most remarkable history, that of the woman who had obtained the child, from beginning to end.

The series of facts, accepting the cabman's statements as honest, and as he had no purpose to serve in deceiving me, I was at once inclined to suppose he spoke the truth – as he did; the series of facts was wonderful from the beginning of the chapter to the end.

The extraordinary list of unusual facts began with a woman, evidently belonging to a good class, being out late at night and hailing a cab. Then followed her inquiry concerning a woman with a very young child. To this succeeds the discovery of the child in the cab, and the ejaculation that Heaven has been good to her; and finally had to be considered the fact of her having thirty pounds in gold with her, and which she offers at once to the cabman for the child.

Accustomed to weigh facts, and trace out clear meanings, something after the manner of lawyers, a habit common to all detectives, before I began in a loose, half-curious way to question Flemps upon the history he had betrayed to me, I had made out a tolerable case against the lady.

As she knew that the woman had passed that way it appeared evident to me that she had seen her, guessing her to be a beggar, at some earlier period of the evening than that at which she addressed the cabman. And as after the cabman refused her for a fare she expressed great joy at hearing the crying of the infant, the inference stood that her despair at the cabman's refusal was in some way connected with the child itself.

Continuing out this reasoning – and custom was so ready within me that the process was finished before the cabman had – I came to the conclusion, after duly balancing the fact of her having with her thirty pounds in gold, and her bringing the cabman with it, that for some reason unknown she had pressing need for a child. I felt certain that she had seen the woman in an earlier part of the evening, that she had set out to overtake the woman, to purchase the child off her, if possible, and that meeting the cab, the driver of which could have no knowledge of her, she had hailed him in the hope of more speedily overtaking the woman and child.

The questions, as a detective, I wished answered were these –

Who was she?

Why did she act as she did?

Where was she?

At once I apprehended I should have little difficulty in ascertaining where she was, provided she still lived in the district, and provided the cabman could give me some clue by which to identify her.

For I may tell you at once that I saw crime in the whole of this business. Children are not bought in the dark in the midst of fear and trembling, if all is clear and honest sailing.

So pretending to be really interested in the story, which I was, I began putting questions.

"Did you ever learn anything more?"

"Nothink," said he.

And his wife, of course, responded and repeated.

"You never saw the woman again?"

"Never."

Echoed by Mrs. F. I will leave her repeats out from this time forth.

"How long ago did it happen? You interest me so much!"

"Five years this blessed July."

"Then it was in the July of 1858." I knew that by the date of Little Fourpenny's death.

"It was."

[I should here point out to the reader that though I put this singular case, 'Tenant for Life,' as the leading narrative in my book, it is one of the later of my more remarkable cases.]

"You are quite sure about the milestone?" I said.

"Quite," he replied.

"What kind of a woman was she?"

"Which," the cabman continued, "I could no more say nor I could fly – save she was wildish-looking, and had large black eyes, and was an out-and-out lady."

"Did she – pardon my being so curious – did she have any peculiarity which you remarked?"

"Any pecooliarity? No, not as I am aweer on."

"No mark – no way with her which was uncommon?"

"None sumdever," said the cabman. "Ha! I year 'er now. 'Firty poun's,' says she, which I could hardly unnerstand 'er at fust; 'firty poun's for that child,' says she, 'firty poun's.' But what 'ave you started for, my dear?" he asked me.

"Which," here his wife added, "well she may start, pore dear, with you a tellin' about Littl Fourpenny in a way to child 'er blood."

Now, the fact is, I had started because I thought I saw the end of a good clue. We detective have quite, a handbook of the science of our trade, and we know every line by heart. One o the chief chapters in that unwritten book is the one devoted to identification. The uninitiate would be surprised to learn how many ways we have of identification by certain marks, certai ways, certain personal peculiarities – but above all, by the unnumbered modes of speaking the form of speaking, the subjects spoken of, and above all the impediments or peculiarities o speech. For instance, if we are told a party we are after always misplaces the 'w' and 'v,' we ar inclined to let a suspected person pass who answers in all other ways to the description, excep in this case of the 'v' and 'w.' We know that no cunning, no dexterity would enable the man w are seeking to prevent the exhibition of this imperfection, even if he were on his guard, which h never is. He may change dress, voice, look, appearance, but never his mode of speaking – never his pronunciation.

Now, amongst our list of speech-imperfections is one where there is an impossibility to pronounce the troublesome 'th' and where this difficult sound is replaced by an 'f,' or a 'd,' or sometimes by one or the other, according to the construction of the word.

This imperfection I hoped I had discovered to be distinguishable as belonging to the woman who had purchased the child.

"Do you mean, Mr. Flemps," I said, – "do you mean to say that the woman mid *firty* instead of *thirty*? How odd."

"'Firty' says she, and that were the reason why I could not comprehend 'er at fust. 'Firty' says she; an' it was on'y when the gold chinked as I knowed what she meant."

"And you have never seen nor heard from her any more?"

"It wasn't likely as she would, if you'd a seen her go off as she did."

"And which way did she go?"

"Why a co'rse as I met her, my dear, and as she was coming from somewhere to foller the young woman with the kid, she backed to'ards London, and I 'ad to pass 'er afore I left her behind, an' she never so much as looked at me."

I did not ask any more questions.

I suppose I grew silent; and especially so when we got in the cab and were driving once more borne.

Indeed, Mrs. Flemps said she had no doubt that he had quite upset me with their tale of Little Fourpenny.

"When we reached the milestone, however, Mrs, F. was as full of the subject as ever; and I need not say that – though perhaps I said little – I was very hard at work putting this and that together.

After we had passed the milestone, every house on each side of the way had a strange fascination for me. I hungered after every house as it was left behind me, fancying each might be the one which sheltered the infant.

That I would work it out I determined.

So far I had these facts:

1. The woman must have lived near the road, or she would not have seen the beggar and her child, provided these latter had been on the high road when seen by the former.

2. The time which had elapsed between seeing the woman and meeting the cabman could not have been very great, or she never would have hoped to find the mother and child.

3. The occurrence had only taken place five years previously, and therefore the woman might not have moved out of the neighbourhood.

4. The purchase of the child in such a manner suggested it was to be used for the purpose of deception – in all probability to replace another.

5. Therefore, deception being practised somebody was injured – in all probability an heir.

6. The woman was not needy, or she could not have offered thirty pounds in gold to a stranger, and evidently at a very short notice for it was clear there could have been no demand for the child when she saw it with the mother.

7. Whoever she was she had the far from ordinary failure of speech which consists of an inability to utter the sound of 'th.'

8. Finally, and most importantly, *I had dates.*

Poor Flemps and his wife – they little thought what a serpent of detection they had been nourishing in their cab. I believe they thought I was a person living on my small property, and helping my income out by a little light millinery.

With the information I had already obtained, I determined to try and sift the matter to the bottom; and I may as well state that, not having anything on my hands at that time, I set to work on the Monday morning, telling Mrs. Flemps that I had some business to look after, and being wished luck from the very bottom of her heart by that cajoled woman.

I took a lodging in the first place as near that milestone as I could find one – it was a sweet little country room, with honeysuckle round each window.

I may at once say that the first part of my work was very easy.

Within two days of my arrival at my little lodging at the honeysuckle cottage, I had found out enough to justify me in continuing the search.

As I have said, I could have no reason to doubt the cabman, because he could have no object in deceiving me. But evidence is what detectives live upon.

The first thing I did was to find traces, if possible, of the mother.

It will be remembered that the mother showed great sorrow at losing the child, and that yet she never knocked at the cabman's door. The inference I took was this, that as she had shown love for the child, and as she had never sought to see it after parting with it, that she had been prevented by one of two catastrophes – either she had gone mad, or she had died.

Where was I to make inquiries?

Clearly of the first relieving officer who lived past the milestone, at which she had parted with the child, and in the opposite direction to that which the cab had taken – for I know much of those poor mothers – they always flee from their children when they have parted from them, whether this parting be by the road of murder, or by desertion, or by the coming of some good Samaritan (like the cabman) who, having no children of his own, is willing to accept a child who to its maternal mother is a burden.

I went past the milestone, made inquiries and in time found the relieving officer's house. I was answered in double quick time. I think the man supposed I was a relation, and that perhaps I would gain him some credit by reimbursing the parish, through his activity, its miserable outlay in burying the poor woman.

For she was dead.

Circumstances pointed so absolutely to her as the woman who had parted with her child, that I had no reasonable doubt about my conclusion.

In that month of July, on the night of the 15th, a woman was brought in a cart to the officer's door. The man who drove stated that he found the woman lying in the road, and that had not his horse known she was there before he did, she must have been rim over.

The woman was taken to the union infirmary, and that place she only left for the grave.

She never recovered her senses while at the union hospital. She was found, upon her regaining half consciousness, to be suffering from fever, and as she had but very recently become a mother (not more than a fortnight) the loss of her child made the attempt to overcome that fever quite futile.

She died on the tenth day it appeared, and she had not spoken at her death for three.

[I should perhaps here remark that I am condensing in this page the statements of the relieving officer and a pauper woman who was nurse in the workhouse hospital.]

I was at no loss to understand that this speechlessness was due to opium, which my experience had already taught me is given in all cases where a fever-patient has no chance of life, and in order to still those ravings which would only make the death more terrible.

But during the preceding week she had said enough to convince me, upon hearing reported, that she was the mother of the child. She had called out for her baby, pressing her poor breasts as she did so, and frequently she had shrieked that she heard the cab far, far away in the distance.

I returned to my little cottage lodging not over and above pleased. If there is one thing which foils us detectives more certainly than another, it is death.

Here we have no power. Distance is to us nothing – but we cannot get to the other side of the tomb. Time we care little for, seeing that during life memory more or less holds good. Secrecy we laugh at in all shapes but that of the grave.

It is death which foils us and frequently stops a case when it is so nearly complete as to induce the inexperienced to suppose that it is perfect.

I saw at once that I had lost my chief witness – the mother.

Now came the question – was the child itself alive?

If dead, there was end of my inquiry.

However detectives never give up cases; it is the cases which give up the detectives.

It now became necessary to ascertain what children were born in the milestone district in the month of July, 1858, for I have already shown that the purchaser of the child must have come from somewhere in the neighbourhood of her purchase, and I have hinted that a child purchased under such circumstances as those set about the sale of the child in question, presupposes that the infant is to be used in a surreptitious manner, and in a mode therefore, *prima facie* as the lawyers say, which is, in all probability, illegal, by acting detrimentally upon some one who benefits by the child's death.

To ascertain what children had been born in the district during that month of July, was as easy a task as to convince myself that the child in question had been registered as a new birth by the woman who had purchased him of the cabman.

The reader has in all probability made out such a suppositive case as I did, and to the following effect:

The woman-purchaser saw the mother and child an hour or more before she met the cabman, and had some conversation with her.

This supposition was confirmed by the knowledge I obtained that this woman, found in the road, had a couple of half-crowns in the pocket of her dress.

It will be remembered that she refused Flemps's money.

Between the time of seeing the woman and bargaining with the cabman, it may readily be supposed that a pressing demand for a newly born child had become manifest, when the woman recalled to her mind the beggar and child she had seen, hoped the poor creature's poverty would be her temptress's opportunity, and so set out to find her; when a chain of circumstances, which the ordinary reader would call romantic, but which I, as a detective, am enabled to say is equaled daily in any one of many shapes, led to her possession of the infant.

I searched two registers, and made such inquiries as I thought would be useful. Happily in both cases I had to deal not with the registrar, but with his deputy, who is, as a rule, the more manageable man. We detectives have much to do with registrars in all of their three capacities.

I knew that in all probability I had to deal with, what we call in my profession, *family* people. It was no tradesman's wife or sister I had to deal with. The cabman had said she was a real lady, (your cabman is one who by his daily experience has a good eye at guessing the condition of a fare), and the immediate command of thirty pounds told me that money was easy with her.

My readers know that the profession or trade of the father is always mentioned in the registration of birth; and therein I had a clue to the father or alleged father.

The probability stood that he would be represented as a 'gentleman.'

There were three births I found, after both registers were examined, in that month, in the registration of which the father was set out as 'gentleman.'

The addresses in each case I copied – giving, I need not say, some very plausible excuse for so doing; my acts being of course illustrated with several silver portraits of her majesty the Queen.

And here I would urge upon the reader that he need feel no tittle of respect for my work so far. To this point it had been the plainest and simplest operation in which a detective could be employed. Registers were invented for the use of detectives. They are a medicine in the prosecution of our cures of social disorder.

Indeed it may be said the value of the detective lies not so much in discovering facts, as in putting them together, and finding out what they mean.

Before the day was out I dropped two of my extracts from the registers as valueless. The third I kept, feeling pretty sure it related to the right business, because of two facts with which I made myself acquainted before the day was over. The first of these lay in the discovery that the house at which the birth in question had been alleged to take place was within nine hundred yards of the milestone, where this business had commenced; the second, that the mother of the child had died in giving it birth.

I felt pretty certain that I was on the right road at last, but before I consulted my lawyer (most detectives of any standing necessarily have their attorneys, who of course are very useful to men and women of my calling), I determined to be quite certain I was not wasting my time, and to be well assured I was not about to waste my money; for it often happens that a detective, like any other trader, has to lay out money before he can see more.

Learning that the household consisted of the infant – an heiress, then five years of age – the father, and his sister, I fixed my suspicions immediately upon the latter, as the woman who had purchased the child.

If she were the woman, I knew I had the power of convicting her, in my own mind, by hearing her speak; for it will be remembered that I have said that imperfection of speech is one of the surest means of detection open to the use of a high-class detective.

Of course I easily gained access to the house. It is the peculiar advantage of women detectives, and one which in many cases gives them an immeasurable value beyond that of their male friends, that they can get into houses outside which the ordinary men detectives could barely stand without being suspected.

Thoroughly do I remember my first excuse – we detectives have many – such as the character of a servant, an inquiry after same supposed mutual friend, or after needle-work, a reference from some poor person in the neighbourhood, a respectful inquiry concerning the neighbourhood to which the detective represents herself as a stranger. I introduced mysel as a milliner and dressmaker who had just come to the neighbourhood, and, with the help o an effective card, which I always carry, and which is as good as a skeleton-key in opening bi doors, soon I reached the lady's presence.

Before she spoke I recognised her by the large black eyes which the cabman had noted oven in the night time.

She had not spoken half-a-dozen words before she betrayed herself; she used the lette 'f' or 'v' where the sound 'th' should properly have been pronounced as 'Ve day is fine,' fo 'The day, etc.'

This mal-pronunciation may read very marked in print, but in conversation it may be use for a long time without its being remarked. The hearer may feel that there is somethin

:ong with the language he is hearing, but he will have to watch very attentively before he scovers where the fault lies, unless he has been previously put upon his guard.

I had.

I went away; and I remember as I left the room I was invited to return and make another visit.

I did.

Thus far all was clear.

I had, I felt, found the house – the purchaser of the child – and the child herself, for the infant ıs a girl.

What I had now to find out was the reason the child had been appropriated, and who if ıybody had suffered by that appropriation.

It was now time to consult with my attorney. Who he is and what name he goes by are atters of no consequence to the reader. Those who know him will recognise that gentleman-·law by one bit of description – he has the smallest, softest, and whitest hand in his profession.

I put the full case before him in a confidential way of business – names, dates, places, spicions, conclusions, all set out in fair order.

"I think I see it," said he, "but I wont give an opinion today. Call in a week."

"Oh, dear me, no!" said I, "my dear M—, I can't wait a week. I'll call in three days."

I called on the third day – early in the morning.

The attorney gave me a nod, said he was very busy, couldn't wait a moment, and then chatted ith me for twenty minutes. I should say rather he held forth, for I could barely get a word in lgeways; but what he says is generally worth listening to.

He wanted further information: he desired to know the maiden name of the wife and the ace of her marriage to Mr. Shedleigh – which I will suppose the name of the family concerned his affair.

I was to let him know these further particulars, and come again in three more days.

At first sight this was a little difficult. Singularly enough, the road to this information I und to be very simple, for as a preliminary step, ascertaining from the turnpike-man in that :ighbourhood where Mrs. Shedleigh had been buried, I visited her tomb, in the hope perhaps at her family name and place of settlement might appear on the stone, which often happens nongst the wives of gentry.

In this lady's case no mention was made either of her family name or place of residence, ıt nevertheless I did not leave the cemetery without the power of furnishing my lawyer with formation quite as good as he required.

The lady had been buried in a private vault at the commencement of the catacombs, and the ›ffin was to be seen through the gratings of a gateway, upon which was fixed a coat of arms engraved brass.

Of course as a detective, who has to be informed on a good many points, I knew that the ·ms must refer to the deceased, and therefore I surprised the catacomb keeper considerably hen, later in the day, I spoke once more with him, and told him I wanted to take a rubbing of ıe brass plate in question.

The request being unusual, the usual difficulties of suspicion and prejudice were thrown in ıy way. But it is surprising how much suspicion and prejudice can be bought for five shillings, ıd to curtail this portion of my narrative I may at once say I took away with me an exact copy : the late lady's coat-of-arms. I need not say how this was done. Any one knows how to take facsimile of an engraved surface by putting a sheet of paper on it, and rubbing a morsel of ıarcoal, or black chalk over the paper. The experiment can be tried on the next embossed ›ver, with a sheet of notepaper and a trifle of lead pencil.

This rubbing I took to the lawyer, and then I waited three days.

He had enough to tell me by the end of the second.

In the simplest and most natural way in the world, he had discovered a reason for the appropriation of the child, and not only had that information been obtained, but the name of the man injured by the act, and his interest in the whole business was at the command of the attorney.

We neither of us complimented the other on his discoveries, each being aware that the other had but put in force, the principles and ordinary rules of his business.

I had gained my knowledge by reference to registers, he his by first consulting a book of the lauded gentry and their arms, and secondly by the outlay of a shilling and an inspection of a will in the keeping of the authorities at Doctors' Commons.

The lawyer had found the arms as copied by me from the tomb-gate in a book of landed gentry, had learnt an estate passed from the possession of Sir John Shirley in 1856, by death, and into the ownership of his daughter, an heiress, and wife of Newton Shedleigh, Esq. The entry further showed that the lady, Shirley Shedleigh, had died in 1857, and that by her marriage settlements the property descended upon her children. A child of this lady, named after her Shirley Shedleigh, was then the possessor of the estates, which were large, while the father, Newton Shedleigh, as sole surviving trustee, controlled the property.

So the matter stood.

"I can see it all," said the lawyer, who, I am bound to say, passed over my industry in the business as though it had never existed. "I can see it all. The defendant, Newton Shedleigh, marries an heiress, who, by her marriage settlement, maintains possession of her estate through trustees. As in ordinary cases, these estates devolve upon her children, supposing her to have any, and that they outlive her. But here comes the nicety of the question. If she have children, and they all die before her – granted that her husband outlives her, he, by right of the birth of his and her children, becomes a tenant for life in her possessions, though by the settlement, in event of the wife dying without children to inherit her property, it passes to her father's brother."

"Well?" said I.

"The motive for a supposititious heir is evident. The lady dies in childbed, as the dates of her death and of the birth of her assumed child testify – in all probability her infant is born dead, and therefore the mother dying without having given the father a just claim to the tenantage for life – by the conditions of the settlement the property would at once upon the death of the wife, pass to her uncle, her father's brother. To avoid this, the beggar-woman's child has been made to take the place of the dead infant. The case is about as clear as any I have put together."

"But—" Here I stopped.

"Well?"

"Your argument suggests accomplices."

"Yes."

"Four – the father, his sister, the doctor, and the nurse."

"Four, at least," said the lawyer.

"Do you know, or have you heard of the true owner of the estates?"

The reader will observe that I and the lawyer had already given in a verdict in the case.

"I do not know him – I have made two or three enquiries. He is Sir Nathaniel, Shirley. From what I can hear he does not bear a very good name, though it is quite impossible, I hear, to bring any charge against him."

"This will cost money," I said.

"It will cost money," echoed the lawyer, I have always noticed that when a lawyer has anything not too agreeable to say, generally he echoes what you yourself observe.

"Is he rich?"

"Who?" asks the lawyer, with that love of precision which irritates any woman, even when she is a detective.

"Sir Nathaniel Shirley."

"I hear not."

"Who, then, is to pay expenses?"

"Who is to pay expenses?" says the lawyer, repeating my words. And then, after a pause, as though to show he made a difference between my own words and his, he adds – "Expenses there certainly will be."

"Shall we speak to Sir Nathaniel at once?"

"*You* can speak to Sir Nathaniel at once. As for me, I shall wait till the baronet speaks to me."

"Oh!" said I.

"Yes," replied, my attorney, softly turning over a heavy stick of sealing wax, such as, in all my detective experience, I never saw equalled out of a law-office.

It stood clear that the case was to be left in my hands till it was plain sailing, and then the lawyer would take the helm. I have noticed that the law gentlemen with whom I have had to do are much given to this cautious mode of doing business.

We detectives, who know how much depends upon risk and audacity, are perhaps inclined to look rather meanly upon this cautiousness, knowing as we do that if we were as fearful of taking steps we should never gain a crust.

"I'll see you again, Mr. M—, in a few days."

"Well," said he, looking a little alarmed I thought, "whatever you do don't drop it; turn the matter over in your mind, and let me see you again in three days."

"Thank you," said I; "I'll come when I want you."

I think I noticed a little mixture of surprise and satisfaction on the lawyer's countenance – surprise that I showed some independence, satisfaction by virtue of the intimation my words conveyed that I did not mean to abandon the case.

Abandon the case!

Good as many of the cases in which I had been engaged might have been, I knew that not one had been so near my fame, and, in a small way, my fortune, as this; for I may tell you we detectives are like actors, or singers, or playwrights, who are always hoping for some distinction which shall carry them to the top of their particular tree.

I had saved some money, for I am not extravagant; and though my necessary expenses were large, I had for some years earned good money, and had laid by a trifle, and so I determined myself to find the money which was required to begin and carry on this inquiry.

So far I had got together only facts. Now I had to prove them.

To do this, it was necessary that I should gain an entry into the house.

I had, as the reader knows, planted my first attempt by calling at the house and presenting at the outset a small written card, setting out that I was Miss Gladden, a milliner and dressmaker, who went out by the day or week.

This ruse practised with success upon Mrs. Flemps, and resulting in two caps and a bonnet for that lady, I had always exorcised; indeed, I may say, that I took lessons as an improver in both those trades, in order the better to carry on my actual business, which, I will repeat here once again, is a necessary occupation, however much it may be despised.

If this world lost all its detectives it would very soon complainingly find out their absence, and wish them, or some of them, back again.

But I could not wait till Miss Shedleigh sent for me, even supposing that she remembered me and my application. Even this supposition was questionable.

It therefore became necessary to tout that lady once again. I sent up to the house a specimen of my work, and with it a letter to the effect that my funds were running low and I was becoming uneasy.

The answer returned was that I could come up to the house on the following day at nine in the morning.

I was there to time.

The house was very splendid – magnificently appointed; and the number of servants told of very considerable wealth.

The lady of the house, this Miss Catherine Shedleigh, was one of the pleasantest and most delightful of women – calm, amiable, serene, and possessing that ability to make people at home about her which is a most rare quality, and which we detectives know sufficiently well how to appreciate.

I was located in the housekeepers room, and I was soon surrounded with work.

I had not been in the mansion two hours before I saw the little girl upon whose birth so much had depended.

She was a very pleasant child – nothing very remarkable; and her age, as given by the housekeeper, tallied exactly with the cabman's story.

The arrival of the child, who, to look upon, was comely without being pretty, gave me that opportunity for which I was waiting, I had felt pretty sure I should soon see the heiress; knowing that if children are not desirous of seeing new faces in a house, their younger nurses always are.

"The little missy has lost her mother, hasn't she?" I asked the housekeeper, an open-faced and a candid-spoken woman. Somehow we close-mouthed detectives have a great respect for open, candid-speaking people.

"Yes," said the housekeeper. "Miss Shedleigh never knew her mamma."

"Indeed! How was that? Will you kindly pass me the white wax? Thank you."

"Mrs. Shedleigh died, in childbed."

"Dear me, poor lady!" said I. Then, after a pause, I asked, "Did you know her, ma'am?"

The housekeeper looked up for the moment, a little offended. She soon regained her ordinary amiability, and replied –

"Yes, I was housekeeper to her mother, and afterwards to her father, up to the time of her marriage, and we both came to this house together."

"Ha! Then you wore present at her death, poor lady."

"Pardon me, my dear," the old lady continued. "I do not think there is any need to pity my lady – as I always called her after her mother's, Lady Shirley's death – she was sufficiently good not to fear death over much."

"Did she die peaceably, may I ask, Mrs. Dumarty?"

"I was assured she did."

"Oh, you were not present, Mrs. Dumarty?"

"No, my dear, I was not; and I shall never forgive myself for having been away at the time. But the fact is, that we did not expect any addition to the family for fully two months from the time when the poor dear lady suffered; and I – I shall never forgive myself – had gone down home into the country to see our relations – I mean mine and my lady's, we both coming from one part."

"Oh!" I said, balked; for it was clear, as far as she herself was concerned, Mrs. Bumarty was valueless as one of my witnesses.

"There never was such an unfortunate business as that; and dear me, my dear, talking about it has so confused me that I think I must have made a wrong seam! Yes, I have – it's two different lengths!"

"But the lady was not alone?" said I.

"No, not alone," replied the housekeeper; and then she broke off from the tone of voice she was using, and said, in a higher key, "But you do seem strangely interested in the family?"

"O dear, no," said I; "but it is a way of mine when I am working for a family, I beg your pardon, and will not offend again."

The old lady nodded her head seriously as she pursed up her lips and began to unrip the seam she had foundered on; but she was not silent for long. Soon she began to speak again; and as a kind of apology for having been a little severe, she became more communicative than she had hitherto shown herself.

"My lady was not alone," she said, "though more might have been about her. For instance, Mr. Shedleigh was away from home, though to be sure his sister was in the way."

"What! Was he not in the house when his wife died?"

"No, poor dear; and I'm told that when he learnt the catastrophe – by electric telegraph – he was near broken-hearted, and mayhap he would have been had it not been for the little daughter. It upset him so he could not travel for two days. I learnt the news by electric telegraph, and I shall never forgive myself that I was away."

Here was information!

It was clear, if the housekeeper was to be believed, and she could have no aim in deceiving me, that the father was as ignorant as Sir Nathaniel Shirley of the real state of the case.

"Do you think," said I, leading up to another line in the case – "Do you think the doctor who attended the lady was a clever man?"

"Bless you, my dear," said the housekeeper; and I began to notice that she was becoming gratified rather than angry at the interest I was taking in the family. "Dr. Ellkins was the cleverest of medical men."

"Was?" I said, interrogatively.

"Dead," the housekeeper replied, in a kind of fatalistic voice. "He was never a very strong man, I should say, and he nought never to have tried the journey. He went to Madeiry, my dear, and in Madeiry he died."

So here was another of the four witnesses upon whom I relied beyond detection.

"Perhaps the nurse neglected the poor lady," I said, turning to another branch of my case.

"Ah me!" said the old housekeeper, "that could not be, for it was all so sudden and unexpected, and the death followed the birth so soon that she was not sent for till hours after my poor lady lay dead. The only one she had to help her in her trouble was her dear sister, Miss Shedleigh, who saw her through all her trouble. Miss Shedleigh herself narrowly escaped with her life, and she has been like a mother to our little darling ever since."

So, of those four supposed witnesses to the birth, one only existed who could be of use to me in unravelling the secret; that one was she who had been entirely guilty of the fraud – the sister-in-law of the late lady, and sister of the self-supposing father, whom I now looked upon to be in all probability as certainly deceived as Sir Nathaniel Shirley himself. He had not reached home till two days after the death of the lady, and therefore two days, at least, after the supposed birth of the child which now stood as the heiress to the property, which was very large.

The father was not in the house at the time of the birth or death.

The nurse had not been sent for.

The doctor was dead.

The sister-in-law alone remained. How could I approach her? It was she whose interest it w chiefly to be silent. She would be on her guard, and I could hope for nothing from her.

I began to see my chances of success getting narrower and narrower.

But I did not despair.

That same evening, after I had left the mansion for the night, I went down to the house which Dr. Ellkins had lived, having learnt the address of the housekeeper, and I found tha was still in the occupation of a medical man, who, to be here short, was he who had purchas Dr. Ellkins's business of that gentleman, when he decided upon leaving England.

To inquire if Dr. Ellkins had had an assistant, and, if so, where he could be found, w child's play.

No; Dr. Ellkins had had no assistant.

I had thanked the doctor's housekeeper for her information, and was turning away, whe blushed for myself at the omission I had made when she remarked – "The doctor had a 'prentic

"And where is he?" I asked.

"Dear me, mum, how ever should I know! At one o' the 'spitals up in London I suppo leastways, I know he said he was a going to a 'spital, and likewise to be a Guy."

This statement gave me courage, for I had had some experience of medical students. Havi had a case in which one ultimately became my prisoner, I knew that when this young man h said he was going to be a Guy he meant he was about to become a student at Guy's Hosp over London Bridge.

"What was his name?" I asked.

"Dear me, mum! I do hope he's got in no trouble – his chief fault, while he was with us, bei dancing – which were his fascination."

"No; no trouble. I want to ask him a question."

"Blessed be!" said the old lady; his name was George Geffins – a young man with the redd hair, which he were ever trying to change, and it comin'

out the brighter for what he did to that same."

Saying I would call again (I never did), I left the old housekeeper.

That same night I sent up word to the housekeeper at Shirley House, as Mr. Shedleig mansion was called, that I should not be able to be with her on the following day, and when t next sun rose it found me in London.

I was soon at Guy's Hospital, and within a quarter of an hour of seeing the building I h learnt that a Mr. George Geffins was a student at that place, and the porter, with a grin, h given me his private address.

It was then half-past nine o'clock, and upon reaching the house and getting into the passa I guessed that Mr. Geffins was at breakfast by the clicking of a spoon against a cup or sauc which I heard distinctly. When the landlady said a lady wanted to see him, the clicking of t spoon ended.

Accustomed to hear with more than ordinary acuteness – for I have the belief that the sens may be sharpened up to any extent – I heard Mr. Geffins say–

"Why the devil didn't you say I was out?"

Then he bawled – "Is that you, Matilda?"

"No," said I; "it's not Matilda."

"Ho!" said he; (it struck me he spoke in a relieved tone) – "Ho!" – coming to the door; "th who the devil are you, ma'am?"

It further struck me, and I am willing to admit it, that when he saw me, the gentleman in question betrayed no extraordinary inclination to become better acquainted.

The disinclination was the more marked when I said I had come upon business.

He was a dissipated looking young man, and it appeared to me lived about three years in one twelve-month.

However, he asked me into his parlour – the most forlorn and furniture-damaged apartment which I ever entered – and then awkwardly he asked me, his land-lady having quitted the room with a disturbed air, "What I wanted." He put 'the' and a strong word between 'what' and 'I,' but I refrain from quoting it.

"You were a pupil of Dr. Ellkins?"

"Oh, yes," he said, with a relieved air.

"You were so in 1858?"

"In 1858."

By this time, having got over his evident dread of me, he was beginning to suspect me, I saw.

"I only want to know whether you remember the birth of a child at Shirley House in the July of that year?"

"What, Mrs, Shedleigh's child? Oh, yes, I remember specially. What on earth are you asking me this for?"

"Simply because I want to find out the date of some business which relates personally to me, and which I can tell of once I know the date of the birth of Mr. Shedleigh's daughter."

"Well, I can tell you," said Mr. Geffins, "by as odd a chance as ever you heard. Sit down, ma'am, and excuse me going on with my breakfast; I've got to get to lecture by ten."

I sat down. It is the first lesson of a detective to oblige a victim; his second is to accept that victim's hospitality if he offers it. Nothing opens a man's or woman's mouth so readily as allowing him or her to fill yours.

"Will you take a cup of tea?" he asked.

I did immediately.

"Bless my soul," said he, "I remember the day only too well – the 15th of July it was – for well I remember seeing it on the summons paper – 'That on the said fifteenth of July, 1858, you did wilfully and of malice afore thought, etc.' You see the fact stood, it was our guv's old housekeeper's birthday, and I had promised her a surprise, and she got it in the shape of a whole bundle of crackers, all set alight at once just under her window. And the constable passing at that time, why I got summoned, and had to pay five shillings fine and thirteen shillings costs – well I remember the date. I have got the summons now. I remember it was the governor going up to Shirley House which gave me the, chance of firing 'em. But by Jove," he continue, taking a great bite out of his dry toast, "I must be quick, or I shall never be in time for lecture."

"Excuse me, sir," I continued, "but I want to hear every particular, about times. At what hour did Dr. Ellkins come home from Shirley House?"

"I think it was about ten – and at eleven he was rung up and had to go back to the house again!"

"Ha, exactly!" I said. "Now comes the point which especially interests me. I know he returned to the house, or I never could have wanted to know anything about this matter. May I ask why he returned to the house, or what excuse he made to you when he left his house? Did he say he was going back to Shirley House?"

"Oh yes! and I am quite sure he did go there, because it was the groom who came down for him."

"Is it possible? I wish you would tell me all about it!" I said in an eager tone, "seeing as you must I am indeed most interested in the details."

"Well now, look you here," and I must confess the lad improved upon acquaintance exactly as an ugly dog frequently will; "I'll tell you all about it. Ellkins was not expected to be up at the big house on that job for a good two months, and therefore you may guess he was rather surprised when he was sentfor at ten p.m., on the 15th of July. He came back before eleven, and I remember I asked him if it was all right, and I remember he said no, and it never was likely to be all right."

"What did he mean by that?" I asked.

"Well, you are not, easily shocked, are you?"

"No," I said, looking the young man plainly in the face.

I cannot reproduce the statement he made, but it ran plainly to the effect that Mrs. Shedleigh had not given birth to a living child, and that it was highly improbable that such could ever be the case.

Now this was the very information I wanted, but it would not have done to show this was the case, so I said, in as impatient a tone as I could assume –

"But, now, I want to know what was the time when the doctor again went to the house – if ever he went at all, which I doubt."

I must have completely thrown the young man off his guard as to my real attempt, for he set his cup down, and speaking in a far more gentlemanly tone than any he had yet used, he said –

"Oh, but I assure you that he did go to the house, and returned in about three hours. He looked amazingly upset, I assure you, and when I asked him if anything was amiss he replied Mrs. Shedleigh was dead. He said no more, and went into his room without wishing me goodnight, which for him was a very extraordinary thing to do – he being rather a civil man. Well, you may judge of my surprise the next morning when old Mother Smack – I beg your pardon, when the doctor's housekeeper said to me, 'So there's an heiress up at the great house. I suppose we shall have rare doings? Well, it was so; and when I asked the doctor he told me to hold my tongue, and added another birth had taken place. Then he begged I would say nothing about the affair, nor have I until now. But it matters little now, for I might talk about it, and damage the poor old doctor's reputation over so, and he would not feel it, for he has left the faculty and gone up above; let's hope for his diploma. You see, he had made a mistake, and I was afraid to say anything about it, for perhaps he helped the poor lady into her coffin – doctors *do* do that sort of thing sometimes, and it can't be helped; but really I hope, ma'am, you've got no more questions to ask me, and I hope I have been of service to you. If I stop any longer I shall be too late for lecture, and there'll be no end of a row."

Well, no, I replied, he had not been of much use to me, but I thanked him all the same, and would he allow me to call upon him again?

His jaw dropped. Well, he said, he did not care much to have women about his room, for that sort of thing got about and did a fellow no good, but I might come again, and – for *he* did not want to know my name – and would I kindly send in the name of Walker? I would remember the name – "Walker, you know." But really he *must* be off.

And so saying he bolted, leaving me in the parlour and actually alone with his landlady's silver spoons.

I had learnt far more than he supposed, more than even he, doctor as he was, had ever suspected, and I had no need to call upon him again, although at the time I suspected I should have to surprise him by appearing in my true character, and being instrumental in subpoenaing him as a witness.

What had I learnt in addition to what I already knew of the case?

More, far more than I can openly tell my readers, and yet they must be put in possession of y discovery in some more or less circumlocutory manner.

Know then that nature can bear such evidence of the inability of certain women to become others of living children, that long after death, even hundreds of years after death, if the eleton be perfect, medical men could swear that such an incapacity had existed.

With the knowledge I gained I knew that I had the proof of Miss Shedleigh's guilt in my vn hands.

An examination of the remains of the late body would set the question at rest and the bman if he could identify her, as I had no doubt he could, would bring home the guilt to her she denied it.

What should I do?

My actual duty was at once to inform the legal heir Sir Nathaniel Shirley, of my discovery. But here was he?

This I could most readily find out, in all probability, by returning to Shirley House and aking further inquiries.

* * *

pon reaching the mansion early on the following morning I could not help looking upon it ith a kind of awe, the knowledge being strong within me that only a short previous time it had een to me only as other houses.

The housekeeper welcomed me with a cheerfulness which went to my heart, but I told yself I was to remember that I had to deal with justice not pity.

The end of the detective's work is justice, and if he knows his place he must not look beyond at end.

What I was thoroughly to understand in this business of a 'tenant for life' was this – that by fraud people were enjoying property to which they had no claim. This was a state of things hich I, as a detective, had a right to set right, and this was the work I intended to complete.

I little thought how sincerely I was to wish I had never moved in this business – that I had ever questioned the cabman's wife, and never followed up these inquiries.

It appeared I had given great satisfaction by the work I had completed, and Miss Shedleigh ad pleasantly said to the housekeeper that I was a 'needle and thread treasure.'

I presume it was this success which paved the way to the housekeeper's familiarity. Let that e as it may, it is certain this morning she answered most of my questions – questions which esulted so absolutely out of her own remarks that she could have no suspicion I was cross-xamining her, poor dear old lady.

I learnt very much during that long day's work as I sat in the housekeeper's room.

To begin with the master of the house – the house-keeper said he was a most 'welcome' aster, but 'crotchetty, my dear;' and a question or so put me in possession of his crotchetiness, hich took no other shape than the endeavour to reap double as much wheat to the acre as had ver been raised by the most advanced farmers.

"Miss Shedleigh says," continued the housekeeper, "that her devoted brother hopes if he ucceeds to annihilate starvation – which our miss very truly says must be the case if he doubles ne quantity of wheat in the land; seeing that then it will be so plentiful that people will not want read, as they do now."

I own that this statement touched me; for though I may be a detective, I am still a woman. struck me as good and beautiful that a man should work all his life for the benefit of his fellow-men; and this the master of Shirley House certainly did, if the house-keeper's stateme were truthful. I saw no reason to doubt her words.

Every day throughout the year, I learnt, he was hard at work making experiments either c the land or in a kind of chemist's shop which it appeared he had in the mansion.

He took no pleasure, dressed plainly, ate sparingly, and slept little.

"Was he happy?" I asked.

"How can he be off being happy," said the old housekeeper, wise in her simple experienc "when all his life is spent in trying to help in the happiness of others?"

I changed the subject. "Was he fond of his daughter?" I asked.

It appeared he was devoted to his daughter in a plain, simple way; but that he had given h up almost wholly to the care of his sister.

"Had he loved his wife very much?" I asked.

For a moment the old housekeeper looked as about to assert her dignity again, but apparent she thought better of it, for she smiled and said –

"Yes, my dear; but she was fonder of him."

"Indeed!" I said.

"Yes, though he was almost old enough to be her father. She was but twenty when sh died, my dear; and very beautiful she looked, I do assure you, and like a woman who ha done her duty. She loved him, my dear, because he was trying to do good to the world; an though she was so much younger than her husband it made not the least difference, my de – it made not the least difference, I assure you. And when my lady was dead, she looked lik a woman who had done her duty."

"Did her family approve of the match, ma'am?" I said, "if I may make so bold as to as the question?"

"My lady had only her father to consult, my dear; for the only other relation to the fami was Sir Thomas's brother, now Sir Nathaniel, who was far away at the time, and who was n welcome visitor down in Rutlandshire, where we come from Mr. Shedleigh lives near Londo to attend the societies, and to be amongst gentlemen of science."

"Do you ever see Sir Nathaniel, now?" I asked, going on with my stitching.

"Oh, no, we never see him; Mr. Shedleigh and he are not getting on well together, thoug it's my impression our gentleman allows him an income, and a larger one than Sir Thom paid him."

"But – though perhaps you will think I am impudent in asking questions?"

"Not at all," the housekeeper said; "by no means. You have done that last piece beautifully

"Then I was going to ask, how is it that, Sir Nathaniel did not got the estates with the titl for I thought estates and titles generally went together?"

Said the housekeeper, "So they do, my dear, but in our case it was different. Sir Thoma did not inherit the estates from his father, but made the money which purchased them b banking, for he was a banker, and the greater part of the money he began with he had from first wife, for they were poor as a family, the sixth baronet having spent everything he coul spend, and that is the reason Sir Thomas left all the estates to his daughter, for which I kno Sir Nathaniel never forgave him – never."

"Where is Sir Nathaniel?" I asked.

"He lives, my dear, though I must say you are very curious about him, for the best part a Brighton for he has been a terrible man, and his health is not what it ought to be – but for a that he looks a gentleman, and to speak to, he is one."

"What has he done amiss?" I asked.

But here the housekeeper failed in her reply. She could only adduce very vague and faint rumours, all of which tended to prejudice me in favour of the man to whom I knew it was my duty to submit a history of my discoveries.

"That there must be something bad about Sir Nathaniel is certain," said the housekeeper, "or surely he would be welcome here; and he is not welcome here, though from here, I am pretty well sure, he gets what enables him to live as he does – the life of a gentleman."

There was then a pause. I broke it by saying –

"Was Mr. Shedleigh rich when he married your young lady?"

"As compared with my lady, my dear – no, but as not compared with her he was well to do – very well to do. People down in our parts, of course, said my young lady, a heiress, and beautiful, had thrown herself away; but that was nonsense, my dear, for never was woman happier."

And so the morning wore away. Each moment I picked up some new little fact that might be useful to me; but this is certain, that by the time the house-keeper's dinner arrived, my opinion of the brother and sister Shedleigh was much softened, and I began to look with some doubt in the direction of Sir Nathaniel; for there never was a truer remark than the observation that every grain of scandal helps to weigh down a character.

I may say at once that I remained working more than a week at Shirley House, and by the seventh day my opinion of the Shedleighs was very much altered for the better.

For you must note that we police officers see so much of the worst side of humanity, that, instead of following out a Christian principle, and believing all men to be honest till we find them out to be thieves, we believe all men to be thieves till we are certain they are honest people. Hence, when I dropped upon what I call my great changeling case, I supposed, quite as a matter of course, that I had to do with a crime – as undoubtedly I had; but it should be added at once that I found the crime tinged with a character of almost nobleness. It was crime, nevertheless.

However much I might find my opinion of the Shedleighs improved, I never once wavered in my determination of ultimately informing Sir Nathaniel of the means by which he had been defrauded. This was but justice.

* * *

For a week I worked in that house, and during that time I had amide opportunities of convincing myself of the characters of the people in it, and of obtaining all particulars which might be useful to me, and about which the housekeeper was able to yield me any information.

It will perhaps be well to condense at this point the work of that week.

In the first place, I think I have said that Sir Nathaniel only inherited the title; the property left by Sir Thomas Shirley to his daughter being made by himself in his capacity of banker. That property consisted of no less than four large landed estates, the income from which was accumulating at what may be called compound interest.

And it was during this week that, by a suggestion from my attorney, the case appeared in another light from that in which it had previously stood. The existence of the little girl and heiress kept the father from the enjoyment of the full income yielded by his late wife's property, which he would have possessed had the child died. It was, therefore, clear that in substituting a living child for the dead infant, and caring for that child, something more was meant than fraud. It was clear that if the desire to obtain the life-possession of the property, and this desire alone, had been the motive for fraud, a person or persons who could commit such an act would not be very delicate in removing the substituted child, or, at all events, in turning her to the best possible advantage. Yet this latter benefit had not been taken for the supposed father actually made no claim upon his supposed daughter's estate, but left the whole of the yearly income to accumulate. (This fact we learnt with some difficulty.)

This discovery, into the particulars of which I need not go, as they are not necessary to the elucidation of my case nor very creditable to myself, tended still more to stagger me in, my first conviction that the motive for the substitution of the living for the dead child arose in the desire to keep possession of the property.

During that week, I saw Miss Shedleigh twice. Each time I was working at some kind of needlework.

"Good morning," she said. (She was going out.)

"Does not working so many hours make your head ache?"

"No, thank you," I replied.

"The garden is quite open to you when you wish to walk," she said.

And this was how I came to see Mr. Shedleigh; for taking advantage of that permission to use the garden, and grounds (detectives must take all the advantages offered them and all they can otherwise obtain), I came upon him examining several patches of wheat of various kinds, and with which produce it appeared to me the garden was half filled.

He was a wonderfully pleasant, open-faced man, with dark, deep eyes, and an extraordinarily sweet, loving expression of countenance – something like that of a very young and high-class Jewess.

As detectives are always asking questions about everything which they see and cannot understand, it may be readily guessed that I asked what was meant by growing wheat in a garden.

The answer I obtained made me still more desirous of clearing away that first conviction of mine, to the effect that the substitution of the one child for the other was a crime of greed.

It was from my general informant, the housekeeper, then, I learnt Mr. Shedleigh passed his whole time (in winter in the laboratory, in spring, summer, and autumn in his garden and various trial-fields on the various estates) in making experiments with wheat and other cereals, with a view to increasing the average yield of wheat per acre – I see I have here indulged in a repetition.

It is not often that criminals try to be so good to their fellow-men – if they did, or could, they would be happier – and, therefore, the probability of Mr. Shedleigh being a criminal became still more faint as I learnt this good trait of his character. My experience is this, that a man or woman who tries to benefit society is rarely bad at bottom – if either were, he or she would not think of any other than him or herself.

Mr. Shedleigh spoke very pleasantly to me, asking me what I thought of this and that, and taking his garden-glove off in order to pull me some strawberries.

I think I went back to the house a little ashamed of myself, and possibly had I come upon an unexpected looking-glass, I might have blushed for Miss Gladden and for her work.

But I never wavered for one minute in my determination to deal out justice, to see Sir Nathaniel and let him know all. I should not have been fitted to my trade had I allowed myself at any time to be turned from my duty by pity, or any argument based on expediency.

The second time I saw Miss Shedleigh I was going home to my small lodging for the night. Said she, – "There is a person living near you – a Mrs. Blenham, I think she is called – who, I believe, is in very poor circumstances, but who hides her poverty out of respect for the better days she has passed through. I wish you would find out the true state of her case. You could perhaps manage it much better than myself."

I did manage it, and I had the pleasure and the pain of seeing Miss Shedleigh doing that best of woman's work, an act of necessary charity.

I had previously learnt from the housekeeper that Miss Shedleigh passed almost all her time in looking after the wants and the children of the parish.

To be plain – these Shedleighs appeared to be about as good folk as any I had ever come across.

And it was I who was to throw down the house!

I was sick of my work by the end of the week, and perhaps, without being sentimental, I may admit that I had made up my mind that I would make no money by it. My legitimate expenses, a return of what I had laid out, and no more. This was my determination with reference to money matters, and one in which I meant to be resolute when dealing with Sir Nathaniel. For I assure you we detectives are able to have consciences, and to deal in points of honour.

At the end of that week I had my plans set out, and I left Shirley House with some downheartedness, thoroughly well knowing that the next time I entered the place it would be in my true character.

Within six hours from saying 'good evening' to Miss Shedleigh I was at Brighton, and in presence of Sir Nathaniel Shirley.

I had sent up word that a person of the name of Gladden (that is the name I assume most frequently while in my business) wanted to see him, and I am bound to say that the answer I heard him send down was anything but complimentary.

I was not baffled of course.

I sent up a card on which I had written 'Shirley House business.'

"Tell her to come up," I heard him say.

And up 'she' went.

From the moment I saw him I didn't like him. In outward appearance a gentleman beyond any doubt. But he belonged to a class of men, I could see at a glance, who never say a rude thing to your face, and never think a kind one either before your countenance or behind your back.

Self! – You could see that in every feature. Gentlemanly selfishness, no doubt; yet nevertheless perfect greed not withstanding. With some people it calls for far less an effort to be civil than brutal, as conversely many a harsh speaking man has a heart as tender as that of a good woman.

"What do you want?" he said, in a civil tone, as I entered the room, but not looking towards me.

"To see you," I said, in as civil a tone as I could adopt, and shutting the door as I spoke.

He looked at me quickly. He had those shifting eyes which can look at no one or thing for five seconds together. I have often wondered if such people can even look steadily at their own reflections from a glass.

"Who are you, pray?"

"I am a detective," said I.

I saw him visibly shrink in his chair. Woman as I was, I suppose he thought I was a man in that disguise.

He recovered himself in a moment, but I noticed that the skin about his lips went black, and that the lips themselves became of a muddy white.

"Indeed," he said; and by the time he spoke he was, as to his words, quite collected.

Have I said he was about fifty? He was near that age. His hair was thin, and turning grey, but be brought it over his forehead nattily, and curled it effectively. He dressed very young, and in the latest fashion.

"I have come," I said, "to give you some information."

"Go on."

"When Mrs, Shedleigh died, she left a daughter."

"Go on."

I knew by the tone of the words, though they were said with great good breeding, that he was already bored.

"At least," I continued, "it was supposed she died, leaving a daughter."

He was about to start, but he thought a great deal better of it, and remained quiet. I saw, however, that the darkness about his lips increased.

"In fact," I continued, "she did not leave a daughter."

By this time he had quite conquered his agitation, and I am prepared to declare that till the remainder of our interview he never betrayed the least emotion. Whether this callousness was the result of disease or determination I have never been able to decide.

"What did she leave?" he asked.

"No children whatever."

"Ho! – Then you mean to say that Shirley property is mine?"

"Yes."

He turned in his chair, and looked hard at me, I saw he was used to such battles as had experienced him in gaining victories.

"And you know all about it?"

"All about it."

"Why do you come to me?"

"Because you are the proper person to come to."

"Why haven't you gone to them?"

"Who do you mean?" I asked.

"The Shedleighs," he replied.

"I have just left Shirley House," was my answer.

"I thought so," he added, dropping back in his chair; and harsh as this answer may appear, I can assure the reader it was uttered in the softest tones.

"Why," I urged, "how could I have learnt the particulars of this business without going to the house?"

"How much?" he asked, speaking as civilly as ever.

"How much?"

"Yes," he continued, "how much? I suppose, my dear creature – for I accept what you say, and agree that you really are a detective – I suppose you will make your market between me and those Shedleigh people. You have been to them, and now you come to me. How much? I dare say we can manage it. I suppose you will want it in writing?"

"You moan. Sir Nathaniel, what reward do I expect for the information?"

"That's it, my dear creature – how, much? and let me know at once. I suppose I should have to pay more than the Shedleighs if your news is true."

"I beg your pardon," I replied; "but the Shedleighs know nothing at all about the discovery I have made, and I have come to you at once – I have only known the truth of this matter less than a couple of weeks."

This was strictly the truth.

"Ha! I see; you are going to them after leaving me, I don't blame you – rather admire you, in fact. Decided clever woman, if you can carry the affair through. Come, whatever they offer to you to keep the discovery dark I'll pay you double to make it as clear as you can against them – what do you say to that?"

"Excuse me," I said, and I am bound to admit I already felt as though I should like to get out into the fresh sea air once more; "but I do not care to make money for tills work."

He turned and looked at me without any excitement, but with an expression on his face which clearly meant – "Is she a fool, or is she fooling me?"

"All I should require," said I, "would be the return of the money I have laid out, and payment for my time at the ordinary pay I receive from the Government."

"Ha! – exactly," he replied – the expression of his face had changed the moment I began to speak of my reimbursements – "you must have the money you have laid out returned to you, with interest, but first, my dear creature, prove to me that you are really speaking reasonably."

"I shall have to go into long particulars," I said.

He looked calmly at me; then he said –

"You will not perhaps mind much if I smoke, will you?"

"No," I replied, wishing myself, still more heartily, in the fresh air; for I remember it struck me that I was speaking to a being neither alive nor dead, to a kind of man who was neither fit for the grave nor the world. I think I never approached such a passionless human being.

However, it was my business to tell him of his good fortune, if indeed all kinds of fortune were not the same to him.

I began the case exactly as it occurred to me, commencing with the cabman, Flemps, and so working to the culminating point in the evidence of the medical student, George Geffins.

The only interruption he made was to ask the addresses of the cabman and the student. After writing down each, he said, "Yes!" and again became perfectly motionless.

"You know now as much as I do," I said, at last.

And I am willing to admit that I was heartily sick of my man. I apprehend I felt that kind of disappointment and ashamed anger which a man would experience who found that the answer to his offer of marriage was a blank stare.

"I suppose I can do nothing till Monday?"

"What?" I asked.

It will be remembered it was late on Saturday night.

"Nothing till Monday?"

"May I ask, Sir Nathanial," said I, "what you intend to do on Monday?"

"Why I suppose, give them into custody."

"Custody?" I asked.

"Of course; what else is there to do? They have been robbing me for five years, and these people disserve to be punished. What else can I do than give them into custody?"

For a moment, it need hardly be said, it was a difficult for me to find any reply. At last I said –

"No, Sir Nathaniel, the Shedleighs will not have robbed you, because you will recall that I have told you Mr. Shedleigh has not touched any of the income arising from the Shirley estates."

"But I am not to know that. Much better give them into custody, detective, and see what comes of it."

I confess I never had anticipated any conduct approaching such cool, business-like mercilessness as this. I had designed a dozen ways of setting to work in this matter during the week, each more considerate than the previous mode as those seven days came to a termination – not one of them approached the idea of giving Mr. and Miss Shedleigh into custody.

"I do not think I would, Sir Nathaniel; much better think it over," I replied.

"Can't see what there is to think over," said the baronet. "They've robbed me, and therefore the only thing to do is – give them into custody."

"You had better sleep on it, sir," said I, "I'll see you on, Monday morning, if you please."

"Why not tomorrow?" he asked; "why not go up tomorrow and give them both into custody? I certainly shall."

"Thank you, Sir Nathaniel," said I, and I fancy I spoke a little resentfully; "I do not care to do anything but rest tomorrow, and I am quite sure that the business is not very pressing."

"Not pressing, when they have been robbing me? What nonsense you are talking, my dear creature. Well, if you like, Monday," he said, after he had gone to the window and looked out at the night. "It will be fine tomorrow, and I may well have the day here as not. Good night, detective."

"Good night."

"Here, ma'am, though, you have not given me your address."

I gave him a card, but not one word. I believe in my own mind I was beginning to quarrel with him.

"This is your right card, I suppose, ma'am?"

"Of course it is!"

"And you're not fooling me, my dear creature!"

"No; what could I gain by fooling you?"

This answer appeared to satisfy him.

"Where are you stopping in Brighton, detective?"

I gave him the name of a little public-house in the town at which I had rested on several occasions.

"Good night," I said, going towards the door.

Something I suppose in the tone struck even his dull senses.

"If you want any money, or that sort of thing," said he, "I can let you have some." The most positive expression I had yet seen on his face I had now the power of remarking. "I'm not a rich man, you can pull along till tomorrow with—"

And here, with some exertion of a slow will, he took half-a-sovereign out of his *porte-monnaie*.

I had brought him news which was to put some thousands a year in his pocket.

"No, thank you," I said, hurriedly, and thereupon I left the room.

I did not directly go to the little house I have mentioned.

I crossed the parade, and began traversing the cliff walk.

To those who have walked on a summer moonlight night high up on the Brighton cliff, with the light wind whispering as it courses by, the soft sea kissing the rattling shingle beneath, I have no need to tell how all those natural, gentle sounds increased, and at the same time saddened, the mental pain I was suffering.

He had not uttered a word of thanks – he had not shown a spark of gratitude for his good fortune. Mind, I was not wounded in my vanity by the omission of any expression of gratitude to me, but I was pained that he showed no gratitude whatever. His good fortune came, and he took it as a right. I know that I could not avoid associating him with a certain monkey I had seen at the Zoological Gardens. This animal – and I watched him for an hour during that holiday of mine – stood still, holding out his hand without appearing to think of what he was doing, and when anything was put in his palm, he closed his fingers upon it, shoved the goody in his mouth, and without looking at the donor, or without testifying any knowledge of the gift, again he dropped his hand out between the bars of his cage. He took what came – what more could be wanted of him?

I had done my duty as an honest detective, and I was, as I do not mind confessing, since I am out of the business, sorry I had completed it.

Let me add here, at once, since I have said I have retired from the practice of detection, that I did not effect that retirement on the money I made in that profession. I had a small income left me, which of course now I enjoy. Detectives rarely make fortunes.

When I reached the little inn to which I have already twice referred, I made inquiries touching Sir Nathaniel Shirley, and I need not say I heard no good of him. I do not assert that I discovered any positive harm concerning him, but people spoke of him with a kind of reserve, as though their sense of justice and their prejudices were pulling different ways. What, however, I did ascertain certainly agreed with the man. He had a good income, yet he was rarely out of debt. I could understand that. He never could refuse himself what that personage desired to possess; and, though he spent all his income, no one could say who was the better for it. He always had his worth for his money, and the impression appeared to be that he rarely lost in the game of life. Unquestionably, from what I heard, he was frequently made to pay very dear where he had to pay beforehand for his pleasure – but he had it. No one could give him a good word, yet at the same time not a witness was to be found who could pronounce upon him a down-right bad verdict.

I am accustomed to fall asleep the moment I get to bed, being healthy, and, as the world goes, honest and clear in my conscience. But that night I could not fall off.

The idea of Sir Nathaniel going up to town and arresting the brother and sister, just after the manner of a machine, kept me hopelessly awake. I felt it was no use appealing to his mercy – I might just as well have harangued the steam hammer in Woolwich Dockyard.

It was a nightmare of itself to imagine Mr. Shedleigh taken away from his good work of trying to make the abundant earth more fruitful – to conceive of Miss Shedleigh divorced from her poor, from her lady-life, and locked up in a prison cell.

What was to be done?

And I fell asleep only when I had quite decided what was to be done. I determined to go up in the morning by the first train, hurry to Shirley House, warn and save them. Such an act was no breach of duty. My work was to obtain Sir Nathaniel his heritage, not to punish Mr. and Miss Shedleigh.

I was awake betimes, though I had slept but for a short period, and getting up with a new sense of imprisonment and weight upon me, I made for the station, and before eleven I was in London.

Taking a cab, I reached the neighbourhood of Shirley House, and there for the first time I faced fairly the enormous difficulty I had to encounter.

I saw her as she was leaving the church. She had a very plain black prayer-book in her hand, and as she came out into the porch, a smile spread upon her face as she addressed first me and then another of those she saw.

She was one of the simplest and most unaffected ladies I ever knew.

She saw me, and nodded.

As she did so, a lady came up and touched her on the arm.

But it was absolutely necessary that I should warn her, so I went up to her and said –

"Miss Shedleigh, may I speak with you?"

"Certainly," she replied, with extreme frankness.

"I mean up at the house."

"Oh, call when you like."

"Can I come now?"

She looked at me a little eagerly I marked, and then she said smilingly – "Will not tomorrow do?"

"No," I replied; and it is evident I must have spoken wistfully, for she turned slightly pale.

"Come up at three," she said. "I shall be quite disengaged."

I bowed, and was falling behind her, when she turned quickly, and said, with some little asperity that I marked –

"Is anything the matter?"

"Nothing but what can be repaired," I said, smiling, for I saw it would not do to alarm her.

But between that time and three o'clock I had discovered new cause for alarm. I saw by reference to my 'Bradshaw' (a book with which the library of a detective is never unprovided) that an express train left Brighton directly after church-time. What if Sir Nathaniel should send for me at the Brighton address I had given? – and what if, finding me gone, he should take that express train and hurry on to Shirley House, with a policeman as his companion?

He was quite capable of such an act I felt sure, but I hoped, on the other hand, that his natural laziness, and his cynical belief that I had more to gain than lose by him, would together prompt him to refrain from making inquiries about me.

If he, however, did take the one p.m. train, it was perfectly competent for him to be at Shirley House by three, the after-lunch hour appointed by Miss Shedleigh for my interview with her. And I desire here to remark that this lady must have been one of most unusual kindness and consideration to give way to my request – I who was almost a stranger to her, and to agree to see me on that day which those ladies most devoted to their poor look upon as private, and to be passed without interference.

The time between one and three was not past very pleasantly.

At three I stood on the door-stops of Shirley House.

I confess I was ashamed of the work I had in hand.

When I came to the room in which I knew I should find her, I declare I was afraid to follow the man, and when being in the chamber, the servant had left it, and she had said, "And pray, my dear, what is it that is so important that it cannot wait till tomorrow?" I had for a few moments no power to answer.

"I am afraid," said I, "you will not feel very great pleasure in what I have to say."

"Let me hear it," she replied, with a fine, delicate smile.

"I learnt a secret of your life quite by chance two weeks since."

"A secret of my life!" she said, after a pause, during which she hesitated, and evidently tried to reassure herself, though she turned paler at the moment.

"Poor thing," thought I, "it is clear she has but one great secret, which indeed is one no longer."

"Yes," I replied, "and I must speak to you about it."

Here there came a little feeling of pride to her support, and she said, though very softly and coolly –

"Must?"

"Must," I echoed.

"Pray," she continued, speaking a little highly, "to whom am I addressing myself, that I hear such a word as – *must*?"

"I am a detective," said I, using the phrase which I have so frequently uttered when secrecy has been no longer needful.

"A detective?" she said, evidently not knowing what such an officer was, and yet too unerringly guessing.

"Yes," I continued, "one of the secret police."

She started, and muttered something to herself. She uttered no cry, no exclamation of fear; indeed my long experience assures me that in the majority of cases where a sudden and terrible surprise comes upon people, the shock is so great that they generally receive the news with but little expression of their feelings. It appears as though shock rather stupefies than excites.

In a very few moments she became comparatively calm.

"What do you want?" she said.

"Indeed," I answered, "to save you."

"From what?"

"From the consequences of my duty."

She looked at me intently, and at last she smiled.

"True," she said, "you have your duty to perform as well as others. What does this conversation mean?"

"It means, Miss Shedleigh," I said, "that I know the little girl who is in this house is not Mr. Shedleigh's child."

She thought she had prepared herself for the worst, but she had not.

She trembled, and uttered a short, sharp cry, which touched one's very heart.

"There can be no doubt about it," I said, desirous of preventing her from the attempt to fence with me and my information. "The cabman from whom you obtained the little girl pointed out the very spot where he placed the child in your arms. Pray do not fancy the case could not be proved. The doctor, Dr. Ellkins, may be dead, but he said enough to an apprentice he had, and whom I have seen, to show that the late lady could not have been the mother of the little girl who goes by her name. Avoid any proceedings which might be terrible. I do not know, if you denied everything, but that Mrs. Shedleigh's remains might be brought in evidence against you."

These words, as partially I intended they should, shocked her inexpressibly.

"Surely they could not so outrage my poor sister's grave?"

"Indeed you are mistaken," I said; "the law knows no pity while the truth is doubtful."

"But – but what would you have me do?"

"Confess all to Sir Nathaniel Shirley."

"Sir Nathaniel – do you know him?"

She was now truly alarmed. But she did not betray any wild excitement, such as I believe most people would suppose she would have shown.

"I left him only last night!"

A blank, deadly expression, or rather want of expression, stole over her face.

"Then all is indeed lost," said she.

"No; not yet," I replied.

"Woman, you come from him she said, in a lone of weeping defiance, if that term can be comprehended.

"No, indeed," I replied, "I have come of my own will to warn you against Sir Nathaniel."

"And yet you have come so recently from him."

Then catching, as the drowning man at the shadow of himself on the surface of the water, she said – "Perhaps *he* does not know all?"

"He does," I said, woefully; "all, even to the addresses of the people necessary to prove his case."

"And you furnished him with this power?"

"I did. I grieve to say I was forced to do so."

"Oh, woman, woman! If you did but know what you have done."

"I have done what it was but justice to do."

"You have done a wretched thing," she said. "Sir Nathaniel will have no mercy upon me and I must suffer – I alone must suffer."

"Mr. Shedleigh," said I; "had not he better know–"

"Know? Know what?"

"Why, that the – the fraud has been discovered."

"Woman, he thinks the child his."

"What! He has heard nothing of the truth?"

"Nothing; the deception was practised on him in pity, and now you come, after four years' peace, and may perhaps kill him."

"But," said I, apologetically, "remember you have deprived Sir Nathaniel Shirley of his property."

"Sir Nathaniel – Sir Nathaniel," she repeated; it were well for him that he should never be rich, and well for him that what was done was well done."

I shook my head. I knew that right was right, and that the property was by law the baronet's.

"Sir Nathaniel," she cried, beating her right foot upon the ground – by this time all fear for herself was past – "Sir Nathaniel, had he obtained the property, would have been a beggar by this time, whereas he would never have been unprovided for had you not learnt my secret. Now he will take the estates, though, if the wish of the late owner, my sister-in-law, could be consulted, I know she would keep every poor acre from her uncle. Oh, woman, woman, if you could but judge of the injury you have done!"

"I shall have a quiet conscience, Miss Shedleigh, whatever happens," I said; "but it will be quieter if you will but let me, who have been the means of bringing destruction near you – if you will but let me save you. I am afraid of Sir Nathaniel, he seems so merciless."

"First hear me," she said. "Before you speak again you shall hear my excuse for my conduct – hear me, nor speak till I have finished. I know not by what terrible chance it has happened that you should learn a secret which I thought lay hidden in my sister's grave and my heart. How you have pieced your information together I am unable to imagine, but since you know so much I would have you know the rest, and in learning it, believe that I am to be as much pitied as to be blamed."

I bowed, feeling rather that I was the poor lady's prisoner than she in a measure mine.

"You know my brother's wife brought a dead child into the world; you know that that child, being dead when born, in event of my sister-in-law's death her property could not be enjoyed by her husband for life, simply because the child had not breathed. It was she who put it into my head first. My sister's distress came upon us very suddenly, weeks before we expected, and no preparations had been made. When she learnt that she could not be a mother, news which she inferred rather than learnt, I believe the humiliation felt by her was so great that it led to her death, as certainly as that before she died she prayed Heaven to send her a child to comfort her husband after she was gone, for from the moment the doctor left her she never believed she would rise from her bed again.

It was when she cried out that many a poor woman would be glad to find a home for her puny child, that the idea came upon me of the woman and infant I had seen pass the house about nine, as I came in at the south gate, and to whom I had spoken. I gave that poor woman some silver, pitying her much when she told me her child was barely a fortnight old.

"Perhaps I had no right to speak of this mother and child to my sister, for she was now quite herself at any moment from the time the doctor left to the moment of her death – perhaps I should not have excited her already excited brain. But no sooner did she comprehend what I said than she cried that heaven had heard her prayer, and bade me go and seek the woman. I refused at first, but she looked so powerful that it seemed to me as though she was inspired, and so I said yes, I would go, and I went quickly from the house and down the road, in the direction which the poor woman had taken.

"And when I heard the child crying from within that miserable common cab, I also thought that Heaven had had pity on us. I know now how guilty I was – how very guilty I was.

"I had not left the house twenty minutes when I was returning with the child, and when I came into her room, carrying the infant, I found her still alone, though I had taken no precautions to keep her by herself. She cried out, saying Heaven had been kind, and declaring how a good angel had brought it to me.

"There was no one in the house to see my act. It was the free-school fête day, and the servants, with the exception of one, were at Velvet Dell, three miles away – the only girl that had remained at home had gone down to the surgery with the doctor.

"Before a quarter past ten, at which time the servants came trooping home – they had been given to ten, and there had been nobody to send for them during that terrible hour-and-a-half – before a quarter past ten she was dying in the presence of Dr. Ellkins, who looked much confused and puzzled.

"Even then I felt the enormity of the crime in which I had engaged – I did indeed. Even then I felt that had I opposed my sister's wild idea instead of having fostered it, she herself would never have laid such injunctions upon me as she did.

"It was before the doctor arrived for the second time – and the moment the lady's maid returned with the medicine, I sent her back for the medical man – it was before Dr. Ellkins came again that she had commanded me to swear that I would never tell the truth about the child, she saying – 'Heaven sent it, Heaven sent it, though it was but a poor woman's daughter.'

"She told me," the poor lady continued, looking eagerly in my face – it was now half-past three, as I saw by the great French clock on the mantel piece, so that if Sir Nathaniel had come up by the one p.m. train he would soon be at Shirley House – "she told me that it would break down Newton – Newton is Mr. Shedleigh – if he lost both her and his child together, and that he was doing the world good, and that nothing must stop his work. You know," she continued, breaking off, "she married my brother because she rather admired his intellect than himself.

"She said also I should save a poor child from destitution, and finally she declared that she willed that her uncle should not have her property – that he was wicked and wasteful, and that her husband ought to have it to do good with.

"And then, as I heard the ring at the hall-door, and as she knew it was the doctor returned, she raised her right hand, looked wildly at me, and said – 'I command – in the name of God.'

"She never spoke aloud again. She only whispered messages to her husband, and taking the doctor's head between her hands, whispered something to him which made the poor gentleman tremble.

"Then she died as the servants came trooping into the house from the school treat.

"I knew how wrong I had been long before the next day. But when I looked at her still face, my dear, I could not disobey her; and I felt more unable to oppose her last wishes when our housekeeper, Mrs. Dumarty, whispered to me that she looked in her sleep as though *she* had done her duty.

"I know how wicked it all was, but as the years have rolled on I hoped I had done all for the best. My brother, when he came home at the end of those two days, found a deep consolation in the little child – and I could not tell him he was weeping over a stranger.

"I fell very ill myself, my dear, after the burial, and they thought it was grief which had overpowered me. But I am afraid it was more my conscience than my sorrow, though I am sure I loved my sister very dearly.

"As the years have gone on I have thought I had done all for the best. Sir Nathaniel has received a large income yearly from me; for I came into a good property very soon after Mrs. Shedleigh's death. And I have made my will in his favour, so that he could never have been poor through my action – whereas had he inherited the estates he would soon have wasted them for he is quite a prodigal.

"Now you know all. You tell me, my poor woman, you wish to save me. How can you?"

Long before the good lady asked me that woeful question, I had hung my head in sorrow and regret.

Don't suppose we detectives have no soft places in our hearts because we are obliged to steel them against the daily wickedness we have to encounter. It is not long since that one Tom White, a detective of the R Division, was shocked by seeing a young thief, whom he was pursuing, fall dead at his feet. Tom White never was the thing after that; so he must have had some soft place in his heart, poor fellow.

I confess I was sorry I had shown Sir Nathaniel the cards he now held.

Could I save her?

I was determined to do my best.

"Well?" she said, a little wearily, and coming to me, she put her hand lightly on my shoulder.

I confess I never felt a hand rest so heavily upon me, though her touch was as delicate as that of the lady she must have always been.

"I am very sorry—" I said.

"There is no need," she replied.

"And very much ashamed—"

"Why, my dear? *You* have done your duty, whatever I may have omitted."

"I would rather be you," I said.

I confess these replies of mine wore sentimental for a detective. Still, as they were uttered, I repeat them.

And lo! as I spoke, there came a sudden, fierce, imperious peal upon the great gate-bell.

As I glanced at the great clock, and read a quarter to four, I felt certain the visitor was Sir Nathaniel.

He did not even send a card up; only his name, with the statement that he must see either Mr. or Miss Shedleigh.

The man added that he had replied his master was out in the grounds, but that his lady was in the house.

Positively Sir Nathaniel felt himself already so much master that he had not waited for permission to come upstairs.

"Good day, Catherine," said the baronet, entering; "I heard you were in, and so I did not wait for the man coming down again."

The coward! he was afraid she would gain the more advantage the longer the time before he saw her.

As he spoke, he glanced at me as though I stood his enemy, he had held out his hand to me, taken what I offered without remark (like my friend the ring-tailed at the gardens), and now he was ready to snarl because he supposed I had nothing more to give.

When the man had left the room, he turned to me and said the following words, in as sweet a tone as he would have used for inquiring after my health.

"I thought I should find you here, you baggage!"

"Sir!" said I, and I think I was justified in the exclamation.

"Now, you don't get from me a rap," he said, still in a sweet voice, but with one of the ugliest countenances ever I remember to have remarked.

It is certain he was a miserable tyrant – infinitely more dangerous to his friends (if he bad any) than to his enemies.

"And what have you got to say?" he asked, turning to Miss Shedleigh.

"What have you?" she asked, and her voice was as surprisingly steady as her manner was collected.

"You know what I have come for."

"Yes," she said, quite gently.

"So I have found you out at last?" he said.

It was clear he bad passed me over in the matter as though I had never known of it.

Here I looked at him – perhaps a little keenly – and then it was that I noticed the blackness I had marked on the previous night round his mouth was still more observable as he stood confronting his niece's sister-in-law, and with as ugly a look of victory upon his face as a man could wear.

"One moment!" here I interposed.

"Well?" he said, speaking sweetly, but looking at me as though I was one of the worst kind of dogs.

"I'm not wanted here. I will leave the room."

"You will do no such thing!" said he, brave I presume because he had but to do with a couple of women.

"Indeed!" said I, "take care. You know I'm a police-officer; impede me in the execution of my duty at your peril. I say I am not wanted here, and I think fit to leave the room."

As I moved towards him another change in his face became apparent. Whether it was that he turned more generally pallid, and so he looked darker about the mouth – or whether the blackness around his lips did increase, it is certain that a change occurred.

He stood in my way till I came near him, and then he fell back almost as though I had touched him.

I left the room, but before I did so, I said to Miss Shedleigh – "I shall be outside. If you call to me I shall hear you. Don't be afraid of this gentleman."

Then I left the room.

What was said I never learnt.

The need of my attendance was brought about by a scream on the part of the lady, whereupon I thought fit to run into the room, where I found—

But before I reach that last scone but one in this narrative I should make the reader acquainted with some observations I made.

Upon reaching the corridor beyond the room in which the war was to be fought out, I found myself near a window which, with the ordinary eyes of a detective, I knew must be in a plane with the windows of the room I had just left, simply because the view from it was such as I had noticed, without much intention of doing so (for observation of all before him becomes a habit with the detective), from those openings.

The whole of these windows looked over the sweep before the house, which was enclosed by a wall in front, and two heavy solid wooden gates. In each gate, however, was a wicket, one of which was open, and through it I saw the faces of two men who were peering from the cab, the top of which only I could see beyond the wall and gates.

Faintly as I saw their faces, and under such disadvantages, I recognised one of them as that of a policeman known to me.

Beyond any question the other individual was also an officer.

So, he had shown no sign of mercy. He had not sought to compromise with the Shedleighs, by having an interview with them. Cruel as he was, he had brought down two policemen with him, and it struck me at once that it was the time necessary for the procuring of these officers which accounted for the half hour's grace he had shown before he arrived. To arrest Miss Shedleigh at an earlier hour than that at which now he was proceeding to accomplish that act, he must have got up early in the morning – a piece of severity which, doubtless, he could not force upon himself, though it was to lead the earlier to the exhibition of his cruelty.

I had been watching the faces through the open window – for it was the end of July, fine weather – and the gate-wicket, and without being seen myself, for about two minutes, when I heard the officer I knew say –

"There he is – he's coming."

It was not much above a whisper, but the breeze set my way, and my ears are uncommonly fine and sharp; indeed, I believe it is admitted that we women detectives are enabled to educate our five senses to a higher pitch than are our male competitors.

Clearly, the officers could see across the gardens, and round by the house over the grounds, whilst I was only to make observations in an opposite direction.

But in a moment I heard a clear light voice singing lowly and sweetly. I recognised it in a moment for that of the master of the house.

There was no sound but the rustle of the light wind (twittering the leaves and rippling patches of wheat) to interfere with his voice, and indeed it seemed to me as though the murmur made with his voice a sweet chorus.

He came round by the house, the volume of his voice increasing as he did so, and then he passed away on the other side, his voice dying away till the note of the wind was louder than his hymn.

The policemen followed him with their sight as far as they could, and if you have seen a cat lose a mouse you can comprehend the style of look upon the officers faces as their charge went round the corner of his own house.

I suppose this episode had taken up about two minutes of time.

But this is only guesswork.

Suddenly a quick, sharp, shrill scream.

Then – silence.

As I heard the officers leaping from the cab and crunching over the gravel, I ran forward and broke in rather than opened the door.

There lay Sir Nathaniel on his face.

Two or three yards away from him knelt Miss Shedleigh, her hands as tightly clasped as they could be, and pressed against the wall.

I may say at once – he was dead.

Afterwards, when the lady could speak calmly, she told me she had been certain it was death as he fell. She knew the family disease had grasped him – that fell heart disease which had killed his brother, which had helped in a measure to destroy his niece, Mrs. Shedleigh.

She declared she saw upon his face as he fell that expression which she had seen in death upon the countenance of her sister-in-law, and of that lady's father, at whose bedside she had been at the time of his death.

The policemen, I need not say, were in the house almost before I entered the room, into which they got quite as soon as the servants.

But before they had reached their client's dead side I had found a line of conduct to take.

The baronet was deceased. Very well – then all things were as they were before I told him of what was, perhaps, his good fortune, though he died over it; for, from what I heard, I doubt if he would have expired in his own bed but in a government one, had he been at liberty much longer to carry on his very bad life.

This question only stood in my way –

Had he told the police the exact state of affairs?

I guessed he had refrained from doing so. I felt sure he was a man who would say no more than was needed. It could not have been necessary to report at the station the history I had given him.

The course I took will perhaps be most quickly understood by a report of the words I used.

You may guess that the officer of the two who knew me was considerably taken aback by finding me in the room when he entered it.

"Blackman," said I, when the doctor had been, when he had pronounced his opinion (which did not take long), and when there was breathing time for the household once more – "Blackman, what on earth were you here for?"

"He brought us."

The emphasis on 'he' plainly proved it was the dead man which was meant.

"What did he say?"

"Why, that he wanted to give his brother and his sister-in-law into custody for robbing him."

"Yes – he was mad," said I.

Blackman turned all manner of colours.

"Lord!" said he, turning at last quite red, "and to think that though I thought him such a queer customer, and the job such a queer job – to think as I didn't see that. Of course, G. (I am called G. by the force), *you* is here on that business?"

"Precisely," said I.

"Of course – *I* see it all."

"Of course you do," said I.

And it is astonishing how my explanation was accepted by all concerned in the inquest, and even by the general public.

[I have not much hesitation in telling this tale, however, for now, by certain events, no one has been wronged by the substituted child for she has played her part out in the play of this world.]

Sir Nathaniel's pocket-book, however, gave me a fright, for it contained the addresses of Flemps the cabman, and Mr. Geffins the medical student. However, Miss Shedleigh was out of the way when the cabman gave his evidence, she having been a witness at the opening inquiry (together with myself), and the cabman offering his evidence at the adjourned examination. Flemps's evidence was not full. He had to look at the deceased gentleman for identification, and his evidence ran to this effect – "Which if ever I sord the gent afore, take my badge away and give me three months."

I was out of the way when this evidence was adduced, nor did I show myself when the following witness, Mr. Geffins, deposed that he had never seen the "subject before in life."

Sir Nathaniel's medical adviser was called, and I have no doubt this gentleman, of great note – for Sir Nathaniel would have everything of the best of its kind, from his medical advisor to his blacking – I have no doubt that this gentleman considerably tended to close the inquiry quickly. He deposed, with some degree of pain evidently, a condition which gave his statement more weight, that the deceased gentleman had been suffering for some time from disease of the heart – a family complaint; that this disease had been much accelerated in its progress by the loose mode of life in which the baronet had lived, and that he had warned him only a few previous days to avoid any great excitement, as it might be dangerous. "I added," said the witness, "that if Sir Nathaniel kept himself quiet he might live into a given old age – a result of which there was a possibility, but little probability."

Hearing this evidence, to which was added that of the post-mortem examination, I could readily comprehend why his face, and especially the skin about his month, assumed such appearances as they did each time I saw him; and I could also understand how thoroughly well-fitted by nature he was to agree with his doctor's direction to avoid excitement.

It was clear his was a nature where selfishness provokes a man, habitually callous and insensible, till his natural licentiousness moved and carried him beyond himself.

I say I have no doubt the medical evidence against Sir Nathaniel blunted the inquiry – a result not proceeding from any wilful hoodwinking of justice, but simply from the fact that human judgment must be made up of previous impressions. When men hear a dead man has been bad, they surely are not so desirous of talking over his coffin as they would be did they learn he had lived an honourable life.

The coroner's "Oh!" showed how much even an old legal official could be impressed by a witness deposing against the gentleman on trial. I know that coroner. He is not a very moral man, but he offered that hypocrisy of faultiness, open respect for virtue.

Miss Shedleigh's evidence, under my direction, had been given to the effect that Sir Nathaniel came about money matters; that when he fell he was about to seek Mr. Shedleigh, and that she had run forward entreating him not to carry out his intention.

And when the coroner and the jury learnt that Sir Nathaniel had for some years been supported by the Shedleighs, Miss Shedleigh was asked no more questions.

My tale of a 'Tenant for Life' is done. It has been told to show how simple a thing may lead to most important consequences. Had I not taken that ride in Flemps's cab on a Sunday, I never could have learnt that Sir Nathaniel Shirley was the actual heir to the Shirley estates.

When the little girl died (about eight months since) Mr. Shedleigh gave up the estates to the next heir after Sir Nathaniel. As it had never been proved that the child was not his, he by law was Tenant for Life; but he waved his right, not because he had learnt the secret of his sister's life – for we kept it to ourselves – but because he felt that the only owner of the Shirley property should be one who claimed to be of the Shirley pedigree.

So it all came right at last, and no man was punished in order to procure justice.

The Anthropologist at Large

R. Austin Freeman

THORNDYKE WAS NOT a newspaper reader. He viewed with extreme disfavour all scrappy and miscellaneous forms of literature, which, by presenting a disorderly series of unrelated items of information, tended, as he considered, to destroy the habit of consecutive mental effort.

"It is most important," he once remarked to me, "habitually to pursue a definite train of thought, and to pursue it to a finish, instead of flitting indolently from one uncompleted topic to another, as the newspaper reader is so apt to do. Still, there is no harm in a daily paper – so long as you don't read it."

Accordingly, he patronized a morning paper, and his method of dealing with it was characteristic. The paper was laid on the table after breakfast, together with a blue pencil and a pair of office shears. A preliminary glance through the sheets enabled him to mark with the pencil those paragraphs that were to be read, and these were presently cut out and looked through, after which they were either thrown away or set aside to be pasted in an indexed book.

The whole proceeding occupied, on an average, a quarter of an hour.

On the morning of which I am now speaking he was thus engaged. The pencil had done its work, and the snick of the shears announced the final stage. Presently he paused with a newly-excised cutting between his fingers, and, after glancing at it for a moment, he handed it to me.

"Another art robbery," he remarked. "Mysterious affairs, these – as to motive, I mean. You can't melt down a picture or an ivory carving, and you can't put them on the market as they stand. The very qualities that give them their value make them totally unnegotiable."

"Yet I suppose," said I, "the really inveterate collector – the pottery or stamp maniac, for instance – will buy these contraband goods even though he dare not show them."

"Probably. No doubt the *cupiditas habendi*, the mere desire to possess, is the motive force rather than any intelligent purpose—"

The discussion was at this point interrupted by a knock at the door, and a moment later my colleague admitted two gentlemen. One of these I recognized as a Mr. Marchmont, a solicitor, for whom we had occasionally acted; the other was a stranger – a typical Hebrew of the blonde type – good-looking, faultlessly dressed, carrying a bandbox, and obviously in a state of the most extreme agitation.

"Good-morning to you, gentlemen," said Mr. Marchmont, shaking hands cordially. "I have brought a client of mine to see you, and when I tell you that his name is Solomon Löwe, it will be unnecessary for me to say what our business is."

"Oddly enough," replied Thorndyke, "we were, at the very moment when you knocked, discussing the bearings of his case."

"It is a horrible affair!" burst in Mr. Löwe. "I am distracted! I am ruined! I am in despair!"

He banged the bandbox down on the table, and flinging himself into a chair, buried his face in his hands.

"Come, come," remonstrated Marchmont, "we must be brave, we must be composed. Tell Dr. Thorndyke your story, and let us hear what he thinks of it."

He leaned back in his chair, and looked at his client with that air of patient fortitude that comes to us all so easily when we contemplate the misfortunes of other people.

"You must help us, sir," exclaimed Löwe, starting up again – "you must, indeed, or I shall go mad. But I shall tell you what has happened, and then you must act at once. Spare no effort and no expense. Money is no object – at least, not in reason," he added, with native caution. He sat down once more, and in perfect English, though with a slight German accent, proceeded volubly: "My brother Isaac is probably known to you by name."

Thorndyke nodded.

"He is a great collector, and to some extent a dealer – that is to say, he makes his hobby a profitable hobby."

"What does he collect?" asked Thorndyke.

"Everything," replied our visitor, flinging his hands apart with a comprehensive gesture – "everything that is precious and beautiful – pictures, ivories, jewels, watches, objects of art and *vertu* – everything. He is a Jew, and he has that passion for things that are rich and costly that has distinguished our race from the time of my namesake Solomon onwards. His house in Howard Street, Piccadilly, is at once a museum and an art gallery. The rooms are filled with cases of gems, of antique jewellery, of coins and historic relics – some of priceless value – and the walls are covered with paintings, every one of which is a masterpiece. There is a fine collection of ancient weapons and armour, both European and Oriental; rare books, manuscripts, papyri, and valuable antiquities from Egypt, Assyria, Cyprus, and elsewhere. You see, his taste is quite catholic, and his knowledge of rare and curious things is probably greater than that of any other living man. He is never mistaken. No forgery deceives him, and hence the great prices that he obtains; for a work of art purchased from Isaac Löwe is a work certified as genuine beyond all cavil."

He paused to mop his face with a silk handkerchief, and then, with the same plaintive volubility, continued:

"My brother is unmarried. He lives for his collection, and he lives with it. The house is not a very large one, and the collection takes up most of it; but he keeps a suite o rooms for his own occupation, and has two servants – a man and wife – to look after him The man, who is a retired police sergeant, acts as caretaker and watchman; the woman a housekeeper and cook, if required, but my brother lives largely at his club. And now I com to this present catastrophe."

He ran his fingers through his hair, took a deep breath, and continued:

"Yesterday morning Isaac started for Florence by way of Paris, but his route was nc certain, and he intended to break his journey at various points as circumstances determinec Before leaving, he put his collection in my charge, and it was arranged that I should occup his rooms in his absence. Accordingly, I sent my things round and took possession.

"Now, Dr. Thorndyke, I am closely connected with the drama, and it is my custom spend my evenings at my club, of which most of the members are actors. Consequently, am rather late in my habits; but last night I was earlier than usual in leaving my club, fc I started for my brother's house before half-past twelve. I felt, as you may suppose, tl responsibility of the great charge I had undertaken; and you may, therefore, imagine n horror, my consternation, my despair, when, on letting myself in with my latchkey, I four a police-inspector, a sergeant, and a constable in the hall. There had been a robbery, sir, in my brief absence, and the account that the inspector gave of the affair was briefly this:

"While taking the round of his district, he had noticed an empty hansom proceeding in leisurely fashion along Howard Street. There was nothing remarkable in this, but when, about ten minutes later, he was returning, and met a hansom, which he believed to be the same, proceeding along the same street in the same direction, and at the same easy pace, the circumstance struck him as odd, and he made a note of the number of the cab in his pocket-book. It was 72,863, and the time was 11.35.

"At 11.45 a constable coming up Howard Street noticed a hansom standing opposite the door of my brother's house, and, while he was looking at it, a man came out of the house carrying something, which he put in the cab. On this the constable quickened his pace, and when the man returned to the house and reappeared carrying what looked like a portmanteau, and closing the door softly behind him, the policeman's suspicions were aroused, and he hurried forward, hailing the cabman to stop.

"The man put his burden into the cab, and sprang in himself. The cabman lashed his horse, which started off at a gallop, and the policeman broke into a run, blowing his whistle and flashing his lantern on to the cab. He followed it round the two turnings into Albemarle Street, and was just in time to see it turn into Piccadilly, where, of course, it was lost. However, he managed to note the number of the cab, which was 72,863, and he describes the man as short and thick-set, and thinks he was not wearing any hat.

"As he was returning, he met the inspector and the sergeant, who had heard the whistle, and on his report the three officers hurried to the house, where they knocked and rang for some minutes without any result. Being now more than suspicious, they went to the back of the house, through the mews, where, with great difficulty, they managed to force a window and effect an entrance into the house.

"Here their suspicions were soon changed to certainty, for, on reaching the first-floor, they heard strange muffled groans proceeding from one of the rooms, the door of which was locked, though the key had not been removed. They opened the door, and found the caretaker and his wife sitting on the floor, with their backs against the wall. Both were bound hand and foot, and the head of each was enveloped in a green-baize bag; and when the bags were taken off, each was found to be lightly but effectively gagged.

"Each told the same story. The caretaker, fancying he heard a noise, armed himself with a truncheon, and came downstairs to the first-floor, where he found the door of one of the rooms open, and a light burning inside. He stepped on tiptoe to the open door, and was peering in, when he was seized from behind, half suffocated by a pad held over his mouth, pinioned, gagged, and blindfolded with the bag.

"His assailant – whom he never saw – was amazingly strong and skilful, and handled him with perfect ease, although he – the caretaker – is a powerful man, and a good boxer and wrestler. The same thing happened to the wife, who had come down to look for her husband. She walked into the same trap, and was gagged, pinioned, and blindfolded without ever having seen the robber. So the only description that we have of this villain is that furnished by the constable."

"And the caretaker had no chance of using his truncheon?" said Thorndyke.

"Well, he got in one backhanded blow over his right shoulder, which he thinks caught the burglar in the face; but the fellow caught him by the elbow, and gave his arm such a twist that he dropped the truncheon on the floor."

"Is the robbery a very extensive one?"

"Ah!" exclaimed Mr. Löwe, "that is just what we cannot say. But I fear it is. It seems that my brother had quite recently drawn out of his bank four thousand pounds in notes and gold. These little transactions are often carried out in cash rather than by cheque" – here I caught a twinkle in Thorndyke's eye – "and the caretaker says that a few days ago Isaac brought home several parcels, which were put away temporarily in a strong cupboard. He seemed to be very pleased with his new acquisitions, and gave the caretaker to understand that they were of extraordinary rarity and value.

"Now, this cupboard has been cleared out. Not a vestige is left in it but the wrappings of the parcels, so, although nothing else has been touched, it is pretty clear that goods to the value of four thousand pounds have been taken; but when we consider what an excellent buyer my brother is, it becomes highly probable that the actual value of those things is two or three times that amount, or even more. It is a dreadful, dreadful business, and Isaac will hold me responsible for it all."

"Is there no further clue?" asked Thorndyke. "What about the cab, for instance?"

"Oh, the cab," groaned Löwe – "that clue failed. The police must have mistaken the number. They telephoned immediately to all the police stations, and a watch was set, with the result that number 72,863 was stopped as it was going home for the night. But it then turned out that the cab had not been off the rank since eleven o'clock, and the driver had been in the shelter all the time with several other men. But there is a clue; I have it here."

Mr. Löwe's face brightened for once as he reached out for the bandbox.

"The houses in Howard Street," he explained, as he untied the fastening, "have small balconies to the first-floor windows at the back. Now, the thief entered by one of these windows, having climbed up a rain-water pipe to the balcony. It was a gusty night, as you will remember, and this morning, as I was leaving the house, the butler next door called to me and gave me this; he had found it lying in the balcony of his house."

He opened the bandbox with a flourish, and brought forth a rather shabby billycock hat.

"I understand," said he, "that by examining a hat it is possible to deduce from it, not only the bodily characteristics of the wearer, but also his mental and moral qualities, his state of health, his pecuniary position, his past history, and even his domestic relations and the peculiarities of his place of abode. Am I right in this supposition?"

The ghost of a smile flitted across Thorndyke's face as he laid the hat upon the remains of the newspaper. "We must not expect too much," he observed. "Hats, as you know, have a way of changing owners. Your own hat, for instance" (a very spruce, hard felt), "is a new one, I think."

"Got it last week," said Mr. Löwe.

"Exactly. It is an expensive hat, by Lincoln and Bennett, and I see you have judiciousl written your name in indelible marking-ink on the lining. Now, a new hat suggests discarded predecessor. What do you do with your old hats?"

"My man has them, but they don't fit him. I suppose he sells them or gives them away

"Very well. Now, a good hat like yours has a long life, and remains serviceable lon after it has become shabby; and the probability is that many of your hats pass from owne to owner; from you to the shabby-genteel, and from them to the shabby ungenteel. An it is a fair assumption that there are, at this moment, an appreciable number of tramp and casuals wearing hats by Lincoln and Bennett, marked in indelible ink with the nam S. Löwe; and anyone who should examine those hats, as you suggest, might draw som very misleading deductions as to the personal habits of S. Löwe."

Mr. Marchmont chuckled audibly, and then, remembering the gravity of the occasion, suddenly became portentously solemn.

"So you think that the hat is of no use, after all?" said Mr. Löwe, in a tone of deep disappointment.

"I won't say that," replied Thorndyke. "We may learn something from it. Leave it with me, at any rate; but you must let the police know that I have it. They will want to see it, of course."

"And you will try to get those things, won't you?" pleaded Löwe.

"I will think over the case. But you understand, or Mr. Marchmont does, that this is hardly in my province. I am a medical jurist, and this is not a medico-legal case."

"Just what I told him," said Marchmont. "But you will do me a great kindness if you will look into the matter. Make it a medico-legal case," he added persuasively.

Thorndyke repeated his promise, and the two men took their departure.

For some time after they had left, my colleague remained silent, regarding the hat with a quizzical smile. "It is like a game of forfeits," he remarked at length, "and we have to find the owner of 'this very pretty thing.'" He lifted it with a pair of forceps into a better light, and began to look at it more closely.

"Perhaps," said he, "we have done Mr. Löwe an injustice, after all. This is certainly a very remarkable hat."

"It is as round as a basin," I exclaimed. "Why, the fellow's head must have been turned in a lathe!"

Thorndyke laughed. "The point," said he, "is this. This is a hard hat, and so must have fitted fairly, or it could not have been worn; and it was a cheap hat, and so was not made to measure. But a man with a head that shape has got to come to a clear understanding with his hat. No ordinary hat would go on at all.

"Now, you see what he has done – no doubt on the advice of some friendly hatter. He has bought a hat of a suitable size, and he has made it hot – probably steamed it. Then he has jammed it, while still hot and soft, on to his head, and allowed it to cool and set before removing it. That is evident from the distortion of the brim. The important corollary is, that this hat fits his head exactly – is, in fact, a perfect mould of it; and this fact, together with the cheap quality of the hat, furnishes the further corollary that it has probably only had a single owner.

"And now let us turn it over and look at the outside. You notice at once the absence of old dust. Allowing for the circumstance that it had been out all night, it is decidedly clean. Its owner has been in the habit of brushing it, and is therefore presumably a decent, orderly man. But if you look at it in a good light, you see a kind of bloom on the felt, and through this lens you can make out particles of a fine white powder which has worked into the surface."

He handed me his lens, through which I could distinctly see the particles to which he referred.

"Then," he continued, "under the curl of the brim and in the folds of the hatband, where the brush has not been able to reach it, the powder has collected quite thickly, and we can see that it is a very fine powder, and very white, like flour. What do you make of that?"

"I should say that it is connected with some industry. He may be engaged in some factory or works, or, at any rate, may live near a factory, and have to pass it frequently."

"Yes; and I think we can distinguish between the two possibilities. For, if he only passes the factory, the dust will be on the outside of the hat only; the inside will be protected by his head. But if he is engaged in the works, the dust will be inside, too, as the hat will hang on a peg in the dust-laden atmosphere, and his head will also be powdered, and so convey the dust to the inside."

He turned the hat over once more, and as I brought the powerful lens to bear upon the dark lining, I could clearly distinguish a number of white particles in the interstices of the fabric.

"The powder is on the inside, too," I said.

He took the lens from me, and, having verified my statement, proceeded with the examination. "You notice," he said, "that the leather head-lining is stained with grease, and this staining is more pronounced at the sides and back. His hair, therefore, is naturally greasy, or he greases it artificially; for if the staining were caused by perspiration, it would be most marked opposite the forehead."

He peered anxiously into the interior of the hat, and eventually turned down the head-lining; and immediately there broke out upon his face a gleam of satisfaction.

"Ha!" he exclaimed. "This is a stroke of luck. I was afraid our neat and orderly friend had defeated us with his brush. Pass me the small dissecting forceps, Jervis."

I handed him the instrument, and he proceeded to pick out daintily from the space behind the head-lining some half a dozen short pieces of hair, which he laid, with infinite tenderness, on a sheet of white paper.

"There are several more on the other side," I said, pointing them out to him.

"Yes, but we must leave some for the police," he answered, with a smile. "They must have the same chance as ourselves, you know."

"But surely," I said, as I bent down over the paper, "these are pieces of horsehair!"

"I think not," he replied; "but the microscope will show. At any rate, this is the kind of hair I should expect to find with a head of that shape."

"Well, it is extraordinarily coarse," said I, "and two of the hairs are nearly white."

"Yes; black hairs beginning to turn grey. And now, as our preliminary survey has given such encouraging results, we will proceed to more exact methods; and we must waste no time, for we shall have the police here presently to rob us of our treasure."

He folded up carefully the paper containing the hairs, and taking the hat in both hands, as though it were some sacred vessel, ascended with me to the laboratory on the next floor.

"Now, Polton," he said to his laboratory assistant, "we have here a specimen for examination and time is precious. First of all, we want your patent dust-extractor."

The little man bustled to a cupboard and brought forth a singular appliance, of his own manufacture, somewhat like a miniature vacuum cleaner. It had been made from a bicycle foot-pump, by reversing the piston-valve, and was fitted with a glass nozzle and a smal detachable glass receiver for collecting the dust, at the end of a flexible metal tube.

"We will sample the dust from the outside first," said Thorndyke, laying the hat upon th work-bench. "Are you ready, Polton?"

The assistant slipped his foot into the stirrup of the pump and worked the handl vigorously, while Thorndyke drew the glass nozzle slowly along the hat-brim under the curle edge. And as the nozzle passed along, the white coating vanished as if by magic, leaving th felt absolutely clean and black, and simultaneously the glass receiver became clouded ove with a white deposit.

"We will leave the other side for the police," said Thorndyke, and as Polton cease pumping he detached the receiver, and laid it on a sheet of paper, on which he wrote i pencil, "Outside," and covered it with a small bell-glass. A fresh receiver having been fitted o the nozzle was now drawn over the silk lining of the hat, and then through the space behir the leather head-lining on one side; and now the dust that collected in the receiver was muc of the usual grey colour and fluffy texture, and included two more hairs.

"And now," said Thorndyke, when the second receiver had been detached and set asid "we want a mould of the inside of the hat, and we must make it by the quickest method; the is no time to make a paper mould. It is a most astonishing head," he added, reaching dov from a nail a pair of large callipers, which he applied to the inside of the hat; "six inches and nine-tenths long by six and six-tenths broad, which gives us" – he made a rapid calculation on a scrap of paper – "the extraordinarily high cephalic index of 95·6."

Polton now took possession of the hat, and, having stuck a band of wet tissue-paper round the inside, mixed a small bowl of plaster-of-Paris, and very dexterously ran a stream of the thick liquid on to the tissue-paper, where it quickly solidified. A second and third application resulted in a broad ring of solid plaster an inch thick, forming a perfect mould of the inside of the hat, and in a few minutes the slight contraction of the plaster in setting rendered the mould sufficiently loose to allow of its being slipped out on to a board to dry.

We were none too soon, for even as Polton was removing the mould, the electric bell, which I had switched on to the laboratory, announced a visitor, and when I went down I found a police-sergeant waiting with a note from Superintendent Miller, requesting the immediate transfer of the hat.

"The next thing to be done," said Thorndyke, when the sergeant had departed with the bandbox, "is to measure the thickness of the hairs, and make a transverse section of one, and examine the dust. The section we will leave to Polton – as time is an object, Polton, you had better imbed the hair in thick gum and freeze it hard on the microtome, and be very careful to cut the section at right angles to the length of the hair – meanwhile, we will get to work with the microscope."

The hairs proved on measurement to have the surprisingly large diameter of 1/135 of an inch – fully double that of ordinary hairs, although they were unquestionably human. As to the white dust, it presented a problem that even Thorndyke was unable to solve. The application of reagents showed it to be carbonate of lime, but its source for a time remained a mystery.

"The larger particles," said Thorndyke, with his eye applied to the microscope, "appear to be transparent, crystalline, and distinctly laminated in structure. It is not chalk, it is not whiting, it is not any kind of cement. What can it be?"

"Could it be any kind of shell?" I suggested. "For instance—"

"Of course!" he exclaimed, starting up; "you have hit it, Jervis, as you always do. It must be mother-of-pearl. Polton, give me a pearl shirt-button out of your oddments box."

The button was duly produced by the thrifty Polton, dropped into an agate mortar, and speedily reduced to powder, a tiny pinch of which Thorndyke placed under the microscope.

"This powder," said he, "is, naturally, much coarser than our specimen, but the identity of character is unmistakable. Jervis, you are a treasure. Just look at it."

I glanced down the microscope, and then pulled out my watch. "Yes," I said, "there is no doubt about it, I think; but I must be off. Anstey urged me to be in court by 11.30 at the latest."

With infinite reluctance I collected my notes and papers and departed, leaving Thorndyke diligently copying addresses out of the Post Office Directory.

My business at the court detained me the whole of the day, and it was near upon dinner-time when I reached our chambers. Thorndyke had not yet come in, but he arrived half an hour later, tired and hungry, and not very communicative.

"What have I done?" he repeated, in answer to my inquiries. "I have walked miles of dirty pavement, and I have visited every pearl-shell cutter's in London, with one exception, and I have not found what I was looking for. The one mother-of-pearl factory that remains, however, is the most likely, and I propose to look in there tomorrow morning. Meanwhile, we have completed our data, with Polton's assistance. Here is a tracing of our friend's skull taken from the mould; you see it is an extreme type of brachycephalic skull, and markedly asymmetrical. Here is a transverse section of his hair, which is quite circular – unlike yours or mine, which would be oval. We have the mother-of-pearl dust from the outside of the hat, and from the inside similar dust mixed with various fibres and a few granules of rice starch. Those are our data."

"Supposing the hat should not be that of the burglar after all?" I suggested.

"That would be annoying. But I think it is his, and I think I can guess at the nature of the art treasures that were stolen."

"And you don't intend to enlighten me?"

"My dear fellow," he replied, "you have all the data. Enlighten yourself by the exercise of your own brilliant faculties. Don't give way to mental indolence."

I endeavoured, from the facts in my possession, to construct the personality of the mysterious burglar, and failed utterly; nor was I more successful in my endeavour to guess at the nature of the stolen property; and it was not until the following morning, when we had set out on our quest and were approaching Limehouse, that Thorndyke would revert to the subject.

"We are now," he said, "going to the factory of Badcomb and Martin, shell importers and cutters, in the West India Dock Road. If I don't find my man there, I shall hand the facts over to the police, and waste no more time over the case."

"What is your man like?" I asked.

"I am looking for an elderly Japanese, wearing a new hat or, more probably, a cap, and having a bruise on his right cheek or temple. I am also looking for a cab-yard; but here we are at the works, and as it is now close on the dinner-hour, we will wait and see the hands come out before making any inquiries."

We walked slowly past the tall, blank-faced building, and were just turning to re-pass it when a steam whistle sounded, a wicket opened in the main gate, and a stream of workmen – each powdered with white, like a miller – emerged into the street. We halted to watch the men as they came out, one by one, through the wicket, and turned to the right or left towards their homes or some adjacent coffee-shop; but none of them answered to the description that my friend had given.

The outcoming stream grew thinner, and at length ceased; the wicket was shut with a bang, and once more Thorndyke's quest appeared to have failed.

"Is that all of them, I wonder?" he said, with a shade of disappointment in his tone; bu even as he spoke the wicket opened again, and a leg protruded. The leg was followed by a back and a curious globular head, covered with iron-grey hair, and surmounted by a clot cap, the whole appertaining to a short, very thick-set man, who remained thus, evident talking to someone inside.

Suddenly he turned his head to look across the street; and immediately I recognized, b the pallid yellow complexion and narrow eye-slits, the physiognomy of a typical Japanes The man remained talking for nearly another minute; then, drawing out his other leg, h turned towards us; and now I perceived that the right side of his face, over the promine cheekbone, was discoloured as though by a severe bruise.

"Ha!" said Thorndyke, turning round sharply as the man approached, "either this is o man or it is an incredible coincidence." He walked away at a moderate pace, allowing th Japanese to overtake us slowly, and when the man had at length passed us, he increased h speed somewhat, so as to maintain the distance.

Our friend stepped along briskly, and presently turned up a side street, whither w followed at a respectful distance, Thorndyke holding open his pocket-book, and appeari to engage me in an earnest discussion, but keeping a sharp eye on his quarry.

"There he goes!" said my colleague, as the man suddenly disappeared – "the house with the green window-sashes. That will be number thirteen."

It was; and, having verified the fact, we passed on, and took the next turning that would lead us back to the main road.

Some twenty minutes later, as we were strolling past the door of a coffee-shop, a man came out, and began to fill his pipe with an air of leisurely satisfaction. His hat and clothes were powdered with white like those of the workmen whom we had seen come out of the factory. Thorndyke accosted him.

"Is that a flour-mill up the road there?"

"No, sir; pearl-shell. I work there myself."

"Pearl-shell, eh?" said Thorndyke. "I suppose that will be an industry that will tend to attract the aliens. Do you find it so?"

"No, sir; not at all. The work's too hard. We've only got one foreigner in the place, and he ain't an alien – he's a Jap."

"A Jap!" exclaimed Thorndyke. "Really. Now, I wonder if that would chance to be our old friend Kotei – you remember Kotei?" he added, turning to me.

"No, sir; this man's name is Futashima. There was another Jap in the works, a chap named Itu, a pal of Futashima's, but he's left."

"Ah! I don't know either of them. By the way, usen't there to be a cab-yard just about here?"

"There's a yard up Rankin Street where they keep vans and one or two cabs. That chap Itu works there now. Taken to horseflesh. Drives a van sometimes. Queer start for a Jap."

"Very." Thorndyke thanked the man for his information, and we sauntered on towards Rankin Street. The yard was at this time nearly deserted, being occupied only by an ancient and crazy four-wheeler and a very shabby hansom.

"Curious old houses, these that back on to the yard," said Thorndyke, strolling into the enclosure. "That timber gable, now," pointing to a house, from a window of which a man was watching us suspiciously, "is quite an interesting survival."

"What's your business, mister?" demanded the man in a gruff tone.

"We are just having a look at these quaint old houses," replied Thorndyke, edging towards the back of the hansom, and opening his pocket-book, as though to make a sketch.

"Well, you can see 'em from outside," said the man.

"So we can," said Thorndyke suavely, "but not so well, you know."

At this moment the pocket-book slipped from his hand and fell, scattering a number of loose papers about the ground under the hansom, and our friend at the window laughed joyously.

"No hurry," murmured Thorndyke, as I stooped to help him to gather up the papers – which he did in the most surprisingly slow and clumsy manner. "It is fortunate that the ground is dry." He stood up with the rescued papers in his hand, and, having scribbled down a brief note, slipped the book in his pocket.

"Now you'd better mizzle," observed the man at the window.

"Thank you," replied Thorndyke, "I think we had;" and, with a pleasant nod at the custodian, he proceeded to adopt the hospitable suggestion.

"Mr. Marchmont has been here, sir, with Inspector Badger and another gentleman," said Polton, as we entered our chambers. "They said they would call again about five."

"Then," replied Thorndyke, "as it is now a quarter to five, there is just time for us to have a wash while you get the tea ready. The particles that float in the atmosphere of Limehouse are not all mother-of-pearl."

Our visitors arrived punctually, the third gentleman being, as we had supposed, Mr. Solomon Löwe. Inspector Badger I had not seen before, and he now impressed me as showing a tendency to invert the significance of his own name by endeavouring to "draw" Thorndyke; in which, however, he was not brilliantly successful.

"I hope you are not going to disappoint Mr. Löwe, sir," he commenced facetiously. "You have had a good look at that hat – we saw your marks on it – and he expects that you will be able to point us out the man, name and address all complete." He grinned patronizingly at our unfortunate client, who was looking even more haggard and worn than he had been on the previous morning.

"Have you – have you made any – discovery?" Mr Löwe asked with pathetic eagerness.

"We examined the hat very carefully, and I think we have established a few facts of some interest."

"Did your examination of the hat furnish any information as to the nature of the stolen property, sir?" inquired the humorous inspector.

Thorndyke turned to the officer with a face as expressionless as a wooden mask.

"We thought it possible," said he, "that it might consist of works of Japanese art, such as netsukes, paintings, and such like."

Mr. Löwe uttered an exclamation of delighted astonishment, and the facetiousness faded rather suddenly from the inspector's countenance.

"I don't know how you can have found out," said he. "We have only known it half an hour ourselves, and the wire came direct from Florence to Scotland Yard."

"Perhaps you can describe the thief to us," said Mr. Löwe, in the same eager tone.

"I dare say the inspector can do that," replied Thorndyke.

"Yes, I think so," replied the officer. "He is a short strong man, with a dark complexion and hair turning grey. He has a very round head, and he is probably a workman engaged at some whiting or cement works. That is all we know; if you can tell us any more, sir, we shall be very glad to hear it."

"I can only offer a few suggestions," said Thorndyke, "but perhaps you may find them useful. For instance, at 13, Birket Street, Limehouse, there is living a Japanese gentleman named Futashima, who works at Badcomb and Martin's mother-of-pearl factory. I think that if you were to call on him, and let him try on the hat that you have, it would probably fit him."

The inspector scribbled ravenously in his notebook, and Mr. Marchmont – an old admirer of Thorndyke's – leaned back in his chair, chuckling softly and rubbing his hands.

"Then," continued my colleague, "there is in Rankin Street, Limehouse, a cab-yard where another Japanese gentleman named Itu is employed. You might find out where Itu was the night before last; and if you should chance to see a hansom cab there – number 22,481 – have a good look at it. In the frame of the number-plate you will find six small holes. Those holes may have held brads, and the brads may have held a false number card. At any rate, you might ascertain where that cab was at 11.30 the night before last. That is all I have to suggest."

Mr. Löwe leaped from his chair. "Let us go – now – at once – there is no time to be lost. A thousand thanks to you, doctor – a thousand million thanks. Come!"

He seized the inspector by the arm and forcibly dragged him towards the door, and a few moments later we heard the footsteps of our visitors clattering down the stairs.

"It was not worth while to enter into explanations with them," said Thorndyke, as the footsteps died away – "nor perhaps with you?"

"On the contrary," I replied, "I am waiting to be fully enlightened."

"Well, then, my inferences in this case were perfectly simple ones, drawn from well-known thropological facts. The human race, as you know, is roughly divided into three groups – the ack, the white, and the yellow races. But apart from the variable quality of colour, these races ve certain fixed characteristics associated especially with the shape of the skull, of the eye-ckets, and the hair.

"Thus in the black races the skull is long and narrow, the eye-sockets are long and narrow, d the hair is flat and ribbon-like, and usually coiled up like a watch-spring. In the white races e skull is oval, the eye-sockets are oval, and the hair is slightly flattened or oval in section, and nds to be wavy; while in the yellow or Mongol races, the skull is short and round, the eye-ckets are short and round, and the hair is straight and circular in section. So that we have, in e black races, long skull, long orbits, flat hair; in the white races, oval skull, oval orbits, oval ir; and in the yellow races, round skull, round orbits, round hair.

"Now, in this case we had to deal with a very short round skull. But you cannot argue from ces to individuals; there are many short-skulled Englishmen. But when I found, associated ith that skull, hairs which were circular in section, it became practically certain that the dividual was a Mongol of some kind. The mother-of-pearl dust and the granules of rice starch om the inside of the hat favoured this view, for the pearl-shell industry is specially connected ith China and Japan, while starch granules from the hat of an Englishman would probably be heat starch.

"Then as to the hair: it was, as I mentioned to you, circular in section, and of very large ameter. Now, I have examined many thousands of hairs, and the thickest that I have ever seen me from the heads of Japanese; but the hairs from this hat were as thick as any of them. But e hypothesis that the burglar was a Japanese received confirmation in various ways. Thus, he as short, though strong and active, and the Japanese are the shortest of the Mongol races, and ry strong and active.

"Then his remarkable skill in handling the powerful caretaker – a retired police-sergeant suggested the Japanese art of ju-jitsu, while the nature of the robbery was consistent with e value set by the Japanese on works of art. Finally, the fact that only a particular collection as taken, suggested a special, and probably national, character in the things stolen, while eir portability – you will remember that goods of the value of from eight to twelve thousand ounds were taken away in two hand-packages – was much more consistent with Japanese than hinese works, of which the latter tend rather to be bulky and ponderous. Still, it was nothing t a bare hypothesis until we had seen Futashima – and, indeed, is no more now. I may, after l, be entirely mistaken."

He was not, however; and at this moment there reposes in my drawing-room an ancient etsuke, which came as a thank-offering from Mr. Isaac Löwe on the recovery of the booty om a back room in No. 13, Birket Street, Limehouse. The treasure, of course, was given in e first place to Thorndyke, but transferred by him to my wife on the pretence that but for y suggestion of shell-dust the robber would never have been traced. Which is, on the face of preposterous.

Twenty Column Inches

Michael Martin Garrett

RAYMOND REYNOLDS, a disheveled and rather loosely put together fellow wearing Stetson of timeworn black felt, panicked as the door behind him creaked open. He pluck the smoking joint stuffed with sticky sativa from his lips, smooshed it into the ashtray besi the back door of the Detweiler County municipal building, and hoped his eyes weren't ove bloodshot. Luckily, his new companion was not a member of the police force housed in t same building, but an older woman with an elaborately-coiffed mahogany mane in an oversiz trench coat and impenetrable sunglasses. Ray breathed a sigh of relief, but then cursed hims for wasting weed. That was some good shit he just smashed into the pile of butts and ash.

The woman, standing beside him and watching the rain pour down on the municipal l produced a pack of cigarettes from insider her coat. She extended the pack toward Ray, w shook his head.

"No thanks. Don't smoke."

She cocked an eyebrow and looked at the hand-rolled wrapping Ray had just extinguished the ashtray, but merely shrugged and brought a cigarette to her red-painted lips. Ray turned h collar up and pulled his hat down, preparing to venture forth into the rain. He had to get ba to the newsroom to write up the county commissioners meeting. His editor wanted twer column inches, which Ray had tried to warn against. Nothing interesting ever happened wi the commissioners.

"Reynolds, right?" Ray turned to look at her. "We should talk."

"Should we?"

"I have a story for you." Her voice creaked like a rusted hinge.

"Well, greetings before business, as my dad used to say." Ray extended his hand. "Raymo Reynolds, crime reporter, Haroldston Herald." The woman grimaced, sucking down cigaret smoke. He frowned and retracted his hand. "You see, how greetings usually go, is one pers introduces themselves, then the other person goes, you see…"

"But I'm not important."

"Oh? Well, we got that in common."

The woman let out something halfway between a scoff and a chuckle. "Aren't you cleve She smirked in a peculiar way, the right half of her mouth curling upwards while the l remained inert.

"Not that I don't appreciate it," Ray said, "but flattery won't convince me to write whatever is you say you got for me."

"What would?"

Ray shrugged. "Dropping this silly lil' act couldn't hurt?"

Her eyebrows rose above the rims of her sunglasses. "Couldn't hurt *you*, maybe."

"Uh-huh. Look." He folded his arms. "Even off the record, I don't take tips from people wo tell me their name."

"I could be...an *anonymous* source."

"Yeah, that ain't how that works. You want to talk, you put your name to it. And *then*, if you ask nice, I won't put it in print."

A long moment slipped past as rain drip-dropped against the asphalt. Just as Ray was prepared to walk away, the woman sighed. "Abigail." Ray made little circles with his hand, as if reeling in a fishing line. "Connors."

"Uh-*huh*. Abigail Connors," extending his hand again, "pleased to make your acquaintance." The woman took his hand limply in her own.

"Charmed," she said.

"So what's the story, morning glory?"

She exhaled sharply from her nose, sending twin plumes of acrid smoke wafting toward him. "You know Allen Harbaugh, of course."

Ray nodded. He was the chair of the Detweiler County Commissioners, a squat and balding man with a monotone drawl who seemed determined to make each meeting of the board as dreadfully dull as possible. "Do you know," she asked, "what he did before his retirement, and subsequent election?"

"Construction."

"Founder of Harbaugh Construction, as a matter of fact, who just so happen to have been awarded every lucrative county contract since his election..."

Ray adjusted his hat. "Yeah, we looked into that a while back. He stepped down from the position before he even ran for office. Even talked off the record to a lawyer. Said it shouldn't be an issue, so long as he had removed himself from his business interests."

"You think these contracts are coincidence?"

He shrugged. "I mean, if they bid the lowest, they bid the lowest, y'know?"

She shook her head. "I'd expect better from the fourth estate." She flicked the butt to the ground and walked past him, turning her collar against the rain. "Follow the money, Reynolds."

After she turned the corner, Ray plucked his joint from the ashtray, brushed off a dusting of ash, and reignited it. The smoke, previously tinged with a floral sweetness, tasted now of tar.

* * *

The next afternoon, Ray sat in the driver's seat of his battered Bronco puffing on a joint in the parking lot outside the municipal building, slowly filling the cabin with sticky-sweet smoke as he watched rain-swollen clouds roll eastward across the Pennsylvania sky. In one of his jean pockets was a folded sheet of paper, detailing his Right-to-Know request for any and all documents related to the county's contracts with Harbaugh Construction. In the other was a sandwich baggie stuffed with half an ounce of maryjane.

He returned his gaze to his phone. He'd been scrolling through the Harbaugh Construction Facebook page for nearly twenty minutes, not quite sure what he was looking for, if anything. Wait. There. He paused to look at a photo that caught his eye. It had been posted five years ago, on the company's 30 year anniversary, and showed Allen Harbaugh and his staff posing with rigid smiles on their first day at work three decades earlier. Beside Harbaugh, clinging to his arm like tinsel to a Christmas tree, was a woman with a peculiar smirk. Only the right side of her mouth smiled, while the left stayed still. All she was missing was a trench coat and an oversized pair of sunglasses.

"Hey there, Abigail..."

Funny thing was, there were no Connors in the area, at least not that Ray knew. He didn't know everyone exactly, but kept tabs on who had beef with whom, tracking generations-long familial disputes that spilled over into his beat with some regularity. If there was a feud between the Harbaughs and another family, like these alleged Connors, Ray wagered he'd already have known about it.

A sharp rapping at his window interrupted his musings. Ray choked on a lungful of hot smoke. Looking over, he saw a thin-lipped and prematurely gray-headed figure in a cheap suit: David Wells, county administrator, a beleaguered bureaucrat who spent his days shuffling paperwork for the commissioners. Ray unlocked his Bronco doors.

"Christ, Reynolds, have a little courtesy, huh?" Wells said, waving his hand in an ill-fated attempt to dissipate the cloud of pungent smoke that filled the truck. "I gotta go back in the office."

Ray was too preoccupied with regurgitating his lungs to respond. He pulled the bag of weed from his pocket and tossed it in Wells' lap. The bureaucrat placed a wad of twenties in his cup holder. He moved to exit the truck, but Ray held up a finger.

"What? The longer I sit here, the more I smell like getting fired."

"I have something else for you," Ray wheezed, "but first..." He showed him the photo on his phone and pointed to the woman. "Do you know her?"

"Harbaugh's ex-wife? Sure. Why?"

Ray coughed, then smiled. "No reason." He pulled the papers from his other pocket and passed them to Wells. "These are for you."

Wells took them and read the request over. He rolled his eyes. "What are you after, Ray?" He shrugged. "You know, I could probably get away with denying this request for being overly broad. *Any and all* documents on Harbaugh contracts? County's been working with them for years."

Ray nodded, tapping his fingers together in front of his mouth. "Funny. That's also as long as I been sellin' you the dankest shit in town."

Wells grimaced. "Mmm."

"Come on. Isn't this, like, your job?"

"*Part* of my job. You have any idea how much time this'll take me?" Ray stuck out his lip in an exaggerated pout. Wells sighed. "Fine. Just give me a bit of time. I'll get you the records. Just don't go sticking my name in anything."

"No worries, my guy. Off the record."

* * *

Two weeks passed before Wells got Ray what he'd formally requested pursuant to state law longer than the law technically allotted. Ray could see what it had taken so long. The folder, held together by an oversized rubber band, was thick enough to stop a bullet.

"My magnum opus," Wells said when he handed it over, again sitting in Ray's passenger seat "Think this can get me a discount off my next order?"

Ray shook his head. "Technically, trading favors is a violation of my professional ethics..."

"And dealing to sources isn't?" Ray raised a finger to respond, but paused. He had a poin Wells pressed on. "I'm not sure what you're looking for in there, but if this has anything to d with Eleanor, I'd watch yourself."

"Eleanor?"

"Harbaugh's ex. The one you'd asked about. She's been trying to stir up trouble for him ever since they split. Sent out mailers during his reelection campaign accusin' him of being a RINO."

"Musta been a messy divorce."

"Left her for another woman," Wells nodded. "Don't see his new wife around much anymore, though."

"Tell you the truth, Eleanor mighta had sumptin to do with my curiosity."

"Careful. Whatever story she said she had for you, it ain't outta the goodness of her heart."

"So? It never is. But that don't mean it ain't true."

He started reading through the folder that night, sitting on the collection of lumps he called a couch with joint in hand and a well-worn copy of *At Folsom Prison* spinning on his turntable. There were hundreds of pages of bids, contracts, and records of payments, dating back decades. After several hours of squinting at the undersized font through the smoke and lamplight, a pattern began to emerge.

The county had worked on and off with Harbaugh Construction since the company's founding in 1979. They'd often submitted bids for projects, but were rarely the lowest bidder. But after Harbaugh was elected to the board of county commissioners in 2005, the frequency of contracts skyrocketed. In fact, Ray noticed, they were still only the lowest bidder maybe a third of the time, but received nearly every contract for which they had entered a bid. Things weren't adding up, namely, the dollar signs. In almost every case, the county was paying out somewhere in the neighborhood of fifteen to twenty percent more than what was listed in the bids, contracts, or invoices. According to his napkin math, over $600,000 of taxpayer funds had vanished into the aether over the last fourteen years. Another $400,000 or so could've been saved if the county had contracted out to lower bidders in the first place. Ray wasn't a lawyer, but if it looks like embezzlement and quacks like embezzlement…

He cracked his knuckles, opened his laptop, and got to work. He sent a message to Harbaugh's official county email address requesting an interview on a story he was working on 'concerning discrepancies related to the county's contracts with Harbaugh Construction.' Three joints later, he had the bones of the most interesting county commissioner story he'd ever written, at twenty five column inches.

* * *

Twenty-six joints, four emails, three days, and two voicemails later, Ray still hadn't heard from Harbaugh. He'd already waited long enough. Maybe too long. Eleanor had already earned her own folder in his inbox for her messages inquiring about the story, all signed 'Abigail Connors.' For all he knew, she had already pulled her femme fatale act with WKKA, the local Fox affiliate, who would probably fall for the schtick. More importantly, his editor would have his guts for garters if they beat him to the story. But there was no way Ray could, in good conscience, go to print without some kind of comment from the man himself. Even an official 'no comment' from Harbaugh or, more likely, from his lawyer, would be enough. Time for the nuclear option. His stomach turned at the thought, but, as his dad used to say, half the job was just showing up. One of many lessons Ray wished he'd listened to when he was younger.

It was a brisk Saturday afternoon lit by cold, pale sunlight when Ray pulled up outside of Harbaugh's Victorian manor on what passed for the ritzy side of Haroldston, the Detweiler County seat, where the neatly-manicured lawns and water features this side of Main Street stood in stark contrast to the entropy that had slowly engulfed the rest of town over the preceding decades. But the pale green paint of Harbaugh's home had grown peeled and faded, the gutters stuffed with dead leaves, and the lawn wildly unkempt, as if he'd given up on maintaining the outward appearance of wealth his neighbors on either side still enjoyed.

Ray had burned down a joint on the way over to calm his nerves, which had accomplished the exact opposite. He now imagined escalating scenarios wherein Harbaugh, desperate, at the end of his rope, pulled a gun on him. Maybe he should bring the folder. He repeated a familiar mantra. *I'm probably just being paranoid.* Ten deep breaths later, he left his Bronco, crossed the street, and rang the bell.

The door opened. Harbaugh, one of the few people Ray knew shorter than him, peered up at him through the crack in the doorway.

"Reynolds," he said simply, as if he'd been expecting him.

"Afternoon, Commissioner Harbaugh. I'm here to—"

"I know why you're here, and I have no comment." Harbaugh opened the door. He wore an ash-grey terry robe over a plain white t-shirt and sweats. "But what's done is done. Might as well come in." He walked off, leaving the door open behind him. Ray entered. Harbaugh poked his head into the foyer from around the corner and pointed to a mat on the floor. "Shoes." Ray obliged, leaving his father's beat-up black leather cowboy boots beside the door.

Hesitatingly, he followed in his sockfeet from the foyer to a living room lined by potted ferns and framed oil paintings of barns, farms, and landscapes. Past a granite-topped breakfast bar, Ray could see into a spacious kitchen, where a grey-headed woman in white sat at the kitchen table beside a portly nurse who raised a spoonful of soup to the old woman's mouth, gently encouraged her to receive the food, and watched carefully as she swallowed. Her eyes, bright but unfocused, circled aimlessly until they landed on Ray.

"Oh, hi," she smiled. "Who are you?"

"This is Raymond Reynolds," Harbaugh answered before Ray could. "He's a friend from work."

The woman nodded, a wide smile splitting her face in two. "I'm Barbara," she said to Ray. "Do you want to have lunch with me?"

"Oh, I, uh…" Ray stammered, but the woman looked away as he tried to answer. She turned back to him and smiled again.

"Hi! ...who are you? I'm Barbara."

Ray looked at Harbaugh, who sat now on the couch with his hands folded in front of his face. "Chris?" The nurse looked at him. "Can you take Barb and give us a moment? We need to talk privately. Business, you know." The nurse nodded, stood from the table, and helped Barbara to her feet. She followed the nurse, led gently by the arm, down the hall into the recesses of the home. Ray sat opposite Harbaugh, removed his hat, and laid it beside him Harbaugh lowered his hands and folded them in his lap, frowning at Ray.

"This can be off the record, I hope."

Ray nodded. "So, Barbara, is she…?"

"My wife."

"After Eleanor?"

Harbaugh looked down, smiled darkly to himself. "Shoulda figured you'd met he Probably came to you even." He looked back up at Ray, who said nothing. "It's okay. understand. Part of her never moved on after the divorce. That's her right, I suppose. Di a lot of wrong by her."

"Commissioner—"

"Allen, please." He gestured to the couch. Ray took a seat.

"...Allen, I'm sorry, but that's not what I'm here about."

The commissioner sighed and nodded. "I know. I got your messages. Maybe I just wanted to think the problem would go away if I ignored it." He shook his head. "Guess I'll never learn."

Ray sat there for a moment, employing the old reporter's trick of letting the silence force the subject into speaking, but Harbaugh remained quiet, his brow furrowed contemplatively. Ray squirmed on the cloud-soft cushion, nervously curling and uncurling his toes inside his socks. Still Allen said nothing, staring sadly at his socks.

"I obtained a number of county records that, near as I can tell, show that a *lot* of taxpayer funds were overpaid to Harbaugh Construction. Funds that weren't on the invoices the company submitted. Funds that disappeared somewhere. Anything you want to say about what that's all about?"

Harbaugh smiled, but there was no joy in the grin. "What does it look like?"

"Well, it doesn't look good," Ray said. Harbaugh looked up at him, his grey eyes steely and cold. The smile melted. "And the public will probably draw their own conclusions."

Harbaugh exhaled from his nose and rested his head against the back of the couch, staring impassively at the ceiling. "'Spose I should call up my attorney at some point."

"Yeah. Probably," Ray agreed.

Harbaugh leaned forward again, rubbed his face with his hands. "Do you know what it's like to watch someone die while they're still alive?"

Ray nodded. "Yes," he said, quietly.

"So you understand?"

Ray said nothing.

"You need to understand. You need to understand what's at stake, what you're doing," Harbaugh said. "You said this is all off the record?" The reporter nodded. "Not that it matters," the commissioner continued, his voice taking on an icy edge, "not that you care, but when Barb first started showing signs, forgetting little things, gettin' all confused over nothin', I just wanted to pretend it was gonna be okay. Just a little lie to get through the day."

"Sure. I tell a few myself."

"But it kept getting worse, until the truth became bigger than the lie. I had to do something." Harbaugh gazed desperately, almost pleadingly, at Ray. "So I did. Alright? I did what I had to do. Who are you to tell what I should've done?"

"I'm just trying to tell the truth," Ray said. "And I'm sorry about Barbara. Really, I am. But what do you want from me, just don't publish the story?"

"Well," he raised his empty, well-calloused hands, "Your words."

"Look, this is *public* money. And a shit ton of it."

Harbaugh leaned back, crossed his legs, and looked down the long hall Barbara and the nurse had disappeared down. His eyes grew red and wet. Ray wondered if they were crocodile tears on his behalf.

"I'm sorry," Ray said, hunched over, shaking his head. "But this is going in the paper."

Harbaugh, his cheeks flushed, wiped sweat from his brow, despite the humming of the air conditioner in the window. "I'm sure we could... come to some kind of arrangement. Make it worth your while..."

Ray thought about all the things in his life that were nearly empty: his bank account, his gas tank, his pantry, his stomach. But still he shook his head.

"But," Harbaugh's lips began to tremble, but his voice was steady and sharp, "think about what'll happen to Barb if you—"

"You want to lay this on me? You made your choices. Not me. You knew what you were doing," Ray said, crossing his arms.

Harbaugh's lips quit their trembling and anger flashed in his eyes. "This is the problem with you people," he said. "Never taking responsibility for the lies you tell, the agendas you push. The *lives* you *ruin*."

"Ohohohokay," Ray genuinely laughed. "It's like that. Alright. The only lie I'd be telling is if I let this sleeping dog alone." He stood up, grabbing his hat from the cushion beside him. "And the only mistakes I'm responsible for are mine. Tell you what, I've made more of 'em than I've had hot dinners and I carry 'em around like an albatross 'round my neck every damn day. So best lawyer up and learn to blame yourself, 'cause I don't need the weight of your fuck-ups too."

They smoldered at each for a long, quiet moment, Harbaugh still sitting with and Ray standing, their arms both crossed. Harbaugh rose to his full height, about to Ray's nose, sneering.

"Get the hell out of my house."

"Sure," Ray said, donning his Stetson. "You got it. Thanks for your time, and help with this story."

The sound of Barbara's laughter echoed from down the hall. Harbaugh looked toward the sound, the lines of his face softening instinctively. Ray made for the door, but kept slipping as he hurriedly tried to slip on his boots. Harbaugh came into the foyer as Ray was sitting on the floor, awkwardly yanking his pull-straps. Ray stood up, trying to play it cool, and reached for the handle.

"Wait," Harbaugh said. "Who was it?"

"Wha?"

"You said you knew what it was like. To watch someone die, still living."

Ray stood quiet and still as a statue.

"Who was it?"

He opened the door, stepped through, and pulled it closed behind him as he left. Back in his Bronco, he sat silently for a long time, not smoking, not moving, not thinking. He eventually pulled a joint from his glovebox and lit up as he opened his laptop and pulled up the latest version of the article. He added a single line to the end: "When contacted, Harbaugh declined to comment." He fired off the story.

Ray closed the laptop and tossed it into the passenger seat. He thought, for the first time in a long time, about his mother. She'd forgotten his name, then her own. All the years he wasted drugging and drinking and rambling around the commonwealth, they hadn't spoken. He hadn't so much as called. She'd never seen him in uniform after joining the Navy. And by the time he finally came back home, the chance had passed forever, just one more in a long line of regrets that followed Ray through the long, languid years of his life like a shadow. He wiped his face. When had he started crying?

By the time he got back to his apartment, Ray had navigated himself back to a comfortable and familiar emptiness. A reply was waiting in his inbox from his editor. Apparently the story was too long. She wanted him to cut it down to twenty column inches.

Ray sighed and lit up a joint.

Missing: Page Thirteen

Anna Katherine Green

Chapter I

“**ONE MORE!** Just one more well-paying affair, and I promise to stop; really and truly to stop.”

“But, Puss, why one more? You have earned the amount you set for yourself, – or very nearly, – and though my help is not great, in three months I can add enough—”

“No, you cannot, Arthur. You are doing well; I appreciate it; in fact, I am just delighted to have you work for me in the way you do, but you cannot, in your position, make enough in three months, or in six, to meet the situation as I see it. Enough does not satisfy me. The measure must be full, heaped up, and running over. Possible failure following promise must be provided for. Never must I feel myself called upon to do this kind of thing again. Besides, I have never got over the Zabriskie tragedy. It haunts me continually. Something new may help to put it out of my head. I feel guilty. I was responsible—”

“No, Puss. I will not have it that you were responsible. Some such end was bound to follow a complication like that. Sooner or later he would have been driven to shoot himself—”

“But not her.”

“No, not her. But do you think she would have given those few minutes of perfect understanding with her blind husband for a few years more of miserable life?”

Violet made no answer; she was too absorbed in her surprise. Was this Arthur? Had a few weeks' work and a close connection with the really serious things of life made this change in him? Her face beamed at the thought, which seeing, but not understanding what underlay this evidence of joy, he bent and kissed her, saying with some of his old nonchalance:

“Forget it, Violet; only don't let anyone or anything lead you to interest yourself in another affair of the kind. If you do, I shall have to consult a certain friend of yours as to the best way of stopping this folly. I mention no names. Oh! you need not look so frightened. Only behave; that's all.”

“He's right,” she acknowledged to herself, as he sauntered away; “altogether right.”

Yet because she wanted the extra money—

* * *

The scene invited alarm, – that is, for so young a girl as Violet, surveying it from an automobile some time after the stroke of midnight. An unknown house at the end of a heavily shaded walk, in the open doorway of which could be seen the silhouette of a woman's form leaning eagerly forward with arms outstretched in an appeal for help! It vanished while she looked, but the effect remained, holding her to her seat for one startled moment. This seemed strange, for she had anticipated adventure. One is not summoned from a private ball to ride a dozen miles into the country on an errand of investigation, without some expectation of encountering the mysterious and the tragic. But Violet Strange, for all her many experiences, was of a most susceptible nature, and for the instant in which that door stood open, with only the memory of that expectant figure to disturb the faintly lit vista of the hall beyond, she felt that grip upon the throat which comes from an indefinable fear which no words can explain and no plummet sound.

But this soon passed. With the setting of her foot to ground, conditions changed and her emotions took on a more normal character. The figure of a man now stood in the place held by the vanished woman, and it was not only that of one she knew but that of one whom she trusted – a friend whose very presence gave her courage. With this recognition came a better understanding of the situation, and it was with a beaming eye and unclouded features that she tripped up the walk to meet the expectant figure and outstretched hand of Roger Upjohn.

"You here!" she exclaimed, amid smiles and blushes, as he drew her into the hall.

He at once launched forth into explanations mingled with apologies for the presumption he had shown in putting her to this inconvenience. There was trouble in the house – great trouble. Something had occurred for which an explanation must be found before morning, or the happiness and honour of more than one person now under this unhappy roof would be wrecked. He knew it was late – that she had been obliged to take a long and dreary ride alone, but her success with the problem which had once come near wrecking his own life had emboldened him to telephone to the office and – "But you are in ball-dress," he cried in amazement. "Did you think—"

"I came from a ball. Word reached me between the dances. I did not go home. I had been bidden to hurry."

He looked his appreciation, but when he spoke it was to say:

"This is the situation. Miss Digby—"

"The lady who is to be married tomorrow?"

"Who *hopes* to be married tomorrow."

"How, *hopes*?"

"Who *will* be married tomorrow, if a certain article lost in this house tonight can be found before any of the persons who have been dining here leave for their homes."

Violet uttered an exclamation.

"Then, Mr. Cornell—" she began.

"Mr. Cornell has our utmost confidence," Roger hastened to interpose. "But the article missing is one which he might reasonably desire to possess and which he alone of all present had the opportunity of securing. You can therefore see why he, with his pride – the pride of a man not rich, engaged to marry a woman who is – should declare that unless his innocence is established before daybreak, the doors of St. Bartholomew will remain shut tomorrow."

"But the article lost – what is it?"

"Miss Digby will give you the particulars. She is waiting to receive you," he added with a gesture towards a half-open door at their right.

Violet glanced that way, then cast her looks up and down the hall in which they stood.

"Do you know that you have not told me in whose house I am? Not hers, I know. She lives in the city."

"And you are twelve miles from Harlem. Miss Strange, you are in the Van Broecklyn mansion, famous enough you will acknowledge. Have you never been here before?"

"I have been by here, but I recognized nothing in the dark. What an exciting place for an investigation!"

"And Mr. Van Broecklyn? Have you never met him?"

"Once, when a child. He frightened me *then*."

"And may frighten you now; though I doubt it. Time has mellowed him. Besides, I have prepared him for what might otherwise occasion him some astonishment. Naturally he would not look for just the sort of lady investigator I am about to introduce to him."

She smiled. Violet Strange was a very charming young woman, as well as a keen prober of odd mysteries.

The meeting between herself and Miss Digby was a sympathetic one. After the first inevitable shock which the latter felt at sight of the beauty and fashionable appearance of the mysterious little being who was to solve her difficulties, her glance, which under other circumstances might have lingered unduly upon the piquant features and exquisite dressing of the fairy-like figure before her, passed at once to Violet's eyes in whose steady depths beamed an intelligence quite at odds with the coquettish dimples which so often misled the casual observer in his estimation of a character singularly subtle and well-poised.

As for the impression she herself made upon Violet – it was the same she made upon everyone. No one could look long at Florence Digby and not recognize the loftiness of her spirit and the generous nature of her impulses. In person she was tall, and as she leaned to take Violet's hand, the difference between them brought out the salient points in each, to the great admiration of the one onlooker.

Meantime for all her interest in the case in hand, Violet could not help casting a hurried look about her, in gratification of the curiosity incited by her entrance into a house signalized from its foundation by such a series of tragic events. The result was disappointing. The walls were plain, the furniture simple. Nothing suggestive in either, unless it was the fact that nothing was new, nothing modern. As it looked in the days of Burr and Hamilton so it looked today, even to the rather startling detail of candles which did duty on every side in place of gas.

As Violet recalled the reason for this the fascination of the past seized upon her imagination. There was no knowing where this might have carried her, had not the feverish gleam in Miss Digby's eyes warned her that the present held its own excitement. Instantly, she was all attention and listening with undivided mind to that lady's disclosures.

They were brief and to the following effect:

The dinner which had brought some half-dozen people together in this house had been given in celebration of her impending marriage. But it was also in a way meant as a compliment to one of the other guests, a Mr. Spielhagen, who, during the week, had succeeded in demonstrating to a few experts the value of a discovery he had made which would transform a great industry.

In speaking of this discovery, Miss Digby did not go into particulars, the whole matter being far beyond her understanding; but in stating its value she openly acknowledged that it was in the line of Mr. Cornell's own work, and one which involved calculations and a formula which, if prematurely disclosed, would invalidate the contract Mr. Spielhagen hoped to make, and thus destroy his present hopes.

Of this formula but two copies existed. One was locked up in a safe-deposit vault in Boston, the other he had brought into the house on his person, and it was the latter which was now missing, it having been abstracted during the evening from a manuscript of sixteen or more sheets, under circumstances which he would now endeavour to relate.

Mr. Van Broecklyn, their host, had in his melancholy life but one interest which could be called at all absorbing. This was for explosives. As a consequence, much of the talk at the dinner-table had been on Mr. Spielhagen's discovery, and the possible changes it might introduce into this especial industry. As these, worked out from a formula kept secret from the trade, could not but affect greatly Mr. Cornell's interests, she found herself listening intently, when Mr. Van Broecklyn, with an apology for his interference, ventured to remark that if Mr. Spielhagen had made a valuable discovery in this line, so had he, and one which he had substantiated by many experiments. It was not a marketable one, such as Mr. Spielhagen's was, but in his work upon the same, and in the tests which he had been led to make, he had discovered certain instances he would gladly name, which demanded exceptional procedure to be successful. If Mr. Spielhagen's method did not allow for these exceptions, nor make suitable provision for them, then Mr. Spielhagen's method would fail more times than it would succeed. Did it so allow and so provide? It would relieve him greatly to learn that it did.

The answer came quickly. Yes, it did. But later and after some further conversation, Mr. Spielhagen's confidence seemed to wane, and before they left the dinner-table, he openly declared his intention of looking over his manuscript again that very night, in order to be sure that the formula therein contained duly covered all the exceptions mentioned by Mr. Van Broecklyn.

If Mr. Cornell's countenance showed any change at this moment, she for one had not noticed it; but the bitterness with which he remarked upon the other's good fortune in having discovered this formula of whose entire success he had no doubt, was apparent to everybody, and naturally gave point to the circumstances which a short time afterward associated him with the disappearance of the same.

The ladies (there were two others besides herself) having withdrawn in a body to the music-room, the gentlemen all proceeded to the library to smoke. Here, conversation loosed from the one topic which had hitherto engrossed it, was proceeding briskly, when Mr. Spielhagen, with a nervous gesture, impulsively looked about him and said:

"I cannot rest till I have run through my thesis again. Where can I find a quiet spot? I won't be long; I read very rapidly."

It was for Mr. Van Broecklyn to answer, but no word coming from him, every eye turned his way, only to find him sunk in one of those fits of abstraction so well known to his friends, and from which no one who has this strange man's peace of mind at heart ever presumes to rouse him.

What was to be done? These moods of their singular host sometimes lasted half an hour, and Mr. Spielhagen had not the appearance of a man of patience. Indeed he presently gave proof of the great uneasiness he was labouring under, for noticing a door standing ajar on the other side of the room, he remarked to those around him:

"A den! and lighted! Do you see any objection to my shutting myself in there for a few minutes?"

No one venturing to reply, he rose, and giving a slight push to the door, disclosed a small room exquisitely panelled and brightly lighted, but without one article of furniture in it, not even a chair.

"The very place," quoth Mr. Spielhagen, and lifting a light cane-bottomed chair from the many standing about, he carried it inside and shut the door behind him.

Several minutes passed during which the man who had served at table entered with a tray on which were several small glasses evidently containing some choice liqueur. Finding his master fixed in one of his strange moods, he set the tray down and, pointing to one of the glasses, said:

"That is for Mr. Van Broecklyn. It contains his usual quieting powder." And urging the gentlemen to help themselves, he quietly left the room.

Mr. Upjohn lifted the glass nearest him, and Mr. Cornell seemed about to do the same when he suddenly reached forward and catching up one farther off started for the room in which Mr. Spielhagen had so deliberately secluded himself.

Why he did all this – why, above all things, he should reach across the tray for a glass instead of taking the one under his hand, he can no more explain than why he has followed many another unhappy impulse. Nor did he understand the nervous start given by Mr. Spielhagen at his entrance, or the stare with which that gentleman took the glass from his hand and mechanically drank its contents, till he saw how his hand had stretched itself across the sheet of paper he was reading, in an open attempt to hide the lines visible between his fingers. Then indeed the intruder flushed and withdrew in great embarrassment, fully conscious of his indiscretion but not deeply disturbed till Mr. Van Broecklyn, suddenly arousing and glancing down at the tray placed very near his hand, remarked in some surprise: "Dobbs seems to have forgotten me." Then indeed, the unfortunate Mr. Cornell realized what he had done. It was the glass intended for his host which he had caught up and carried into the other room – the glass which he had been told contained a drug. Of what folly he had been guilty, and how tame would be any effort at excuse!

Attempting none, he rose and with a hurried glance at Mr. Upjohn who flushed in sympathy at his distress, he crossed to the door he had so lately closed upon Mr. Spielhagen. But feeling his shoulder touched as his hand pressed the knob, he turned to meet the eye of Mr. Van Broecklyn fixed upon him with an expression which utterly confounded him.

"Where are you going?" that gentleman asked.

The questioning tone, the severe look, expressive at once of displeasure and astonishment, were most disconcerting, but Mr. Cornell managed to stammer forth:

"Mr. Spielhagen is in here consulting his thesis. When your man brought in the cordial, I was awkward enough to catch up your glass and carry it in to Mr. Spielhagen. He drank it and I – I am anxious to see if it did him any harm."

As he uttered the last word he felt Mr. Van Broecklyn's hand slip from his shoulder, but no word accompanied the action, nor did his host make the least move to follow him into the room.

This was a matter of great regret to him later, as it left him for a moment out of the range of every eye, during which he says he simply stood in a state of shock at seeing Mr. Spielhagen still sitting there, manuscript in hand, but with head fallen forward and eyes closed; dead, asleep or – he hardly knew what; the sight so paralyzed him.

Whether or not this was the exact truth and the whole truth, Mr. Cornell certainly looked very unlike himself as he stepped back into Mr. Van Broecklyn's presence; and he was only partially reassured when that gentleman protested that there was no real harm in the drug, and that Mr. Spielhagen would be all right if left to wake naturally and without shock. However, as his present attitude was one of great discomfort, they decided to carry him back and lay him on the library lounge. But before doing this, Mr. Upjohn drew from his flaccid grasp the precious manuscript, and carrying it into the larger room placed it on a remote table, where it remained undisturbed till Mr. Spielhagen, suddenly coming to himself at the end of some fifteen minutes, missed the sheets from his hand, and bounding up, crossed the room to repossess himself of them.

His face, as he lifted them up and rapidly ran through them with ever-accumulating anxiety, told them what they had to expect.

The page containing the formula was gone!

* * *

Violet now saw her problem.

Chapter II

THERE WAS NO DOUBT about the loss I have mentioned; all could see that page 13 was not there. In vain a second handling of every sheet, the one so numbered was not to be found. Page 14 met the eye on the top of the pile, and page 12 finished it off at the bottom, but no page 13 in between, or anywhere else.

Where had it vanished, and through whose agency had this misadventure occurred? No one could say, or, at least, no one there made any attempt to do so, though everybody started to look for it.

But where look? The adjoining small room offered no facilities for hiding a cigar-end, much less a square of shining white paper. Bare walls, a bare floor, and a single chair for furniture, comprised all that was to be seen in this direction. Nor could the room in which they then stood be thought to hold it, unless it was on the person of some one of them. Could this be the explanation of the mystery? No man looked his doubts; but Mr. Cornell, possibly divining the general feeling, stepped up to Mr. Van Broecklyn and in a cool voice, but with the red burning hotly on either cheek, said so as to be heard by everyone present:

"I demand to be searched – at once and thoroughly."

A moment's silence, then the common cry:

"We will all be searched."

"Is Mr. Spielhagen sure that the missing page was with the others when he sat down in the adjoining room to read his thesis?" asked their perturbed host.

"Very sure," came the emphatic reply. "Indeed, I was just going through the formula itself when I fell asleep."

"You are ready to assert this?"

"I am ready to swear it."

Mr. Cornell repeated his request.

"I demand that you make a thorough search of my person. I must be cleared, and instantly, of every suspicion," he gravely asserted, "or how can I marry Miss Digby tomorrow?"

After that there was no further hesitation. One and all subjected themselves to the ordeal suggested; even Mr. Spielhagen. But this effort was as futile as the rest. The lost page was not found.

What were they to think? What were they to do?

There seemed to be nothing left to do, and yet some further attempt must be made towards the recovery of this important formula. Mr. Cornell's marriage and Mr. Spielhagen's business success both depended upon its being in the latter's hands before six in the morning, when he was engaged to hand it over again to a certain manufacturer sailing for Europe on an early steamer.

Five hours!

Had Mr. Van Broecklyn a suggestion to offer? No, he was as much at sea as the rest.

Simultaneously look crossed look. Blankness was on every face.

"Let us call the ladies," suggested one.

It was done, and however great the tension had been before, it was even greater when Miss Digby stepped upon the scene. But she was not a woman to be shaken from her poise even by a crisis of this importance. When the dilemma had been presented to her and the full situation grasped, she looked first at Mr. Cornell and then at Mr. Spielhagen, and quietly said:

"There is but one explanation possible of this matter. Mr. Spielhagen will excuse me, but he is evidently mistaken in thinking that he saw the lost page among the rest. The condition into which he was thrown by the unaccustomed drug he had drank, made him liable to hallucinations. I have not the least doubt he thought he had been studying the formula at the time he dropped off to sleep. I have every confidence in the gentleman's candour. But so have I in that of Mr. Cornell," she supplemented, with a smile.

An exclamation from Mr. Van Broecklyn and a subdued murmur from all but Mr. Spielhagen testified to the effect of this suggestion, and there is no saying what might have been the result if Mr. Cornell had not hurriedly put in this extraordinary and most unexpected protest:

"Miss Digby has my gratitude," said he, "for a confidence which I hope to prove to be deserved. But I must say this for Mr. Spielhagen. He was correct in stating that he was engaged in looking over his formula when I stepped into his presence with the glass of cordial. If you were not in a position to see the hurried way in which his hand instinctively spread itself over the page he was reading, I was; and if that does not seem conclusive to you, then I feel bound to state that in unconsciously following this movement of his, I plainly saw the number written on the top of the page, and that number was – 13."

A loud exclamation, this time from Spielhagen himself, announced his gratitude and corresponding change of attitude toward the speaker.

"Wherever that damned page has gone," he protested, advancing towards Cornell with outstretched hand, "you have nothing to do with its disappearance."

Instantly all constraint fled, and every countenance took on a relieved expression. *But the problem remained.*

Suddenly those very words passed someone's lips, and with their utterance Mr. Upjohn remembered how at an extraordinary crisis in his own life, he had been helped and an equally difficult problem settled, by a little lady secretly attached to a private detective agency. If she could only be found and hurried here before morning, all might yet be well. He would make the effort. Such wild schemes sometimes work. He telephoned to the office and—

Was there anything else Miss Strange would like to know?

Chapter III

MISS STRANGE, thus appealed to, asked where the gentlemen were now.

She was told that they were still all together in the library; the ladies had been sent home.

"Then let us go to them," said Violet, hiding under a smile her great fear that here was an affair which might very easily spell for her that dismal word, *failure*.

So great was that fear that under all ordinary circumstances she would have had no thought for anything else in the short interim between this stating of the problem and her speedy entrance among the persons involved. But the circumstances of this case were so far from ordinary, or rather let me put it in this way, the setting of the case was so very extraordinary, that she scarcely thought of the problem before her, in her great interest in the house through whose rambling halls she was being so carefully guided. So much that was tragic and heartrending had occurred here. The Van Broecklyn name, the Van Broecklyn history, above all the Van Broecklyn tradition, which made the house unique in the country's annals, all made an appeal to her imagination, and centred her thoughts on what she saw about her. There was a door which no man ever opened – had never opened since Revolutionary times – should she see it? Should she know it if she did see it? Then Mr. Van Broecklyn himself! Just to meet him, under any conditions and in any place, was an event. But to meet him here, under the pall of his own mystery! No wonder she had no words for her companions, or that her thoughts clung to this anticipation in wonder and almost fearsome delight.

His story was a well-known one. A bachelor and a misanthrope, he lived absolutely alone save for a large entourage of servants, all men and elderly ones at that. He never visited. Though he now and then, as on this occasion, entertained certain persons under his roof, he declined every invitation for himself, avoiding even, with equal strictness, all evening amusements of whatever kind, which would detain him in the city after ten at night. Perhaps this was to ensure no break in his rule of life never to sleep out of his own bed. Though he was a man well over fifty he had not spent, according to his own statement, but two nights out of his own bed since his return from Europe in early boyhood, and those were in obedience to a judicial summons which took him to Boston.

This was his main eccentricity, but he had another which is apparent enough from what has already been said. He avoided women. If thrown in with them during his short visits into town, he was invariably polite and at all times companionable, but he never sought them out, nor had gossip, contrary to its usual habit, ever linked his name with one of the sex.

Yet he was a man of more than ordinary attraction. His features were fine and his figure impressive. He might have been the cynosure of all eyes had he chosen to enter crowded drawing-rooms, or even to frequent public assemblages, but having turned his back upon everything of the kind in his youth, he had found it impossible to alter his habits with advancing years; nor was he now expected to. The position he had taken was respected. Leonard Van Broecklyn was no longer criticized.

Was there any explanation for this strangely self-centred life? Those who knew him best seemed to think so. In the first place he had sprung from an unfortunate stock. Events of an unusual and tragic nature had marked the family of both parents. Nor had his parents themselves been exempt from this seeming fatality. Antagonistic in tastes and temperament, they had dragged on an unhappy existence in the old home, till both natures rebelled, and a separation ensued which not only disunited their lives but sent them to opposite sides of the globe never to return again. At least, that was the inference drawn from the peculiar circumstances attending the event. On the morning of one never-to-be-forgotten day, John Van Broecklyn, the grandfather of the present representative of the family, found the following note from his son lying on the library table:

Father:

Life in this house, or any house, with her is no longer endurable. One of us must go. The mother should not be separated from her child. Therefore it is I whom you will never see again. Forget me, but be considerate of her and the boy.

William.

Six hours later another note was found, this time; from the wife:

Father:

Tied to a rotting corpse what does one do? Lop off one's arm if necessary to rid one of the contact. As all love between your son and myself is dead, I can no longer live within the sound of his voice. As this is his home, he is the one to remain in it. May our child reap the benefit of his mother's loss and his father's affection.

Rhoda.

Both were gone, and gone forever. Simultaneous in their departure, they preserved each his own silence and sent no word back. If the one went East and the other West, they may have met on the other side of the globe, but never again in the home which sheltered their boy. For him and for his grandfather they had sunk from sight in the great sea of humanity, leaving them stranded on an isolated and mournful shore. The grandfather steeled himself to the double loss, for the child's sake; but the boy of eleven succumbed. Few of the world's great sufferers, of whatever age or condition, have mourned as this child mourned, or shown the effects of his grief so deeply or so long. Not till he had passed his majority did the line, carved in one day in his baby forehead, lose any of its intensity; and there are those who declare that even later than that, the midnight stillness of the house was disturbed from time to time by his muffled shriek of "Mother! Mother!" sending the servants from the house, and adding one more horror to the many which clung about this accursed mansion.

Of this cry Violet had heard, and it was that and the door – But I have already told you about the door which she was still looking for, when her two companions suddenly halted, and she found herself on the threshold of the library, in full view of Mr. Van Broecklyn and his two guests.

Slight and fairy-like in figure, with an air of modest reserve more in keeping with her youth and dainty dimpling beauty than with her errand, her appearance produced an astonishment which none of the gentlemen were able to disguise. This the clever detective, with a genius for social problems and odd elusive cases! This darling of the ball-room in satin and pearls! Mr. Spielhagen glanced at Mr. Carroll, and Mr. Carroll at Mr. Spielhagen, and both at Mr. Upjohn, in very evident distrust. As for Violet, she had eyes only for Mr. Van Broecklyn who stood before her in a surprise equal to that of the others but with more restraint in its expression.

She was not disappointed in him. She had expected to see a man, reserved almost to the point of austerity. And she found his first look even more awe-compelling than her imagination had pictured; so much so indeed, that her resolution faltered, and she took a quick step backward; which seeing, he smiled and her heart and hopes grew warm again. That he could smile, and smile with absolute sweetness, was her great comfort when later – But I am introducing you too hurriedly to the catastrophe. There is much to be told first.

I pass over the preliminaries, and come at once to the moment when Violet, having listened to a repetition of the full facts, stood with downcast eyes before these gentlemen, complaining in some alarm to herself:

"They expect me to tell them now and without further search or parley just where this missing page is. I shall have to balk that expectation without losing their confidence. But how?"

Summoning up her courage and meeting each inquiring eye with a look which seemed to carry a different message to each, she remarked very quietly:

"This is not a matter to guess at. I must have time and I must look a little deeper into the facts just given me. I presume that the table I see over there is the one upon which Mr. Upjohn laid the manuscript during Mr. Spielhagen's unconsciousness."

All nodded.

"Is it – I mean the table – in the same condition it was then? Has nothing been taken from it except the manuscript?"

"Nothing."

"Then the missing page is not there," she smiled, pointing to its bare top. A pause, during which she stood with her gaze fixed on the floor before her. She was thinking and thinking hard.

Suddenly she came to a decision. Addressing Mr. Upjohn she asked if he were quite sure that in taking the manuscript from Mr. Spielhagen's hand he had neither disarranged nor dropped one of its pages.

The answer was unequivocal.

"Then," she declared, with quiet assurance and a steady meeting with her own of every eye, "as the thirteenth page was not found among the others when they were taken from this table, nor on the persons of either Mr. Carroll or Mr. Spielhagen, it is still in that inner room."

"Impossible!" came from every lip, each in a different tone. "That room is absolutely empty."

"May I have a look at its emptiness?" she asked, with a naïve glance at Mr. Van Broecklyn.

"There is positively nothing in the room but the chair Mr. Spielhagen sat on," objected that gentleman with a noticeable air of reluctance.

"Still, may I not have a look at it?" she persisted, with that disarming smile she kept for great occasions.

Mr. Van Broecklyn bowed. He could not refuse a request so urged, but his step was slow and his manner next to ungracious as he led the way to the door of the adjoining room and threw it open.

Just what she had been told to expect! Bare walls and floors and an empty chair! Yet she did not instantly withdraw, but stood silently contemplating the panelled wainscoting surrounding her, as though she suspected it of containing some secret hiding-place not apparent to the eye.

Mr. Van Broecklyn, noting this, hastened to say:

"The walls are sound, Miss Strange. They contain no hidden cupboards."

"And that door?" she asked, pointing to a portion of the wainscoting so exactly like the rest that only the most experienced eye could detect the line of deeper colour which marked an opening.

For an instant Mr. Van Broecklyn stood rigid, then the immovable pallor, which was one of his chief characteristics, gave way to a deep flush, as he explained:

"There was a door there once; but it has been permanently closed. With cement," he forced himself to add, his countenance losing its evanescent colour till it shone ghastly again in the strong light.

With difficulty Violet preserved her show of composure. "*The* door!" she murmured to herself. "I have found it. The great historic door!" But her tone was light as she ventured to say:

"Then it can no longer be opened by your hand or any other?"

"It could not be opened with an axe."

Violet sighed in the midst of her triumph. Her curiosity had been satisfied, but the problem she had been set to solve looked inexplicable. But she was not one to yield easily to discouragement. Marking the disappointment approaching to disdain in every eye but Mr. Upjohn's, she drew herself up – (she had not far to draw) and made this final proposal.

"A sheet of paper," she remarked, "of the size of this one cannot be spirited away, or dissolved into thin air. It exists; it is here; and all we want is some happy thought in order to find it. I acknowledge that that happy thought has not come to me yet, but sometimes I get it in what may seem to you a very odd way. Forgetting myself, I try to assume the individuality of the person who has worked the mystery. If I can think with his thoughts, I possibly may follow him in his actions. In this case I should like to make believe for a few moments that I am Mr. Spielhagen" (with what a delicious smile she said this). "I should like to hold his thesis in my hand and be interrupted in my reading by Mr. Cornell offering his glass of cordial; then I should like to nod and slip off mentally into a deep sleep. Possibly in that sleep the dream may come which will clarify the whole situation. Will you humour me so far?"

A ridiculous concession, but finally she had her way; the farce was enacted and they left her as she had requested them to do, alone with her dreams in the small room.

Suddenly they heard her cry out, and in another moment she appeared before them, the picture of excitement.

"Is this chair standing exactly as it did when Mr. Spielhagen occupied it?" she asked.

"No," said Mr. Upjohn, "it faced the other way."

She stepped back and twirled the chair about with her disengaged hand.

"So?"

Mr. Upjohn and Mr. Spielhagen both nodded, so did the others when she glanced at them.

With a sign of ill-concealed satisfaction, she drew their attention to herself; then eagerly cried:

"Gentlemen, look here!"

Seating herself, she allowed her whole body to relax till she presented the picture of one calmly asleep. Then, as they continued to gaze at her with fascinated eyes, not knowing what to expect, they saw something white escape from her lap and slide across the floor till it touched and was stayed by the wainscot. It was the top page of the manuscript she held, and as some inkling of the truth reached their astonished minds, she sprang impetuously to her feet and, pointing to the fallen sheet, cried:

"Do you understand now? Look where it lies, and then look here!"

She had bounded toward the wall and was now on her knees pointing to the bottom of the wainscot, just a few inches to the left of the fallen page.

"A crack!" she cried, "under what was once the door. It's a very thin one, hardly perceptible to the eye. But see!" Here she laid her finger on the fallen paper and drawing it towards her, pushed it carefully against the lower edge of the wainscot. Half of it at once disappeared.

"I could easily slip it all through," she assured them, withdrawing the sheet and leaping to her feet in triumph. "You know now where the missing page lies, Mr. Spielhagen. All that remains is for Mr. Van Broecklyn to get it for you."

Chapter IV

THE CRIES OF MINGLED astonishment and relief which greeted this simple elucidation of the mystery were broken by a curiously choked, almost unintelligible, cry. It came from the man thus appealed to, who, unnoticed by them all, had started at her first word and gradually, as action followed action, withdrawn himself till he now stood alone and in an attitude almost of defiance behind the large table in the centre of the library.

"I am sorry," he began, with a brusqueness which gradually toned down into a forced urbanity as he beheld every eye fixed upon him in amazement, "that circumstances forbid my being of assistance to you in this unfortunate matter. If the paper lies where you say, and I see no other explanation of its loss, I am afraid it will have to remain there for this night at least. The cement in which that door is embedded is thick as any wall; it would take men with pickaxes, possibly with dynamite, to make a breach there wide enough for anyone to reach in. And we are far from any such help."

In the midst of the consternation caused by these words, the clock on the mantel behind his back rang out the hour. It was but a double stroke, but that meant two hours after midnight and had the effect of a knell in the hearts of those most interested.

"But I am expected to give that formula into the hands of our manager before six o'clock in the morning. The steamer sails at a quarter after."

"Can't you reproduce a copy of it from memory?" someone asked; "and insert it in its proper place among the pages you hold there?"

"The paper would not be the same. That would lead to questions and the truth would come out. As the chief value of the process contained in that formula lies in its secrecy, no explanation I could give would relieve me from the suspicions which an acknowledgment of the existence of a third copy, however well hidden, would entail. I should lose my great opportunity."

Mr. Cornell's state of mind can be imagined. In an access of mingled regret and despair, he cast a glance at Violet, who, with a nod of understanding, left the little room in which they still stood, and approached Mr. Van Broecklyn.

Lifting up her head, – for he was very tall, – and instinctively rising on her toes the nearer to reach his ear, she asked in a cautious whisper:

"Is there no other way of reaching that place?"

She acknowledged afterwards, that for one moment her heart stood still from fear, such a change took place in his face, though she says he did not move a muscle. Then, just when she was expecting from him some harsh or forbidding word, he wheeled abruptly away from her and crossing to a window at his side, lifted the shade and looked out. When he returned, he was his usual self so far as she could see.

"There is a way," he now confided to her in a tone as low as her own, "but it can only be taken by a child."

"Not by me?" she asked, smiling down at her own childish proportions.

For an instant he seemed taken aback, then she saw his hand begin to tremble and his lips twitch. Somehow – she knew not why – she began to pity him, and asked herself as she felt rather than saw the struggle in his mind, that here was a trouble which if once understood would greatly dwarf that of the two men in the room behind them.

"I am discreet," she whisperingly declared. "I have heard the history of that door – how it was against the tradition of the family to have it opened. There must have been some very dreadful reason. But old superstitions do not affect me, and if you will allow me to take the way you mention, I will follow your bidding exactly, and will not trouble myself about anything but the recovery of this paper, which must lie only a little way inside that blocked-up door."

Was his look one of rebuke at her presumption, or just the constrained expression of a perturbed mind? Probably, the latter, for while she watched him for some understanding of his mood, he reached out his hand and touched one of the satin folds crossing her shoulder.

"You would soil this irretrievably," said he.

"There is stuff in the stores for another," she smiled. Slowly his touch deepened into pressure. Watching him she saw the crust of some old fear or dominant superstition melt under her eyes, and was quite prepared, when he remarked, with what for him was a lightsome air:

"I will buy the stuff, if you will dare the darkness and intricacies of our old cellar. I can give you no light. You will have to feel your way according to my direction."

"I am ready to dare anything."

He left her abruptly.

"I will warn Miss Digby," he called back. "She shall go with you as far as the cellar."

Chapter V

VIOLET IN HER short career as an investigator of mysteries had been in many a situation calling for more than womanly nerve and courage. But never – or so it seemed to her at the time – had she experienced a greater depression of spirit than when she stood with Miss Digby before a small door at the extreme end of the cellar, and understood that here was her road – a road which once entered, she must take alone.

First, it was such a small door! No child older than eleven could possibly squeeze through it. But she was of the size of a child of eleven and might possibly manage that difficulty.

Secondly: there are always some unforeseen possibilities in every situation, and though she had listened carefully to Mr. Van Broecklyn's directions and was sure that she knew them by heart, she wished she had kissed her father more tenderly in leaving him that night for the ball, and that she had not pouted so undutifully at some harsh stricture he had made. Did this mean fear? She despised the feeling if it did.

Thirdly: She hated darkness. She knew this when she offered herself for this undertaking; but she was in a bright room at the moment and only imagined what she must now face as a reality. But one jet had been lit in the cellar and that near the entrance. Mr. Van Broecklyn seemed not to need light, even in his unfastening of the small door which Violet was sure had been protected by more than one lock.

Doubt, shadow, and a solitary climb between unknown walls, with only a streak of light for her goal, and the clinging pressure of Florence Digby's hand on her own for solace – surely the prospect was one to tax the courage of her young heart to its limit. But she had promised, and she would fulfil. So with a brave smile she stooped to the little door, and in another moment had started on her journey.

For journey the shortest distance may seem when every inch means a heart-throb and one grows old in traversing a foot. At first the way was easy; she had but to crawl up a slight incline with the comforting consciousness that two people were within reach of her voice, almost within sound of her beating heart. But presently she came to a turn, beyond which her fingers failed to reach any wall on her left. Then came a step up which she stumbled, and farther on a short flight, each tread of which she had been told to test before she ventured to climb it, lest the decay of innumerable years should have weakened the wood too much to bear her weight. One, two, three, four, five steps! Then a landing with an open space beyond. Half of her journey was done. Here she felt she could give a minute to drawing her breath naturally, if the air, unchanged in years, would allow her to do so. Besides, here she had been enjoined to do a certain thing and to do it according to instructions. Three matches had been given her and a little night candle. Denied all light up to now, it was at this point she was to light her candle and place it on the floor, so that in returning she should not miss the staircase and get a fall. She had promised to do this, and was only too happy to see a spark of light scintillate into life in the immeasurable darkness.

She was now in a great room long closed to the world, where once officers in Colonial wars had feasted, and more than one council had been held. A room, too, which had seen more than one tragic happening, as its almost unparalleled isolation proclaimed. So much Mr. Van Broecklyn had told her, but she was warned to be careful in traversing it and not upon any pretext to swerve aside from the right-hand wall till she came to a huge mantelpiece. This passed, and a sharp corner turned, she ought to see somewhere in the dim spaces before her a streak of vivid light shining through the crack at the bottom of the blocked-up door. The paper should be somewhere near this streak.

All simple, all easy of accomplishment, if only that streak of light were all she was likely to see or think of. If the horror which was gripping her throat should not take shape! If things would remain shrouded in impenetrable darkness, and not force themselves in shadowy suggestion upon her excited fancy! But the blackness of the passageway through which she had just struggled, was not to bc found here. Whether it was the effect of that small flame flickering at the top of the staircase behind her, or of some change in her own powers of seeing, surely there was a difference in her present outlook. Tall shapes were becoming visible – the air was no longer blank – she could see – Then suddenly she saw why. In the wall high up on her right was a window. It was small and all but invisible, being covered on the outside with vines, and on the inside with the cobwebs of a century. But some small gleams from the starlight night came through, making phantasms out of ordinary things, which unseen were horrible enough, and half seen choked her heart with terror.

"I cannot bear it," she whispered to herself even while creeping forward, her hand upon the wall. "I will close my eyes" was her next thought. "I will make my own darkness," and with a spasmodic forcing of her lids together, she continued to creep on, passing the mantelpiece, where she knocked against something which fell with an awful clatter.

This sound, followed as it was by that of smothered voices from the excited group awaiting the result of her experiment from behind the impenetrable wall she should be nearing now if she had followed her instructions aright, freed her instantly from her fancies; and opening her eyes once more, she cast a look ahead, and to her delight, saw but a few steps away, the thin streak of bright light which marked the end of her journey.

It took her but a moment after that to find the missing page, and picking it up in haste from the dusty floor, she turned herself quickly about and joyfully began to retrace her steps. Why, then, was it that in the course of a few minutes more her voice suddenly broke into a wild, unearthly shriek, which ringing with terror burst the bounds of that dungeon-like room, and sank, a barbed shaft, into the breasts of those awaiting the result of her doubtful adventure, at either end of this dread no-thoroughfare.

What had happened?

If they had thought to look out, they would have seen that the moon – held in check by a bank of cloud occupying half the heavens – had suddenly burst its bounds and was sending long bars of revealing light into every uncurtained window.

Chapter VI

Florence Digby, in her short and sheltered life, had possibly never known any very great or deep emotion. But she touched the bottom of extreme terror at that moment, as with her ears still thrilling with Violet's piercing cry, she turned to look at Mr. Van Broecklyn, and beheld the instantaneous wreck it had made of this seemingly strong man. Not till he came to lie in his coffin would he show a more ghastly countenance; and trembling herself almost to the point of falling, she caught him by the arm and sought to read in his face what had happened. Something disastrous she was sure; something which he had feared and was partially prepared for, yet which in happening had crushed him. Was it a pitfall into which the poor little lady had fallen? If so – But he is speaking – mumbling low words to himself. Some of them she can hear

He is reproaching himself – repeating over and over that he should never have taken such a chance; that he should have remembered her youth – the weakness of a young girl's nerve. He had been mad, and now – and now—

With the repetition of this word his murmuring ceased. All his energies were now absorbed in listening at the low door separating him from what he was agonizing to know – a door impossible to enter, impossible to enlarge – a barrier to all help – an opening whereby sound might pass but nothing else save her own small body, now lying – where?

"Is she hurt?" faltered Florence, stooping, herself, to listen. "Can you hear anything – anything?"

For an instant he did not answer; every faculty was absorbed in the one sense; then slowly and in gasps he began to mutter:

"I think – I hear – *something*. Her step – no, no, no step. All is as quiet as death; not a sound, – not a breath – she has fainted. O God! O God! Why this calamity on top of all!"

He had sprung to his feet at the utterance of this invocation, but next moment was down on his knees again, listening – listening.

Never was silence more profound; they were hearkening for murmurs from a tomb. Florence began to sense the full horror of it all, and was swaying helplessly when Mr. Van Broecklyn impulsively lifted his hand in an admonitory Hush! and through the daze of her faculties a small far sound began to make itself heard, growing louder as she waited, then becoming faint again, then altogether ceasing only to renew itself once more, till it resolved into an approaching step, faltering in its course, but coming ever nearer and nearer.

"She's safe! She's not hurt!" sprang from Florence's lips in inexpressible relief; and expecting Mr. Van Broecklyn to show an equal joy, she turned toward him, with the cheerful cry.

"Now if she has been so fortunate as to find that missing page, we shall all be repaid for our fright."

A movement on his part, a shifting of position which brought him finally to his feet, but he gave no other proof of having heard her, nor did his countenance mirror her relief. "It is as if he dreaded, instead of hailed, her return," was Florence's inward comment as she watched him involuntarily recoil at each fresh token of Violet's advance.

Yet because this seemed so very unnatural, she persisted in her efforts to lighten the situation, and when he made no attempt to encourage Violet in her approach, she herself stooped and called out a cheerful welcome which must have rung sweetly in the poor little detective's ears.

A sorry sight was Violet, when, helped by Florence she finally crawled into view through the narrow opening and stood once again on the cellar floor. Pale, trembling, and soiled with the dust of years, she presented a helpless figure enough, till the joy in Florence's face recalled some of her spirit, and, glancing down at her hand in which a sheet of paper was visible, she asked for Mr. Spielhagen.

"I've got the formula," she said. "If you will bring him, I will hand it over to him here."

Not a word of her adventure; nor so much as one glance at Mr. Van Broecklyn, standing far back in the shadows.

* * *

Nor was she more communicative, when, the formula restored and everything made right with Mr. Spielhagen, they all came together again in the library for a final word.

"I was frightened by the silence and the darkness, and so cried out," she explained in answer to their questions. "Anyone would have done so who found himself alone in so musty a place," she added, with an attempt at lightsomeness which deepened the pallor on Mr. Van Broecklyn's cheek, already sufficiently noticeable to have been remarked upon by more than one.

"No ghosts?" laughed Mr. Cornell, too happy in the return of his hopes to be fully sensible of the feelings of those about him. "No whispers from impalpable lips or touches from spectre hands? Nothing to explain the mystery of that room so long shut up that even Mr. Van Broecklyn declares himself ignorant of its secret?"

"Nothing," returned Violet, showing her dimples in full force now.

"If Miss Strange had any such experiences – if she has anything to tell worthy of so marked a curiosity, she will tell it now," came from the gentleman just alluded to, in tones so stern and strange that all show of frivolity ceased on the instant. "Have you anything to tell, Miss Strange?"

Greatly startled, she regarded him with widening eyes for a moment, then with a move towards the door, remarked, with a general look about her:

"Mr. Van Broecklyn knows his own house, and doubtless can relate its histories if he will. I am a busy little body who having finished my work am now ready to return home, there to wait for the next problem which an indulgent fate may offer me."

She was near the threshold – she was about to take her leave, when suddenly she felt two hands fall on her shoulder, and turning, met the eyes of Mr. Van Broecklyn burning into her own.

"*You saw!*" dropped in an almost inaudible whisper from his lips.

The shiver which shook her answered him better than any word.

With an exclamation of despair, he withdrew his hands, and facing the others now standing together recovered some of his self-possession:

"I must ask for another hour of your company. I can no longer keep my sorrow to myself. A dividing line has just been drawn across my life, and I must have the sympathy of someone who knows my past, or I shall go mad in my self-imposed solitude. Come back, Miss Strange. You of all others have the prior right to hear."

Chapter VII

"I shall have to begin," said he, when they were all seated and ready to listen, "by giving you some idea, not so much of the family tradition, as of the effect of this tradition upon all who bore the name of Van Broecklyn. This is not the only house, even in America, which contains a room shut away from intrusion. In England there are many. But there is this difference between most of them and ours. No bars or locks forcibly held shut the door we were forbidden to open. The command was enough; that and the superstitious fear which such a command, attended by a long and unquestioning obedience, was likely to engender.

"I know no more than you do why some early ancestor laid his ban upon this room. But from my earliest years I was given to understand that there was one latch in the house which was never to be lifted; that any fault would be forgiven sooner than that; that the honour of the whole family stood in the way of disobedience, and that I was to preserve that honour to my dying day. You will say that all this is fantastic, and wonder that sane people in these modern times should subject themselves to such a ridiculous restriction, especially when no good reason was alleged, and the very source of the tradition from which it sprung forgotten. You are right; but if you look long into human nature, you will see that the bonds which hold the firmest are not material ones – that an idea will make a man and mould a character – that it lies at the source of all heroisms and is to be courted or feared as the case may be.

"For me it possessed a power proportionate to my loneliness. I don't think there was ever a more lonely child. My father and mother were so unhappy in each other's companionship at one or other of them was almost always away. But I saw little of either even when they ere at home. The constraint in their attitude toward each other affected their conduct ward me. I have asked myself more than once if either of them had any real affection for e. To my father I spoke of her; to her of him; and never pleasurably. This I am forced to y, or you cannot understand my story. Would to God I could tell another tale! Would to od I had such memories as other men have of a father's clasp, a mother's kiss – but no! y grief, already profound, might have become abysmal. Perhaps it is best as it is; only, I might ve been a different child, and made for myself a different fate – who knows.

"As it was, I was thrown almost entirely upon my own resources for any amusement. This led e to a discovery I made one day. In a far part of the cellar behind some heavy casks, I found ittle door. It was so low – so exactly fitted to my small body, that I had the greatest desire to ter it. But I could not get around the casks. At last an expedient occurred to me. We had an d servant who came nearer loving me than anyone else. One day when I chanced to be alone the cellar, I took out my ball and began throwing it about. Finally it landed behind the casks, d I ran with a beseeching cry to Michael, to move them.

"It was a task requiring no little strength and address, but he managed, after a few herculean forts, to shift them aside and I saw with delight my way opened to that mysterious little door. ıt I did not approach it then; some instinct deterred me. But when the opportunity came for e to venture there alone, I did so, in the most adventurous spirit, and began my operations by ding behind the casks and testing the handle of the little door. It turned, and after a pull or o the door yielded. With my heart in my mouth, I stooped and peered in. I could see nothing a black hole and nothing more. This caused me a moment's hesitation. I was afraid of the dark had always been. But curiosity and the spirit of adventure triumphed. Saying to myself that I as Robinson Crusoe exploring the cave, I crawled in, only to find that I had gained nothing. It as as dark inside as it had looked to be from without.

"There was no fun in this, so I crawled back and when I tried the experiment again, it was ith a bit of candle in my hand, and a surreptitious match or two. What I saw, when with a ry trembling little hand I had lighted one of the matches, would have been disappointing to ost boys, but not to me. The litter and old boards I saw in odd corners about me were full possibilities, while in the dimness beyond I seemed to perceive a sort of staircase which ight lead – I do not think I made any attempt to answer that question even in my own mind, ıt when, after some hesitation and a sense of great daring, I finally crept up those steps, I member very well my sensation at finding myself in front of a narrow closed door. It suggested o vividly the one in Grandfather's little room – the door in the wainscot which we were ever to open. I had my first real trembling fit here, and at once fascinated and repelled by this ostruction I stumbled and lost my candle, which, going out in the fall, left me in total darkness d a very frightened state of mind. For my imagination, which had been greatly stirred by my vn vague thoughts of the forbidden room, immediately began to people the space about me ith ghoulish figures. How should I escape them, how ever reach my own little room again, ndetected and in safety?

"But these terrors, deep as they were, were nothing to the real fright which seized me when, e darkness finally braved, and the way found back into the bright, wide-open halls of the ouse, I became conscious of having dropped something besides the candle. My match-box as gone – not *my* match-box, but my grandfather's which I had found lying on his table and rried off on this adventure, in all the confidence of irresponsible youth. To make use of it r a little while, trusting to his not missing it in the confusion I had noticed about the house at morning, was one thing; to lose it was another. It was no common box. Made of gold and cherished for some special reason well known to himself, I had often heard him say that some d I would appreciate its value and be glad to own it. And I had left it in that hole and at any minu he might miss it – possibly ask for it! The day was one of torment. My mother was away or shut u in her room. My father – I don't know just what thoughts I had about him. He was not to be see either, and the servants cast strange looks at me when I spoke his name. But I little realized th blow which had just fallen upon the house in his definite departure, and only thought of my ow trouble, and of how I should meet my grandfather's eye when the hour came for him to draw m to his knee for his usual goodnight.

"That I was spared this ordeal for the first time this very night first comforted me, then add to my distress. He had discovered his loss and was angry. On the morrow he would ask me f the box and I would have to lie, for never could I find the courage to tell him where I had bee Such an act of presumption he would never forgive, or so I thought as I lay and shivered in my litt bed. That his coldness, his neglect, sprang from the discovery just made that my mother as we as my father had just fled the house forever was as little known to me as the morning calami I had been given my usual tendance and was tucked safely into bed; but the gloom, the silen which presently settled upon the house had a very different explanation in my mind from the re one. My sin (for such it loomed large in my mind by this time) coloured the whole situation ar accounted for every event.

"At what hour I slipped from my bed on to the cold floor, I shall never know. To me it seeme to be in the dead of night; but I doubt if it were more than ten. So slowly creep away the momen to a wakeful child. I had made a great resolve. Awful as the prospect seemed to me, – frightene as I was by the very thought, – I had determined in my small mind to go down into the cellar, ar into that midnight hole again, in search of the lost box. I would take a candle and matches, th time from my own mantel-shelf, and if everyone was asleep, as appeared from the deathly quiet the house, I would be able to go and come without anybody ever being the wiser.

"Dressing in the dark, I found my matches and my candle and, putting them in one of m pockets, softly opened my door and looked out. Nobody was stirring; every light was out except solitary one in the lower hall. That this still burned conveyed no meaning to my mind. How cou I know that the house was so still and the rooms so dark because everyone was out searching f some clue to my mother's flight? If I had looked at the clock – but I did not; I was too intent upo my errand, too filled with the fever of my desperate undertaking, to be affected by anything no bearing directly upon it.

"Of the terror caused by my own shadow on the wall as I made the turn in the hall below, I hav as keen a recollection today as though it happened yesterday. But that did not deter me; nothir deterred me, till safe in the cellar I crouched down behind the casks to get my breath again befor entering the hole beyond.

"I had made some noise in feeling my way around these casks, and I trembled lest thes sounds had been heard upstairs! But this fear soon gave place to one far greater. Other sound were making themselves heard. A din of small skurrying feet above, below, on every side of m Rats! rats in the wall! rats on the cellar bottom! How I ever stirred from the spot I do not know, bu when I did stir, it was to go forward, and enter the uncanny hole.

"I had intended to light my candle when I got inside; but for some reason I went stumblin along in the dark, following the wall till I got to the steps where I had dropped the box. Here light was necessary, but my hand did not go to my pocket. I thought it better to climb the step first, and softly one foot found the tread and then another. I had only three more to climb an then my right hand, now feeling its way along the wall, would be free to strike a match. I climbe the three steps and was steadying myself against the door for a final plunge, when somethin happened – something so strange, so unexpected, and so incredible that I wonder I did not shriek aloud in my terror. The door was moving under my hand. It was slowly opening inward. I could feel the chill made by the widening crack. Moment by moment this chill increased; the gap was growing – a presence was there – a presence before which I sank in a small heap upon the landing. Would it advance? Had it feet – hands? Was it a presence which could be felt?

"Whatever it was, it made no attempt to pass, and presently I lifted my head only to quake anew at the sound of a voice – a human voice – my mother's voice – so near me that by putting out my arms I might have touched her.

"She was speaking to my father. I knew it from the tone. She was saying words which, little understood as they were, made such a havoc in my youthful mind that I have never forgotten them.

"'I have come!' she said. 'They think I have fled the house and are looking far and wide for me. We shall not be disturbed. Who would think of looking here for either you or me?'

"Here! The word sank like a plummet in my breast. I had known for some few minutes that I was on the threshold of the forbidden room; but they were *in* it. I can scarcely make you understand the tumult which this awoke in my brain. Somehow, I had never thought that any such braving of the house's law would be possible.

"I heard my father's answer, but it conveyed no meaning to me. I also realized that he spoke from a distance, – that he was at one end of the room while we were at the other. I was presently to have this idea confirmed, for while I was striving with all my might and main to subdue my very heart-throbs so that she would not hear me or suspect my presence, the darkness – I should rather say the blackness of the place yielded to a flash of lightning – heat lightning, all glare and no sound – and I caught an instantaneous vision of my father's figure standing with gleaming things about him, which affected me at the moment as supernatural, but which, in later years, I decided to have been weapons hanging on a wall.

"She saw him too, for she gave a quick laugh and said they would not need any candles; and then, there was another flash and I saw something in his hand and something in hers, and though I did not yet understand, I felt myself turning deathly sick and gave a choking gasp which was lost in the rush she made into the centre of the room, and the keenness of her swift low cry.

"'*Garde-toi!* for only one of us will ever leave this room alive!'

"A duel! a duel to the death between this husband and wife – this father and mother – in this hole of dead tragedies and within the sight and hearing of their child! Has Satan ever devised a scheme more hideous for ruining the life of an eleven-year-old boy!

"Not that I took it all in at once. I was too innocent and much too dazed to comprehend such hatred, much less the passions which engendered it. I only knew that something horrible – something beyond the conception of my childish mind – was going to take place in the darkness before me; and the terror of it made me speechless; would to God it had made me deaf and blind and dead!

"She had dashed from her corner and he had slid away from his, as the next fantastic gleam which lit up the room showed me. It also showed the weapons in their hands, and for a moment I felt reassured when I saw these were swords, for I had seen them before with foils in their hands practising for exercise, as they said, in the great garret. But the swords had buttons on them, and this time the tips were sharp and shone in the keen light.

"An exclamation from her and a growl of rage from him were followed by movements I could scarcely hear, but which were terrifying from their very quiet. Then the sound of a clash. The swords had crossed.

"Had the lightning flashed forth then, the end of one of them might have occurred. But the darkness remained undisturbed, and when the glare relit the great room again, they were already far apart. This called out a word from him; the one sentence he spoke – I can never forget it:

"'Rhoda, there is blood on your sleeve; I have wounded you. Shall we call it off and fly, as the poor creatures in there think we have, to the opposite ends of the earth?'

"I almost spoke; I almost added my childish plea to his for them to stop – to remember me and stop. But not a muscle in my throat responded to my agonized effort. Her cold, clear 'No!' fell before my tongue was loosed or my heart freed from the ponderous weight crushing it.

"'I have vowed and *I* keep my promises,' she went on in a tone quite strange to me. 'What would either's life be worth with the other alive and happy in this world?'

"He made no answer; and those subtle movements – shadows of movements I might almost call them – recommenced. Then there came a sudden cry, shrill and poignant – had Grandfather been in his room he would surely have heard it – and the flash coming almost simultaneously with its utterance, I saw what has haunted my sleep from that day to this, my father pinned against the wall, sword still in hand, and before him my mother, fiercely triumphant, her staring eyes fixed on his and –

"Nature could bear no more; the band loosened from my throat; the oppression lifted from my breast long enough for me to give one wild wail and she turned, saw (heaven sent its flashes quickly at this moment) and recognizing my childish form, all the horror of her deed (or so I have fondly hoped) rose within her, and she gave a start and fell full upon the point upturned to receive her.

"A groan; then a gasping sigh from him, and silence settled upon the room and upon my heart and so far as I knew upon the whole created world.

* * *

"That is my story, friends. Do you wonder that I have never been or lived like other men?"

After a few moments of sympathetic silence, Mr. Van Broecklyn went on to say:

"I don't think I ever had a moment's doubt that my parents both lay dead on the floor o that great room. When I came to myself – which may have been soon, and may not have beer for a long while – the lightning had ceased to flash, leaving the darkness stretching like blank pall between me and that spot in which were concentrated all the terrors of which m imagination was capable. I dared not enter it. I dared not take one step that way. My instinc was to fly and hide my trembling body again in my own bed; and associated with this, in fac dominating it and making me old before my time, was another – never to tell; never to le anyone, least of all my grandfather – know what that forbidden room now contained. I felt i an irresistible sort of way that my father's and mother's honour was at stake. Besides, terrc held me back; I felt that I should die if I spoke. Childhood has such terrors and such heroism Silence often covers in such, abysses of thought and feeling which astonish us in later year There is no suffering like a child's, terrified by a secret it dare not for some reason disclose.

"Events aided me. When, in desperation to see once more the light and all the thing which linked me to life – my little bed, the toys on the windowsill, my squirrel in its cage – forced myself to retraverse the empty house, expecting at every turn to hear my father's voic or come upon the image of my mother – yes, such was the confusion of my mind, though knew well enough even then that they were dead and that I should never hear the one or se the other. I was so benumbed with the cold in my half-dressed condition, that I woke in a fev ext morning after a terrible dream which forced from my lips the cry of 'Mother! Mother!' – ıly that.

"I was cautious even in delirium. This delirium and my flushed cheeks and shining eyes led em to be very careful to me. I was told that my mother was away from home; and when after o days of search they were quite sure that all efforts to find either her or my father were likely prove fruitless, that she had gone to Europe where we would follow her as soon as I was ell. This promise, offering as it did, a prospect of immediate release from the terrors which ere consuming me, had an extraordinary effect upon me. I got up out of my bed saying that vas well now and ready to start on the instant. The doctor, finding my pulse equable, and my hole condition wonderfully improved, and attributing it, as was natural, to my hope of soon ining my mother, advised my whim to be humoured and this hope kept active till travel and tercourse with children should give me strength and prepare me for the bitter truth ultimately vaiting me. They listened to him and in twenty-four hours our preparations were made. We w the house closed – with what emotions surging in one small breast, I leave you to imagine – d then started on our long tour. For five years we wandered over the continent of Europe, my andfather finding distraction, as well as myself, in foreign scenes and associations.

"But return was inevitable. What I suffered on re-entering this house, God and my sleepless llow alone know. Had any discovery been made in our absence; or would it be made now that novation and repairs of all kinds were necessary? Time finally answered me. My secret was fe and likely to continue so, and this fact once settled, life became endurable, if not cheerful. nce then I have spent only two nights out of this house, and they were unavoidable. When y grandfather died I had the wainscot door cemented in. It was done from this side and e cement painted to match the wood. No one opened the door nor have I ever crossed its reshold. Sometimes I think I have been foolish; and sometimes I know that I have been very se. My reason has stood firm; how do I know that it would have done so if I had subjected yself to the possible discovery that one or both of them might have been saved if I had sclosed instead of concealed my adventure."

* * *

pause during which white horror had shone on every face; then with a final glance at Violet, said:

"What sequel do you see to this story, Miss Strange? I can tell the past, I leave you to picture e future."

Rising, she let her eye travel from face to face till it rested on the one awaiting it, when she swered dreamily:

"If some morning in the news column there should appear an account of the ancient and storic home of the Van Broecklyns having burned to the ground in the night, the whole untry would mourn, and the city feel defrauded of one of its treasures. But there are five rsons who would see in it the sequel which you ask for."

When this happened, as it did happen, some few weeks later, the astonishing discovery was ade that no insurance had been put upon this house. Why was it that after such a loss Mr. Van oecklyn seemed to renew his youth? It was a constant source of comment among his friends.

Sir Robert's Gargoyle

Philip Brian Hall

Whenever it rained heavily, The Very Reverend Geoffrey Syme went out to the cathedral close and got wet. Neighbours scurrying to shelter would see him staring anxiously up at the acres of lead-sheathed roof, fretting about the gargoyles.

Centuries of English weather had dangerously weakened the stone figures and Geoffrey could no longer put off the issue of their replacement. As dean, he chaired the Restoration Committee's monthly meetings in the chapter house. Sitting quietly beneath the lofty, vaulted ceiling, he'd often mused on those who'd occupied the wooden benches before him. Upon what important debates had light from these colourful stained-glass windows fallen? But now it was his turn.

"Back in the thirteenth century," he said, introducing the vexed topic at the end of the agenda, "the gargoyles were carved as representations of wealthy local gentry and merchants who'd contributed to the cathedral's building costs. It was intended as a mark of popular gratitude for their munificence."

"But sandstone being what it is," Derek Mason, the architect, interjected, "erosion is now so severe we can't make out enough of a likeness to copy."

"Of course," Geoffrey continued optimistically, "we ourselves could imitate the founders by offering portrait sculptures to modern benefactors who might help defray this considerable expense."

"Intolerable betrayal!" The angry voice of Lady Agatha, Dowager Countess of Eggesford, cut through the quiet of the assembly. Whenever anyone overlooked the role of the Fortescues in local history, the countess could be relied upon to remind them of it. Her hearers cringed as the all-too-familiar commanding tones rang out.

"My ancestor, Sir Robert Fortescue, personally bore the whole cost of the crossing vault and the lower tower. In consequence, his gargoyle occupies a place of honour over the south transept. I must insist it is replaced with a similar likeness."

"But we don't *know* what he looked like," Mason repeated stolidly.

"Since I'm his direct descendant, we may assume a strong family resemblance," Lady Agatha retorted.

Argument raged back and forth, occasional explosions of temper echoing from the walls. If the original architects had intended the octagonal chapter house arrangement to promote concord, on this occasion it lacked the desired effect.

Eventually, sensing likely rebellion among the other members, Geoffrey called a halt. Sufficient unto the day was the evil thereof. Everyone could agree to the decision being postponed until the following month.

For a whole week thereafter, daily notes hand-written on embossed, cream paper were delivered to the deanery by the countess' chauffeur. Each reminded Geoffrey of the role a Fortescue had played in the upkeep of the cathedral at various periods of its long history.

The first letter reminded him, as though the fact were not already burned into his memory, that Sir Robert Fortescue, the co-founder, died while on crusade and had no known tomb or memorial other than his gargoyle.

The third note drew attention to the execution of the then Baron Eggesford in 1648, his punishment for hiding the cathedral's plate from marauding Roundheads. Geoffrey knew this story well. According to Her Ladyship, the rebels would have melted down the silver and used it to buy more guns with which to assail good King Charles I of blessed memory.

After the Restoration, however, the plate was never recovered. Scurrilous rumours soon spread that, far from being a hero, the baron had stolen it. If so, he'd not lived to enjoy his ill-gotten gains, but no other plausible explanation could be offered. Locally, the disappearance of the plate became the most celebrated unsolved crime of the seventeenth, or indeed any other, century. The baron entered history as a notorious thief and blasphemer, though that wasn't how Lady Agatha told it.

To each of the missives, Geoffrey replied politely by post.

The following week the bishop called round to the deanery, bringing news that Lambeth Palace had been in touch. Her Ladyship was badgering His Grace the Archbishop. They wanted something done. The bishop said it would be good if Lambeth Palace didn't have cause to complain again.

Geoffrey redoubled his epistolary efforts, unfortunately, without success. The bishop called round once more. Something *must* be done.

Reluctantly Geoffrey climbed into his elderly Morris Minor and drove to Eggesford Hall.

The countess received him in her stately Elizabethan drawing room. Around the walls, portraits of Fortescues of bygone ages brooded over the nervous visitor.

"I wonder, Your Ladyship, if we might seek a compromise," Geoffrey suggested. "Perhaps we could replace Sir Robert's gargoyle with a medieval likeness and replace the others with portraits of modern benefactors?"

"Would the modern benefactors be happy to appear in medieval dress, Dean?"

"Well, I doubt it, Your Ladyship."

"So my ancestor would look silly as the only one?"

"Oh, I'm sure no-one would ever think that, Your Ladyship"

"Of course they would, Dean, in time. After all, it occurred to me at once!"

A week later the archdeacon reported that Eggesford Hall's gardeners had been instructed to refuse the traditional weekly supply of fresh spring flowers for the cathedral's decoration.

The ladies of the Women's Rural Institute, who were very proud of their flower arrangements, wanted to know what the dean was going to do about it. Geoffrey tried to explain. The ladies appealed to the bishop. The bishop angrily insisted. Not only must something be done, it must be done *soon*.

Geoffrey was at his wits' end. He'd no more hope of changing her Ladyship's mind than had Canute of holding back the tide. There seemed no salvation in sight. But he reckoned without Lord Eggesford's celebrated crime.

On Maundy Thursday, shortly after midnight, during a violent electrical storm, the cathedral was struck by lightning. From the window of Geoffrey's bedroom in the deanery no structural damage could be seen but, since Geoffrey wasn't able to sleep, he decided to get up and walk over to the cathedral to be sure.

His small, black-and-white Jack Russell terrier, Benjamin, lately skulking beneath the bed, decided after due philosophical consideration it was better to sally forth with his master and appear brave rather than remain cowering inside the deanery alone.

Geoffrey dressed quickly, putting on a raincoat over his cassock. Across the dark cathedral close, all lights were extinguished and only fitful moonlight illuminated the path. Now and then ragged, fast-drifting clouds obscured even this. The wind piped a mournful note. Crisp night air smelled of damp earth, primroses, daffodils and new beginnings.

Scattered, heavy drops of rain began to fall upon the gravel path and plop loudly on to lawns fresh from their first mowing of the year. As the rain increased, Geoffrey and Benjamin quickened their pace, arriving at the west porch just as a torrential downpour began.

Opening the small hatch let into the massive timbers, Geoffrey stepped into the nave, removed his raincoat and folded it over the dark-oak back of the nearest pew. He tried several electric switches. None worked.

Yet it was not totally dark within. Inconstant, flickering moonlight was admitted by the stained glass of the tall, Curvilinear Gothic windows of the aisles and the earlier Geometrical tracery of the clerestory windows high above the nave. A clearly-lit path along the central aisle threw into shadow the pews on either side, as though to beckon onward towards the altar the two dishevelled refugees from the fury of the storm.

No rubble had fallen, as far as Geoffrey could see, but his eyes were caught by flitting shadows crossing and re-crossing the clerestory window embrasures. Momentarily he experienced a stab of fright.

He took a deep breath to calm himself. Horseshoe bats in considerable numbers had long since taken up residence above the organ loft.

The dean and his dog went on towards the central crossing, where additional moonlight entered through the transept and tower windows.

Benjamin suddenly stopped, hunkered down and gave a low growl. The hair stood up all along his back. Geoffrey paused and looked down at him.

"What's up, Benji old chap?"

The dog growled softly again, showing no inclination to advance and clearly intending his whispered vocal warning solely for the ears of his master rather than the deterrence of any intruder.

"I know, you don't like the thunder. But it can't hurt you, old chap."

The dog did not seem to find this reassuring.

"The Saxons used to say it was the noise of the gods playing skittles."

That was evidently the last straw, even for a Jack Russell who considered himself quite bold for a small dog. The master must deal with the intruders on his own; in this emergency it was every dog for himself. Benjamin turned tail and scuttled back to the west porch as fast as his little legs would carry him.

"Benji! Come back here you terrible coward you!" Geoffrey called after him.

The dog made no reply save a brief, mournful whine from his hiding place in the safety of the shadows.

Geoffrey decided to collect his dog on the way back. He continued into the crossing looked into the choir and the north transept seeing nothing amiss, then made his wa towards the south transept, from which an internal door gave admission to the cloister.

Opening the door, he paused and listened. Was that a soft note or two of music from somewhere outside?

Perhaps just the wind in the trees.

No. There it was again; the quiet, solemn susurration of a Gregorian Chant, a sound so redolent of the history of the cathedral. It was a simple, repetitive, unaccompanied setting of *Dies Irae,* the evocative Latin poem Geoffrey knew so well.

Captivated by the beauty of the singing, Geoffrey forgot to be alarmed. He found it easy to suppose an innocent explanation. Perhaps someone had been caught in the rain and taken shelter, perhaps someone carrying one of those little modern devices allegedly capable of playing a thousand tunes.

But as Geoffrey opened the door, he seemed transported into the distant past. Directly ahead of him, beyond the central garden, where strangely no rain was falling, appeared the source of the music, an archaic procession making its solemn way behind the far colonnade of the cloister.

Rope girdles swaying in time to the rhythm of the chant, their sandals pattering across stone floors, a long line of black-robed monks, each bearing a lighted candle between hands clasped reverently in prayer, shuffled along in single file. The leaders of the procession had already passed through the open door of the chapter house.

Incredibly, the latest arrivals were emerging into existence one at a time from a bricked-up door in the cloister which at one time had given access to the long-since demolished monastic dorter.

Quantus tremor est futurus,
Quando Judex est venturus,
Cuncta stricte discussurus!

What terror shall come when the strict judge of all things appears!

Geoffrey knew holy terror indeed. He understood instinctively he was witness to no modern mummery. Here before him were the cathedral's original builders. Their black robes denoted Cluniacs, the strict offspring of the Benedictine Order.

Yet somehow he knew he was not, as though through a window, looking in upon the thirteenth century. This procession was happening now, a ghostly visitation traversing the vast expanse of centuries as though it offered no greater obstacle than he himself encountered between one transept and the other.

Geoffrey's mind, like his body, froze into immobility. Hovering on the threshold between the natural and the supernatural, he became simply an observer while the miracle passed before his eyes.

Bringing up the rear of the procession, carrying a flask of holy water and wearing around his neck a pale-coloured stole of office, walked a superior monk Geoffrey reckoned must be the prior, the head of the original house.

At the door of the chapter house, this figure turned and looked straight at Geoffrey, who stood rooted to the spot in the transept doorway. The ghostly monk beckoned.

Under the spectral gaze, Geoffrey's heart almost failed within him. Had the builders come to reclaim their property? But the cathedral had been Anglican for almost five centuries; why now? And why on earth appear to him, a mere dean?

Struggling to raise his trembling right hand, he pointed in fearful inquiry towards himself. The ghost nodded slowly, beckoned again, then turned and passed into the chapter house.

Geoffrey would not flee, though terror screamed in his head. He forced paralysed limbs into motion, nervously gathering into his left hand the small crucifix that hung around his neck on a simple silver chain.

The chapter house doorway had been left open. For him? He stumbled towards it, anxiety crippling his steps so he tottered like a drunken man.

The *Dies Irae* ended, as if on a long sigh, leaving silence within the chapter house. Geoffrey wondered if he would enter and find it empty. Strangely he found himself hoping it would not be so. He didn't understand all this; more than anything he *wanted* to understand.

Salutate fratres mei. A single deep voice from within.

Salutem fratrem nostrum. Many voices in unison.

Pax vobiscum.

Et quoque tecum.

Pater noster,

Qui es in caelis...

In the Anglican Church, the service hadn't been conducted in Latin since the days of Henry VIII. This didn't mean Geoffrey was ignorant of the lovely rolling cadences of The Lord's Prayer. He couldn't possibly be afraid of beings who spoke those words so reverently, not even if those beings were without substance, fabricated from the very ether itself. Whatever awaited him within the chapter house, he must enter.

His own voice joining the ghostly congregation in their recitation, Geoffrey stepped through the door. All around the octagonal chamber, severe, black-robed monks stood in front of the wooden benches, looking inward, heads bowed, each holding his candle, intoning the time-honoured words.

In his black cassock, Geoffrey might have been a Cluniac himself. Quietly he drew the door partly-closed behind him and moved to stand against the wall, in the shadows before the first window.

The prayer ended. The prior stepped forward into the centre of the chamber. He looked all around the gathered monks until, finally, his eyes came to rest on Geoffrey. He nodded slowly. Then in his deep voice, he began a lilting chant.

Pater, adestis gratias tibi agimus vitam fratris nostrorum defuncti Roberti Fortescu, miles crucis...

Father we are gathered here to thank thee for the life of our departed brother Robert Fortescue, knight of the cross...

When the prior reached the end of his eulogy, he poured water from his flask into the palm of his hand and splashed it three times on the floor in front of him. Looking down where the drops fell, Geoffrey was astonished to see, set into the flagstones of the floor, a recumbent bas-relief sculpture of a knight in armour, hands folded in prayer across his breast, a sword by his side, a small dog beneath his feet.

But something puzzled him. For twenty years he'd attended meetings in this chapter house. He knew it as well as any man possibly could. But tonight something was different. The walls had somehow grown higher. Turning his head to look back at the door through which he'd entered, he understood. Why had he not noticed straight away? Inside the door, two steps descended to the floor of the chamber.

* * *

Geoffrey awoke chilled, cramped and uncomfortably reclining on a bench within the chapter house. The first streaks of dawn were already brightening the coloured glass of the windows and casting the shadows of Gothic tracery across the floor. At his feet, Benjamin was tugging at his shoelaces, making little growling noises, indicating his need to go outside.

Geoffrey rose stiffly to his feet and stretched his aching back. Remembering the events of the night, he shook his head in wonder. Had it all been a dream? Not possible. Both he and his dog were in the chapter house, not in his bedroom in the deanery.

Looking back at the door, Geoffrey saw no steps. Surely that shouldn't surprise him? There were no steps. Yet last night there'd been steps. If he'd been dreaming, why should he have dreamed steps where none existed?

Before leaving the chapter house he walked to the centre of the chamber and looked at the floor where the prior had let fall the drops of holy water. There was nothing to be seen. But Geoffrey could not possibly let this matter rest.

Outside the south transept, Benjamin scampered away towards the shrubbery in the close. Looking after him, Geoffrey spotted the chunky figure of Derek Mason striding purposefully towards him in the early morning light.

"Good morning, Geoffrey," Derek called. "I came early to see what'd been hit, but I see you've found the damage already.

"What's that?" Geoffrey's mind was still full of the mysterious happenings of the night before. He was unsure for what achievement Derek was giving him credit.

"Sir Robert's gargoyle," Derek replied. "That's what's left of it at your feet."

Geoffrey looked down. The shattered fragments of the sandstone gargoyle lay before him: here a mailed body, there an almost-faceless head with a wide-gaping mouth, smaller pieces scattered over the pathway. Looking up towards the crenelations he saw a jagged hole where the force of the lightning had blasted the figure free from its crumbling mortar.

Geoffrey had never been given any sign by God. He'd never expected one. He was not some great leader, no pagan emperor to be converted by a miraculous sign in the sky, no Arthurian knight to be granted sight of the Holy Grail. Yet on this fresh, rain-washed spring morning, as the cathedral he loved shone clean and bright in the first rays of the rising sun, he knew as certainly as any of the giants of history where his right road lay.

"Derek, we must get a couple of crowbars and some trowels from the maintenance store."

The architect gave him a curious look. "I hope you're not thinking we can climb up there and fix the damage ourselves!"

"No, no. We don't need the tools here. We need them in the chapter house. Tell me, what's underneath the flagstones in there?"

"Sand, I should think. That's what they normally used to lay the flags level."

"Then we'll also need a wheelbarrow to put the sand in. Don't worry, I haven't suddenly gone mad," he added, seeing the look of alarm on Derek's face. "We're not undertaking a major excavation. But something strange has happened and I have to see what's underneath the central flagstones. Please just trust me."

* * *

"I felt it only right I should bring you the news straight away," Geoffrey said, accepting a cup of tea from the housemaid and taking a seat in one of the countess' comfortable old armchairs in front of a good log fire. "I haven't even told the bishop yet, though I expect the news will reach him before I get back."

"What news, exactly?" The steely-eyed dowager inquired. "Do try to calm yourself, Dean. Begin at the beginning. You say it somehow dawned on you the floor of the chapter house had been raised without any record of the fact being made." She sipped her own tea and gave him a puzzled look. "Well I grant you that's a remarkable thing but not, I suspect, enough to send you rushing out here to see me on the very day of the discovery."

"No, Your Ladyship, but what will be of great interest to you is when this seems to have been done and by whom."

"Go on."

"Less than a foot down beneath the flagstones in the centre of the chapter house, we came upon the remains of a leather bag. Inside was a parcel wrapped in velvet. The material was brittle and crumbled almost into dust when we touched it, but we could tell it was originally intended to protect precious contents."

"How fascinating. And what were those contents, Dean?"

"A complete set of mid-seventeenth century silver communion salvers, each weighing close to a pound and each inscribed in Latin *Donum dedit Carolus, Dominus Eggesfordi, Anno Domini MDCXL.* The gift of Charles, Lord Eggesford, in the year of Our Lord 1640."

The countess started to her feet. "The cathedral's lost plate!"

"The very same, Your Ladyship. All intact and well-preserved, thanks to the dry environment in which they were stored. Lord Eggesford hid them carefully. Having donated them to the cathedral himself, he'd no intention of allowing them to be seized by his enemies and used against his king. He went mute to the scaffold rather than reveal their whereabouts."

"I *knew* it," Lady Agatha whispered, a tone of voice Geoffrey had never heard from her before. "The slander-mongers said he'd stolen them, but I *knew* that could not be so."

"And you were right, Your Ladyship"

A strange change came over the countess' face. She shook her head sadly. "Dean, how long have we known each other? Do you think you could perhaps bring yourself to call me Agatha? And perhaps I may call you Geoffrey?"

"Your Ladyship... I mean, Agatha, I'd be very pleased."

"But Geoffrey, I don't understand. To create a dry storage environment? That was the only reason he raised the whole floor? To me, that seems rather a drastic measure, albeit with the best of intentions."

"There was a reason, Your... Agatha, why he couldn't bury the silver beneath the original floor level. There were tombs set into the floor. We've uncovered two and the edge of a third. I think we'll find several of the founders are buried there, each beneath a bas-relief in their likeness. Because of the raised floor, the tombs were hidden from the image-smashers of the Commonwealth era."

"We know what the founders looked like after all!" Lady Agatha clapped her hands in delight. Then a shadow crossed her face. "All but poor Robert."

"You will, I'm sure, forgive me for saying this, Agatha, but in this one case you're wrong His tomb is in the very centre. It seems he returned from crusade only to die shortly afterwards from a fever he'd caught abroad. He was greatly mourned and buried with much ceremony. A solemn procession of Cluniac monks sang the most moving *Dies Irae* I've ever heard..." Geoffrey stopped himself. He'd said too much.

"And you heard it how, exactly, Geoffrey?" Lady Agatha asked quietly.

"Ah... I suppose you might say I was shown a mystery," he conceded.

Lady Agatha smiled. Something else he'd not seen before. "You know, Geoffrey, I am afraid I have become an old battle-axe."

"Oh no..."

"Don't lie to me, it's unbecoming in a man of the cloth. I've fought for the honour of my family so long I've lost sight of all the other things of importance in this world. I've become a mean-spirited, narrow-minded old woman."

Geoffrey fluttered his hands in half-hearted denial.

"Yet in one day, without any fighting, you've done more for the reputation of the Fortescues than I've done in all the years since my husband died."

"I am glad I could be of some service," Geoffrey said modestly.

"Geoffrey, I'm going to retire from the Restoration Committee. I can see things are perfectly safe in your hands. In fact, I've had it in mind for a long time to write a book about the Fortescues and the cathedral. I must make a start before it's too late."

"That does sound like a valuable project."

"Aha! Don't think you escape so easily. You'll come and take tea with me regularly. We'll be two old folks talking together about... something we both love. You can tell me all about this mystery of yours. And I... I shall try to listen. I see now I need to learn from you. Will you do that for me, Geoffrey?"

"Your Ladyship... Agatha," Geoffrey stood up, smiling broadly. "Do you know? I'd be absolutely delighted."

Open House

E.E. King

OLD MISS LAVINIA looked at the long staircase and sighed. It was time to move and she knew it. She'd lived in the house at 2659 Flower Lane since she'd been a bride, over fifty-five years ago. The stairs had been nothing then. Now, they rose up before her – a personal Everest.

She looked out at her lilacs. She didn't imagine that there would be lilacs in her new house. It would be a small one-story without peaks or valleys.

She called two of the realtors she'd seen smiling out at her from the for-sale signs that dotted the neighborhood like tiny billboards.

Kate and Josh Simons arrived to inspect her home. They were not as young, good looking, or thin as they'd been in their picture, but so nice. So friendly!

"Such a great old house," Kate said.

"We'll move some of your furniture into the garage," Josh said. "It will make the house appear more spacious."

"But my things," old Miss Lavinia cried, wringing her hands.

"They are *so* lovely," Kate patted her veined hands with smooth pudgy fingers. "Don't worry, Josh will be *very* careful." And he was.

It was odd having her mother's china cabinet in the garage. She circumnavigated the empty space. It seemed daring somehow, this change, as if she was embarking on a voyage of discovery.

The first open house was set for Saturday.

"It's good to bake bread, or cookies the night before, so that the house smells welcoming," Kate said. "But just boiling cinnamon in water will do the trick."

I'll make the lemon cookies my mother used to, thought Miss Lavinia. *They made the house smell delicious.* She smiled, remembering the citrus-scented mornings and the lazy summers of her youth. She spent the day baking – something she had not done in a long time. She couldn't wait to have Kate taste them.

On Saturday she was so nervous! Thank goodness Kate was there to help.

"These cookies are *so* fabulous," Kate crunched one, careful not to drop any crumbs on the newly vacuumed carpet. "Don't worry about a thing. It will be fine." And it was.

Miss Lavinia sat in her parlor, door open. The breeze wafted in, soft and curious, stroking her ankles and arms, making her feel almost young. It had been so long since she'd sat by an open door waiting for visitors. She hadn't realized how solitary she had become, how isolated. First, her husband, Terrance, had been killed in the war. Then, but so gradually and steadily she hadn't even noticed, all her friends had died or moved away, one by one, fading like the scent of the lilacs in the garden, leaving her alone in a flowerless world.

"Hello?" A girl peeped around the door. "What is that marvelous smell?" she said, just as Miss Lavinia had imagined someone would.

"It's my mother's lemon drop cookies," Miss Lavinia said. "Won't you have one?"

"How lovely," the girl said, holding out her hand. "I'm Margie, this is my fiancé Ken."

Margie was pretty, but not in the flashy way some girls were. She was sweet and respectful. You could tell she'd been brought up well.

Ken had brown hair the color of damp sand at low tide. His eyes were blue, serious, and kind.

"Why, you look just like my husband, Terrance, when he was young," Miss Lavinia blurted out, without even considering if that was a proper thing to say.

"Ma'am, if I weren't already engaged, I'd marry you in a heartbeat," he said. "Those cookies alone should garner you a slew of suitors." He bent over her small hand and brushed it gently with his lips. Miss Lavinia flushed.

"I must get your recipe for those luscious cookies," Margie said when they were leaving. And when Miss Lavinia copied it out in her spidery hand, Margie kissed her cheek.

There must have been a dozen people in and out that Saturday. All commented on the wonderful smell of Miss Lavinia's cookies. They chatted, complemented her house and garden. A few even stayed for tea. When the open house ended, Miss Lavinia was tired, but happier than she had been in years.

And so it continued for two months. All week Miss Lavinia would bake, preparing for her open house. She began to work in the garden again, slowly at first. But gradually growing stronger. After a few weeks, she even managed to dig out the old, dead rose bush. It left a hole in the yard, which she planned to fill with a white lilac.

Every Saturday- and sometimes half of Sunday – she would sit in the parlor, welcoming visitors and showing them around. All the lonely years after Terrance had died, all the decades since her friends had passed away condensed, like an accordion closing. They vanished without leaving even a memory. Only the early years and these later ones remained like bookends, the solid pillars of a happy life.

* * *

Miss Lavinia was in the kitchen, rolling up cinnamon squares when the phone rang, shattering the calm of the swirling dough.

"We have a buyer," Kate announced, not even saying hello. Not even saying her name. Her voice seemed brisk and sharp. So different from the kind, concerned Kate, Miss Lavinia expected.

"What?" Miss Lavinia said. She'd forgotten the end goal. She'd become used to a week of baking and a weekend of visitors. Life was rich and full again. Even the long stairs had become manageable – just a bit of exertion that was probably good for her.

"Who wants it?"

"A Mr. Forbes. He's seen the house on our website and wants to redo it."

"What do you mean?" Miss Lavinia said.

"He's a contractor, he buys homes and remodels them."

"He's never even been here?" Miss Lavinia asked.

"He's more interested in the property than the home. He plans a teardown. But he's willing to pay top dollar."

"I think he should see the house," Miss Lavinia said.

"It's really not necessary," Kate said.

It's not fair, Miss Lavinia thought. *Just when life is good again. Some man – some stranger – wants to destroy my home.*

"He can come and make an offer in person," she said.

Miss Lavinia knew just what this Mr. Forbes would be like. He would be like the generals in the war, the ones who never left their big, leather chairs in their big, airy offices. The ones who unthinkingly, unfeelingly sent young men like her Terrance to do the killing for them.

And what was outcome? Only more wars and more sorrow. More tears and more widows. She tightened her lips and marched into the kitchen, baking with a fierce determination, as if sugar and lemon zest could have more impact than bullets, or tanks.

Mr. Forbes bustled into her home late Friday, looking exactly as she'd imagined. He was big and swaggering. His lips were fat and moist. A sad, thin fringe of grey circled his bald head, like an adolescent's attempt at a mustache.

He did not comment on the lemon, chocolate, cinnamon goodness of the air or the newly blooming, wild, red poppies, or the porcelain-delicate lilies of the valley in the garden. No, instead he shuffled over to the table – her table – and sat down without even asking, just as if he already owned the place. He opened an olive-green leather folder and pulled out a sheath of papers.

Miss Lavinia did not believe in green leather. It was unnatural, displaying a lack of taste, a dearth of refinement.

"All you need to do is sign here," he said.

"But I'm not ready to sell," Miss Lavinia said.

"I'm paying well over market price," Mr. Forbes snarled. "You're not going to get a better deal."

"I need to think it over," Miss Lavinia cried.

"The house has been on the market for months. You don't need to think, you need to sign," and he pressed an enormous silver pen into her trembling hands.

"Here." He pointed to a blank space at the bottom of the tightly typed page.

"And here, and here."

"All right," she said, "But we need to make a toast and celebrate."

"I don't have a 'lotta time, lady. I'm a busy man."

"I'm sure you are," Miss Lavinia said. "But I will only sign if we can have a toast and some sweets. I have never sold a house before. It's the civilized thing to do."

Miss Lavinia doubted if Mr. Forbes was civilized, but she knew that a man so fat could never resist chocolate – at least not hers. She brought out her lemon cookies and carefully rolled chocolate crumbles.

"Just taste one," she said, pouring them each a tiny glass of sherry.

For a big man, he went down fast.

The lily-of-the-valley powder had an almost instantaneous effect. Mr. Forbes tumbled onto the floor foaming at the mouth. His face grew red, then purple, then gradually white. His moaning and drooling stopped and he ceased moving.

At first, she thought she'd chop him up and bury him in pieces, but just severing his little finger required all her force, and besides, there was so much blood. It was much easier, though it still took three days of lifting, and shoving, and resting, and thrusting to maneuver his remains into Terrance's old wheelbarrow, push him into the garden and curl his body into the hole where roses had once bloomed, but she managed. It was midweek. No one came by. There were no open houses planned as the house had ostensibly been sold. She burned his papers and clothes in the fireplace. She hadn't used it for more years than she could remember, but now, after a hard day of sawing and digging, she enjoyed sitting at night by its warm, orange glow.

Kate called on Friday. "Have you heard from Mr. Forbes?"

"Wasn't he going to come over to sign the papers?" Miss Lavinia asked.

"Yes, didn't he show up?"

"No, he must have changed his mind."

"That's odd," said Kate. "He seemed so definite."

"It's a mystery," Miss Lavinia agreed. "I guess we'll just have to put the house back on the market. I'll start cooking right away."

She grated up lemon peel and dried up some more lily of the valley, wondering when she would have to prepare her next chocolate crumble.

The Seven of Hearts

Maurice Leblanc

I AM FREQUENTLY asked this question: "How did you make the acquaintance of Arsène Lupin?"

My connection with Arsène Lupin was well known. The details that I gather concerning that mysterious man, the irrefutable facts that I present, the new evidence that I produce, the interpretation that I place on certain acts of which the public has seen only the exterior manifestations without being able to discover the secret reasons or the invisible mechanism, all establish, if not an intimacy, at least amicable relations and regular confidences.

But how did I make his acquaintance? Why was I selected to be his historiographer? Why I, and not some one else?

The answer is simple: chance alone presided over my choice; my merit was not considered. It was chance that put me in his way. It was by chance that I was participant in one of his strangest and most mysterious adventures; and by chance that I was an actor in a drama of which he was the marvelous stage director; an obscure and intricate drama, bristling with such thrilling events that I feel a certain embarrassment in undertaking to describe it.

The first act takes place during that memorable night of 22 June, of which so much has already been said. And, for my part, I attribute the anomalous conduct of which I was guilty on that occasion to the unusual frame of mind in which I found myself on my return home. I had dined with some friends at the Cascade restaurant, and, the entire evening, whilst we smoked and the orchestra played melancholy waltzes, we talked only of crimes and thefts, and dark and frightful intrigues. That is always a poor overture to a night's sleep.

The Saint-Martins went away in an automobile. Jean Daspry – that delightful, heedless Daspry who, six months later, was killed in such a tragic manner on the frontier of Morocco – Jean Daspry and I returned on foot through the dark, warm night. When we arrived in front of the little house in which I had lived for a year at Neuilly, on the boulevard Maillot, he said to me:

"Are you afraid?"

"What an idea!"

"But this house is so isolated…no neighbors…vacant lots…. Really, I am not a coward, and yet—"

"Well, you are very cheering, I must say."

"Oh! I say that as I would say anything else. The Saint-Martins have impressed me with their stories of brigands and thieves."

We shook hands and said goodnight. I took out my key and opened the door.

"Well, that is good," I murmured, "Antoine has forgotten to light a candle."

Then I recalled the fact that Antoine was away; I had given him a short leave of absence. Forthwith, I was disagreeably oppressed by the darkness and silence of the night. I ascended the stairs on tiptoe, and reached my room as quickly as possible; then, contrary to my usual habit, I turned the key and pushed the bolt.

The light of my candle restored my courage. Yet I was careful to take my revolver from its case – a large, powerful weapon – and place it beside my bed. That precaution completed my reassurance. I laid down and, as usual, took a book from my night-table to read myself to sleep. Then I received a great surprise. Instead of the paper-knife with which I had marked my place on the preceding, I found an envelope, closed with five seals of red wax. I seized it eagerly. It was addressed to me, and marked: "Urgent."

A letter! A letter addressed to me! Who could have put it in that place? Nervously, I tore open the envelope, and read:

"From the moment you open this letter, whatever happens, whatever you may hear, do not move, do not utter one cry. Otherwise you are doomed."

I am not a coward, and, quite as well as another, I can face real danger, or smile at the visionary perils of imagination. But, let me repeat, I was in an anomalous condition of mind, with my nerves set on edge by the events of the evening. Besides, was there not, in my present situation, something startling and mysterious, calculated to disturb the most courageous spirit?

My feverish fingers clutched the sheet of paper, and I read and re-read those threatening words: "Do not move, do not utter one cry. Otherwise, you are doomed."

"Nonsense!" I thought. "It is a joke; the work of some cheerful idiot."

I was about to laugh – a good loud laugh. Who prevented me? What haunting fear compressed my throat?

At least, I would blow out the candle. No, I could not do it. "Do not move, or you are doomed," were the words he had written.

These auto-suggestions are frequently more imperious than the most positive realities; but why should I struggle against them? I had simply to close my eyes. I did so.

At that moment, I heard a slight noise, followed by crackling sounds, proceeding from a large room used by me as a library. A small room or antechamber was situated between the library and my bedchamber.

The approach of an actual danger greatly excited me, and I felt a desire to get up, seize my revolver, and rush into the library. I did not rise; I saw one of the curtains of the left window move. There was no doubt about it: the curtain had moved. It was still moving. And I saw – oh! I saw quite distinctly – in the narrow space between the curtains and the window, a human form; a bulky mass that prevented the curtains from hanging straight. And it is equally certain that the man saw me through the large meshes of the curtain. Then, I understood the situation. His mission was to guard me while the others carried away their booty. Should I rise and seize my revolver? Impossible! He was there! At the least movement, at the least cry, I was doomed.

Then came a terrific noise that shook the house; this was followed by lighter sounds, two or three together, like those of a hammer that rebounded. At least, that was the impression formed in my confused brain. These were mingled with other sounds, thus creating a veritable uproar which proved that the intruders were not only bold, but felt themselves secure from interruption.

They were right. I did not move. Was it cowardice? No, rather weakness, a total inability to move any portion of my body, combined with discretion; for why should I struggle? Behind that man, there were ten others who would come to his assistance. Should I risk my life to save a few tapestries and bibelots?

Throughout the night, my torture endured. Insufferable torture, terrible anguish! The noises had stopped, but I was in constant fear of their renewal. And the man! The man who was guarding me, weapon in hand. My fearful eyes remained cast in his direction. And my heart beat! And a profuse perspiration oozed from every pore of my body!

Suddenly, I experienced an immense relief; a milk-wagon, whose sound was familiar to me, passed along the boulevard; and, at the same time, I had an impression that the light of a new day was trying to steal through the closed window-blinds.

At last, daylight penetrated the room; other vehicles passed along the boulevard; and all the phantoms of the night vanished. Then I put one arm out of the bed, slowly and cautiously. My eyes were fixed upon the curtain, locating the exact spot at which I must fire; I made an exact calculation of the movements I must make; then, quickly, I seized my revolver and fired.

I leaped from my bed with a cry of deliverance, and rushed to the window. The bullet had passed through the curtain and the window-glass, but it had not touched the man – for the very good reason that there was none there. Nobody! Thus, during the entire night, I had been hypnotized by a fold of the curtain. And, during that time, the malefactors....Furiously, with an enthusiasm that nothing could have stopped, I turned the key, opened the door, crossed the antechamber, opened another door, and rushed into the library. But amazement stopped me on the threshold, panting, astounded, more astonished than I had been by the absence of the man. All the things that I supposed had been stolen, furniture, books, pictures, old tapestries, everything was in its proper place.

It was incredible. I could not believe my eyes. Notwithstanding that uproar, those noises of removal.... I made a tour, I inspected the walls, I made a mental inventory of all the familiar objects. Nothing was missing. And, what was more disconcerting, there was no clue to the intruders, not a sign, not a chair disturbed, not the trace of a footstep.

"Well! Well!" I said to myself, pressing my hands on my bewildered head, "surely I am not crazy! I hear something!"

Inch by inch, I made a careful examination of the room. It was in vain. Unless I could consider this as a discovery: Under a small Persian rug, I found a card – an ordinary playing card. It was the seven of hearts; it was like any other seven of hearts in French playing-cards, with this slight but curious exception: The extreme point of each of the seven red spots or hearts was pierced by a hole, round and regular as if made with the point of an awl.

Nothing more. A card and a letter found in a book. But was not that sufficient to affirm that I had not been the plaything of a dream?

* * *

Throughout the day, I continued my searches in the library. It was a large room, much too large for the requirements of such a house, and the decoration of which attested the bizarre taste of its founder. The floor was a mosaic of multicolored stones, formed into large symmetrical designs. The walls were covered with a similar mosaic, arranged in panels, Pompeiian allegories, Byzantine compositions, frescoes of the Middle Ages. A Bacchus bestriding a cask. An emperor wearing a gold crown, a flowing beard, and holding a sword in his right hand.

Quite high, after the style of an artist's studio, there was a large window – the only one in the room. That window being always open at night, it was probable that the men had entered through it, by the aid of a ladder. But, again, there was no evidence. The bottom of the ladder would have left some marks in the soft earth beneath the window; but there were none. Nor were there any traces of footsteps in any part of the yard.

I had no idea of informing the police, because the facts I had before me were so absurd and inconsistent. They would laugh at me. However, as I was then a reporter on the staff of the 'Gil Blas,' I wrote a lengthy account of my adventure and it was published in the paper on the second day thereafter. The article attracted some attention, but no one took it seriously. They regarded it as a work of fiction rather than a story of real life. The Saint-Martins rallied me. But Daspry, who took an interest in such matters, came to see me, made a study of the affair, but reached no conclusion.

A few mornings later, the door-bell rang, and Antoine came to inform me that a gentleman desired to see me. He would not give his name. I directed Antoine to show him up. He was a man of about forty years of age with a very dark complexion, lively features, and whose correct dress, slightly frayed, proclaimed a taste that contrasted strangely with his rather vulgar manners. Without any preamble, he said to me – in a rough voice that confirmed my suspicion as to his social position:

"Monsieur, whilst in a café, I picked up a copy of the 'Gil Blas,' and read your article. It interested me very much.

"Thank you."

"And here I am."

"Ah!"

"Yes, to talk to you. Are all the facts related by you quite correct?"

"Absolutely so."

"Well, in that case, I can, perhaps, give you some information."

"Very well; proceed."

"No, not yet. First, I must be sure that the facts are exactly as you have related them."

"I have given you my word. What further proof do you want?"

"I must remain alone in this room."

"I do not understand," I said, with surprise.

"It's an idea that occurred to me when reading your article. Certain details established an extraordinary coincidence with another case that came under my notice. If I am mistaken, I shall say nothing more. And the only means of ascertaining the truth is by my remaining in the room alone."

What was at the bottom of this proposition? Later, I recalled that the man was exceedingly nervous; but, at the same time, although somewhat astonished, I found nothing particularly abnormal about the man or the request he had made. Moreover, my curiosity was aroused; so I replied:

"Very well. How much time do you require?"

"Oh! three minutes – not longer. Three minutes from now, I will rejoin you."

I left the room, and went downstairs. I took out my watch. One minute passed. Two minutes. Why did I feel so depressed? Why did those moments seem so solemn and weird? Two minutes and a half.... Two minutes and three quarters. Then I heard a pistol shot.

I bounded up the stairs and entered the room. A cry of horror escaped me. In the middle of the room, the man was lying on his left side, motionless. Blood was flowing from a wound in his forehead. Near his hand was a revolver, still smoking.

But, in addition to this frightful spectacle, my attention was attracted by another object. At two feet from the body, upon the floor, I saw a playing-card. It was the seven of hearts. I picked it up. The lower extremity of each of the seven spots was pierced with a small round hole.

* * *

A half-hour later, the commissary of police arrived, then the coroner and the chief of the Sûreté, Mon. Dudouis. I had been careful not to touch the corpse. The preliminary inquiry was very brief, and disclosed nothing. There were no papers in the pockets of the deceased; no name upon his clothes; no initial upon his linen; nothing to give any clue to his identity. The room was in the same perfect order as before. The furniture had not been disturbed. Yet this man had not come to my house solely for the purpose of killing himself, or because he considered my place the most convenient one for his suicide! There must have been a motive for his act of despair, and that motive was, no doubt, the result of some new fact ascertained by him during the three minutes he was alone.

What was that fact? What had he seen? What frightful secret had been revealed to him? There was no answer to these questions. But, at the last moment, an incident occurred that appeared to us of considerable importance. As two policemen were raising the body to place it on a stretcher, the left hand thus being disturbed, a crumpled card fell from it. The card bore these words: "Georges Andermatt, 37 Rue de Berry."

What did that mean? Georges Andermatt was a rich banker in Paris, the founder and president of the Metal Exchange which had given such an impulse to the metallic industries in France. He lived in princely style; was the possessor of numerous automobiles, coaches, and an expensive racing-stable. His social affairs were very select, and Madame Andermatt was noted for her grace and beauty.

"Can that be the man's name?" I asked.

The chief of the Sûreté leaned over him.

"It is not he. Mon. Andermatt is a thin man, and slightly grey."

"But why this card?"

"Have you a telephone, monsieur?"

"Yes, in the vestibule. Come with me."

He looked in the directory, and then asked for number 415.21.

"Is Mon. Andermatt at home?....Please tell him that Mon. Dudouis wished him to come at once to 102 Boulevard Maillot. Very important."

Twenty minutes later, Mon. Andermatt arrived in his automobile. After the circumstances had been explained to him, he was taken in to see the corpse. He displayed considerable emotion, and spoke, in a low tone, and apparently unwillingly:

"Etienne Varin," he said.

"You know him?"

"No...or, at least, yes...by sight only. His brother..."

"Ah! he has a brother?"

"Yes, Alfred Varin. He came to see me once on some matter of business...I forget what it was."

"Where does he live?"

"The two brothers live together – rue de Provence, I think."

"Do you know any reason why he should commit suicide?"

"None."

"He held a card in his hand. It was your card with your address."

"I do not understand that. It must have been there by some chance that will be disclosed by the investigation."

A very strange chance, I thought; and I felt that the others entertained the same impression.

I discovered the same impression in the papers next day, and amongst all my friends with whom I discussed the affair. Amid the mysteries that enveloped it, after the double discovery of the seven of hearts pierced with seven holes, after the two inscrutable events that had happened in my house, that visiting card promised to throw some light on the affair. Through it, the truth may be revealed. But, contrary to our expectations, Mon. Andermatt furnished no explanation. He said:

"I have told you all I know. What more can I do? I am greatly surprised that my card should be found in such a place, and I sincerely hope the point will be cleared up."

It was not. The official investigation established that the Varin brothers were of Swiss origin, had led a shifting life under various names, frequenting gambling resorts, associating with a band of foreigners who had been dispersed by the police after a series of robberies in which their participation was established only by their flight. At number 24 rue de Provence, where the Varin brothers had lived six years before, no one knew what had become of them.

I confess that, for my part, the case seemed to me so complicated and so mysterious that I did not think the problem would ever be solved, so I concluded to waste no more time upon it. But Jean Daspry, whom I frequently met at that period, became more and more interested in it each day. It was he who pointed out to me that item from a foreign newspaper which was reproduced and commented upon by the entire press. It was as follows:

"The first trial of a new model of submarine boat, which is expected to revolutionize naval warfare, will be given in presence of the former Emperor at a place that will be kept secret until the last minute. An indiscretion has revealed its name; it is called 'The Seven-of-Hearts.'"

The Seven-of-Hearts! That presented a new problem. Could a connection be established between the name of the sub-marine and the incidents which we have related? But a connection of what nature? What had happened here could have no possible relation with the sub-marine.

"What do you know about it?" said Daspry to me. "The most diverse effects often proceed from the same cause."

Two days later, the following foreign news item was received and published:

"It is said that the plans of the new sub-marine 'Seven-of-Hearts' were prepared by French engineers, who, having sought, in vain, the support of their compatriots, subsequently entered into negotiations with the British Admiralty, without success."

I do not wish to give undue publicity to certain delicate matters which once provoked considerable excitement. Yet, since all danger of injury therefrom has now come to an end, I must speak of the article that appeared in the 'Echo de France,' which aroused so much comment at that time, and which threw considerable light upon the mystery of the Seven-of-Hearts. This is the article as it was published over the signature of Salvator:

THE AFFAIR OF THE SEVEN OF HEARTS. A CORNER OF THE VEIL RAISED.

We will be brief. Ten years ago, a young mining engineer, Louis Lacombe, wishing to devote his time and fortune to certain studies, resigned his position he then held, and rented number 102 boulevard Maillot, a small house that had been recently built and decorated for an Italian count. Through the agency of the Varin brothers of Lausanne, one of whom assisted in the preliminary experiments and the other acted as financial agent, the young engineer was introduced to Georges Andermatt, the founder of the Metal Exchange.

After several interviews, he succeeded in interesting the banker in a submarine boat on which he was working, and it was agreed that as soon as the invention was perfected, Mon. Andermatt would use his influence with the Minister of Marine to obtain a series of trials under the direction of the government. For two years, Louis Lacombe was a frequent visitor at Andermatt's house, and he submitted to the banker the various improvements he made upon his original plans, until one day, being satisfied with the perfection of his work, he asked Mon. Andermatt to communicate with the Minister of Marine. That day, Louis Lacombe dined at Mon. Andermatt's house. He left there about half-past eleven at night. He has not been seen since.

A perusal of the newspapers of that date will show that the young man's family caused every possible inquiry to be made, but without success; and it was the general opinion that Louis Lacombe – who was known as an original and visionary youth – had quietly left for parts unknown.

Let us accept that theory – improbable, though it be, – and let us consider another question, which is a most important one for our country: What has become of the plans of the sub-marine? Did Louis Lacombe carry them away? Are they destroyed?

After making a thorough investigation, we are able to assert, positively, that the plans are in existence, and are now in the possession of the two brothers Varin. How did they acquire such a possession? That is a question not yet determined; nor do we know why they have not tried to sell them at an earlier date. Did they fear that their title to them would be called in question? If so, they have lost that fear, and we can announce definitely, that the plans of Louis Lacombe are now the property of foreign power, and we are in a position to publish the correspondence that passed between the Varin brothers and the representative of that power. The 'Seven-of-Hearts' invented by Louis Lacombe has been actually constructed by our neighbor.

Will the invention fulfill the optimistic expectations of those who were concerned in that treacherous act?"

And a post-script adds:

Later. – Our special correspondent informs us that the preliminary trial of the 'Seven-of-Hearts' has not been satisfactory. It is quite likely that the plans sold and delivered by the Varin brothers did not include the final document carried by Louis Lacombe to Mon. Andermatt on the day of his disappearance, a document that was indispensable to a thorough understanding of the invention. It contained a summary of the final conclusions of the inventor, and estimates and figures not contained in the other papers. Without this document, the plans are incomplete; on the other hand, without the plans, the document is worthless.

Now is the time to act and recover what belongs to us. It may be a difficult matter, but we rely upon the assistance of Mon. Andermatt. It will be to his interest to explain his conduct which has hitherto been so strange and inscrutable. He will explain not only why he concealed these facts at the time of the suicide of Etienne Varin, but also why he has never revealed the disappearance of the paper – a fact well known to him. He will tell why, during the last six years, he paid spies to watch the movements of the Varin brothers. We expect from him, not only words, but acts. And at once. Otherwise—

The threat was plainly expressed. But of what did it consist? What whip was Salvator, the anonymous writer of the article, holding over the head of Mon. Andermatt?

An army of reporters attacked the banker, and ten interviewers announced the scornful manner in which they were treated. Thereupon, the 'Echo de France' announced its position in these words:

"Whether Mon. Andermatt is willing or not, he will be, henceforth, our collaborator in the work we have undertaken."

* * *

Daspry and I were dining together on the day on which that announcement appeared. That evening, with the newspapers spread over my table, we discussed the affair and examined it from every point of view with that exasperation that a person feels when walking in the dark and finding himself constantly falling over the same obstacles. Suddenly, without any warning whatsoever, the door opened and a lady entered. Her face was hidden behind a thick veil. I rose at once and approached her.

"Is it you, monsieur, who lives here?" she asked.

"Yes, madame, but I do not understand—"

"The gate was not locked," she explained.

"But the vestibule door?"

She did not reply, and it occurred to me that she had used the servants' entrance. How did she know the way? Then there was a silence that was quite embarrassing. She looked at Daspry, and I was obliged to introduce him. I asked her to be seated and explain the object of her visit. She raised her veil, and I saw that she was a brunette with regular features and, though not handsome, she was attractive – principally, on account of her sad, dark eyes.

"I am Madame Andermatt," she said.

"Madame Andermatt!" I repeated, with astonishment.

After a brief pause, she continued with a voice and manner that were quite easy and natural:

"I have come to see you about that affair – you know. I thought I might be able to obtain some information—"

"Mon Dieu, madame, I know nothing but what has already appeared in the papers. But if you will point out in what way I can help you..."

"I do not know...I do not know."

Not until then did I suspect that her calm demeanor was assumed, and that some poignant grief was concealed beneath that air of tranquility. For a moment, we were silent and embarrassed. Then Daspry stepped forward, and said:

"Will you permit me to ask you a few questions?"

"Yes, yes," she cried. "I will answer."

"You will answer...whatever those questions may be?"

"Yes."

"Did you know Louis Lacombe?" he asked.

"Yes, through my husband."

"When did you see him for the last time?"

"The evening he dined with us."

"At that time, was there anything to lead you to believe that you would never see him again?"

"No. But he had spoken of a trip to Russia – in a vague way."

"Then you expected to see him again?"

"Yes. He was to dine with us, two days later."

"How do you explain his disappearance?"

"I cannot explain it."

"And Mon. Andermatt?"

"I do not know."

"Yet the article published in the 'Echo de France' indicates—"

"Yes, that the Varin brothers had something to do with his disappearance."

"Is that your opinion?"

"Yes."

"On what do you base your opinion?"

"When he left our house, Louis Lacombe carried a satchel containing all the papers relating to his invention. Two days later, my husband, in a conversation with one of the Varin brothers, learned that the papers were in their possession."

"And he did not denounce them?"

"No."

"Why not?"

"Because there was something else in the satchel – something besides the papers of Louis Lacombe."

"What was it?"

She hesitated; was on the point of speaking, but, finally, remained silent. Daspry continued:

"I presume that is why your husband has kept a close watch over their movements instead of informing the police. He hoped to recover the papers and, at the same time, that compromising article which has enabled the two brothers to hold over him threats of exposure and blackmail."

"Over him, and over me."

"Ah! over you, also?"

"Over me, in particular."

She uttered the last words in a hollow voice. Daspry observed it; he paced to and fro for a moment, then, turning to her, asked:

"Had you written to Louis Lacombe?"

"Of course. My husband had business with him—"

"Apart from those business letters, had you written to Louis Lacombe.... other letters? Excuse my insistence, but it is absolutely necessary that I should know the truth. Did you write other letters?"

"Yes," she replied, blushing.

"And those letters came into the possession of the Varin brothers?"

"Yes."

"Does Mon. Andermatt know it?"

"He has not seen them, but Alfred Varin has told him of their existence and threatened to publish them if my husband should take any steps against him. My husband was afraid.... of a scandal."

"But he has tried to recover the letters?"

"I think so; but I do not know. You see, after that last interview with Alfred Varin, and after some harsh words between me and my husband in which he called me to account – we live as strangers."

"In that case, as you have nothing to lose, what do you fear?"

"I may be indifferent to him now, but I am the woman that he has loved, the one he would still love – oh! I am quite sure of that," she murmured, in a fervent voice, "he would still love me if he had not got hold of those cursed letters—"

"What! Did he succeed?....But the two brothers still defied him?"

"Yes, and they boasted of having a secure hiding-place."

"Well?"

"I believe my husband discovered that hiding-place."

"Well?"

"I believe my husband has discovered that hiding-place."

"Ah! where was it?"

"Here."

"Here!" I cried in alarm.

"Yes. I always had that suspicion. Louis Lacombe was very ingenious and amused himself in his leisure hours, by making safes and locks. No doubt, the Varin brothers were aware of that fact and utilized one of Lacombe's safes in which to conceal the letters.... and other things, perhaps."

"But they did not live here," I said.

"Before you came, four months ago, the house had been vacant for some time. And they may have thought that your presence here would not interfere with them when they wanted to get the papers. But they did not count on my husband, who came here on the night of 22 June, forced the safe, took what he was seeking, and left his card to inform the two brothers that he feared them no more, and that their positions were now reversed. Two days later, after reading the article in the 'Gil Blas,' Etienne Varin came here, remained alone in this room, found the safe empty, and…killed himself."

After a moment, Daspry said:

"A very simple theory.… Has Mon. Andermatt spoken to you since then?"

"No."

"Has his attitude toward you changed in any way? Does he appear more gloomy, more anxious?"

"No, I haven't noticed any change."

"And yet you think he has secured the letters. Now, in my opinion, he has not got those letters, and it was not he who came here on the night of 22 June."

"Who was it, then?"

"The mysterious individual who is managing this affair, who holds all the threads in his hands, and whose invisible but far-reaching power we have felt from the beginning. It was he and his friends who entered this house on 22 June; it was he who discovered the hiding-place of the papers; it was he who left Mon. Andermatt's card; it is he who now holds the correspondence and the evidence of the treachery of the Varin brothers."

"Who is he?" I asked, impatiently.

"The man who writes letters to the 'Echo de France'...Salvator! Have we not convincing evidence of that fact? Does he not mention in his letters certain details that no one could know, except the man who had thus discovered the secrets of the two brothers?"

"Well, then," stammered Madame Andermatt, in great alarm, "he has my letters also, and it is he who now threatens my husband. Mon Dieu! What am I to do?"

"Write to him," declared Daspry. "Confide in him without reserve. Tell him all you know and all you may hereafter learn. Your interest and his interest are the same. He is not working against Mon. Andermatt, but against Alfred Varin. Help him."

"I Iow?"

"Has your husband the document that completes the plans of Louis Lacombe?"

"Yes."

"Tell that to Salvator, and, if possible, procure the document for him. Write to him at once. You risk nothing."

The advice was bold, dangerous even at first sight, but Madame Andermatt had no choice. Besides, as Daspry had said, she ran no risk. If the unknown writer were an enemy, that step would not aggravate the situation. If he were a stranger seeking to accomplish a particular purpose, he would attach to those letters only a secondary importance. Whatever might happen, it was the only solution offered to her, and she, in her anxiety, was only too glad to act on it. She thanked us effusively, and promised to keep us informed.

In fact, two days later, she sent us the following letter that she had received from Salvator:

"Have not found the letters, but I will get them. Rest easy. I am watching everything. S."

I looked at the letter. It was in the same handwriting as the note I found in my book on the night of 22 June.

Daspry was right. Salvator was, indeed, the originator of that affair.

* * *

We were beginning to see a little light coming out of the darkness that surrounded us, and an unexpected light was thrown on certain points; but other points yet remained obscure – for instance, the finding of the two seven-of-hearts. Perhaps I was unnecessarily concerned about those two cards whose seven punctured spots had appeared to me under such startling circumstances! Yet I could not refrain from asking myself: What role will they play in the drama? What importance do they bear? What conclusion must be drawn from the fact that the submarine constructed from the plans of Louis Lacombe bore the name of 'Seven-of-Hearts'?

Daspry gave little thought to the other two cards; he devoted all his attention to another problem which he considered more urgent; he was seeking the famous hiding-place.

"And who knows," said he, "I may find the letters that Salvator did not find – by inadvertence perhaps. It is improbable that the Varin brothers would have removed from a spot, which they deemed inaccessible, the weapon which was so valuable to them."

And he continued to search. In a short time, the large room held no more secrets for him, so he extended his investigations to the other rooms. He examined the interior and the exterior the stones of the foundation, the bricks in the walls; he raised the slates of the roof.

One day, he came with a pickaxe and a spade, gave me the spade, kept the pickaxe, pointed to the adjacent vacant lots, and said: "Come."

I followed him, but I lacked his enthusiasm. He divided the vacant land into several sections which he examined in turn. At last, in a corner, at the angle formed by the walls of two neighboring proprietors, a small pile of earth and gravel, covered with briers and grass attracted his attention. He attacked it. I was obliged to help him. For an hour, under a hot sun, we labored without success. I was discouraged, but Daspry urged me on. His ardor was as strong as ever.

At last, Daspry's pickaxe unearthed some bones – the remains of a skeleton to which some scraps of clothing still hung. Suddenly, I turned pale. I had discovered, sticking in the earth, a small piece of iron cut in the form of a rectangle, on which I thought I could see red spots. I stooped and picked it up. That little iron plate was the exact size of a playing-card, and the red spots, made with red lead, were arranged upon it in a manner similar to the seven-of-hearts, and each spot was pierced with a round hole similar to the perforations in the two playing cards.

"Listen, Daspry, I have had enough of this. You can stay if it interests you. But I am going."

Was that simply the expression of my excited nerves? Or was it the result of a laborious task executed under a burning sun? I know that I trembled as I walked away, and that I went to bed, where I remained forty-eight hours, restless and feverish, haunted by skeletons that danced around me and threw their bleeding hearts at my head.

Daspry was faithful to me. He came to my house every day, and remained three or four hours, which he spent in the large room, ferreting, thumping, tapping.

"The letters are here, in this room," he said, from time to time, "they are here. I will stake my life on it."

On the morning of the third day I arose – feeble yet, but cured. A substantial breakfast cheered me up. But a letter that I received that afternoon contributed, more than anything else, to my complete recovery, and aroused in me a lively curiosity. This was the letter:

Monsieur,

The drama, the first act of which transpired on the night of 22 June, is now drawing to a close. Force of circumstances compel me to bring the two principal actors in that drama face to face, and I wish that meeting to take place in your house, if you will be so kind as to give me the use of it for this evening from nine o'clock to eleven. It will be advisable to give your servant leave of absence for the evening, and, perhaps, you will be so kind as to leave the field open to the two adversaries. You will remember that when I visited your house on the night of 22 June, I took excellent care of your property. I feel that I would do you an injustice if I should doubt, for one moment, your absolute discretion in this affair. Your devoted,

SALVATOR

I was amused at the facetious tone of his letter and also at the whimsical nature of his request. There was a charming display of confidence and candor in his language, and nothing in the world could have induced me to deceive him or repay his confidence with ingratitude.

I gave my servant a theatre ticket, and he left the house at eight o'clock. A few minutes later, Daspry arrived. I showed him the letter.

"Well?" said he.

"Well, I have left the garden gate unlocked, so anyone can enter."

"And you – are you going away?"

"Not at all. I intend to stay right here."

"But he asks you to go—"

"But I am not going. I will be discreet, but I am resolved to see what takes place."

"Ma foi!" exclaimed Daspry, laughing, "you are right, and I shall stay with you. I shouldn
like to miss it."

We were interrupted by the sound of the door-bell.

"Here already?" said Daspry, "twenty minutes ahead of time! Incredible!"

I went to the door and ushered in the visitor. It was Madame Andermatt. She was fair and nervous, and in a stammering voice, she ejaculated:

"My husband…is coming…he has an appointment…they intend to give him the letters…

"How do you know?" I asked.

"By chance. A message came for my husband while we were at dinner. The servant gav it to me by mistake. My husband grabbed it quickly, but he was too late. I had read it."

"You read it?"

"Yes. It was something like this: 'At nine o'clock this evening, be at Boulevard Maill with the papers connected with the affair. In exchange, the letters.' So, after dinner, hastened here."

"Unknown to your husband?"

"Yes."

"What do you think about it?" asked Daspry, turning to me.

"I think as you do, that Mon. Andermatt is one of the invited guests."

"Yes, but for what purpose?"

"That is what we are going to find out."

I led the men to a large room. The three of us could hide comfortably behind the velv chimney-mantle, and observe all that should happen in the room. We seated ourselv there, with Madame Andermatt in the centre.

The clock struck nine. A few minutes later, the garden gate creaked upon its hinges. confess that I was greatly agitated. I was about to learn the key to the mystery. The startlin events of the last few weeks were about to be explained, and, under my eyes, the last batt was going to be fought. Daspry seized the hand of Madame Andermatt, and said to her:

"Not a word, not a movement! Whatever you may see or hear, keep quiet!"

Some one entered. It was Alfred Varin. I recognized him at once, owing to the clos resemblance he bore to his brother Etienne. There was the same slouching gait; the sam cadaverous face covered with a black beard.

He entered with the nervous air of a man who is accustomed to fear the presence traps and ambushes; who scents and avoids them. He glanced about the room, and I ha the impression that the chimney, masked with a velvet portière, did not please him. H took three steps in our direction, when something caused him to turn and walk towa the old mosaic king, with the flowing beard and flamboyant sword, which he examine minutely, mounting on a chair and following with his fingers the outlines of the shoulde and head and feeling certain parts of the face. Suddenly, he leaped from the chair an walked away from it. He had heard the sound of approaching footsteps. Mon. Anderma appeared at the door.

"You! You!" exclaimed the banker. "Was it you who brought me here?"

"I? By no means," protested Varin, in a rough, jerky voice that reminded me of h brother, "on the contrary, it was your letter that brought me here."

"My letter?"

"A letter signed by you, in which you offered—"

"I never wrote to you," declared Mon. Andermatt.

"You did not write to me!"

Instinctively, Varin was put on his guard, not against the banker, but against the unknown enemy who had drawn him into this trap. A second time, he looked in our direction, then walked toward the door. But Mon. Andermatt barred his passage.

"Well, where are you going, Varin?"

"There is something about this affair I don't like. I am going home. Good evening."

"One moment!"

"No need of that, Mon. Andermatt. I have nothing to say to you."

"But I have something to say to you, and this is a good time to say it."

"Let me pass."

"No, you will not pass."

Varin recoiled before the resolute attitude of the banker, as he muttered:

"Well, then, be quick about it."

One thing astonished me; and I have no doubt my two companions experienced a similar feeling. Why was Salvator not there? Was he not a necessary party at this conference? Or was he satisfied to let these two adversaries fight it out between themselves? At all events, his absence was a great disappointment, although it did not detract from the dramatic strength of the situation.

After a moment, Mon. Andermatt approached Varin and, face to face, eye to eye, said:

"Now, after all these years and when you have nothing more to fear, you can answer me candidly: What have you done with Louis Lacombe?"

"What a question! As if I knew anything about him!"

"You do know! You and your brother were his constant companions, almost lived with him in this very house. You knew all about his plans and his work. And the last night I ever saw Louis Lacombe, when I parted with him at my door, I saw two men slinking away in the shadows of the trees. That, I am ready to swear to."

"Well, what has that to do with me?"

"The two men were you and your brother."

"Prove it."

"The best proof is that, two days later, you yourself showed me the papers and the plans that belonged to Lacombe and offered to sell them. How did these papers come into your possession?"

"I have already told you, Mon. Andermatt, that we found them on Louis Lacombe's table, the morning after his disappearance."

"That is a lie!"

"Prove it."

"The law will prove it."

"Why did you not appeal to the law?"

"Why? Ah! Why—" stammered the banker, with a slight display of emotion.

"You know very well, Mon. Andermatt, if you had the least certainty of our guilt, our little threat would not have stopped you."

"What threat? Those letters? Do you suppose I ever gave those letters a moment's thought?"

"If you did not care for the letters, why did you offer me thousands of francs for their return? And why did you have my brother and me tracked like wild beasts?"

"To recover the plans."

"Nonsense! You wanted the letters. You knew that as soon as you had the letters in your possession, you could denounce us. Oh! no, I couldn't part with them!"

He laughed heartily, but stopped suddenly, and said:

"But, enough of this! We are merely going over old ground. We make no headway. We had better let things stand as they are."

"We will not let them stand as they are," said the banker, "and since you have referred to the letters, let me tell you that you will not leave this house until you deliver up those letters."

"I shall go when I please."

"You will not."

"Be careful, Mon. Andermatt. I warn you—"

"I say, you shall not go."

"We will see about that," cried Varin, in such a rage that Madame Andermatt could not suppress a cry of fear. Varin must have heard it, for he now tried to force his way out. Mon. Andermatt pushed him back. Then I saw him put his hand into his coat pocket.

"For the last time, let me pass," he cried.

"The letters, first!"

Varin drew a revolver and, pointing it at Mon. Andermatt, said:

"Yes or no?"

The banker stooped quickly. There was the sound of a pistol-shot. The weapon fell from Varin's hand. I was amazed. The shot was fired close to me. It was Daspry who had fired it at Varin, causing him to drop the revolver. In a moment, Daspry was standing between the two men, facing Varin; he said to him, with a sneer:

"You were lucky, my friend, very lucky. I fired at your hand and struck only the revolver."

Both of them looked at him, surprised. Then he turned to the banker, and said:

"I beg your pardon, monsieur, for meddling in your business; but, really, you play a very poor game. Let me hold the cards."

Turning again to Varin, Daspry said:

"It's between us two, comrade, and play fair, if you please. Hearts are trumps, and I play the seven."

Then Daspry held up, before Varin's bewildered eyes, the little iron plate, marked with the seven red spots. It was a terrible shock to Varin. With livid features, staring eyes, and an air of intense agony, the man seemed to be hypnotized at the sight of it.

"Who are you?" he gasped.

"One who meddles in other people's business, down to the very bottom."

"What do you want?"

"What you brought here tonight."

"I brought nothing."

"Yes, you did, or you wouldn't have come. This morning, you received an invitation to come here at nine o'clock, and bring with you all the papers held by you. You are here. Where are the papers?"

There was in Daspry's voice and manner a tone of authority that I did not understand; his manner was usually quite mild and conciliatory. Absolutely conquered, Varin placed his hand on one of his pockets, and said:

"The papers are here."

"All of them?"

"Yes."

"All that you took from Louis Lacombe and afterwards sold to Major von Lieben?"

"Yes."

"Are these the copies or the originals?"

"I have the originals."

"How much do you want for them?"

"One hundred thousand francs."

"You are crazy," said Daspry. "Why, the major gave you only twenty thousand, and that was like money thrown into the sea, as the boat was a failure at the preliminary trials."

"They didn't understand the plans."

"The plans are not complete."

"Then, why do you ask me for them?"

"Because I want them. I offer you five thousand francs – not a sou more."

"Ten thousand. Not a sou less."

"Agreed," said Daspry, who now turned to Mon. Andermatt, and said:

"Monsieur will kindly sign a check for the amount."

"But...I haven't got—"

"Your check-book? Here it is."

Astounded, Mon. Andermatt examined the check-book that Daspry handed to him.

"It is mine," he gasped. "How does that happen?"

"No idle words, monsieur, if you please. You have merely to sign."

The banker took out his fountain pen, filled out the check and signed it. Varin held out his hand for it.

"Put down your hand," said Daspry, "there is something more." Then, to the banker, he said: "You asked for some letters, did you not?"

"Yes, a package of letters."

"Where are they, Varin?"

"I haven't got them."

"Where are they, Varin?"

"I don't know. My brother had charge of them."

"They are hidden in this room."

"In that case, you know where they are."

"How should I know?"

"Was it not you who found the hiding-place? You appear to be as well informed...as Salvator."

"The letters are not in the hiding-place."

"They are."

"Open it."

Varin looked at him, defiantly. Were not Daspry and Salvator the same person? Everything pointed to that conclusion. If so, Varin risked nothing in disclosing a hiding-place already known.

"Open it," repeated Daspry.

"I have not got the seven of hearts."

"Yes, here it is," said Daspry, handing him the iron plate. Varin recoiled in terror, and cried:

"No, no, I will not."

"Never mind," replied Daspry, as he walked toward the bearded king, climbed on a chair and applied the seven of hearts to the lower part of the sword in such a manner that the edges of the iron plate coincided exactly with the two edges of the sword. Then, with the assistance of an awl which he introduced alternately into each of the seven holes, he pressed upon seven of the little mosaic stones. As he pressed upon the seventh one, a clicking sound was heard, and the entire bust of the King turned upon a pivot, disclosing a large opening lined with steel. It was really a fire-proof safe.

"You can see, Varin, the safe is empty."

"So I see. Then, my brother has taken out the letters."

Daspry stepped down from the chair, approached Varin, and said:

"Now, no more nonsense with me. There is another hiding-place. Where is it?"

"There is none."

"Is it money you want? How much?"

"Ten thousand."

"Monsieur Andermatt, are those letters worth ten thousand francs to you?"

"Yes," said the banker, firmly.

Varin closed the safe, took the seven of hearts and placed it again on the sword at the same spot. He thrust the awl into each of the seven holes. There was the same clicking sound, but this time, strange to relate, it was only a portion of the safe that revolved on the pivot, disclosing quite a small safe that was built within the door of the larger one. The packet of letters was here, tied with a tape, and sealed. Varin handed the packet to Daspry. The latter turned to the banker, and asked:

"Is the check ready, Monsieur Andermatt?"

"Yes."

"And you have also the last document that you received from Louis Lacombe – the one that completes the plans of the sub-marine?"

"Yes."

The exchange was made. Daspry pocketed the document and the checks, and offered the packet of letters to Mon. Andermatt.

"This is what you wanted, Monsieur."

The banker hesitated a moment, as if he were afraid to touch those cursed letters that he had sought so eagerly. Then, with a nervous movement, he took them. Close to me, I heard a moan. I grasped Madame Andermatt's hand. It was cold.

"I believe, monsieur," said Daspry to the banker, "that our business is ended. Oh! no thanks. It was only by a mere chance that I have been able to do you a good turn. Goodnight."

Mon. Andermatt retired. He carried with him the letters written by his wife to Louis Lacombe.

"Marvelous!" exclaimed Daspry, delighted. "Everything is coming our way. Now, we have only to close our little affair, comrade. You have the papers?"

"Here they are – all of them."

Daspry examined them carefully, and then placed them in his pocket.

"Quite right. You have kept your word," he said.

"But—"

"But what?"

"The two checks? The money?" said Varin, eagerly.

"Well, you have a great deal of assurance, my man. How dare you ask such a thing?"

"I ask only what is due to me."

"Can you ask pay for returning papers that you stole? Well, I think not!"

Varin was beside himself. He trembled with rage; his eyes were bloodshot.

"The money…the twenty thousand…" he stammered.

"Impossible! I need it myself."

"The money!"

"Come, be reasonable, and don't get excited. It won't do you any good."

Daspry seized his arm so forcibly, that Varin uttered a cry of pain. Daspry continued:

"Now, you can go. The air will do you good. Perhaps you want me to show you the way. Ah yes, we will go together to the vacant lot near here, and I will show you a little mound of earth and stones and under it—"

"That is false! That is false!"

"Oh! no, it is true. That little iron plate with the seven spots on it came from there. Louis Lacombe always carried it, and you buried it with the body – and with some other things that will prove very interesting to a judge and jury."

Varin covered his face with his hands, and muttered:

"All right, I am beaten. Say no more. But I want to ask you one question. I should like to know—"

"What is it?"

"Was there a little casket in the large safe?"

"Yes."

"Was it there on the night of 22 June?"

"Yes."

"What did it contain?"

"Everything that the Varin brothers had put in it – a very pretty collection of diamonds and pearls picked up here and there by the said brothers."

"And did you take it?"

"Of course I did. Do you blame me?"

"I understand…it was the disappearance of that casket that caused my brother to kill himself."

"Probably. The disappearance of your correspondence was not a sufficient motive. But the disappearance of the casket…. Is that all you wish to ask me?"

"One thing more: your name?"

"You ask that with an idea of seeking revenge."

"Parbleu! The tables may be turned. Today, you are on top. Tomorrow—"

"It will be you."

"I hope so. Your name?"

"Arsène Lupin."

"Arsène Lupin!"

The man staggered, as though stunned by a heavy blow. Those two words had deprived him of all hope.

Daspry laughed, and said:

"Ah! did you imagine that a Monsieur Durand or Dupont could manage an affair like this? No, it required the skill and cunning of Arsène Lupin. And now that you have my name, go and prepare your revenge. Arsène Lupin will wait for you."

Then he pushed the bewildered Varin through the door.

"Daspry! Daspry!" I cried, pushing aside the curtain. He ran to me.

"What? What's the matter?"

"Madame Andermatt is ill."

He hastened to her, caused her to inhale some salts, and, while caring for her, questioned me:

"Well, what did it?"

"The letters of Louis Lacombe that you gave to her husband."

He struck his forehead and said:

"Did she think that I could do such a thing! But, of course she would. Imbecile that I am!"

Madame Andermatt was now revived. Daspry took from his pocket a small package exactly similar to the one that Mon. Andermatt had carried away.

"Here are your letters, Madame. These are the genuine letters."

"But…the others?"

"The others are the same, rewritten by me and carefully worded. Your husband will not find anything objectionable in them, and will never suspect the substitution since they were taken from the safe in his presence."

"But the handwriting—"

"There is no handwriting that cannot be imitated."

She thanked him in the same words she might have used to a man in her own social circle, so I concluded that she had not witnessed the final scene between Varin and Arsène Lupin. But the surprising revelation caused me considerable embarrassment. Lupin! My club companion was none other than Arsène Lupin. I could not realize it. But he said, quite at his ease:

"You can say farewell to Jean Daspry."

"Ah!"

"Yes, Jean Daspry is going on a long journey. I shall send him to Morocco. There, he may find a death worthy of him. I may say that that is his expectation."

"But Arsène Lupin will remain?"

"Oh! Decidedly. Arsène Lupin is simply at the threshold of his career, and he expects—"

I was impelled by curiosity to interrupt him, and, leading him away from the hearing of Madame Andermatt, I asked:

"Did you discover the smaller safe yourself – the one that held the letters?"

"Yes, after a great deal of trouble. I found it yesterday afternoon while you were asleep. And yet, God knows it was simple enough! But the simplest things are the ones that usually escape our notice." Then, showing me the seven of hearts, he added: "Of course I had guessed that, in order to open the larger safe, this card must be placed on the sword of the mosaic king."

"How did you guess that?"

"Quite easily. Through private information, I knew that fact when I came here on the evening of 22 June—"

"After you left me—"

"Yes, after turning the subject of our conversation to stories of crime and robbery which were sure to reduce you to such a nervous condition that you would not leave your bed, but would allow me to complete my search uninterrupted."

"The scheme worked perfectly."

"Well, I knew when I came here that there was a casket concealed in a safe with a secret lock and that the seven-of-hearts was the key to that lock. I had merely to place the card upon the spot that was obviously intended for it. An hour's examination showed me where the spot was."

"One hour!"

"Observe the fellow in mosaic."

"The old emperor?"

"That old emperor is an exact representation of the king of hearts on all playing cards."

"That's right. But how does the seven of hearts open the larger safe at one time and the smaller safe at another time? And why did you open only the larger safe in the first instance? I mean on the night of 22 June."

"Why? Because I always placed the seven of hearts in the same way. I never changed the position. But, yesterday, I observed that by reversing the card, by turning it upside down, the arrangement of the seven spots on the mosaic was changed."

"Parbleu!"

"Of course, parbleu! But a person has to think of those things."

"There is something else: you did not know the history of those letters until Madame Andermatt—"

"Spoke of them before me? No. Because I found in the safe, besides the casket, nothing but the correspondence of the two brothers which disclosed their treachery in regard to the plans."

"Then it was by chance that you were led, first, to investigate the history of the two brothers, and then to search for the plans and documents relating to the sub-marine?"

"Simply by chance."

"For what purpose did you make the search?"

"Mon Dieu!" exclaimed Daspry, laughing, "how deeply interested you are!"

"The subject fascinates me."

"Very well, presently, after I have escorted Madame Andermatt to a carriage, and dispatched a short story to the 'Echo de France,' I will return and tell you all about it."

He sat down and wrote one of those short, clear-cut articles which served to amuse and mystify the public. Who does not recall the sensation that followed that article produced throughout the entire world?

"Arsène Lupin has solved the problem recently submitted by Salvator. Having acquired possession of all the documents and original plans of the engineer Louis Lacombe, he has placed them in the hands of the Minister of Marine, and he has headed a subscription list for the purpose of presenting to the nation the first submarine constructed from those plans. His subscription is twenty thousand francs."

"Twenty thousand francs! The checks of Mon. Andermatt?" I exclaimed, when he had given me the paper to read.

"Exactly. It was quite right that Varin should redeem his treachery."

* * *

And that is how I made the acquaintance of Arsène Lupin. That is how I learned that Jean Daspry, a member of my club, was none other than Arsène Lupin, gentleman-thief. That is how I formed very agreeable ties of friendship with that famous man, and, thanks to the confidence with which he honored me, how I became his very humble and faithful historiographer.

The Whittaker-Chambers Method

Or, Mulligan's Last Mystery

Tom Mead

IN THE WARM, restful summer of 1960, Hester Queeg wrote her first and only fan letter. Like a lot of fan letters, it was long and a little cloying but it was completely sincere. She wrote it to Calvin Mulligan, the mystery writer – maybe you remember the name? No one reads him much these days, but in certain circles he is remembered fondly. I suppose the problem is that his kind of story seems pretty dated now – locked room mysteries, where lords and ladies in country houses get killed by daggers made of ice, or strangled in the snow by a killer who leaves no footprints.

Hester, who lived peacefully in a suburb of San Francisco, had plenty to occupy her time. She had given up her work as a secretary when she got pregnant the second time, and now she was a happy housewife nearing forty, with a hard-working husband and two boisterous kids. She spent her days among friends, and shopping at the local mart, and cooking and washing clothes and whatever else you might expect of a professional housewife. To look at her, you would not know she had a dark side.

Oftentimes she could be seen puttering along the tree-lined streets in her wood-panelled station wagon, with the back seats occupied by bulging grocery bags. You might see a woman like that and not even recognise her predilection for murder. But tucked in one of those grocery bags, more often than not, you might spy a lurid magazine cover peeping out: *Black Mask* or *Murder!* or *Midnight Mystery*.

Hester was an aficionado of crime, and in the last throes of that lambent summer, she came across a story that startled her more than she cared to admit. It was her favourite style – a classic golden age locked room mystery – and it was by Calvin Mulligan. But this piece, 'The Clue of the Cartesian Mirror,' was unlike anything she had encountered before. She read it in a single sitting, at the kitchen table, and when she was finished she found herself almost breathless at the effortless invention. She was convinced it was the greatest mystery story she had ever read. That is why she took up her pad and pen and began in her neatest cursive hand to write the fan letter.

She mailed it the following morning – sending it care of *Midnight Mystery Magazine* before reading the story through a second time and shaking her head in wonderment. The letter arrived at *MMM* HQ in San Diego, where it was promptly forwarded to the author's home address. But Calvin Mulligan never got to read it.

Mystery Writer Slain! Shrieked the headline of the local paper. Hester, however, did not immediately make the connection. The headline photograph depicted a distinguished elderly lady; the sort of society grand dame largely thought to have died out with the nineteenth century. But when she read the first paragraph, Hester's heart punched her chest like a fist.

Police reports indicate that Mildred Nash, 78, author of several popular mysteries under the name Calvin Mulligan, was found dead in the study of her Noe Valley home last night. Noe Valley! Hester had no idea her idol had lived so close.

The following day, on her way back from the grocery store, Hester took a quick detour. Soon enough she spotted the house she had recognised from the newspaper photograph: an immense stone edifice perched between swaying willow trees. It had a romantic, gothic desolation to it. Even more so, considering the macabre fate of its occupant. Hester turned off the car engine and studied the house for a moment. In less than a minute, she was marching up the driveway.

You may wonder *how* she gained access to the house, and the clutch of suspects? How else for a homely housewife but to use her innate charm? One thing Hester had never lost over the years was her disarming warmth. When she rapped on the door of the late Mildred Nash's house she did not quite know what she was going to say, but she knew it would be good and it would do the trick.

"Hello," she said to the middle-aged woman who peered suspiciously out at her through the screen door. "My name is Hester Queeg. I just wanted to tell you how very very sorry I am about Mrs. Nash."

A pause. "Were you a friend of hers?" The voice was brittle as glass. The woman wore black, to match her hair, which had been slashed into a brutal bob.

"More an admirer," Hester answered. "She really was one of the greats."

"Oh, she was wasn't she?" said the woman, easing open the screen door and ushering Hester inside. "One of the very best writers, and the very best *people*. I worked for her for nearly fifty years. I don't know what I'll do now she's gone. How did you know her?"

"Through her work," Hester replied instantly, "it was pure hero worship."

The other woman smiled, and her face was sad and lined with grey shadow. "My name is Mrs. Friedland. I'm the housekeeper here." They shook hands. "Now...can I get you some tea?"

Once she was inside the late author's home, Hester found her curiosity whetted further. Mrs. Friedland took her into an old-fashioned kitchen (copper pans and a lead-lined basin) and seated her at a varnished wooden table. At the far end of the room was what appeared to be a wooden serving hatch, but Hester recognised it as an old-style dumbwaiter.

"I still can't believe it," said Mrs. Friedland.

"Death always comes as a shock," Hester answered sagely.

"No!" the older woman almost snapped. "No, you don't understand. Of course, how could you? Even the papers haven't got hold of the full story yet."

"What do you mean?"

The kettle had begun to whistle. As Mrs. Friedland poured the tea she began to explain.

For perhaps a month before her death, Mildred Nash had been the target of a malicious poison pen campaign. The letters were a sinister portrait of a troubled mind. The threats they contained were oblique but no less unpleasant for that. They were typed on an Olivetti typewriter, similar (but distinct) from the one in Mildred's own office. Difficult to trace, as it was a standard model available from all retail outlets. (This foxed Hester immediately – in her brand of mystery there would usually be one retailer in the state offering that brand of writer, with a carefully-maintained log of sales and buyers.)

"Somebody wanted her dead," Mrs. Friedland concluded.

Hester sipped her tea. "You can't be saying it was *murder*?"

Mrs. Friedland was deathly pale and funereally serious. "That is exactly what I'm saying. And what's more, Detective Kemble agrees with me."

In her most maternal tones, Hester said: "I think you'd better tell me everything."

True enough, as the housekeeper laid out the scenario it sounded like the most elaborate of fictional mysteries: perhaps from fear, Mildred Nash had taken to locking herself in first-floor study during the day. On the evening she died, she had left the key in the lock. Likewise, the two wide dormer windows were impenetrable: they were painted shut some years ago, and even if they *could* be opened, this would be impossible without leaving some trace flakes of paint on the carpet, or some such. And yet, when the body was found, she displayed clear signs of poisoning. Foam about the mouth, a faint bluish tinge about the lips and fingertips – not to mention the grotesque contortion of her aged frame. Evidently, this was not a natural death.

"*Could* anyone have poisoned her?" Hester asked.

"Mrs. Nash had just finished her evening meal. I delivered it to her myself. But I can tell you for a fact there was nothing untoward in the food. It was clam chowder, her favourite. Oh, and a glass of water."

"Could she have taken the poison some other way?"

Mrs. Friedland gave an indulgent chuckle. "I don't think you understand. Mrs. Nash had been in that room of hers all day. She hadn't once set foot outside. She hadn't *eaten* anything either. I was the only one who cooked for her – she wouldn't have had it any other way. She was old-fashioned and set in her ways. I always felt kind of sorry for her. She struggled when she was young, what with the epilepsy and all."

"Oh," said Hester, "I never realised the poor lady was epileptic."

"They never understood it when she was young. But as she aged, medical advancements were made."

"So she was taking medication?"

"Potassium bromide, from her doctor. But that couldn't have been what killed her. She'd been taking it for years. Maybe even since she was a little girl."

"Then maybe the food you prepared *was* tampered with in some way?"

But the housekeeper shook her head. "That may be what that mean-spirited Lauren wants you to think. But it's impossible, believe me."

Hester's brow was furrowed. "Lauren…?"

"Oh!" Hester turned in her seat. Standing in the doorway was a startled-looking girl of about twenty-three. "Who are you?"

"My name is Hester Queeg."

"Well I guess Friedland has told you about me already. I'm Lauren. Mildred's niece." She came over and they shook hands. Lauren was young and pretty – a real Mamie van Doren. She wore a figure-hugging dress in sun-yellow and studied Hester through fluttering, opalescent eyes.

"Do you live here Lauren?"

"I used to. That is, till Aunt Mildred died. Now I'm homeless."

"What do you mean?"

"Everything – this house, the fortune – it all goes to Friedland."

"You mean, your aunt didn't make some kind of allowance for you?"

"Nothing. Isn't that right, Friedland?"

The housekeeper's jaw was clenched. "I could almost feel sorry for you, Lauren. If you'd eve done anything but leech off your aunt in your whole miserable life."

Lauren gave an unpleasant laugh. "You see how she talks to me? Pretty damn suspicious. I'v a good mind to tell Detective Kemble…"

"Oh, stop," Mrs. Friedland hissed. "You know full well I could no more have poisoned th chowder than you could."

"Is it true?" Hester asked Lauren. "Your aunt only ate one meal that day, and it was the one that killed her?"

Lauren nodded.

"Who prepared the food?"

"I did." It was Mrs. Friedland, and the statement was almost a confrontation. "And I can tell you there was nothing wrong with the food. Miss Nash can vouch for that herself."

Hester turned to Lauren, who was studying her shoes. "Yes," the girl conceded with some reluctance, "there was nothing wrong with the food."

"But how can you be sure?"

"I was here while it was being prepared. And...I tasted it."

Hester blinked. "You *tasted* it?"

Mrs. Friedland cut in: "A fatuous remark is what she made – saying 'how do I know you haven't put poison in her food?'"

"Yes. That's what I said. But it was only a joke."

"Joke or not, I won't have anyone saying that about my food. So I handed her the plate and a fork, and I said 'go ahead – taste!'"

"And you did?"

Lauren nodded slowly. "I took a forkful."

"Took a forkful and she ate it in front of me. And not just that – she took a sip of the water too."

"Then what happened?"

"I watched Friedland put the food in the dumbwaiter."

"And then?"

"And then? Then nothing. She pressed the button and it buzzed away, up to the second storey. It was delivered right into Aunt Mildred's study, and she ate it all up and then she died."

"Do you mind if I...?" Hester got up and walked over to the dumbwaiter. She poked her head inside and examined the simple cubic wooden frame on which the food was placed, and which was carried upward by a system of pulleys, guided by small steel wheels. It was very much a relic of the nineteenth century, even down to the ornate inlaid patterns in the wood. It ran on electric now – but even *that* was archaic and dust-caked.

Mrs. Friedland seemed to read her mind. "It may be old," she said, but it gets the job done. There's nothing wrong with that dumbwaiter at all. In fact, we had the repairman out just last month to replace a faulty connection. So it really is in tip-top shape. It's a simple enough mechanism – the food goes *here*, you press this button and it's carried upstairs."

"Straight up to Mrs. Nash's room," Hester reiterated, "which was locked on the inside."

Mrs. Friedland and Lauren nodded.

The next instant, Hester was jolted from her reverie by a hammering on the door.

Mrs. Friedland, now flustered, hurried out to answer. She returned to the kitchen with two men. One, a tall matinee-idol type in a trench coat, was leading another sweaty stick-insect of a man by his necktie. It did not take Hester long to deduce that the matinee idol was the famous "Detective Kemble."

"I found this fella wandering out in the grounds," he said. "He says he's a friend of Mrs. Nash. Can you vouch for him?"

Hester studied the other man. A miserable round head, with strands of oily hair smeared across it. A suit that pinched under the arms and bulged a little around the belly. But in his buttonhole, a freshly-picked carnation.

"Oh, Kemble," sighed Lauren irreverently, "what *have* you been doing out there? That's Eustace Hyburn. He was Mildred's agent."

Kemble, flummoxed, looked to Mrs. Friedland for confirmation. The housekeeper was nodding. "It's true, Detective. That's Mr. Hyburn. And he *was* Mrs. Nash's literary agent."

"See?" snapped the little fellow, "I told you, didn't I?"

"That's as maybe," said Hester, serenely, "but agents have been known to murder their authors, you know."

Silence fell. "Really," Eustace eventually spluttered, "why would I want to kill my most popular author? It'd be like slitting the throat of the goose that lays the golden egg."

"I read a lot of fiction," said Hester, "and I know for a fact that sometimes dying is the best career move a writer can make. It sends sales figures through the roof."

"In the short term. But long-term I'd have been a lot better off if Mildred had lived to produce more novels."

Hester thought about this. "So the only way a murder would be financially viable would be if you had real threats of monetary problems."

"I'm sorry," cut in Detective Kemble, "am I missing something? Just who might you be, ma'am?"

"My name is Hester Queeg," she announced, "and I'm just leaving."

* * *

Within the week, the death of Mildred Nash, was being hallooed by the tabloids as an ingenious locked-room murder. This wasn't Hester's doing – she hadn't told a soul. But these things have a way of getting out. And it caused ripples right the way through town.

While shopping for groceries, Hester spotted a stand on which were propped an array of the late author's work – pristine paperbacks heaped high like goldbricks. When she met a couple o girlfriends for coffee in Stacey's Diner, all the waitress could talk about was Mildred Nash. "Jus think," she said as she dribbled coffee from a murky percolator into a row of mugs, "we had a famous writer under our noses all this time and we never even knew it."

Hester nodded thoughtfully. "The way I understand it," said Hester's coffee-companion Karen, "there's no way the food could have been poisoned in the kitchen. It had to be th dumbwaiter, some trickery that was rigged up."

"That's just murder-mystery nonsense," said her other companion Claire, "it was suicide c course. Apparently her books weren't selling too well. Maybe she had debts."

"But they never found a bottle, did they? If she poisoned herself, there would have been bottle."

With worrying synchronicity, the women turned to glare at Hester. "*You've* been out ther honey – what's the story?"

Hester sighed. "There's nothing in the dumbwaiter. The two women were together th whole time after the meal went up to Mrs. Nash. When they found her dead, they called th police straight away. There was no opportunity for any booby trap to be planted or removed."

"Well," said Claire smugly, "there you are. Suicide."

"But…" Hester continued between sips, "if Mrs. Nash poisoned her own food, *there wou have been a bottle*."

It was a messy case. A puzzle to rival even the most daring invention of Calvin Mulligan. Th food was prepared by Mrs. Friedland in the kitchen, tasted by Lauren, and then placed into th dumbwaiter where it went straight up to Mildred Nash, who promptly ate it and died of as-y undetermined poisoning.

Hester couldn't stop thinking about it. She thought about it when she awoke the following morning, and ambled blearily out into the bathroom. Her husband was awake early, and he had left a scattering of tell-tale dark chin-hairs in the sink from his morning shave. Hester tutted, and then looked at herself in the mirror. She would look better, she reasoned, after a mug of coffee.

Down in the kitchen of her own home – so modern and yet meagre compared to the house out in Noe Valley where Mildred Nash died – Hester prepared the coffee and, while she was waiting for it to cool, she peered through the window at the quiet street outside. It was not yet eight o' clock, and the neighbourhood had not yet come to life. From the window she saw Georgie Loomis, who'd just had his thirteenth birthday, walking the family dogs. Not one but two Great Danes, and excitable, tails thumping like rotor blades as they wrenched the poor bewildered boy along. Hester turned away from the comic spectacle of the boy being wrenched out of view by the slobbering dogs. She had been struck by a thought.

When the kids had gone to school, and her husband to work, Hester did not immediately head for the grocery store. She had a few other errands to take care of. In the first place, she called on her friend Karen, who ran an antique store a few blocks away. Once she had got what she wanted there, she headed for the public library. There she startled the librarian by requesting "any books you have on toxic chemicals." Then she drove out to Noe Valley once more.

When she got there, she was surprised to find the quiet street lined with police cars. As she began to make her way up the driveway toward the old house, Detective Kemble jogged over to stop her.

"What's going on Detective?" she asked innocently.

"We're just about to arrest Mrs. Friedland."

"But why?"

"We searched her room. Tucked in the bottom of the wardrobe we found a typewriter. It matches exactly the letters Mildred received."

Hester shook her head. "No, no, no..."

"What? You think she's innocent?"

"This is straight out of a mystery story, can't you see that Detective?"

When he spoke, he was stern. "But it's *not* a mystery story, Mrs. Queeg. It's real life."

Hester sighed. "Can I speak with you, Detective? In private, I mean?"

They went out into the garden – it was blissful and serene, with perfect view of the sparkling bay. Hester took a moment to gather herself. "You need to forget about these letters. They have no bearing on Mildred's death whatsoever."

"How can you say that?"

"It was obvious to me right from the beginning that Lauren was the one who wrote those letters. She was the only one who had any reason to, because of course all of Mildred's estate goes to Mrs. Friedland. Lauren's idea was to frame Mrs. Friedland, and convince Mildred to change her will."

"But the typewriter..."

"Lauren had plenty of opportunity to use Mrs. Friedland's typewriter. No doubt Mrs. Friedland recognised the writing straight away when she saw one of the notes. But of course, she couldn't say anything. She knew she was being framed, and she knew why too. But she daren't risk her position in the household by saying anything."

Kemble lit up a cigarette. "What you're saying makes a kind of sense. But Mildred never did change her will."

"No. And she never intended to. That's why I would advise you to forget about the letters. They have no bearing on her death."

"Who does that leave us then? The agent?"

"He had no motive. No money worries that might have been alleviated by Mildred's death and the sudden spike in sales that would create."

Now, Kemble jabbed out the cigarette angrily on the trunk of a sycamore tree. "Then who?"

Hester gave a little smile. "Come back to the house. I want to show you something."

They headed for the kitchen, where Hester made straight for the dumbwaiter. "I got the idea when I was cleaning out the sink at home," she began with child-like enthusiasm. "My husband is a wonderful man but he *will* not learn to clean up after himself when he's done shaving in the morning. So as soon as I step into the bathroom I find a sink dusted with tiny black hairs. I guess my mind works in kind of a funny way, because that got me thinking about the *act* of shaving. You know, the friction of a blade against the skin – it's kind of scary when you think about it. And that's what turned me onto the dumbwaiter."

With a flourish, she produced from her handbag a crisp white handkerchief. This she unfolded and laid flat on the tray of the dumbwaiter. "This is an authentic nineteenth century construction. See the inlay here? That's nearly a hundred years old. A friend of mine owns an antique dealers and knows about this kind of thing. Pretty, isn't it? She tells me that back in the day the cabinetmakers, usually Pennsylvania Germans like my grandpa, would make the grooves with a blade then pour molten liquid into the groove to create the finish. But not just any liquid – they used molten *sulfur*."

Then she held the 'call' button down with her thumb and they waited as the contraption buzzed all the way up to the second floor. When it returned, Hester carefully retrieved the handkerchief and laid it on the table. "Look," she said.

Kemble did as instructed. Squinting at the white cotton, he noticed a dusting of fine grey specks distributed evenly across the surface of the material. "What is it?" he demanded.

"Listen to this," she said, with a hint of pride. "I know how it happened. When you think about it, there's only one possible way. One of the first things I found out about the case was that the dumbwaiter had been recently repaired. But I misunderstood what Mrs. Friedland told me. When she said it was a "faulty connection" I assumed it was the circuitry that had malfunctioned, but it wasn't. It was the pulley system overhead. In other words, the ropes and guiding tracks directly above the dumbwaiter itself. The talk of the 'connection' made me think of electrics – but it was the *rope* that had to be replaced. And it was replaced. But when I saw poor Georgie Loomis struggling with two almighty Great Danes when he was out walking them this morning, I started thinking that the ropes we have nowadays might not necessarily fit too well with an old-style dumbwaiter. If anything, they might be *too* strong. In other words, they may create a lot of friction when they scrape against the old, rotting wood of the dumbwaiter itself. And the friction may begin to slice off tiny fragments of the wood whenever the contraption is used, and leave a sprinkle of fine shavings on whatever is placed on the tray. Ordinarily, this would be a nuisance, but it wouldn't be deadly. But in the case of Mildred Nash, it was a little different.

"We know the poor lady took Potassium Bromide as a remedy for her seizures – that's what the glass of water with the food was for. And the bromine in her medication has a nasty chemical reaction when it comes into contact with sulfur. In *water*, the molecules combine and you get none other than *hydrobromic acid*. I guess I don't need to tell you that it's a lethal substance. But the reaction wouldn't take place until the sulfur, the bromine and the water *are* came into contact, which didn't take place until Mildred consumed the pill after her meal. And *that* combination is what killed her."

Lombard looked at her, nonplussed. "Is that some kind of joke?"

"It's science, Detective. Basic chemistry."

"But it's *impossible*..."

Hester spoke severely: "It certainly is not. In fact it's the only solution to the problem that's even slightly possible. If the poison was there in the kitchen, then Lauren would have tasted it too. So it must have been the shavings which dropped into the glass *while the tray was moving up*. Then when poor Mrs. Nash took her pill after her meal, the reaction happened and she died."

Kemble was shaking his head, muttering. Hester caught the word 'impossible' again. "'Improbable' is the word you're looking for. And I can't help that, Detective. If it's the truth, it's the truth."

"It's improbable all right – damned improbable. Hell of a way for an old lady to go."

Now Hester smiled. "But don't you see, Detective? It's perfect. All her life, Mildred Nash sought to create a method for a perfect murder. And, without meaning to, she did. It was a perfect murder for one simple reason: *because it wasn't a murder at all*."

The Case of the Dixon Torpedo

Arthur Morrison

HEWITT WAS VERY apt, in conversation, to dwell upon the many curious chances and coincidences that he had observed, not only in connection with his own cases, but also in matters dealt with by the official police, with whom he was on terms of pretty regular, and, indeed, friendly, acquaintanceship. He has told me many an anecdote of singular happenings to Scotland Yard officials with whom he has exchanged experiences. Of Inspector Nettings, for instance, who spent many weary months in a search for a man wanted by the American Government, and in the end found, by the merest accident (a misdirected call), that the man had been lodging next door to himself the whole of the time; just as ignorant, of course, as was the inspector himself as to the enemy at the other side of the party-wall. Also of another inspector, whose name I can not recall, who, having been given rather meager and insufficient details of a man whom he anticipated having great difficulty in finding, went straight down the stairs of the office where he had received instructions, and actually *fell over* the man near the door, where he had stooped down to tie his shoe-lace! There were cases, too, in which, when a great and notorious crime had been committed, and various persons had been arrested on suspicion, some were found among them who had long been badly wanted for some other crime altogether. Many criminals had met their deserts by venturing out of their own particular line of crime into another; often a man who got into trouble over something comparatively small found himself in for a startlingly larger trouble, the result of some previous misdeed that otherwise would have gone unpunished. The ruble note-forger Mirsky might never have been handed over to the Russian authorities had he confined his genius to forgery alone. It was generally supposed at the time of his extradition that he had communicated with the Russian Embassy, with a view to giving himself up – a foolish proceeding on his part, it would seem, since his whereabouts, indeed even his identity as the forger, had not been suspected. He *had* communicated with the Russian Embassy, it is true, but for quite a different purpose, as Martin Hewitt well understood at the time. What that purpose was is now for the first time published.

* * *

The time was half-past one in the afternoon, and Hewitt sat in his inner office examining and comparing the handwriting of two letters by the aid of a large lens. He put down the lens and glanced at the clock on the mantel-piece with a premonition of lunch; and as he did so his clerk quietly entered the room with one of those printed slips which were kept for the announcement of unknown visitors. It was filled up in a hasty and almost illegible hand, thus:

***Name of visitor**: F. Graham Dixon.*
***Address**: Chancery Lane.*
***Business**: Private and urgent.*

"Show Mr. Dixon in," said Martin Hewitt.

Mr. Dixon was a gaunt, worn-looking man of fifty or so, well, although rather carelessly, dressed, and carrying in his strong, though drawn, face and dullish eyes the look that characterizes the life-long strenuous brain-worker. He leaned forward anxiously in the chair which Hewitt offered him, and told his story with a great deal of very natural agitation.

"You may possibly have heard, Mr. Hewitt – I know there are rumors – of the new locomotive torpedo which the government is about adopting; it is, in fact, the Dixon torpedo, my own invention, and in every respect – not merely in my own opinion, but in that of the government experts – by far the most efficient and certain yet produced. It will travel at least four hundred yards farther than any torpedo now made, with perfect accuracy of aim (a very great desideratum, let me tell you), and will carry an unprecedentedly heavy charge. There are other advantages – speed, simple discharge, and so forth – that I needn't bother you about. The machine is the result of many years of work and disappointment, and its design has only been arrived at by a careful balancing of principles and means, which are expressed on the only four existing sets of drawings. The whole thing, I need hardly tell you, is a profound secret, and you may judge of my present state of mind when I tell you that one set of drawings has been stolen."

"From your house?"

"From my office, in Chancery Lane, this morning. The four sets of drawings were distributed thus: Two were at the Admiralty Office, one being a finished set on thick paper, and the other a set of tracings therefrom; and the other two were at my own office, one being a penciled set, uncolored – a sort of finished draft, you understand – and the other a set of tracings similar to those at the Admiralty. It is this last set that has gone. The two sets were kept together in one drawer in my room. Both were there at ten this morning; of that I am sure, for I had to go to that very drawer for something else when I first arrived. But at twelve the tracings had vanished."

"You suspect somebody, probably?"

"I can not. It is a most extraordinary thing. Nobody has left the office (except myself, and then only to come to you) since ten this morning, and there has been no visitor. And yet the drawings are gone!"

"But have you searched the place?"

"Of course I have! It was twelve o'clock when I first discovered my loss, and I have been turning the place upside down ever since – I and my assistants. Every drawer has been emptied, every desk and table turned over, the very carpet and linoleum have been taken up, but there is not a sign of the drawings. My men even insisted on turning all their pockets inside out, although I never for a moment suspected either of them, and it would take a pretty big pocket to hold the drawings, doubled up as small as they might be."

"You say your men – there are two, I understand – had neither left the office?"

"Neither; and they are both staying in now. Worsfold suggested that it would be more satisfactory if they did not leave till something was done toward clearing the mystery up, and, although, as I have said, I don't suspect either in the least, I acquiesced."

"Just so. Now – I am assuming that you wish me to undertake the recovery of these drawings?"

The engineer nodded hastily.

"Very good; I will go round to your office. But first perhaps you can tell me something about your assistants – something it might be awkward to tell me in their presence, you know. Mr. Worsfold, for instance?"

"He is my draughtsman – a very excellent and intelligent man, a very smart man, indeed, and, I feel sure, quite beyond suspicion. He has prepared many important drawings for me (he has been with me nearly ten years now), and I have always found him trustworthy. But, of course, the temptation in this case would be enormous. Still, I can not suspect Worsfold. Indeed, how can I suspect anybody in the circumstances?"

"The other, now?"

"His name's Ritter. He is merely a tracer, not a fully skilled draughtsman. He is quite a decent young fellow, and I have had him two years. I don't consider him particularly smart, or he would have learned a little more of his business by this time. But I don't see the least reason to suspect him. As I said before, I can't reasonably suspect anybody."

"Very well; we will get to Chancery Lane now, if you please, and you can tell me more as we go."

"I have a cab waiting. What else can I tell you?"

"I understand the position to be succinctly this: The drawings were in the office when you arrived. Nobody came out, and nobody went in; and *yet* they vanished. Is that so?"

"That is so. When I say that absolutely nobody came in, of course I except the postman. He brought a couple of letters during the morning. I mean that absolutely nobody came past the barrier in the outer office – the usual thing, you know, like a counter, with a frame of ground glass over it."

"I quite understand that. But I think you said that the drawings were in a drawer in your *own* room – not the outer office, where the draughtsmen are, I presume?"

"That is the case. It is an inner room, or, rather, a room parallel with the other, and communicating with it; just as your own room is, which we have just left."

"But, then, you say you never left your office, and yet the drawings vanished – apparently by some unseen agency – while you were there in the room?"

"Let me explain more clearly." The cab was bowling smoothly along the Strand, and the engineer took out a pocket-book and pencil. "I fear," he proceeded, "that I am a little confused in my explanation – I am naturally rather agitated. As you will see presently, my offices consist of three rooms, two at one side of a corridor, and the other opposite – thus." He made a rapid pencil sketch.

"In the outer office my men usually work. In the inner office I work myself. These rooms communicate, as you see, by a door. Our ordinary way in and out of the place is by the door of the outer office leading into the corridor, and we first pass through the usual lifting flap in the barrier. The door leading from the *inner* office to the corridor is always kept locked on the inside, and I don't suppose I unlock it once in three months. It has not been unlocked all the morning. The drawer in which the missing drawings were kept, and in which I saw them at ten o'clock this morning, is at the place marked D; it is a large chest of shallow drawers in which the plans lie flat."

"I quite understand. Then there is the private room opposite. What of that?"

"That is a sort of private sitting-room that I rarely use, except for business interviews of a very private nature. When I said I never left my office, I did not mean that I never stirred out of the inner office. I was about in one room and another, both the outer and the inner offices, and once I went into the private room for five minutes, but nobody came either in or out of any of the rooms at that time, for the door of the private room was wide open, and I was standing at the book-case (I had gone to consult a book), just inside the door, with a full view of the doors opposite. Indeed, Worsfold was at the door of the outer office most of the short time. He came to ask me a question."

"Well," Hewitt replied, "it all comes to the simple first statement. You know that nobody left the place or arrived, except the postman, who couldn't get near the drawings, and yet the drawings went. Is this your office?"

The cab had stopped before a large stone building. Mr. Dixon alighted and led the way to the first-floor. Hewitt took a casual glance round each of the three rooms. There was a sort of door in the frame of ground glass over the barrier to admit of speech with visitors. This door Hewitt pushed wide open, and left so.

He and the engineer went into the inner office. "Would you like to ask Worsfold and Ritter any questions?" Mr. Dixon inquired.

"Presently. Those are their coats, I take it, hanging just to the right of the outer office door, over the umbrella stand?"

"Yes, those are all their things – coats, hats, stick, and umbrella."

"And those coats were searched, you say?"

"Yes."

"And this is the drawer – thoroughly searched, of course?"

"Oh, certainly; every drawer was taken out and turned over."

"Well, of course I must assume you made no mistake in your hunt. Now tell me, did anybody know where these plans were, beyond yourself and your two men?"

"As far as I can tell, not a soul."

"You don't keep an office boy?"

"No. There would be nothing for him to do except to post a letter now and again, which Ritter does quite well for."

"As you are quite sure that the drawings were there at ten o'clock, perhaps the thing scarcely matters. But I may as well know if your men have keys of the office?"

"Neither. I have patent locks to each door and I keep all the keys myself. If Worsfold or Ritter arrive before me in the morning they have to wait to be let in; and I am always present myself when the rooms are cleaned. I have not neglected precautions, you see."

"No. I suppose the object of the theft – assuming it is a theft – is pretty plain: the thief would offer the drawings for sale to some foreign government?"

"Of course. They would probably command a great sum. I have been looking, as I need hardly tell you, to that invention to secure me a very large fortune, and I shall be ruined, indeed, if the design is taken abroad. I am under the strictest engagements to secrecy with the Admiralty, and not only should I lose all my labor, but I should lose all the confidence reposed in me at headquarters; should, in fact, be subject to penalties for breach of contract, and my career stopped forever. I can not tell you what a serious business this is for me. If you can not help me, the consequences will be terrible. Bad for the service of the country, too, of course."

"Of course. Now tell me this: It would, I take it, be necessary for the thief to *exhibit* these drawings to anybody anxious to buy the secret – I mean, he couldn't describe the invention by word of mouth."

"Oh, no, that would be impossible. The drawings are of the most complicated description, and full of figures upon which the whole thing depends. Indeed, one would have to be a skilled expert to properly appreciate the design at all. Various principles of hydrostatics, chemistry, electricity, and pneumatics are most delicately manipulated and adjusted, and the smallest error or omission in any part would upset the whole. No, the drawings are necessary to the thing, and they are gone."

At this moment the door of the outer office was heard to open and somebody entered. The door between the two offices was ajar, and Hewitt could see right through to the glass door left open over the barrier and into the space beyond. A well-dressed, dark, bushy-bearded man stood there carrying a hand-bag, which he placed on the ledge before him. Hewitt raised his hand to enjoin silence. The man spoke in a rather high-pitched voice and with a slight accent. "Is Mr. Dixon now within?" he asked.

"He is engaged," answered one of the draughtsmen; "very particularly engaged. I am afraid you won't be able to see him this afternoon. Can I give him any message?"

"This is two – the second time I have come today. Not two hours ago Mr. Dixon himself tells me to call again. I have a very important – very excellent steam-packing to show him that is very cheap and the best of the market." The man tapped his bag. "I have just taken orders from the largest railway companies. Can not I see him, for one second only? I will not detain him."

"Really, I'm sure you can't this afternoon; he isn't seeing anybody. But if you'll leave your name—"

"My name is Hunter; but what the good of that? He ask me to call a little later, and I come, and now he is engaged. It is a very great pity." And the man snatched up his bag and walking-stick, and stalked off, indignantly.

Hewitt stood still, gazing through the small aperture in the doorway.

"You'd scarcely expect a man with such a name as Hunter to talk with that accent, would you?" he observed, musingly. "It isn't a French accent, nor a German; but it seems foreign. You don't happen to know him, I suppose?"

"No, I don't. He called here about half-past twelve, just while we were in the middle of our search and I was frantic over the loss of the drawings. I was in the outer office myself, and told him to call later. I have lots of such agents here, anxious to sell all sorts of engineering appliances. But what will you do now? Shall you see my men?"

"I think," said Hewitt, rising – "I think I'll get you to question them yourself."

"Myself?"

"Yes, I have a reason. Will you trust me with the 'key' of the private room opposite? I will go over there for a little, while you talk to your men in this room. Bring them in here and shut the door; I can look after the office from across the corridor, you know. Ask them each to detail his exact movements about the office this morning, and get them to recall each visitor who has been here from the beginning of the week. I'll let you know the reason of this later. Come across to me in a few minutes."

Hewitt took the key and passed through the outer office into the corridor.

Ten minutes later Mr. Dixon, having questioned his draughtsmen, followed him. He found Hewitt standing before the table in the private room, on which lay several drawings on tracing-paper.

"See here, Mr. Dixon," said Hewitt, "I think these are the drawings you are anxious about?"

The engineer sprang toward them with a cry of delight. "Why, yes, yes," he exclaimed, turning them over, "every one of them! But where – how – they must have been in the place after all, then? What a fool I have been!"

Hewitt shook his head. "I'm afraid you're not quite so lucky as you think, Mr. Dixon," he said. "These drawings have most certainly been out of the house for a little while. Never mind how – we'll talk of that after. There is no time to lose. Tell me – how long would it take a good draughtsman to copy them?"

"They couldn't possibly be traced over properly in less than two or two and a half long days of very hard work," Dixon replied with eagerness.

"Ah! then it is as I feared. These tracings have been photographed, Mr. Dixon, and our task is one of every possible difficulty. If they had been copied in the ordinary way, one might hope to get hold of the copy. But photography upsets everything. Copies can be multiplied with such amazing facility that, once the thief gets a decent start, it is almost hopeless to checkmate him. The only chance is to get at the negatives before copies are taken. I must act at once; and I fear, between ourselves, it may be necessary for me to step very distinctly over the line of the law in the matter. You see, to get at those negatives may involve something very like house-breaking. There must be no delay, no waiting for legal procedure, or the mischief is done. Indeed, I very much question whether you have any legal remedy, strictly speaking."

"Mr. Hewitt, I implore you, do what you can. I need not say that all I have is at your disposal. I will guarantee to hold you harmless for anything that may happen. But do, I entreat you, do everything possible. Think of what the consequences may be!"

"Well, yes, so I do," Hewitt remarked, with a smile. "The consequences to me, if I were charged with house-breaking, might be something that no amount of guarantee could mitigate. However, I will do what I can, if only from patriotic motives. Now, I must see your tracer, Ritter. He is the traitor in the camp."

"Ritter? But how?"

"Never mind that now. You are upset and agitated, and had better not know more than is necessary for a little while, in case you say or do something unguarded. With Ritter I must take a deep course; what I don't know I must appear to know, and that will seem more likely to him if I disclaim acquaintance with what I do know. But first put these tracings safely away out of sight."

Dixon slipped them behind his book-case.

"Now," Hewitt pursued, "call Mr. Worsfold and give him something to do that will keep him in the inner office across the way, and tell him to send Ritter here."

Mr. Dixon called his chief draughtsman and requested him to put in order the drawings in the drawers of the inner room that had been disarranged by the search, and to send Ritter, as Hewitt had suggested.

Ritter walked into the private room with an air of respectful attention. He was a puffy-faced, unhealthy-looking young man, with very small eyes and a loose, mobile mouth.

"Sit down, Mr. Ritter," Hewitt said, in a stern voice. "Your recent transactions with your friend Mr. Hunter are well known both to Mr. Dixon and myself."

Ritter, who had at first leaned easily back in his chair, started forward at this, and paled.

"You are surprised, I observe; but you should be more careful in your movements out of doors if you do not wish your acquaintances to be known. Mr. Hunter, I believe, has the drawings which Mr. Dixon has lost, and, if so, I am certain that you have given them to him. That, you know, is theft, for which the law provides a severe penalty."

Ritter broke down completely and turned appealingly to Mr. Dixon.

"Oh, sir," he pleaded, "it isn't so bad, I assure you. I was tempted, I confess, and hid the drawings; but they are still in the office, and I can give them to you – really, I can."

"Indeed?" Hewitt went on. "Then, in that case, perhaps you'd better get them at once. Just go and fetch them in; we won't trouble to observe your hiding-place. I'll only keep this door open, to be sure you don't lose your way, you know – down the stairs, for instance."

The wretched Ritter, with hanging head, slunk into the office opposite. Presently he reappeared, looking, if possible, ghastlier than before. He looked irresolutely down the corridor, as if meditating a run for it, but Hewitt stepped toward him and motioned him back to the private room.

"You mustn't try any more of that sort of humbug," Hewitt said with increased severity. "The drawings are gone, and you have stolen them; you know that well enough. Now attend to me. If you received your deserts, Mr. Dixon would send for a policeman this moment, and have you hauled off to the jail that is your proper place. But, unfortunately, your accomplice, who calls himself Hunter – but who has other names besides that – as I happen to know – has the drawings, and it is absolutely necessary that these should be recovered. I am afraid that it will be necessary, therefore, to come to some arrangement with this scoundrel – to square him, in fact. Now, just take that pen and paper, and write to your confederate as I dictate. You know the alternative if you cause any difficulty."

Ritter reached tremblingly for the pen.

"Address him in your usual way," Hewitt proceeded. "Say this: 'There has been an alteration in the plans.' Have you got that? 'There has been an alteration in the plans. I shall be alone here at six o'clock. Please come, without fail.' Have you got it? Very well; sign it, and address the envelope. He must come here, and then we may arrange matters. In the meantime, you will remain in the inner office opposite."

The note was written, and Martin Hewitt, without glancing at the address, thrust it into his pocket. When Ritter was safely in the inner office, however, he drew it out and read the address. "I see," he observed, "he uses the same name, Hunter; 27 Little Carton Street, Westminster, is the address, and there I shall go at once with the note. If the man comes here, I think you had better lock him in with Ritter, and send for a policeman – it may at least frighten him. My object is, of course, to get the man away, and then, if possible, to invade his house, in some way or another, and steal or smash his negatives if they are there and to be found. Stay here, in any case, till I return. And don't forget to lock up those tracings."

* * *

It was about six o'clock when Hewitt returned, alone, but with a smiling face that told of good fortune at first sight.

"First, Mr. Dixon," he said, as he dropped into an easy chair in the private room, "let me ease your mind by the information that I have been most extraordinarily lucky; in fact, I think you have no further cause for anxiety. Here are the negatives. They were not all quite dry when I – well, what? – stole them, I suppose I must say; so that they have stuck together a bit, and probably the films are damaged. But you don't mind that, I suppose?"

He laid a small parcel, wrapped in a newspaper, on the table. The engineer hastily tore away the paper and took up five or six glass photographic negatives, of a half-plate size, which were damp, and stuck together by the gelatine films in couples. He held them, one after another, up to the light of the window, and glanced through them. Then, with a great sigh of relief, he placed them on the hearth and pounded them to dust and fragments with the poker.

For a few seconds neither spoke. Then Dixon, flinging himself into a chair, said:

"Mr. Hewitt, I can't express my obligation to you. What would have happened if you had failed, I prefer not to think of. But what shall we do with Ritter now? The other man hasn't been here yet, by the by."

"No; the fact is I didn't deliver the letter. The worthy gentleman saved me a world of trouble by taking himself out of the way." Hewitt laughed. "I'm afraid he has rather got himself into a mess by trying two kinds of theft at once, and you may not be sorry to hear that his attempt on your torpedo plans is likely to bring him a dose of penal servitude for something else. I'll tell you what has happened.

"Little Carton Street, Westminster, I found to be a seedy sort of place – one of those old streets that have seen much better days. A good many people seem to live in each house – they are fairly large houses, by the way – and there is quite a company of bell-handles on each doorpost, all down the side like organ-stops. A barber had possession of the ground floor front of No. 27 for trade purposes, so to him I went. 'Can you tell me,' I said, 'where in this house I can find Mr. Hunter?' He looked doubtful, so I went on: 'His friend will do, you know – I can't think of his name; foreign gentleman, dark, with a bushy beard.'

"The barber understood at once. 'Oh, that's Mirsky, I expect,' he said. 'Now, I come to think of it, he has had letters addressed to Hunter once or twice; I've took 'em in. Top floor back.'

"This was good so far. I had got at 'Mr. Hunter's' other alias. So, by way of possessing him with the idea that I knew all about him, I determined to ask for him as Mirsky before handing over the letter addressed to him as Hunter. A little bluff of that sort is invaluable at the right time. At the top floor back I stopped at the door and tried to open it at once, but it was locked. I could hear somebody scuttling about within, as though carrying things about, and I knocked again. In a little while the door opened about a foot, and there stood Mr. Hunter – or Mirsky, as you like – the man who, in the character of a traveler in steam-packing, came here twice today. He was in his shirt-sleeves, and cuddled something under his arm, hastily covered with a spotted pocket-handkerchief.

"'I have called to see M. Mirsky," I said, 'with a confidential letter—'

"'Oh, yas, yas,' he answered hastily; 'I know – I know. Excuse me one minute.' And he rushed off down-stairs with his parcel.

"Here was a noble chance. For a moment I thought of following him, in case there might be something interesting in the parcel. But I had to decide in a moment, and I decided on trying the room. I slipped inside the door, and, finding the key on the inside, locked it. It was a confused sort of room, with a little iron bedstead in one corner and a sort of rough boarded inclosure in another. This I rightly conjectured to be the photographic dark-room, and made for it at once.

"There was plenty of light within when the door was left open, and I made at once for the drying-rack that was fastened over the sink. There were a number of negatives in it, and I began hastily examining them one after another. In the middle of this our friend Mirsky returned and tried the door. He rattled violently at the handle and pushed. Then he called.

"At this moment I had come upon the first of the negatives you have just smashed. The fixing and washing had evidently only lately been completed, and the negative was drying on the rack. I seized it, of course, and the others which stood by it.

"'Who are you, there, inside?' Mirsky shouted indignantly from the landing. 'Why for you go in my room like that? Open this door at once, or I call the police!'

"I took no notice. I had got the full number of negatives, one for each drawing, but I was not by any means sure that he had not taken an extra set; so I went on hunting down the rack. There were no more, so I set to work to turn out all the undeveloped plates. It was quite possible, you see, that the other set, if it existed, had not yet been developed.

"Mirsky changed his tune. After a little more banging and shouting I could hear him kneel down and try the key-hole. I had left the key there, so that he could see nothing. But he began talking softly and rapidly through the hole in a foreign language. I did not know it in the least, but I believe it was Russian. What had led him to believe I understood Russian I could not at the time imagine, though I have a notion now. I went on ruining his stock of plates. I found several boxes, apparently of new plates, but, as there was no means of telling whether they were really unused or were merely undeveloped, but with the chemical impress of your drawings on them, I dragged every one ruthlessly from its hiding-place and laid it out in the full glare of the sunlight – destroying it thereby, of course, whether it was unused or not.

"Mirsky left off talking, and I heard him quietly sneaking off. Perhaps his conscience was not sufficiently clear to warrant an appeal to the police, but it seemed to me rather probable at the time that that was what he was going for. So I hurried on with my work. I found three dark slides – the parts that carried the plates in the back of the camera, you know – one of them fixed in the camera itself. These I opened, and exposed the plates to ruination as before. I suppose nobody ever did so much devastation in a photographic studio in ten minutes as I managed.

"I had spoiled every plate I could find, and had the developed negatives safely in my pocket, when I happened to glance at a porcelain washing-well under the sink. There was one negative in that, and I took it up. It was *not* a negative of a drawing of yours, but of a Russian twenty-ruble note!"

This *was* a discovery. The only possible reason any man could have for photographing a bank-note was the manufacture of an etched plate for the production of forged copies. I was almost as pleased as I had been at the discovery of *your* negatives. He might bring the police now as soon as he liked; I could turn the tables on him completely. I began to hunt about for anything else relating to this negative.

"I found an inking-roller, some old pieces of blanket (used in printing from plates), and in a corner on the floor, heaped over with newspapers and rubbish, a small copying-press. There was also a dish of acid, but not an etched plate or a printed note to be seen. I was looking at the press, with the negative in one hand and the inking-roller in the other, when I became conscious of a shadow across the window. I looked up quickly, and there was Mirsky hanging over from some ledge or projection to the side of the window, and staring straight at me, with a look of unmistakable terror and apprehension.

"The face vanished immediately. I had to move a table to get at the window, and by the time I had opened it there was no sign or sound of the rightful tenant of the room. I had no doubt now of his reason for carrying a parcel down-stairs. He probably mistook me for another visitor he was expecting, and, knowing he must take this visitor into his room, threw the papers and rubbish over the press, and put up his plates and papers in a bundle and secreted them somewhere down-stairs, lest his occupation should be observed.

"Plainly, my duty now was to communicate with the police. So, by the help of my friend the barber down-stairs, a messenger was found and a note sent over to Scotland Yard. I awaited, of course, for the arrival of the police, and occupied the interval in another look round – finding nothing important, however. When the official detective arrived, he recognized at once the importance of the case. A large number of forged Russian notes have been put into circulation on the Continent lately, it seems, and it was suspected that they came from London. The Russian Government have been sending urgent messages to the police here on the subject.

"Of course I said nothing about your business; but, while I was talking with the Scotland Yard man, a letter was left by a messenger, addressed to Mirsky. The letter will be examined, of course, by the proper authorities, but I was not a little interested to perceive that the envelope bore the Russian imperial arms above the words 'Russian Embassy.' Now, why should Mirsky communicate with the Russian Embassy? Certainly not to let the officials know that he was carrying on a very extensive and lucrative business in the manufacture of spurious Russian notes. I think it is rather more than possible that he wrote – probably before he actually got your drawings – to say that he could sell information of the highest importance, and that this letter was a reply. Further, I think it quite possible that, when I asked for him by his Russian name and spoke of 'a confidential letter,' he at once concluded that *I* had come from the embassy in answer to his letter. That would account for his addressing me in Russian through the key-hole; and, of course, an official from the Russian Embassy would be the very last person in the world whom he would like to observe any indications of his little etching experiments. But, anyhow, be that as it may," Hewitt concluded, "your drawings are safe now, and if once Mirsky is caught, and I think it likely, for a man in his shirt-sleeves, with scarcely any start, and, perhaps, no money about him, hasn't a great chance to get away – if he is caught, I say, he will probably get something handsome at St. Petersburg in the way of imprisonment, or Siberia, or what not; so that you will be amply avenged."

"Yes, but I don't at all understand this business of the drawings even now. How in the world were they taken out of the place, and how in the world did you find it out?"

"Nothing could be simpler; and yet the plan was rather ingenious. I'll tell you exactly how the thing revealed itself to me. From your original description of the case many people would consider that an impossibility had been performed. Nobody had gone out and nobody had come in, and yet the drawings had been taken away. But an impossibility is an impossibility, after all, and as drawings don't run away of themselves, plainly somebody had taken them, unaccountable as it might seem. Now, as they were in your inner office, the only people who could have got at them besides yourself were your assistants, so that it was pretty clear that one of them, at least, had something to do with the business. You told me that Worsfold was an excellent and intelligent draughtsman. Well, if such a man as that meditated treachery, he would probably be able to carry away the design in his head – at any rate, a little at a time – and would be under no necessity to run the risk of stealing a set of the drawings. But Ritter, you remarked, was an inferior sort of man. 'Not particularly smart,' I think, were your words – only a mechanical sort of tracer. *He* would be unlikely to be able to carry in his head the complicated details of such designs as yours, and, being in a subordinate position, and continually overlooked, he would find it impossible to make copies of the plans in the office. So that, to begin with, I thought I saw the most probable path to start on.

"When I looked round the rooms, I pushed open the glass door of the barrier and left the door to the inner office ajar, in order to be able to see any thing that *might* happen in any part of the place, without actually expecting any definite development. While we were talking, as it happened, our friend Mirsky (or Hunter – as you please) came into the outer office, and my attention was instantly called to him by the first thing he did. Did you notice anything peculiar yourself?"

"No, really, I can't say I did. He seemed to behave much as any traveler or agent might."

"Well, what I noticed was the fact that as soon as he entered the place he put his walking-stick into the umbrella-stand over there by the door, close by where he stood, a most unusual thing for a casual caller to do, before even knowing whether you were in. This made me watch him closely. I perceived with increased interest that the stick was exactly of the same kind and pattern as one already standing there, also a curious thing. I kept my eyes carefully on those sticks, and was all the more interested and edified to see, when he left, that he took the *other* stick – not the one he came with – from the stand, and carried it away, leaving his own behind. I might have followed him, but I decided that more could be learned by staying, as, in fact, proved to be the case. This, by the by, is the stick he carried away with him. I took the liberty of fetching it back from Westminster, because I conceive it to be Ritier's property."

Hewitt produced the stick. It was an ordinary, thick Malacca cane, with a buck-horn handle and a silver band. Hewitt bent it across his knee and laid it on the table.

"Yes," Dixon answered, "that is Ritter's stick. I think I have often seen it in the stand. But what in the world—"

"One moment; I'll just fetch the stick Mirsky left behind." And Hewitt stepped across the corridor.

He returned with another stick, apparently an exact fac-simile of the other, and placed it by the side of the other.

"When your assistants went into the inner room, I carried this stick off for a minute or two. I knew it was not Worsfold's, because there was an umbrella there with his initial on the handle. Look at this."

Martin Hewitt gave the handle a twist and rapidly unscrewed it from the top. Then it was seen that the stick was a mere tube of very thin metal, painted to appear like a Malacca cane.

"It was plain at once that this was no Malacca cane – it wouldn't bend. Inside it I found your tracings, rolled up tightly. You can get a marvelous quantity of thin tracing-paper into a small compass by tight rolling."

"And this – this was the way they were brought back!" the engineer exclaimed. "I see that clearly. But how did they get away? That's as mysterious as ever."

"Not a bit of it! See here. Mirsky gets hold of Ritter, and they agree to get your drawings and photograph them. Ritter is to let his confederate have the drawings, and Mirsky is to bring them back as soon as possible, so that they sha'n't be missed for a moment. Ritter habitually carries this Malacca cane, and the cunning of Mirsky at once suggests that this tube should be made in outward fac-simile. This morning Mirsky keeps the actual stick, and Ritter comes to the office with the tube. He seizes the first opportunity – probably when you were in this private room, and Worsfold was talking to you from the corridor – to get at the tracings, roll them up tightly, and put them in the tube, putting the tube back into the umbrella-stand. At half-past twelve, or whenever it was, Mirsky turns up for the first time with the actual stick and exchanges them, just as he afterward did when he brought the drawings back."

"Yes, but Mirsky came half an hour after they were – Oh, yes, I see. What a fool I was! I was forgetting. Of course, when I first missed the tracings, they were in this walking-stick, safe enough, and I was tearing my hair out within arm's reach of them!"

"Precisely. And Mirsky took them away before your very eyes. I expect Ritter was in a rare funk when he found that the drawings were missed. He calculated, no doubt, on your not wanting them for the hour or two they would be out of the office."

"How lucky that it struck me to jot a pencil-note on one of them! I might easily have made my note somewhere else, and then I should never have known that they had been away."

"Yes, they didn't give you any too much time to miss them. Well, I think the rest pretty clear. I brought the tracings in here, screwed up the sham stick and put it back. You identified the tracings and found none missing, and then my course was pretty clear, though it looked difficult. I knew you would be very naturally indignant with Ritter, so, as I wanted to manage him myself, I told you nothing of what he had actually done, for fear that, in your agitated state, you might burst out with something that would spoil my game. To Ritter I pretended to know nothing of the return of the drawings or *how* they had been stolen – the only things I did know with certainty. But I *did* pretend to know all about Mirsky – or Hunter – when, as a matter of fact, I knew nothing at all, except that he probably went under more than one name. That put Ritter into my hands completely. When he found the game was up, he began with a lying confession. Believing that the tracings were still in the stick and that we knew nothing of their return, he said that they had not been away, and that he would fetch them – as I had expected he would. I let him go for them alone, and, when he returned, utterly broken up by the discovery that they were not there, I had him altogether at my mercy. You see, if he had known that the drawings were all the time behind your book-case, he might have brazened it out, sworn that the drawings had been there all the time, and we could have done nothing with him. We couldn't have sufficiently frightened him by a threat of prosecution for theft, because there the things were in your possession, to his knowledge.

"As it was he answered the helm capitally: gave us Mirsky's address on the envelope, and wrote the letter that was to have got him out of the way while I committed burglary, if that disgraceful expedient had not been rendered unnecessary. On the whole, the case has gone very well."

"It has gone marvellously well, thanks to yourself. But what shall I do with Ritter?"

"Here's his stick – knock him down-stairs with it, if you like. I should keep the tube, if I were you, as a memento. I don't suppose the respectable Mirsky will ever call to ask for it. But I should certainly kick Ritter out of doors – or out of window, if you like – without delay."

Mirsky was caught, and, after two remands at the police-court, was extradited on the charge of forging Russian notes. It came out that he had written to the embassy, as Hewitt had surmised, stating that he had certain valuable information to offer, and the letter which Hewitt had seen delivered was an acknowledgment, and a request for more definite particulars. This was what gave rise to the impression that Mirsky had himself informed the Russian authorities of his forgeries. His real intent was very different, but was never guessed.

* * *

"I wonder," Hewitt has once or twice observed, "whether, after all, it would not have paid the Russian authorities better on the whole if I had never investigated Mirsky's little note factory. The Dixon torpedo was worth a good many twenty-ruble notes."

Scoop!

Trixie Nisbet

SHEEP SLIPS FROM CLIFF TOP.

No, I was sure I'd used that before. I pressed delete then tried again. ANOTHER SHEEP FALLS OFF CLIFF. I felt like banging my head against a wall. No matter how I phrased it, I couldn't make the headline exciting. And as a front-page story, it was dire.

It wasn't even original. I'm not sure who's the more stupid – the sheep or old Tom the farmer. The field slopes deceptively down to the cliff edge and so many sheep have slipped in wet weather I'm surprised a kebab shop hasn't opened a branch on the under-cliff walkway.

No, scrap that. The idea of *fast*-food in Peacehaven is unthinkable. Everything, and I mean *everything*, in this town crawls slower than a snail's pace.

Alice for example – she shuffled past the doorway of the cupboard I like to call my office. She was carrying a mug of tea in one hand and a plate of custard creams in the other. Alice was never far from tea and biscuits.

"Struggling?" she asked. She gazed in at my front-page layout, displayed on the screen. "Not another sheep – poor thing."

I'd found a picture on the internet of a big-eyed ewe, groomed and cleaned like somebody's pet. I hoped it would evoke a sympathetic reaction in the readers. But realistically I knew it was hopeless. Another hardly-stunning front page for the 'Peacehaven Chronicle'.

I pinched a biscuit from Alice's plate. "Does nothing happen in this town?" I moaned. "Ever?"

"It's a haven of peace," said Alice. "What more could you want?"

"Some real *news* wouldn't go amiss." I'd lost count of the falling sheep. And it was hardly news the first time. I felt suddenly trapped by the cramped space around me. "How am I going to make a name for myself, Alice? I'm not likely to have this story syndicated in the nationals."

"You're too ambitious for this place, Jason." Alice snatched the plate back out of my reach. "Tell you what..." Her face wrinkled into a conspiratorial grin. "Make something up. Vernon would never know."

Alice withdrew back to her desk and a pile of newspaper admin. She's a good sort, Alice – for an oldie.

She was right of course. Old Vernon, the editor, doesn't worry about the so-called news features. He pretty much leaves that all to me – that's what I'm paid my pittance of a wage for, apparently. All he's concerned about are the advertisers – it's their revenue that keeps the paper going – that, and the property pull-out section. There is always a good turn-over of bungalows in Peacehaven; keeps the estate agents busy. Well, it's about the only beneficial effect of living in a retirement town where everyone, except me, is about ninety. Perhaps I could do a feature on the supermarket queues at Cost-Save; about the Saturday morning jams of white-haired biddies on their mobility scooters.

No. Suddenly the sheep seemed quite interesting after all.

In my desperate search for headlines, I'd taken to calling the local police station every week, and even Mrs. Seedy of the local Neighbourhood Watch. Surely there would be some crime worthy of a mention, something to get the fogies in a froth.

Last week we ran with POLICE READY FOR ACTION. A catchy enough heading. But the story: how harshly the police would treat any speeding over the new humps by the charity shop, was marred by the fact that nobody had actually sped over the humps, yet. Still it was no doubt comforting to know that it would be treated seriously – if it ever happened.

"What's the lead story this week?" Vernon's doughnut of grey hair appeared around the doorway, the glow of my desk lamp glinted off his monk-like bald patch.

I managed an apathetic gesture at the screen.

"You know, we should start a campaign for a fence," said Vernon shuffling forward. "Next time it could be some poor holiday maker, unfamiliar with the paths and fields." Vernon nodded to himself with approval, sucking thoughtfully on his dentures. "That would generate a lot of local attention. We could organise a petition to the council. Look into it would you, Jason." He waved at the screen. "And it would add another layer of interest to your sheep feature."

I slumped in my chair and groaned. For a start – *holiday makers?* Brighton is less than ten miles along the coast, chock-a-block with visitor attractions. No visitor in their right mind would dream of stopping here, unless they were lost.

And anyway, these local-paper campaigns never work. I could imagine another headline in three years' time: CHRONICLE *STILL* CAMPAIGNING FOR CLIFF FENCE. *Three years' time!* The thought sank like a block of lead into my numbed brain. Surely, I'd have moved on to something more interesting by then. That or this crummy time-warped town would have driven me mental.

I decided then that it was time for lunch; I needed a beer.

* * *

As it happened, the sheep was relegated to the bottom of page four, under HILDA'S HOROSCOPES. That was another of my duties. 'Hilda' was a battered shoe box, full of second hand predictions we'd bought from a bankrupt American glossy. Each week I'd select twelve, more-or-less at random. It kept the gullible readers happy, and filled another half page. Occasionally I would rig my own star sign to predict an unexpected treat or perhaps a vast inheritance. Anything to nudge fate in my favour; nothing worked. Somehow my horoscope is *always* wrong – even if I select it myself.

I decided to adjust Aries, the ram. In deference to the sheep, I typed-up a paragraph which basically said look before you leap, or you could expect a downfall. That amused me; I love a play on words – anything to brighten up a dead-end job like this.

The front page was given over to the great teabag scandal. I had been in the local Cost-Save, trying to find a sandwich with some taste to it among the soft bread cheese or ham best sellers, when old Arthur announced the robbery. A whole crate of teabags was missing, apparently. It was a sensation for at least twenty minutes; you'd have thought someone had pinched the crown jewels! Searches were made, but to no avail. I offered to help, and got Arthur's opinion on the youth of today who were, no doubt, to blame for this outrageous theft.

What youth? I looked at the plodders in the bright Cost-Save aisles; everyone here was well beyond their best-before date. But OUTRAGE AT LOCAL SHOP made for quite a catchy headline.

Incidentally, I'd glimpsed the missing crate in the back of the shop's little delivery van. Old Arthur would come across it in his own time, but I wasn't going to let that spoil a good story. Yeah, I could have said something, but by then I was desperate. And, now I come to think of it, by not speaking out, that was the first time that I'd directly affected the front-page story.

I didn't realise then what it would lead to…

* * *

The next week was dire as well. I actually considered herding another sheep towards the cliff edge. I'd already influenced the news about the robbery – and I suppose that's what made me think of the can of green spray paint I had somewhere in the garage.

GRAFITI VANDAL AT BUS STOP was the next headline, with a page of flabbergasted comment from locals, incensed, poor things, about the disgraceful daubings of frogs that had appeared over night on the bus shelter.

I'd intended some sort of alien – little green men – story. But frogs would do. Take it from me; it's not easy to draw with spray paint.

That sustained some fury in the letters page. Some blamed kids from the neighbouring town, venturing – God knows why – over the hill with cans of paint. Mrs. Seedy from Neighbourhood Watch even blamed the French, and the police gave ominous warnings that spray-painting frogs would not be tolerated.

The following week had the cleaning of the bus shelter. I was there in the biting wind to report and take photos. The mayor was wheeled out for the occasion, to show the gravity of the incident. He posed on the coast road, with one of the just-passing-through buses in the background, in full chain and disapproving scowl. That filled page three, while the front page puzzled over who'd taken a hammer to all the garden gnomes in Edith Avenue.

I've always hated gnomes, gaudy grinning things. What have they got to be happy about in a dreary dump like this? I crept out after dark; I needn't have worried about being seen, everyone goes to bed about nine anyway. I swung my hammer and the little distorted figures shattered like flower pots over the neat front lawns and clipped hedges. One looked fat and pompous, like the mayor, another like Mrs. Seedy. I imagined all the irritating people in this town, one by one, as the painted faces caved in. The redundant police force, farmer Tom, old Vernon, even admin Alice.

Not a bad evening's work for a front page. OK, it would never make the nationals – but it *was* a story. I got a quote from a biddy who assumed 'yobs' were to blame. YOBS SMASH GNOMES was the headline, which neatly directed suspicion away from me.

From then on, Peacehaven positively seethed with minor incident; usually on a Tuesday night, just before my Wednesday deadline.

Flowers were stolen from gardens, and the old tree that devastatingly fell through the library window was found to have been sawn through.

"You know, Jason," said old Vernon. "I've just had a call from Mr King, the librarian; he wantec to congratulate Hilda on her horoscope."

I feigned interested ignorance. Strangely enough, Sagittarians had been told to expect a windfall at work. I couldn't resist that. But it may have been this prophetic embellishment whicl made old Vernon suspect. He was suddenly more interested in my material – wanted to know m sources – how I found out about these just-before-deadline dramas.

I fobbed him off of course. Easy. Some flannel about the police web site and the ever-quotable Mrs. Seedy.

Vernon seemed pacified.

I never for a moment thought he'd follow me.

I'd discovered that Peacehaven is the perfect place for anyone up to a spot of mischief. Late in the evening everyone is tucked-up indoors, shutters shut, and bolts bolted and both pubs are empty long before closing time. So it was no surprise that, on that night, the cliff-top path was virtually deserted. I stood for a while in the sea breeze, while a lonely dog walker dawdled past. Far below, the surge and hiss of the sea was magnified in the near silence. A full moon turned the steep line of chalky cliffs to silver, looking as if some chisel-jawed sea monster had bitten chunks out of the coastline. The dog walker turned a corner; no one about. No one to see me loitering with an old rag soaked in paraffin.

Does anywhere else in the world still have a hardware shop that sells paraffin? The stuff stinks, so I had the rag sealed in a Cost-Save sandwich bag. I strolled to the post box at the end of the promenade, where the cliff path meets the sheep field, and fed the rag into the letter slot. I'd intended a small fire, and actually the smoke it caused was quite dramatic. Pity I couldn't take any pictures, but I knew with a bit of suggestion Mrs. Seedy would provide a dramatic quote about the flames and public danger.

I was cutting across the field toward home when Vernon appeared.

The moon gleamed on his bald patch and I felt my heart lurch painfully in my chest. How much had he seen?

"Jason." That's all he said, slowly shaking his head. Just one word. But the disappointment and disapproval in his voice, as they say, spoke volumes.

* * *

That week was my best headline so far. DEATH PLUNGE – Newspaper editor found dead at the bottom of cliff. I was very careful with the wording, stressing the opinion that this was a tragic accident – and it was made all the more poignant because of the cliff safety campaign poor old Vernon was running in the paper at the time.

That was the first of my stories to make the nationals, quite a scoop, and to my surprise it paid well too.

I'm editor now as well as news reporter. I've got a proper office, and being my own boss, I can safely report on whatever I want – without suspicion.

Alice is thinking of moving away now. "I used to love Peacehaven, Jason," she'd say. "But it's changed recently. It's not the quiet little place I used to know." I'll have to get another admin girl – a newer model, so that's no bad thing. It's all change for the better, now that I'm in charge at the Chronicle.

It turned out that Vernon's death was, in fact, the first of a series of bizarre (and profitable) catastrophes to befall the sleepy town of Peacehaven.

And I can still remember selecting my horoscope that week, randomly, as usual, from Hilda the shoe box. Seems like, on that one occasion, my horoscope proved to be correct after all. *Events this week steer you onto a new path. Seize the opportunity; it could change your life forever.*

For once, Hilda, I couldn't have put it better myself.

A Day's Folly

Baroness Orczy

Chapter I

I DON'T THINK that anyone ever knew that the real eludication of the extraordinary mystery known to the newspaper-reading public as the 'Somersetshire Outrage' was evolved in my own dear lady's quick, intuitive brain.

As a matter of fact, to this day – as far as the public is concerned – the Somersetshire outrage never was properly explained; and it is a very usual thing for those busybodies who are so fond of criticising the police to point to that case as an instance of remarkable incompetence on the part of our detective department.

A young woman named Jane Turner, a visitor at Weston-super-Mare, had been discovered one afternoon in a helpless condition, bound and gagged, and suffering from terror and inanition, in the bedroom which she occupied in a well-known apartment-house of that town. The police had been immediately sent for, and as soon as Miss Turner had recovered she gave what explanation she could of the mysterious occurrence.

She was employed in one of the large drapery shops in Bristol, and was spending her annual holiday at Weston-super-Mare. Her father was the local butcher at Banwell – a village distant about four miles from Weston – and it appears that somewhere near one o'clock in the afternoon of Friday, the 3rd of September, she was busy in her bedroom putting a few things together in a handbag, preparatory to driving out to Banwell, meaning to pay her parents a week-end visit.

There was a knock at her door, and a voice said, "It's me, Jane – may I come in?"

She did not recognise the voice, but somehow thought that it must be that of a friend, so she shouted, "Come in!"

This was all that the poor thing recollected definitely, for the next moment the door was thrown open, someone rushed at her with amazing violence, she heard the crash of a falling table and felt a blow on the side of her head, whilst a damp handkerchief was pressed to her nose and mouth.

Then she remembered nothing more.

When she gradually came to her senses she found herself in the terrible plight in which Mrs. Skeward – her landlady – discovered her twenty-four hours later.

When pressed to try and describe her assailant, she said that when the door was thrown open she thought that she saw an elderly woman in a wide mantle and wearing bonnet and veil, but that, at the same time, she was quite sure, from the strength and brutality of the onslaught, that she was attacked by a man. She had no enemies, and no possessions worth stealing; but her hand-bag, which, however, only contained few worthless trifles, had certainly disappeared.

The people of the house, on the other hand, could throw but little light on the mystery which surrounded this very extraordinary and seemingly purposeless assault.

Mrs. Skeward only remembered that on Friday Miss Turner told her that she was just off to Banwell, and would be away for the week-end; but that she wished to keep her room on, against her return on the Monday following.

That was somewhere about half-past twelve o'clock, at the hour when luncheons were being got ready for the various lodgers; small wonder, therefore, that no one in the busy apartment-house took much count of the fact that Miss Turner was not seen to leave the house after that, and no doubt the wretched girl would have been left for several days in the pitiable condition in which she was ultimately found but for the fact that Mrs. Skeward happened to be of the usual grasping type common to those of her kind.

Weston-super-Mare was over-full that week-end, and Mrs. Skeward, beset by applicants for accommodation, did not see why she should not let her absent lodger's room for the night or two that the latter happened to be away, and thus get money twice over for it.

She conducted a visitor up to Miss Turner's room on the Saturday afternoon, and, throwing open the door – which, by the way, was not locked – was horrified to see the poor girl half-sitting, half-slipping off the chair to which she had been tied with a rope, whilst a woolen shawl was wound round the lower part of her face.

As soon as she had released the unfortunate victim, Mrs. Skeward sent for the police, and it was through the intelligent efforts of Detective Parsons – a local man – that a few scraps of very hazy evidence were then and there collected.

First, there was the question of the elderly female in the wide mantle, spoken of by Jane Turner as her assailant. It seems that someone answering to that description had called on the Friday at about one o'clock, and asked to see Miss Turner. The maid who answered the door replied that she thought Miss Turner had gone to Banwell.

"Oh!" said the old dame, "she won't have started yet. I am Miss Turner's mother, and I was to call for her so that we might drive out together."

"Then p'r'aps Miss Turner is still in her room," suggested the maid. "Shall I go and see?"

"Don't trouble," replied the woman; "I know my way. I'll go myself."

Whereupon the old dame walked past the servant, crossed the hall and went upstairs. No one saw her come down again, but one of the lodgers seems to have heard a knock at Jane Turner's door, and the female voice saying, "It's me, Jane – may I come in?"

What happened subsequently, who the mysterious old female was, and how and for what purpose she assaulted Jane Turner and robbed her of a few valueless articles, was the puzzle which faced the police then, and which – so far as the public is concerned – has never been solved. Jane Turner's mother was in bed at the time suffering from a broken ankle and unable to move. The elderly woman was, therefore, an impostor, and the search after her – though keen and hot enough at the time, I assure you – has remained, in the eyes of the public, absolutely fruitless. But of this more anon.

On the actual scene of the crime there was but little to guide subsequent investigation. The rope with which Jane Turner had been pinioned supplied no clue; the wool shawl was Miss Turner's own, snatched up by the miscreant to smother the girl's screams; on the floor was a handkerchief, without initial or laundry mark, which obviously had been saturated with chloroform; and close by a bottle which had contained the anæsthetic. A small table was overturned, and the articles which had been resting upon it were lying all around – such as a vase which had held a few flowers, a box of biscuits, and several issues of the *West of England Times.*

And nothing more. The miscreant, having accomplished his fell purpose, succeeded evidently in walking straight out of the house unobserved; his exit being undoubtedly easily managed owing to it being the busy luncheon hour.

Various theories were, of course, put forward by some of our ablest fellows at the Yard; the most likely solution being the guilt or, at least, the complicity of the girl's sweetheart, Arthur Cutbush – a ne'er-do-well, who spent the greater part of his time on race-courses. Inspector Danvers, whom the chief had sent down to assist the local police, declared that Jane Turner herself suspected her sweetheart, and was trying to shield him by stating she possessed nothing of any value; whereas, no doubt, the young blackguard knew that she had some money, and had planned this amazing *coup* in order to rob her of it.

Danvers was quite chagrined when, on investigation, it was proved that Arthur Cutbush had gone to the York races three days before the assault, and never left that city until the Saturday evening, when a telegram from Miss Turner summoned him to Weston.

Moreover, the girl did not break off her engagement with young Cutbush, and thus the total absence of motive was a serious bar to the likelihood of the theory.

Then it was the Chief sent for Lady Molly. No doubt he began to feel that here, too, was a case where feminine tact and my lady's own marvellous intuition might prove more useful than the more approved methods of the sterner sex.

Chapter II

"OF COURSE, there is a woman in the case, Mary," said Lady Molly to me, when she came home from the interview with the chief, "although they all pooh-pooh that theory at the Yard, and declare that the female voice – to which the only two witnesses we have are prepared to swear – was a disguised one."

"You think, then, that a woman assaulted Jane Turner?"

"Well," she replied somewhat evasively, "if a man assumes a feminine voice, the result is a high-pitched, unnatural treble; and that, I feel convinced, would have struck either the maid or the lodger, or both, as peculiar."

This was the train of thought which my dear lady and I were following up, when, with that sudden transition of manner so characteristic of her, she said abruptly to me:

"Mary, look out a train for Weston-super-Mare. We must try to get down there tonight."

"Chief's orders?" I asked.

"No – mine," she replied laconically. "Where's the A B C?"

Well, we got off that self-same afternoon, and in the evening we were having dinner at the Grand Hotel, Weston-super-Mare.

My dear lady had been pondering all through the journey, and even now she was singularly silent and absorbed. There was a deep frown between her eyes, and every now and then the luminous, dark orbs would suddenly narrow, and the pupils contract as if smitten with a sudden light.

I was not a little puzzled as to what was going on in that active brain of hers, but my experience was that silence on my part was the surest card to play.

Lady Molly had entered our names in the hotel book as Mrs. Walter Bell and Miss Granard from London; and the day after our arrival there came two heavy parcels for her under that name. She had them taken upstairs to our private sitting-room, and there we undid them together.

To my astonishment they contained stacks of newspapers: as far as I could see at a glance back numbers of the *West of England Times* covering a whole year.

"Find and cut out the 'Personal' column of every number, Mary," said Lady Molly to me. 'll look through them on my return. I am going for a walk, and will be home by lunch time."

I knew, of course, that she was intent on her business and on that only, and as soon as she ad gone out I set myself to the wearisome task which she had allotted me. My dear lady was idently working out a problem in her mind, the solution of which she expected to find in a ack number of the *West of England Times*.

By the time she returned I had the "Personal" column of some three hundred numbers the paper neatly filed and docketed for her perusal. She thanked me for my promptitude ith one of her charming looks, but said little, if anything, all through luncheon. After that eal she set to work. I could see her studying each scrap of paper minutely, comparing one ith the other, arranging them in sets in front of her, and making marginal notes on them l the while.

With but a brief interval for tea, she sat at her table for close on four hours, at the end of hich she swept all the scraps of paper on one side, with the exception of a few which she ept in her hand. Then she looked up at me, and I sighed with relief.

My dear lady was positively beaming.

"You have found what you wanted?" I asked eagerly.

"What I expected," she replied.

"May I know?"

She spread out the bits of paper before me. There were six altogether, and each of these olumns had one paragraph specially marked with a cross.

"Only look at the paragraphs which I have marked," she said.

I did what I was told. But if in my heart I had vaguely hoped that I should then and there e confronted with the solution of the mystery which surrounded the Somersetshire outrage, was doomed to disappointment.

Each of the marked paragraphs in the "Personal" columns bore the initials H. S. H., and eir purport was invariably an assignation at one of the small railway stations on the line etween Bristol and Weston.

I suppose that my bewilderment must have been supremely comical, for my lady's rippling ugh went echoing through the bare, dull hotel sitting-room.

"You don't see it, Mary?" she asked gaily.

"I confess I don't," I replied. "It completely baffles me."

"And yet," she said more gravely, "those few silly paragraphs have given me the clue to the ysterious assault on Jane Turner, which has been puzzling our fellows at the Yard for over ree weeks."

"But how? I don't understand."

"You will, Mary, directly we get back to town. During my morning walk I have learnt all that want to know, and now these paragraphs have set my mind at rest."

Chapter III

HE NEXT day we were back in town.

Already, at Bristol, we had bought a London morning paper, which contained in its centre ge a short notice under the following startling headlines:

THE SOMERSETSHIRE OUTRAGE
AMAZING DISCOVERY BY THE POLICE AN UNEXPECTED CLUE

The article went on to say:

> *We are officially informed that the police have recently obtained knowledge of certain facts which establish beyond a doubt the motive of the brutal assault committed on the person of Miss Jane Turner. We are not authorised to say more at present than that certain startling developments are imminent.*

On the way up my dear lady had initiated me into some of her views with regard to the case itself, which at the chief's desire she had now taken entirely in hand, and also into her immediate plans, of which the above article was merely the preface.

She it was who had 'officially informed' the Press Association, and, needless to say, the news duly appeared in most of the London and provincial dailies.

How unerring was her intuition, and how well thought out her scheme, was proved within the next four-and-twenty hours in our own little flat, when our Emily, looking somewhat important and awed, announced Her Serene Highness the Countess of Hohengebirg.

H. S. H. – the conspicuous initials in the 'Personal' columns of the *West of England Times*! You may imagine how I stared at the exquisite apparition – all lace and chiffon and roses – which the next moment literally swept into our office, past poor, open-mouthed Emily.

Had my dear lady taken leave of her senses when she suggested that this beautiful young woman with the soft, fair hair, with the pleading blue eyes and childlike mouth, had anything to do with a brutal assault on a shop girl?

The young Countess shook hands with Lady Molly and with me, and then, with a deep sigh, she sank into the comfortable chair which I was offering her.

Speaking throughout with great diffidence, but always in the gentle tones of a child that knows it has been naughty, she began by explaining that she had been to Scotland Yard, where a very charming man – the chief, I presume – had been most kind and sent her hither, where he promised her she would find help and consolation in her dreadful, dreadful trouble.

Encouraged by Lady Molly, she soon plunged into her narrative: a pathetic tale of her own frivolity and foolishness.

She was originally Lady Muriel Wolfe-Strongham, daughter of the Duke of Weston, and when scarce out of the schoolroom had met the Grand Duke of Starkburg-Nauheim, who fell in love with her and married her. The union was a morganatic one, the Grand Duke conferring on his English wife the title of the Countess of Hohengebirg and the rank of Serene Highness.

It seems that, at first, the marriage was a fairly happy one, in spite of the bitter animosity o the mother and sister of the Grand Duke: the Dowager Grand Duchess holding that all Englis girls were loud and unwomanly, and the Princess Amalie, seeing in her brother's marriage a serious bar to the fulfilment of her own highly ambitious matrimonial hopes.

"They can't bear me, because I don't knit socks and don't know how to bake almond cakes," said her dear little Serene Highness, looking up with tender appeal at Lady Molly's grave and beautiful face; "and they will be so happy to see a real estrangement between my husban and myself."

It appears that last year, while the Grand Duke was doing his annual cure at Marienbad, th Countess of Hohengebirg went to Folkestone for the benefit of her little boy's health. She staye at one of the Hotels there merely as any English lady of wealth might do – with nurses and he own maid, of course, but without the paraphernalia and nuisance of her usual German retinu

Whilst there she met an old acquaintance of her father's, a Mr. Rumboldt, who is a ric financier, it seems, and who at one time moved in the best society, but whose reputation ha greatly suffered recently, owing to a much talked of divorce case which brought his name into unenviable notoriety.

Her Serene Highness, with more mopping of her blue eyes, assured Lady Molly that over at Schloss Starkburg she did not read the English papers, and was therefore quite unaware that Mr. Rumboldt, who used to be a *persona grata* in her father's house, was no longer a fit and proper acquaintance for her.

"It was a very fine morning," she continued with gentle pathos, "and I was deadly dull at Folkestone. Mr. Rumboldt persuaded me to go with him on a short trip on his yacht. We were to cross over to Boulogne, have luncheon there, and come home in the cool of the evening."

"And, of course, something occurred to disable the yacht," concluded Lady Molly gravely, as the lady herself had paused in her narrative.

"Of course," whispered the little Countess through her tears.

"And, of course, it was too late to get back by the ordinary afternoon mail boat?"

"That boat had gone an hour before, and the next did not leave until the middle of the night."

"So you had perforce to wait until then, and in the meanwhile you were seen by a girl named Jane Turner, who knew you by sight, and who has been blackmailing you ever since."

"How did you guess that?" ejaculated Her Highness, with a look of such comical bewilderment in her large, blue eyes that Lady Molly and I had perforce to laugh.

"Well," replied my dear lady after awhile, resuming her gravity, "we have a way in our profession of putting two and two together, haven't we? And in this case it was not very difficult. The assignations for secret meetings at out-of-the-way railway stations which were addressed to H. S. H. in the columns of the *West of England Times* recently, gave me one clue, shall we say? The mysterious assault on a young woman, whose home was close to those very railway stations as well as to Bristol Castle – your parents' residence, where you have frequently been staying of late, was another piece that fitted in the puzzle; whilst the number of copies of the *West of England Times* that were found in that same young woman's room helped to draw my thoughts to her. Then your visit to me Today – it is very simple, you see."

"I suppose so," said H. S. H. with a sigh. "Only it is worse even than you suggest, for that horrid Jane Turner, to whom I had been ever so kind when I was a girl, took a snapshot of me and Mr. Rumboldt standing on the steps of Hôtel des Bains at Boulogne. I saw her doing it and rushed down the steps to stop her. She talked quite nicely then – hypocritical wretch! – and said that perhaps the plate would be no good when it was developed, and if it were she would destroy it. I was not to worry; she would contrive to let me know through the agony column of the *West of England Times*, which – as I was going home to Bristol Castle to stay with my parents – I could see every day, but she had no idea I should have minded, and all that sort of rigmarole. Oh! she is a wicked girl, isn't she, to worry me so?"

And once again the lace handkerchief found its way to the most beautiful pair of blue eyes I think I have ever seen. I could not help smiling, though I was really very sorry for the silly, emotional, dear little thing.

"And instead of reassurance in the *West of England Times*, you found a demand for a secret meeting at a country railway station?"

"Yes! And when I went there – terrified lest I should be seen – Jane Turner did not meet me herself. Her mother came and at once talked of selling the photograph to my husband or to my mother-in-law. She said it was worth four thousand pounds to Jane, and that she had advised her daughter not to sell it to me for less."

"What did you reply?"

"That I hadn't got four thousand pounds," said the Countess ruefully; "so after a lot of argument it was agreed that I was to pay Jane two hundred and fifty pounds a year out of my dress allowance. She would keep the negative as security, but promised never to let anyone see it so long as she got her money regularly. It was also arranged that whenever I stayed with my parents at Bristol Castle, Jane would make appointments to meet me through the columns of the *West of England Times*, and I was to pay up the instalments then just as she directed."

I could have laughed, if the whole thing had not been so tragic, for truly the way this silly, harmless little woman had allowed herself to be bullied and blackmailed by a pair of grasping females was beyond belief.

"And this has been going on for over a year," commented Lady Molly gravely.

"Yes, but I never met Jane Turner again: it was always her mother who came."

"You knew her mother before that, I presume?"

"Oh, no. I only knew Jane because she had been sewing-maid at the Castle some few years ago."

"I see," said Lady Molly slowly. "What was the woman like whom you used to meet at the railway stations, and to whom you paid over Miss Turner's money?"

"Oh, I couldn't tell you what she was like. I never saw her properly."

"Never saw her properly?" ejaculated Lady Molly, and it seemed to my well-trained ears as if there was a ring of exultation in my dear lady's voice.

"No," replied the little Countess ruefully. "She always appointed a late hour of the evening, and those little stations on that line are very badly lighted. I had such difficulties getting away from home without exciting comment, and used to beg her to let me meet her at a more convenient hour. But she always refused."

Lady Molly remained thoughtful for a while; then she asked abruptly:

"Why don't you prosecute Jane Turner for blackmail?"

"Oh, I dare not – I dare not!" ejaculated the little Countess, in genuine terror. "My husband would never forgive me, and his female relations would do their best afterwards to widen the breach between us. It was because of the article in the London newspaper about the assault on Jane Turner – the talk of a clue and of startling developments – that I got terrified, and went to Scotland Yard. Oh, no! no! no! Promise me that my name won't be dragged into this case. It would ruin me for ever!"

She was sobbing now; her grief and fear were very pathetic to witness, and she moaned through her sobs:

"Those wicked people know that I daren't risk an exposure, and simply prey on me like vampires because of that. The last time I saw the old woman I told her that I would confess everything to my husband – I couldn't bear to go on like this. But she only laughed; she knew should never dare."

"When was this?" asked Lady Molly.

"About three weeks ago – just before Jane Turner was assaulted and robbed of the photographs

"How do you know she was robbed of the photographs?"

"She wrote and told me so," replied the young Countess, who seemed strangely awed now b my dear lady's earnest question. And from a dainty reticule she took a piece of paper, which bor traces of many bitter tears on its crumpled surface. This she handed to Lady Molly, who took from her. It was a type-written letter, which bore no signature. Lady Molly perused it in silenc first, then read its contents out aloud to me:

"To H.S.H. the Countess of Hohengebirg.

"You think I have been worrying you the past twelve months about your adventure wi Mr. Rumboldt in Boulogne. But it was not me; it was one who has power over me, and wh knew about the photograph. He made me act as I did. But whilst I kept the photo you were safe. Now he has assaulted me and nearly killed me, and taken the negative away. I can, and will, get it out of him again, but it will mean a large sum down. Can you manage one thousand pounds?"

"When did you get this?" asked Lady Molly.

"Only a few days ago," replied the Countess. "And oh! I have been enduring agonies of doubt and fear for the past three weeks, for I had heard nothing from Jane since the assault, and I wondered what had happened."

"You have not sent a reply, I hope."

"No. I was going to, when I saw the article in the London paper, and the fear that all had been discovered threw me into such a state of agony that I came straight up to town and saw the gentleman at Scotland Yard, who sent me on to you. Oh!" she entreated again and again, "you won't do anything that will cause a scandal! Promise me – promise me! I believe I should commit suicide rather than face it – and I could find a thousand pounds."

"I don't think you need do either," said Lady Molly. "Now, may I think over the whole matter quietly to myself," she added, "and talk it over with my friend here? I may be able to let you have some good news shortly."

She rose, intimating kindly that the interview was over. But it was by no means that yet, for there was still a good deal of entreaty and a great many tears on the one part, and reiterated kind assurances on the other. However when, some ten minutes later, the dainty clouds of lace and chiffon were finally wafted out of our office, we both felt that the poor, harmless, unutterably foolish little lady looked distinctly consoled and more happy than she had been for the past twelve months.

Chapter IV

"YES! SHE has been an utter little goose," Lady Molly was saying to me an hour later when we were having luncheon; "but that Jane Turner is a remarkably clever girl."

"I suppose you think, as I do, that the mysterious elderly female, who seems to have impersonated the mother all through, was an accomplice of Jane Turner's, and that the assault was a put-up job between them," I said. "Inspector Danvers will be delighted – for this theory is a near approach to his own."

"H'm!" was all the comment vouchsafed on my remark.

"I am sure it was Arthur Cutbush, the girl's sweetheart, after all," I retorted hotly, "and you'll see that, put to the test of sworn evidence, his alibi at the time of the assault itself won't hold good. Moreover, now," I added triumphantly, "we have knowledge which has been lacking all along – the motive."

"Ah!" said my lady, smiling at my enthusiasm, "that's how you argue, Mary, is it?"

"Yes, and in my opinion the only question in doubt is whether Arthur Cutbush acted in collusion with Jane Turner or against her."

"Well, suppose we go and elucidate that point – and some others – at once," concluded Lady Molly as she rose from the table.

She decided to return to Bristol that same evening. We were going by the 8.50 p.m., and I was just getting ready – the cab being already at the door – when I was somewhat startled by the sudden appearance into my room of an old lady, very beautifully dressed, with snow-white hair dressed high above a severe, interesting face.

A merry, rippling laugh issuing from the wrinkled mouth, and a closer scrutiny on my part, soon revealed the identity of my dear lady, dressed up to look like an extremely dignified *grande dame* of the old school, whilst a pair of long, old-fashioned earrings gave a curious, foreign look to her whole appearance.

I didn't quite see why she chose to arrive at the Grand Hotel, Bristol, in that particular disguise, nor why she entered our names in the hotel book as Grand Duchess and Princess Amalie von Starkburg, from Germany; nor did she tell me anything that evening.

But by the next afternoon, when we drove out together in a fly, I was well up in the *rôle* which I had to play. My lady had made me dress in a very rich black silk dress of her own, and ordered me to do my hair in a somewhat frumpish fashion, with a parting, and a "bun" at the back. She herself looked more like Royalty travelling incognito than ever, and no wonder small children and tradesmen's boys stared open-mouthed when we alighted from our fly outside one of the mean-looking little houses in Bread Street.

In answer to our ring, a smutty little servant opened the door, and my lady asked her if Miss Jane Turner lived here and if she were in.

"Yes, Miss Turner lives here, and it bein' Thursday and early closin' she's home from business."

"Then please tell her," said Lady Molly in her grandest manner, "that the Dowager Grand Duchess of Starkburg-Nauheim and the Princess Amalie desire to see her."

The poor little maid nearly fell backwards with astonishment. She gasped an agitated "Lor!" and then flew down the narrow passage and up the steep staircase, closely followed by my dear lady and myself.

On the first-floor landing the girl, with nervous haste, knocked at a door, opened it and muttered half audibly:

"Ladies to see you, miss!"

Then she fled incontinently upstairs. I have never been able to decide whether that little girl thought that we were lunatics, ghosts, or criminals.

But already Lady Molly had sailed into the room, where Miss Jane Turner apparently had been sitting reading a novel. She jumped up when we entered, and stared open-eyed at the gorgeous apparitions. She was not a bad-looking girl but for the provoking, bold look in her black eyes, and the general slatternly appearance of her person.

"Pray do not disturb yourself, Miss Turner," said Lady Molly in broken English, as she sank into a chair, and beckoned me to do likewise. "Pray sit down – I vill be brief. You have a compromising photograph – is it not? – of my daughter-in-law ze Countess of Hohengebirg. I am ze Grand Duchess of Starkburg-Nauheim – zis is my daughter, ze Princess Amalie. We are here incognito. You understand? Not?"

And, with inimitable elegance of gesture, my dear lady raised a pair of 'starers' to her eyes and fixed them on Jane Turner's quaking figure.

Never had I seen suspicion, nay terror, depicted so plainly on a young face, but I will do the girl the justice to state that she pulled herself together with marvellous strength of will.

She fought down her awed respect of this great lady; or rather shall I say that the British middle class want of respect for social superiority, especially if it be foreign, now stood her in good stead.

"I don't know what you are talking about," she said with an arrogant toss of the head.

"Zat is a lie, is it not?" rejoined Lady Molly calmly, as she drew from her reticule the typewritten letter which Jane Turner had sent to the Countess of Hohengebirg. "Zis you wrote to my daughter-in-law; ze letter reached me instead of her. It interests me much. I vill give you two tousend pounds for ze photograph of her and Mr. – er – Rumboldt. You vill sell it to me for zat, is it not?"

The production of the letter had somewhat cowed Jane's bold spirit. But she was still defiant

"I haven't got the photograph here," she said.

"Ah, no! but you vill get it – yes?" said my lady, quietly replacing the letter in her reticule. "In ze letter you offer to get it for tousend pound. I vill give you two tousend. Today is a holiday for you. You vill get ze photograph from ze gentleman – not? And I vill vait here till you come back."

Whereupon she rearranged her skirts round her and folded her hands placidly, like one prepared to wait.

"I haven't got the photograph," said Jane Turner, doggedly, "and I can't get it Today . The – the person who has it doesn't live in Bristol."

"No? Ah! but quite close, isn't it?" rejoined my lady, placidly. "I can vait all ze day."

"No, you shan't!" retorted Jane Turner, whose voice now shook with obvious rage or fear – I knew not which. "I can't get the photograph Today – so there! And I won't sell it to you – I won't. I don't want your two thousand pounds. How do I know you are not an imposter?"

"From zis, my good girl," said Lady Molly, quietly; "that if I leave zis room wizout ze photograph, I go straight to ze police with zis letter, and you shall be prosecuted by ze Grand Duke, my son, for blackmailing his wife. You see, I am not like my daughter-in-law; I am not afraid of a scandal. So you vill fetch ze photograph – isn't it? I and ze Princess Amalie vill vait for it here. Zat is your bedroom – not?" she added, pointing to a door which obviously gave on an inner room. "Vill you put on your hat and go at once, please? Two tousend pound or two years in prison – you have ze choice – isn't it?"

Jane Turner tried to keep up her air of defiance, looking Lady Molly full in the face; but I who watched her could see the boldness in her eyes gradually giving place to fear, and then to terror and even despair; the girl's face seemed literally to grow old as I looked at it – pale, haggard, and drawn – whilst Lady Molly kept her stern, luminous eyes fixed steadily upon her.

Then, with a curious, wild gesture, which somehow filled me with a nameless fear, Jane Turner turned on her heel and ran into the inner room.

There followed a moment of silence. To me it was tense and agonising. I was straining my ears to hear what was going on in that inner room. That my dear lady was not as callous as she wished to appear was shown by the strange look of expectancy in her beautiful eyes.

The minutes sped on – how many I could not afterwards have said. I was conscious of a clock ticking monotonously over the shabby mantelpiece, of an errand boy outside shouting at the top of his voice, of the measured step of the cab horse which had brought us hither being walked up and down the street.

Then suddenly there was a violent crash, as of heavy furniture being thrown down. I could not suppress a scream, for my nerves by now were terribly on the jar.

"Quick, Mary – the inner room!" said Lady Molly. "I thought the girl might do that."

I dared not pause in order to ask what "that" meant, but flew to the door.

It was locked.

"Downstairs – quick!" commanded my lady. "I ordered Danvers to be on the watch outside."

You may imagine how I flew, and how I blessed my dear lady's forethought in the midst of her daring plan, when, having literally torn open the front door, I saw Inspector Danvers in plain clothes, calmly patrolling the street. I beckoned to him – he was keeping a sharp look-out – and together we ran back into the house.

Fortunately, the landlady and the servant were busy in the basement, and had neither heard the crash nor seen me run in search of Danvers. My dear lady was still alone in the dingy parlour, stooping against the door of the inner room, her ear glued to the keyhole.

"Not too late, I think," she whispered hurriedly. "Break it open, Danvers."

Danvers, who is a great, strong man, soon put his shoulder to the rickety door, which yielded to the first blow.

The sight which greeted us filled me with horror, for I had never seen such a tragedy before. The wretched girl, Jane Turner, had tied a rope to a ring in the ceiling, which I suppose at one time held a hanging lamp; the other end of that rope she had formed into a slip-noose, and passed round her neck.

She had apparently climbed on to a table, and then used her best efforts to end her life by kicking the table away from under her. This was the crash which we had heard, and which had caused us to come to her rescue. Fortunately, her feet had caught in the back of a chair close by; the slip-noose was strangling her, and her face was awful to behold, but she was not dead.

Danvers soon got her down. He is a first-aid man, and has done these terrible jobs before. As soon as the girl had partially recovered, Lady Molly sent him and me out of the room. In the dark and dusty parlour, where but a few moments ago I had played my small part in a grim comedy, I now waited to hear what the sequel to it would be.

Danvers had been gone some time, and the shades of evening were drawing in; outside, the mean-looking street looked particularly dreary. It was close on six o'clock when at last I heard the welcome rustle of silks, the opening of a door, and at last my dear lady – looking grave but serene – came out of the inner room, and, beckoning to me, without a word led the way out of the house and into the fly, which was still waiting at the door.

"We'll send a doctor to her," were her first words as soon as we were clear of Bread Street. "But she is quite all right now, save that she wants a sleeping draught. Well, she has been punished enough, I think. She won't try her hand at blackmailing again."

"Then the photograph never existed?" I asked amazed.

"No; the plate was a failure, but Jane Turner would not thus readily give up the idea of getting money out of the poor, pusillanimous Countess. We know how she succeeded in terrorizing that silly little woman. It is wonderful how cleverly a girl like that worked out such a complicated scheme, all alone."

"All alone?"

"Yes; there was no one else. She was the elderly woman who used to meet the Countess, and who rang at the front door of the Weston apartment-house. She arranged the whole of the *mise en scène* of the assault on herself, all alone, and took everybody in with it – it was so perfectly done. She planned and executed it because she was afraid that the little Countess would be goaded into confessing her folly to her husband, or to her own parents, when a prosecution for blackmail would inevitably follow. So she risked everything on a big *coup*, and almost succeeded in getting a thousand pounds from Her Serene Highness, meaning to reassure her, as soon as she had the money, by the statement that the negative and prints had been destroyed. But the appearance of the Grand Duchess of Starkburg-Nauheim this afternoon frightened her into an act of despair. Confronted with the prosecution she dreaded and with the prison she dared not face, she, in a mad moment, attempted to take her life."

"I suppose now the whole matter will be hushed up."

"Yes," replied Lady Molly with a wistful sigh. "The public will never know who assaulted Jane Turner."

She was naturally a little regretful at that. But it was a joy to see her the day when she was able to assure Her Serene Highness the Countess of Hohengebirg that she need never again fear the consequences of that fatal day's folly.

The Fordwych Castle Mystery

Baroness Orczy

CAN YOU wonder that, when some of the ablest of our fellows at the Yard were at their wits' ends to know what to do, the chief instinctively turned to Lady Molly?

Surely the Fordwych Castle Mystery, as it was universally called, was a case which more than any other required feminine tact, intuition, and all those qualities of which my dear lady possessed more than her usual share.

With the exception of Mr. McKinley, the lawyer, and young Jack d'Alboukirk, there were only women connected with the case.

If you have studied Debrett at all, you know as well as I do that the peerage is one of those old English ones which date back some six hundred years, and that the present Lady d'Alboukirk is a baroness in her own right, the title and estates descending to heirs-general. If you have perused that same interesting volume carefully, you will also have discovered that the late Lord d'Alboukirk had two daughters, the eldest, Clementina Cecilia – the present Baroness, who succeeded him – the other, Margaret Florence, who married in 1884 Jean Laurent Duplessis, a Frenchman whom Debrett vaguely describes as 'of Pondicherry, India,' and of whom she had issue two daughters, Henriette Marie, heir now to the ancient barony of d'Alboukirk of Fordwych, and Joan, born two years later.

There seems to have been some mystery or romance attached to this marriage of the Honourable Margaret Florence d'Alboukirk to the dashing young officer of the Foreign Legion. Old Lord d'Alboukirk at the time was British Ambassador in Paris, and he seems to have had grave objections to the union, but Miss Margaret, openly flouting her father's displeasure, and throwing prudence to the winds, ran away from home one fine day with Captain Duplessis, and from Pondicherry wrote a curt letter to her relatives telling them of her marriage with the man she loved best in all the world. Old Lord d'Alboukirk never got over his daughter's wilfulness. She had been his favourite, it appears, and her secret marriage and deceit practically broke his heart. He was kind to her, however, to the end, and when the first baby girl was born and the young pair seemed to be in straitened circumstances, he made them an allowance until the day of his daughter's death, which occurred three years after her elopement, on the birth of her second child.

When, on the death of her father, the Honourable Clementina Cecilia came into the title and fortune, she seemed to have thought it her duty to take some interest in her late sister's eldest child, who, failing her own marriage, and issue, was heir to the barony of d'Alboukirk. Thus it was that Miss Henriette Marie Duplessis came, with her father's consent, to live with her aunt at Fordwych Castle. Debrett will tell you, moreover, that in 1901 she assumed the name of d'Alboukirk, in lieu of her own, by royal licence. Failing her, the title and estate would devolve firstly on her sister Joan, and subsequently on a fairly distant cousin, Captain John d'Alboukirk, at present a young officer in the Guards.

According to her servants, the present Baroness d'Alboukirk is very self-willed, but otherwise neither more nor less eccentric than any north-country old maid would be who had such an exceptional position to keep up in the social world. The one soft trait in her otherwise not very lovable character is her great affection for her late sister's child. Miss Henriette Duplessis d'Alboukirk has inherited from her French father dark eyes and hair and a somewhat swarthy complexion, but no doubt it is from her English ancestry that she has derived a somewhat masculine frame and a very great fondness for all outdoor pursuits. She is very athletic, knows how to fence and to box, rides to hounds, and is a remarkably good shot.

From all accounts, the first hint of trouble in that gorgeous home was coincident with the arrival at Fordwych of a young, very pretty girl visitor, who was attended by her maid, a half-caste woman, dark-complexioned and surly of temper, but obviously of dog-like devotion towards her young mistress. This visit seems to have come as a surprise to the entire household at Fordwych Castle, her ladyship having said nothing about it until the very morning that the guests were expected. She then briefly ordered one of the housemaids to get a bedroom ready for a young lady, and to put up a small camp-bedstead in an adjoining dressing-room. Even Miss Henriette seems to have been taken by surprise at the announcement of this visit, for, according to Jane Taylor, the housemaid in question, there was a violent word-passage between the old lady and her niece, the latter winding up an excited speech with the words:

"At any rate, aunt, there won't be room for both of us in this house!" After which she flounced out of the room, banging the door behind her.

Very soon the household was made to understand that the newcomer was none other than Miss Joan Duplessis, Miss Henriette's younger sister. It appears that Captain Duplessis had recently died in Pondicherry, and that the young girl then wrote to her aunt, Lady d'Alboukirk, claiming her help and protection, which the old lady naturally considered it her duty to extend to her.

It appears that Miss Joan was very unlike her sister, as she was and fair, more English-looking than foreign, and had pretty, dainty ways which soon endeared her to the household. The devotion existing between her and the half-caste woman she had brought from India was, moreover, unique.

It seems, however, that from the moment these newcomers came into the house, dissensions, often degenerating into violent quarrels, became the order of the day. Henriette seemed to have taken a strong dislike to her younger sister, and most particularly to the latter's dark attendant, who was vaguely known in the house as Roonah.

That some events of serious import were looming ahead, the servants at Fordwych were prett sure. The butler and footmen at dinner heard scraps of conversation which sounded very ominous There was talk of 'lawyers,' of 'proofs,' of 'marriage and birth certificates,' quickly suppressec when the servants happened to be about. Her ladyship looked terribly anxious and worried, anc she and Miss Henriette spent long hours closeted together in a small boudoir, whence proceedec ominous sounds of heartrending weeping on her ladyship's part, and angry and violent word from Miss Henriette.

Mr. McKinley, the eminent lawyer from London, came down two or three times to Fordwyct and held long conversations with her ladyship, after which the latter's eyes were very swolle and red. The household thought it more than strange that Roonah, the Indian servant, wa almost invariably present at these interviews between Mr. McKinley, her ladyship, and Miss Joar Otherwise the woman kept herself very much aloof; she spoke very little, hardly took any notice c anyone save of her ladyship and her young mistress, and the outbursts of Miss Henriette's tempe seemed to leave her quite unmoved. A strange fact was that she had taken a sudden and gre fancy for frequenting a small Roman Catholic convent chapel which was distant about half a mi from the Castle, and presently it was understood that Roonah, who had been a Parsee, had bee converted by the attendant priest to the Roman Catholic faith.

All this happened, mind you, within the last two or three months; in fact, Miss Joan had been in the Castle exactly twelve weeks when Captain Jack d'Alboukirk came to pay his cousin one of his periodical visits. From the first he seems to have taken a great fancy to his cousin Joan, and soon everyone noticed that this fancy was rapidly ripening into love. It was equally certain that from that moment dissensions between the two sisters became more frequent and more violent; the generally accepted opinion being that Miss Henriette was jealous of Joan, whilst Lady d'Alboukirk herself, for some unexplainable reason, seems to have regarded this love-making with marked disfavour.

Then came the tragedy.

One morning Joan ran downstairs, pale, and trembling from head to foot, moaning and sobbing as she ran:

"Roonah! – my poor old Roonah! – I knew it – I knew it!"

Captain Jack happened to meet her at the foot of the stairs. He pressed her with questions, but the girl was unable to speak. She merely pointed mutely to the floor above. The young man, genuinely alarmed, ran quickly upstairs; he threw open the door leading to Roonah's room, and there, to his horror, he saw the unfortunate woman lying across the small camp-bedstead, with a handkerchief over her nose and mouth, her throat cut.

The sight was horrible.

Poor Roonah was obviously dead.

Without losing his presence of mind, Captain Jack quietly shut the door again, after urgently begging Joan to compose herself, and try to keep up, at any rate until the local doctor could be sent for and the terrible news gently broken to Lady d'Alboukirk.

The doctor, hastily summoned, arrived some twenty minutes later. He could but confirm Joan's and Captain Jack's fears. Roonah was indeed dead – in fact, she had been dead some hours.

Chapter II

FROM THE very first, mind you, the public took a more than usually keen interest in this mysterious occurrence. The evening papers on the very day of the murder were ablaze with flaming headlines such as:

THE TRAGEDY AT FORDWYCH CASTLE
MYSTERIOUS MURDER OF AN IMPORTANT WITNESS GRAVE CHARGES AGAINST PERSONS IN HIGH LIFE

and so forth.

As time went on, the mystery deepened more and more, and I suppose Lady Molly must have had an inkling that sooner or later the chief would have to rely on her help and advice, for she sent me down to attend the inquest, and gave me strict orders to keep eyes and ears open for every detail in connection with the crime – however trivial it might seem. She herself remained in town, awaiting a summons from the chief.

The inquest was held in the dining-room of Fordwych Castle, and the noble hall was crowded to its utmost when the coroner and jury finally took their seats, after having viewed the body of the poor murdered woman upstairs.

The scene was dramatic enough to please any novelist, and an awed hush descended over the crowd when, just before the proceedings began, a door was thrown open, and in walked

– stiff and erect – the Baroness d'Alboukirk, escorted by her niece, Miss Henriette, and closely followed by her cousin, Captain Jack, of the Guards.

The old lady's face was as indifferent and haughty as usual, and so was that of her athletic niece. Captain Jack, on the other hand, looked troubled and flushed. Everyone noted that, directly he entered the room, his eyes sought a small, dark figure that sat silent and immovable beside the portly figure of the great lawyer, Mr. Hubert McKinley. This was Miss Joan Duplessis, in a plain black stuff gown, her young face pale and tear-stained.

Dr. Walker, the local practitioner, was, of course, the first witness called. His evidence was purely medical. He deposed to having made an examination of the body, and stated that he found that a handkerchief saturated with chloroform had been pressed to the woman's nostrils, probably while she was asleep, her throat having subsequently been cut with a sharp knife; death must have been instantaneous, as the poor thing did not appear to have struggled at all.

In answer to a question from the coroner, the doctor said that no great force or violence would be required for the gruesome deed, since the victim was undeniably unconscious when it was done. At the same time it argued unusual coolness and determination.

The handkerchief was produced, also the knife. The former was a bright-coloured one, stated to be the property of the deceased. The latter was a foreign, old-fashioned hunting-knife, one of a panoply of small arms and other weapons which adorned a corner of the hall. It had been found by Detective Elliott in a clump of gorse on the adjoining golf links. There could be no question that it had been used by the murderer for his fell purpose, since at the time it was found it still bore traces of blood.

Captain Jack was the next witness called. He had very little to say, as he merely saw the body from across the room, and immediately closed the door again and, having begged his cousin to compose herself, called his own valet and sent him off for the doctor.

Some of the staff of Fordwych Castle were called, all of whom testified to the Indian woman's curious taciturnity, which left her quite isolated among her fellow-servants. Miss Henriette's maid, however, Jane Partlett, had one or two more interesting facts to record. She seems to have been more intimate with the deceased woman than anyone else, and on one occasion, at least, had quite a confidential talk with her.

"She talked chiefly about her mistress," said Jane, in answer to a question from the coroner, "to whom she was most devoted. She told me that she loved her so, she would readily die for her. Of course, I thought that silly like, and just mad, foreign talk, but Roonah was very angry when I laughed at her, and then she undid her dress in front, and showed me some papers which were sown in the lining of her dress. 'All these papers my little missee's fortune,' she said to me. 'Roonah guard these with her life. Someone must kill Roonah before taking them from her!'

"This was about six weeks ago," continued Jane, whilst a strange feeling of awe seemed to descend upon all those present whilst the girl spoke. "Lately she became much more silent, and, on my once referring to the papers, she turned on me savage like and told me to hold my tongue."

Asked if she had mentioned the incident of the papers to anyone, Jane replied in the negative.

"Except to Miss Henriette, of course," she added, after a slight moment of hesitation.

Throughout all these preliminary examinations Lady d'Alboukirk, sitting between her cousin Captain Jack and her niece Henriette, had remained quite silent in an erect attitude expressive of haughty indifference. Henriette, on the other hand, looked distinctly bored. Once or twice she had yawned audibly, which caused quite a feeling of anger against her among the spectators. Such callousness in the midst of so mysterious a tragedy, and when her own sister as obviously in such deep sorrow, impressed everyone very unfavourably. It was well known at the young lady had had a fencing lesson just before the inquest in the room immediately low that where Roonah lay dead, and that within an hour of the discovery of the tragedy she as calmly playing golf.

Then Miss Joan Duplessis was called.

When the young girl stepped forward there was that awed hush in the room which usually falls on an attentive audience when the curtain is about to rise on the crucial act of a dramatic play. ut she was calm and self-possessed, and wonderfully pathetic-looking in her deep black and with e obvious lines of sorrow which the sad death of a faithful friend had traced on her young face.

In answer to the coroner, she gave her name as Joan Clarissa Duplessis, and briefly stated that ntil the day of her servant's death she had been a resident at Fordwych Castle, but that since then e had left that temporary home, and had taken up her abode at the d'Alboukirk Arms, a quiet tle hostelry on the outskirts of the town.

There was a distinct feeling of astonishment on the part of those who were not aware of this ct, and then the coroner said kindly:

"You were born, I think, in Pondicherry, in India, and are the younger daughter of Captain and rs. Duplessis, who was own sister to her ladyship?"

"I was born in Pondicherry," replied the young girl, quietly, "and I am the only legitimate child the late Captain and Mrs. Duplessis, own sister to her ladyship."

A wave of sensation, quickly suppressed by the coroner, went through the crowd at these ords. The emphasis which the witness had put on the word "legitimate" could not be mistaken, nd everyone felt that here must lie the clue to the, so far impenetrable, mystery of the Indian oman's death.

All eyes were now turned on old Lady d'Alboukirk and on her niece Henriette, but the two dies were carrying on a whispered conversation together, and had apparently ceased to take any rther interest in the proceedings.

"The deceased was your confidential maid, was she not?" asked the coroner, after a slight pause.

"Yes."

"She came over to England with you recently?"

"Yes; she had to accompany me in order to help me to make good my claim to being my late other's only legitimate child, and therefore the heir to the barony of d'Alboukirk."

Her voice had trembled a little as she said this, but now, as breathless silence reigned in e room, she seemed to make a visible effort to control herself, and, replying to the coroner's uestion, she gave a clear and satisfactory account of her terrible discovery of her faithful servant's eath. Her evidence had lasted about a quarter of an hour or so, when suddenly the coroner put e momentous question to her:

"Do you know anything about the papers which the deceased woman carried about her erson, and reference to which has already been made?"

"Yes," she replied quietly; "they were the proofs relating to my claim. My father, Captain uplessis, had in early youth, and before he met my mother, contracted a secret union with a alf-caste woman, who was Roonah's own sister. Being tired of her, he chose to repudiate her – e had no children – but the legality of the marriage was never for a moment in question. After at, he married my mother, and his first wife subsequently died, chiefly of a broken heart; but er death only occurred two months after the birth of my sister Henriette. My father, I think, had een led to believe that his first wife had died some two years previously, and he was no doubt ery much shocked when he realised what a grievous wrong he had done our mother. In order to end matters somewhat, he and she went through a new form of marriage – a legal one this time

– and my father paid a lot of money to Roonah's relatives to have the matter hushed up. Less than a year after this second – and only legal – marriage, I was born and my mother died."

"Then these papers of which so much has been said – what did they consist of?"

"There were the marriage certificates of my father's first wife – and two sworn statements as to her death, two months the birth of my sister Henriette; one by Dr. Rénaud, who was at the time a well-known medical man in Pondicherry, and the other by Roonah herself, who had held her dying sister in her arms. Dr. Rénaud is dead, and now Roonah has been murdered, and all the proofs have gone with her – "

Her voice broke in a passion of sobs, which, with manifest self-control, she quickly suppressed. In that crowded court you could have heard a pin drop, so great was the tension of intense excitement and attention.

"Then those papers remained in your maid's possession? Why was that?" asked the coroner.

"I did not dare to carry the papers about with me," said the witness, while a curious look of terror crept into her young face as she looked across at her aunt and sister. "Roonah would not part with them. She carried them in the lining of her dress, and at night they were all under her pillow. After her – her death, and when Dr. Walker had left, I thought it my duty to take possession of the papers which meant my whole future to me, and which I desired then to place in Mr. McKinley's charge. But, though I carefully searched the bed and all the clothing by my poor Roonah's side, I did not find the papers. They were gone."

I won't attempt to describe to you the sensation caused by the deposition of this witness. All eyes wandered from her pale young face to that of her sister, who sat almost opposite to her, shrugging her athletic shoulders and gazing at the pathetic young figure before her with callous and haughty indifference.

"Now, putting aside the question of the papers for the moment," said the coroner, after a pause, "do you happen to know anything of your late servant's private life? Had she an enemy, or perhaps a lover?"

"No," replied the girl; "Roonah's whole life was centred in me and in my claim. I had often begged her to place our papers in Mr. McKinley's charge, but she would trust no one. I wish she had obeyed me," here moaned the poor girl involuntarily, "and I should not have lost what means my whole future to me, and the being who loved me best in all the world would not have been so foully murdered."

Of course, it was terrible to see this young girl thus instinctively, and surely unintentionally, proffering so awful an accusation against those who stood so near to her. That the whole case had become hopelessly involved and mysterious, nobody could deny. Can you imagine the mental picture formed in the mind of all present by the story, so pathetically told, of this girl who had come over to England in order to make good her claim which she felt to be just, and who, in one fell swoop, saw that claim rendered very difficult to prove through the dastardly murder of her principal witness?

That the claim was seriously jeopardised by the death of Roonah and the disappearance of the papers, was made very clear, mind you, through the statements of Mr. McKinley, the lawyer. He could not say very much, of course, and his statements could never have been taken as actual proof because Roonah and Joan had never fully trusted him and had never actually placed the proofs c the claim in his hands. He certainly had seen the marriage certificate of Captain Duplessis's wife and a copy of this, as he very properly stated, could easily be obtained. The woman seems to have died during the great cholera epidemic of 1881, when, owing to the great number of deaths which occurred, the deceit and concealment practised by the natives at Pondicherry, and the supineness of the French Government, death certificates were very casually and often incorrectly made out

Roonah had come over to England ready to swear that her sister had died in her arms two months after the birth of Captain Duplessis's eldest child, and there was the sworn testimony of Dr. Rénaud, since dead. These affidavits Mr. McKinley had seen and read.

Against that, the only proof which now remained of the justice of Joan Duplessis's claim was the fact that her mother and father went through a second form of marriage some time the birth of their first child, Henriette. This fact was not denied, and, of course, it could be easily proved, if necessary, but even then it would in no way be conclusive. It implied the presence of a doubt in Captain Duplessis's mind, a doubt which the second marriage ceremony may have served to set at rest; but it in no way established the illegitimacy of his eldest daughter.

In fact, the more Mr. McKinley spoke, the more convinced did everyone become that the theft of the papers had everything to do with the murder of the unfortunate Roonah. She would not part with the proofs which meant her mistress's fortune, and she paid for her devotion with her life.

Several more witnesses were called after that. The servants were closely questioned, the doctor was recalled, but, in spite of long and arduous efforts, the coroner and jury could not bring a single real fact to light beyond those already stated.

The Indian woman had been murdered!

The papers which she always carried about her body had disappeared.

Beyond that, nothing! An impenetrable wall of silence and mystery!

The butler at Fordwych Castle had certainly missed the knife with which Roonah had been killed from its accustomed place on the morning after the murder had been committed, but not before, and the mystery further gained in intensity from the fact that the only purchase of chloroform in the district had been traced to the murdered woman herself.

She had gone down to the local chemist one day some two or three weeks previously, and shown him a prescription for cleansing the hair which required some chloroform in it. He gave her a very small quantity in a tiny bottle, which was subsequently found empty on her own dressing-table. No one at Fordwych Castle could swear to having heard any unaccustomed noise during that memorable night. Even Joan, who slept in the room adjoining that where the unfortunate Roonah lay, said she had heard nothing unusual. But then, the door of communication between the two rooms was shut, and the murderer had been quick and silent.

Thus this extraordinary inquest drew to a close, leaving in its train an air of dark suspicion and of unexplainable horror.

The jury returned a verdict of "Wilful murder against some person or persons unknown," and the next moment Lady d'Alboukirk rose, and, leaning on her niece's arm, quietly walked out of the room.

Chapter III

TWO OF OUR best men from the Yard, Pegram and Elliott, were left in charge of the case. They remained at Fordwych (the little town close by), as did Miss Joan, who had taken up her permanent abode at the d'Alboukirk Arms, whilst I returned to town immediately after the inquest. Captain Jack had rejoined his regiment, and apparently the ladies of the Castle had resumed their quiet, luxurious life just the same as heretofore. The old lady led her own somewhat isolated, semi-regal life; Miss Henriette fenced and boxed, played hockey and golf, and over the fine Castle and its haughty inmates there hovered like an ugly bird of prey the threatening presence of a nameless suspicion.

The two ladies might choose to flout public opinion, but public opinion was dead against them. No one dared formulate a charge, but everyone remembered that Miss Henriette had, on the very morning of the murder, been playing golf in the field where the knife was discovered, and that if Miss Joan Duplessis ever failed to make good her claim to the barony of d'Alboukirk, Miss Henriette would remain in undisputed possession. So now, when the ladies drove past in the village street, no one doffed a cap to salute them, and when at church the parson read out the sixth commandment, "Thou shalt do no murder," all eyes gazed with fearsome awe at the old Baroness and her niece.

Splendid isolation reigned at Fordwych Castle. The daily papers grew more and more sarcastic at the expense of the Scotland Yard authorities, and the public more and more impatient.

Then it was that the chief grew desperate and sent for Lady Molly, the result of the interview being that I once more made the journey down to Fordwych, but this time in the company of my dear lady, who had received from headquarters to do whatever she thought right in the investigation of the mysterious crime.

She and I arrived at Fordwych at 8.0 p.m., after the usual long wait at Newcastle. We put up at the d'Alboukirk Arms, and, over a hasty and very bad supper, Lady Molly allowed me a brief insight into her plans.

"I can see every detail of that murder, Mary," she said earnestly, "just as if I had lived at the Castle all the time. I know exactly where our fellows are wrong, and why they cannot get on. But, although the chief has given me a free hand, what I am going to do is so irregular that if I fail I shall probably get my immediate , whilst some of the disgrace is bound to stick to you. It is not too late – you may yet draw back, and leave me to act alone."

I looked her straight in the face. Her dark eyes were gleaming; there was the power of second sight in them, or of marvelous intuition of "men and things."

"I'll follow your lead, my Lady Molly," I said quietly.

"Then go to bed now," she replied, with that strange transition of manner which to me was so attractive and to everyone else so unaccountable.

In spite of my protest, she refused to listen to any more talk or to answer any more questions, and, perforce, I had to go to my room. The next morning I saw her graceful figure, immaculately dressed in a perfect tailor-made gown, standing beside my bed at a very early hour.

"Why, what is the time?" I ejaculated, suddenly wide awake.

"Too early for you to get up," she replied quietly. "I am going to early Mass at the Roman Catholic convent close by."

"To Mass at the Roman Catholic convent?"

"Yes. Don't repeat all my words, Mary; it is silly, and wastes time. I have introduced myself in the neighbourhood as the American, Mrs. Silas A. Ogen, whose motor has broken down and is being repaired at Newcastle, while I, its owner, amuse myself by viewing the beauties of the neighbourhood. Being a Roman Catholic, I go to Mass first, and, having met Lady d'Alboukirk once in London, I go to pay her a respectful visit afterwards. When I come back we will have breakfast together. You might try in the meantime to scrape up an acquaintance with Miss Joan Duplessis, who is still staying here, and ask her to join us at breakfast."

She was gone before I could make another remark, and I could but obey her instantly to the letter.

An hour later I saw Miss Joan Duplessis strolling in the hotel garden. It was not difficult to pass the time of day with the young girl, who seemed quite to brighten up at having someone to talk to . We spoke of the weather and so forth, and I steadily avoided the topic of the Fordwych Castle tragedy until the return of Lady Molly at about ten o'clock. She came back looking just as smart, just as self-possessed, as when she had started three hours earlier. Only I, who knew her so well, noted the glitter of triumph in her eyes, and knew that she had not failed. She was accompanied by Pegram, who, however, immediately left her side and went straight into the hotel, whilst she joined us in the garden, and, after a few graceful words, introduced herself to Miss Joan Duplessis and asked her to join us in the coffee-room upstairs.

The room was empty and we sat down to table, I quivering with excitement and awaiting events. Through the open window I saw Elliott walking rapidly down the village street. Presently the waitress went off, and I being too excited to eat or speak, Lady Molly carried on a running conversation with Miss Joan, asking her about her life in India and her father, Captain Duplessis. Joan admitted that she had always been her father's favourite.

"He never liked Henriette, somehow," she explained.

Lady Molly asked her when she had first known Roonah.

"She came to the house when my mother died," replied Joan, "and she had charge of me as a baby." At Pondicherry no one had thought it strange that she came as a servant into an officer's house where her own sister had reigned as mistress. Pondicherry is a French settlement, and manners and customs there are often very peculiar.

I ventured to ask her what were her future plans.

"Well," she said, with a great touch of sadness, "I can, of course, do nothing whilst my aunt is alive. I cannot force her to let me live at Fordwych or to acknowledge me as her heir. After her death, if my sister does assume the title and fortune of d'Alboukirk," she added, whilst suddenly a strange look of vengefulness – almost of hatred and cruelty – marred the child-like expression of her face, "then I shall revive the story of the tragedy of Roonah's death, and I hope that public opinion – "

She paused here in her speech, and I, who had been gazing out of the window, turned my eyes on her. She was ashy-pale, staring straight before her; her hands dropped the knife and fork which she had held. Then I saw the Pegram had come into the room, that he had come up to the table and placed a packet of papers in Lady Molly's hand.

I saw it all as in a flash!

There was a loud cry of despair like an animal at bay, a shrill cry, followed by a deep one from Pegram of "No, you don't," and before anyone could prevent her, Joan's graceful young figure stood outlined for a short moment at the open window.

The next moment she had disappeared into the depth below, and we heard a dull thud which nearly froze the blood in my veins.

Pegram ran out of the room, but Lady Molly sat quite still.

"I have succeeded in clearing the innocent," she said quietly; "but the guilty has meted out to herself her own punishment."

"Then it was she?" I murmured, horror-struck.

"Yes. I suspected it from the first," replied Lady Molly calmly. "It was this conversion of Roonah to Roman Catholicism and her consequent change of manner which gave me the first clue."

"But why – why?" I muttered.

"A simple reason, Mary," she rejoined, tapping the packet of papers with her delicate hand; and, breaking open the string that held the letters, she laid them out upon the table. "The whole thing was a fraud from beginning to end. The woman's marriage certificate was all right, of course, but I mistrusted the genuineness of the other papers from the moment that I heard that Roonah would not part with them and would not allow Mr. McKinley to have charge of them. I am sure that the idea at first was merely one of blackmail. The papers were only to be the means of extorting money from the old lady, and there was no thought of taking them into court.

"Roonah's part was, of course, the important thing in the whole case, since she was here prepared to swear to the actual date of the first Madame Duplessis's death. The initiative, of course, may have come either from Joan or from Captain Duplessis himself, out of hatred for the family who would have nothing to do with him and his favourite younger daughter. That, of course, we shall never know. At first Roonah was a Parsee, with a dog-like devotion to the girl whom she had nursed as a baby, and who no doubt had drilled her well into the part she was to play. But presently she became a Roman Catholic – an ardent convert, remember, with all a Roman Catholic's fear of hell-fire. I went to the convent this morning. I heard the priest's sermon there, and I realised what an influence his eloquence must have had over poor, ignorant, superstitious Roonah. She was still ready to die for her young mistress, but she was no longer prepared to swear to a lie for her sake. After Mass I called at Fordwych Castle. I explained my position to old Lady d'Alboukirk, who took me into the room where Roonah had slept and died. There I found two things," continued Lady Molly, as she opened the elegant reticule which still hung upon her arm, and placed a big key and a prayer-book before me.

"The key I found in a drawer of an old cupboard in the dressing-room where Roonah slept, with all sorts of odds and ends belonging to the unfortunate woman, and going to the door which led into what had been Joan's bedroom, I found that it was locked, and that this key fitted into the lock. Roonah had locked that door herself on her own side – I knew now that I was right in my surmise. The prayer-book is a Roman Catholic one. It is heavily thumbmarked there, where false oaths and lying are denounced as being deadly sins for which hell-fire would be the punishment. Roonah, terrorised by fear of the supernatural, a new convert to the faith, was afraid of committing a deadly sin.

"Who knows what passed between the two women, both of whom have come to so violent and terrible an end? Who can tell what prayers, tears, persuasions Joan Duplessis employed from the time she realised that Roonah did not mean to swear to the lie which would have brought her mistress wealth and glamour until the awful day when she finally understood that Roonah would no longer even hold her tongue, and devised a terrible means of silencing her for ever?

"With this certainty before me, I ventured on my big . I was so sure, you see. I kept Joan talking in here whilst I sent Pegram to her room with orders to break open the locks of her hand-bag and dressing-case. There! – I told you that if I was wrong I would probably be dismissed the force for irregularity, as of course I had no right to do that; but if Pegram found the papers there where I felt sure they would be, we could bring the murderer to justice. I know my own sex pretty well, don't I, Mary? I knew that Joan Duplessis had not destroyed – never would destroy – those papers."

Even as Lady Molly spoke we could hear heavy tramping outside the passage. I ran to the door, and there was met by Pegram.

"She is quite dead, miss," he said. "It was a drop of forty feet, and a stone pavement down below."

The guilty had indeed meted out her own punishment to herself!

Lady d'Alboukirk sent Lady Molly a cheque for £5,000 the day the whole affair was made known to the public.

I think you will say that it had been well earned. With her own dainty hands my dear lady had lifted the veil which hung over the tragedy of Fordwych Castle, and with the finding of the papers in Joan Duplessis's dressing-bag, and the unfortunate girl's suicide, the murder of the Indian woman was no longer a mystery.

The Murder at Troyte's Hill

Catherine Louisa Pirkis

"GRIFFITHS, of the Newcastle Constabulary, has the case in hand," said Mr. Dyer; "those Newcastle men are keen-witted, shrewd fellows, and very jealous of outside interference. They only sent to me under protest, as it were, because they wanted your sharp wits at work inside the house."

"I suppose throughout I am to work with Griffiths, not with you?" said Miss Brooke.

"Yes; when I have given you in outline the facts of the case, I simply have nothing more to do with it, and you must depend on Griffiths for any assistance of any sort that you may require."

Here, with a swing, Mr. Dyer opened his big ledger and turned rapidly over its leaves till he came to the heading 'Troyte's Hill' and the date 'September 6th.'

"I'm all attention," said Loveday, leaning back in her chair in the attitude of a listener.

"The murdered man," resumed Mr. Dyer, "is a certain Alexander Henderson – usually known as old Sandy – lodge-keeper to Mr. Craven, of Troyte's Hill, Cumberland. The lodge consists merely of two rooms on the ground floor, a bedroom and a sitting-room; these Sandy occupied alone, having neither kith nor kin of any degree. On the morning of September 6th, some children going up to the house with milk from the farm, noticed that Sandy's bed-room window stood wide open. Curiosity prompted them to peep in; and then, to their horror, they saw old Sandy, in his night-shirt, lying dead on the floor, as if he had fallen backwards from the window. They raised an alarm; and on examination, it was found that death had ensued from a heavy blow on the temple, given either by a strong fist or some blunt instrument. The room, on being entered, presented a curious appearance. It was as if a herd of monkeys had been turned into it and allowed to work their impish will. Not an article of furniture remained in its place: the bed-clothes had been rolled into a bundle and stuffed into the chimney; the bedstead – a small iron one – lay on its side; the one chair in the room stood on the top of the table; fender and fire-irons lay across the washstand, whose basin was to be found in a farther corner, holding bolster and pillow. The clock stood on its head in the middle of the mantelpiece; and the small vases and ornaments, which flanked it on either side, were walking, as it were, in a straight line towards the door. The old man's clothes had been rolled into a ball and thrown on the top of a high cupboard in which he kept his savings and whatever valuables he had. This cupboard, however, had not been meddled with, and its contents remained intact, so it was evident that robbery was not the motive for the crime. At the inquest, subsequently held, a verdict of 'willful murder' against some person or persons unknown was returned. The local police are diligently investigating the affair, but, as yet, no arrests have been made. The opinion that at present prevails in the neighbourhood is that the crime has been perpetrated by some lunatic, escaped or otherwise and enquiries are being made at the local asylums as to missing or lately released inmates. Griffiths, however, tells me that his suspicions set in another direction."

"Did anything of importance transpire at the inquest?"

"Nothing specially important. Mr. Craven broke down in giving his evidence when he alluded to the confidential relations that had always subsisted between Sandy and himself, and spoke of the last time that he had seen him alive. The evidence of the butler, and one or two of the female servants, seems clear enough, and they let fall something of a hint that Sandy was not altogether a favourite among them, on account of the overbearing manner in which he used his influence with his master. Young Mr. Craven, a youth of about nineteen, home from Oxford for the long vacation, was not present at the inquest; a doctor's certificate was put in stating that he was suffering from typhoid fever, and could not leave his bed without risk to his life. Now this young man is a thoroughly bad sort, and as much a gentleman-blackleg as it is possible for such a young fellow to be. It seems to Griffiths that there is something suspicious about this illness of his. He came back from Oxford on the verge of delirium tremens, pulled round from that, and then suddenly, on the day after the murder, Mrs. Craven rings the bell, announces that he has developed typhoid fever and orders a doctor to be sent for."

"What sort of man is Mr. Craven senior?"

"He seems to be a quiet old fellow, a scholar and learned philologist. Neither his neighbours nor his family see much of him; he almost lives in his study, writing a treatise, in seven or eight volumes, on comparative philology. He is not a rich man. Troyte's Hill, though it carries position in the county, is not a paying property, and Mr. Craven is unable to keep it up properly. I am told he has had to cut down expenses in all directions in order to send his son to college, and his daughter from first to last has been entirely educated by her mother. Mr. Craven was originally intended for the church, but for some reason or other, when his college career came to an end, he did not present himself for ordination – went out to Natal instead, where he obtained some civil appointment and where he remained for about fifteen years. Henderson was his servant during the latter portion of his Oxford career, and must have been greatly respected by him, for although the remuneration derived from his appointment at Natal was small, he paid Sandy a regular yearly allowance out of it. When, about ten years ago, he succeeded to Troyte's Hill, on the death of his elder brother, and returned home with his family, Sandy was immediately installed as lodge-keeper, and at so high a rate of pay that the butler's wages were cut down to meet it."

"Ah, that wouldn't improve the butler's feelings towards him," ejaculated Loveday.

Mr. Dyer went on: "But, in spite of his high wages, he doesn't appear to have troubled much about his duties as lodge-keeper, for they were performed, as a rule, by the gardener's boy, while he took his meals and passed his time at the house, and, speaking generally, put his finger into every pie. You know the old adage respecting the servant of twenty-one years' standing: 'Seven years my servant, seven years my equal, seven years my master.' Well, it appears to have held good in the case of Mr. Craven and Sandy. The old gentleman, absorbed in his philological studies, evidently let the reins slip through his fingers, and Sandy seems to have taken easy possession of them. The servants frequently had to go to him for orders, and he carried things, as a rule, with a high hand."

"Did Mrs. Craven never have a word to say on the matter?"

"I've not heard much about her. She seems to be a quiet sort of person. She is a Scotch missionary's daughter; perhaps she spends her time working for the Cape mission and that sort of thing."

"And young Mr. Craven: did he knock under to Sandy's rule?"

"Ah, now you're hitting the bull's eye and we come to Griffiths' theory. The young man and Sandy appear to have been at loggerheads ever since the Cravens took possession of Troyte's Hill. As a schoolboy Master Harry defied Sandy and threatened him with his hunting-crop; and subsequently, as a young man, has used strenuous endeavours to put the old servant in his place. On the day before the murder, Griffiths says, there was a terrible scene between the two, in which the young gentleman, in the presence of several witnesses, made use of strong language and threatened the old man's life. Now, Miss Brooke, I have told you all the circumstances of the case so far as I know them. For fuller particulars I must refer you to Griffiths. He, no doubt, will meet you at Grenfell – the nearest station to Troyte's Hill, and tell you in what capacity he has procured for you an entrance into the house. By-the-way, he has wired to me this morning that he hopes you will be able to save the Scotch express tonight."

Loveday expressed her readiness to comply with Mr. Griffiths' wishes.

"I shall be glad," said Mr. Dyer, as he shook hands with her at the office door, "to see you immediately on your return – that, however, I suppose, will not be yet awhile. This promises, I fancy, to be a longish affair?" This was said interrogatively.

"I haven't the least idea on the matter," answered Loveday. "I start on my work without theory of any sort – in fact, I may say, with my mind a perfect blank."

And anyone who had caught a glimpse of her blank, expressionless features, as she said this, would have taken her at her word.

Grenfell, the nearest post-town to Troyte's Hill, is a fairly busy, populous little town – looking south towards the black country, and northwards to low, barren hills. Pre-eminent among these stands Troyte's Hill, famed in the old days as a border keep, and possibly at a still earlier date as a Druid stronghold.

At a small inn at Grenfell, dignified by the title of "The Station Hotel," Mr. Griffiths, of the Newcastle constabulary, met Loveday and still further initiated her into the mysteries of the Troyte's Hill murder.

"A little of the first excitement has subsided," he said, after preliminary greetings had been exchanged; "but still the wildest rumours are flying about and repeated as solemnly as if they were Gospel truths. My chief here and my colleagues generally adhere to their first conviction, that the criminal is some suddenly crazed tramp or else an escaped lunatic, and they are confident that sooner or later we shall come upon his traces. Their theory is that Sandy, hearing some strange noise at the Park Gates, put his head out of the window to ascertain the cause and immediately had his death blow dealt him; then they suppose that the lunatic scrambled into the room through the window and exhausted his frenzy by turning things generally upside down. They refuse altogether to share my suspicions respecting young Mr. Craven."

Mr. Griffiths was a tall, thin-featured man, with iron-grey hair, but so close to his head that it refused to do anything but stand on end. This gave a somewhat comic expression to the upper portion of his face and clashed oddly with the melancholy look that his mouth habitually wore.

"I have made all smooth for you at Troyte's Hill," he presently went on. "Mr. Craven is not wealthy enough to allow himself the luxury of a family lawyer, so he occasionally employs the services of Messrs. Wells and Sugden, lawyers in this place, and who, as it happens, have, off and on, done a good deal of business for me. It was through them I heard that Mr. Craven was anxious to secure the assistance of an amanuensis. I immediately offered your services, stating that you were a friend of mine, a lady of impoverished means, who would gladly undertake the duties for the munificent sum of a guinea a month, with board and lodging. The old gentleman at once jumped at the offer, and is anxious for you to be at Troyte's Hill at once."

Loveday expressed her satisfaction with the programme that Mr. Griffiths had sketched for her, then she had a few questions to ask.

"Tell me," she said, "what led you, in the first instance, to suspect young Mr. Craven of the crime?"

"The footing on which he and Sandy stood towards each other, and the terrible scene that occurred between them only the day before the murder," answered Griffiths, promptly. "Nothing of this, however, was elicited at the inquest, where a very fair face was put on Sandy's relations with the whole of the Craven family. I have subsequently unearthed a good deal respecting the private life of Mr. Harry Craven, and, among other things, I have found out that on the night of the murder he left the house shortly after ten o'clock, and no one, so far as I have been able to ascertain, knows at what hour he returned. Now I must draw your attention, Miss Brooke, to the fact that at the inquest the medical evidence went to prove that the murder had been committed between ten and eleven at night."

"Do you surmise, then, that the murder was a planned thing on the part of this young man?"

"I do. I believe that he wandered about the grounds until Sandy shut himself in for the night, then aroused him by some outside noise, and, when the old man looked out to ascertain the cause, dealt him a blow with a bludgeon or loaded stick, that caused his death."

"A cold-blooded crime that, for a boy of nineteen?"

"Yes. He's a good-looking, gentlemanly youngster, too, with manners as mild as milk, but from all accounts is as full of wickedness as an egg is full of meat. Now, to come to another point – if, in connection with these ugly facts, you take into consideration the suddenness of his illness, I think you'll admit that it bears a suspicious appearance and might reasonably give rise to the surmise that it was a plant on his part, in order to get out of the inquest."

"Who is the doctor attending him?"

"A man called Waters; not much of a practitioner, from all accounts, and no doubt he feels himself highly honoured in being summoned to Troyte's Hill. The Cravens, it seems, have no family doctor. Mrs. Craven, with her missionary experience, is half a doctor herself, and never calls in one except in a serious emergency."

"The certificate was in order, I suppose?"

"Undoubtedly. And, as if to give colour to the gravity of the case, Mrs. Craven sent a message down to the servants, that if any of them were afraid of the infection they could at once go to their homes. Several of the maids, I believe, took advantage of her permission, and packed their boxes. Miss Craven, who is a delicate girl, was sent away with her maid to stay with friends at Newcastle, and Mrs. Craven isolated herself with her patient in one of the disused wings of the house."

"Has anyone ascertained whether Miss Craven arrived at her destination at Newcastle?"

Griffiths drew his brows together in thought.

"I did not see any necessity for such a thing," he answered. "I don't quite follow you. What do you mean to imply?"

"Oh, nothing. I don't suppose it matters much: it might have been interesting as a side-issue." She broke off for a moment, then added:

"Now tell me a little about the butler, the man whose wages were cut down to increase Sandy's pay."

"Old John Hales? He's a thoroughly worthy, respectable man; he was butler for five or six years to Mr. Craven's brother, when he was master of Troyte's Hill, and then took duty under this Mr. Craven. There's no ground for suspicion in that quarter. Hales's exclamation when he heard of the murder is quite enough to stamp him as an innocent man: 'Serve the old idiot right,' he cried: 'I couldn't pump up a tear for him if I tried for a month of Sundays!' Now I take it, Miss Brooke, a guilty man wouldn't dare make such a speech as that!"

"You think not?"

Griffiths stared at her. "I'm a little disappointed in her," he thought. "I'm afraid her powers have been slightly exaggerated if she can't see such a straight-forward thing as that."

Aloud he said, a little sharply, "Well, I don't stand alone in my thinking. No one yet has breathed a word against Hales, and if they did, I've no doubt he could prove an *alibi* without any trouble, for he lives in the house, and everyone has a good word for him."

"I suppose Sandy's lodge has been put into order by this time?"

"Yes; after the inquest, and when all possible evidence had been taken, everything was put straight."

"At the inquest it was stated that no marks of footsteps could be traced in any direction?"

"The long drought we've had would render such a thing impossible, let alone the fact that Sandy's lodge stands right on the gravelled drive, without flower-beds or grass borders of any sort around it. But look here, Miss Brooke, don't you be wasting your time over the lodge and its surroundings. Every iota of fact on that matter has been gone through over and over again by me and my chief. What we want you to do is to go straight into the house and concentrate attention on Master Harry's sick-room, and find out what's going on there. What he did outside the house on the night of the 6th, I've no doubt I shall be able to find out for myself. Now, Miss Brooke, you've asked me no end of questions, to which I have replied as fully as it was in my power to do; will you be good enough to answer one question that I wish to put, as straightforwardly as I have answered yours? You have had fullest particulars given you of the condition of Sandy's room when the police entered it on the morning after the murder. No doubt, at the present moment, you can see it all in your mind's eye – the bedstead on its side, the clock on its head, the bed-clothes half-way up the chimney, the little vases and ornaments walking in a straight line towards the door?"

Loveday bowed her head.

"Very well, now will you be good enough to tell me what this scene of confusion recalls to your mind before anything else?"

"The room of an unpopular Oxford freshman after a raid upon it by undergrads," answered Loveday promptly.

Mr. Griffiths rubbed his hands.

"Quite so!" he ejaculated. "I see, after all, we are one at heart in this matter, in spite of a little surface disagreement of ideas. Depend upon it, by-and-bye, like the engineers tunnelling from different quarters under the Alps, we shall meet at the same point and shake hands. By-the-way, I have arranged for daily communication between us through the postboy who takes the letters to Troyte's Hill. He is trustworthy, and any letter you give him for me will find its way into my hands within the hour."

It was about three o'clock in the afternoon when Loveday drove in through the park gates of Troyte's Hill, past the lodge where old Sandy had met with his death. It was a pretty little cottage, covered with Virginia creeper and wild honeysuckle, and showing no outward sign of the tragedy that had been enacted within.

The park and pleasure-grounds of Troyte's Hill were extensive, and the house itself was a somewhat imposing red brick structure, built, possibly, at the time when Dutch William's taste had grown popular in the country. Its frontage presented a somewhat forlorn appearance, its centre windows – a square of eight – alone seeming to show signs of occupation. With the exception of two windows at the extreme end of the bedroom floor of the north wing, where, possibly, the invalid and his mother were located, and two windows at the extreme end of the ground floor of the south wing, which Loveday ascertained subsequently were those of Mr. Craven's study, not a single window in either wing owned blind or curtain. The wings were extensive, and it was easy to understand that at the extreme end of the one the fever patient would be isolated from the rest of the household, and that at the extreme end of the other Mr. Craven could secure the quiet and freedom from interruption which, no doubt, were essential to the due prosecution of his philological studies.

Alike on the house and ill-kept grounds were present the stamp of the smallness of the income of the master and owner of the place. The terrace, which ran the length of the house in front, and on to which every window on the ground floor opened, was miserably out of repair: not a lintel or door-post, window-ledge or balcony but what seemed to cry aloud for the touch of the painter. "Pity me! I have seen better days," Loveday could fancy written as a legend across the red-brick porch that gave entrance to the old house.

The butler, John Hales, admitted Loveday, shouldered her portmanteau and told her he would show her to her room. He was a tall, powerfully-built man, with a ruddy face and dogged expression of countenance. It was easy to understand that, off and on, there must have been many a sharp encounter between him and old Sandy. He treated Loveday in an easy, familiar fashion, evidently considering that an amanuensis took much the same rank as a nursery governess – that is to say, a little below a lady's maid and a little above a house-maid.

"We're short of hands, just now," he said, in broad Cumberland dialect, as he led the way up the wide stair case. "Some of the lasses downstairs took fright at the fever and went home. Cook and I are single-handed, for Moggie, the only maid left, has been told off to wait on Madam and Master Harry. I hope you're not afeared of fever?"

Loveday explained that she was not, and asked if the room at the extreme end of the north wing was the one assigned to "Madam and Master Harry."

"Yes," said the man; "it's convenient for sick nursing; there's a flight of stairs runs straight down from it to the kitchen quarters. We put all Madam wants at the foot of those stairs and Moggie herself never enters the sick-room. I take it you'll not be seeing Madam for many a day, yet awhile."

"When shall I see Mr. Craven? At dinner tonight?"

"That's what naebody could say," answered Hales. "He may not come out of his study till past midnight; sometimes he sits there till two or three in the morning. Shouldn't advise you to wait till he wants his dinner – better have a cup of tea and a chop sent up to you. Madam never waits for him at any meal."

As he finished speaking he deposited the portmanteau outside one of the many doors opening into the gallery.

"This is Miss Craven's room," he went on; "cook and me thought you'd better have it, as it would want less getting ready than the other rooms, and work is work when there are so few hands to do it. Oh, my stars! I do declare there is cook putting it straight for you now." The last sentence was added as the opened door laid bare to view, the cook, with a duster in her hand, polishing a mirror; the bed had been made, it is true, but otherwise the room must have been much as Miss Craven left it, after a hurried packing up.

To the surprise of the two servants Loveday took the matter very lightly.

"I have a special talent for arranging rooms and would prefer getting this one straight for myself," she said. "Now, if you will go and get ready that chop and cup of tea we were talking about just now, I shall think it much kinder than if you stayed here doing what I can so easily do for myself."

When, however, the cook and butler had departed in company, Loveday showed no disposition to exercise the 'special talent' of which she had boasted.

She first carefully turned the key in the lock and then proceeded to make a thorough and minute investigation of every corner of the room. Not an article of furniture, nor an ornament or toilet accessory, but what was lifted from its place and carefully scrutinized. Even the ashes in the grate, the debris of the last fire made there, were raked over and well looked through.

This careful investigation of Miss Craven's late surroundings occupied in all about three quarters of an hour, and Loveday, with her hat in her hand, descended the stairs to see Hales crossing the hall to the dining-room with the promised cup of tea and chop.

In silence and solitude she partook of the simple repast in a dining-hall that could with ease have banqueted a hundred and fifty guests.

"Now for the grounds before it gets dark," she said to herself, as she noted that already the outside shadows were beginning to slant.

The dining-hall was at the back of the house; and here, as in the front, the windows, reaching to the ground, presented easy means of egress. The flower-garden was on this side of the house and sloped downhill to a pretty stretch of well-wooded country.

Loveday did not linger here even to admire, but passed at once round the south corner of the house to the windows which she had ascertained, by a careless question to the butler, were those of Mr. Craven's study.

Very cautiously she drew near them, for the blinds were up, the curtains drawn back. A side glance, however, relieved her apprehensions, for it showed her the occupant of the room, seated in an easy-chair, with his back to the windows. From the length of his outstretched limbs he was evidently a tall man. His hair was silvery and curly, the lower part of his face was hidden from her view by the chair, but she could see one hand was pressed tightly across his eyes and brows. The whole attitude was that of a man absorbed in deep thought. The room was comfortably furnished, but presented an appearance of disorder from the books and manuscripts scattered in all directions. A whole pile of torn fragments of foolscap sheets, overflowing from a waste-paper basket beside the writing-table, seemed to proclaim the fact that the scholar had of late grown weary of, or else dissatisfied with his work, and had condemned it freely.

Although Loveday stood looking in at this window for over five minutes, not the faintest sign of life did that tall, reclining figure give, and it would have been as easy to believe him locked in sleep as in thought.

From here she turned her steps in the direction of Sandy's lodge. As Griffiths had said, it was graveled up to its doorstep. The blinds were closely drawn, and it presented the ordinary appearance of a disused cottage.

A narrow path beneath over-arching boughs of cherry-laurel and arbutus, immediately facing the lodge, caught her eye, and down this she at once turned her footsteps.

This path led, with many a wind and turn, through a belt of shrubbery that skirted the frontage of Mr. Craven's grounds, and eventually, after much zig-zagging, ended in close proximity to the stables. As Loveday entered it, she seemed literally to leave daylight behind her.

"I feel as if I were following the course of a circuitous mind," she said to herself as the shadows closed around her. "I could not fancy Sir Isaac Newton or Bacon planning or delighting in such a wind-about-alley as this!"

The path showed greyly in front of her out of the dimness. On and on she followed it; here and there the roots of the old laurels, struggling out of the ground, threatened to trip her up. Her eyes, however, had now grown accustomed to the half-gloom, and not a detail of her surroundings escaped her as she went along.

A bird flew from out the thicket on her right hand with a startled cry. A dainty little frog leaped out of her way into the shrivelled leaves lying below the laurels. Following the movements of this frog, her eye was caught by something black and solid among those leaves. What was it? A bundle – a shiny black coat? Loveday knelt down, and using her hands to assist her eyes, found that they came into contact with the dead, stiffened body of a beautiful black retriever. She parted, as well as she was able, the lower boughs of the evergreens, and minutely examined the poor animal. Its eyes were still open, though glazed and bleared, and its death had, undoubtedly, been caused by the blow of some blunt, heavy instrument, for on one side its skull was almost battered in.

"Exactly the death that was dealt to Sandy," she thought, as she groped hither and thither beneath the trees in hopes of lighting upon the weapon of destruction.

She searched until increasing darkness warned her that search was useless. Then, still following the zig-zagging path, she made her way out by the stables and thence back to the house.

She went to bed that night without having spoken to a soul beyond the cook and butler. The next morning, however, Mr. Craven introduced himself to her across the breakfast-table. He was a man of really handsome personal appearance, with a fine carriage of the head and shoulders, and eyes that had a forlorn, appealing look in them. He entered the room with an air of great energy, apologized to Loveday for the absence of his wife, and for his own remissness in not being in the way to receive her on the previous day. Then he bade her make herself at home at the breakfast-table, and expressed his delight in having found a coadjutor in his work.

"I hope you understand what a great – a stupendous work it is?" he added, as he sank into a chair. "It is a work that will leave its impress upon thought in all the ages to come. Only a man who has studied comparative philology as I have for the past thirty years, could gauge the magnitude of the task I have set myself."

With the last remark, his energy seemed spent, and he sank back in his chair, covering his eyes with his hand in precisely the same attitude as that in which Loveday had seen him over-night, and utterly oblivious of the fact that breakfast was before him and a stranger-guest seated at table. The butler entered with another dish. "Better go on with your breakfast," he whispered to Loveday, "he may sit like that for another hour."

He placed his dish in front of his master.

"Captain hasn't come back yet, sir," he said, making an effort to arouse him from his reverie.

"Eh, what?" said Mr. Craven, for a moment lifting his hand from his eyes.

"Captain, sir – the black retriever," repeated the man.

The pathetic look in Mr. Craven's eyes deepened.

"Ah, poor Captain!" he murmured; "the best dog I ever had."

Then he again sank back in his chair, putting his hand to his forehead.

The butler made one more effort to arouse him.

"Madam sent you down a newspaper, sir, that she thought you would like to see," he shouted almost into his master's ear, and at the same time laid the morning's paper on the table beside his plate.

"Confound you! Leave it there," said Mr. Craven irritably. "Fools! Dolts that you all are! With your trivialities and interruptions you are sending me out of the world with my work undone!"

And again he sank back in his chair, closed his eyes and became lost to his surroundings.

Loveday went on with her breakfast. She changed her place at table to one on Mr. Craven's right hand, so that the newspaper sent down for his perusal lay between his plate and hers. It was folded into an oblong shape, as if it were wished to direct attention to a certain portion of a certain column.

A clock in a corner of the room struck the hour with a loud, resonant stroke. Mr. Craven gave a start and rubbed his eyes.

"Eh, what's this?" he said. "What meal are we at?" He looked around with a bewildered air. "Eh! – who are you?" he went on, staring hard at Loveday. "What are you doing here? Where's Nina? – Where's Harry?"

Loveday began to explain, and gradually recollection seemed to come back to him.

"Ah, yes, yes," he said. "I remember; you've come to assist me with my great work. You promised, you know, to help me out of the hole I've got into. Very enthusiastic, I remember they said you were, on certain abstruse points in comparative philology. Now, Miss – Miss – I've forgotten your name – tell me a little of what you know about the elemental sounds of speech that are common to all languages. Now, to how many would you reduce those elemental sounds – to six, eight, nine? No, we won't discuss the matter here, the cups and saucers distract me. Come into my den at the other end of the house; we'll have perfect quiet there."

And utterly ignoring the fact that he had not as yet broken his fast, he rose from the table, seized Loveday by the wrist, and led her out of the room and down the long corridor that led through the south wing to his study.

But seated in that study his energy once more speedily exhausted itself.

He placed Loveday in a comfortable chair at his writing-table, consulted her taste as to pens, and spread a sheet of foolscap before her. Then he settled himself in his easy-chair, with his back to the light, as if he were about to dictate folios to her.

In a loud, distinct voice he repeated the title of his learned work, then its sub-division, then the number and heading of the chapter that was at present engaging his attention. Then he put his hand to his head. "It's the elemental sounds that are my stumbling-block," he said. "Now, how on earth is it possible to get a notion of a sound of agony that is not in part a sound of terror? or a sound of surprise that is not in part a sound of either joy or sorrow?"

With this his energies were spent, and although Loveday remained seated in that study from early morning till daylight began to fade, she had not ten sentences to show for her day's work as amanuensis.

Loveday in all spent only two clear days at Troyte's Hill.

On the evening of the first of those days Detective Griffiths received, through the trustworthy post-boy, the following brief note from her:

I have found out that Hales owed Sandy close upon a hundred pounds, which he had borrowed at various times. I don't know whether you will think this fact of any importance. – L.B.

Mr. Griffiths repeated the last sentence blankly. "If Harry Craven were put upon his defence, his counsel, I take it, would consider the fact of first importance," he muttered. And for the remainder of that day Mr. Griffiths went about his work in a perturbed state of mind, doubtful whether to hold or to let go his theory concerning Harry Craven's guilt.

The next morning there came another brief note from Loveday which ran thus:

As a matter of collateral interest, find out if a person, calling himself Harold Cousins, sailed two days ago from London Docks for Natal in the Bonnie Dundee?

To this missive Loveday received, in reply, the following somewhat lengthy dispatch:

I do not quite see the drift of your last note, but have wired to our agents in London to carry out its suggestion. On my part, I have important news to communicate. I have found out what Harry Craven's business out of doors was on the night of the murder, and at my instance a warrant has been issued for his arrest. This warrant it will be my duty to serve on him in the course of today. Things are beginning to look very black against him, and I am convinced his illness is all a sham. I have seen Waters, the man who is supposed to be attending him, and have driven him into a corner and made him admit that he has only seen young Craven once – on the first day of his illness – and that he gave his certificate entirely on the strength of what Mrs. Craven told him of her son's condition. On the occasion of this, his first and only visit, the lady, it seems, also told him that it would not be necessary for him to continue his attendance, as she quite felt herself competent to treat the case, having had so much experience in fever cases among the blacks at Natal.

As I left Waters's house, after eliciting this important information, I was accosted by a man who keeps a low-class inn in the place, McQueen by name. He said that he wished to speak to me on a matter of importance. To make a long story short, this McQueen stated that on the night of the sixth, shortly after eleven o'clock, Harry Craven came to his house, bringing with him a valuable piece of plate – a handsome epergne – and requested him to lend him a hundred pounds on it, as he hadn't a penny in his pocket. McQueen complied with his request to the extent of ten sovereigns, and now, in a fit of nervous terror, comes to me to confess himself a receiver of stolen goods and play the honest man! He says he noticed that the young gentleman was very much agitated as he made the request, and he also begged him to mention his visit to no one. Now, I am curious to learn how Master Harry will get over the fact that he passed the lodge at the hour at which the murder was most probably committed; or how he will get out of the dilemma of having repassed the lodge on his way back to the house, and not noticed the wide-open window with the full moon shining down on it?

Another word! Keep out of the way when I arrive at the house, somewhere between two and three in the afternoon, to serve the warrant. I do not wish your professional capacity to get wind, for you will most likely yet be of some use to us in the house.

S.G.

Loveday read this note, seated at Mr. Craven's writing-table, with the old gentleman himself reclining motionless beside her in his easy-chair. A little smile played about the corners of her mouth as she read over again the words – "for you will most likely yet be of some use to us in the house."

Loveday's second day in Mr. Craven's study promised to be as unfruitful as the first. For fully an hour after she had received Griffiths' note, she sat at the writing-table with her pen in her hand, ready to transcribe Mr. Craven's inspirations. Beyond, however, the phrase, muttered with closed eyes – "It's all here, in my brain, but I can't put it into words" – not a half-syllable escaped his lips.

At the end of that hour the sound of footsteps on the outside gravel made her turn her head towards the window. It was Griffiths approaching with two constables. She heard the hall door opened to admit them, but, beyond that, not a sound reached her ear, and she realized how fully she was cut off from communication with the rest of the household at the farther end of this unoccupied wing.

Mr. Craven, still reclining in his semi-trance, evidently had not the faintest suspicion that so important an event as the arrest of his only son on a charge of murder was about to be enacted in the house.

Meantime, Griffiths and his constables had mounted the stairs leading to the north wing, and were being guided through the corridors to the sick-room by the flying figure of Moggie, the maid.

"Hoot, mistress!" cried the girl, "here are three men coming up the stairs – policemen, every one of them – will ye come and ask them what they be wanting?"

Outside the door of the sick-room stood Mrs. Craven – a tall, sharp-featured woman with sandy hair going rapidly grey.

"What is the meaning of this? What is your business here?" she said haughtily, addressing Griffiths, who headed the party.

Griffiths respectfully explained what his business was, and requested her to stand on one side that he might enter her son's room.

"This is my daughter's room; satisfy yourself of the fact," said the lady, throwing back the door as she spoke.

And Griffiths and his confrères entered, to find pretty Miss Craven, looking very white and scared, seated beside a fire in a long flowing robe de chambre.

Griffiths departed in haste and confusion, without the chance of a professional talk with Loveday. That afternoon saw him telegraphing wildly in all directions, and dispatching messengers in all quarters. Finally he spent over an hour drawing up an elaborate report to his chief at Newcastle, assuring him of the identity of one, Harold Cousins, who had sailed in the *Bonnie Dundee* for Natal, with Harry Craven, of Troyte's Hill, and advising that the police authorities in that far-away district should be immediately communicated with.

The ink had not dried on the pen with which this report was written before a note, in Loveday's writing, was put into his hand.

Loveday evidently had had some difficulty in finding a messenger for this note, for it was brought by a gardener's boy, who informed Griffiths that the lady had said he would receive a gold sovereign if he delivered the letter all right.

Griffiths paid the boy and dismissed him, and then proceeded to read Loveday's communication.

It was written hurriedly in pencil, and ran as follows:

> *Things are getting critical here. Directly you receive this, come up to the house with two of your men, and post yourselves anywhere in the grounds where you can see and not be seen. There will be no difficulty in this, for it will be dark by the time you are able to get there. I am not sure whether I shall want your aid tonight, but you had better keep in the grounds until morning, in case of need; and above all, never once lose sight of the study windows." (This was underscored.) "If I put a lamp*

with a green shade in one of those windows, do not lose a moment in entering by that window, which I will contrive to keep unlocked.

Detective Griffiths rubbed his forehead – rubbed his eyes, as he finished reading this.

"Well, I daresay it's all right," he said, "but I'm bothered, that's all, and for the life of me I can't see one step of the way she is going."

He looked at his watch: the hands pointed to a quarter past six. The short September day was drawing rapidly to a close. A good five miles lay between him and Troyte's Hill – there was evidently not a moment to lose.

At the very moment that Griffiths, with his two constables, were once more starting along the Grenfell High Road behind the best horse they could procure, Mr. Craven was rousing himself from his long slumber, and beginning to look around him. That slumber, however, though long, had not been a peaceful one, and it was sundry of the old gentleman's muttered exclamations, as he had started uneasily in his sleep, that had caused Loveday to open, and then to creep out of the room to dispatch, her hurried note.

What effect the occurrence of the morning had had upon the household generally, Loveday, in her isolated corner of the house, had no means of ascertaining. She only noted that when Hales brought in her tea, as he did precisely at five o'clock, he wore a particularly ill-tempered expression of countenance, and she heard him mutter, as he set down the tea-tray with a clatter, something about being a respectable man, and not used to such 'goings on.'

It was not until nearly an hour and a half after this that Mr. Craven had awakened with a sudden start, and, looking wildly around him, had questioned Loveday who had entered the room.

Loveday explained that the butler had brought in lunch at one, and tea at five, but that since then no one had come in.

"Now that's false," said Mr. Craven, in a sharp, unnatural sort of voice; "I saw him sneaking round the room, the whining, canting hypocrite, and you must have seen him, too! Didn't you hear him say, in his squeaky old voice: 'Master, I knows your secret – '" He broke off abruptly, looking wildly round. "Eh, what's this?" he cried. "No, no, I'm all wrong – Sandy is dead and buried – they held an inquest on him, and we all praised him up as if he were a saint."

"He must have been a bad man, that old Sandy," said Loveday sympathetically.

"You're right! You're right!" cried Mr. Craven, springing up excitedly from his chair and seizing her by the hand. "If ever a man deserved his death, he did. For thirty years he held that rod over my head, and then – ah where was I?"

He put his hand to his head and again sank, as if exhausted, into his chair.

"I suppose it was some early indiscretion of yours at college that he knew of?" said Loveday, eager to get at as much of the truth as possible while the mood for confidence held sway in the feeble brain.

"That was it! I was fool enough to marry a disreputable girl – a barmaid in the town – and Sandy was present at the wedding, and then—" Here his eyes closed again and his mutterings became incoherent.

For ten minutes he lay back in his chair, muttering thus; "A yelp – a groan," were the only words Loveday could distinguish among those mutterings, then suddenly, slowly and distinctly, he said, as if answering some plainly-put question: "A good blow with the hammer and the thing was done."

"I should like amazingly to see that hammer," said Loveday; "do you keep it anywhere at hand?"

His eyes opened with a wild, cunning look in them.

"Who's talking about a hammer? I did not say I had one. If anyone says I did it with a hammer, they're telling a lie."

"Oh, you've spoken to me about the hammer two or three times," said Loveday calmly; "the one that killed your dog, Captain, and I should like to see it, that's all."

The look of cunning died out of the old man's eye – "Ah, poor Captain! splendid dog that! Well, now, where were we? Where did we leave off? Ah, I remember, it was the elemental sounds of speech that bothered me so that night. Were you here then? Ah, no! I remember. I had been trying all day to assimilate a dog's yelp of pain to a human groan, and I couldn't do it. The idea haunted me – followed me about wherever I went. If they were both elemental sounds, they must have something in common, but the link between them I could not find; then it occurred to me, would a well-bred, well-trained dog like my Captain in the stables, there, at the moment of death give an unmitigated currish yelp; would there not be something of a human note in his death-cry? The thing was worth putting to the test. If I could hand down in my treatise a fragment of fact on the matter, it would be worth a dozen dogs' lives. So I went out into the moonlight – ah, but you know all about it – now, don't you?"

"Yes. Poor Captain! Did he yelp or groan?"

"Why, he gave one loud, long, hideous yelp, just as if he had been a common cur. I might just as well have let him alone; it only set that other brute opening his window and spying out on me, and saying in his cracked old voice: 'Master, what are you doing out here at this time of night?'"

Again he sank back in his chair, muttering incoherently with half-closed eyes.

Loveday let him alone for a minute or so; then she had another question to ask.

"And that other brute – did he yelp or groan when you dealt him his blow?"

"What, old Sandy – the brute? He fell back – Ah, I remember, you said you would like to see the hammer that stopped his babbling old tongue – now didn't you?"

He rose a little unsteadily from his chair, and seemed to drag his long limbs with an effort across the room to a cabinet at the farther end. Opening a drawer in this cabinet, he produced, from amidst some specimens of strata and fossils, a large-sized geological hammer.

He brandished it for a moment over his head, then paused with his finger on his lip.

"Hush!" he said, "we shall have the fools creeping in to peep at us if we don't take care." And to Loveday's horror he suddenly made for the door, turned the key in the lock, withdrew it and put it into his pocket.

She looked at the clock; the hands pointed to half-past seven. Had Griffiths received her note at the proper time, and were the men now in the grounds? She could only pray that they were.

"The light is too strong for my eyes," she said, and rising from her chair, she lifted the green-shaded lamp and placed it on a table that stood at the window.

"No, no, that won't do," said Mr. Craven; "that would show everyone outside what we're doing in here." He crossed to the window as he spoke and removed the lamp thence to the mantelpiece.

Loveday could only hope that in the few seconds it had remained in the window it had caught the eye of the outside watchers.

The old man beckoned to Loveday to come near and examine his deadly weapon. "Give it a good swing round," he said, suiting the action to the word, "and down it comes with a splendid crash." He brought the hammer round within an inch of Loveday's forehead.

She started back.

"Ha, ha," he laughed harshly and unnaturally, with the light of madness dancing in his eyes now; "did I frighten you? I wonder what sort of sound you would make if I were to give you a little tap just there." Here he lightly touched her forehead with the hammer. "Elemental, of course, it would be, and—"

Loveday steadied her nerves with difficulty. Locked in with this lunatic, her only chance lay in gaining time for the detectives to reach the house and enter through the window.

"Wait a minute," she said, striving to divert his attention; "you have not yet told me what sort of an elemental sound old Sandy made when he fell. If you'll give me pen and ink, I'll write down a full account of it all, and you can incorporate it afterwards in your treatise."

For a moment a look of real pleasure flitted across the old man's face, then it faded. "The brute fell back dead without a sound," he answered; "it was all for nothing, that night's work; yet not altogether for nothing. No, I don't mind owning I would do it all over again to get the wild thrill of joy at my heart that I had when I looked down into that old man's dead face and felt myself free at last! Free at last!" his voice rang out excitedly – once more he brought his hammer round with an ugly swing.

"For a moment I was a young man again; I leaped into his room – the moon was shining full in through the window – I thought of my old college days, and the fun we used to have at Pembroke – topsy turvey I turned everything—" He broke off abruptly, and drew a step nearer to Loveday. "The pity of it all was," he said, suddenly dropping from his high, excited tone to a low, pathetic one, "that he fell without a sound of any sort." Here he drew another step nearer. "I wonder – " he said, then broke off again, and came close to Loveday's side. "It has only this moment occurred to me," he said, now with his lips close to Loveday's ear, "that a woman, in her death agony, would be much more likely to give utterance to an elemental sound than a man."

He raised his hammer, and Loveday fled to the window, and was lifted from the outside by three pairs of strong arms.

"I thought I was conducting my very last case – I never had such a narrow escape before!" said Loveday, as she stood talking with Mr. Griffiths on the Grenfell platform, awaiting the train to carry her back to London. "It seems strange that no one before suspected the old gentleman's sanity – I suppose, however, people were so used to his eccentricities that they did not notice how they had deepened into positive lunacy. His cunning evidently stood him in good stead at the inquest."

"It is possible" said Griffiths thoughtfully, "that he did not absolutely cross the very slender line that divided eccentricity from madness until after the murder. The excitement consequent upon the discovery of the crime may just have pushed him over the border. Now, Miss Brooke, we have exactly ten minutes before your train comes in. I should feel greatly obliged to you if you would explain one or two things that have a professional interest for me."

"With pleasure," said Loveday. "Put your questions in categorical order and I will answer them."

"Well, then, in the first place, what suggested to your mind the old man's guilt?"

"The relations that subsisted between him and Sandy seemed to me to savour too much of fear on the one side and power on the other. Also the income paid to Sandy during Mr. Craven's absence in Natal bore, to my mind, an unpleasant resemblance to hush-money."

"Poor wretched being! And I hear that, after all, the woman he married in his wild young days died soon afterwards of drink. I have no doubt, however, that Sandy sedulously kept up the fiction of her existence, even after his master's second marriage. Now fo nother question: how was it you knew that Miss Craven had taken her brother's place in ne sick-room?"

"On the evening of my arrival I discovered a rather long lock of fair hair in the unswept replace of my room, which, as it happened, was usually occupied by Miss Craven. It at once ccurred to me that the young lady had been cutting off her hair and that there must be me powerful motive to induce such a sacrifice. The suspicious circumstances attending her rother's illness soon supplied me with such a motive."

"Ah! that typhoid fever business was very cleverly done. Not a servant in the house, I verily elieve, but who thought Master Harry was upstairs, ill in bed, and Miss Craven away at her iends' in Newcastle. The young fellow must have got a clear start off within an hour of the urder. His sister, sent away the next day to Newcastle, dismissed her maid there, I hear, on the ea of no accommodation at her friends' house – sent the girl to her own home for a holiday nd herself returned to Troyte's Hill in the middle of the night, having walked the five miles om Grenfell. No doubt her mother admitted her through one of those easily-opened front indows, cut her hair and put her to bed to personate her brother without delay. With Miss raven's strong likeness to Master Harry, and in a darkened room, it is easy to understand that e eyes of a doctor, personally unacquainted with the family, might easily be deceived. Now, iss Brooke, you must admit that with all this elaborate chicanery and double dealing going on, was only natural that my suspicions should set in strongly in that quarter."

"I read it all in another light, you see," said Loveday. "It seemed to me that the mother, nowing her son's evil proclivities, believed in his guilt, in spite, possibly, of his assertions of nocence. The son, most likely, on his way back to the house after pledging the family plate, ad met old Mr. Craven with the hammer in his hand. Seeing, no doubt, how impossible it ould be for him to clear himself without incriminating his father, he preferred flight to Natal giving evidence at the inquest."

"Now about his alias?" said Mr. Griffiths briskly, for the train was at that moment steaming to the station. "How did you know that Harold Cousins was identical with Harry Craven, and ad sailed in the *Bonnie Dundee*?"

"Oh, that was easy enough," said Loveday, as she stepped into the train; "a newspaper sent own to Mr. Craven by his wife, was folded so as to direct his attention to the shipping list. In it saw that the *Bonnie Dundee* had sailed two days previously for Natal. Now it was only natural connect Natal with Mrs. Craven, who had passed the greater part of her life there; and it was asy to understand her wish to get her scapegrace son among her early friends. The alias under hich he sailed came readily enough to light. I found it scribbled all over one of Mr. Craven's riting pads in his study; evidently it had been drummed into his ears by his wife as his son's ias, and the old gentleman had taken this method of fixing it in his memory. We'll hope that e young fellow, under his new name, will make a new reputation for himself – at any rate, he'll ave a better chance of doing so with the ocean between him and his evil companions. Now s goodbye, I think."

"No," said Mr. Griffiths; "it's au revoir, for you'll have to come back again for the assizes, and ve the evidence that will shut old Mr. Craven in an asylum for the rest of his life."

The Black Bag Left on a Door Step

Catherine Louisa Pirkis

"IT'S A BIG thing," said Loveday Brooke, addressing Ebenezer Dyer, chief of the well-know detective agency in Lynch Court, Fleet Street; "Lady Cathrow has lost £30,000 worth of jeweller if the newspaper accounts are to be trusted."

"They are fairly accurate this time. The robbery differs in few respects from the usu run of country-house robberies. The time chosen, of course, was the dinner-hour, when th family and guests were at table and the servants not on duty were amusing themselves i their own quarters. The fact of its being Christmas Eve would also of necessity add to th business and consequent distraction of the household. The entry to the house, however, i this case was not effected in the usual manner by a ladder to the dressing-room window, b through the window of a room on the ground floor – a small room with one window ar two doors, one of which opens into the hall, and the other into a passage that leads by th back stairs to the bedroom floor. It is used, I believe, as a sort of hat and coat room by th gentlemen of the house."

"It was, I suppose, the weak point of the house?"

"Quite so. A very weak point indeed. Craigen Court, the residence of Sir George and Lac Cathrow, is an oddly-built old place, jutting out in all directions, and as this window looked o upon a blank wall, it was filled in with stained glass, kept fastened by a strong brass catch, ar never opened, day or night, ventilation being obtained by means of a glass ventilator fitted the upper panes. It seems absurd to think that this window, being only about four feet fro the ground, should have had neither iron bars nor shutters added to it; such, however, wa the case. On the night of the robbery, someone within the house must have deliberately, ar of intention, unfastened its only protection, the brass catch, and thus given the thieves ea entrance to the house."

"Your suspicions, I suppose, centre upon the servants?"

"Undoubtedly; and it is in the servants' hall that your services will be required. The thieve whoever they were, were perfectly cognizant of the ways of the house. Lady Cathrow's jewelle was kept in a safe in her dressing-room, and as the dressing-room was over the dining-roor Sir George was in the habit of saying that it was the 'safest' room in the house. (Note th pun, please; Sir George is rather proud of it). By his orders the window of the dining-roo immediately under the dressing-room window was always left unshuttered and without blir during dinner, and as a full stream of light thus fell through it on to the outside terrace, it wou have been impossible for anyone to have placed a ladder there unseen."

"I see from the newspapers that it was Sir George's invariable custom to fill his house ar give a large dinner on Christmas Eve."

"Yes. Sir George and Lady Cathrow are elderly people, with no family and few relatives, ar have consequently a large amount of time to spend on their friends."

"I suppose the key of the safe was frequently left in the possession of Lady Cathrow's maid

"Yes. She is a young French girl, Stephanie Delcroix by name. It was her duty to clear the dressing-room directly after her mistress left it; put away any jewellery that might be lying about, lock the safe, and keep the key till her mistress came up to bed. On the night of the robbery, however, she admits that, instead of so doing, directly her mistress left the dressing-room, she ran down to the housekeeper's room to see if any letters had come for her, and remained chatting with the other servants for some time – she could not say for how long. It was by the half-past-seven post that her letters generally arrived from St. Omer, where her home is."

"Oh, then, she was in the habit of thus running down to enquire for her letters, no doubt, and the thieves, who appear to be so thoroughly cognizant of the house, would know this also."

"Perhaps; though at the present moment I must say things look very black against the girl. Her manner, too, when questioned, is not calculated to remove suspicion. She goes from one fit of hysterics into another; contradicts herself nearly every time she opens her mouth, then lays it to the charge of her ignorance of our language; breaks into voluble French; becomes theatrical in action, and then goes off into hysterics once more."

"All that is quite Français, you know," said Loveday. "Do the authorities at Scotland Yard lay much stress on the safe being left unlocked that night?"

"They do, and they are instituting a keen enquiry as to the possible lovers the girl may have. For this purpose they have sent Bates down to stay in the village and collect all the information he can outside the house. But they want someone within the walls to hob-nob with the maids generally, and to find out if she has taken any of them into her confidence respecting her lovers. So they sent to me to know if I would send down for this purpose one of the shrewdest and most clear-headed of my female detectives. I, in my turn, Miss Brooke, have sent for you – you may take it as a compliment if you like. So please now get out your notebook, and I'll give you sailing orders."

Loveday Brooke, at this period of her career, was a little over thirty years of age, and could be best described in a series of negations.

She was not tall, she was not short; she was not dark, she was not fair; she was neither handsome nor ugly. Her features were altogether nondescript; her one noticeable trait was a habit she had, when absorbed in thought, of dropping her eyelids over her eyes till only a line of eyeball showed, and she appeared to be looking out at the world through a slit, instead of through a window.

Her dress was invariably black, and was almost Quaker-like in its neat primness.

Some five or six years previously, by a jerk of Fortune's wheel, Loveday had been thrown upon the world penniless and all but friendless. Marketable accomplishments she had found she had none, so she had forthwith defied convention, and had chosen for herself a career that had cut her off sharply from her former associates and her position in society. For five or six years she drudged away patiently in the lower walks of her profession; then chance, or, to speak more precisely, an intricate criminal case, threw her in the way of the experienced head of the flourishing detective agency in Lynch Court. He quickly enough found out the stuff she was made of, and threw her in the way of better-class work – work, indeed, that brought increase of pay and of reputation alike to him and to Loveday.

Ebenezer Dyer was not, as a rule, given to enthusiasm; but he would at times wax eloquent over Miss Brooke's qualifications for the profession she had chosen.

"Too much of a lady, do you say?" he would say to anyone who chanced to call in question those qualifications. "I don't care twopence-halfpenny whether she is or is not a lady. I only know she is the most sensible and practical woman I ever met. In the first place, she has the faculty – so rare among women – of carrying out orders to the very letter: in the second place, she has a clear, shrewd brain, unhampered by any hard-and-fast theories; thirdly, and most important item of all, she has so much common sense that it amounts to genius – positively to genius, sir."

But although Loveday and her chief as a rule, worked together upon an easy and friendly footing, there were occasions on which they were wont, so to speak, to snarl at each other.

Such an occasion was at hand now.

Loveday showed no disposition to take out her notebook and receive her 'sailing orders.'

"I want to know," she said, "If what I saw in one newspaper is true – that one of the thieves before leaving, took the trouble to close the safe-door, and to write across it in chalk: 'To be let, unfurnished'?"

"Perfectly true; but I do not see that stress need be laid on the fact. The scoundrels often do that sort of thing out of insolence or bravado. In that robbery at Reigate, the other day, they went to a lady's Davenport, took a sheet of her notepaper, and wrote their thanks on it for her kindness in not having had the lock of her safe repaired. Now, if you will get out your notebook—"

"Don't be in such a hurry," said Loveday calmly: "I want to know if you have seen this?" She leaned across the writing-table at which they sat, one either side, and handed to him a newspaper cutting which she took from her letter-case.

Mr. Dyer was a tall, powerfully-built man with a large head, benevolent bald forehead and a genial smile. That smile, however, often proved a trap to the unwary, for he owned a temper so irritable that a child with a chance word might ruffle it.

The genial smile vanished as he took the newspaper cutting from Loveday's hand.

"I would have you to remember, Miss Brooke," he said severely, "that although I am in the habit of using dispatch in my business, I am never known to be in a hurry; hurry in affairs I take to be the especial mark of the slovenly and unpunctual."

Then, as if still further to give contradiction to her words, he very deliberately unfolded her slip of newspaper and slowly, accentuating each word and syllable, read as follows:

"Singular Discovery. A black leather bag, or portmanteau, was found early yesterday morning by one of Smith's newspaper boys on the doorstep of a house in the road running between Easterbrook and Wreford, and inhabited by an elderly spinster lady. The contents of the bag include a clerical collar and necktie, a Church Service, a book of sermons, a copy of the works of Virgil, a *facsimile* of Magna Charta, with translations, a pair of black kid gloves, a brush and comb, some newspapers, and several small articles suggesting clerical ownership. On the top of the bag the following extraordinary letter, written in pencil on a long slip of paper, was found:

> *'The fatal day has arrived. I can exist no longer. I go hence and shall be no more seen. But I would have Coroner and Jury know that I am a sane man, and a verdict of temporary insanity in my case would be an error most gross after this intimation. I care not if it is felo de se, as I shall have passed all suffering. Search diligently for my poor lifeless body in the immediate neighbourhood – on the cold heath, the rail, or the river by yonder bridge – a few moments will decide how I shall depart. If I had walked aright I might have been a power in the Church of which I am now an unworthy member and priest; but the damnable sin of gambling got hold on me, and betting has been my ruin, as it has been the ruin of thousands who have preceded me. Young man, shun the bookmaker and the race-course as you would shun the devil and hell. Farewell, chums of Magdalen. Farewell, and take warning. Though I can claim relationship with a Duke, a Marquess, and a Bishop, and though I am the son of a noble woman, yet am I a tramp and an outcast, verily*

and indeed. Sweet death, I greet thee. I dare not sign my name. To one and all, farewell. O, my poor Marchioness mother, a dying kiss to thee. R.I.P.'

"The police and some of the railway officials have made a 'diligent search' in the ighbourhood of the railway station, but no 'poor lifeless body' has been found. The lice authorities are inclined to the belief that the letter is a hoax, though they are still vestigating the matter."

In the same deliberate fashion as he had opened and read the cutting, Mr. Dyer folded d returned it to Loveday.

"May I ask," he said sarcastically, "what you see in that silly hoax to waste your and my luable time over?"

"I wanted to know," said Loveday, in the same level tones as before, "if you saw anything it that might in some way connect this discovery with the robbery at Craigen Court?"

Mr. Dyer stared at her in utter, blank astonishment.

"When I was a boy," he said sarcastically as before, "I used to play at a game called hat is my thought like?' Someone would think of something absurd – say the top of the onument – and someone else would hazard a guess that his thought might be – say the e of his left boot, and that unfortunate individual would have to show the connection tween the toe of his left boot and the top of the monument. Miss Brooke, I have no wish repeat the silly game this evening for your benefit and mine."

"Oh, very well," said Loveday, calmly; "I fancied you might like to talk it over, that was all. ve me my 'sailing orders,' as you call them, and I'll endeavour to concentrate my attention the little French maid and her various lovers."

Mr. Dyer grew amiable again.

"That's the point on which I wish you to fix your thoughts," he said; "you had better start Craigen Court by the first train tomorrow – it's about sixty miles down the Great Eastern e. Huxwell is the station you must land at. There one of the grooms from the Court will eet you, and drive you to the house. I have arranged with the housekeeper there – Mrs. lliams, a very worthy and discreet person – that you shall pass in the house for a niece of rs, on a visit to recruit, after severe study in order to pass board-school teachers' exams. turally you have injured your eyes as well as your health with overwork; and so you n wear your blue spectacles. Your name, by the way, will be Jane Smith – better write it wn. All your work will be among the servants of the establishment, and there will be no cessity for you to see either Sir George or Lady Cathrow – in fact, neither of them have en apprised of your intended visit – the fewer we take into our confidence the better. I've doubt, however, that Bates will hear from Scotland Yard that you are in the house, and ll make a point of seeing you."

"Has Bates unearthed anything of importance?"

"Not as yet. He has discovered one of the girl's lovers, a young farmer of the name Holt; but as he seems to be an honest, respectable young fellow, and entirely above spicion, the discovery does not count for much."

"I think there's nothing else to ask," said Loveday, rising to take her departure. "Of urse, I'll telegraph, should need arise, in our usual cipher."

The first train that left Bishopsgate for Huxwell on the following morning included, nong its passengers, Loveday Brooke, dressed in the neat black supposed to be appropriate servants of the upper class. The only literature with which she had provided herself in der to beguile the tedium of her journey was a small volume bound in paper boards, and entitled, "The Reciter's Treasury." It was published at the low price of one shilling, and seemed specially designed to meet the requirements of third-rate amateur reciters at penny readings.

Miss Brooke appeared to be all-absorbed in the contents of this book during the first half of her journey. During the second, she lay back in the carriage with closed eyes, and motionless as if asleep or lost in deep thought.

The stopping of the train at Huxwell aroused her, and set her collecting together her wraps.

It was easy to single out the trim groom from Craigen Court from among the country loafers on the platform. Someone else beside the trim groom at the same moment caught her eye – Bates, from Scotland Yard, got up in the style of a commercial traveler, and carrying the orthodox "commercial bag" in his hand. He was a small, wiry man, with red hair and whiskers, and an eager, hungry expression of countenance.

"I am half-frozen with cold," said Loveday, addressing Sir George's groom; "if you'll kindly take charge of my portmanteau, I'd prefer walking to driving to the Court."

The man gave her a few directions as to the road she was to follow, and then drove off with her box, leaving her free to indulge Mr. Bate's evident wish for a walk and confidential talk along the country road.

Bates seemed to be in a happy frame of mind that morning.

"Quite a simple affair, this, Miss Brooke," he said: "a walk over the course, I take it, with you working inside the castle walls and I unearthing without. No complications as yet have arisen, and if that girl does not find herself in jail before another week is over her head, my name is not Jeremiah Bates."

"You mean the French maid?"

"Why, yes, of course. I take it there's little doubt but what she performed the double duty of unlocking the safe and the window too. You see I look at it this way, Miss Brooke: all girls have lovers, I say to myself, but a pretty girl like that French maid, is bound to have double the number of lovers than the plain ones. Now, of course, the greater the number of lovers, the greater the chance there is of a criminal being found among them. That's plain as a pikestaff, isn't it?"

"Just as plain."

Bates felt encouraged to proceed.

"Well, then, arguing on the same lines, I say to myself, this girl is only a pretty, silly thing not an accomplished criminal, or she wouldn't have admitted leaving open the safe door give her rope enough and she'll hang herself. In a day or two, if we let her alone, she'll b bolting off to join the fellow whose nest she has helped to feather, and we shall catch th pair of them 'twixt here and Dover Straits, and also possibly get a clue that will bring us o the traces of their accomplices. Eh, Miss Brooke, that'll be a thing worth doing?"

"Undoubtedly. Who is this coming along in this buggy at such a good pace?"

The question was added as the sound of wheels behind them made her look round.

Bates turned also. "Oh, this is young Holt; his father farms land about a couple of mile from here. He is one of Stephanie's lovers, and I should imagine about the best of the lo But he does not appear to be first favourite; from what I hear someone else must hav made the running on the sly. Ever since the robbery I'm told the young woman has give him the cold shoulder."

As the young man came nearer in his buggy he slackened pace, and Loveday could n but admire his frank, honest expression of countenance.

"Room for one – can I give you a lift?" he said, as he came alongside of them.

And to the ineffable disgust of Bates, who had counted upon at least an hour's confidential talk with her, Miss Brooke accepted the young farmer's offer, and mounted beside him in his buggy.

As they went swiftly along the country road, Loveday explained to the young man that her destination was Craigen Court, and that as she was a stranger to the place, she must trust to him to put her down at the nearest point to it that he would pass.

At the mention of Craigen Court his face clouded.

"They're in trouble there, and their trouble has brought trouble on others," he said a little bitterly.

"I know," said Loveday sympathetically; "it is often so. In such circumstances as these suspicions frequently fastens on an entirely innocent person."

"That's it! that's it!" he cried excitedly; "if you go into that house you'll hear all sorts of wicked things said of her, and see everything setting in dead against her. But she's innocent. I swear to you she is as innocent as you or I are."

His voice rang out above the clatter of his horse's hoots. He seemed to forget that he had mentioned no name, and that Loveday, as a stranger, might be at a loss to know to whom he referred.

"Who is guilty Heaven only knows," he went on after a moment's pause; "it isn't for me to give an ill name to anyone in that house; but I only say she is innocent, and that I'll stake my life on."

"She is a lucky girl to have found one to believe in her, and trust her as you do," said Loveday, even more sympathetically than before.

"Is she? I wish she'd take advantage of her luck, then," he answered bitterly. "Most girls in her position would be glad to have a man to stand by them through thick and thin. But not she! Ever since the night of that accursed robbery she has refused to see me – won't answer my letters – won't even send me a message. And, great Heavens! I'd marry her tomorrow, if I had the chance, and dare the world to say a word against her."

He whipped up his pony. The hedges seemed to fly on either side of them, and before Loveday realized that half her drive was over, he had drawn rein, and was helping her to alight at the servants' entrance to Craigen Court.

"You'll tell her what I've said to you, if you get the opportunity, and beg her to see me, if only for five minutes?" he petitioned before he re-mounted his buggy. And Loveday, as she thanked the young man for his kind attention, promised to make an opportunity to give his message to the girl.

Mrs. Williams, the housekeeper, welcomed Loveday in the servants' hall, and then took her to her own room to pull off her wraps. Mrs. Williams was the widow of a London tradesman, and a little beyond the average housekeeper in speech and manner.

She was a genial, pleasant woman, and readily entered into conversation with Loveday. Tea was brought in, and each seemed to feel at home with the other. Loveday in the course of this easy, pleasant talk, elicited from her the whole history of the events of the day of the robbery, the number and names of the guests who sat down to dinner that night, together with some other apparently trivial details.

The housekeeper made no attempt to disguise the painful position in which she and every one of the servants of the house felt themselves to be at the present moment.

"We are none of us at our ease with each other now," she said, as she poured out hot tea for Loveday, and piled up a blazing fire. "Everyone fancies that everyone else is suspecting him or her, and trying to rake up past words or deeds to bring in as evidence. The whole house seems under a cloud. And at this time of year, too; just when everything as a rule is at its merriest!" and here she gave a doleful glance to the big bunch of holly and mistletoe hanging from the ceiling.

"I suppose you are generally very merry downstairs at Christmas time?" said Loveday. "Servants' balls, theatricals, and all that sort of thing?"

"I should think we were! When I think of this time last year and the fun we all had, I can scarcely believe it is the same house. Our ball always follows my lady's ball, and we have permission to ask our friends to it, and we keep it up as late as ever we please. We begin our evening with a concert and recitations in character, then we have a supper and then we dance right on till morning; but this year!" – she broke off, giving a long, melancholy shake of her head that spoke volumes.

"I suppose," said Loveday, "some of your friends are very clever as musicians or reciters?"

"Very clever indeed. Sir George and my lady are always present during the early part of the evening, and I should like you to have seen Sir George last year laughing fit to kill himself at Harry Emmett dressed in prison dress with a bit of oakum in his hand, reciting the "Noble Convict!" Sir George said if the young man had gone on the stage, he would have been bound to make his fortune."

"Half a cup, please," said Loveday, presenting her cup. "Who was this Harry Emmett then – a sweetheart of one of the maids?"

"Oh, he would flirt with them all, but he was sweetheart to none. He was footman to Colonel James, who is a great friend of Sir George's, and Harry was constantly backwards and forwards bringing messages from his master. His father, I think, drove a cab in London, and Harry for a time did so also; then he took it into his head to be a gentleman's servant, and great satisfaction he gave as such. He was always such a bright, handsome young fellow and so full of fun, that everyone liked him. But I shall tire you with all this; and you, of course, want to talk about something so different;" and the housekeeper sighed again, as the thought of the dreadful robbery entered her brain once more.

"Not at all. I am greatly interested in you and your festivities. Is Emmett still in the neighbourhood? I should amazingly like to hear him recite myself."

"I'm sorry to say he left Colonel James about six months ago. We all missed him very much at first. He was a good, kind-hearted young man, and I remember he told me he was going away to look after his dear old grandmother, who had a sweet-stuff shop somewhere or other, but where I can't remember."

Loveday was leaning back in her chair now, with eyelids drooped so low that she literally looked out through "slits" instead of eyes.

Suddenly and abruptly she changed the conversation.

"When will it be convenient for me to see Lady Cathrow's dressing-room?" she asked.

The housekeeper looked at her watch. "Now, at once," she answered: "it's a quarter to five now and my lady sometimes goes up to her room to rest for half an hour before she dresses for dinner."

"Is Stephanie still in attendance on Lady Cathrow?" Miss Brooke asked as she followed the housekeeper up the back stairs to the bedroom floor.

"Yes, Sir George and my lady have been goodness itself to us through this trying time, and they say we are all innocent till we are proved guilty, and will have it that none of our duties are to be in any way altered."

"Stephanie is scarcely fit to perform hers, I should imagine?"

"Scarcely. She was in hysterics nearly from morning till night for the first two or three days ter the detectives came down, but now she has grown sullen, eats nothing and never speaks vord to any of us except when she is obliged. This is my lady's dressing-room, walk in please."

Loveday entered a large, luxuriously furnished room, and naturally made her way straight to e chief point of attraction in it – the iron safe fitted into the wall that separated the dressing-om from the bedroom.

It was a safe of the ordinary description, fitted with a strong iron door and Chubb lock. And ross this door was written with chalk in characters that seemed defiant in their size and ldness, the words: "To be let, unfurnished."

Loveday spent about five minutes in front of this safe, all her attention concentrated upon e big, bold writing.

She took from her pocket-book a narrow strip of tracing-paper and compared the writing it, letter by letter, with that on the safe door. This done she turned to Mrs. Williams and ofessed herself ready to follow her to the room below.

Mrs. Williams looked surprised. Her opinion of Miss Brooke's professional capabilities ffered considerable diminution.

"The gentlemen detectives," she said, "spent over an hour in this room; they paced the floor, ey measured the candles, they—"

"Mrs. Williams," interrupted Loveday, "I am quite ready to look at the room below." Her anner had changed from gossiping friendliness to that of the business woman hard at work her profession.

Without another word, Mrs. Williams led the way to the little room which had proved itself be the "weak point" of the house.

They entered it by the door which opened into a passage leading to the back-stairs of the use. Loveday found the room exactly what it had been described to her by Mr. Dyer. It needed second glance at the window to see the ease with which anyone could open it from the tside, and swing themselves into the room, when once the brass catch had been unfastened.

Loveday wasted no time here. In fact, much to Mrs. Williams's surprise and disappointment, e merely walked across the room, in at one door and out at the opposite one, which opened o the large inner hall of the house.

Here, however, she paused to ask a question:

"Is that chair always placed exactly in that position?" she said, pointing to an oak chair that od immediately outside the room they had just quitted.

The housekeeper answered in the affirmative. It was a warm corner. "My lady" was particular at everyone who came to the house on messages should have a comfortable place to wait in.

"I shall be glad if you will show me to my room now," said Loveday, a little abruptly; "and ll you kindly send up to me a county trade directory, if, that is, you have such a thing in e house?"

Mrs. Williams, with an air of offended dignity, led the way to the bedroom quarters once ore. The worthy housekeeper felt as if her own dignity had, in some sort, been injured by e want of interest Miss Brooke had evinced in the rooms which, at the present moment, she nsidered the "show" rooms of the house.

"Shall I send someone to help you unpack?" she asked, a little stiffly, at the door of veday's room.

"No, thank you; there will not be much unpacking to do. I must leave here by the first up-in tomorrow morning."

"Tomorrow morning! Why, I have told everyone you will be here at least a fortnight!"

"Ah, then you must explain that I have been suddenly summoned home by telegram. I'm sure I can trust you to make excuses for me. Do not, however, make them before supper-time. I shall like to sit down to that meal with you. I suppose I shall see Stephanie then?"

The housekeeper answered in the affirmative, and went her way, wondering over the strange manners of the lady whom, at first, she had been disposed to consider "such a nice, pleasant, conversable person!"

At supper-time, however, when the upper-servants assembled at what was, to them, the pleasantest meal of the day, a great surprise was to greet them.

Stephanie did not take her usual place at table, and a fellow-servant, sent to her room to summon her returned, saying that the room was empty, and Stephanie was nowhere to be found.

Loveday and Mrs. Williams together went to the girl's bed-room. It bore its usual appearance: no packing had been done in it, and, beyond her hat and jacket, the girl appeared to have taken nothing away with her.

On enquiry, it transpired that Stephanie had, as usual, assisted Lady Cathrow to dress for dinner; but after that not a soul in the house appeared to have seen her.

Mrs. Williams thought the matter of sufficient importance to be at once reported to her master and mistress; and Sir George, in his turn, promptly dispatched a messenger to Mr. Bates, at the "King's Head," to summon him to an immediate consultation.

Loveday dispatched a messenger in another direction – to young Mr. Holt, at his farm, giving him particulars of the girl's disappearance.

Mr. Bates had a brief interview with Sir George in his study, from which he emerged radiant. He made a point of seeing Loveday before he left the Court, sending a special request to her that she would speak to him for a minute in the outside drive.

Loveday put her hat on, and went out to him. She found him almost dancing for glee.

"Told you so! told you so! Now, didn't I, Miss Brooke?" he exclaimed. "We'll come upon her traces before morning, never fear. I'm quite prepared. I knew what was in her mind al along. I said to myself, when that girl bolts it will be after she has dressed my lady for dinne – when she has two good clear hours all to herself, and her absence from the house won' be noticed, and when, without much difficulty, she can catch a train leaving Huxwell fo Wreford. Well, she'll get to Wreford safe enough; but from Wreford she'll be followed ever step of the way she goes. Only yesterday I set a man on there – a keen fellow at this sort o thing – and gave him full directions; and he'll hunt her down to her hole properly. Take nothing with her, do you say? What does that matter? She thinks she'll find all she want where she's going – 'the feathered nest' I spoke to you about this morning. Ha! ha! Wel instead of stepping into it, as she fancies she will, she'll walk straight into a detective's arm and land her pal there into the bargain. There'll be two of them netted before anothe forty-eight hours are over our heads, or my name's not Jeremiah Bates."

"What are you going to do now?" asked Loveday, as the man finished his long speech.

"Now! I'm back to the "King's Head" to wait for a telegram from my colleague Wreford. Once he's got her in front of him he'll give me instructions at what point t meet him. You see, Huxwell being such an out-of-the-way place, and only one tra leaving between 7.30 and 10.15, makes us really positive that Wreford must be the gir destination and relieves my mind from all anxiety on the matter."

"Does it?" answered Loveday gravely. "I can see another possible destination for the girl – the stream that runs through the wood we drove past this morning. Good night, Mr. Bates, it's cold out here. Of course so soon as you have any news you'll send it up to Sir George."

The household sat up late that night, but no news was received of Stephanie from any quarter. Mr. Bates had impressed upon Sir George the ill-advisability of setting up a hue and cry after the girl that might possibly reach her ears and scare her from joining the person whom he was pleased to designate as her 'pal.'

"We want to follow her silently, Sir George, silently as, the shadow follows the man," he had said grandiloquently, "and then we shall come upon the two, and I trust upon their booty also." Sir George in his turn had impressed Mr. Bates's wishes upon his household, and if it had not been for Loveday's message, dispatched early in the evening to young Holt, not a soul outside the house would have known of Stephanie's disappearance.

Loveday was stirring early the next morning, and the eight o'clock train for Wreford numbered her among its passengers. Before starting, she dispatched a telegram to her chief in Lynch Court. It read rather oddly, as follows:

Cracker fired. Am just starting for Wreford. Will wire to you from there. L.B.

Oddly though it might read, Mr. Dyer did not need to refer to his cipher book to interpret it. 'Cracker fired' was the easily remembered equivalent for 'clue found' in the detective phraseology of the office.

"Well, she has been quick enough about it this time!" he soliquised as he speculated in his own mind over what the purport of the next telegram might be.

Half an hour later there came to him a constable from Scotland Yard to tell him of Stephanie's disappearance and the conjectures that were rife on the matter, and he then, not unnaturally, read Loveday's telegram by the light of this information, and concluded that the clue in her hands related to the discovery of Stephanie's whereabouts as well as to that of her guilt.

A telegram received a little later on, however, was to turn this theory upside down. It was, like the former one, worded in the enigmatic language current in the Lynch Court establishment, but as it was a lengthier and more intricate message, it sent Mr. Dyer at once to his cipher book.

"Wonderful! She has cut them all out this time!" was Mr. Dyer's exclamation as he read and interpreted the final word.

In another ten minutes he had given over his office to the charge of his head clerk for the day, and was rattling along the streets in a hansom in the direction of Bishopsgate Station.

There he was lucky enough to catch a train just starting for Wreford.

"The event of the day," he muttered, as he settled himself comfortably in a corner seat, 'will be the return journey when she tells me, bit by bit, how she has worked it all out."

It was not until close upon three o'clock in the afternoon that he arrived at the old-fashioned market town of Wreford. It chanced to be cattle-market day, and the station was crowded with drovers and farmers. Outside the station Loveday was waiting for him, as she had told him in her telegram that she would, in a four-wheeler.

"It's all right," she said to him as he got in; "he can't get away, even if he had an idea that we were after him. Two of the local police are waiting outside the house door with a warrant for his arrest, signed by a magistrate. I did not, however, see why the Lynch Court office should not have the credit of the thing, and so telegraphed to you to conduct the arrest."

They drove through the High Street to the outskirts of the town, where the shops became intermixed with private houses let out in offices. The cab pulled up outside one of these, and two policemen in plain clothes came forward, and touched their hats to Mr. Dyer.

"He's in there now, sir, doing his office work," said one of the men pointing to a door, just within the entrance, on which was printed in black letters, "The United Kingdom Cab-drivers' Beneficent Association." "I hear however, that this is the last time he will be found there, as a week ago he gave notice to leave."

As the man finished speaking, a man, evidently of the cab-driving fraternity, came up the steps. He stared curiously at the little group just within the entrance, and then chinking his money in his hand, passed on to the office as if to pay his subscription.

"Will you be good enough to tell Mr. Emmett in there," said Mr. Dyer, addressing the man, "that a gentleman outside wishes to speak with him."

The man nodded and passed into the office. As the door opened, it disclosed to view an old gentleman seated at a desk apparently writing receipts for money. A little in his rear at his right hand, sat a young and decidedly good-looking man, at a table on which were placed various little piles of silver and pence. The get-up of this young man was gentleman-like, and his manner was affable and pleasant as he responded, with a nod and a smile, to the cab-driver's message.

"I sha'n't be a minute," he said to his colleague at the other desk, as he rose and crossed the room towards the door.

But once outside that door it was closed firmly behind him, and he found himself in the centre of three stalwart individuals, one of whom informed him that he held in his hand a warrant for the arrest of Harry Emmett on the charge of complicity in the Craigen Court robbery, and that he had "better come along quietly, for resistance would be useless."

Emmett seemed convinced of the latter fact. He grew deadly white for a moment, then recovered himself.

"Will someone have the kindness to fetch my hat and coat," he said in a lofty manner. "I don't see why I should be made to catch my death of cold because some other people have seen fit to make asses of themselves."

His hat and coat were fetched, and he was handed into the cab between the two officials.

"Let me give you a word of warning, young man," said Mr. Dyer, closing the cab door and looking in for a moment through the window at Emmett. "I don't suppose it's a punishable offence to leave a black bag on an old maid's doorstep, but let me tell you, if it had not been for that black bag you might have got clean off with your spoil."

Emmett, the irrepressible, had his answer ready. He lifted his hat ironically to Mr. Dyer; "You might have put it more neatly, guv'nor," he said; "if I had been in your place I would have said: 'Young man, you are being justly punished for your misdeeds; you have been taking off your fellow-creatures all your life long, and now they are taking off you.'"

Mr. Dyer's duty that day did not end with the depositing of Harry Emmett in the local jail. The search through Emmett's lodgings and effects had to be made, and at this he was naturally present. About a third of the lost jewellery was found there, and from this it was consequently concluded that his accomplices in the crime had considered that he had borne a third of the risk and of the danger of it.

Letters and various memoranda discovered in the rooms, eventually led to the detection of those accomplices, and although Lady Cathrow was doomed to lose the greater part of her valuable property, she had ultimately the satisfaction of knowing that each one of the thieves received a sentence proportionate to his crime.

It was not until close upon midnight that Mr. Dyer found himself seated in the train, facing Miss Brooke, and had leisure to ask for the links in the chain of reasoning that had led her in so remarkable a manner to connect the finding of a black bag, with insignificant contents, with an extensive robbery of valuable jewellery.

Loveday explained the whole thing, easily, naturally, step by step in her usual methodical manner.

"I read," she said, "as I dare say a great many other people did, the account of the two things in the same newspaper, on the same day, and I detected, as I dare say a great many other people did not, a sense of fun in the principal actor in each incident. I notice while all people are agreed as to the variety of motives that instigate crime, very few allow sufficient margin for variety of character in the criminal. We are apt to imagine that he stalks about the world with a bundle of deadly motives under his arm, and cannot picture him at his work with a twinkle in his eye and a keen sense of fun, such as honest folk have sometimes when at work at their calling."

Here Mr. Dyer gave a little grunt; it might have been either of assent or dissent.

Loveday went on:

"Of course, the ludicrousness of the diction of the letter found in the bag would be apparent to the most casual reader; to me the high falutin sentences sounded in addition strangely familiar; I had heard or read them somewhere I felt sure, although where I could not at first remember. They rang in my ears, and it was not altogether out of idle curiosity that I went to Scotland Yard to see the bag and its contents, and to copy, with a slip of tracing paper, a line or two of the letter. When I found that the handwriting of this letter was not identical with that of the translations found in the bag, I was confirmed in my impression that the owner of the bag was not the writer of the letter; that possibly the bag and its contents had been appropriated from some railway station for some distinct purpose; and, that purpose accomplished, the appropriator no longer wished to be burthened with it, and disposed of it in the readiest fashion that suggested itself. The letter, it seemed to me, had been begun with the intention of throwing the police off the scent, but the irrepressible spirit of fun that had induced the writer to deposit his clerical adjuncts upon an old maid's doorstep had proved too strong for him here, and had carried him away, and the letter that was intended to be pathetic ended in being comic."

"Very ingenious, so far," murmured Mr. Dyer: "I've no doubt when the contents of the bag are widely made known through advertisements a claimant will come forward, and your theory be found correct."

"When I returned from Scotland Yard," Loveday continued, "I found your note, asking me to go round and see you respecting the big jewel robbery. Before I did so I thought it best to read once more the newspaper account of the case, so that I might be well up in its details. When I came to the words that the thief had written across the door of the safe, 'To be Let, Unfurnished,' they at once connected themselves in my mind with the 'dying kiss to my Marchioness Mother,' and the solemn warning against the race-course and the book-maker, of the black-bag letter-writer. Then, all in a flash, the whole thing became clear to me. Some two or three years back my professional duties necessitated my frequent attendance at certain low class penny-readings, given in the South London slums. At these penny-readings young shop-assistants, and others of their class, glad of an opportunity for exhibiting their accomplishments, declaim with great vigour; and, as a rule, select pieces which their very mixed audience might be supposed to appreciate. During my attendance at these meetings, it seemed to me that one book of selecte readings was a great favourite among the reciters, and I took the trouble to buy it. Here it is."

Here Loveday took from her cloak-pocket "The Reciter's Treasury," and handed it t her companion.

"Now," she said, "if you will run your eye down the index column you will find the titles c those pieces to which I wish to draw your attention. The first is 'The Suicide's Farewell;' th second, 'The Noble Convict;' the third, 'To be Let, Unfurnished.'"

"By Jove! so it is!" ejaculated Mr. Dyer.

"In the first of these pieces, 'The Suicide's Farewell,' occur the expressions with which th black-bag letter begins – 'The fatal day has arrived,' etc., the warnings against gambling, an the allusions to the 'poor lifeless body.' In the second, 'The Noble Convict,' occur the allusion to the aristocratic relations and the dying kiss to the marchioness mother. The third piece, 'T be Let, Unfurnished,' is a foolish little poem enough, although I dare say it has often raised laugh in a not too-discriminating audience. It tells how a bachelor, calling at a house to enquir after rooms to be let unfurnished, falls in love with the daughter of the house, and offers he his heart, which, he says, is to be let unfurnished. She declines his offer, and retorts that sh thinks his head must be to let unfurnished, too. With these three pieces before me, it was nc difficult to see a thread of connection between the writer of the black-bag letter and the thie who wrote across the empty safe at Craigen Court. Following this thread, I unearthed the stor of Harry Emmett – footman, reciter, general lover and scamp. Subsequently I compared th writing on my tracing paper with that on the safe-door, and, allowing for the difference betwee a bit of chalk and a steel nib, came to the conclusion that there could be but little doubt but wha both were written by the same hand. Before that, however, I had obtained another, and what consider the most important, link in my chain of evidence – how Emmett brought his cleric dress into use."

"Ah, how did you find out that now?" asked Mr. Dyer, leaning forward with his elbows o his knees.

"In the course of conversation with Mrs. Williams, whom I found to be a most communicativ person, I elicited the names of the guests who had sat down to dinner on Christmas Eve. The were all people of undoubted respectability in the neighbourhood. Just before dinner wa announced, she said, a young clergyman had presented himself at the front door, asking t speak with the Rector of the parish. The Rector, it seems, always dines at Craigen Court o Christmas Eve. The young clergyman's story was that he had been told by a certain clergyma whose name he mentioned, that a curate was wanted in the parish, and he had traveled dow from London to offer his services. He had been, he said, to the Rectory and had been told by th servants where the Rector was dining, and fearing to lose his chance of the curacy, had followe him to the Court. Now the Rector had been wanting a curate and had filled the vacancy only th previous week; he was a little inclined to be irate at this interruption to the evening's festivitie and told the young man that he didn't want a curate. When, however, he saw how disappointe the poor young fellow looked – I believe he shed a tear or two – his heart softened; he tol him to sit down and rest in the hall before he attempted the walk back to the station, and sai he would ask Sir George to send him out a glass of wine. the young man sat down in a cha immediately outside the room by which the thieves entered. Now I need not tell you who th young man was, nor suggest to your mind, I am sure, the idea that while the servant went t fetch him his wine, or, indeed, so soon as he saw the coast clear, he slipped into that little roor and pulled back the catch of the window that admitted his confederates, who, no doubt, that very moment were in hiding in the grounds. The housekeeper did not know whether th meek young curate had a black bag with him. Personally I have no doubt of the fact, nor that it contained the cap, cuffs, collar, and outer garments of Harry Emmett, which were most likely redonned before he returned to his lodgings at Wreford, where I should say he repacked the bag with its clerical contents, and wrote his serio-comic letter. This bag, I suppose, he must have deposited in the very early morning, before anyone was stirring, on the door step of the house in the Easterbrook Road."

Mr. Dyer drew a long breath. In his heart was unmitigated admiration for his colleague's skill, which seemed to him to fall little short of inspiration. By-and-by, no doubt, he would sing her praises to the first person who came along with a hearty good will; he had not, however, the slightest intention of so singing them in her own ears – excessive praise was apt to have a bad effect on the rising practitioner.

So he contented himself with saying:

"Yes, very satisfactory. Now tell me how you hunted the fellow down to his diggings?"

"Oh, that was mere ABC work," answered Loveday. "Mrs. Williams told me he had left his place at Colonel James's about six months previously, and had told her he was going to look after his dear old grandmother, who kept a sweet stuff-shop; but where she could not remember. Having heard that Emmett's father was a cab-driver, my thoughts at once flew to the cabman's vernacular – you know something of it, no doubt – in which their provident association is designated by the phase, 'the dear old grandmother,' and the office where they make and receive their payments is styled 'the sweet stuff-shop.'"

"Ha, ha, ha! And good Mrs. Williams took it all literally, no doubt?"

"She did; and thought what a dear, kind-hearted fellow the young man was. Naturally I supposed there would be a branch of the association in the nearest market town, and a local trades' directory confirmed my supposition that there was one at Wreford. Bearing in mind where the black bag was found, it was not difficult to believe that young Emmett, possibly through his father's influence and his own prepossessing manners and appearance, had attained to some position of trust in the Wreford branch. I must confess I scarcely expected to find him as I did, on reaching the place, installed as receiver of the weekly moneys. Of course, I immediately put myself in communication with the police there, and the rest I think you know."

Mr. Dyer's enthusiasm refused to be longer restrained.

"It's capital, from first to last," he cried; "you've surpassed yourself this time!"

"The only thing that saddens me," said Loveday, "is the thought of the possible fate of that poor little Stephanie."

Loveday's anxieties on Stephanie's behalf were, however, to be put to flight before another twenty-four hours had passed. The first post on the following morning brought a letter from Mrs. Williams telling how the girl had been found before the night was over, half dead with cold and fright, on the verge of the stream running through Craigen Wood – 'found too' – wrote the housekeeper, 'by the very person who ought to have found her, young Holt, who was, and is so desperately in love with her. Thank goodness! At the last moment her courage failed her, and instead of throwing herself into the stream, she sank down, half-fainting, beside it. Holt took her straight home to his mother, and there, at the farm, she is now, being taken care of and petted generally by everyone.'

The I's Have It

Annette Siketa

Chapter I

SITTING IN HIS OFFICE in the Rockford police station, Detective Inspector John Simmonds tossed the evening paper onto his desk. "I will never understand it," he admitted to Detective Mike Furrow, a recently arrived subordinate. "The more gruesome and outlandish a murder, the more the public lap it up, and the media are only too happy to feed the voracious appetite." He pointed to a headline. 'Is society safe?' "It's difficult enough to catch a serial killer, without the public's paranoia being fed into the bargain." He peered into his lukewarm cup of tea. "The Rockford Ripper indeed!"

The so-called 'Rockford Ripper' had murdered seven high profile women to date, the more notable being Charlene Tusset, youngest daughter of local peer Sir Edward Tusset. The others were two dynastic heiresses, three socialites, and the fiancée of an upwardly mobile politician. All had been injected with an undiluted narcotic - presumably to render them helpless, and then while still alive, their face and hair had been hacked to pieces. In addition, they had been sexually assaulted but not raped. Arguably, their eventual strangulation was a merciful end.

Clues were few and far between. Several dark brown hairs had been found near the bodies, but DNA revealed they came from a wig. Nor was there a social link, for although some of the victims had attended the same functions, none were close friends. Apart from being successful and attractive, there was no tangible connection between the women.

According to the experts, the killer was defined by three I's. Invisibility – he thinks he blended into the background. Invincibility – in that he was too clever to be caught. Lastly, and paradoxically, he suffered from a massive inferiority complex. By targeting the elite, he was trying to prove – though goodness knew to whom, that by having the power of life over death, he was far superior than his victim. Outwardly, he was ordinary to the point of blandness. Inwardly, he was completely insane.

Following the death of Charlene Tusset, security surrounding Rockford's social elite had rapidly increased. And yet in spite of the heightened awareness and the increased police patrols, the murders had continued, and now the media were baying for blood.

Furrow looked at the headline. "I don't know what else you can do, sir. Witness statements have been checked and double checked, alibis incontrovertibly verified and anyone with even the smallest link to a victim has been interviewed."

Inspector Simmonds picked up his cup. "And yet we're getting nowhere." He took a drink of tea. "Ouch!" He winced and clutched his jaw.

"Your tooth?" asked the subordinate sympathetically. The inspector's fondness for desserts was well known amongst his troops, and the eruption of a molar was not helping matters. "There's a dentist around the corner. Why don't you nip round and have it seen too? Its not like we'll be making an arrest anytime soon."

* * *

Like most people, Inspector Simmonds had a morbid fear of dentists, and twenty minutes later when he sat in the dreaded black chair, he tried to think of anything that would distract him from needles and novocaine. His gaze fell on a child's drawing pinned to a wall. It depicted a horse and rider about to jump a fence. There was also a colourful array of unlikely looking flowers, and for clouds, the young hand had drawn an irregular series of concentric circles.

"Your daughter's?" he slurred to the dentist, who with instrument in hand, was ready to pull the tooth.

"No, just a grateful patient. Now, open wide, this won't hurt a bit."

* * *

When the Inspector returned to the station a short time later, there was a very determined look on his face. Still with the gauze pad in his mouth, he closed the door of his office and re-read every document on the murders, and some three hours later he knew the identity of the killer. However, there wasn't a shred of proof.

The following morning, he discussed an audacious plan with the Chief Constable. Unfortunately, 'Operation Blindside' was barely legal, and so to prevent any potential cry of 'entrapment, the Chief Constable insisted on the inclusion of a creditable outsider who was wholly disconnected from the case. Inspector Simmonds protested vehemently but could have saved his breath. His superior already had someone in mind, and four days later the killer was caught.

Chapter II

WITH ONE exception, Tilly Bellingham did not know any of her guests. However, they certainly knew her, or more accurately, her name. A British born heiress who lived primarily in Australia, she was in Rockford on a private visit and staying at the exquisite home of a famous, movie producer cousin. To show her – albeit late, support for her social brethren, she had decided to hold a dinner party. Such was her reputation that it would have been social suicide to refuse the invitation.

Tilly turned on the six o'clock news. She watched as Patrick Thomas Evans, a 26-year-old plumber described as a loner, was led into court.

"He doesn't look much like the photofit," she murmured, and along with a hired cook, continued preparations.

The guest list - four middle aged couples and two elderly singles, was a good representation of Rockford's elite. Brushing her waist-length blonde hair, Tilly tried to calculate their combined worth, but gave up when her head began to spin.

The first to arrive were David and Tessa Marks. Her father was a long-standing councillor and one time Rockford mayor. David Marks was a renowned architect. His long public battle with the tax department, which he had won the previous week, had made him an accountants' hero.

Next to arrive, and all in one car, were Billy and Christie Pascoe, and Paul and Sarah Hopkins. Christie, being a non- drinker, was the designated driver. This was not unusual, for in addition to salacious gossip, Billy had a reputation for hard drinking, and from the way he stumbled out of the car, it was clear that he had already indulged in pre-dinner drinks.

He had made his fortune in private security, and his clientele included some very prominent names, including Sir Edward Tusset. He was also a notorious lethario, renowned for his constant change of secretaries.

Paul and Sarah Hopkins were childhood sweethearts. After leaving school, they had worked long and hard to establish a business and now owned a national chain of supermarkets. Although timid by nature, Sarah was an impeccable hostess, and an invitation to her summer barbecues was a 'must' on the social calendar. As one socialite cattily proclaimed, "Nobody can cook a sausage like Sarah."

The two singles - Colonel Edward Beeton and Mrs. Ada Harris, arrived separately but simultaneously. Colonel Beeton had retired from the Foreign Office some five years earlier, and was one of those 'insiders ' who knew more than was perhaps good for him. Mrs. Harris was plump and pink-cheeked and incredibly 'nosey'. She was also related to Sir Edward Tusset, father of the ill fated, Charlene.

The last to arrive - Vladimir and Angelica Putzin, were the type of couple who attracted speculation. They had moved to Rockford shortly before the first murder, and although their wealth had provided an entrance into society, many of the elite had still not taken them to their gold-plated bosoms. The main problem was that they were too plain and conservative to be typical Russian immigrants. It pleased the gossip mongers to have Vladimir connected to the Russian mafia, and Angelica, with her mass of flaming red curls, to be the biggest Madam in the Soviet bloc, providing everything from mail order brides to white slaves.

The Putzin's were too bemused by this description to correct it. The truth was that, like many fleeing oppression, they had arrived in the country penniless, and after working hard and taking several extraordinary risks, they now owned a vast electronics conglomerate.

* * *

Christie Pascoe sipped a glass of mineral water. "Thank goodness the police have finally arrested the fiend. I don't know about you, Tessa, but I for one will now sleep soundly."

Tessa Marks, her fair hair and complexion accentuated by a bottle green dress, raised a perfectly plucked eyebrow. "I think its a little early to be relaxing. I mean, how do we know the police have the right man?"

"What do you mean, 'now sleep soundly'?" said Billy Pascoe, coming forward to join the conversation. "You always sleep soundly. I can never wake you up."

Christie looked at her husband with icy indifference. "That's because whenever you deign to come to bed, you're practically comatose." She smiled acidly and turned back to Tessa. "We can all rest easy, the police wouldn't dare arrest the wrong man. Now, if you'll excuse me, I must go and discover who that distinguished looking gentleman is." She waltzed away in a haze of lemon chiffon, her smooth glossy shoulder length blonde hair a credit to Clairol.

Tessa took an unsteady gulp of her gin & tonic. "Do you think she's right, Billy? I wish I could feel as confident."

Billy slipped an arm around her waist, his breath reeking of stale whiskey. "Well, if the police have it wrong, I'll be happy to come and tuck you into bed."

Tessa did not know which repulsed her the most - his slimy touch or his overture of adultery. She was no shrinking violet, and as she pushed his hand away, she wondered why Christie put up with him.

"If you would excuse me," she said curtly, "I must powder my nose," and as she walked away, Billy watched her with lustful eyes.

Her husband and Paul Hopkins were standing at a small but well-stocked bar. "Congratulations, David. You certainly scored one for the underdogs."

David lit a small cigar. "Typical government department. All the paperwork was correct, but some lazy bastard hadn't processed it properly. What gets me is that if I hadn't put up a fight, I might now be sharing a cell with that murderer."

Paul grinned. "And in all likelihood attracting a sentence just as long." He looked around for his wife. Sarah had just entered the room. Her fresh lipstick and designer tousled black hair were a clear signal as to her recent locale. She literally bumped into Christie Pascoe, who was heading towards Colonel Beeton. "Do you know who the oldies are?" said Paul, surreptitiously wafting the cigar smoke away.

David followed his gaze. "If I remember from the introductions, the old boy is a Colonel Beeton, and the old girl is a Mrs. Harris. She is, or should I say, was, a distant relative of Charlene Tusset. Another drink?"

Mrs. Harris, who was chatting to the Colonel, broke off and smiled as Sarah and Christie approached. "I hope you ladies feel much safer now that this dreadful man has been caught."

Sarah let out a nervous giggle. "My husband said that those people are like mice - where there's one, there's another. I sincerely hope he's wrong."

"Of course he is," said Christie insistently. "I was just saying to Tessa that the police wouldn't dare arrest the wrong man."

Colonel Beeton raised a grey bushy eyebrow. "Oh? Just because the police have someone in custody, doesn't guarantee it's the right person. It is very easy to jump to conclusions. No doubt the police have been inundated with all sorts of information, some false, some genuine but irrelevant, and some that lay between the two. Then there's those deranged people who will confess to just about anything. I don't envy the investigators a jot."

Sarah's blue eyes widened in alarm. She grasped a strand of her long black hair and twined it around her fingers. "But…but that would mean he's still out there."

Mrs. Harris patted her arm. "Please, don't be frightened. In such cases, the police rarely make mistakes."

Sarah tried not to look skittish. However, the hair around her hand was twisted so tight that it was affecting circulation. Consequently, her fingers were white and waxy, almost cadaverous. "Tilly said you're a relative of Charlene's, so I suppose if you're satisfied then I should be too. Even so, I won't be happy till he's in prison."

Mrs. Harris breathed a sigh of lament. "I am by way of being a distant cousin of her father's. Such a beautiful and gifted girl. Did either of you know her?"

"Speaking for myself," said Christie, "I only knew her slightly. Even though many of us move in the same circles, we are not overly intimate with each other."

Mrs. Harris nodded in understanding. "It's like an extended family. You have relatives aplenty, and every now and then you gather together for weddings and the such like. You are polite and courteous, exchanging information or even snippets of family gossip, but you are not bosom companions."

Christie raised her mineral water in salute. "Exactly."

"And you, Mrs. Hopkins?" prompted Mrs. Harris. "Did you know my poor Charlene?"

"I only met her once. Charlene was organising a children's picnic, and as Paul is in consumables, she approached him about donating the food." Sarah paused, and with her eyes firmly locked on her husband, added in a girlish voice, "He was extremely generous, as usual."

Though Sarah's tone had been soft and affectionate, her last statement could also have been interpreted as criticism. Not wishing to step onto what might be 'delicate ground', Mrs. Harris changed the subject.

"The Russian guests look rather lonely. Do you know them?"

"Only by reputation," answered Christie. "They haven't been in Rockford very long." Sarah and the Colonel proffered similar replies.

"The poor things. Perhaps I should try and cheer them up," and as Mrs. Harris moved away, her place was taken by Tessa Marks, who was rubbing her hands and shivering.

"What's wrong?" asked Christie, noticing the goose bumps on Tessa's arms.

Tessa lowered her voice. "When you go to the bathroom, take a coat. There's a problem with the window. Tilly just told me that its jammed open."

"I noticed that too," said Sarah, releasing her twisted hair. It dangled below her neck like a tightly coiled spring. She flexed her bloodless fingers. "But, compared with your recent tax problem, an open window doesn't even rate a mention. But, I do empathise with you. Paul had a terrible problem with a frozen food supplier and it took months to sort it out."

Tessa narrowed her eyes, her tone cold and cutting. "I don't think fish fingers compares to being almost prosecuted for something you didn't do."

Sarah's cheeks flushed scarlet. "No…no," she said timidly, "I suppose not."

Seeing that the colonel was looking a little bored, Christie changed the subject. "Colonel, are you and Mrs. Harris also related?"

"Not in the slightest. I am by way of an old friend of Tilly's father." He leaned forward and whispered mischievously, "I suspect I was only invited here to make up the numbers." He looked across the room. "Speaking of which, Mrs. Harris seems to have conquered Russia."

Though it had been many years since Mrs. Harris had conversed in Russian, she managed to exchange pleasantries in the native tongue. "I'm sorry, Mr. Putzin," she went on, breaking into English with a chuckle, "but that's the extent of my Russian."

"It is gratifying that someone would make the effort," he complimented. "Where did you learn it?"

"I once lived in a boarding house with several Russian students, and on cold winter nights, they would sit around the fire and reminisce."

Vladimir Putzin smiled wistfully. "Oh, how that brings back memories. I often think of my childhood in Moscow. My entire family, including innumerable aunts and cousins, were all crammed into one room. We had nothing, absolutely nothing, and yet we were rich in love and joy."

"I know exactly what you mean," said Mrs. Harris. "I was a war baby, and although times were extremely hard, I think it built character. Most of the people in this room wouldn't know what real poverty was. Do you know anyone here?"

"I have collaborated with Mr. Pascoe on several projects. He's in security and I'm in electronics. I have heard of Mr. Hopkins and Mr. Marks of course, but this is the first time I've met them."

Mrs. Harris glanced at Angelica Putzin. As yet, the overly coiffed alleged 'madam' had not uttered a word. Perhaps, thought Mrs. Harris, she doesn't understand English, and that red hair is either a very bad dye job or a wig. Now, isn't that strange? I haven't seen a wig in years, and yet tonight I've seen two of them...possibly three.

* * *

Tilly entered the room. After the initial introductions, she had withdrawn to finish dressing, and she looked spectacular. Her low-cut heavily embellished burgundy velvet dress set off her long blonde hair to perfection. In the Hollywood of the 1950's, the colour would have been termed, 'platinum.'

Everyone adjourned to the dining room. The Pascoes' and the Putzins' with the Colonel between them, sat on one side of the table, while the Marks' and Hopkins' and Mrs. Harris were on the other, with Tilly at the head.

As though by silent consent, the conversation was kept to general topics. Nobody spoke of murder. However, towards the end of the dinner, it inevitably turned to the day's dramatic event.

Paul Hopkins said to the colonel, "You've given my wife the impression that the police may have arrested the wrong man."

The Colonel cleared his throat. "I was simply suggesting that just because someone has been arrested, it doesn't mean it's the right person."

"You think there's room for doubt?"

"Just because a person may behave or dress a little oddly, doesn't automatically make them a killer."

"Yes, but how do the police know when they have the right man?" said Christie. She glanced at Tessa, who was trying to look interested, even though the foot rubbing her leg under the table was not her husbands. "Do they have some kind of formula?"

"Killers come in all shapes and sizes," said the colonel. "As a matter of fact, I have a photograph of one that will prove the point."

"Really?" said Christie excitedly. "Could we see it?"

"Let me tell you the story first. It..." The colonel stopped and glanced round the table. "On second thoughts, perhaps I shouldn't. Its quite gruesome."

Amidst a chorus of protest, Sarah Hopkins looked rather queasy. Her husband said, "Perhaps, Colonel, you could tone it down. I'm sure my wife would like to hear the story, but she has no stomach for horror."

The Colonel smiled at Sarah before beginning, "This story takes place when I was stationed in India in the early 1950's. The killer was very clever, much cleverer than our man if newspaper reports are to be believed."

"Did you catch him?" interrupted Billy Pascoe, who was now considerably the worse for wear.

Christie shot him a withering look. "Shut up, Billy."

The colonel continued, "The killer stalked his victims with precision. He knew exactly when to strike. It began with the disappearance of two small children from an impoverished village. At first, we thought they'd been abducted or sold as child brides, a practice that was, and unfortunately still is, very common. Yet there was something in the mother's distress that convinced us otherwise, and so a search was launched. Two days later, we found what remained of their heads.

"Well, one after another, 12 people were murdered. They were horribly mutilated, and yet despite the wealth of material, no useful clues were found." The Colonel produced a photograph from his wallet. "But like most killers he made a mistake. He was caught and executed on the spot."

The picture was passed around the table. Tilly gasped in surprise. Paul Hopkins barely glanced at it, and without showing it to his wife, gave it to Mrs. Harris. David and Tessa Marks both wrinkled their noses', and Billy Pascoe roared with laughter.

"I thought you were talking about a person!" he said between guffaws.

Christie snatched the photo out of her husband's hand. She stared incredulously and then exclaimed, "It's a fucking tiger!"

The room fell uncomfortably silent. The outburst of vulgarity had seemingly corrupted the convivial atmosphere. Tilly was clearly embarrassed, Paul Hopkins averted his eyes, Sarah Hopkins covered her mouth with a handkerchief, while Mrs. Harris and the Colonel both looked at the ceiling. David Marks tut-tutted, while Tessa, who was rapidly losing patience with Billy's amorous foot, simply shrugged.

The Putzins' spoke in Russian and then Vladimir said, "If you would excuse us, Tilly. My wife has a headache and I have an early plane to catch. Thank you for a wonderful evening."

As Tilly escorted them out, Billy Pascoe rounded on his wife. His words might have been slurred but his meaning was very clear.

"Now look what you've done - stupid whore! Not only have you offended the guests, but you've insulted our hostess."

"How dare you! You're nothing *but* offensive! How stupid do you think I am? Did you really think I believed those excuses about inefficient secretaries? Tell me, my supposed loyal and faithful husband, how many bastards have you fathered?"

Having heard the acrimonious exchange from the front door, Tilly quickly returned and said diplomatically, "I'll bring the coffee."

Glaring at her husband, Christie snatched up her handbag. "I'll give you a hand. The air around me has suddenly become stale."

* * *

Deep within the bowels of the Rockford police station, Patrick Thomas Evans was tucking into an exceptionally spicy chicken vindaloo, his reward for an Oscar-winning performance. Detective Mike Furrow's vast experience in amateur dramatics had made him perfect for the role.

Inspector Simmonds, who had a similar meal in front of him, put down a walkie-talkie. "Well, that's one couple out of the picture, not that either were in the running."

"By comparison, I had the easy part," said Constable Furrow. "I don't envy them a bit. I'm not sure I could sit down to dinner with a killer, serial or otherwise."

Inspector Simmonds sucked a plump piece of rice from between his teeth. "I wish we could have bugged the house. To mix metaphors, we dangled a carrot, and now it's up to the killer to take the bait."

"And if the killer doesn't bite?"

John Simmonds picked up a pappadum. "Then I'll be retiring much earlier than expected."

* * *

Billy Pascoe tried to laugh off the incident. "Sorry about that. My wife's still upset over this killer business," and squinting through bloodshot eyes, successfully grabbed the whiskey decanter.

The colonel returned the photograph to his wallet, Sarah Hopkins rummaged in her handbag, while to ease the tension, Mrs. Harris changed the subject.

"Mr. Hopkins," she said, "I understand you're a great contributor to philanthropic causes. How do you choose which ones?"

"A sceptic might say that I choose the ones that will generate the most publicity, but really, I judge each on their merits."

"Like my poor Charlene's?"

"Charlene was extremely dedicated to her causes. You know, I think I must be the only person who, because of our charity connection, had contact with all seven victims. But, before you get the wrong idea, let me state that I was out of town when several of the murders occurred." Paul Hopkins suddenly stopped and stared at the wall, as though a thought had just occurred to him. "Sorry, Mrs. Harris, I just remembered something. Worthy Causes? Do you have one in mind?"

Mrs. Harris smiled. "I can think of several, but that's not why I asked the question. I like learning what makes people tick. What appeals to one person, another may regard with disgust."

Ignoring Billy's incoherent drunken muttering, the others engaged in desultory conversation. In the kitchen, Christie Pascoe was trying to mend her broken dignity.

"I'm very sorry, Tilly. Arguing in front of your guests was unforgivable. Now, where did I put my handbag? I'm sure I brought it with me. Ah, there it is."

She brushed passed Tilly as she went to a bench. Tilly, who was preparing percolated coffee, quickly glanced over her shoulder and then turned back.

"Don't worry about the outburst. We all need to blow off steam once in a while."

Tilly and Christie were of similar age, and as true kindred spirits were rare in the 'elite', Christie considered that she'd found a friend. She therefore spoke candidly. "I don't know how I've put up with him all these years," said Christie, withdrawing a hairbrush from her handbag. "But there again, I suppose it's better than being alone. Do you have someone special?"

Tilly poured the coffee into a silver pot. "Not particularly. I have always been an independent woman."

"Take it from me," said Christie, who was vigorously brushing her hair, "stay single and enjoy yourself. I know at least a dozen men who would be happy to take you to dinner. Give me a ring next week and I'll throw some phone numbers your way."

Tilly picked up the first of two trays. "Thank you, but I am very happy as I am. Would you carry the other tray for me?"

They returned to the dining room and distributed the coffee. Sarah Hopkins had finally closed her handbag, a clean handkerchief in her hand. Tessa Marks had won the battle against Billy's roving foot, but only because he was now too drunk to bother.

"Colonel," said Christie, resuming her seat, "what happened to the tiger?"

"Well, after I shot it, it was…erm…eaten."

David Marks said incredulously, "Are you saying that you ate the beast who ate…" he left the sentence unfinished.

"Not me personally, but in some remote tribes, its part of a cleansing ritual to eat the carcass of a killer animal."

Mrs. Harris suddenly looked ill. "Tilly, my dear," she said throatily, "could you point me in the direction of the bathroom?"

"Of course. Come with me," and as they left the table, Sarah rummaged in her handbag again.

* * *

The colonel was very apologetic when Tilly and Mrs. Harris returned to the dining room. "I'm not usually squeamish," said Mrs. Harris. "Its just that the image you conjured up was a little…erm…disturbing."

Stifling a yawn, Paul Hopkins whispered to Sarah, "We'll have coffee and then leave," to which announcement she looked very relieved.

Half an hour later, and after Christie had declined a lift home and poured Billy into a taxi instead, everyone had gone.

Chapter III

THE HOODED and darkly clad figure took advantage of sporadic cloud cover to climb through the bathroom window. Shafts of moonlight lit the way. It also bounced off Tilly's long blonde hair as it cascaded over the side of the bed.

As the figure paused to uncork a syringe, the needle glinted in the lunar light. Then, with cat-like movements, the figure attempted to inject Tilly's arm. But, instead of flesh, the needle hit something hard.

"I don't think you want to do that," said a voice from behind. The light snapped on and the figure instantly lunged at Mrs. Harris, who swiftly stepped aside to reveal a stern faced Inspector Simmonds standing in the doorway.

* * *

Dawn was breaking when Inspector Simmonds, his face drawn with fatigue, entered his office. "Singing like a bird," he announced, "but nothing I can use in court."

"Would you like me to try?" said Mrs. Harris. "To put it metaphorically, some nuts are harder to crack than others. It's simply a question of using the right hammer."

"Nuts is right!" He rubbed his eyes and sighed. He still did not know who Mrs. Harris actually was, nor had she volunteered any information. The Chief Constable's faith in her however, was absolute. "Alright, give it your best shot, but I hope you don't have a delicate constitution."

* * *

Mrs. Harris entered the interview room. Two uniformed policewomen were sitting behind a defiant looking Sarah Hopkins.

She glared at the elderly woman as she said, "I suppose you think you can do better than that bumbling Inspector? I will not sit here and be questioned by a common housewife. Besides, you cant prove a thing." She patted her hair and spoke as if ordering strawberries at Wimbledon. "Would you call me a taxi? I really must get to the hairdressers."

Mrs. Harris smiled indulgently. "The police don't need a confession to prove your guilt. Nor will natural hair stay spiralled like a corkscrew, at least, not without a dirth of hairspray. When did you start wearing a wig?"

Sarah's cheeks flushed with colour, but whether from anger or embarrassment was unclear. "None of your damned business!" She suddenly leaned forward, her eyes sparkling with malice. "I've heard about dried up women like you. What's your fancy? Little boys, little girls, or do you fantasise about a rich toy boy?"

* * *

Mrs. Harris smiled as she folded her hands. She had found the hammer with which to crack the nut – vanity. "You are hardly in a position to be making demands, but then, that's what all this has been about. Position, envy, and humiliation. Allow me to tell you a fairytale."

"I don't want to hear your grubby fantasy." Then, sounding rather like Queen Victoria, Sarah added, "You are dismissed."

"Once upon a time," Mrs. Harris went on, "there was a bright young grocer with a head for business. He soon became successful and gave those he loved, especially his childhood sweetheart, everything they had ever wanted. Time passed, and he began to associate with other businesses, garnering fame and fortune along the way. His sweetheart, now his wife, tried to blend-in, but being from common stock as it were, she was extremely naïve in the ways of the elite.

"Compounding the issue was the fact that, the ever increasing circles to which she was now attached, had made their fortunes from more exciting means. A vein of jealousy began to blossom, especially towards the glamorous wives. They were streets ahead in superiority, and seemingly without effort, were indulged and admired. They were the antithesis of the rich & powerful, to which the wife could not possibly hope to compete, and despite her own privileged position, developed an inferiority complex."

Sarah crossed her arms and spoke petulantly. "Me? Inferior? Utter nonsense."

"Ah, but I haven't finished yet. Then, into her seething mass of resentment came a pair of Russian immigrants. Unlike the grocer's wife, who'd struggled for years for acceptance, this plain and conservative couple were welcomed with open arms. In effect, they were put on the pedestal she covetously craved."

"They have no breeding and no right to be rich. They should have stayed in Russia amongst the potatoes. Pedestal indeed! They're nothing but a pair of court jesters suitable only for amusement."

Mrs. Harris ignored the racial taunt. "Jealousy can manifest in many ways. These women had humiliated you, so why not humiliate them back? However, while hideously disfiguring their faces', you developed a weakness - a fetish if you like, for hair, and while the colonel was telling us about the tiger, you cut off two chunks of Tilly's hair."

"Is that it?" asked Sarah scornfully. "Some bimbo loses a bit of hair and that makes me a killer? Don't make me laugh."

"Deny it all you want," said Mrs. Harris coolly, "but there is sufficient evidence to prove the point."

"What evidence?" asked Sarah quickly, and for the first time there was an edge to her voice.

"You had a pair of nail scissors hidden in your handkerchief, but you were so obsessed with acquiring a piece of Tilly's hair that you didn't notice it was a wig. Later, when I pretended to be ill and Tilly escorted me to the bathroom, she checked her hair. Incidentally, the policewoman who impersonated Tilly played her part to perfection, though I do think the dummy in the bed did not do justice to her figure."

Sarah was too engrossed in survival to process the revelation. "All circumstantial," she declared.

Mrs. Harris shrugged. "And then there's the jammed window, which wasn't really jammed. It was one of those trifles that always give rise to comment, and it would be human nature not to try and close it. So, as a safety precaution..." and here Mrs. Harris almost smiled, "...after everyone had gone home, the windowsill was sprinkled with toner from a photocopier. Being black and in the dark, nobody would see it. Your clothes are now being tested."

"I suppose you think you're very clever?" said Sarah peevishly, but her mocking tone lacked conviction.

"On the contrary, it was Inspector Simmonds who worked it out. Most serial killers are men, and you did a good job of creating that illusion. Then, quite by chance, he saw a child's drawing with concentric circles for clouds, and once he shifted focus from a man to a woman, the common denominator via your husband, was you. I believe your husband realised this when we were discussing Charlene. He was out of town when several murders occurred, but you were not."

There was a long silence in which Sarah began to cry, but the tears were for herself and not her victims. Mrs. Harris had no sympathy, and standing up to leave, she could not resist a parting shot.

"There are other points of course, but no doubt your lawyers and psychiatrists will freely spend your husband's hard earned money to disprove them."

* * *

Inspector Simmonds slowly shook his head. "So, once again, the green-eyed monster has raised its ugly head. Those poor women, and it was all unnecessary."

"In a round about way," said Mrs. Harris, "Sarah is also a victim. Wealth and happiness were always within her grasp, but bitterness and envy prevented her from seeing it."

Inspector Simmonds said reflectively, "We sailed dangerously close to entrapment."

"I disagree. Nobody forced her to return to the house with a syringe full of cocaine. Speaking of which, how did you persuade the real Tilly Bellingham to co-operate?"

The Inspector grinned roguishly. "She's my niece. But, talking of relations, how do you know the Chief Constable? He was quite adamant to have you involved."

Mrs. Harris's blue eyes twinkled as she said, "The less you know, the better."

As she picked up her handbag and prepared to leave, Inspector Simmonds had a curious sense of emptiness. The old lady had been extraordinarily brave, and the end of the association felt as though a favourite relative was about to emigrate.

"Perhaps I can take you to dinner to show my appreciation. I know a really good Indian restaurant."

Mrs. Harris smiled benignly. "No, thank you, Inspector. I've had quite enough of formal dinners."

Murder on the Lunar Commute

B. David Spicer

LEOPOLD KALTENBACH sat in his cabin sipping coffee from a wide porcelain cup and watched the stars whirling outside the windows of the lunar ferry. When he could tear his gaze away from the stars, he'd try to concentrate on his crossword puzzle, but this one had him stumped. A six-letter word for *a permanent ending*. Smiling, he penciled in the word *retire*. He finished his coffee and rang the conductor for another. A few minutes later, he heard a tentative knock on the cabin door.

"Enter." His smile faltered when he saw the porter's face. "Everything all right, Martin?"

Martin, who rarely had a single strand of his blond hair out of place, wrung his hands nervously. "No, sir, I'm afraid not. I've been instructed to bring you to the comm compartment. A call is waiting for you."

Kaltenbach didn't hesitate. He dropped his puzzle book onto the little table next to his coffee cup, and stood. "Certainly." He followed Martin up the narrow hall to the front of the ferry, where he stepped into a small room that had two chairs, a table and a monitor on the wall. The sound-proof door closed behind him and he took a seat in front of the monitor. He tapped the screen, opening the comm link.

"Leopold." Director Whitt, looking as grim as only a policeman can, attempted a smile but gave up half way through it.

Kaltenbach shook his head. "I'm not coming back, Whitt. I'm really retiring this time."

Whitt held up his hands in surrender. "I'm not asking you to come back to the force, Leo, but there is something I need you to do."

"What is it?"

"There's been a murder, and I need you to take charge of the investigation until I can get another officer on the scene."

Kaltenbach threw a huge sigh at Whitt. "Where was it, Tycho City? I'm leaving for Mars in two days, so I don't have much time to spend crawling all over the moon."

"You won't have to. The murder happened on the ferry. You're sitting about ten yards away from the scene of the crime."

Kaltenbach rubbed his hand over his thin white hair. "That's interesting, who was the victim?"

Whitt squinted at a clipboard. "The engineer, a fella named McTavish."

"Do you think the perp was a passenger, or a member of the crew?"

"Crew member. The passenger areas are pretty well covered with cameras, I'm told the crew areas are not. For obvious safety reasons, passengers can't get into the crew areas, which is where the murder happened. That part of the ship is zero-G, all of which points to a member of the crew."

Kaltenbach made a sour face. "Whitt, you know how much I hate zero-G. It makes me queasy."

"Sorry, Leo. Just secure the scene, see what you can figure out, and pass your findings on to the authorities in Tycho City. Consider your status as an officer reactivated until then."

"*Temporarily* reactivated. I'll be on that flight to Syria Planum."

Whitt grinned beneath his whiskers. "Of course, Leo, of course."

Kaltenbach terminated the transmission and scowled at the blank screen for a moment before exiting the tiny room. Martin stood waiting in the hallway. "I'm to investigate the situation, Martin. I'll need access to the crew area."

"Of course, sir. If you'll follow me." He led Kaltenbach to the transition passage. The ferry consisted of two sections, the passenger section, which spun to create artificial gravity, and the crew section which dispensed with such luxuries and remained in zero-G. The transition passage connected the two sections and allowed one to transition from zero-G to to normal gravity or vice versa. Martin placed his six-inch long brass passkey, that was really more of a lever, into the transition passage lock, and gave it a twist, which started it spinning until it matched the spin of the passenger compartment. Kaltenbach stepped into it once it seemed to have stooped moving relative to the passenger section, and moved up the corridor until he made it to the halfway point, at which point he took hold of the handrail and looked back toward the conductor. "Go ahead, Martin."

"Good luck with your investigation, sir. Murder is a bad business."

"That it is."

Martin turned the key again, and the transition corridor began to slow its spin, which reduced the gravity holding Kaltenbach's feet to the floor. Within a few seconds he floated free of the deck, as weightless as everybody else in the crew section. He held onto the handrail and pulled himself forward with a tiny tug. At the door of the crew section, he stopped his forward motion by grasping the handrail tightly, and activated the door, which opened with a whoosh.

A woman with intense blue eyes and short brown hair hovered just inside the door, upside-down from Kaltenbach's perspective. "You must be the cop." She tapped the wall and spun to face him right-side-up. "I'm Captain Bree Conners."

"Leopold Kaltenbach."

Her eyebrows rose. "*The* detective Kaltenbach?"

"Yes, *the temporarily re-instated* detective Kaltenbach. I'll need to know everything that happened, I'll need to interview every crew member, and I'll need to see where the body was found. I understand that it happened in the zero-G portion of the ship?"

"Yeah, we found him in the galley." She launched herself by tapping a foot against the wall, soaring toward a compartment with practiced grace.

"What was his name?"

"Travis McTavish, but we all just called him Meatball."

"Why?"

"Because he was a goof, always had a joke, never took anything seriously." She thumbed a switch and opened the door to the galley. "Be careful, there's still blood in the air. I'd hate for you to inhale any of it."

The galley looked more like a locker room than a kitchen. Instead of the tables and chairs one would expect to find in a normal-gravity galley, this room featured several rows of drawers, each containing dehydrated foodstuffs in leak-proof containers. Anything that got away would simply float around in the room like annoying insects. This included the late Travis 'Meatball' McTavish's blood, which swarmed around the room in tiny crimson clouds.

"Who found the victim?"

Captain Connors ran her fingers through her hair. "I did. Does that make me the prime suspect?

"Not necessarily. Who else is in the crew?"

"There are four members in a standard lunar ferry crew. The captain, who is the primary pilot, the co-pilot, who is the auxiliary systems officer, the engineer, and the nurse."

"What about the conductors and the cooks in the passenger compartment?"

She shook her head. "They're not really part of the crew. They're employed by a contract agency, not the ferry line"

"I see. Who are the crew members?"

"The co-pilot is Kelley, she's on the flight deck now. The nurse is Lengete. He's in the infirmary with Meatball's body. I separated them so they couldn't discuss the matter. I didn't want them influencing each other's story."

"Would they lie for each other?" Kaltenbach waved away a passing blob of blood.

"We've been together a long time, we're like a family in a lot of ways, dysfunctional, quarrelsome, infinitely annoying. If this was a question of stolen cookies, I'd say yes, but since it's a question of murder, I'd think not."

"You're not certain?"

Connors shrugged. "How can I be? One of my friends apparently killed another one of my friends. Evidently, I don't know at least one of them as well as I thought I did."

Kaltenbach pulled himself out of the galley, followed by Connors, who closed the door behind them. He glanced around the compartment. "Is there a room I can use to conduct the interviews of the crew?"

She opened a door beneath them and gestured for him to enter. "Sure, this is my office." She floated into the room and pointed out a desk with a chair bolted to the floor on either side of it. "I find that sometimes you just want to sit in a chair." Matching deed to word, she sat in one of the chairs and fastened a seatbelt to hold her to it, and Kaltenbach did the same on the opposite side of the desk. "You want to start with me?"

Kaltenbach nodded. He fished a data-pad out of his pocket and opened a new file and began making notes. "When did you last see McTavish alive?"

"About twelve hours ago, just before my shift on the flight deck began. He told me there was some sort of intermittent power glitch in the passenger compartment that he wanted to check out, just a minor inconvenience, but he was bored and thought he'd see what he could do. I told him that was fine with me. That was the last conversation I had with him."

"Is it usual for the crew to enter the passenger section while the ferry is underway?"

Connors shrugged. "Not really, but sometimes it happens. In general, after the ferry leaves *Verne Station*, there's no need for anyone to cross between the two sections, so nobody does."

"What happened then?"

"I went to the flight deck, relieved Kelley, and started my turn at the helm. Each shift is twelve hours long. When my shift ended, Kelley took over and I went to the galley for something to eat. I opened the door and found Meatball."

"He was already dead when you found him?"

Connors nodded, but seemed unable to speak just then.

"Then what did you do?"

"I called Lengete immediately, but I knew it was too late. I served on a frigate during The War, I know what death looks like. When Lengete confirmed that Meatball was dead, I called it in. Protocol in all emergencies is that the ferry captain call the destination authorities, in this case, the Lunar Constabulary Authority, instead of the authorities on Earth. I guess they called you. That's all I know."

"Thank you, captain. That's all I need from you for now. Could you please send in Mr. Lengete?"

"Sure thing." She unbuckled her seatbelt and flung herself up and out of the room. Kaltenbach watched her with a hand pressed over his stomach. He swallowed a couple of times, and apparently decided not to throw up just yet.

Lengete drifted down into the room and buckled himself into the seat opposite Kaltenbach. "Are you okay? You're looking a little peaked."

"My stomach doesn't tolerate zero-G very well."

"I can give you something for the nausea if you'd like."

Kaltenbach waved that off. "Maybe later. You're Lengete?"

"I am. Paul Lengete, RN."

Kaltenbach picked up the data-pad and tapped in a few notes then looked at Lengete. "Tell me about Meatball."

"He was a good guy, always joking around, had a comeback for anything anybody said. He was a good engineer, kept this bucket space-worthy. Even though he was always worried about money, he'd give you the shirt off his back."

"He had money trouble?"

Lengete made a face. "Not really, he made enough to pay his bills, but he wanted more out of life. He'd talk about getting a gig on the Earth-Saturn run because it payed so well, but he didn't like the idea of spending two years in hibernation at a time."

"When did you last see him?"

Lengete closed his eyes and rubbed his nose for a moment. "About four hours before Bree found him in the galley. He was coming out of the access hatch to the environmental control systems."

"What was he doing in there?"

Lengete shrugged. "I never thought to ask. He was the engineer, so he was always crawling around somewhere, fixing this or that. He looked like he'd gotten in a fight with an ash bucket and lost."

Kaltenbach leaned forward on the desk. "You mean he was dirty?"

"Oh yeah, he was filthy. Covered in thick, black dust."

"Have you seen him like that before? Since he was always clambering into the engines and such?"

He rubbed his nose again. "Well, I've seen him dirty before, but today he was dirtier than usual. Maybe dirtier than I've ever seen him be."

"Tell me what you found when Captain Connors called you to the galley."

Lengete took a deep breath and exhaled slowly. "When I opened the door, I found Meatball spinning in the middle of the room. Lots of blood. He'd been struck in the head with a blunt object. Twice. He died of blunt-force trauma to the head."

"Couldn't it have been an accident?"

"If there had been a single wound, I'd say it was possible, though still highly improbable. Two virtually identical wounds that close together? No way."

Kaltenbach tapped halfheartedly on his data-pad. "Why not? It's not at all possible?"

"No. It's not possible." Lengete's voice was firm. "Everything in that galley, everything in the zero-G section of the ship, is designed to reduce accidental injuries. Look closely at the galley, there aren't any protruding edges anywhere. Somebody hit him."

"What kind of weapon do you think was used by the killer?"

"Something with an edge."

"Would it have to be heavy?"

Lengete frowned and shook his head. "Not in zero-G. Even pipe-wrenches are weightless."

"Was he still dirty?"

"No. He must have had a shower before going into the galley."

"Thank you, Mr. Lengete. I think that's all I need from you just now. Please send Ms. Kelley in, thank you."

Lengete raised his arms above his head and was halfway out of the room before his legs left the floor.

Several minutes passed before a pink-haired head popped into the room. "You're the detective?" She dropped into the room headfirst, then spun around and ended up sitting in the chair with her legs crossed, as if such acrobatics came as naturally as walking. Maybe, in her case, they did.

"Yes, I'm Detective Kaltenbach."

"The bigshot gumshoe who caught that *Wall Street Mangler* guy?"

"The same."

She grinned. "Wow! You're famous!" Her eyes shared the same cotton-candy pink as her hair, and they sparkled as she floated above the chair. "Like, so-so-so famous!"

"I am. So, what do you do on the ship?"

"I'm the aux-sys-off. I fly the ship sometimes, but mostly I watch readouts, which is so-so-so boring."

"What kind of readouts?"

"All the sys displays, navi positions, engine outputs. The whole encyclopedia."

"Were there any interesting readouts today? Something less than boring?"

"Just a glitchy sensor or two. Lost a few subsystems for a while, nothing horrid at all."

"What subsystems did you lose?" He pecked at the data-pad.

"Lost environmental con for a while, then security con for a while. Meaty took care of it though."

"What can you tell me about Meatball?"

"He's so-so-so dead! Which is so-so-so sad." She looked like she might cry. "He wasn't horrid. I liked him, big brother-wise, not boyfriend-wise. He gave me giggles. I like giggles."

"Don't we all. Did you see him today?"

She scrunched up her elfin face, and found a spot on the desk to scrutinize. "Yeah-yeah. I called him about the glitches, and he fixed them. Took hours though. For-ev-er in watching-readout-time."

"You actually saw him, or just spoke to him on the comm?"

"I saw him go into the tunnel. I barked at him 'cause he got me all wet."

Kaltenbach tilted his head to one side. "How did he do that?"

"His hair was all wet, he came up close to me and shook it, so it got all over me. So-so-so rude, but he just laughed and laughed until I got the giggles and laughed too."

"Interesting. Did you see him after that?"

"No. I went to sleep. Cap'n Bree woke me up to call Luna two hours later. I was gutted, so-so-so sad."

"Who else did you call? Earth?"

"No, only Luna. Nobody else."

"So nobody outside of the crew knew of the murder until the lunar authorities called me?"

"Nope!"

"Are you certain?"

She frowned. "Sure I'm certain, Mr. Famous detective."

Kaltenbach unbuckled his seatbelt and floated up toward the door. "Thank you, that'll be all or now!"

Kelley came up along side of him. "I'm done?"

"Yes. How long can you leave the flight deck unattended?"

"Twenty-minutes according to rules-n-regs, but half an hour is okay too."

"Can you have the captain meet us near the environmental access controls."

She spun in circles, such was her excitement. "You're going all bloodhound, aren't ya!"

"Please bring the captain!" He watched her flit away, then found the infirmary. He had Lengete lead him to the place where he'd last seen Meatball alive. The captain and Kelley joined them a few minutes later.

"What's this all about, Kaltenbach?" Captain Connors looked annoyed.

"I believe I know who murdered your engineer."

"Who-who-who?" Kelley seemed to bounce from floor to ceiling with every syllable.

Kaltenbach held up an index finger. "We'll get to that in a moment. First, I'd like to establish *why* he was murdered." He slid open the crawlspace that led to the environmental control machinery. "I think we'll find something interesting in there." He looked at the crew, and they looked at each other.

The captain finally spoke. "I'll go in." She flung herself into the compartment with practiced ease. The others hovered outside the hatch, waiting for her to reappear.

Kelley, unable to wait any longer, poked her head into the compartment and shouted in her piping, high-pitched voice. "Well? You're so-so-so slow!"

Finally, Connors emerged, dripping wet and dragging a duffel bag behind her. "I found this stuffed in the air-exchange shaft."

Kaltenbach, who'd brought rubber gloves with him from the infirmary, donned them and carefully unzipped the bag. Inside were hundreds of small octagonal bits of metal. He opened it enough for everybody to have a good look, but then closed it before any of the octagons could float free of the bag. "Mr. McTavish died because someone wanted this bag of loot all to their self."

Lengete frowned. "What are they?"

Everyone looked at Kaltenbach, who only smiled. "These bits of metal are made of platinum, and I believe they've been liberated from the ships' environmental systems. Those systems catalyze one gas into another one. The resulting gases are mostly carbon dioxide, and water vapor. The water vapor is collected to be used by both the crew and passengers. I believe Mr. McTavish purposefully disabled the sensors to allow him time to remove the platinum from the environmental system, that was when Mr. Lengete saw him, covered in black dust. The carbon dioxide is processed into breathable oxygen, and carbon. When Meatball came out of the environmental system hatch he was covered in black carbon which would have been in the areas immediately surrounding the platinum. That was four hours before his death."

Lengete shook his head. "Why wouldn't he just put that bag with his belongings and take it with him when we got to Luna. It's not like he would have been searched when we got there."

"Because he didn't have to. His buyer is on board this ship as we speak."

Everyone stared at Kaltenbach, waiting but not speaking, so he continued. "I think he met his partner, but something went wrong. So, instead of handing off the platinum, he hid it in the environmental compartment, where nobody would be likely to find it. He came out of it dripping wet, just as the captain did just now because with some or all of the platinum removed, the water would have freely floated in that compartment, thereby giving him the 'shower' that Mr. Lengete assumed Meatball had taken. That was two hours before he died."

Kelley almost burst from excitement. "But who-who-who is his partner?"

"Tell me, Ms. Kelley, when was the security system offline? Would it have covered the last four hours of Meatball's life?"

She counted it up on her fingertips. "Yeah-yeah-yeah!"

"During that outage, what security systems were disabled?"

"All of them!"

"So, there would have been no entries made in any of the security logs?"

"Nope, none-none-none!"

"Then, I'm afraid we don't have the evidence we need to determine who the killer is, not yet."

Half an hour later Kaltenbach slammed the door to the comm compartment not even caring that it didn't close all the way. He keyed in the Lunar Constabulary Authority comm code, and requested Director Whitt. "It's all a mess Whitt. There's no evidence at all. No apparent motive, not even an opportunity. I plan on dropping this in your lap as soon as we dock at *Copernicus Station*."

Whitt's whiskers twitched. "Just calm down, Leo. I won't have a single officer available until 0800. I'll need you to stay onboard until then."

"That's four more hours! No thank you. I'm retiring, effective today. I'll escort the crew off the ship at Copernicus, then I'm out. Retired. Permanently." He terminated the link and sat scowling at the screen for several minutes before finally returning to his cabin. He picked up his puzzle book and shoved it into his pocket before storming out of the room.

Kaltenback hovered in the dark, finally hearing the door open. He switched on the light of McTavish's room and watched Martin's face contort in surprise. "What are you doing here?"

"I might ask you the same question, Martin. Then again, I already know why you're here. You're too late, the platinum's already gone. You killed McTavish for no reason."

"I don't know what you're talking about."

"I think you do. You told me with your own mouth. 'Murder is a bad business,' you said. You're right, it is, but you could only have known there was a murder in the crew section if you'd done it yourself. Nobody in the passenger section had any idea that anything was amiss in the fore-section. Might as well fess up, Martin. They're searching your cabin as we speak. McTavish's blood is undoubtedly on your clothing somewhere. Fluids in zero-G get everywhere."

"You. Why did you have to be on this trip?" He scowled at Kaltenbach.

"You hit him on your head with your passkey didn't you?"

Martin pulled it out of his pocket and twirled it on its hefty chain. "It makes a surprisingly effective weapon. When I couldn't get all the money right away, Meatball got cold feet and tried to back out. He said he was gonna put it all back in the environmental system! Such a waste! We could have both made a lot of dough. I just needed more time, but he was a coward."

"So he had to die?"

"Oh yes, and so do you, Kaltenbach." He drew back to strike Kaltenbach with the key, but Whitt and his officers crashed into the room, knocking Martin against the wall, then handcuffing him. They dragged his struggling, but still weightless body out of the room.

Kaltenbach frowned at Whitt. "You're a terrible actor."

Grinning, Whitt extended his hand. "Thanks, Leo. Nice to see you in action one last time."

"Yes, one last time."

Kaltenbach left the ferry and sat in the lobby of Copernicus Station. A stranger sat next to him. First time on Luna?"

"No, I'm a native."

"How nice. Inbound or outbound?"

"I'm going to Mars for a while."

"Oh? On vacation?"

"A *temporary* retirement." He pulled out his puzzle book and reread the last clue he'd filled in. A six-letter word for *a permanent ending*. He erased his first answer and wrote in its place the word *murder*.

Just the Fax

Nancy Sweetland

MARCY MARCH sat at her computer, gazing dreamily out the window. She was thinking up the next steamy love scene for her friend Alfred Doolittle to weave into the sexy romance novels he wrote as Wendy Winsome. That is, the novels were sexy when Marcy got through beefing up his bland he-and-she-meet-and-fight-and-fall-in-love stories. Marcy's fax machine toggled a sensuous 'brrrp' and spit out a paper. Good, she thought, Alfred must have finished his final chapter.

The small print at the top of the sheet listed the date, Alfred's name, and 16:29, nautical time Marcy translated to 4:29 p.m. Alfred's usual cover sheet was missing. This transmission was mostly blank, but spotted with smudges along the left side. It read: 'MARCY: HELP! IT DOESN'T WORK FOR UNCLE FRED TO DIE OF A HEART ATTACK.' Smaller print followed: 'You told me so, and now I believe it, but what can I do? Answer, please. NOW.'

Marcy made a face. Uncle Fred was a character in *Love along the Nile*, Alfred/Wendy's latest romance. Alfred always consulted Marcy to help develop his plots. In fact, the books were actually written more by Marcy than either of them admitted.

"I *told* Alfred not to murder anyone in that story," mumbled Marcy. "Now he's stuck with dead Fred and wants *me* to fix it."

Marcy frowned over the fax. Alfred was usually so neat – the smudges weren't like him at all. He must have been messing with a stamp pad, or putting in a printer ribbon.

"Fred's dead, and that's that," Marcy faxed back. "Bury him in style or get rid of him altogether. He didn't add to the story, anyway." Her machine hummed; magically her answer appeared on Alfred's fax a few seconds later.

But it wasn't Alfred who carefully pulled the paper from the machine. Alfred Doolittle, aka Wendy Winsome, lay across his computer keyboard in a darkening pool of blood, and he wasn't going to write any more stories ever, sexy or not. The person who received Marcy's fax placed it carefully in Alfred's hand as though he had pulled it from the machine himself, stepped calmly around Alfred's already cooling body and walked out.

* * *

"Miss March?" The man at her door flipped open his badge case. "Detective Pierce. I'd like to ask you a few questions."

Eyebrows raised, Marcy looked beyond him at the undistinguished car parked against the curb, glad her nosy neighbors wouldn't recognize it as police.

"Come in. What's this about?" Marcy led him into the living room. "Sit?"

"No, thanks. You're acquainted with Alfred Doolittle?"

Marcy's eyebrows went up again. "Sure. We work together. Not here, by fax and phone. Why?"

"When did you last see him?"

Marcy thought a minute. "Last Friday. We met for a fish fry."

"But you've communicated with him since then."

"Oh, sure." Marcy explained their working relationship. "In fact, my last fax from him was today. Four twenty-nine, to be exact."

Detective Pierce raised *his* eyebrows. "Four twenty-nine, exactly? Of course. The fax machine prints it on the paper. That's a help."

"For what? What's Alfred done?"

The detective hesitated for a moment. "It's not what *he's* done, Miss March. It's what's been done to *him*. He's dead. Murdered."

Marcy stepped back, her mouth agape. "You're joking. Alfred's like...like a friendly puppy. That's why he couldn't write good love scenes, he's just a cuddler. Who'd *kill* him?"

"Somebody with an ax to grind. Actually, somebody with an ax. Or a sharp, heavy instrument like one. Not a pretty sight."

* * *

Across town, Bryce Colton held his celebratory glass of wine up to catch the light. Beautiful. Almost the color of blood. It had been too easy, sending the fax after Doolittle had been dead for more than two hours. What a stroke of luck that Alfred had been just ready to send the fax when Bryce bludgeoned him; something so simple as a printed time line would alibi his perfect crime.

Bryce had then turned up the air conditioning in Alfred's tiny office to stall normal body deterioration in the late summer heat. He'd previously arranged to meet Candy King for a drink at Porter's Pub, and lagged there more than two hours. Then he told her he had to make a private call from his car phone, but he'd be right back to pick her up for dinner. Candy waited, as he knew she would.

It took only twenty minutes to speed back to Doolittle's, reset the air conditioner, send Alfred's fax and receive Marcy's in return, and get out. With a rock-solid alibi from Candy and the bartender at Porter's from a few minutes after Bryce had actually clobbered Doolittle on through early evening, he was home free.

Too bad the shrimp's sister just happened to be Bryce Colton's wife, but that couldn't be helped. Colton toasted himself again. Ever since Doolittle's books had become best-sellers, Colton had hated him. Damn, the man couldn't even write them himself, had to call on Marcy March to provide the *real* emotion. Yet Doolittle's Winsome books fairly flew off the shelves, while Colton's erudite, involved fiction was repeatedly rejected.

Now, maybe, with less of Doolittle's fluff to distract them, editors would look more favorably at Colton's serious work. *Dissecting the Future* would sell, he knew it. Colton's old camping hatchet had been scrubbed clean and tossed into the swiftly flowing river as Colton drove over the bridge on the uninhabited back way to return to Porter's Pub. Garbage was thrown into the river all the time; if the hatchet was ever found, it would be washed clean, with no connection to anything.

Colton pulled a crumpled sheet of paper and a small computer disk out of his pocket. 'Love along the Nile,' he read from the label. He laughed aloud. "Soon to become 'Love in the Landfill.' Goodbye forever, Wendy Winsome." He tossed the disk and the paper into the direct chute to his building's incinerator.

* * *

After Detective Pierce left, Marcy made a soothing cup of tea and stared out her kitchen window. Alfred was so quiet, so unassuming...who hated Alfred that much? To bash his head in? Such a *bloody* way. *Love along the Nile* was all but finished. Actually, she could finish it herself; it wouldn't take much to delete dead Fred from her disk copy, add a little more steam, and let Wendy Winsome go out in a last hurrah.

* * *

"No, we haven't made any progress." Detective Pierce looked wearily across his desk at Marcy. "We know Doolittle was alive at the time he sent you the fax. His place is so isolated, no one saw anything that afternoon. If his sister hadn't dropped in when she got back to town, he'd be lying there yet. Have you thought of anyone who wanted him dead?"

Marcy shook her head. "There's a couple of people at the monthly Writer's group who don't really care for Alfred, he is – was – such an odd little man. Since we work together, they wouldn't say anything against him to me, even if they hated his good fortune with the Wendy Winsome books."

"Wendy Winsome? Really?" Pierce's surprise was evident. "He was her? My wife *dotes* on those books."

"Many women do," said Marcy, wishing the royalties were hers instead of just getting one-time fees for writing the love scenes. She got up. "I'd like to help."

"Be my guest. We're stumped."

* * *

Marcy's passion was reading mystery novels. She usually spotted the perpetrator halfway through the book. If I can do that, she thought, I ought to be able to figure out who killed Alfred.

But real life wasn't as easy as fiction. Maybe if she wrote it all down, it would come clear. She began typing:

> *He was a small man, who scuttled when he walked, and peered through thick, smeary glasses. Alfred Doolittle was nobody's hero, in person. But on paper, he was every character: hero and heroine, villain, mother, father, child. His books are every author's dream: repeat sellers.*
>
> *Alfred's old house sits in ten wooded acres. His office – a small, made-over kitchen pantry – has state of the art computer, printer and phone-fax machines. Super-controlled air conditioning keeps everything working properly.*
>
> *Alfred was devoted to his sister Ethel. She is married to Bryce Colton, a ladies' man so slick you could slide off him if you got too close, though I never heard Alfred say anything derogatory about him. Bryce also writes, far more scholarly tomes. Bryce can't stand Alfred.*

Marcy stopped typing. Did Bryce actually *hate* Alfred? Enough to kill? Surely Detective Pierce had questioned him, but maybe Bryce would open up to Marcy, as one writer to another.

She made a face at the prospect. Bryce, who considered himself above criticism, hadn't come to writers' meetings since Amelia Grant had highly praised Alfred/ Wendy's last book. Marcy turned off her computer and drove downtown.

His office door proclaimed 'Bryce Colton, Consultant.' What kind of consultant, it didn't say.

She knocked once and walked in to a flurry of movement as Bryce's secretary turned her back and quickly fumbled with her blouse buttons while he pretended to search the bookcase behind her desk.

"Sorry to interrupt."

"Oh, no interruption, Marcy," Bryce said smoothly, pulling out a book. "I was just looking something up."

Something up his secretary's skirt, most likely. "Can we talk? Privately?"

Bryce checked his watch. "For a minute. I've got to go help Ethel with the arrangements."

"You're going to bury Alfred already?"

"Why not?" Bryce shrugged. "It's clear how he died. The police have all the information. Whoever did it is long gone." Bryce motioned Marcy into his office and settled her in a leather chair. "Now, what can I do for you?"

"First, tell me how Ethel is taking this. And then tell me where you were yesterday afternoon, for starters."

Bryce raised his eyebrows. "Doing some sleuthing, are we, Miss March?" He leaned back complacently. "Ethel is devastated, of course. I'm sorry about Alfred, and it's no secret I detested the little shrimp, but the police know I was with Candy King at Porter's Pub from about two until early evening. I know you and Alfred are – were – friends, but I don't think my whereabouts is any of your concern."

Marcy rose. "Maybe not. But Alfred's death does concern me. There was no reason for it."

Bryce made a disparaging sound. "There's always a reason for everything. Now, I really must go. Ethel needs me."

Marcy walked out past the busily typing secretary, thinking, is it just because I don't like Bryce, or does he have something to hide?

* * *

"I'll have the salmon salad," Marcy said to the heavily made up waitress at the Salad Kitchen. The lunch crowd was gone. "And I'd like to talk with you for a moment, if you have time. You're Candy King, aren't you?"

"Yeah. Whatsit to you? You a cop?"

"No way."

Candy pursed her too-red lips. "Let me put your order in. Then I got only a minute." She hung the order ticket on a revolving wheel over the kitchen pass-through and plunked down across from Marcy. "What."

"Bryce Colton says you were with him yesterday afternoon."

"I already told the cops I was. At Porter's Pub."

"All afternoon?"

"Yeah..." she paused. "'Cept for a phone call he had to make from his car. We had dinner later."

"He didn't leave you alone, at all?"

"Just that little, for the call." Candy frowned. "Why?"

Marcy sighed. "Just wondered."

Candy got up. "That all? Your salad's ready."

The usually excellent salad tasted like disappointment.

Back at her computer, Marcy typed in her encounter with Candy, and wondered whether she had really thought Candy was going to hang Bryce. But something about him didn't ring true; she wasn't sure just what it was. Maybe his insincere concern.

Marcy looked again at the last fax she had received.

Looked closer.

The smudges.

Two of them were just smudges. But the third...it was a definite fingerprint. Not really clear, but...

Marcy picked up the phone. "Detective Pierce, did you find the original of Alfred Doolittle's fax to me in his office?"

"Just a minute." Marcy heard Pierce shuffle through papers. "Not listed here, why?"

"Because it should have been. He would have sent it just before he was killed. I sent my answer right back, within minutes."

A pause. "Right. Wasn't there, though. Not anywhere."

"What about a computer disk marked 'Love along the Nile'"?

More shuffling. "No. Lots of others, but not that one."

"I have something to show you. I'll be right down."

* * *

Pierce looked closely at the smudges. "Yes, they do look like prints, but only one might be clear enough to identify."

"Want to know what I think?"

"Sure."

"I think they're blood, not ink. I think the killer sent the fax after Alfred was dead. Maybe for quite a while."

Pierce raised his brows. "But the time of death – 4:19 or thereabouts, clicks with the body temp, give or take."

"I've thought about that. But Alfred's tiny office had a powerful air conditioner. What if the killer turned the temperature way down to make it seem he was killed later?"

Pierce rubbed his chin. "Possible."

"Could you check something for me?"

"If I can."

"See if any calls were made from Bryce Colton's car phone about the time Alfred's fax was sent?"

"You've got an idea about all this?"

"Just a hunch."

Minutes later, Pierce said, "No calls."

Marcy nodded. "Candy told me he was gone just long enough to make an 'important' call. I think he killed Alfred earlier, met her, then zipped back to Alfred's, sent me the already-prepared fax but bloodied his fingers doing it. He couldn't take time to make another original. He waited for my answer, and scooted back to Porter's to cover his tracks."

"What about the murder weapon? The computer disk? The messed-up original fax?"

"He's smart. He got rid of them all. But, if this print is clear enough to match with his, we might find something at his office building."

"What makes you so sure? Even without checking the print with Colton's?"

"Because," said Marcy, "look where the prints are on this fax I received. He put the fax into the machine with his *left* hand. Bryce Colton is a lefty. Alfred was right handed."

* * *

The clear print matched Bryce Colton's left thumb. *Love along the Nile* was, like the other Wendy Winsome books, a bestseller. And Marcy March, through Alfred Doolittle's will, received the rights to continue to publish under the Winsome name.

She'd solved the mystery of Alfred's death…by simply studying the fax.

Raven Nevermore

Louise Taylor

WHOEVER INVITED Beverly Buckshire to join the Pauper's Poetry Circle should be poisoned. Inexplicably, that 'whoever' turned out to be Les West (aka DJ Dare).

With a name like 'Les West', did he actually need a hip pseudonym? That was just one irritating feature about Les. Others included the phony 'ghetto' speak he veered into (particularly embarrassing when Walter Havel-Smith was present). Annabelle knew for a fact that Les came from a solid farming family in rural Vermont and was surviving in Paris on a tiny trust fund. Further annoyances included his love of clove cigarettes and the punk rock clothing that only drew attention to his flaccid body. Nothing quite said *old* like a belly sagging over the waist of torn skinny jeans. That said, Les produced beautiful verse. And he had great eyes.

Why Beverly Buckshire? If any two people had less in common, it was Les and Beverly. She was champagne and caviar (albeit, the trashy Euro kind) while Les was corn nuts and beer. Yet not only did Les invite Beverly to join the poetry circle (without asking anyone beforehand), but the whole damn group (again, inexplicably!) had embraced her.

Beverly's first poem, *Ode to a Croissant,* received an unprecedented round of applause and she had ingratiated herself ever since to the point that they now met at her swanky townhouse instead of Annabelle's tiny flat. The plates piled with pastries (including, of course, croissants) served with strong Indian tea and a full open bar no doubt played a pivotal role in seducing the threadbare group.

Annabelle's standing slipped a peg with each meeting. For years, she had hosted their meetings, her cramped living room arranged solely for the comfort of their weekly gatherings. Then one cold Saturday Beverly offered the spacious abode she shared with husband Graham after the heat went out in Annabelle's building. Annabelle still fumed when she recalled the group's unbridled admiration over Beverly's richly appointed home. She thought they were paupers and proud of it! Yet from the blissful expressions as they settled in front of Beverly's roaring fireplace coddling snifters of Cognac, she saw that she was wrong.

Beverly also encroached on Annabelle's other role – that of chief critic. While Annabelle's poems weren't the cleverest (and certainly not the most published) she liked to think tha the criticism she offered, designed to draw the best out of each writer, was valued. The group had an unspoken agreement whereby Annabelle spoke first after each reading, drawing from careful notes she took. Beverly had started leading the critiques with her own uninformed analyses, leaping in during the tiny split-second Annabelle needed to gather her thoughts.

Besides poaching the roles of hostess and critic, Beverly had the Havel-Smiths firml in her thrall since inviting Walter to lead a writer's retreat she was organizing in a Loir valley chateau. Honestly, the woman moved faster than mold in a Normandy outhouse

At their most recent gathering, not only did Beverly not *get* Annabelle's poem *Rave Awaits* (nine months in the writing!) but she had the gall to pronounce it 'gloomy

Annabelle seethed through Beverly's insulting critique and returning home after to a fifth-floor walk-up the size of Beverly's bathroom hadn't helped matters.

The Havel-Smiths usually pointed out the better features of Annabelle's work, but they were too busy preparing for their Loire Valley retreat. Instead, after Beverly's ignorant assault, the group had to listen to Dirk Austin's pedantic comparison with that other famous raven (as if Annabelle would attempt to highjack Poe!) until the group was glassy eyed with boredom.

Poe hadn't taken out a patent on ravens, had he? Other writers were still free to mention them as far as Annabelle knew. Yet Dirk droned on, quoting Poe line and verse until Annabelle felt like a cheap fraud. Meanwhile Les coolly sucked on his clove cigarette, looking faintly amused and above it all. What an imposter! Annabelle had seen him stuff two croissants into his coat pocket when he thought no one was looking. Martha Wainwright, too timid as usual to forward an opinion, sat perched on her chair, her lank mushroom-colored hair drooping in her face.

"*Quoth the raven 'Nevermore!'*" Dirk wound up, looking triumphantly around the room.

'Nevermore' am I coming to this group,' Annabelle thought bitterly, though she said nothing.

But back she came. Without the poetry group, Annabelle's weekends yawned as empty as Death Valley in August. Her hotel job was dreary, but it paid the bills and filled her week. The weekends were more troublesome.

So here she was again, resentfully watching as Beverly, squashed into a pumpkin-colored silk trouser suit that flattered her auburn hair, held court, assigning each member to one of the seats she had carefully arranged around a magnificent ebony coffee table. Annabelle deliberately took the chair designated for Les. Beverly looked askance but said nothing.

Ladurée macaroons were in abundance today, Annabelle's favorite, though she'd be damned if she let Beverly know that. Taking her cue from Les and the croissants, she covertly wrapped her napkin around a copious pile and stuffed them into her handbag.

The group typically discussed one or two pieces of verse per meeting. This week, Tim Lemon had reluctantly agreed to read. After a few minutes of chatter, Tim passed around copies of *Kansas City Waitress*. He had been trying 'to work out the knots' since last February. What started out as a morsel of folksy Americana had transmuted over time into a pretentious, overwrought rendering of what boiled down to little more than a cheesy one-night stand. Perhaps the only one he had experienced in his nineteen years, so understandably important to Tim, he had yet to convince the reader of the transcendental significance of a quickie in a coffee shop during a snow storm. Although Annabelle would never say so. Certainly not in those terms. One had to focus on the *positive*. One had to *encourage*.

Dirk somehow beat both Annabelle and Beverly to the punch when Tim finished reading, launching into a dry monologue on winter power outages in the mid-west. Annabelle zoned out. If she gave up the poetry group, what could she do with her weekends? While she didn't particularly enjoy helping tourists navigate their way to the Louvre, her job was busy and the days went by fast. She should have got in with one of the bigger hotels years ago. It was too late in the game now. She'd be lucky if she could hang on to her job until retirement. She wondered if she could convince the other receptionists to share the coveted higher-paying weekend shift. She supposed she could try volunteer work again, although serving soup to smelly old homeless people had proved much less satisfying than she'd imagined. She could possibly go back to church. She wondered if they'd forgotten the incident with Iris Dagoune. Not that everyone believed what happened was Annabelle's fault. After all, it had been ruled an accident. In any case, everybody knew that Annabelle had been in charge of cleaning the silver for years. Iris had come out of nowhere. Officially nobody had actually *banned* Annabelle from attending the church, although the pastor had hinted…oh, dear God, was Dirk singing *Wichita Lineman?*

"And the Wichita Lineman…is still on the roooooaaad!"

There was an embarrassed silence as Dirk wound up, his snow white hair glistening under the chandelier Beverly had lit against the darkening sky.

"Anyhow," Tim started after an awkward pause. "What I'm *trying* to convey…"

"The *problem*," Beverly interrupted abruptly. "Actually, one of *many* problems, as far as I can see…" she continued with a little chuckle.

Annabelle cringed. It had taken Tim months to screw up the courage to show his poem to the group. Criticism should be delivered with a gentle hand, not dumped over the author's head like a bucket of icy water. Even the word 'problem' was, well, problematic. Annabelle would have chosen 'challenge'. But Beverly knew nothing of the subtle courtesies the group had honed over the years. The room fell silent as Beverly continued her scathing assault.

Tim put on a brave face, even snickering when Beverly suggest he find a more sophisticated synonym for 'boobs', yet Annabelle knew he was wounded by the relentless diatribe. How could he not be? She had to do something.

"Well, I have to disagree," she began when Beverly finally finished, peering over her reading glasses to give Tim a conspiratorial wink. "*Kansas City Waitress* is definitely getting somewhere. The only *problem,"* here she gave Beverly a withering look, "is that not everyone was part of the group when we first heard the poem. Even Tim will admit that what began as an exposé of a sordid little tryst of no real interest to anyone (I'm sure even the waitress has long forgotten it!)"– Beverly wasn't the only one who could be witty – "is emerging as an exploration of American misogyny and male entitlement. Most young men would not have the courage to expose their own vulgarity and naïveté. It takes bravery to reveal such ignorance, such shallowness. Such stupidity, really. I say, *bravo*."

Annabelle looked around. Dirk still had a pleased-looking smile plastered on his face from his song. Martha's face wore its typical question mark of worry. Les was dozing off in his chair. Tim, meanwhile, was clenching his jaw hard enough to shatter his teeth. His face shone with fury.

Was Beverly *blind*? Could she not she see how she stepped on toes and hurt feelings? After another awkward pause, during which Annabelle imagined the others reflecting on the ingenuity of her critique, Dirk broke the silence.

"So who's next?" He said, merrily clapping his large worn hands.

* * *

Annabelle wasn't surprised when no one volunteered on the heels of Beverly's insensitive remarks. As Martha studied the battered tips of her pale blue ballerinas, Annabelle's hear sank. She had overheard the young woman confide to Tim that she was ready to present he first poem as they were pulling on their coats at the end of their last gathering. Annabell was looking forward to hearing Martha's work. Still waters ran deep, after all. It would be welcome relief after the shallow pools of Tim's *Waitress* and Beverly's *Croissant*. But Marth remained stubbornly silent.

"If no one else has anything, I've tweaked *Ode to a Croissant* a bit," Beverly said dainti when no one replied. Seriously? Heedless of the ill feelings she had aroused, Beverly wa keen to step back into the limelight. What a narcissist! Annabelle could not bear to s through another reading of the cloying *Croissant,* a poem that plundered every French stereotype ever propagated, from the grumpy café waiter to the chic *Parisienne.* As Beverly was pulling out her work, Les came to the rescue.

"I have something I'd kinda like to read," he drawled in what Annabelle knew from years of observation was a false display of modesty. Still, Les possessed a unique perspective and was the most published of the rag-tag group. Only Walter Havel-Smith came close, with a verse that appeared in *Granta* six years earlier, and from which he still drew mileage, including now, it appeared a gig at Beverly's fancy Loire Valley writer's retreat for bored housewives. Annabelle wondered whether he was getting paid.

Beverly, clearly annoyed as the group enthusiastically turned toward Les, managed to recover quickly.

"Ooh, yes, please," she cozied, batting her eyelashes at Les.

As Les prepared to read, there came a sharp rap at the door. As Dirk went to answer, Annabelle witnessed another flicker of irritation cross Beverly's heavily made-up features. This was *her* salon after all; she should have the privilege of welcoming guests. But *oblivious* was Dirk's middle name.

As Walter and Patricia Havel-Smith swept into the room, it was Les' turn to look peeved. He could do without their donnish presence. Les didn't know about anyone else, but he was relieved when the pompous couple didn't show. With them out of the way, Les could reign as group intellectual without endless quibbling over some of the more dubious facts he sprinkled throughout his work. While the Havel-Smiths considered these discussions 'spirited' and 'enlightening', Les resented the constant querying of his knowledge. He recalled with particular ire a lengthy debate over whether Hume was truly an atheist following the reading of Les' poem *Lumière.* When the Havel-Smiths were absent, Les could get some peace. Beverly Buckshire and Tim were too stupid to dispute any of his facts, Annabelle too gaga, and the other one too timid. Only Dirk might pose a problem, but then who actually listened to Dirk? While his *Thistles in January* had stunned the group with its sensitivity and grace, Dirk hadn't presented anything new in three years. Les often wondered if Dirk wasn't in the early stages of dementia.

Annabelle also felt irritable at the arrival of the Havel-Smiths. Where the hell were they when *Raven Awaits* was being plucked apart? If they weren't going to show up on a regular basis, they should just quit.

After much blustering, the robust Havel-Smiths were comfortably ensconced, laden with tea and a heaping plate of macaroons, including, Les noticed with vexation, the last of the chocolate ones, over which Patricia's hand was now hovering.

"Les was just about to read something new," Annabelle informed Walter, who raised his eyebrows in a way that Les interpreted as condescending. Seething inside, he gave Walter a steely look, then, shaking the mop of graying curls from his eyes, made his expression go blank and prepared to read.

Though he signed it DJ Dare, *X into Y* was pure Les: a work of showy intelligentsia interwoven with explicit imagery and raw emotion, which swept the listener around the world, examining *en route* the isolation and grief that united humanity in the face of the inescapable solitude of death. By the time he wrapped up, Annabelle was breathless.

Now *that* was poetry.

"I don't think Zaranj is actually in Afghanistan," Walter ventured after a brief silence. "It's on the *border* with Afghanistan, but it's in Iran."

Patricia, the other half of the rotund Havel-Smith couple, could only nod in agreement, her mouth stuffed with the chocolate macaroon.

Annabelle felt a twinge of anger. Les had just exposed the human condition – in some sort of folkloric verse, no less – and Walter and Patricia wanted to nitpick.

"It's in Afghanistan," Les said flatly.

"Was that haiku?" Beverly gushed. No one in the group missed the intimate squeeze she gave Les' knee.

"Uh…I don't think so," Tim ventured. An English major doing a year abroad, Tim wasn't sure what verse Les used, but he knew it wasn't haiku.

"Oh, the Afghans," bemoaned Dirk. "First attacked from the outside and now being destroyed from within." His craggy face took on the faraway look he had when working up a monologue.

"Zaranj is in Afghanistan. Look on a map," Les snapped. "The form is an ancient Afghan verse called Landay. As for the Afghans, a lot of their troubles they've brought on themselves." With that, Les lit up a clove cigarette.

Patricia Havel-Smith waved dramatically at the smoke. Les rolled his eyes and blew a lungful directly at her.

'Looks like I'm not the only one who's fed up,' Annabelle reflected. Maybe she could lure Les away and form a splinter group. They could bring Tim and Martha with them. She gave Les a sympathetic look, turning her thin mouth down in a little moue. He studiously ignored her. That Les, he was a moody one. Great talents often were.

Patricia Havel-Smith tore herself away from the macaroons long enough to offer an opinion.

"While there are certainly some great ideas in the piece, I'm not sure if the form is really suitable."

Walter nodded his large black head in agreement.

"I don't know much about *form*," interceded Beverly, "but I know I like what I heard. Why, I almost feel like I've been to Afghanistan and forced to wear a burka while there!"

Les tried not to look pleased at this last comment, which to Annabelle's ears sounded vaguely lascivious. Well, two could play at that game. Beverly didn't know who she was dealing with. Annabelle and Les went way back. Nothing had actually happened yet between them, but there had more than a few sparks over the years. Annabelle was almost certain his poem *Muse* was about her.

"I was swept away," she began breathlessly, giving Les a coy glance. But Les was locked into a smoldering gaze with Beverly, their eyes shining with desire. Annabelle's comment hung in the air, prim and cloying. "Undo my stays and fetch the smelling salts!" could have been her follow-up line.

While the rest of the group feasted voyeuristically on the mortifying moment, Annabelle sat perfectly still as a hurricane of emotions writhed through her. Disappointment gave way to betrayal followed by rage. The silence was broken by Dirk, who cleared his throat.

"The burka," he began in a lecturing voice, "takes different styles and forms according to the interpretation of the Quran…and of course local customs."

But nobody cared about the burka. Everyone wanted to know more about the obvious liaison between confirmed bachelor Les and the married Beverly Buckshire.

"But you should know about burkas, Beverly," Dirk said abruptly, uncharacteristic venom tainting his voice. "Your husband spent a lot of time in that part of the world, back in the day as they say."

"He was in Kuwait for seven years," Amana conceded uncomfortably.

"He certainly was," Dirk confirmed, now openly hostile.

The Havel-Smiths exchanged bewildered glances. Annabelle recalled a rumor she had heard about Dirk losing his fortune in an oil swindle a decade ago. Had Buckshire been involved? Why would Dirk make a fuss about it now?

But Dirk had regained control of his emotions and returned to the topic of the burka. "Why *blue* in Afghanistan? One might ask."

Les and Beverly? Annabelle couldn't believe it! Beverly wasn't his type, what with her corporate spouse lifestyle, her big Jackie-O hair and the glossy Hermes scarves she used to hide her crepey neck. Les was practically an anarchist. He'd only hook up with someone like Beverly to literally screw the system.

More importantly, surely Les wouldn't be so crass to destroy the unspoken affinity between them by parading an affair before Annabelle's eyes. She couldn't have been mistaken all these years. The small gestures, the subtle flatteries, the lingering glances. Had she imagined all that? Or had Beverly managed to undo years of patient, steady building with her brash, bosomy ways? She was clearly a woman used to getting what she wanted; one glance around her opulent flat made that clear. Besides, what middle-aged woman wouldn't enjoy an encounter with a starving artist boy-toy like Les? One final fling before the ravishes of age put her out to pasture.

Poor Les! Although he played the weary cynic, he didn't know when he was being duped. Beverly would play with him like a yo-yo, dumping him the minute he became dull. Annabelle had come across plenty of Beverlys in her day: bored ex-pat housewives with too much time and money. Paris was crawling with them.

"Where are you planning on submitting it?" Martha Wainwright was addressing her question to Les. Before he could respond, Beverly had clapped her hands together. "Graham has a friend at the *New Yorker*," she announced. "He's going to forward it for Les."

So *that's* what it was all about. Les would shag a sheep to get published in the *New Yorker*. Annabelle hid her smirk. That Les – he really *was* a bad boy! Beverly was going to crash and burn!

But by the next week, Les seemed deeper under Beverly's spell. Entering in a battered black leather trench, he gave Beverly a frankly lustful smile. The Havel-Smiths were also unusually warm to their hostess, while monosyllabic Tim kissed her hand and even Dirk had gotten over his resentment of the previous week. Beverly appeared indifferent to the ingratiating gestures as she flitted about like an agitated butterfly. Only Martha remained her usual tepid self.

It was the last Saturday of the month and tradition held that they study a well-known work. It was Martha's first turn to select a poem. Annabelle could only imagine the agonies the girl had endured trying to come up with something that wouldn't make Les sneer or Walter torpedo her with his patronizing comments.

In fact, Martha made a bold choice and presented it with surprising confidence. Annabelle vaguely recalled William Blake's *A Poison Tree* from her undergraduate years. The poem was some sort of Christian allegory – the kind of thing that hadn't captured her interest back then. Today, however, she listened with an interest that became infused with alarm as Martha read aloud in her gentle voice.

I was angry with my friend:
I told my wrath, my wrath did end.
I was angry with my foe:

I told it not, my wrath did grow.

And I watered it in fears
Night and morning with my tears,
And I sunned it with smiles
And with soft deceitful wiles.

And it grew both day and night,
Till it bore an apple bright,
And my foe beheld it shine,
And he knew that it was mine,--

And into my garden stole
When the night had veiled the pole;
In the morning, glad, I see
My foe outstretched beneath the tree.

Throughout the reading, Annabelle sensed Martha glancing at her.

The message hidden in the chosen verse was easy to interpret. It was a cry for help! Beverly was obviously the 'foe'.

What was Martha saying? Did she wish Beverly harm? Annabelle realized she'd thought only of herself and how Beverly had compromised her own standing in the group. She didn't realize things had become so bad for the others, too. She couldn't bear to think of young Martha's or Tim's budding enthusiasm for writing extinguished by the over-bearing redhead. Beverly was destroying the group! Look at how she'd ripped apart Tim's poem -- Martha didn't dare show her work now. Even mild-mannered Dirk had a problem with Beverly. And then there was Les! Les was the last straw.

Annabelle would be doing the whole damn group a favor by getting rid of Beverly. But *how*? She'd wormed her way into the very heart of the group. Maybe the Havel-Smiths could be brought to reason. After all, they were the most intelligent. But they barely showed up anymore. Besides, Beverly had won them over with her writer's retreat. They were scarcely likely to bite the hand that was feeding them. Patricia was already talking about holding regular paying writing workshops after the retreat. It was a travesty! The Pauper's Poetry Circle had sold out and they were all too shallow and greedy to admit it. It was up to Annabelle to save them. Hadn't their philosophy always been that money couldn't compare to art and noble values and what-not? The group had limped along for the past eleven years and Annabelle would be damned if she'd let Beverly sweep in and destroy it now. Money could not buy everything! She would be doing the Pauper's Poetry Circle a favor by getting rid of Beverly. But *how*?

Desperate measures called for desperate actions.

* * *

It was an exciting week for Annabelle. After poring a dusty tome in the chemistry section of the local library, she spent an afternoon travelling to a seedy internet cafe on the other side of the city where she could be anonymous. Her eyes darted around the dingy café as she made a furtive online purchase, her credit card held close to her chest. It was risky, but she had no choice.

She was surprised when a tattered little parcel showed up in her mailbox nine days later. She thought it would be weeks, if it came at all. It was all turning out to be so easy. It was as if the universe wanted her to do it. Putting her plot into action would be the trickiest part.

As if by providence, at the next meeting, Beverly surprised them with large pitchers of homemade eggnog. Christmas was still a month away but the group was breaking for the holidays and would not reconvene until mid-January. Annabelle missed the weekly get-together during the holidays but she pretended to be excited over the prospect of festivities, travel, family and friends. Maybe she would take herself to London. If only she had a companion to go with. Her mind turned to a familiar daydream: she and Les holidaying in London – poking around bookshops, stopping for tea, sharing a sagging bed in a quaint little B&B they could chuckle over later. She was sure they had been building toward just such a relationship until Beverly waltzed in and snagged Les from under her nose. Well, that would soon be over.

Beverly plied her guests with drink the moment they walked through the door. For once they weren't obliged to take assigned seats, but stood around talking, holding elegant crystal tumblers filled with the milky beverage, helping themselves from plates of minced pies and Christmas cake. Annabelle avoided imbibing the bourbon-heavy drink. She needed a clear head for what was to come. The others had no such qualms. Even Martha was drinking up, her pale face already reddening from the combination of alcohol and the heat that radiated from an open fireplace where scented logs burned merrily.

Annabelle patted the pocket of her cardigan. The vial was there, holding the pale blue liquid she had carefully prepared the night before. She awaited an opportunity to put her plan into action.

Beverly unwittingly assisted Annabelle by staining the rim of her glass with unmistakable orange lipstick. Annabelle watched Beverly place her tumbler on the mantel piece while she poked at the burning logs. She just needed one moment alone. This was miraculously afforded a short while later when Dirk, already on his third eggnog, stumbled sideways into Beverly's Christmas tree.

While the others rushed over to assist Dirk as he lay entangled amongst the tree ornaments, Annabelle took a deep breath, her heart pounding in her ears, and removed the vial from her pocket. She undid the small rubber stopper and carefully emptied the contents into Beverly's glass on the mantel piece. She quickly topped up the glass with more eggnog, pouring shakily from the heavy pitcher. She gave the concoction a quick stir with her finger. Smoothing her graying bob, she poured herself a large glass of eggnog to steady her nerves, then settled into her favorite seat, a leather wingback Chippendale. She would miss this chair.

She was forcing her tense muscles to relax when there came a fresh commotion. Walter and Les had squared off and were swinging punches at each other.

"Liar!" Walter spat at Les in response to something Annabelle hadn't heard.

Beverly shrieked as a side table of figurines crashed to the floor.

Annabelle leapt to her feet. Placing herself between the two men, she smiled inwardly. Her flushed cheeks and trembling hands might now be blamed on the brawl. She never imagined it would be so easy. It was as if God himself wanted her to take out Beverly.

It took a while to calm the group down, but Annabelle was damned if she would let the gathering be sidetracked from their annual tradition of listening to a genuine recording of Dylan Thomas reciting *A Child's Christmas in Wales*. There was only one distraction she was willing to put up with today, and that was the expiration of Beverly Buckshire. If she had mixed the formula correctly, Beverly would go quickly, without expelling a lot of messy bodily fluids. It was supposed to be like drifting off to sleep…forever.

As the group took their seats to listen to the poem, Les and Walter glared at each other across the coffee table. Annabelle sat stiffly, her mouth pursed. She was tired of playing policeman. If people weren't willing to abide by the rules, perhaps they *should* disband. She said as much and plenty more, taking each member to task for their various infractions. Dirk was disruptive and distracted, Les was arrogant and mercenary. She wanted to say 'unfaithful' or even 'sluttish' but she couldn't have *that* conversation at group level. They'd have a talk later. In the meantime, the Havel-Smiths weren't committed, Tim was crude, and Martha needed to participate more if she wanted to stay in the Pauper's Poetry Circle. She couldn't bring herself to address Beverly and hoped nobody noticed. But the others she willingly reprimanded. Why must it fall to Annabelle to keep the group in line each time? It was *painful* for her! The others listened meekly. When she was done, Annabelle rewarded herself with a large swig of eggnog. Was it her imagination, or did Les smirk at Walter as she swallowed the pungent brew?

Fifteen minutes later Annabelle was feeling more than woozy. What was the trace of orange on the rim of her glass, she wondered blearily as her head started spinning.

At Beverly's urging, she loosened her skirt clasp and lay down on the sofa. In the background she heard mumbling. At one point she thought she heard Martha Wainwright murmur, "*It shouldn't be much longer*". Then everything went black.

* * *

The police – you'd think they'd seen it all. After all, plenty of people went public these days. But a suicide during a Christmas party, for Christ's sake? They found the concoction in Annabelle's tiny kitchen next to a notebook open to her poem *Raven Awaits*. It was obviously a suicide confession.

* * *

After the holidays, the group reconvened. Martha brought her first poem to read aloud. Dirk discussed the verse he had started composing during the holiday break. The Havel-Smiths were downright jolly – the stint at the chateau had brought them lucrative new business. Tim had added a few earthy descriptions to *Kansas City Waitress* and was thinking of sending it to Playpen magazine's forum. Les' poem *X into Y* would be appearing in the *New Yorker* in May. Beverly and Les sat together holding hands. Everyone felt free – untethered. They decided the poetry group needed a fresh name. As they toasted each other, Dirk came up with the perfect moniker: Raven Nevermore. The Raven Nevermore Poetry Group.

Discovering Rex

Edgar Wallace

IN THE OFFICE of the Public Prosecutor was a young lawyer named Keddler, for whom the prospects were of the brightest until he grew impatient with the type of evidence which was supplied him by the painstaking but unimaginative constabulary, and went out single-handed to better their efforts. And he succeeded so remarkably well that a reluctant Commissioner of Police admitted his superiority as a detective and offered him a post at New Scotland Yard.

This offer was enthusiastically accepted, but since the regulations do not admit of amateur police work and he found himself relegated to the legal department, where his work consisted of preparing statements of evidence for his successor at the P.P. office to examine, he resigned at the end of six months. To return to his former position was, at the time, impossible, and against the advice of his friends and in face of solemn warnings from his old chief, he opened an office in the city of London, describing himself as an 'Investigating Agent.'

Despite the gloomy predictions of his associates, John Keddler grew both opulent and famous. The opulence was welcome, but the fame was embarrassing, not that John was unduly modest, but because it led on three occasions to his identification at a moment when it was vitally necessary that he should be unknown to the persons who detected him.

Starting on a small job for the Midland and County Bank, a matter of a forged acceptance, in which the real police had failed to satisfy the bank, he enlarged his clientele until he found himself working amicably with Scotland Yard in the matter of Rex Jowder, alias Tom the Toy, alias Lambert Sollon.

Rex was wanted urgently by several police departments for insurance fraud, impersonation, theft, forgery, and general larceny, but only the insurance fraud was really important because it involved a well-known Chicago house in a loss of 700,000 dollars, which they were anxious to recover before Rex, who was notoriously careless when he handled other people's money, dissipated his fortune in riotous living. John Keddler was commissioned by the London agents of the company to bring about this desirable result, but unfortunately the lean, shrewd thief had learnt from an indiscreet newspaper that John was his principal danger, and had spent two days waiting in the country lane in which the detective's modest little house was situated, and one dark night when John descended from his car to open the gates of his demesne, six pounds weight of sand had fallen upon his shoulder. The sand was enclosed in a sausage-shaped bag, and it was intended for his neck.

Taken at this disadvantage Keddler was almost helpless and would have ceased to worry Mr. Jowder until the inevitable give and take of the Day of Judgment, only the assailant had placed himself in an unfavorable position to follow up his attack, though it was helpful to him that the red rear light of the car reflected on the polished steel of the gun John pulled mechanically.

He dived to the cover of a hedge and ran, and John Keddler had been so respectabl brought up that he hesitated to scandalize the neighborhood by discharging firearms t the public danger. In some respects John Keddler was a slave of convention. But this mil adventure served to concentrate his mind and attention still more closely upon the case c Rex Jowder, and so well did he work that at the end of a week there was a police raid upo a certain safe deposit in the city, and there was discovered the bulk of the stolen mone which the misguided Jowder had cached (as he believed) beyond the fear of discovery.

Why this raid was carried out is a story made up of John's instinct, a drunken man, frightened woman (Rex was strong for ladies' society), and an indiscreet reference, repeate by his terrorized lady friend, to a mysterious key which hung about his neck. He would hav been captured also, only the police were a little over-elaborate in their preparations.

With his money gone, the fruit of two years' clever and dangerous work, Rex Jowde became something more than annoyed. Before him was a life sentence, and standing at th focal point of his misfortune was one John Keddler. From the point of view of the insuranc company whose gratitude he had earned, John was not a 'good life.'

"What about Jowder?" asked his confidential clerk.

"Jowder can wait," said John. "As a matter of fact I am not very much interested in th man any longer."

But the man was very much interested in John, and he was content to wait too, thoug his waiting had to be done in a mean Lambeth lodging.

As for John Keddler, he accepted in a joyous holiday spirit the commission whic followed the loss of Lady Bresswell's jewelry, for Lady Bresswell lived on the Lake of Comc and John was partial to the Italian lakes. Incidentally this visit was to introduce him to th Marchessa Della Garda – that unhappy lady.

From the first the wisdom of Mona Harringay's marriage bristled with notes c interrogation – those little sickles that trim the smothering overgrowth of truth.

There was no doubt that the Della Garda family hated the Marchessa with a hatred bor of an enormous disappointment. They referred to Mona as 'The Señora Pelugnera' (the affected Spanish by virtue of their descent from the Borgias), and 'Mrs. Hairdresser' wa adopted to keep fresh the ghastly fact that Mona's father was the very rich proprietor c Harringay's Elixir for the Hair.

The marriage was in every way an amazing one, for Giocomi was no impoverishe third cousin of the real nobility. Head of the Della Garda clan and immensely wealth the ordinary excuses and explanations of a marriage between an Italian marquis and th daughter of a rich American were wanting. They had met in Harringay's Long Island hom where Giocomi was a guest. He was making his first long absence from the Continent c Europe. Therefore he was home-sick and miserable when he met Mona, and their marriag was the natural reaction. She, for her part, was fascinated by his good looks and a littl overwhelmed by the impetuosity of his wooing. The wedding was the social event of brilliant season.

Not until the liner was clear of Sandy Hook did Giocomi Della Garda emerge from hi delirium, and face the certainty of his relatives' wrath. For all his good looks and his perfec manners, he was not a nice young man. He had, in particular, a weakness for approva one of the most fatal to which the human soul is liable, and the nearer to Genoa the vesse came, the more and more he resented the existence of a wife who had already surrendere her mystery, that lure which had led Giocomi into so many adventures, but which ha never before yielded him a wife.

Mona, Marchessa Della Garda, realized the bleak failure of her life long before she came home to the cold, oppressive atmosphere of the gloomy palace which had housed sixteen generations of the family. Neither the cold majesty of the Pallacco Della Garda, nor the exotic splendors of the Villa Mendoza, set amidst the loveliness of Lake Como, brought compensation to a disillusioned heart-sick girl. But her one and only visit to the Como home was not without its consequences. Lady Bresswell, a grateful and somewhat voluble lady (her lost jewels recovered without the scandal which would have attended the investigations of the police), was showing John Keddler the glories of the lake. They had brought her ladyship's expensive motor-boat to a rest near Cadenabbia, and the servants were spreading lunch when round a tiny headland came a boat, the sole occupant of which was a girl.

She pulled with long, steady strokes and seemed oblivious to their presence, although she only passed them a dozen yards away.

John Keddler, a man to whom all women were very much alike, gazed at her fascinated. The sun in her russet gold hair, the appealing sadness of her delicate face, the sweep of her perfect figure, took his breath away. It was as though he had seen a vision of some other world.

He watched her until she brought the boat to a white landing-stage, and stepping out and tying the boat, had disappeared behind a great fuchsia bush.

Then he heaved a long sigh, and like a man waking from a dream turned to meet the laughing eyes of his hostess.

"Who was that?" he asked, almost in a whisper.

"I've told you twice, Mr. Keddler," smiled Lady Bresswell, "but you were so absorbed that you didn't hear me. She is lovely, isn't she?"

"Who is she?"

"The Marchessa Della Garda, an American girl who married Giocomi – poor dear. Giocomi is rather a beast."

"Oh," said John, and that was all he said.

Sixteen generations on her father's side of hairdressers, general workers, coal-miners, and peasants had supplied Mona Della Garda with the capacity for endurance and patience, but on her mother's side, she went back to some quick-drawing folks who had made the lives of successive western sheriffs exasperatingly lively, and when, some six months after John Keddler had seen her, Giocomi followed a flagrant breach of his marriage vows by boxing her ears, she took a pistol from the drawer of her dressing-table.

There was excellent reason for this act, for Giocomi was weeping with rage at her mild reproach and had flung off to his room in search of a hunting-crop. Following him went Pietro Roma, his valet, also in tears, for this man worshipped the young Marchessa and would have died for her. It nearly happened that he did, for in frenzy at his interference, Giocomi clubbed him into insensibility with the heavy end of the stock. He never used the whip.

The major-domo of his establishment, attending the cracked head of the valet, heard a shot and mistook it for the crack of a whip, until the Marchessa came downstairs wearing a heavy carriage coat over her evening dress and carrying her jewel-case in her hand. Even then, he did no more than wonder why the illustrious lady should go abroad on a night of storm.

Later came doctors, examining magistrates, and, one by one, white-faced Della Gardas to take counsel together. More than a week passed and Giocomi Della Garda was laid away in the dingy family vaults of SS. Theresa and Joseph, before the name of John Keddler was mentioned.

It came about that news reached Rome of Pietro Roma, who disappeared with a broken head the day after his master's death and had been seen in London.

"If she is in London too," said Philip Della Garda thoughtfully, "you may be sure that she will never be discovered. The English and Americans work hand in hand, and they will do everything that is humanly possible to cover up her tracks. I am all for employing the man Keddler.

He recovered Lady Bresswell's jewelry last summer, and even at the British Embassy they speak of him with respect."

Prince Paolo Crecivicca, his kinsman, stroked his white beard.

"I shall never be happy until this woman is brought to trial," he said, "and I agree that this infernal rascal, Pietro, is probably in communication with her, for, according to Dellimono, he was the man who betrayed to 'The Hairdresser' poor Giocomi's little affair with the Scala girl, and these vulgarians would be on terms of friendship. Employ Mr. Keddler by all means. Wire to him at once."

John Keddler arrived in Rome thirty-six hours later – no miracle this, with the London-Paris, Paris-Milan, Milan-Rome air services in full operation. Though he answered the summons in such a hurry that Philip Della Garda not unnaturally believed he was eager for the job, he displayed no remarkable enthusiasm for the undertaking. Particularly was this apathy noticeable after all that Prince Crecivicca described as the 'unfortunate facts' were revealed.

"In England, of course, she would be acquitted," he said, a little stiffly, "and even in Italy – do you think it is wise to bring this matter before your courts? The publicity... the scandal...?"

Philip Della Garda showed his small teeth in a smile.

"We are superior to public opinion," he said smugly. "Had this happened two hundred years ago we would have dealt with the Hairdresser without invoking the assistance of the courts. As it is—"

As it was explained by the Della Gardas in chorus, this woman must be subjected to the humiliations of a trial, whatever be the jurors' verdict.

"Of course," said John politely. "Have you a photograph of the lady?"

Not until then did he realize that he had been sent to track the woman of his dreams – the woman who had no name to him but "The Girl in the Boat." They saw him frown and a queer expression come to his face.

"I will do my best," he said.

When he had gone, leaving his employers with a sense of dissatisfaction, Philip Della Garda, accounted by his friends as something of a sportsman, had an inspiration.

"Quis custodiet ipsos custodes?" he demanded pedantically. "I will go to London myself."

Passing through Paris, Keddler was seen by a journalist who happened to be on the aviation ground, and it was his speculative note on the occurrence which Mona Della Garda read in her Battersea lodging:

> *Among the famous people who now use the air express for their continental travels is Mr. John Keddler, the well-known private detective. Mr. Keddler, in an interview, says he finds the air-way an invaluable boon. He had been called to Rome in connection with the Della Garda murder, and was able to make the*

return journey in a little over twenty- four hours – a journey which ordinarily would have taken four to five days. He left immediately for London, and hopes to bring about the arrest of the Marchessa in a very short time.

Of course, John Keddler said nothing about the Della Garda murder, or his hopes. He had grunted a "good afternoon" at the enterprising press agent of the Aviation Company, and there began and ended the interview – but Mona Della Garda, reading this paragraph, fell into a blind panic.

For now, the sustaining heat of righteous anger had departed from her, and the strain of the sixteen barber generations – they had been law-abiding and for the most part timorous barbers, with exalted views on the sanctity of human life – was asserting its pull. Murder in any degree was to them merely a phenomenon of the Sunday newspapers, as remote from reality as the moons of Saturn.

"I wonder, miss, if you ever read them agony columns in the newspapers!" asked Mrs. Flemmish one morning.

Mrs. Flemmish was her landlady and a woman from the Wessex borders of Devon, a woman of rolled sleeves and prodigious energy, whose stoves were brighter than the panels of limousines.

Mona had found her room by accident and was perfectly served, for Mrs. Flemmish had unbounded faith in the spoken word of her sex, and never doubted that 'Miss Smith' was a young lady who wrote for the press. Mona had to excuse her feverish interest in the daily newspapers.

"Yes – yes," said Mona, going white. She lost her color readily in these days, and her frequent pallors gave her delicate face a fragility which Mrs. Flemmish in secret accepted as a symptom of lung trouble.

"I'd like to know who this 'Dad' is who keeps on advertising to 'M.', telling her to communicant – communicate, I mean, with him. Where's Long Island, miss?"

"In – in America," said the girl hurriedly, "near New York."

"I suppose she's run away from home," ruminated Mrs. Flemmish. "Girls be girls all over the world – but she ought to let her father know, don't ye think so, Miss Smith?"

Mona nodded. How could she let him know, other than by letter, and a letter was on its way. Mr. Harringay would pass that epistle in mid-ocean, for he had caught the first east-bound liner, a greatly distracted man.

If she could only get into touch with the devoted Pietro. The poor fellow was in London, searching for her – a mad search, since he would be followed, and he could not find her without also betraying her.

A thought came to her on the third evening after the return of John Keddler. There had been some reference to Pietro in the newspapers. A reporter had found him amongst the outcast and homeless on the Thames Embankment one night, and had secured a 'good story' from him. Perhaps he slept there every night? She would search for him. A man's help might save her – even the help of this poor devoted servant.

"I am going out tonight, Mrs. Flemmish," she said.

Mrs. Flemmish made a little grimace.

"It's not a good night for ye, mum," she shook her head. "There's one of them Lunnon fogs workin' up. Did ye read the paper tonight about the Eye-talian lady, miss?"

Mona's heart almost stopped beating.

"N—no," she said; "is there any fresh – which Italian lady?" she asked.

Mrs. Flemmish had settled herself down in the chintz-covered arm- chair and was stirring the fire economically.

"They a' set a detective on her, poor creature," she said. "Do you think 'twas her father that put the advertisement in the paper?"

Mona had a grip of herself now.

"Perhaps," she answered steadily, and Mrs. Flemmish, staring in the orange depths of the fire, nodded.

"If I were her, her bein' a rich young woman, I know what I'd do, ees fay!"

Mona frowned. She had never looked to this sturdy country woman for a solution to her agonizing problems.

"What would you do?" she asked slowly.

"I'd marry a young Englishman," nodded Mrs. Flemmish. "My man were in a lawyer's office an' clever he was, as all the Welsh people are, an' often he's told me that you can't arrest an Englishwoman in England for a crime in foreign parts."

The girl could only stare. That solution had not occurred to her, and if it had, she would have rejected it, for even the enthusiastic scientist is not prone to repeat the experiment which cost him everything short of life by its failure.

"Her has money, by all accounts," said the woman, feeling furtively between the bars of the fire to dislodge a glowing piece of slate. "Her could buy a husband and divorce him, and even when she was divorced her'd be safe."

Mona stood for a long time pinching her red lips in thought, and Mrs. Flemmish turned her head to see if she was still there, a movement that startled the girl into activity.

"I'll go now, Mrs. Flemmish," she said hastily. "I have the key...."

A light yellow mist lay upon the streets, which were crowded even at this late hour, for it was Christmas week, as the cheery contents of the shop windows showed. Great blobs of golden light looming through the fog marked the blazing windows of the stores, and she passed through a road lined with stalls that showed vivid coloring under the flaring, pungent naphtha lamps.

She checked a sob that rose in her throat at the memory of other Christmas weeks, and hurried her pace, glad, at last, to reach the bleakness of the bridge that crossed a gray void where the river had been.

A taxi-cab carried her to the West End, and this she dismissed in the darkest corner of Trafalgar Square, making her way on foot toward Northumberland Avenue. She had to pass under the brilliant portico lights of the Grand Hotel, and had disappeared into the gloom beyond, before the young man who was standing on the step waiting for his car, realized it was she.

She heard his startled exclamation, and looking back in affright, recognizing Philip Della Garda, ran. Swiftly, blindly through the thickening fog she flew, crossing the wide thoroughfare and turning backward into Graven Street.

Philip Della Garda!

He hated London in the best of seasons. There could be only one incentive to his presence in the raw of December, and she was terrified. They would arrest her and take her back to Italy and a lifelong imprisonment. She had heard stories, horrifying stories, of the Italian prisons, where the convicted murderers were buried in an underground cell away from light and human companionship in the very silence of death. None spoke to them, neither guardian nor priest They lived speechless until the thick darkness drove them mad.

She could have shrieked; the terror thus magnified by the uncanny mirk in which she now moved had assumed a new and more hideous significance.

Marriage could save her! It was this mad panic thought that sent her hurrying along the Strand, peering into the faces of men who loomed from the nothingness of the fog and passed, none dreaming of her quest. There were men who leered at her, men who stared resentfully at the eager scrutiny she gave them in the fractional space of a second that the light allowed.

And then the inspiration came, and she hurried down a steep slippery street to the Thames Embankment. The benches were already filled with huddled figures, so wrapped in their thread-bare coats that it was almost impossible to tell that they were human.

"May I speak to you?"

Her heart was beating a stifling tattoo as she sat down in the one unoccupied space which Providence had left by the side of the man whose face she had glimpsed in the light thrown by a passing tramway car.

Instantly she had made her decision. There was a certain refinement revealed in the lean face, a sense of purpose which seemed out of tune with his situation. He did not answer her, but drew more closely to the wreck that slumbered noisily at his side.

"I—I don't know how to begin," she said breathlessly, "but I'm in great trouble. I—I must tell you the truth; the police are searching for me for something I did in Italy—"

She stopped, physically unable to go on.

"The police are searching for you, are they?" There was an undercurrent of amusement in the man's words. "Well, I sympathize with you – I'm being sought for at this particular moment."

She shrank back almost imperceptibly, but he noticed the movement and laughed. She recovered herself. She must go on now to the bitter end.

"Are you British?" she asked, and after a second's hesitation he nodded. "Are you married?" He shook his head. "If I gave you money – a lot of money, would you – would you marry me – at once?"

He half turned and stared at her.

"Why?" he asked.

"Because if—if I became British by marriage they would not arrest me. I only want your name – I will pay you – anything, anything!"

Her voice was husky, and the underlying fear in it was not to be mistaken.

"I see," he said; "you want to be naturalized by marriage. That's the idea?"

She nodded.

"Could it be done – quickly?"

The man rubbed his chin.

"I think it could be done," he said. "Tomorrow is Thursday. If I gave notice we could marry Saturday – where do you live?"

She told him and he rubbed his chin again.

"It might be done," he said. "I've got a sort of claim to Battersea. If I—anyway you can meet me at the registrar's on Saturday at twelve. What is your name?"

She told him that and gave him the other particulars he asked. He seemed to be thinking the matter over, for he did not speak for a long time. A policeman strolled past, flashing his lantern in their direction, and he dropped his head.

"There is one thing I want to say," said Mona desperately. It took all her courage to tell him this. "I only want your name. When – when it is all over I shall divorce you... you understand?"

"H'm," said the man, and got up.

"Let's walk along," he said. "I'll take you as far as Westminster Bridge, and you don't mind if I cross the road occasionally; it might be very awkward if I met a certain person, if I was with you."

The man kept close to the parapet, Mona nodded, and they were abreast of Cleopatra's Needle when he caught her arm and drew her to the recess. The fog had lifted and he had seen a tall saunterer walking near the kerb and scrutinizing the sleepers on the bench.

The searcher did not see them, and the man at Mona's side looked after him.

"If you weren't here," he said softly, "I'd have settled an old score with that gentleman."

He left her at the end of the Embankment and Mona went home, not daring to think. The next day was a day of torture. She was placing her life in the hands of a man who, by his own confession, was a fugitive from justice. And yet... she must do it, she must, she must, she told herself vehemently.

That morning the newspapers had given greater prominence to the Della Garda murder. There was an interview with Philip Della Garda, who had seen her and had told of his recognition in half a column of closely set type. From this newspaper, too, she had a clue as to the identity of her future husband. She found it in a note dealing with the activities of John Keddler.

"Mr. Keddler, who has been commissioned by the Della Garda family to assist the police in their search, is also on the track of Rex Jowder, an international swindler, supposed to be of British origin, who is wanted for frauds both in London and New York."

In a flash it came to her. That saunterer was Keddler – the man who was tracking her down, and her chosen husband was an international swindler! She wrung her hands in despair, and for a second wavered in her resolution.

Nevertheless, a sleepless night spent in a painful weighing of this advantage against that peril, brought her to the registrar's office.

She carried with her a large portion of the money she had brought from Italy – happily, in view of a flight from the tyrannies of Giocomi Della Garda, she had kept a considerable sum in the house. She realized with consternation that she had fixed no sum; would he be satisfied with the four thousand pounds she brought to him? But what did that matter? Once she was married, she would be free to communicate with her father, and he would satisfy the most extravagant demands of her husband.

There was only one fear in her heart as she walked through the pelting rain to the dingy little office. Would the man repent of his bargain – or worse, would he be unable to keep the appointment? Both aspects of her doubt were cleared as soon as she set foot in the outer lobby of the office. He was waiting, looking more presentable than she had expected. His raincoat was buttoned to the chin and she thought him good looking in the daylight.

"I had the certificate made out in your maiden name," he said in a low voice. "It makes no difference to the legality of the marriage."

She nodded, and opening a door, they stepped into a chilly-looking office, and to the presence of an elderly man who sat writing slowly and laboriously at a big desk.

He glanced up over his spectacles.

"Oh yes – Mr. – er—" He looked helplessly at the certificate he was filling. "Yes – yes, I won't keep you young people longer than a few moments."

They sat down and Mona utilized the respite.

"Here is the money," she whispered, and pushed a roll of notes into his outstretched hand.

He took the notes without any great display of interest and coolly slipped them into the pocket of his raincoat without troubling to count them.

Presently the old man rose and beckoned them.

As in a dream Mona Della Garda heard his monotonous voice, and then a ring was pressed upon her cold finger.

"That's that," said her husband cheerfully. "Now come along and have some food – you look half dead."

She stared from him to the golden circlet on her hand.

"But—but I don't want to go with you," she stammered in her agitation. "It was understood... I leave you now... but you must tell me where I can find you."

"Young lady," the man's voice was not unkind, "I have taken a few risks for you and you must do something for me. There is a gentleman waiting in the rain for me; he has been trailing me all the morning, and my only chance of escaping a disagreeable occurrence is in your companionship."

"But I don't want..." she began, and seeing his face, "very well, I will go with you to a restaurant."

He nodded and they went out in the rain together. Three paces they had taken when there was a sound like the sharp crack of a whip. Something like an angry bee in terrific flight snapped past Mona's face, and her husband leapt at a man who was standing half a dozen paces away. Again came the explosion, but this time the bullet went high, and in a second she was the terrified spectator of two men at grips.

The struggle did not last long. Three policemen came from nowhere and one of the men was seized. The other came back to her wiping the mud from his coat.

"I didn't think he was such a blackguard," he said.

She could only look at him in wide-eyed fear.

"Who was he?" she gasped.

"A fellow named Rex Jowder," said her husband; "he's been looking for me for a month."

"Then you...?"

"I'm John Keddler," he smiled, "and I think I've lost a good client. Come along and lunch and I'll tell you how you can get your divorce – I'm a bit of a lawyer, you know. Besides which I'd like to return all that money you gave me."

* * *

Whether or not, in the complicated terms of the Extradition Treaty between Italy and Britain, Mona Keddler could have been tried in London for a crime committed in Rome, no jurist would commit himself to say. John Keddler in his wisdom did not challenge a decision. He had an interview with his furious employer, who threatened and stormed – and went home. Mona he sent to a place of safety until the storm blew over; but the storm was the mildest of breezes.

The winter turned to spring and the spring to summer. The Italian Government notified all persons concerned that the Della Garda 'affair' would be regarded as a lamentable family tragedy, for which nobody could be held liable; and the summer came to autumn again before Mona Keddler sailed for New York.

The question of divorce, in spite of many meetings at luncheon, dinner, and tea-tables, had never been properly discussed by either. It was not until the evening before she sailed for New York that Mona Keddler asked the question that had puzzled her so through the six months of her curiously pleasant married life.

"I cannot quite understand, Jack, why you did it," she said.

"Did what?"

She hesitated.

"Married me," she said. "It has practically ruined your career, for I don't see just how we can divorce one another without... well, without unpleasantness. The divorce laws are so horribly strict in England. And you are married – without a wife. It was selfish, miserably selfish of me to let you do it – but why did you?"

He was unusually grave.

"For the last reason in the world you would suspect," he said.

"But what?" she asked.

Here he was adamantine.

"I'll keep my mystery," he said, "but I'll write my reason in a letter, if you swear you will not break the seal of the envelope until your ship is on the high seas."

She promised, and he watched the Olympic drift from the pier at Southampton with a little ache at his heart that nothing could assuage – watched until the trim figure on the promenade deck and the handkerchief she waved were indistinguishable from other figures and other wildly waving handkerchiefs.

Then he went back to town, heavy hearted, feeling that life was almost done with.

At that moment Mona Keddler was reading for the fortieth time the scrawled words in pencil:

"Because I loved you from the day I saw you rowing on the Lake of Como."

Her trunks were piled on the deck and she was watching the low-lying shores of France with a light in her eyes which no man had ever seen.

John Keddler had forgotten that the ship called at Cherbourg on the outward voyage.

A Mouthful of Murder

Elise Warner

"CLOSE THE DOOR, Clyde." Though Wendy Flite's reedy soprano made my ears ring; Clyde Potter, the director of the city's Convention and Visitor's Bureau and the man responsible for hiring us, ignored her plea. Glacial blasts of fresh air followed his pudgy body through the exhibition center's entrance and rushed past our bank of registration counters.

I adjusted the name tag clipped to my maroon jacket – it read Augusta Weidenmaier – Staff. Beneath the jacket, required attire for all bureau personnel, a set of thermal underwear kept me feeling snug despite the drop in temperature. Unlike the younger women hired by the bureau, old-timers wore several layers of clothing to keep the draughts at bay. Wendy, poor anemic creature, was wrapped in a goose down coat, beret, scarf, and thermal gloves. How, I wondered, would she ever manage to type a badge?

Clyde's small feet, encased in highly polished, tasseled loafers, took graceful steps – unusual in a man of such bulk – in our direction. A grimace, meant to pass as a smile, drew attention to the shy mustache nestled under his nose. Georgia Lee Wilkes, Clyde's assistant, dogged his heels. Clyde stopped short; Georgia bumped into him, dropping a shopping bag filled with brochures, restaurant guides, and street maps.

"Clumsy," Clyde thundered. Our leader had once performed in amateur theatricals and tended toward extravagant dramatization.

Georgia's complexion flushed a flaming flamingo.

"Lose the coat and hat," Clyde's focus shifted to Wendy Flite.

"Clyde," Wendy said – with more spirit than I would have believed her capable of – "you have no right to dictate our wardrobe. The lobby is colder than a meat locker."

"I can replace you with somebody younger who doesn't mind the cold."

Clyde and Wendy held a staring contest. Clyde won – Wendy needed her paycheck.

Clyde walked past the row of computers, nodding his head, collecting the greetings offered by his hirelings.

"I could just murder that..." Wendy swallowed the rest of her sentence as Clyde retraced his steps.

"Augusta," he said to me, "I need you at the office tomorrow."

"Hello Augusta." Dolores May Bright chirped as she rushed to my side, coffee sloshing in a cardboard container. Dolores had been a Rockette in her salad days. Her legs – Dolores calls them 'gams,' are still good for a woman of seventy-something, but in my opinion, mini-skirts are not proper business attire for any job that doesn't require high kicks and a brass band.

"Taking another break?" Clyde asked after a look at Dolores' costume. "Where's your maroon jacket? I expect all my girls to obey the new dress code. This will cost you a ten-buck fine, my 'Ancient Angel.' Make a note, Georgia."

Georgia uncapped her pen; a squirt of ink splotched Clyde's right shoe.

"You are on probation as of now," Clyde said.

Georgia's weak eyes glared at Dolores.

A smile quivered around the edge of Dolores' mouth. "I'll be sure and wear the maroon jacket on my next job." Dolores took back the apple muffin she had given me and handed it to Clyde. "I'm making goodies specially for you tonight. I'll be by the office tomorrow and we can discuss my assignments for next month."

"The assignments may not be ready by tomorrow." Clyde raised his hand in a Caesar-like farewell and descended the stairs leading to the lower level.

"Clyde eats too much, doesn't he?" Dolores said – more a statement than a question. "He's a prime candidate for a heart attack."

A bus discharged its passengers; a line of attendees formed in front of my computer. I typed their badges and directed them to the printer presided over by Rose LaFleur who presented every badge with a flourish. A residual gesture from years spent working as an acrobat with Ringling Brothers Circus.

When my lunch break came I was glad to sink into a chair in the cafeteria. Forty-five minutes of peace and quiet was…not to be. A bevy of 'Ancient Angels' sat down at my table. My word! I was thinking of my friends just the way Clyde did.

Ethel Watkins, who had, in her youth, ridden bucking broncos in rodeos, said this was her first job in months. She was thinking of going back to the wide-open spaces.

"Lose thirty pounds first," Rose LaFleur advised. "As for me, I may get…married."

"Again?" Dolores May asked. "You've been widowed twice, Rose."

"Third time lucky, Rose said. "We met at the Botanical Gardens. He's a retired chemist and he was admiring the Ricinus Communis – that's where castor oil comes from, girls." Knows all about medicinal herbs. Made me a poultice of plantain leaves on our first date and my arthritis disappeared."

The next day when I arrived at the bureau's office, I found Georgia's temper as foul as the weather.

"You should be doing the filing, Augusta," she said. "It's not fair. You are the temp."

Poor Georgia – the file room was a dismal place with no window and one flickering florescent light.

"Ah, you're early, Augusta," Clyde said. He handed me a scrawled batch of letters and memos. "Fix them up before you type them. You know."

I knew. Clyde's knowledge and use of structure and meaning in generating sentences was sadly deficient; he hired me because I had taught classes in English literature, language and composition before retiring.

"Do you have a band-aid, Augusta?" Clyde asked. "Georgia stuck me with the tip of her umbrella. Miss Butterfingers is dangerous to have around." The candy he popped in his mouth partially stifled a snide laugh. He turned to the second page of a work-sheet leaving a smear of chocolate on the first.

He squinted at the small print. "Here we are. You'll be working at the Hilton Hotel next weekend with my 'Ancient Angels.' You're the youngest of the lot." Clyde tossed another chocolate in his mouth then slowly licked his fingers. "An offering from Rose Lafleur. Want one?" Clyde's offer was half-hearted; he hated sharing his sweets.

"Perhaps after lunch. If you don't mind, I'll just take a minute and powder my nose.

"Bring me a diet coke, Augusta," Clyde said. "Ethel Watkins' chili tends to be a little on the hot side."

"Hello Augusta. I brought a few sweets for Clyde. Is he in a good mood?" Dolores May stepped off the elevator, clutching a small shopping bag just as I reached the restroom. I turned to answer her question but she was already halfway down the hall.

When I returned, copy for the newsletter had been placed next to my computer – a full afternoon's work. Clyde sat slumped at his desk – his complexion pasty. An empty plate that once held Ethel's chili lay on the floor.

"What's wrong," I asked.

"My stomach hurts; must be indigestion. Think I'll spend some time in the toilet." Clyde wobbled out of the office.

Forty-five minutes went by and Clyde hadn't returned. He had over-eaten as usual; I marched to the lavatory feeling exasperated. There was so much work to do.

"Clyde? You've been in there a long time."

"I can't stop throwing up."

"I'm going to call a cab and take you to the emergency room."

The door opened and Clyde stepped towards me than collapsed on the floor. I knelt and felt for his pulse. His extremities were as cold as a tray of ice cubes.

"Clyde, what are you doing on the floor?" Georgia asked. "I have to go to lunch."

"Georgia, don't stand there, call an ambulance. Clyde's pulse is close to nonexistent."

A weak squeak followed by a squawk that turned into a shriek emerged from Georgia's scrawny throat. Her body landed on top of his.

By the time the ambulance delivered both of them to the emergency room, Clyde had left our world.

"Irregularities. Heart," one of the interns said when I inquired.

All Clyde's 'Ancient Angels,' gathered for an afternoon of reminiscing at Dolores May Bright's apartment. Despite his teasing and often rudeness, they seemed fond of the man. Dolores baked apple turnovers; Rose Lafleur brought her chocolates. Ethel Watkins made chili. Wendy Flite's contribution was a bag of apricots and prunes. I supplied the green tea. Our memorial became a party. The ladies gossiped about Clyde's possible replacement and tittered over slightly risqué stories.

"At least Clyde died doing what he enjoyed most," I said. The ladies stared at me. "He loved to eat," I explained, "and you made such delectable cakes and candy for…"

"I'll try just one chocolate," Wendy reached across the table while obviously changing the subject. "I hope I'm not going to be up all night. Chocolate gives me hives and it has caffeine." Wendy poured more water into her cup; a few drops splashed over the rim of her saucer and stained Dolores May's carpet.

"You're so careless, Wendy." Dolores May dropped to her knees and patted the spot with her napkin.

"I didn't do it on purpose," One lonesome tear slid down Wendy's cheek.

"No. Of course you didn't," Rose said. "Don't be so sensitive. Losing Clyde, we're all just a teensy bit over wrought."

"I hate to speak ill of the dead," Dolores May said, "but Clyde had a mean streak. The way he spoke to us."

"I never busted a bronco's spirit, the way Clyde tried to break mine," Ethel Watkins said.

"What about me?" Rose Lafleur asked. "I encouraged that boy; Clyde forgot but I didn't. He kept adding new young people who couldn't care less about the proper way to register attendees. Present company excluded, Augusta. You may be new but if you'll excuse my saying so, you're not that young and you fit in with the rest of us girls. That's why we include you in almost everything we do."

I kept quiet – the ladies were more upset about Clyde's early demise then I realized.

I expected an autopsy would find the cause for Clyde's death, apoplexy or emphysema or, most likely a heart attack; he was grossly overweight.

The following morning, the phone rang just as I was sipping a steaming cup of Darjeeling tea and indulging in a second slice of toast spread with course-cut, Seville orange marmalade.

"Augusta Weidenmaier? Georgia Lee Wilkes speaking. Clyde was poisoned."

"What?"

"No time for chit-chat, Augusta. The police are talking to everyone. As the acting head of the bureau's job center, I expect you all to respect our good name and not spread false rumors. Do not call the office; I will call you with your next assignment."

Poison – the ladies were all atwitter. Clyde wasn't the type who would do himself in; could Clyde have been murdered?

"You were the one who found him, weren't you, Augusta?" I was asked that question more than once. Were my fellow workers looking at me with suspicion? "Who do you think did it?"

The ladies were constantly bringing Clyde treats he craved. Did someone put poison in a cake? Chocolates? Chili? Where would that person obtain poison?

Another week, another trade show at the convention center. I was working the exhibitor's desk at an intimate apparel exhibition. Clyde's murder had not been solved; the registration desks hummed with gossip.

"He must of left my name," the boy said.

"Young man," I said, "no one under sixteen is allowed." I could hear my stomach issuing unladylike noises. Where was Wendy? She was supposed to give me my lunch break.

"My father wants me to work in his booth," the boy said.

"What's your father's name?"

"Daddy. Come on, lady. Be a sport."

"Next," I said and turned away as Wendy straggled toward my counter.

"Sorry. The time just got away from me," Wendy said. "Some of us got together to talk about the pollution in this place. Look at my eyes, pink as a rabbit's." Wendy positioned her face close to mine; I could smell the garlic she ate to ward off the flu. "Augusta, you simply have to sign this petition."

"Lady," the boy interrupted, "I'll be honest with ya. My girl's a model. I just wanna see her."

"Young man, you do not belong here. And please – I want to – not wanna. You must go home and work on your diction and your grammar."

"Give him a badge and get rid of him, Augusta," Wendy said. "The petition is more important."

"I am going to lunch, Wendy."

"Take this with you. Read it while you eat. Page twenty – the article on contaminated air. That's what this petition is all about." Wendy thrust the magazine at me. She was still talking as I walked out of earshot.

I unwrapped my sandwich and pulled Wendy's magazine out of my tote bag. A health magazine, of course. I was about to place it back in my bag when the title of another article caught my eye. "Killer Kernels – Beware the Poisonous Pit."

Fruit pits and seeds, the article said could be toxic. Twenty raw peach or apricot kernels contained enough cyanide to be lethal. A cupful of apple seeds could cause an early demise in someone foolhardy enough to munch them. The fruit of the castor bean plant held mottled brown seeds the size of pinto beans that were six thousand times more poisonous than cyanide. A white powder called ricin could be distilled from the beans.

Cyanide in fruit pits. Wendy had read the article. Dolores May made candy and apple muffins. Rose gardened. Ethel's specialty is chili made with pinto beans. Perhaps she hadn' used pinto beans. Had she used castor beans? Were all of the 'Ancient Angels,' in it together My word!

Later that afternoon, Georgia, dressed in a pinstriped power suit, marched past the row of computer terminals, just as Clyde had done before his involuntary retirement.

"Ladies," Georgia Lee said," "Stop the chatter. The police have made an arrest. Poor Clyde's murderer is..." Georgia paused for dramatic effect. "Ethel Watkins."

Before I knew what was happening, I was chosen to visit Ethel. Despite her prison pallor, she was bearing up. She wore her prison uniform with flare.

"Ethel," I said, "You're looking well despite everything that's happened."

"I have lost a few pounds, Augusta," she said. "Soon I'll be back in the saddle again."

"Ethel, how could you do that to Clyde? He wasn't a gentleman, I admit but..."

"I did not murder Clyde." Ethel shook her head. "How could you think such a thing?"

"The chili," I said. "Ricin was found in his body."

"My recipe does not include poison."

The next day I was back in the Bureau's office. The weather channel had predicted a sunny day; instead we had a major snowstorm. Except for Georgia and myself, the office was empty. I worked at Clyde's desk; thoughts of his murder distracting me from my job. Put on your thinking cap, Augusta, I told myself, if Ethel's chili hadn't poisoned Clyde, what did?

Only Dolores May had visited the office that day but the staff kept Clyde well supplied with goodies he kept in a small refrigerator. Could the police be mistaken? Had it been suicide after all? No. Clyde took too much delight in making others miserable to do away with himself. My head whirled with theories. I needed a break. Best to brave the weather and buy myself a good, hot bowl of soup.

It was snowing harder than ever. I wrapped my scarf around my head and was buttoning my coat when I noticed a stack of health magazines in the closet. One would never believe Georgia read them. Poor thing constantly sniffled – but her name was on the mailing label. I decided to borrow one along with an umbrella I spied buried behind them. No one would my using it for half an hour. I took my gloves from my purse – a Band-Aid had come unwrapped and stuck to one glove. Band-aid. Umbrella. What was the connection?

"Snoop!" Georgia became agitated. Her eyes blinked; her hands tightened into fists. "Give me my umbrella."

My word...the day he was murdered, Georgia stuck Clyde with the tip of her umbrella. His skin had been pierced. Could there have been ricin on the point? Could the murder weapon be in my hand?

Georgia wrenched the umbrella from my grasp. The woman's body had to be pumping adrenalin. She pointed the tip of the umbrella at my heart. I backed away.

Dolores May stepped off the elevator. "Wait until you taste this," Dolores May said. "I found a recipe for peach cake and, despite the weather, I just had to bring it up to Georgia."

Georgia turned; I managed to grab her arm.

"Call the police, Dolores May. It's high time we got Ethel out of jail."

A second autopsy proved my theory. The ricin was in Clyde's system but not in the food he had eaten. Georgia had the motive, the opportunity and the umbrella.

Ethel is not one to hold a grudge. In fact, on visitor's day, Ethel and the other 'Ancient Angels,' are taking a care package to Georgia's prison. Chocolate, chili and a peach cake. My Word!

The Big Bow Mystery

Israel Zangwill

Chapter I

ON A MEMORABLE morning of early December London opened its eyes on a frigid gray mist. There are mornings when King Fog masses his molecules of carbon in serried squadrons in the city, while he scatters them tenuously in the suburbs; so that your morning train may bear you from twilight to darkness. But today the enemy's maneuvering was more monotonous. From Bow even unto Hammersmith there draggled a dull, wretched vapor, like the wraith of an impecunious suicide come into a fortune immediately after the fatal deed. The barometers and thermometers had sympathetically shared its depression, and their spirits (when they had any) were low. The cold cut like a many-bladed knife.

Mrs. Drabdump, of 11 Glover Street, Bow, was one of the few persons in London whom fog did not depress. She went about her work quite as cheerlessly as usual. She had been among the earliest to be aware of the enemy's advent, picking out the strands of fog from the coils of darkness the moment she rolled up her bedroom blind and unveiled the somber picture of the winter morning. She knew that the fog had come to stay for the day at least, and that the gas bill for the quarter was going to beat the record in high-jumping. She also knew that this was because she had allowed her new gentleman lodger, Mr. Arthur Constant, to pay a fixed sum of a shilling a week for gas, instead of charging him a proportion of the actual account for the whole house. The meteorologists might have saved the credit of their science if they had reckoned with Mrs. Drabdump's next gas bill when they predicted the weather and made 'Snow' the favorite, and said that 'Fog' would be nowhere. Fog was everywhere, yet Mrs. Drabdump took no credit to herself for her prescience. Mrs. Drabdump indeed took no credit for anything, paying her way along doggedly, and struggling through life like a wearied swimmer trying to touch the horizon. That things always went as badly as she had foreseen did not exhilarate her in the least.

Mrs. Drabdump was a widow. Widows are not born, but made, else you might have fancied Mrs. Drabdump had always been a widow. Nature had given her that tall, spare form, and that pale, thin-lipped, elongated, hard-eyed visage, and that painfully precise hair, which are always associated with widowhood in low life. It is only in higher circles that women can lose their husbands and yet remain bewitching. The late Mr. Drabdump had scratched the base of his thumb with a rusty nail, and Mrs. Drabdump's foreboding that he would die of lockjaw had not prevented her wrestling day and night with the shadow of Death, as she had wrestled with it vainly twice before, when Katie died of diphtheria and little Johnny of scarlet fever. Perhaps it is from overwork among the poor that Death has been reduced to a shadow.

Mrs. Drabdump was lighting the kitchen fire. She did it very scientifically, as knowing the contrariety of coal and the anxiety of flaming sticks to end in smoke unless rigidly kept up to the mark. Science was a success as usual; and Mrs. Drabdump rose from her knees content, like a Parsee priestess who had duly paid her morning devotions to her deity. Then she started violently, and nearly lost her balance. Her eye had caught the hands of the clock on the mantel. They pointed to fifteen minutes to seven. Mrs. Drabdump's devotion to the kitchen fire invariably terminated at fifteen minutes past six. What was the matter with the clock?

Mrs. Drabdump had an immediate vision of Snoppet, the neighboring horologist, keeping the clock in hand for weeks and then returning it only superficially repaired and secretly injured more vitally "for the good of the trade." The evil vision vanished as quickly as it came, exorcised by the deep boom of St. Dunstan's bells chiming the three-quarters. In its place a great horror surged. Instinct had failed; Mrs. Drabdump had risen at half-past six instead of six. Now she understood why she had been feeling so dazed and strange and sleepy. She had overslept herself.

Chagrined and puzzled, she hastily set the kettle over the crackling coal, discovering a second later that she had overslept herself because Mr. Constant wished to be woke three-quarters of an hour earlier than usual, and to have his breakfast at seven, having to speak at an early meeting of discontented tram-men. She ran at once, candle in hand, to his bedroom. It was upstairs. All 'upstairs' was Arthur Constant's domain, for it consisted of but two mutually independent rooms. Mrs. Drabdump knocked viciously at the door of the one he used for a bedroom, crying, "Seven o'clock, sir. You'll be late, sir. You must get up at once." The usual slumbrous "All right" was not forthcoming; but, as she herself had varied her morning salute, her ear was less expectant of the echo. She went downstairs, with no foreboding save that the kettle would come off second best in the race between its boiling and her lodger's dressing.

For she knew there was no fear of Arthur Constant's lying deaf to the call of duty – temporarily represented by Mrs. Drabdump. He was a light sleeper, and the tram conductors' bells were probably ringing in his ears, summoning him to the meeting. Why Arthur Constant, B. A. – white-handed and white-shirted, and gentleman to the very purse of him – should concern himself with tram-men, when fortune had confined his necessary relations with drivers to cabmen at the least, Mrs. Drabdump could not quite make out. He probably aspired to represent Bow in Parliament; but then it would surely have been wiser to lodge with a landlady who possessed a vote by having a husband alive. Nor was there much practical wisdom in his wish to black his own boots (an occupation in which he shone but little), and to live in every way like a Bow working man. Bow working men were not so lavish in their patronage of water, whether existing in drinking glasses, morning tubs, or laundress' establishments. Nor did they eat the delicacies with which Mrs. Drabdump supplied him, with the assurance that they were the artisan's appanage. She could not bear to see him eat things unbefitting his station. Arthur Constant opened his mouth and ate what his landlady gave him, not first deliberately shutting his eyes according to the formula, the rather pluming himself on keeping them very wide open. But it is difficult for saints to see through their own halos; and in practice an aureola about the head is often indistinguishable from a mist. The tea to be scalded in Mr. Constant's pot, when that cantankerous kettle should boil, was not the coarse mixture of black and green sacred to herself and Mr. Mortlake, of whom the thoughts of breakfast now reminded her. Poor Mr. Mortlake, gone off without any to Devonport, somewhere about four in the fog-thickened darkness of a winter night! Well, she hoped his journey would be duly rewarded, that his perks would be heavy, and that he would make as good a thing out of the "traveling expenses" as rival labor leaders roundly accused him of to other people's faces. She did not grudge him his gains, nor was it her business if, as they alleged, in introducing Mr. Constant to her vacant rooms, his idea was not merely to benefit his landlady. He had done her an uncommon good turn, queer as was the lodger thus introduced. His own apostleship to the sons of toil gave Mrs. Drabdump no twinges of perplexity. Tom Mortlake had been a compositor; and apostleship was obviously a profession better paid and of a higher social status. Tom Mortlake – the hero of a hundred strikes – set up in print on a poster, was unmistakably superior to Tom Mortlake setting up other men's names at a case. Still, the work was not all beer and skittles, and Mrs. Drabdump felt that Tom's latest job was not enviable. She shook his door as she passed it on her way to the kitchen, but there was no response. The street door was only a few feet off down the passage, and a glancc at it dispelled the last hope that Tom had abandoned the journey. The door was unbolted and unchained, and the only security was the latch-key lock. Mrs. Drabdump felt a whit uneasy, though, to give her her due, she never suffered as much as most housewives do from criminals who never come. Not quite opposite, but still only a few doors off, on the other side of the street, lived the celebrated ex-detective, Grodman, and, illogically enough, his presence in the street gave Mrs. Drabdump a curious sense of security, as of a believer living under the shadow of the fane. That any human being of ill-odor should consciously come within a mile of the scent of so famous a sleuth-hound seemed to her highly improbable. Grodman had retired (with a competence) and was only a sleeping dog now; still, even criminals would have sense enough to let him lie.

So Mrs. Drabdump did not really feel that there had been any danger, especially as a second glance at the street door showed that Mortlake had been thoughtful enough to slip the loop that held back the bolt of the big lock. She allowed herself another throb of sympathy for the labor leader whirling on his dreary way toward Devonport Dockyard. Not that he had told her anything of his journey beyond the town; but she knew Devonport had a Dockyard because Jessie Dymond – Tom's sweetheart – once mentioned that her aunt lived near there, and it lay on the surface that Tom had gone to help the dockers, who were imitating their London brethren. Mrs. Drabdump did not need to be told things to be aware of them. She went back to prepare Mr. Constant's superfine tea, vaguely wondering why people were so discontented nowadays. But when she brought up the tea and the toast and the eggs to Mr. Constant's sitting-room (which adjoined his bedroom, though without communicating with it), Mr. Constant was not sitting in it. She lit the gas, and laid the cloth; then she returned to the landing and beat at the bedroom door with an imperative palm. Silence alone answered her. She called him by name and told him the hour, but hers was the only voice she heard, and it sounded strangely to her in the shadows of the staircase. Then, muttering, "Poor gentleman, he had the toothache last night; and p'r'aps he's only just got a wink o' sleep. Pity to disturb him for the sake of them grizzling conductors. I'll let him sleep his usual time," she bore the tea-pot downstairs with a mournful, almost poetic, consciousness, that soft-boiled eggs (like love) must grow cold.

Half-past seven came – and she knocked again. But Constant slept on.

His letters, always a strange assortment, arrived at eight, and a telegram came soon after. Mrs. Drabdump rattled his door, shouted, and at last put the wire under it. Her heart was beating fast enough now, though there seemed to be a cold, clammy snake curling round it. She went downstairs again and turned the handle of Mortlake's room, and went in without knowing why. The coverlet of the bed showed that the occupant had only lain down in his clothes, as if fearing to miss the early train. She had not for a moment expected to find him in the room; yet somehow the consciousness that she was alone in the house with the sleeping Constant seemed to flash for the first time upon her, and the clammy snake tightened its folds round her heart.

She opened the street door, and her eye wandered nervously up and down. It was half-past eight. The little street stretched cold and still in the gray mist, blinking bleary eyes at either end where the street lamps smoldered on. No one was visible for the moment, though smoke was rising from many of the chimneys to greet its sister mist. At the house of the detective across the way the blinds were still down and the shutters up. Yet the familiar, prosaic aspect of the street calmed her. The bleak air set her coughing; she slammed the door to, and returned to the kitchen to make fresh tea for Constant, who could only be in a deep sleep. But the canister trembled in her grasp. She did not know whether she dropped it or threw it down, but there was nothing in the hand that battered again a moment later at the bedroom door. No sound within answered the clamor without. She rained blow upon blow in a sort of spasm of frenzy, scarce remembering that her object was merely to wake her lodger, and almost staving in the lower panels with her kicks. Then she turned the handle and tried to open the door, but it was locked. The resistance recalled her to herself – she had a moment of shocked decency at the thought that she had been about to enter Constant's bedroom. Then the terror came over her afresh. She felt that she was alone in the house with a corpse. She sank to the floor, cowering; with difficulty stifling a desire to scream. Then she rose with a jerk and raced down the stairs without looking behind her, and threw open the door and ran out into the street, only pulling up with her hand violently agitating Grodman's door-knocker. In a moment the first floor window was raised – the little house was of the same pattern as her own – and Grodman's full, fleshy face loomed through the fog in sleepy irritation from under a nightcap. Despite its scowl the ex-detective's face dawned upon her like the sun upon an occupant of the haunted chamber.

"What in the devil's the matter?" he growled. Grodman was not an early bird, now that he had no worms to catch. He could afford to despise proverbs now, for the house in which he lived was his, and he lived in it because several other houses in the street were also his, and it is well for the landlord to be about his own estate in Bow, where poachers often shoot the moon. Perhaps the desire to enjoy his greatness among his early cronies counted for something, too, for he had been born and bred at Bow, receiving when a youth his first engagement from the local police quarters, whence he drew a few shillings a week as an amateur detective in his leisure hours.

Grodman was still a bachelor. In the celestial matrimonial bureau a partner might have been selected for him, but he had never been able to discover her. It was his one failure as a detective. He was a self-sufficing person, who preferred a gas stove to a domestic; but in deference to Glover Street opinion he admitted a female factotum between ten a. m. and ten p. m., and, equally in deference to Glover Street opinion, excluded her between ten p. m. and ten a. m.

"I want you to come across at once," Mrs. Drabdump gasped. "Something has happened to Mr. Constant."

"What! Not bludgeoned by the police at the meeting this morning, I hope?"

"No, no! He didn't go. He is dead."

"Dead?" Grodman's face grew very serious now.

"Yes. Murdered!"

"What?" almost shouted the ex-detective. "How? When? Where? Who?"

"I don't know. I can't get to him. I have beaten at his door. He does not answer."

Grodman's face lit up with relief.

"You silly woman! Is that all? I shall have a cold in my head. Bitter weather. He's dog-tired after yesterday – processions, three speeches, kindergarten, lecture on 'the moon,' article on co-operation. That's his style." It was also Grodman's style. He never wasted words.

"No," Mrs. Drabdump breathed up at him solemnly, "he's dead."

"All right; go back. Don't alarm the neighborhood unnecessarily. Wait for me. Down in five minutes." Grodman did not take this Cassandra of the kitchen too seriously. Probably he knew his woman. His small, bead-like eyes glittered with an almost amused smile as he withdrew them from Mrs. Drabdump's ken, and shut down the sash with a bang. The poor woman ran back across the road and through her door, which she would not close behind her. It seemed to shut her in with the dead. She waited in the passage. After an age – seven minutes by any honest clock – Grodman made his appearance, looking as dressed as usual, but with unkempt hair and with disconsolate side-whisker. He was not quite used to that side-whisker yet, for it had only recently come within the margin of cultivation. In active service Grodman had been clean-shaven, like all members of the profession – for surely your detective is the most versatile of actors. Mrs. Drabdump closed the street door quietly, and pointed to the stairs, fear operating like a polite desire to give him precedence. Grodman ascended, amusement still glimmering in his eyes. Arrived on the landing he knocked peremptorily at the door, crying, "Nine o'clock, Mr. Constant; nine o'clock!" When he ceased there was no other sound or movement. His face grew more serious. He waited, then knocked, and cried louder. He turned the handle, but the door was fast. He tried to peer through the keyhole, but it was blocked. He shook the upper panels, but the door seemed bolted as well as locked. He stood still, his face set and rigid, for he liked and esteemed the man.

"Ay, knock your loudest," whispered the pale-faced woman. "You'll not wake him now."

The gray mist had followed them through the street door, and hovered about the staircase, charging the air with a moist, sepulchral odor.

"Locked and bolted," muttered Grodman, shaking the door afresh.

"Burst it open," breathed the woman, trembling violently all over, and holding her hands before her as if to ward off the dreadful vision. Without another word, Grodman applied his shoulder to the door, and made a violent muscular effort. He had been an athlete in his time, and the sap was yet in him. The door creaked, little by little it began to give, the woodwork enclosing the bolt of the lock splintered, the panels bent upward, the large upper bolt tore off its iron staple; the door flew back with a crash. Grodman rushed in.

"My God!" he cried. The woman shrieked. The sight was too terrible.

* * *

Within a few hours the jubilant news-boys were shrieking "Horrible Suicide in Bow," and "The Star" poster added, for the satisfaction of those too poor to purchase: "A Philanthropist Cuts His Throat."

Chapter II

BUT THE NEWSPAPERS were premature. Scotland Yard refused to prejudge the case despite the penny-a-liners. Several arrests were made, so that the later editions were compelled to soften 'Suicide' into 'Mystery.' The people arrested were a nondescript collection of tramps Most of them had committed other offenses for which the police had not arrested them. One bewildered-looking gentleman gave himself up (as if he were a riddle), but the police would have none of him, and restored him forthwith to his friends and keepers. The number o candidates for each new opening in Newgate is astonishing.

The full significance of this tragedy of a noble young life cut short had hardly time to filte into the public mind, when a fresh sensation absorbed it. Tom Mortlake had been arreste the same day at Liverpool on suspicion of being concerned in the death of his fellow-lodge The news fell like a bombshell upon a land in which Tom Mortlake's name was a househol word. That the gifted artisan orator, who had never shrunk upon occasion from launchin red rhetoric at Society, should actually have shed blood seemed too startling, especially as the blood shed was not blue, but the property of a lovable young middle-class idealist, who had now literally given his life to the Cause. But this supplementary sensation did not grow to a head, and everybody (save a few labor leaders) was relieved to hear that Tom had been released almost immediately, being merely subpoenaed to appear at the inquest. In an interview which he accorded to the representative of a Liverpool paper the same afternoon, he stated that he put his arrest down entirely to the enmity and rancor entertained toward him by the police throughout the country. He had come to Liverpool to trace the movements of a friend about whom he was very uneasy, and he was making anxious inquiries at the docks to discover at what times steamers left for America, when the detectives stationed there in accordance with instructions from headquarters had arrested him as a suspicious-looking character. "Though," said Tom, "they must very well have known my phiz, as I have been sketched and caricatured all over the shop. When I told them who I was they had the decency to let me go. They thought they'd scored off me enough, I reckon. Yes, it certainly is a strange coincidence that I might actually have had something to do with the poor fellow's death, which has cut me up as much as anybody; though if they had known I had just come from the 'scene of the crime,' and actually lived in the house, they would probably have – let me alone." He laughed sarcastically. "They are a queer lot of muddle-heads are the police. Their motto is, 'First catch your man, then cook the evidence.' If you're on the spot you're guilty because you're there, and if you're elsewhere you're guilty because you have gone away. Oh, I know them! If they could have seen their way to clap me in quod, they'd ha' done it. Lucky I know the number of the cabman who took me to Euston before five this morning."

"If they clapped you in quod," the interviewer reported himself as facetiously observing, "the prisoners would be on strike in a week."

"Yes, but there would be so many black-legs ready to take their places," Mortlake flashed back, "that I'm afraid it 'ould be no go. But do excuse me. I am so upset about my friend. I'm afraid he has left England, and I have to make inquiries; and now there's poor Constant gone – horrible! horrible! and I'm due in London at the inquest. I must really run away. Good-by. Tell your readers it's all a police grudge."

"One last word, Mr. Mortlake, if you please. Is it true that you were billed to preside at a great meeting of clerks at St. James' Hall between one and two today to protest against the German invasion?"

"Whew! so I had. But the beggars arrested me just before one, when I was going to wire, and then the news of poor Constant's end drove it out of my head. What a nuisance! Lord, how troubles do come together! Well, good-by, send me a copy of the paper."

Tom Mortlake's evidence at the inquest added little beyond this to the public knowledge of his movements on the morning of the Mystery. The cabman who drove him to Euston had written indignantly to the papers to say that he had picked up his celebrated fare at Bow Railway Station at about half-past four a. m., and the arrest was a deliberate insult to democracy, and he offered to make an affidavit to that effect, leaving it dubious to which effect. But Scotland Yard betrayed no itch for the affidavit in question, and No. 2,138 subsided again into the obscurity of his rank. Mortlake – whose face was very pale below the black mane brushed back from his fine forehead – gave his evidence in low, sympathetic tones. He had known the deceased for over a year, coming constantly across him in their common political and social work, and had found the furnished rooms for him in Glover Street at his own request, they just being to let when Constant resolved to leave his rooms at Oxford House in Bethnal Green and to share the actual life of the people. The locality suited the deceased, as being near the People's Palace.

He respected and admired the deceased, whose genuine goodness had won all hearts. The deceased was an untiring worker; never grumbled, was always in fair spirits, regarded his life and wealth as a sacred trust to be used for the benefit of humanity. He had last seen him at a quarter past nine p. m. on the day preceding his death. He (witness) had received a letter by the last post which made him uneasy about a friend. Deceased was evidently suffering from toothache, and was fixing a piece of cotton-wool in a hollow tooth, but he did not complain. Deceased seemed rather upset by the news he brought, and they both discussed it rather excitedly.

By a Juryman: Did the news concern him?

Mortlake: Only impersonally. He knew my friend, and was keenly sympathetic when one was in trouble.

Coroner: Could you show the jury the letter you received?

Mortlake: I have mislaid it, and cannot make out where it has got to. If you, sir, think it relevant or essential, I will state what the trouble was.

Coroner: Was the toothache very violent?

Mortlake: I cannot tell. I think not, though he told me it had disturbed his rest the night before.

Coroner: What time did you leave him?

Mortlake: About twenty to ten.

Coroner: And what did you do then?

Mortlake: I went out for an hour or so to make some inquiries. Then I returned, and told my landlady I should be leaving by an early train for – for the country.

Coroner: And that was the last you saw of the deceased?

Mortlake (with emotion): The last.

Coroner: How was he when you left him?

Mortlake: Mainly concerned about my trouble.

Coroner: Otherwise you saw nothing unusual about him?

Mortlake: Nothing.

Coroner: What time did you leave the house on Tuesday morning?

Mortlake: At about five and twenty minutes past four.

Coroner: Are you sure that you shut the street door?

Mortlake: Quite sure. Knowing my landlady was rather a timid person, I even slipped the bolt of the big lock, which was usually tied back. It was impossible for any one to get in even with a latch-key.

Mrs. Drabdump's evidence (which, of course, preceded his) was more important, and occupied a considerable time, unduly eked out by Drabdumpian padding. Thus she not only deposed that Mr. Constant had the toothache, but that it was going to last about a week; in tragic-comic indifference to the radical cure that had been effected. Her account of the last hours of the deceased tallied with Mortlake's, only that she feared Mortlake was quarreling with him over something in the letter that came by the nine o'clock post. Deceased had left the house a little after Mortlake, but had returned before him, and had gone straight to his bedroom. She had not actually seen him come in, having been in the kitchen, but she heard his latch-key, followed by his light step up the stairs.

A Juryman: How do you know it was not somebody else? (Sensation, of which the juryman tries to look unconscious.)

Witness: He called down to me over the banisters, and says in his sweetish voice: "Be hextra sure to wake me at a quarter to seven, Mrs. Drabdump, or else I shan't get to my tram meeting.

(Juryman collapses.)

Coroner: And did you wake him?

Mrs. Drabdump (breaking down): Oh, my lud, how can you ask?

Coroner: There, there, compose yourself. I mean did you try to wake him?

Mrs. Drabdump: I have taken in and done for lodgers this seventeen years, my lud, and have always gave satisfaction; and Mr. Mortlake, he wouldn't ha' recommended me otherwise, though I wish to Heaven the poor gentleman had never—

Coroner: Yes, yes, of course. You tried to rouse him?

But it was some time before Mrs. Drabdump was sufficiently calm to explain that though she had overslept herself, and though it would have been all the same anyhow, she had come up to time. Bit by bit the tragic story was forced from her lips – a tragedy that even her telling could not make tawdry. She told with superfluous detail how – when Mr. Grodman broke in the door – she saw her unhappy gentleman lodger lying on his back in bed, stone dead, with a gaping red wound in his throat; how her stronger-minded companion calmed her a little by spreading a handkerchief over the distorted face; how they then looked vainly about and under the bed for any instrument by which the deed could have been done, the veteran detective carefully making a rapid inventory of the contents of the room, and taking notes of the precise position and condition of the body before anything was disturbed by the arrival of gapers or bunglers; how she had pointed out to him that both the windows were firmly bolted to keep out the cold night air; how, having noted this down with a puzzled, pitying shake of the head, he had opened the window to summon the police, and espied in the fog one Denzil Cantercot, whom he called and told to run to the nearest police-station and ask them to send on an inspector and a surgeon. How they both remained in the room till the police arrived, Grodman pondering deeply the while and making notes every now and again, as fresh points occurred to him, and asking her questions about the poor, weak-headed young man. Pressed as to what she meant by calling the deceased "weak-headed," she replied that some of her neighbors wrote him begging letters, though, Heaven knew, they were better off than herself, who had to scrape her fingers to the bone for every penny she earned. Under further pressure from Mr. Talbot, who was watching the inquiry on behalf of Arthur Constant's family, Mrs. Drabdump admitted that the deceased had behaved like a human being, nor was there anything externally eccentric or queer in his conduct. He was always cheerful and pleasant spoken, though certainly soft – God rest his soul. No; he never shaved, but wore all the hair that Heaven had given him.

By a Juryman: She thought deceased was in the habit of locking his door when he went to bed. Of course, she couldn't say for certain. (Laughter.) There was no need to bolt the door as well. The bolt slid upward, and was at the top of the door. When she first let lodgings, her reasons for which she seemed anxious to publish, there had only been a bolt, but a suspicious lodger, she would not call him a gentleman, had complained that he could not fasten his door behind him, and so she had been put to the expense of having a lock made. The complaining lodger went off soon after without paying his rent. (Laughter.) She had always known he would.

The Coroner: Was deceased at all nervous?

Witness: No, he was a very nice gentleman. (A laugh.)

Coroner: I mean did he seem afraid of being robbed?

Witness: No, he was always goin' to demonstrations. (Laughter.) I told him to be careful. I told him I lost a purse with 3s. 2d. myself on Jubilee Day.

Mrs. Drabdump resumed her seat, weeping vaguely.

The Coroner: Gentlemen, we shall have an opportunity of viewing the room shortly.

The story of the discovery of the body was retold, though more scientifically, by Mr. George Grodman, whose unexpected resurgence into the realm of his early exploits excited as keen curiosity as the reappearance "for this occasion only" of a retired prima donna. His book,

"Criminals I Have Caught," passed from the twenty-third to the twenty-fourth edition merely on the strength of it. Mr. Grodman stated that the body was still warm when he found it. He thought that death was quite recent. The door he had had to burst was bolted as well as locked. He confirmed Mrs. Drabdump's statement about the windows; the chimney was very narrow. The cut looked as if done by a razor. There was no instrument lying about the room. He had known the deceased about a month. He seemed a very earnest, simple-minded young fellow who spoke a great deal about the brotherhood of man. (The hardened old man-hunter's voice was not free from a tremor as he spoke jerkily of the dead man's enthusiasms.) He should have thought the deceased the last man in the world to commit suicide.

Mr. Denzil Cantercot was next called. He was a poet. (Laughter.) He was on his way to Mr. Grodman's house to tell him he had been unable to do some writing for him because he was suffering from writer's cramp, when Mr. Grodman called to him from the window of No. 11 and asked him to run for the police. No, he did not run; he was a philosopher. (Laughter.) He returned with them to the door, but did not go up. He had no stomach for crude sensations. (Laughter.) The gray fog was sufficiently unbeautiful for him for one morning. (Laughter.)

Inspector Howlett said: About 9:45 on the morning of Tuesday, 4th December, from information received, he went with Sergeant Runnymede and Dr. Robinson to 11 Glover Street, Bow, and there found the dead body of a young man, lying on his back with his throat cut. The door of the room had been smashed in, and the lock and the bolt evidently forced. The room was tidy. There were no marks of blood on the floor. A purse full of gold was on the dressing-table beside a big book. A hip-bath with cold water stood beside the bed, over which was a hanging bookcase. There was a large wardrobe against the wall next to the door. The chimney was very narrow. There were two windows, one bolted. It was about 18 feet to the pavement. There was no way of climbing up. No one could possibly have got out of the room, and then bolted the doors and windows behind him; and he had searched all parts of the room in which anyone might have been concealed. He had been unable to find any instrument in the room, in spite of exhaustive search, there being not even a penknife in the pockets of the clothes of the deceased, which lay on a chair. The house and the back yard, and the adjacent pavement, had also been fruitlessly searched.

Sergeant Runnymede made an identical statement, saving only that he had gone with Dr. Robinson and Inspector Howlett.

Dr. Robinson, divisional surgeon, said: The deceased was lying on his back, with his throat cut. The body was not yet cold, the abdominal region being quite warm. Rigor mortis had set in in the lower jaw, neck and upper extremities. The muscles contracted when beaten. I inferred that life had been extinct some two or three hours, probably not longer, it might have been less. The bedclothes would keep the lower part warm for some time. The wound, which was a deep one, was 5-1/2 inches from right to left across the throat to a point under the left ear. The upper portion of the windpipe was severed, and likewise the jugular vein. The muscular coating of the carotid artery was divided. There was a slight cut, as if in continuation of the wound, on the thumb of the left hand. The hands were clasped underneath the head. There was no blood on the right hand. The wound could not have been self-inflicted. A sharp instrument had been used, such as a razor. The cut might have been made by a left-handed person. No doubt death was practically instantaneous. I saw no signs of a struggle about the body or the room. I noticed a purse on the dressing-table, lying next to Madame Blavatsky's big book on Theosophy. Sergeant Runnymede drew my attention to the fact that the door had evidently been locked and bolted from within.

By a Juryman: I do not say the cuts could not have been made by a right-handed person. I can offer no suggestion as to how the inflicter of the wound got in or out. Extremely improbable that the cut was self-inflicted. There was little trace of the outside fog in the room.

Police Constable Williams said he was on duty in the early hours of the morning of the 4th inst. Glover Street lay within his beat. He saw or heard nothing suspicious. The fog was never very dense, though nasty to the throat. He had passed through Glover Street about half-past four. He had not seen Mr. Mortlake or anybody else leave the house.

The Court here adjourned, the Coroner and the jury repairing in a body to 11 Glover Street to view the house and the bedroom of the deceased. And the evening posters announced, "The Bow Mystery Thickens."

Chapter III

BEFORE THE INQUIRY was resumed, all the poor wretches in custody had been released on suspicion that they were innocent; there was not a single case even for a magistrate. Clues, which at such seasons are gathered by the police like blackberries off the hedges, were scanty and unripe. Inferior specimens were offered them by bushels, but there was not a good one among the lot. The police could not even manufacture a clue.

Arthur Constant's death was already the theme of every hearth, railway carriage and public house. The dead idealist had points of contact with so many spheres. The East End and West End alike were moved and excited, the Democratic Leagues and the Churches, the Doss-houses and the Universities. The pity of it! And then the impenetrable mystery of it!

The evidence given in the concluding portion of the investigation was necessarily less sensational. There were no more witnesses to bring the scent of blood over the coroner's table; those who had yet to be heard were merely relatives and friends of the deceased, who spoke of him as he had been in life. His parents were dead, perhaps luckily for them; his relatives had seen little of him, and had scarce heard as much about him as the outside world. No man is a prophet in his own country, and, even if he migrates, it is advisable for him to leave his family at home. His friends were a motley crew; friends of the same friend are not necessarily friends of one another. But their diversity only made the congruity of the tale they had to tell more striking. It was the tale of a man who had never made an enemy even by benefiting him, nor lost a friend even by refusing his favors; the tale of a man whose heart overflowed with peace and good will to all men all the year round; of a man to whom Christmas came not once, but three hundred and sixty-five times a year; it was the tale of a brilliant intellect, who gave up to mankind what was meant for himself, and worked as a laborer in the vineyard of humanity, never crying that the grapes were sour; of a man uniformly cheerful and of good courage, living in that forgetfulness of self which is the truest antidote to despair. And yet there was not quite wanting the note of pain to mar the harmony and make it human. Richard Elton, his chum from boyhood, and vicar of Somerton, in Midlandshire, handed to the coroner a letter from the deceased about ten days before his death, containing some passages which the coroner read aloud: "Do you know anything of Schopenhauer? I mean anything beyond the current misconceptions? I have been making his acquaintance lately. He is an agreeable rattle of a pessimist; his essay on 'The Misery of Mankind' is quite lively reading. At first his assimilation of Christianity and Pessimism (it occurs in his essay on 'Suicide') dazzled me as an audacious paradox. But there is truth in it. Verily, the whole creation groaneth and travaileth, and man is a degraded monster, and sin is over all. Ah, my friend, I have shed many of my illusions since I came to this seething hive of misery and wrongdoing. What shall one man's life – a million men's lives – avail against the corruption, the vulgarity and the squalor of civilization? Sometimes

I feel like a farthing rush-light in the Hall of Eblis. Selfishness is so long and life short. And the worst of it is that everybody is so beastly contented. The poor no mc desire comfort than the rich culture. The woman to whom a penny school fee for h child represents an appreciable slice of her income is satisfied that the rich we sh always have with us.

"The real crusted old Tories are the paupers in the Workhouse. The Radical worki men are jealous of their own leaders, and the leaders of one another. Schopenhau must have organized a labor party in his salad days. And yet one can't help feeli that he committed suicide as a philosopher by not committing it as a man. He clai kinship with Buddha, too; though Esoteric Buddhism at least seems spheres remov from the philosophy of 'The Will and the Idea'. What a wonderful woman Madar Blavatsky must be. I can't say I follow her, for she is up in the clouds nearly all t time, and I haven't as yet developed an astral body. Shall I send you on her book? is fascinating.... I am becoming quite a fluent orator. One soon gets into the way it. The horrible thing is that you catch yourself saying things to lead up to 'Chee instead of sticking to the plain realities of the business. Lucy is still doing the galler in Italy. It used to pain me sometimes to think of my darling's happiness whe came across a flat-chested factory girl. Now I feel her happiness is as important a factory girl's."

Lucy, the witness explained, was Lucy Brent, the betrothed of the deceased. T poor girl had been telegraphed for, and had started for England. The witness stat that the outburst of despondency in this letter was almost a solitary one, most of t letters in his possession being bright, buoyant and hopeful. Even this letter end with a humorous statement of the writer's manifold plans and projects for the n year. The deceased was a good Churchman.

Coroner: Was there any private trouble in his own life to account for t temporary despondency?

Witness: Not so far as I am aware. His financial position was exceptionally favorab

Coroner: There had been no quarrel with Miss Brent?

Witness: I have the best authority for saying that no shadow of difference had ev come between them.

Coroner: Was the deceased left-handed?

Witness: Certainly not. He was not even ambidextrous.

A Juryman: Isn't Shoppinhour one of the infidel writers, published by t Freethought Publication Society?

Witness: I do not know who publishes his books.

The Juryman (a small grocer and big raw-boned Scotchman, rejoicing in the nar of Sandy Sanderson and the dignities of deaconry and membership of the committ of the Bow Conservative Association): No equeevocation, sir. Is he not a seculari who has lectured at the Hall of Science?

Witness: No, he is a foreign writer – (Mr. Sanderson was heard to thank Heaven this small mercy) – who believes that life is not worth living.

The Juryman: Were you not shocked to find the friend of a meenister reading su impure leeterature?

Witness: The deceased read everything. Schopenhauer is the author of a syste of philosophy, and not what you seem to imagine. Perhaps you would like to insp the book? (Laughter.)

The Juryman: I would na' touch it with a pitchfork. Such books should be burnt. And this Madame Blavatsky's book – what is that? Is that also pheelosophy?

Witness: No. It is Theosophy. (Laughter.)

Mr. Allen Smith, secretary of the Trammel's Union, stated that he had had an interview with the deceased on the day before his death, when he (the deceased) spoke hopefully of the prospects of the movement, and wrote him out a check for 10 guineas for his union. Deceased promised to speak at a meeting called for a quarter past seven a.m. the next day.

Mr. Edward Wimp, of the Scotland Yard Detective Department, said that the letters and papers of the deceased threw no light upon the manner of his death, and they would be handed back to the family. His Department had not formed any theory on the subject.

The Coroner proceeded to sum up the evidence. "We have to deal, gentlemen," he said, "with a most incomprehensible and mysterious case, the details of which are yet astonishingly simple. On the morning of Tuesday, the 4th inst., Mrs. Drabdump, a worthy, hard-working widow, who lets lodgings at 11 Grover Street, Bow, was unable to arouse the deceased, who occupied the entire upper floor of the house. Becoming alarmed, she went across to fetch Mr. George Grodman, a gentleman known to us all by reputation, and to whose clear and scientific evidence we are much indebted, and got him to batter in the door. They found the deceased lying back in bed with a deep wound in his throat. Life had only recently become extinct. There was no trace of any instrument by which the cut could have been effected; there was no trace of any person who could have effected the cut. No person could apparently have got in or out. The medical evidence goes to show that the deceased could not have inflicted the wound himself. And yet, gentlemen, there are, in the nature of things, two – and only two – alternative explanations of his death. Either the wound was inflicted by his own hand, or it was inflicted by another's. I shall take each of these possibilities separately. First, did the deceased commit suicide? The medical evidence says deceased was lying with his hands clasped behind his head. Now the wound was made from right to left, and terminated by a cut on the left thumb. If the deceased had made it he would have had to do it with his right hand, while his left hand remained under his head – a most peculiar and unnatural position to assume. Moreover, in making a cut with the right hand, one would naturally move the hand from left to right. It is unlikely that the deceased would move his right hand so awkwardly and unnaturally, unless, of course, his object was to baffle suspicion. Another point is that on this hypothesis, the deceased would have had to replace his right hand beneath his head. But Dr. Robinson believes that death was instantaneous. If so, deceased could have had no time to pose so neatly. It is just possible the cut was made with the left hand, but then the deceased was right-handed. The absence of any signs of a possible weapon undoubtedly goes to corroborate the medical evidence. The police have made an exhaustive search in all places where the razor or other weapon or instrument might by any possibility have been concealed, including the bedclothes, the mattress, the pillow, and the street into which it might have been dropped. But all theories involving the willful concealment of the fatal instrument have to reckon with the fact or probability that death was instantaneous, also with the fact that there was no blood about the floor. Finally, the instrument used was in all likelihood a razor, and the deceased did not shave, and was never known to be in possession of any such instrument. If, then, we were to confine ourselves to the medical and police evidence, there would, I think, be little hesitation in dismissing the idea of suicide. Nevertheless, it is well to forget the physical aspect of the case for a moment and to apply our minds to an unprejudiced inquiry into the mental aspect of it. Was there any reason why the deceased should wish to take his own life? He was young, wealthy and popular, loving and loved; life stretched fair before him. He had no vices. Plain living, high thinking, and noble doing were the three guiding stars of his life. If he had had ambition, an illustrious public career was within reach. He was an orator of no mean power, a brilliant and industrious man. His outlook was always on the future – he was always sketching out ways in which he could be useful to his fellow-men. His purse and his time were ever at the command of whosoever could show fair claim upon them. If such a man were likely to end his own life, the science of human nature would be at an end. Still, some of the shadows of the picture have been presented to us. The man had his moments of despondency – as which of us has not? But they seem to have been few and passing. Anyhow, he was cheerful enough on the day before his death. He was suffering, too, from toothache. But it does not seem to have been violent, nor did he complain. Possibly, of course, the pain became very acute in the night. Nor must we forget that he may have overworked himself, and got his nerves into a morbid state. He worked very hard, never rising later than half-past seven, and doing far more than the professional 'labor leader.' He taught and wrote as well as spoke and organized. But on the other hand all witnesses agree that he was looking forward eagerly to the meeting of tram-men on the morning of the 4th inst. His whole heart was in the movement. Is it likely that this was the night he would choose for quitting the scene of his usefulness? Is it likely that if he had chosen it, he would not have left letters and a statement behind, or made a last will and testament? Mr. Wimp has found no possible clue to such conduct in his papers. Or is it likely he would have concealed the instrument? The only positive sign of intention is the bolting of his door in addition to the usual locking of it, but one cannot lay much stress on that. Regarding the mental aspects alone, the balance is largely against suicide; looking at the physical aspects, suicide is well nigh impossible. Putting the two together, the case against suicide is all but mathematically complete. The answer, then, to our first question, Did the deceased commit suicide? is, that he did not."

The coroner paused, and everybody drew a long breath. The lucid exposition had been followed with admiration. If the coroner had stopped now, the jury would have unhesitatingly returned a verdict of "murder." But the coroner swallowed a mouthful of water and went on.

"We now come to the second alternative – was the deceased the victim of homicide? In order to answer that question in the affirmative it is essential that we should be able to form some conception of the *modus operandi*. It is all very well for Dr. Robinson to say the cut was made by another hand; but in the absence of any theory as to how the cut could possibly have been made by that other hand, we should be driven back to the theory of self-infliction, however improbable it may seem to medical gentlemen. Now, what are the facts? When Mrs. Drabdump and Mr. Grodman found the body it was yet warm, and Mr. Grodman, a witness fortunately qualified by special experience, states that death had been quite recent. This tallies closely enough with the view of Dr. Robinson, who, examining the body about an hour later, put the time of death at two or three hours before, say seven o'clock. Mrs. Drabdump had attempted to wake the deceased at a quarter to seven, which would put back the act to a little earlier. As I understand from Dr. Robinson, that it is impossible to fix the time very precisely, death may have very well taken place several hours before Mrs. Drabdump's first attempt to wake deceased. Of course, it may have taken place between the first and second calls, as he may merely have been sound asleep at first; it may also not impossibly have taken place considerably earlier than the first call, for all the physical data seem to prove. Nevertheless, on the whole, I think we shall be least likely to err if we assume the time of death to be half-past six. Gentlemen, let us picture to ourselves No. 11 Glover Street at half-past six. We have seen the house; we know exactly how it is constructed. On the ground floor a front room tenanted by Mr. Mortlake, with two windows giving on the street, both securely bolted; a back room occupied by the landlady; and a kitchen. Mrs. Drabdump did not leave her bedroom till half-past six, so that we may be sure all the various doors and windows have not yet been unfastened; while the season of the year is a guarantee that nothing had been left open. The front door through which Mr. Mortlake has gone out before half-past four, is guarded by the latch-key lock and the big lock. On the upper floor are two rooms – a front room used by deceased for a bedroom, and a back room which he used as a sitting-room. The back room has been left open, with the key inside, but the window is fastened. The door of the front room is not only locked, but bolted. We have seen the splintered mortise and the staple of the upper bolt violently forced from the woodwork and resting on the pin. The windows are bolted, the fasteners being firmly fixed in the catches. The chimney is too narrow to admit of the passage of even a child. This room, in fact, is as firmly barred in as if besieged. It has no communication with any other part of the house. It is as absolutely self-centered and isolated as if it were a fort in the sea or a log-hut in the forest. Even if any strange person is in the house, nay, in the very sitting-room of the deceased, he cannot get into the bedroom, for the house is one built for the poor, with no communication between the different rooms, so that separate families, if need be, may inhabit each. Now, however, let us grant that some person has achieved the miracle of getting into the front room, first floor, 18 feet from the ground. At half-past six, or thereabouts, he cuts the throat of the sleeping occupant. How is he then to get out without attracting the attention of the now roused landlady? But let us concede him that miracle, too. How is he to go away and yet leave the doors and windows locked and bolted from within? This is a degree of miracle at which my credulity must draw the line. No, the room had been closed all night – there is scarce a trace of fog in it. No one could get in or out. Finally, murders do not take place without motive. Robbery and revenge are the only conceivable motives. The deceased had not an enemy in the world; his money and valuables were left untouched. Everything was in order. There were no signs of a struggle. The answer then to our second inquiry – was the deceased killed by another person? – is, that he was not.

"Gentlemen, I am aware that this sounds impossible and contradictory. But it is the facts that contradict themselves. It seems clear that the deceased did not commit suicide. It seems equally clear that the deceased was not murdered. There is nothing for it, therefore, gentlemen, but to return a verdict tantamount to an acknowledgment of our incompetence to come to any adequately grounded conviction whatever as to the means or the manner by which the deceased met his death. It is the most inexplicable mystery in all my experience." (Sensation.)

The Foreman (after a colloquy with Mr. Sandy Sanderson): "We are not agreed, sir. One of the jurors insists on a verdict of "Death from visitation by the act of God.""

Chapter IV

BUT SANDY SANDERSON'S burning solicitude to fix the crime flickered out in the face of opposition, and in the end he bowed his head to the inevitable "open verdict." Then the floodgates of inkland were opened, and the deluge pattered for nine days on the deaf coffin where the poor idealist moldered. The tongues of the Press were loosened, and the leader writers reveled in recapitulating the circumstances of "The Big Bow Mystery," though they could contribute nothing but adjectives to the solution. The papers teemed with letters – it was a kind of Indian summer of the silly season. But the editors could not keep them out, nor cared to. The mystery was the one topic of conversation everywhere – it was on the carpet and the bare boards alike, in the kitchen and the drawing-room. It was discussed with science or stupidity, with aspirates or without. It came up for breakfast with the rolls, and was swept off the supper table with the last crumbs.

No. 11 Glover Street, Bow, remained for days a shrine of pilgrimage. The once sleepy little street buzzed from morning till night. From all parts of the town people came to stare up at the bedroom window and wonder with a foolish look of horror. The pavement was often blocked for hours together, and itinerant vendors of refreshment made it a new market center, while vocalists hastened thither to sing the delectable ditty of the deed without having any voice in the matter. It was a pity the Government did not erect a toll-gate at either end of the street. But Chancellors of the Exchequer rarely avail themselves of the more obvious expedients for paying off the National debt.

Finally, familiarity bred contempt, and the wits grew facetious at the expense of the Mystery. Jokes on the subject appeared even in the comic papers.

To the proverb, "You must not say Boo to a goose," one added, "or else she will explain you the Mystery." The name of the gentleman who asked whether the Bow Mystery was not 'arrowing shall not be divulged. There was more point in "Dagonet's" remark that, if he had been one of the unhappy jurymen, he should have been driven to "suicide." A professional paradox-monger pointed triumphantly to the somewhat similar situation in "the murder in the Rue Morgue," and said that Nature had been plagiarizing again – like the monkey she was – and he recommended Poe's publishers to apply for an injunction. More seriously, Poe's solution was re-suggested by "Constant Reader" as an original idea. He thought that a small organ-grinder's monkey might have got down the chimney with its master's razor, and, after attempting to shave the occupant of the bed, have returned the way it came. This idea created considerable sensation, but a correspondent with a long train of letters draggling after his name pointed out that a monkey small enough to get down so narrow a flue would not be strong enough to inflict so deep a wound. This was disputed by a third writer, and the contest raged so keenly about the power of monkeys' muscles that it was almost taken for granted that a monkey was the guilty party. The bubble was pricked by the pen of "Common Sense," who laconically remarked that no traces of soot or blood had been discovered on the floor, or on the nightshirt, or the counterpane. The "Lancet's" leader on the Mystery was awaited with interest. It said: "We cannot join in the praises that have been showered upon the coroner's summing up. It shows again the evils resulting from having coroners who are not medical men. He seems to have appreciated but inadequately the significance of the medical evidence. He should certainly have directed the jury to return a verdict of murder on that. What was it to do with him that he could see no way by which the wound could have been inflicted by an outside agency? It was for the police to find how that was done. Enough that it was impossible for the unhappy young man to have inflicted such a wound and then have strength and will power enough to hide the instrument and to remove perfectly every trace of his having left the bed for the purpose." It is impossible to enumerate all the theories propounded by the amateur detectives, while Scotland Yard religiously held its tongue. Ultimately the interest on the subject became confined to a few papers which had received the best letters. Those papers that couldn't get interesting letters stopped the correspondence and sneered at the "sensationalism" of those that could. Among the mass of fantasy there were not a few notable solutions, which failed brilliantly, like rockets posing as fixed stars. One was that in the obscurity of the fog the murderer had ascended to the window of the bedroom by means of a ladder from the pavement. He had then with a diamond cut one of the panes away, and effected an entry through the aperture. On leaving he fixed in the pane of glass again (or another which he had brought with him), and thus the room remained with its bolts and locks untouched. On its being pointed out that the panes were too small, a third correspondent showed that that didn't matter, as it was only necessary to insert the hand and undo the fastening, when the entire window could be opened, the process being reversed by the murderer on leaving. This pretty edifice of glass was smashed by a glazier, who wrote to say that a pane could hardly be fixed in from only one side of a window frame, that it would fall out when touched, and that in any case the wet putty could not have escaped detection. A door panel sliced out and replaced was also put forward, and as many trap-doors and secret passages were ascribed to No. 11 Glover Street as if it were a medieval castle. Another of these clever theories was that the murderer was in the room the whole time the police were there – hidden in the wardrobe. Or he had got behind the door when Grodman broke it open, so that he was not noticed in the excitement of the discovery, and escaped with his weapon at the moment when Grodman and Mrs. Drabdump were examining the window fastenings.

Scientific explanations also were to hand to explain how the assassin locked and bolted the door behind him. Powerful magnets outside the door had been used to turn the key and push the bolt within. Murderers armed with magnets loomed on the popular imagination like a new microbe. There was only one defect in this ingenious theory – the thing could not be done. A physiologist recalled the conjurers who swallowed swords – by an anatomical peculiarity of the throat – and said that the deceased might have swallowed the weapon after cutting his own throat. This was too much for the public to swallow. As for the idea that the suicide had been effected with a penknife or its blade, or a bit of steel, which had got buried in the wound, not even the quotation of Shelley's line:

"Makes such a wound, the knife is lost in it,"

could secure it a moment's acceptance. The same reception was accorded to the idea that the cut had been made with a candlestick (or other harmless article) constructed like a sword-stick. Theories of this sort caused a humorist to explain that the deceased had hidden the razor in his hollow tooth! Some kind friend of Messrs. Maskelyne and Cook suggested that they were the only persons who could have done the deed, as no one else could get out of a locked cabinet. But perhaps the most brilliant of these flashes of false fire was the facetious, yet probably half-seriously meant, letter that appeared in the *Pell Mell Press* under the heading of

THE BIG BOW MYSTERY SOLVED

"Sir – You will remember that when the Whitechapel murders were agitating the universe, I suggested that the district coroner was the assassin. My suggestion has been disregarded. The coroner is still at large. So is the Whitechapel murderer. Perhaps this suggestive coincidence will incline the authorities to pay more attention to me this time. The problem seems to be this. The deceased could not have cut his own throat. The deceased could not have had his throat cut for him. As one of the two must have happened, this is obvious nonsense. As this is obvious nonsense I am justified in disbelieving it. As this obvious nonsense was primarily put in circulation by Mrs. Drabdump and Mr. Grodman, I am justified in disbelieving them. In short, sir, what guarantee have we that the whole tale is not a cock-and-bull story, invented by the two persons who first found the body? What proof is there that the deed was not done by these persons themselves, who then went to work to smash the door and

break the locks and the bolts, and fasten up all the windows before they called the police in? I enclose my card, and am, sir, yours truly, One Who Looks Through His Own Spectacles."

("Our correspondent's theory is not so audaciously original as he seems to imagine. Has he not looked through the spectacles of the people who persistently suggested that the Whitechapel murderer was invariably the policeman who found the body? Somebody must find the body, if it is to be found at all. – Ed. P. M. P.")

The editor had reason to be pleased that he inserted this letter, for it drew the following interesting communication from the great detective himself:

THE BIG BOW MYSTERY SOLVED

"Sir – I do not agree with you that your correspondent's theory lacks originality. On the contrary, I think it is delightfully original. In fact it has given me an idea. What that idea is I do not yet propose to say, but if 'One Who Looks Through His Own Spectacles' will favor me with his name and address I shall be happy to inform him a little before the rest of the world whether his germ has borne any fruit. I feel he is a kindred spirit, and take this opportunity of saying publicly that I was extremely disappointed at the unsatisfactory verdict. The thing was a palpable assassination; an open verdict has a tendency to relax the exertions of Scotland Yard. I hope I shall not be accused of immodesty, or of making personal reflections, when I say that the Department has had several notorious failures of late. It is not what it used to be. Crime is becoming impertinent. It no longer knows its place, so to speak. It throws down the gauntlet where once it used to cower in its fastnesses. I repeat, I make these remarks solely in the interest of law and order. I do not for one moment believe that Arthur Constant killed himself, and if Scotland Yard satisfies itself with that explanation, and turns on its other side and goes to sleep again, then, sir, one of the foulest and most horrible crimes of the century will forever go unpunished. My acquaintance with the unhappy victim was but recent; still, I saw and knew enough of the man to be certain (and I hope I have seen and known enough of other men to judge) that he was a man constitutionally incapable of committing an act of violence, whether against himself or anybody else. He would not hurt a fly, as the saying goes. And a man of that gentle stamp always lacks the active energy to lay hands on himself. He was a man to be esteemed in no common degree, and I feel proud to be able to say that he considered me a friend. I am hardly at the time of life at which a man cares to put on his harness again; but, sir, it is impossible that I should ever know a day's rest till the perpetrator of this foul deed is discovered. I have already put myself in communication with the family of the victim, who, I am pleased to say, have every confidence in me, and look to me to clear the name of their unhappy relative from the semi-imputation of suicide. I shall be pleased if anyone who shares my distrust of the authorities, and who has any clue whatever to this terrible mystery, or any plausible suggestion to offer, if, in brief, any 'One who looks through his own spectacles' will communicate with me. If I were asked to indicate the direction in which new clues might be most usefully sought, I should say, in the first instance, anything is valuable that helps us to piece together a complete picture of the manifold activities of the man in the East End. He entered one way or another into the lives of a good many people; is it true that he nowhere made enemies? With

the best intentions a man may wound or offend; his interference may be resented; he may even excite jealousy. A young man like the late Mr. Constant could not have had as much practical sagacity as he had goodness. Whose corns did he tread on? The more we know of the last few months of his life the more we shall know of the manner of his death. Thanking you by anticipation for the insertion of this letter in your valuable columns, I am, sir, yours truly,

"George Grodman."46 Glover Street, Bow."

"P. S. – Since writing the above lines I have, by the kindness of Miss Brent, been placed in possession of a most valuable letter, probably the last letter written by the unhappy gentleman. It is dated Monday, 3 December, the very eve of the murder, and was addressed to her at Florence, and has now, after some delay, followed her back to London where the sad news unexpectedly brought her. It is a letter couched, on the whole, in the most hopeful spirit, and speaks in detail of his schemes. Of course, there are things in it not meant for the ears of the public, but there can be no harm in transcribing an important passage:

"'You seem to have imbibed the idea that the East End is a kind of Golgotha, and this despite that the books out of which you probably got it are carefully labeled "Fiction." Lamb says somewhere that we think of the "Dark Ages" as literally without sunlight, and so I fancy people like you, dear, think of the "East End" as a mixture of mire, misery and murder. How's that for alliteration? Why, within five minutes' walk of me there are the loveliest houses, with gardens back and front, inhabited by very fine people and furniture. Many of my university friends' mouths would water if they knew the income of some of the shop-keepers in the High Road.

"'The rich people about here may not be so fashionable as those in Kensington and Bayswater, but they are every bit as stupid and materialistic. I don't deny, Lucy, I do have my black moments, and I do sometimes pine to get away from all this to the lands of sun and lotus-eating. But, on the whole, I am too busy even to dream of dreaming. My real black moments are when I doubt if I am really doing any good. But yet on the whole my conscience or my self-conceit tells me that I am. If one cannot do much with the mass, there is at least the consolation of doing good to the individual. And, after all, is it not enough to have been an influence for good over one or two human souls? There are quite fine characters hereabout – especially in the women – natures capable not only of self-sacrifice, but of delicacy of sentiment. To have learnt to know of such, to have been of service to one or two of such – is not this ample return? I could not get to St. James' Hall to hear your friend's symphony at the Henschel concert. I have been reading Mme. Blavatsky's latest book, and getting quite interested in occult philosophy. Unfortunately I have to do all my reading in bed, and I don't find the book as soothing a soporific as most new books. For keeping one awake I find Theosophy as bad as toothache....'"

* * *

"Sir – I wonder if anyone besides myself has been struck by the incredible bad taste of Mr. Grodman's letter in your last issue. That he, a former servant of the Department, should publicly insult and run it down can only be charitably

explained by the supposition that his judgment is failing him in his old age. In view of this letter, are the relatives of the deceased justified in entrusting him with any private documents? It is, no doubt, very good of him to undertake to avenge one whom he seems snobbishly anxious to claim as a friend; but, all things considered, should not his letter have been headed 'The Big Bow Mystery Shelved?' I enclose my card, and am, sir,

"Your obedient servant, Scotland Yard."

George Grodman read this letter with annoyance, and, crumpling up the paper, murmured scornfully, "Edward Wimp."

Chapter V

"YES, BUT WHAT will become of the Beautiful?" said Denzil Cantercot.

"Hang the Beautiful!" said Peter Crowl, as if he were on the committee of the Academy. "Give me the True."

Denzil did nothing of the sort. He didn't happen to have it about him.

Denzil Cantercot stood smoking a cigarette in his landlord's shop, and imparting an air of distinction and an agreeable aroma to the close leathery atmosphere. Crowl cobbled away, talking to his tenant without raising his eyes. He was a small, big-headed, sallow, sad-eyed man, with a greasy apron. Denzil was wearing a heavy overcoat with a fur collar. He was never seen without it in public during the winter. In private he removed it and sat in his shirt sleeves. Crowl was a thinker, or thought he was – which seems to involve original thinking anyway. His hair was thinning rapidly at the top, as if his brain was struggling to get as near as possible to the realities of things. He prided himself on having no fads. Few men are without some foible or hobby; Crowl felt almost lonely at times in his superiority. He was a Vegetarian, a Secularist, a Blue Ribbonite, a Republican, and an Anti-Tobacconist. Meat was a fad. Drink was a fad. Religion was a fad. Monarchy was a fad. Tobacco was a fad. "A plain man like me," Crowl used to say, "can live without fads." "A plain man" was Crowl's catchword. When of a Sunday morning he stood on Mile-end Waste, which was opposite his shop – and held forth to the crowd on the evils of kings, priests and mutton chops, the "plain man" turned up at intervals like the "theme" of a symphonic movement. "I am only a plain man and I want to know." It was a phrase that sabered the spider-webs of logical refinement, and held them up scornfully on the point. When Crowl went for a little recreation in Victoria Park on Sunday afternoons, it was with this phrase that he invariably routed the supernaturalists. Crowl knew his Bible better than most ministers, and always carried a minutely-printed copy in his pocket, dogs-eared to mark contradictions in the text. The second chapter of Jeremiah says one thing; the first chapter of Corinthians says another. Two contradictory statements may both be true, but "I am only a plain man, and I want to know." Crowl spent a large part of his time in setting "the word against the word." Cock-fighting affords its votaries no acuter pleasure than Crowl derived from setting two texts by the ears. Crowl had a metaphysical genius which sent his Sunday morning disciples frantic with admiration, and struck the enemy dumb with dismay. He had discovered, for instance, that the Deity could not move, owing to already filling all space. He was also the first to invent, for the confusion of the clerical, the crucial case of a saint dying at the Antipodes contemporaneously with another in London. Both went skyward to heaven, yet the two traveled in directly opposite directions. In all eternity they would never meet. Which, then, got to heaven? Or was there no such place? "I am only a plain man, and I want to know." Preserve us our open spaces; they exist to testify to the incurable interest of humanity in the Unknown and the Misunderstood. Even 'Arry is capable of five minutes' attention to speculative theology, if 'Arriet isn't in a 'urry.

Peter Crowl was not sorry to have a lodger like Denzil Cantercot, who, though a man of parts and thus worth powder and shot, was so hopelessly wrong on all subjects under the sun. In only one point did Peter Crowl agree with Denzil Cantercot – he admired Denzil Cantercot secretly. When he asked him for the True – which was about twice a day on the average – he didn't really expect to get it from him. He knew that Denzil was a poet.

"The Beautiful," he went on, "is a thing that only appeals to men like you. The True is for all men. The majority have the first claim. Till then you poets must stand aside. The True and the Useful – that's what we want. The Good of Society is the only test of things. Everything stands or falls by the Good of Society."

"The Good of Society!" echoed Denzil, scornfully. "What's the Good of Society? The Individual is before all. The mass must be sacrificed to the Great Man. Otherwise the Great Man will be sacrificed to the mass. Without great men there would be no art. Without art life would be a blank."

"Ah, but we should fill it up with bread and butter," said Peter Crowl.

"Yes, it is bread and butter that kills the Beautiful," said Denzil Cantercot bitterly. "Many of us start by following the butterfly through the verdant meadows, but we turn aside—"

"To get the grub," chuckled Peter, cobbling away.

"Peter, if you make a jest of everything, I'll not waste my time on you."

Denzil's wild eyes flashed angrily. He shook his long hair. Life was very serious to him. He never wrote comic verse intentionally.

There are three reasons why men of genius have long hair. One is, that they forget it is growing. The second is, that they like it. The third is, that it comes cheaper; they wear it long for the same reason that they wear their hats long.

Owing to this peculiarity of genius, you may get quite a reputation for lack of twopence. The economic reason did not apply to Denzil, who could always get credit with the profession on the strength of his appearance. Therefore, when street Arabs vocally commanded him to get his hair cut, they were doing no service to barbers. Why does all the world watch over barbers and conspire to promote their interests? Denzil would have told you it was not to serve the barbers, but to gratify the crowd's instinctive resentment of originality. In his palmy days Denzil had been an editor, but he no more thought of turning his scissors against himself than of swallowing his paste. The efficacy of hair has changed since the days of Samson, otherwise Denzil would have been a Hercules instead of a long, thin, nervous man, looking too brittle and delicate to be used even for a pipe-cleaner. The narrow oval of his face sloped to a pointed, untrimmed beard. His linen was reproachable, his dingy boots were down at heel, and his cocked hat was drab with dust. Such are the effects of a love for the Beautiful.

Peter Crowl was impressed with Denzil's condemnation of flippancy, and he hastened to turn off the joke.

"I'm quite serious," he said. "Butterflies are no good to nothing or nobody; caterpillars at least save the birds from starving."

"Just like your view of things, Peter," said Denzil. "Good morning, madam." This to Mrs. Crowl, to whom he removed his hat with elaborate courtesy. Mrs. Crowl grunted and looked at her husband with a note of interrogation in each eye. For some seconds Crowl stuck to his last, endeavoring not to see the question. He shifted uneasily on his stool. His wife coughed grimly. He looked up, saw her towering over him, and helplessly shook his head in a horizontal direction. It was wonderful how Mrs. Crowl towered over Mr. Crowl, even when he stood up in his shoes. She measured half an inch less. It was quite an optical illusion.

"Mr. Crowl," said Mrs. Crowl, "then I'll tell him."

"No, no, my dear, not yet," faltered Peter helplessly; "leave it to me."

"I've left it to you long enough. You'll never do nothing. If it was a question of provin' to a lot of chuckleheads that Jollygee and Genesis, or some other dead and gone Scripture folk that don't consarn no mortal soul, used to contradict each other, your tongue 'ud run thirteen to the dozen. But when it's a matter of takin' the bread out o' the mouths o' your own children, you ain't got no more to say for yourself than a lamppost. Here's a man stayin' with you for weeks and weeks – eatin' and drinkin' the flesh off your bones – without payin' a far—"

"Hush, hush, mother; it's all right," said poor Crowl, red as fire.

Denzil looked at her dreamily. "Is it possible you are alluding to me, Mrs. Crowl?" he said.

"Who then should I be alludin' to, Mr. Cantercot? Here's seven weeks come and gone, and not a blessed 'aypenny have I—"

"My dear Mrs. Crowl," said Denzil, removing his cigarette from his mouth with a pained air, "why reproach me for your neglect?"

"My neglect! I like that!"

"I don't," said Denzil, more sharply. "If you had sent me in the bill you would have had the money long ago. How do you expect me to think of these details?"

"We ain't so grand down here. People pays their way – they don't get no bills," said Mrs. Crowl, accentuating the word with infinite scorn.

Peter hammered away at a nail, as though to drown his spouse's voice.

"It's three pounds fourteen and eight-pence, if you're so anxious to know," Mrs. Crowl resumed. "And there ain't a woman in the Mile End Road as 'ud a-done it cheaper, with bread at fourpence threefarden a quartern and landlords clamorin' for rent every Monday morning almost afore the sun's up and folks draggin' and slidderin' on till their shoes is only fit to throw after brides, and Christmas comin' and seven-pence a week for schoolin'!"

Peter winced under the last item. He had felt it coming – like Christmas. His wife and he parted company on the question of Free Education. Peter felt that, having brought nine children into the world, it was only fair he should pay a penny a week for each of those old enough to bear educating. His better half argued that, having so many children, they ought in reason to be exempted. Only people who had few children could spare the penny. But the one point on which the cobbler-skeptic of the Mile End Road got his way was this of the fees. It was a question of conscience, and Mrs. Crowl had never made application for their remission, though she often slapped her children in vexation instead. They were used to slapping, and when nobody else slapped them they slapped one another. They were bright, ill-mannered brats, who pestered their parents and worried their teachers, and were happy as the Road was long.

"Bother the school fees!" Peter retorted, vexed. "Mr. Cantercot's not responsible for your children."

"I should hope not, indeed, Mr. Crowl," Mrs. Crowl said sternly. "I'm ashamed of you." And with that she flounced out of the shop into the back parlor.

"It's all right," Peter called after her soothingly. "The money'll be all right, mother."

In lower circles it is customary to call your wife your mother; in somewhat superior circles it is the fashion to speak of her as "the wife" as you speak of "the Stock Exchange," or "the Thames," without claiming any peculiar property. Instinctively men are ashamed of being moral and domesticated.

Denzil puffed his cigarette, unembarrassed. Peter bent attentively over his work, making nervous stabs with his awl. There was a long silence. An organ-grinder played a waltz outside, unregarded; and, failing to annoy anybody, moved on. Denzil lit another cigarette. The dirty-faced clock on the shop wall chimed twelve.

"What do you think," said Crowl, "of Republics?"

"They are low," Denzil replied. "Without a Monarch there is no visible incarnation of Authority."

"What! do you call Queen Victoria visible?"

"Peter, do you want to drive me from the house? Leave frivolousness to women, whose minds are only large enough for domestic difficulties. Republics are low. Plato mercifully kept the poets out of his. Republics are not congenial soil for poetry."

"What nonsense! If England dropped its fad of Monarchy and became a Republic tomorrow, do you mean to say that—?"

"I mean to say that there would be no Poet Laureate to begin with."

"Who's fribbling now, you or me, Cantercot? But I don't care a button-hook about poets, present company always excepted. I'm only a plain man, and I want to know where's the sense of givin' any one person authority over everybody else?"

"Ah, that's what Tom Mortlake used to say. Wait till you're in power, Peter, with trade-union money to control, and working men bursting to give you flying angels and to carry you aloft, like a banner, huzzahing."

"Ah, that's because he's head and shoulders above 'em already," said Crowl, with a flash in his sad gray eyes. "Still, it don't prove that I'd talk any different. And I think you're quite wrong about his being spoiled. Tom's a fine fellow – a man every inch of him, and that's a good many. I don't deny he has his weaknesses, and there was a time when he stood in this very shop and denounced that poor dead Constant. 'Crowl,' said he, 'that man'll do mischief. I don't like these kid-glove philanthropists mixing themselves up in practical labor disputes they don't understand.'"

Denzil whistled involuntarily. It was a piece of news.

"I daresay," continued Crowl, "he's a bit jealous of anybody's interference with his influence. But in this case the jealousy did wear off, you see, for the poor fellow and he got quite pals, as everybody knows. Tom's not the man to hug a prejudice. However, all that don't prove nothing against Republics. Look at the Czar and the Jews. I'm only a plain man, but I wouldn't live in Russia not for – not for all the leather in it! An Englishman, taxed as he is to keep up his Fad of Monarchy, is at least king in his own castle, whoever bosses it at Windsor. Excuse me a minute, the missus is callin'."

"Excuse *me* a minute. I'm going, and I want to say before I go – I feel it is only right you should know at once – that after what has passed today I can never be on the same footing here as in the – shall I say pleasant? – days of yore."

"Oh, no, Cantercot. Don't say that; don't say that!" pleaded the little cobbler.

"Well, shall I say unpleasant, then?"

"No, no, Cantercot. Don't misunderstand me. Mother has been very much put to it lately to rub along. You see she has such a growing family. It grows – daily. But never mind her. You pay whenever you've got the money."

Denzil shook his head. "It cannot be. You know when I came here first I rented your top room and boarded myself. Then I learnt to know you. We talked together. Of the Beautiful. And the Useful. I found you had no soul. But you were honest, and I liked you. I went so far as to take my meals with your family. I made myself at home in your back parlor. But the vase has been shattered (I do not refer to that on the mantelpiece), and though the scent of the roses may cling to it still, it can be pieced together – nevermore." He shook his hair sadly and shambled out of the shop. Crowl would have gone after him, but Mrs. Crowl was still calling, and ladies must have the precedence in all polite societies.

Cantercot went straight – or as straight as his loose gait permitted – to 46 Glover Street, and knocked at the door. Grodman's factotum opened it. She was a pock-marked person, with a brickdust complexion and a coquettish manner.

"Oh, here we are again!" she said vivaciously.

"Don't talk like a clown," Cantercot snapped. "Is Mr. Grodman in?"

"No, you've put him out," growled the gentleman himself, suddenly appearing in his slippers. "Come in. What the devil have you been doing with yourself since the inquest? Drinking again?"

"I've sworn off. Haven't touched a drop since—"

"The murder?"

"Eh?" said Denzil Cantercot, startled. "What do you mean?"

"What I say. Since December 4, I reckon everything from that murder, now, as they reckon longitude from Greenwich."

"Oh," said Denzil Cantercot.

"Let me see. Nearly a fortnight. What a long time to keep away from Drink – and Me."

"I don't know which is worse," said Denzil, irritated. "You both steal away my brains."

"Indeed?" said Grodman, with an amused smile. "Well, it's only petty pilfering, after all. What's put salt on your wounds?"

"The twenty-fourth edition of my book."

"Whose book?"

"Well, your book. You must be making piles of money out of 'Criminals I Have Caught.'"

"'Criminals *I* Have Caught,'" corrected Grodman. "My dear Denzil, how often am I to point out that I went through the experiences that make the backbone of my book, not you? In each case I cooked the criminal's goose. Any journalist could have supplied the dressing."

"The contrary. The journeymen of journalism would have left the truth naked. You yourself could have done that – for there is no man to beat you at cold, lucid, scientific statement. But I idealized the bare facts and lifted them into the realm of poetry and literature. The twenty-fourth edition of the book attests my success."

"Rot! The twenty-fourth edition was all owing to the murder! Did you do that?"

"You take one up so sharply, Mr. Grodman," said Denzil, changing his tone.

"No – I've retired," laughed Grodman.

Denzil did not reprove the ex-detective's flippancy. He even laughed a little.

"Well, give me another fiver, and I'll cry 'quits.' I'm in debt."

"Not a penny. Why haven't you been to see me since the murder? I had to write that letter to the 'Pell Mell Press' myself. You might have earned a crown."

"I've had writer's cramp, and couldn't do your last job. I was coming to tell you so on the morning of the—"

"Murder. So you said at the inquest."

"It's true."

"Of course. Weren't you on your oath? It was very zealous of you to get up so early to tell me. In which hand did you have this cramp?"

"Why, in the right, of course."

"And you couldn't write with your left?"

"I don't think I could even hold a pen."

"Or any other instrument, mayhap. What had you been doing to bring it on?"

"Writing too much. That is the only possible cause."

"Oh, I don't know. Writing what?"

Denzil hesitated. "An epic poem."

"No wonder you're in debt. Will a sovereign get you out of it?"

"No; it wouldn't be the least use to me."

"Here it is, then."

Denzil took the coin and his hat.

"Aren't you going to earn it, you beggar? Sit down and write something for me."

Denzil got pen and paper, and took his place.

"What do you want me to write?"

"The Epic Poem."

Denzil started and flushed. But he set to work. Grodman leaned back in his armchair and laughed, studying the poet's grave face.

Denzil wrote three lines and paused.

"Can't remember any more? Well, read me the start."

Denzil read:

"Of man's first disobedience and the fruit
Of that forbidden tree whose mortal taste
Brought death into the world—"

"Hold on!" cried Grodman; "what morbid subjects you choose, to be sure."

"Morbid! Why, Milton chose the same subject!"

"Blow Milton. Take yourself off – you and your Epics."

Denzil went. The pock-marked person opened the street door for him.

"When am I to have that new dress, dear?" she whispered coquettishly.

"I have no money, Jane," he said shortly.

"You have a sovereign."

Denzil gave her the sovereign, and slammed the door viciously. Grodman overheard their whispers, and laughed silently. His hearing was acute. Jane had first introduced Denzil to his acquaintance about two years ago, when he spoke of getting an amanuensis, and the poet had been doing odd jobs for him ever since. Grodman argued that Jane had her reasons. Without knowing them he got a hold over both. There was no one, he felt, he could not get a hold over. All men – and women – have something to conceal, and you have only to pretend to know what it is. Thus Grodman, who was nothing if not scientific.

Denzil Cantercot shambled home thoughtfully, and abstractedly took his place at the Crowl dinner-table.

Chapter VI

MRS. CROWL surveyed Denzil Cantercot so stonily and cut him his beef so savagely that he said grace when the dinner was over. Peter fed his metaphysical genius on tomatoes. He was tolerant enough to allow his family to follow their Fads; but no savory smells ever tempted him to be false to his vegetable loves. Besides, meat might have reminded him too much of his work. There is nothing like leather, but Bow beefsteaks occasionally come very near it.

After dinner Denzil usually indulged in poetic reverie. But today he did not take his nap. He went out at once to "raise the wind." But there was a dead calm everywhere. In vain he asked for an advance at the office of the "Mile End Mirror," to which he contributed scathing leaderettes about vestrymen. In vain he trudged to the city and offered to write the "Ham and Eggs Gazette" an essay on the modern methods of bacon-curing. Denzil knew a great deal about the breeding and slaughtering of pigs, smoke-lofts and drying processes, having for years dictated the policy of the "New Pork Herald" in these momentous matters. Denzil also knew a great deal about many other esoteric matters, including weaving machines, the manufacture of cabbage leaves and snuff, and the inner economy of drain-pipes. He had written for the trade papers since boyhood. But there is great competition on these papers. So many men of literary gifts know all about the intricate technicalities of manufactures and markets, and are eager to set the trade right. Grodman perhaps hardly allowed sufficiently for the step backward that Denzil made when he devoted his whole time for months to "Criminals I Have Caught." It was as damaging as a debauch. For when your rivals are pushing forward, to stand still is to go back.

In despair Denzil shambled toilsomely to Bethnal Green. He paused before the window of a little tobacconist's shop, wherein was displayed a placard announcing:

PLOTS FOR SALE.

The announcement went on to state that a large stock of plots was to be obtained on the premises – embracing sensational plots, humorous plots, love plots, religious plots, and poetic plots; also complete manuscripts, original novels, poems and tales. Apply within.

It was a very dirty-looking shop, with begrimed bricks and blackened woodwork. The window contained some musty old books, an assortment of pipes and tobacco, and a large number of the vilest daubs unhung, painted in oil on Academy boards, and unframed. These were intended for landscapes, as you could tell from the titles. The most expensive was "Chingford Church," and it was marked 1s. 9d. The others ran from 6d. to 1s. 3d., and were mostly representations of Scotch scenery – a loch with mountains in the background, with solid reflections in the water and a tree in the foreground. Sometimes the tree would be in the background. Then the loch would be in the foreground. Sky and water were intensely blue in all. The name of the collection was "Original oil paintings done by hand." Dust lay thick upon everything, as if carefully shoveled on; and the proprietor looked as if he slept in his shop window at night without taking his clothes off. He was a gaunt man with a red nose, long but scanty black locks covered by a smoking cap, and a luxuriant black mustache. He smoked a long clay pipe, and had the air of a broken-down operatic villain.

"Ah, good afternoon, Mr. Cantercot," he said, rubbing his hands, half from cold, half from usage; "what have you brought me?"

"Nothing," said Denzil, "but if you will lend me a sovereign I'll do you a stunner."

The operatic villain shook his locks, his eyes full of pawky cunning. "If you did it after that it would be a stunner."

What the operatic villain did with these plots, and who bought them, Cantercot never knew nor cared to know. Brains are cheap today, and Denzil was glad enough to find a customer.

"Surely you've known me long enough to trust me," he cried.

"Trust is dead," said the operatic villain, puffing away.

"So is Queen Anne," cried the irritated poet. His eyes took a dangerous hunted look. Money he must have. But the operatic villain was inflexible. No plot, no supper.

Poor Denzil went out flaming. He knew not where to turn. Temporarily he turned on his heel again and stared despairingly at the shop window. Again he read the legend:

PLOTS FOR SALE.

He stared so long at this that it lost its meaning. When the sense of the words suddenly flashed upon him again, they bore a new significance. He went in meekly, and borrowed fourpence of the operatic villain. Then he took the 'bus for Scotland Yard. There was a not ill-looking servant girl in the 'bus. The rhythm of the vehicle shaped itself into rhymes in his brain. He forgot all about his situation and his object. He had never really written an epic – except "Paradise Lost" – but he composed lyrics about wine and women and often wept to think how miserable he was. But nobody ever bought anything of him, except articles on bacon-curing or attacks on vestrymen. He was a strange, wild creature, and the wench felt quite pretty under his ardent gaze. It almost hypnotized her, though, and she looked down at her new French kid boots to escape it.

At Scotland Yard Denzil asked for Edward Wimp. Edward Wimp was not on view. Like kings and editors, Detectives are difficult of approach – unless you are a criminal, when you cannot see anything of them at all. Denzil knew of Edward Wimp, principally because of Grodman's contempt for his successor. Wimp was a man of taste and culture. Grodman's interests were entirely concentrated on the problems of logic and evidence. Books about these formed his sole reading; for *belles lettres* he cared not a straw. Wimp, with his flexible intellect, had a great contempt for Grodman and his slow, laborious, ponderous, almost Teutonic methods. Worse, he almost threatened to eclipse the radiant tradition of Grodman by some wonderfully ingenious bits of workmanship. Wimp was at his greatest in collecting circumstantial evidence; in putting two and two together to make five. He would collect together a number of dark and disconnected data and flash across them the electric light of some unifying hypothesis in a way which would have done credit to a Darwin or a Faraday. An intellect which might have served to unveil the secret workings of nature was subverted to the protection of a capitalistic civilization.

By the assistance of a friendly policeman, whom the poet magnetized into the belief that his business was a matter of life and death, Denzil obtained the great detective's private address. It was near King's Cross. By a miracle Wimp was at home in the afternoon. He was writing when Denzil was ushered up three pairs of stairs into his presence, but he got up and flashed the bull's-eye of his glance upon the visitor.

"Mr. Denzil Cantercot, I believe!" said Wimp.

Denzil started. He had not sent up his name, merely describing himself as a gentleman.

"That is my name," he murmured.

"You were one of the witnesses at the inquest on the body of the late Arthur Constant. I have your evidence there." He pointed to a file. "Why have you come to give fresh evidence?"

Again Denzil started, flushing in addition this time. "I want money," he said, almost involuntarily.

"Sit down." Denzil sat. Wimp stood.

Wimp was young and fresh-colored. He had a Roman nose, and was smartly dressed. He had beaten Grodman by discovering the wife Heaven meant for him. He had a bouncing boy, who stole jam out of the pantry without anyone being the wiser. Wimp did what work he could do at home in a secluded study at the top of the house. Outside his chamber of horrors he was the ordinary husband of commerce. He adored his wife, who thought poorly of his intellect, but highly of his heart. In domestic difficulties Wimp was helpless. He could not even tell whether the servant's "character" was forged or genuine. Probably he could not level himself to such petty problems. He was like the senior wrangler who has forgotten how to do quadratics, and has to solve equations of the second degree by the calculus.

"How much money do you want?" he asked.

"I do not make bargains," Denzil replied, his calm come back by this time. "I came to tender you a suggestion. It struck me that you might offer me a fiver for my trouble. Should you do so, I shall not refuse it."

"You shall not refuse it – if you deserve it."

"Good. I will come to the point at once. My suggestion concerns – Tom Mortlake."

Denzil threw out the name as if it were a torpedo. Wimp did not move.

"Tom Mortlake," went on Denzil, looking disappointed, "had a sweetheart." He paused impressively.

Wimp said "Yes?"

"Where is that sweetheart now?"

"Where, indeed?"

"You know about her disappearance?"

"You have just informed me of it."

"Yes, she is gone – without a trace. She went about a fortnight before Mr. Constant's murder."

"Murder? How do you know it was a murder?"

"Mr. Grodman says so," said Denzil, startled again.

"H'm! Isn't that rather a proof that it was suicide? Well, go on."

"About a fortnight before the suicide, Jessie Dymond disappeared. So they tell me in Stepney Green, where she lodged and worked."

"What was she?"

"She was a dressmaker. She had a wonderful talent. Quite fashionable ladies got to know of it. One of her dresses was presented at Court. I think the lady forgot to pay for it; so Jessie's landlady said."

"Did she live alone?"

"She had no parents, but the house was respectable."

"Good-looking, I suppose?"

"As a poet's dream."

"As yours, for instance?"

"I am a poet; I dream."

"You dream you are a poet. Well, well! She was engaged to Mortlake?"

"Oh, yes! They made no secret of it. The engagement was an old one. When he was earning 36s. a week as a compositor they were saving up to buy a home. He worked at Railton and Hockes', who print the 'New Pork Herald.' I used to take my 'copy' into the comps' room, and one day the Father of the Chapel told me all about 'Mortlake and his young woman.' Ye gods!

How times are changed! Two years ago Mortlake had to struggle with my caligraphy – now he is in with all the nobs, and goes to the 'at homes' of the aristocracy."

"Radical M. P.'s," murmured Wimp, smiling.

"While I am still barred from the dazzling drawing-rooms, where beauty and intellect foregather. A mere artisan! A manual laborer!" Denzil's eyes flashed angrily. He rose with excitement. "They say he always was a jabberer in the composing-room, and he has jabbered himself right out of it and into a pretty good thing. He didn't have much to say about the crimes of capital when he was set up to second the toast of 'Railton and Hockes' at the beanfeast."

"Toast and butter, toast and butter," said Wimp genially. "I shouldn't blame a man for serving the two together, Mr. Cantercot."

Denzil forced a laugh. "Yes; but consistency's my motto. I like to see the royal soul immaculate, unchanging, immovable by fortune. Anyhow, when better times came for Mortlake the engagement still dragged on. He did not visit her so much. This last autumn he saw very little of her."

"How do you know?"

"I – I was often in Stepney Green. My business took me past the house of an evening. Sometimes there was no light in her room. That meant she was downstairs gossiping with the landlady."

"She might have been out with Tom?"

"No, sir; I knew Tom was on the platform somewhere or other. He was working up to all hours organizing the eight hours working movement."

"A very good reason for relaxing his sweethearting."

"It was. He never went to Stepney Green on a week night."

"But you always did."

"No – not every night."

"You didn't go in?"

"Never. She wouldn't permit my visits. She was a girl of strong character. She always reminded me of Flora Macdonald."

"Another lady of your acquaintance?"

"A lady I know better than the shadows who surround me; who is more real to me than the women who pester me for the price for apartments. Jessie Dymond, too, was of the race of heroines. Her eyes were clear blue, two wells with Truth at the bottom of each. When I looked into those eyes my own were dazzled. They were the only eyes I could never make dreamy." He waved his hand as if making a pass with it. "It was she who had the influence over me."

"You knew her then?"

"Oh, yes. I knew Tom from the old 'New Pork Herald' days, and when I first met him with Jessie hanging on his arm he was quite proud to introduce her to a poet. When he got on he tried to shake me off."

"You should have repaid him what you borrowed."

"It – it – was only a trifle," stammered Denzil.

"Yes, but the world turns on trifles," said the wise Wimp.

"The world is itself a trifle," said the pensive poet. "The Beautiful alone is deserving of our regard."

"And when the Beautiful was not gossiping with her landlady, did she gossip with you as you passed the door?"

"Alas, no! She sat in her room reading, and cast a shadow—"

"On your life?"

"No; on the blind."

"Always one shadow?"

"No, sir. Once or twice, two."

"Ah, you had been drinking."

"On my life, not. I have sworn off the treacherous wine-cup."

"That's right. Beer is bad for poets. It makes their feet shaky. Whose was the second shadow?"

"A man's."

"Naturally. Mortlake's, perhaps?"

"Impossible. He was still striking eight hours."

"You found out whose? You didn't leave it a shadow of doubt?"

"No; I waited till the substance came out."

"It was Arthur Constant."

"You are a magician! You – you terrify me. Yes, it was he."

"Only once or twice, you say?"

"I didn't keep watch over them."

"No, no, of course not. You only passed casually. I understand you thoroughly."

Denzil did not feel comfortable at the assertion.

"What did he go there for?" Wimp went on.

"I don't know. I'd stake my soul on Jessie's honor."

"You might double your stake without risk."

"Yes, I might! I would! You see her with my eyes."

"For the moment they are the only ones available. When was the last time you saw the two together?"

"About the middle of November."

"Mortlake knew nothing of their meetings?"

"I don't know. Perhaps he did. Mr. Constant had probably enlisted her in his social mission work. I knew she was one of the attendants at the big children's tea in the Great Assembly Hall early in November. He treated her quite like a lady. She was the only attendant who worked with her hands."

"The others carried the cups on their feet, I suppose?"

"No; how could that be? My meaning is that all the other attendants were real ladies, and Jessie was only an amateur, so to speak. There was no novelty for her in handing kids cups of tea. I daresay she had helped her landlady often enough at that – there's quite a bushel of brats below stairs. It's almost as bad as at friend Crowl's. Jessie was a real brick. But perhaps Tom didn't know her value. Perhaps he didn't like Constant to call on her, and it led to a quarrel. Anyhow, she's disappeared, like the snowfall on the river. There's not a trace. The landlady, who was such a friend of hers that Jessie used to make up her stuff into dresses for nothing, tells me that she's dreadfully annoyed at not having been left the slightest clue to her late tenant's whereabouts."

"You have been making inquiries on your own account apparently."

"Only of the landlady. Jessie never even gave her the week's notice, but paid her in lieu of it, and left immediately. The landlady told me I could have knocked her down with a feather. Unfortunately, I wasn't there to do it, for I should certainly have knocked her down for not keeping her eyes open better. She says if she had only had the least suspicion beforehand that the minx (she dared to call Jessie a minx) was going, she'd have known where, or her name would have been somebody else's. And yet she admits that Jessie was looking ill and worried. Stupid old hag!"

"A woman of character," murmured the detective.

"Didn't I tell you so?" cried Denzil eagerly. "Another girl would have let out that she was going. But, no! not a word. She plumped down the money and walked out. The landlady ran upstairs. None of Jessie's things were there. She must have quietly sold them off, or transferred them to the new place. I never in my life met a girl who so thoroughly knew her own mind or had a mind so worth knowing. She always reminded me of the Maid of Saragossa."

"Indeed! And when did she leave?"

"On the 19th of November."

"Mortlake of course knows where she is?"

"I can't say. Last time I was at the house to inquire – it was at the end of November – he hadn't been seen there for six weeks. He wrote to her, of course, sometimes – the landlady knew his writing."

Wimp looked Denzil straight in the eyes, and said, "You mean, of course, to accuse Mortlake of the murder of Mr. Constant?"

"N-n-no, not at all," stammered Denzil, "only you know what Mr. Grodman wrote to the 'Pell Mell.' The more we know about Mr. Constant's life the more we shall know about the manner of his death. I thought my information would be valuable to you, and I brought it."

"And why didn't you take it to Mr. Grodman?"

"Because I thought it wouldn't be valuable to me."

"You wrote 'Criminals I Have Caught.'"

"How – how do you know that?" Wimp was startling him today with a vengeance.

"Your style, my dear Mr. Cantercot. The unique noble style."

"Yes, I was afraid it would betray me," said Denzil. "And since you know, I may tell you that Grodman's a mean curmudgeon. What does he want with all that money and those houses – a man with no sense of the Beautiful? He'd have taken my information, and given me more kicks than ha'pence for it, so to speak."

"Yes, he is a shrewd man after all. I don't see anything valuable in your evidence against Mortlake."

"No!" said Denzil in a disappointed tone, and fearing he was going to be robbed. "Not when Mortlake was already jealous of Mr. Constant, who was a sort of rival organizer, unpaid! A kind of blackleg doing the work cheaper – nay, for nothing."

"Did Mortlake tell you he was jealous?" said Wimp, a shade of sarcastic contempt piercing through his tones.

"Oh, yes! He said to me, 'That man will work mischief. I don't like your kid-glove philanthropists meddling in matters they don't understand.'"

"Those were his very words?"

"His *ipsissima verba*."

"Very well. I have your address in my files. Here is a sovereign for you."

"Only one sovereign! It's not the least use to me."

"Very well. It's of great use to me. I have a wife to keep."

"I haven't," said Denzil with a sickly smile, "so perhaps I can manage on it after all." He took his hat and the sovereign.

Outside the door he met a rather pretty servant just bringing in some tea to her master. He nearly upset her tray at sight of her. She seemed more amused at the *rencontre* than he.

"Good afternoon, dear," she said coquettishly. "You might let me have that sovereign. I do so want a new Sunday bonnet."

Denzil gave her the sovereign, and slammed the hall door viciously when he got to the bottom of the stairs. He seemed to be walking arm-in-arm with the long arm of coincidence. Wimp did not hear the duologue. He was already busy on his evening's report to headquarters. The next day Denzil had a body-guard wherever he went. It might have gratified his vanity had he known it. But tonight he was yet unattended, so no one noted that he went to 46 Glover Street, after the early Crowl supper. He could not help going. He wanted to get another sovereign. He also itched to taunt Grodman. Not succeeding in the former object, he felt the road open for the second.

"Do you still hope to discover the Bow murderer?" he asked the old bloodhound.

"I can lay my hand on him now," Grodman announced curtly.

Denzil hitched his chair back involuntarily. He found conversation with detectives as lively as playing at skittles with bombshells. They got on his nerves terribly, these undemonstrative gentlemen with no sense of the Beautiful.

"But why don't you give him up to justice?" he murmured.

"Ah – it has to be proved yet. But it is only a matter of time."

"Oh!" said Denzil, "and shall I write the story for you?"

"No. You will not live long enough."

Denzil turned white. "Nonsense! I am years younger than you," he gasped.

"Yes," said Grodman, "but you drink so much."

Chapter VII

WHEN WIMP invited Grodman to eat his Christmas plum-pudding at King's Cross Grodman was only a little surprised. The two men were always overwhelmingly cordial when they met, in order to disguise their mutual detestation. When people really like each other, they make no concealment of their mutual contempt. In his letter to Grodman, Wimp said that he thought it would be nicer for him to keep Christmas in company than in solitary state. There seems to be a general prejudice in favor of Christmas numbers, and Grodman yielded to it. Besides, he thought that a peep at the Wimp domestic interior would be as good as a pantomime. He quite enjoyed the fun that was coming, for he knew that Wimp had not invited him out of mere "peace and goodwill."

There was only one other guest at the festive board. This was Wimp's wife's mother's mother, a lady of sweet seventy. Only a minority of mankind can obtain a grandmother-in-law by marrying, but Wimp was not unduly conceited. The old lady suffered from delusions. One of them was that she was a centenarian. She dressed for the part. It is extraordinary what pains ladies will take to conceal their age. Another of Wimp's grandmother-in-law's delusions was that Wimp had married to get her into the family. Not to frustrate his design, she always gave him her company on high-days and holidays. Wilfred Wimp – the little boy who stole the jam – was in great form at the Christmas dinner. The only drawback to his enjoyment was that its sweets needed no stealing. His mother presided over the platters, and thought how much cleverer Grodman was than her husband. When the pretty servant who waited on them was momentarily out of the room, Grodman had remarked that she seemed very inquisitive. This coincided with Mrs. Wimp's own convictions, though Mr. Wimp could never be brought to see anything unsatisfactory or suspicious about the girl, not even though there were faults in spelling in the "character" with which her last mistress had supplied her.

It was true that the puss had pricked up her ears when Denzil Cantercot's name was mentioned. Grodman saw it and watched her, and fooled Wimp to the top of his bent. It was, of course, Wimp who introduced the poet's name, and he did it so casually that Grodman perceived at once that he wished to pump him. The idea that the rival bloodhound should come to him for confirmation of suspicions against his own pet jackal was too funny. It was almost as funny to Grodman that evidence of some sort should be obviously lying to hand in the bosom of Wimp's hand-maiden; so obviously that Wimp could not see it. Grodman enjoyed his Christmas dinner, secure that he had not found a successor after all. Wimp, for his part, contemptuously wondered at the way Grodman's thought hovered about Denzil without grazing the truth. A man constantly about him, too!

"Denzil is a man of genius," said Grodman. "And as such comes under the heading of Suspicious Characters. He has written an Epic Poem and read it to me. It is morbid from start to finish. There is 'death' in the third line. I daresay you know he polished up my book." Grodman's artlessness was perfect.

"No. You surprise me," Wimp replied. "I'm sure he couldn't have done much to it. Look at your letter in the 'Pell Mell.' Who wants more polish and refinement than that showed?"

"Ah, I didn't know you did me the honor of reading that."

"Oh, yes; we both read it," put in Mrs. Wimp. "I told Mr. Wimp it was clever and cogent. After that quotation from the letter to the poor fellow's *fiancée* there could be no more doubt but that it was murder. Mr. Wimp was convinced by it, too, weren't you, Edward?"

Edward coughed uneasily. It was a true statement, and therefore an indiscreet. Grodman would plume himself terribly. At this moment Wimp felt that Grodman had been right in remaining a bachelor. Grodman perceived the humor of the situation, and wore a curious, sub-mocking smile.

"On the day I was born," said Wimp's grandmother-in-law, "over a hundred years ago, there was a babe murdered." Wimp found himself wishing it had been she. He was anxious to get back to Cantercot. "Don't let us talk shop on Christmas Day," he said, smiling at Grodman. "Besides, murder isn't a very appropriate subject."

"No, it ain't," said Grodman. "How did we get on to it? Oh, yes – Denzil Cantercot. Ha! ha! ha! That's curious, for since Denzil wrote 'Criminals I have Caught,' his mind's running on nothing but murders. A poet's brain is easily turned."

Wimp's eye glittered with excitement and contempt for Grodman's blindness. In Grodman's eye there danced an amused scorn of Wimp; to the outsider his amusement appeared at the expense of the poet.

Having wrought his rival up to the highest pitch Grodman slyly and suddenly unstrung him.

"How lucky for Denzil!" he said, still in the same naive, facetious Christmasy tone, "that he can prove an alibi in this Constant affair."

"An alibi!" gasped Wimp. "Really?"

"Oh, yes. He was with his wife, you know. She's my woman of all work, Jane. She happened to mention his being with her."

Jane had done nothing of the kind. After the colloquy he had overheard Grodman had set himself to find out the relation between his two employes. By casually referring to Denzil as "your husband" he so startled the poor woman that she did not attempt to deny the bond. Only once did he use the two words, but he was satisfied. As to the alibi he had not yet troubled her; but to take its existence for granted would upset and discomfort Wimp. For the moment that was triumph enough for Wimp's guest.

"Par," said Wilfred Wimp, "what's a alleybi? A marble?"

"No, my lad," said Grodman, "it means being somewhere else when you're supposed to be somewhere."

"Ah, playing truant," said Wilfred self-consciously; his schoolmaster had often proved an alibi against him. "Then Denzil will be hanged."

Was it a prophecy? Wimp accepted it as such; as an oracle from the gods bidding him mistrust Grodman. Out of the mouths of little children issueth wisdom; sometimes even when they are not saying their lessons.

"When I was in my cradle, a century ago," said Wimp's grandmother-in-law, "men were hanged for stealing horses."

They silenced her with snapdragon performances.

Wimp was busy thinking how to get at Grodman's factotum.

Grodman was busy thinking how to get at Wimp's domestic.

Neither received any of the usual messages from the Christmas Bells.

* * *

The next day was sloppy and uncertain. A thin rain drizzled languidly. One can stand that sort of thing on a summer Bank Holiday; one expects it. But to have a bad December Bank Holiday is too much of a bad thing. Some steps should surely be taken to confuse the weather clerk's chronology. Once let him know that Bank Holiday is coming, and he writes to the company for more water. Today his stock seemed low and he was dribbling it out; at times the wintry sun would shine in a feeble, diluted way, and though the holiday-makers would have preferred to take their sunshine neat, they swarmed forth in their myriads whenever there was a ray of hope. But it was only dodging the raindrops; up went the umbrellas again, and the streets became meadows of ambulating mushrooms.

Denzil Cantercot sat in his fur overcoat at the open window, looking at the landscape in water colors. He smoked an after-dinner cigarette, and spoke of the Beautiful. Crowl was with him. They were in the first floor front, Crowl's bedroom, which, from its view of the Mile End Road, was livelier than the parlor with its outlook on the backyard. Mrs. Crowl was an anti-tobacconist as regards the best bedroom; but Peter did not like to put the poet or his cigarette out. He felt there was something in common between smoke and poetry, over and above their being both Fads. Besides, Mrs. Crowl was sulking in the kitchen. She had been arranging for an excursion with Peter and the children to Victoria Park. She had dreamed of the Crystal Palace, but Santa Claus had put no gifts in the cobbler's shoes. Now she could not risk spoiling the feather in her bonnet. The nine brats expressed their disappointment by slapping one another on the staircases. Peter felt that Mrs. Crowl connected him in some way with the rainfall, and was unhappy. Was it not enough that he had been deprived of the pleasure of pointing out to a superstitious majority the mutual contradictions of Leviticus and the Song of Solomon? It was not often that Crowl could count on such an audience.

"And you still call Nature beautiful?" he said to Denzil, pointing to the ragged sky and the dripping eaves. "Ugly old scarecrow!"

"Ugly she seems today," admitted Denzil. "But what is Ugliness but a higher form of Beauty? You have to look deeper into it to see it; such vision is the priceless gift of the few. To me this wan desolation of sighing rain is lovely as the sea-washed ruins of cities."

"Ah, but you wouldn't like to go out in it," said Peter Crowl. As he spoke the drizzle suddenly thickened into a torrent.

"We do not always kiss the woman we love."

"Speak for yourself, Denzil. I'm only a plain man, and I want to know if Nature isn't a Fad. Hallo, there goes Mortlake! Lord, a minute of this will soak him to the skin."

The labor leader was walking along with bowed head. He did not seem to mind the shower. It was some seconds before he even heard Crowl's invitation to him to take shelter. When he did hear it he shook his head.

"I know I can't offer you a drawing-room with duchesses stuck about it," said Peter, vexed.

Tom turned the handle of the shop door and went in. There was nothing in the world which now galled him more than the suspicion that he was stuck-up and wished to cut old friends. He picked his way through the nine brats who clung affectionately to his wet knees, dispersing them finally by a jet of coppers to scramble for. Peter met him on the stair and shook his hand lovingly and admiringly, and took him into Mrs. Crowl's bedroom.

"Don't mind what I say, Tom. I'm only a plain man, and my tongue will say what comes uppermost! But it ain't from the soul, Tom, it ain't from the soul," said Peter, punning feebly, and letting a mirthless smile play over his sallow features. "You know Mr. Cantercot, I suppose? The poet."

"Oh, yes; how do you do, Tom? Seen the 'New Pork Herald' lately? Not bad, those old times, eh?"

"No," said Tom, "I wish I was back in them."

"Nonsense, nonsense," said Peter, in much concern. "Look at the good you are doing to the working man. Look how you are sweeping away the Fads. Ah, it's a grand thing to be gifted, Tom. The idea of your chuckin' yourself away on a composin' room! Manual labor is all very well for plain men like me, with no gift but just enough brains to see into the realities of things – to understand that we've got no soul and no immortality, and all that – and too selfish to look after anybody's comfort but my own and mother's and the kid's. But men like you and Cantercot – it ain't right that you should be peggin' away at low material things. Not that I think Cantercot's gospel's any value to the masses. The Beautiful is all very well for folks who've got nothing else to think of, but give me the True. You're the man for my money, Mortlake. No reference to the funds, Tom, to which I contribute little enough, Heaven knows; though how a place can know anything, Heaven alone knows. You give us the Useful, Tom; that's what the world wants more than the Beautiful."

"Socrates said that the Useful is the Beautiful," said Denzil.

"That may be," said Peter, "but the Beautiful ain't the Useful."

"Nonsense!" said Denzil. "What about Jessie – I mean Miss Dymond? There's a combination for you. She always reminds me of Grace Darling. How is she, Tom?"

"She's dead!" snapped Tom.

"What?" Denzil turned as white as a Christmas ghost.

"It was in the papers," said Tom; "all about her and the lifeboat."

"Oh, you mean Grace Darling," said Denzil, visibly relieved. "I meant Miss Dymond."

"You needn't be so interested in her," said Tom, surlily. "She don't appreciate it. Ah, the shower is over. I must be going."

"No, stay a little longer, Tom," pleaded Peter. "I see a lot about you in the papers, but very little of your dear old phiz now. I can't spare the time to go and hear you. But I really must give myself a treat. When's your next show?"

"Oh, I am always giving shows," said Tom, smiling a little. "But my next big performance is on the twenty-first of January, when that picture of poor Mr. Constant is to be unveiled at the Bow Break o' Day Club. They have written to Gladstone and other big pots to come down. I do hope the old man accepts. A non-political gathering like this is the only occasion we could both speak at, and I have never been on the same platform with Gladstone."

He forgot his depression and ill-temper in the prospect, and spoke with more animation.

"No, I should hope not, Tom," said Peter. "What with his Fads about the Bible being a Rock, and Monarchy being the right thing, he is a most dangerous man to lead the Radicals. He never lays his ax to the root of anything – except oak trees."

"Mr. Cantycot!" It was Mrs. Crowl's voice that broke in upon the tirade. "There's a gentleman to see you." The astonishment Mrs. Crowl put into the "gentleman" was delightful. It was almost as good as a week's rent to her to give vent to her feelings. The controversial couple had moved away from the window when Tom entered, and had not noticed the immediate advent of another visitor who had spent his time profitably in listening to Mrs. Crowl before asking to see the presumable object of his visit.

"Ask him up if it's a friend of yours, Cantercot," said Peter. It was Wimp. Denzil was rather dubious as to the friendship, but he preferred to take Wimp diluted. "Mortlake's upstairs," he said. "Will you come up and see him?"

Wimp had intended a duologue, but he made no objection, so he, too, stumbled through the nine brats to Mrs. Crowl's bedroom. It was a queer quartette. Wimp had hardly expected to find anybody at the house on Boxing Day, but he did not care to waste a day. Was not Grodman, too, on the track? How lucky it was that Denzil had made the first overtures, so that he could approach him without exciting suspicion.

Mortlake scowled when he saw the detective. He objected to the police – on principle. But Crowl had no idea who the visitor was, even when told his name. He was rather pleased to meet one of Denzil's high-class friends, and welcomed him warmly. Probably he was some famous editor, which would account for his name stirring vague recollections. He summoned the eldest brat and sent him for beer (people would have their Fads), and not without trepidation called down to "Mother" for glasses. "Mother" observed at night (in the same apartment) that the beer money might have paid the week's school fees for half the family.

"We were just talking of poor Mr. Constant's portrait, Mr. Wimp," said the unconscious Crowl; "they're going to unveil it, Mortlake tells me, on the twenty-first of next month at the Bow Break o' Day Club."

"Ah," said Wimp, elated at being spared the trouble of maneuvering the conversation; "mysterious affair that, Mr. Crowl."

"No; it's the right thing," said Peter. "There ought to be some memorial of the man in the district where he worked and where he died, poor chap." The cobbler brushed away a tear.

"Yes, it's only right," echoed Mortlake a whit eagerly. "He was a noble fellow, a true philanthropist. The only thoroughly unselfish worker I've ever met."

"He was that," said Peter; "and it's a rare pattern is unselfishness. Poor fellow, poor fellow. He preached the Useful, too. I've never met his like. Ah, I wish there was a Heaven for him to go to!" He blew his nose violently with a red pocket-handkerchief.

"Well, he's there, if there *is*," said Tom.

"I hope he is," added Wimp fervently; "but I shouldn't like to go there the way he did."

"You were the last person to see him, Tom, weren't you?" said Denzil.

"Oh, no," answered Tom quickly. "You remember he went out after me; at least, so Mrs Drabdump said at the inquest."

"That last conversation he had with you, Tom," said Denzil. "He didn't say anything to you that would lead you to suppose—"

"No, of course not!" interrupted Mortlake impatiently.

"Do you really think he was murdered, Tom?" said Denzil.

"Mr. Wimp's opinion on that point is more valuable than mine," replied Tom, testily. "It may have been suicide. Men often get sick of life – especially if they are bored," he added meaningly.

"Ah, but you were the last person known to be with him," said Denzil.

Crowl laughed. "Had you there, Tom."

But they did not have Tom there much longer, for he departed, looking even worse-tempered than when he came. Wimp went soon after, and Crowl and Denzil were left to their interminable argumentation concerning the Useful and the Beautiful.

Wimp went west. He had several strings (or cords) to his bow, and he ultimately found himself at Kensal Green Cemetery. Being there, he went down the avenues of the dead to a grave to note down the exact date of a death. It was a day on which the dead seemed enviable. The dull, sodden sky, the dripping, leafless trees, the wet spongy soil, the reeking grass – everything combined to make one long to be in a warm, comfortable grave, away from the leaden ennui of life. Suddenly the detective's keen eye caught sight of a figure that made his heart throb with sudden excitement. It was that of a woman in a gray shawl and a brown bonnet standing before a railed-in grave. She had no umbrella. The rain plashed mournfully upon her, but left no trace on her soaking garments. Wimp crept up behind her, but she paid no heed to him. Her eyes were lowered to the grave, which seemed to be drawing them toward it by some strange morbid fascination. His eyes followed hers. The simple headstone bore the name: "Arthur Constant."

Wimp tapped her suddenly on the shoulder.

Mrs. Drabdump went deadly white. She turned round, staring at Wimp without any recognition.

"You remember me, surely," he said. "I've been down once or twice to your place about that poor gentleman's papers." His eye indicated the grave.

"Lor! I remember you now," said Mrs. Drabdump.

"Won't you come under my umbrella? You must be drenched to the skin."

"It don't matter, sir. I can't take no hurt. I've had the rheumatics this twenty year."

Mrs. Drabdump shrank from accepting Wimp's attentions, not so much perhaps because he was a man as because he was a gentleman. Mrs. Drabdump liked to see the fine folks keep their place, and not contaminate their skirts by contact with the lower castes. "It's set wet, it'll rain right into the new year," she announced. "And they say a bad beginnin' makes a worse endin'." Mrs. Drabdump was one of those persons who give you the idea that they just missed being born barometers.

"But what are you doing in this miserable spot, so far from home?" queried the detective.

"It's Bank Holiday," Mrs. Drabdump reminded him in tones of acute surprise. "I always make a hexcursion on Bank Holiday."

Chapter VIII

THE NEW YEAR BROUGHT Mrs. Drabdump a new lodger. He was an old gentleman with a long gray beard. He rented the rooms of the late Mr. Constant, and lived a very retired life. Haunted rooms – or rooms that ought to be haunted if the ghosts of those murdered in them had any self-respect – are supposed to fetch a lower rent in the market. The whole Irish problem might be solved if the spirits of "Mr. Balfour's victims" would only depreciate the value of property to a point consistent with the support of an agricultural population. But Mrs. Drabdump's new lodger paid so much for his rooms that he laid himself open to a suspicion of special interest in ghosts. Perhaps he was a member of the Psychical Society. The neighborhood imagined him another mad philanthropist, but as he did not appear to be doing any good to anybody it relented and conceded his sanity. Mortlake, who occasionally stumbled across him in the passage, did not trouble himself to think about him at all. He was too full of other troubles and cares. Though he worked harder than ever, the spirit seemed to have gone out of him. Sometimes he forgot himself in a fine rapture of eloquence – lashing himself up into a divine resentment of injustice or a passion of sympathy with the sufferings of his brethren – but mostly he plodded on in dull, mechanical fashion. He still made brief provincial tours, starring a day here and a day there, and everywhere his admirers remarked how jaded and overworked he looked. There was talk of starting a subscription to give him a holiday on the Continent – a luxury obviously unobtainable on the few pounds allowed him per week. The new lodger would doubtless have been pleased to subscribe, for he seemed quite to like occupying Mortlake's chamber the nights he was absent, though he was thoughtful enough not to disturb the hardworked landlady in the adjoining room by unseemly noise. Wimp was always a quiet man.

Meantime the 21st of the month approached, and the East End was in excitement. Mr. Gladstone had consented to be present at the ceremony of unveiling the portrait of Arthur Constant, presented by an unknown donor to the Bow Break o' Day Club, and it was to be a great function. The whole affair was outside the lines of party politics, so that even Conservatives and Socialists considered themselves justified in pestering the committee for tickets. To say nothing of ladies. As the committee desired to be present themselves, nine-tenths of the applications for admission had to be refused, as is usual on these occasions. The committee agreed among themselves to exclude the fair sex altogether as the only way of disposing of their womankind who were making speeches as long as Mr. Gladstone's. Each committeeman told his sisters, female cousins and aunts that the other committeemen had insisted on divesting the function of all grace; and what could a man do when he was in a minority of one?

Crowl, who was not a member of the Break o' Day Club, was particularly anxious to hear the great orator whom he despised; fortunately Mortlake remembered the cobbler's anxiety to hear himself, and on the eve of the ceremony sent him a ticket. Crowl was in the first flush of possession when Denzil Cantercot returned, after a sudden and unannounced absence of three days. His clothes were muddy and tattered, his cocked hat was deformed, his cavalier beard was matted, and his eyes were bloodshot. The cobbler nearly dropped the ticket at the sight of him. "Hullo, Cantercot!" he gasped. "Why, where have you been all these days?"

"Terribly busy!" said Denzil. "Here, give me a glass of water. I'm dry as the Sahara."

Crowl ran inside and got the water, trying hard not to inform Mrs. Crowl of their lodger's return. "Mother" had expressed herself freely on the subject of the poet during his absence, and not in terms which would have commended themselves to the poet's fastidious literary sense. Indeed, she did not hesitate to call him a sponger and a low swindler, who had run away to avoid paying the piper. Her fool of a husband might be quite sure he would never set eyes on the scoundrel again. However, Mrs. Crowl was wrong. Here was Denzil back again. And yet Mr. Crowl felt no sense of victory. He had no desire to crow over his partner and to utter that "See! didn't I tell you so?" which is a greater consolation than religion in most of the misfortunes of life. Unfortunately, to get the water, Crowl had to go to the kitchen; and as he was usually such a temperat man, this desire for drink in the middle of the day attracted the attention of the lady i possession. Crowl had to explain the situation. Mrs. Crowl ran into the shop to improve it. Mr. Crowl followed in dismay, leaving a trail of spilled water in his wake.

"You good-for-nothing, disreputable scarecrow, where have—"

"Hush, mother. Let him drink. Mr. Cantercot is thirsty."

"Does he care if my children are hungry?"

Denzil tossed the water greedily down his throat almost at a gulp, as if it were brandy.

"Madam," he said, smacking his lips, "I do care. I care intensely. Few things in life would grieve me more deeply than to hear that a child, a dear little child – the Beautiful in a nutshell – had suffered hunger. You wrong me." His voice was tremulous with the sense of injury. Tears stood in his eyes.

"Wrong you? I've no wish to wrong you," said Mrs. Crowl. "I should like to hang you."

"Don't talk of such ugly things," said Denzil, touching his throat nervously.

"Well, what have you been doin' all this time?"

"Why, what should I be doing?"

"How should I know what became of you? I thought it was another murder."

"What!" Denzil's glass dashed to fragments on the floor. "What do you mean?"

But Mrs. Crowl was glaring too viciously at Mr. Crowl to reply. He understood the message as if it were printed. It ran: "You have broken one of my best glasses. You have annihilated threepence, or a week's school fees for half the family." Peter wished she would turn the lightning upon Denzil, a conductor down whom it would run innocuously. He stooped down and picked up the pieces as carefully as if they were cuttings from the Koh-i-noor. Thus the lightning passed harmlessly over his head and flew toward Cantercot.

"What do I mean?" Mrs. Crowl echoed, as if there had been no interval. "I mean that it would be a good thing if you had been murdered."

"What unbeautiful ideas you have, to be sure!" murmured Denzil.

"Yes; but they'd be useful," said Mrs. Crowl, who had not lived with Peter all these years for nothing. "And if you haven't been murdered what have you been doing?"

"My dear, my dear," put in Crowl, deprecatingly, looking up from his quadrupedal position like a sad dog, "you are not Cantercot's keeper."

"Oh, ain't I?" flashed his spouse. "Who else keeps him I should like to know?"

Peter went on picking up the pieces of the Koh-i-noor.

"I have no secrets from Mrs. Crowl" Denzil explained courteously. "I have been working day and night bringing out a new paper. Haven't had a wink of sleep for three nights."

Peter looked up at his bloodshot eyes with respectful interest.

"The capitalist met me in the street – an old friend of mine – I was overjoyed at the *rencontre* and told him the idea I'd been brooding over for months and he promised to stand all the racket."

"What sort of a paper?" said Peter.

"Can you ask? To what do you think I've been devoting my days and nights but to the cultivation of the Beautiful?"

"Is that what the paper will be devoted to?"

"Yes. To the Beautiful."

"I know," snorted Mrs. Crowl, "with portraits of actresses."

"Portraits? Oh, no!" said Denzil. "That would be the True – not the Beautiful."

"And what's the name of the paper?" asked Crowl.

"Ah, that's a secret, Peter. Like Scott, I prefer to remain anonymous."

"Just like your Fads. I'm only a plain man, and I want to know where the fun of anonymity comes in? If I had any gifts, I should like to get the credit. It's a right and natural feeling, to my thinking."

"Unnatural, Peter; unnatural. We're all born anonymous, and I'm for sticking close to Nature. Enough for me that I disseminate the Beautiful. Any letters come during my absence, Mrs. Crowl?"

"No," she snapped. "But a gent named Grodman called. He said you hadn't been to see him for some time, and looked annoyed to hear you'd disappeared. How much have you let him in for?"

"The man's in my debt," said Denzil, annoyed. "I wrote a book for him and he's taken all the credit for it, the rogue! My name doesn't appear even in the Preface. What's that ticket you're looking so lovingly at, Peter?"

"That's for tonight – the unveiling of Constant's portrait. Gladstone speaks. Awful demand for places."

"Gladstone!" sneered Denzil. "Who wants to hear Gladstone? A man who's devoted his life to pulling down the pillars of Church and State."

"A man's who's devoted his whole life to propping up the crumbling Fads of Religion and Monarchy. But, for all that, the man has his gifts, and I'm burnin' to hear him."

"I wouldn't go out of my way an inch to hear him," said Denzil; and went up to his room, and when Mrs. Crowl sent him up a cup of nice strong tea at tea time, the brat who bore it found him lying dressed on the bed, snoring unbeautifully.

The evening wore on. It was fine frosty weather. The Whitechapel Road swarmed, with noisy life, as though it were a Saturday night. The stars flared in the sky like the lights of celestial costermongers. Everybody was on the alert for the advent of Mr. Gladstone. He must surely come through the Road on his journey from the West Bow-wards. But nobody saw him or his carriage, except those about the Hall. Probably he went by tram most of the way. He would have caught cold in an open carriage, or bobbing his head out of the window of a closed.

"If he had only been a German prince, or a cannibal king," said Crowl bitterly, as he plodded toward the Club, "we should have disguised Mile End in bunting and blue fire. But perhaps it's a compliment. He knows his London, and it's no use trying to hide the facts from him. They must have queer notions of cities, those monarchs. They must fancy everybody lives in a flutter of flags and walks about under triumphal arches, like as if I were to stitch shoes in my Sunday clothes." By a defiance of chronology Crowl had them on today, and they seemed to accentuate the simile.

"And why shouldn't life be fuller of the Beautiful," said Denzil. The poet had brushed the reluctant mud off his garments to the extent it was willing to go, and had washed his face, but his eyes were still bloodshot from the cultivation of the Beautiful. Denzil was accompanying Crowl to the door of the Club out of good-fellowship. Denzil was himself accompanied by Grodman, though less obtrusively. Least obtrusively was he accompanied by his usual Scotland Yard shadows, Wimp's agents. There was a surging nondescript crowd about the Club, and the police, and the door-keeper, and the stewards could with difficulty keep out the tide of the ticketless, through which the current of the privileged had equal difficulty in permeating. The streets all around were thronged with people longing for a glimpse of Gladstone. Mortlake drove up in a hansom (his head a self-conscious pendulum of popularity, swaying and bowing to right and left) and received all the pent-up enthusiasm.

"Well, good-by, Cantercot," said Crowl.

"No, I'll see you to the door, Peter."

They fought their way shoulder to shoulder.

Now that Grodman had found Denzil he was not going to lose him again. He had only found him by accident, for he was himself bound to the unveiling ceremony, to which he had been invited in view of his known devotion to the task of unveiling the Mystery. He spoke to one of the policemen about, who said, "Ay, ay, sir," and he was prepared to follow Denzil, if necessary, and to give up the pleasure of hearing Gladstone for an acuter thrill. The arrest must be delayed no longer.

But Denzil seemed as if he were going in on the heels of Crowl. This would suit Grodman better. He could then have the two pleasures. But Denzil was stopped half-way through the door.

"Ticket, sir!"

Denzil drew himself up to his full height.

"Press," he said, majestically. All the glories and grandeurs of the Fourth Estate were concentrated in that haughty monosyllable. Heaven itself is full of journalists who have overawed St. Peter. But the door-keeper was a veritable dragon.

"What paper, sir?"

"'New Pork Herald,'" said Denzil sharply. He did not relish his word being distrusted.

"'New York Herald,'" said one of the bystanding stewards, scarce catching the sounds. "Pass him in."

And in the twinkling of an eye, Denzil had eagerly slipped inside.

But during the brief altercation Wimp had come up. Even he could not make his face quite impassive, and there was a suppressed intensity in the eyes and a quiver about the mouth. He went in on Denzil's heels, blocking up the doorway with Grodman. The two men were so full of their coming *coups* that they struggled for some seconds, side by side, before they recognized each other. Then they shook hands heartily.

"That was Cantercot just went in, wasn't it, Grodman?" said Wimp.

"I didn't notice," said Grodman, in tones of utter indifference.

At bottom Wimp was terribly excited. He felt that his *coup* was going to be executed under very sensational circumstances. Everything would combine to turn the eyes of the country upon him – nay, of the world, for had not the Big Bow Mystery been discussed in every language under the sun? In these electric times the criminal achieves a cosmopolitan reputation. It is a privilege he shares with few other artists. This time Wimp would be one of them; and, he felt, deservedly so. If the criminal had been cunning to the point of genius in planning the murder, he had been acute to the point of divination in detecting it. Never before had he pieced together so broken a chain. He could not resist the unique opportunity of setting a sensational scheme in a sensational frame-work. The dramatic instinct was strong in him; he felt like a playwright who has constructed a strong melodramatic plot, and has the Drury Lane stage suddenly offered him to present it on. It would be folly to deny himself the luxury, though the presence of Mr. Gladstone and the nature of the ceremony should perhaps have given him pause. Yet, on the other hand, these were the very factors of the temptation. Wimp went in and took a seat behind Denzil. All the seats were numbered, so that everybody might have the satisfaction of occupying somebody else's. Denzil was in the special reserved places in the front row just by the central gangway; Crowl was squeezed into a corner behind a pillar near the back of the hall. Grodman had been honored with a seat on the platform, which was accessible by steps on the right and left, but he kept his eye on Denzil. The picture of the poor idealist hung on the wall behind Grodman's head, covered by its curtain of brown holland. There was a subdued buzz of excitement about the hall, which swelled into cheers every now and again as some gentleman known to fame or Bow took his place upon the platform. It was occupied by several local M. P.'s of varying politics, a number of other Parliamentary satellites of the great man, three or four labor leaders, a peer or two of philanthropic pretensions, a sprinkling of Toynbee and Oxford

Hall men, the president and other honorary officials, some of the family and friends of the deceased, together with the inevitable percentage of persons who had no claim to be there save cheek. Gladstone was late – later than Mortlake, who was cheered to the echo when he arrived, someone starting "For He's a Jolly Good Fellow," as if it were a political meeting. Gladstone came in just in time to acknowledge the compliment. The noise of the song, trolled out from iron lungs, had drowned the huzzahs heralding the old man's advent. The convivial chorus went to Mortlake's head, as if champagne had really preceded it. His eyes grew moist and dim. He saw himself swimming to the Millenium on waves of enthusiasm. Ah, how his brother-toilers should be rewarded for their trust in him!

With his usual courtesy and consideration, Mr. Gladstone had refused to perform the actual unveiling of Arthur Constant's portrait. "That," he said in his postcard, "will fall most appropriately to Mr. Mortlake, a gentleman who has, I am given to understand, enjoyed the personal friendship of the late Mr. Constant, and has co-operated with him in various schemes for the organization of skilled and unskilled classes of labor, as well as for the diffusion of better ideals – ideals of self-culture and self-restraint – among the workingmen of Bow, who have been fortunate, so far as I can perceive, in the possession (if in one case unhappily only temporary possession) of two such men of undoubted ability and honesty to direct their divided counsels and to lead them along a road, which, though I cannot pledge myself to approve of it in all its turnings and windings, is yet not unfitted to bring them somewhat nearer to goals to which there are few of us but would extend some measure of hope that the working classes of this great Empire may in due course, yet with no unnecessary delay, be enabled to arrive."

Mr. Gladstone's speech was an expansion of his postcard, punctuated by cheers. The only new thing in it was the graceful and touching way in which he revealed what had been a secret up till then – that the portrait had been painted and presented to the Bow Break o' Day Club, by Lucy Brent, who in the fulness of time would have been Arthur Constant's wife. It was a painting for which he had sat to her while alive, and she had stifled yet pampered her grief by working hard at it since his death. The fact added the last touch of pathos to the occasion. Crowl's face was hidden behind his red handkerchief; even the fire of excitement in Wimp's eye was quenched for a moment by a tear-drop, as he thought of Mrs. Wimp and Wilfred. As for Grodman, there was almost a lump in his throat. Denzil Cantercot was the only unmoved man in the room. He thought the episode quite too Beautiful, and was already weaving it into rhyme.

At the conclusion of his speech Mr. Gladstone called upon Tom Mortlake to unveil the portrait. Tom rose, pale and excited. His hand faltered as he touched the cord. He seemed overcome with emotion. Was it the mention of Lucy Brent that had moved him to his depths?

The brown holland fell away – the dead stood revealed as he had been in life. Every feature, painted by the hand of Love, was instinct with vitality: the fine, earnest face, the sad kindly eyes, the noble brow seeming still a-throb with the thought of Humanity. A thrill ran through the room – there was a low, undefinable murmur. O, the pathos and the tragedy of it! Every eye was fixed, misty with emotion, upon the dead man in the picture and the living man who stood, pale and agitated, and visibly unable to commence his speech, at the side of the canvas. Suddenly a hand was laid upon the labor leader's shoulder, and there rang through the hall in Wimp's clear, decisive tones the words: "Tom Mortlake, I arrest you for the murder of Arthur Constant!"

Chapter IX

FOR A MOMENT there was an acute, terrible silence. Mortlake's face was that of a corpse the face of the dead man at his side was flushed with the hues of life. To the overstrun nerves of the onlookers, the brooding eyes of the picture seemed sad and stern with menace, and charged with the lightnings of doom.

It was a horrible contrast. For Wimp, alone, the painted face had fuller, more tragical, meanings. The audience seemed turned to stone. They sat or stood – in every variety of attitude – frozen, rigid. Arthur Constant's picture dominated the scene, the only living thing in a hall of the dead.

But only for a moment. Mortlake shook off the detective's hand.

"Boys!" he cried, in accents of infinite indignation, "this is a police conspiracy."

His words relaxed the tension. The stony figures were agitated. A dull, excited hubbub answered him. The little cobbler darted from behind his pillar, and leaped upon a bench. The cords of his brow were swollen with excitement. He seemed a giant overshadowing the hall.

"Boys!" he roared, in his best Victoria Park voice, "listen to me. This charge is a foul and damnable lie."

"Bravo!" "Hear, hear!" "Hooray!" "It is!" was roared back at him from all parts of the room. Everybody rose and stood in tentative attitudes, excited to the last degree.

"Boys!" Peter roared on, "you all know me. I'm a plain man, and I want to know if it's likely a man would murder his best friend."

"No," in a mighty volume of sound.

Wimp had scarcely calculated upon Mortlake's popularity. He stood on the platform, pale and anxious as his prisoner.

"And if he did, why didn't they prove it the first time?"

"Hear, hear!"

"And if they want to arrest him, why couldn't they leave it till the ceremony was over? Tom Mortlake's not the man to run away."

"Tom Mortlake! Tom Mortlake! Three cheers for Tom Mortlake! Hip, hip, hip, hooray!"

"Three groans for the police." "Hoo! Oo! Oo!"

Wimp's melodrama was not going well. He felt like the author to whose ears is borne the ominous sibilance of the pit. He almost wished he had not followed the curtain-raiser with his own stronger drama. Unconsciously the police, scattered about the hall, drew together. The people on the platform knew not what to do. They had all risen and stood in a densely-packed mass. Even Mr. Gladstone's speech failed him in circumstances so novel. The groans died away; the cheers for Mortlake rose and swelled and fell and rose again. Sticks and umbrellas were banged and rattled, handkerchiefs were waved, the thunder deepened. The motley crowd still surging about the hall took up the cheers, and for hundreds of yards around people were going black in the face out of mere irresponsible enthusiasm. At last Tom waved his hand – the thunder dwindled, died. The prisoner was master of the situation.

Grodman stood on the platform, grasping the back of his chair, a curious mocking Mephistophelian glitter about his eyes, his lips wreathed into a half smile. There was no hurry for him to get Denzil Cantercot arrested now. Wimp had made an egregious, a colossal blunder. In Grodman's heart there was a great glad calm as of a man who has strained his sinews to win in a famous match, and has heard the judge's word. He felt almost kindly to Denzil now.

Tom Mortlake spoke. His face was set and stony. His tall figure was drawn up haughtily to its full height. He pushed the black mane back from his forehead with a characteristic gesture. The fevered audience hung upon his lips – the men at the back leaned eagerly forward – the reporters were breathless with fear lest they should miss a word. What would the great labor leader have to say at this supreme moment?

"Mr. Chairman and Gentlemen: It is to me a melancholy pleasure to have been honored with the task of unveiling tonight this portrait of a great benefactor to Bow and a true friend to the laboring classes. Except that he honored me with his friendship while living, and that the aspirations of my life have, in my small and restricted way, been identical with his, there is little reason why this honorable duty should have fallen upon me. Gentlemen, I trust that we shall all find an inspiring influence in the daily vision of the dead, who yet liveth in our hearts and in this noble work of art – wrought, as Mr. Gladstone has told us, by the hand of one who loved him." The speaker paused a moment, his low vibrant tones faltering into silence. "If we humble workingmen of Bow can never hope to exert individually a tithe of the beneficial influence wielded by Arthur Constant, it is yet possible for each of us to walk in the light he has kindled in our midst – a perpetual lamp of self-sacrifice and brotherhood."

That was all. The room rang with cheers. Tom Mortlake resumed his seat. To Wimp the man's audacity verged on the Sublime; to Denzil on the Beautiful. Again there was a breathless hush. Mr. Gladstone's mobile face was working with excitement. No such extraordinary scene had occurred in the whole of his extraordinary experience. He seemed about to rise. The cheering subsided to a painful stillness. Wimp cut the situation by laying his hand again upon Tom's shoulder.

"Come quietly with me," he said. The words were almost a whisper, but in the supreme silence they traveled to the ends of the hall.

"Don't you go, Tom!" The trumpet tones were Peter's. The call thrilled an answering chord of defiance in every breast, and a low, ominous murmur swept through the hall.

Tom rose, and there was silence again. "Boys," he said, "let me go. Don't make any noise about it. I shall be with you again tomorrow."

But the blood of the Break o' Day boys was at fever heat. A hurtling mass of men struggled confusedly from their seats. In a moment all was chaos. Tom did not move. Half-a-dozen men, headed by Peter, scaled the platform. Wimp was thrown to one side, and the invaders formed a ring round Tom's chair. The platform people scampered like mice from the center. Some huddled together in the corners, others slipped out at the rear. The committee congratulated themselves on having had the self-denial to exclude ladies. Mr. Gladstone's satellites hurried the old man off and into his carriage; though the fight promised to become Homeric. Grodman stood at the side of the platform secretly more amused than ever, concerning himself no more with Denzil Cantercot, who was already strengthening his nerves at the bar upstairs. The police about the hall blew their whistles, and policemen came rushing in from outside and the neighborhood. An Irish M. P. on the platform was waving his gingham like a shillalah in sheer excitement, forgetting his new-found respectability and dreaming himself back at Donnybrook Fair. Him a conscientious constable floored with a truncheon. But a shower of fists fell on the zealot's face, and he tottered back bleeding. Then the storm broke in all its fury. The upper air was black with staves, sticks, and umbrellas, mingled with the pallid hailstones of knobby fists. Yells and groans and hoots and battle-cries blent in grotesque chorus, like one of Dvorák's weird diabolical movements. Mortlake stood impassive, with arms folded, making no further effort, and the battle raged round him as the water swirls around some steadfast rock. A posse of police from the back fought their way steadily toward him, and charged up the heights of the platform steps, only to be sent tumbling backward, as their leader was hurled at them like a battering ram. Upon the top of the heap fell he, surmounting the strata of policemen. But others clambered upon them, escalading the platform. A moment more and Mortlake would have been taken, after being well shaken. Then the miracle happened

As when of old a reputable goddess *ex machina* saw her favorite hero in dire peril, straightway she drew down a cloud from the celestial stores of Jupiter and enveloped her fondling in kindly night, so that his adversary strove with the darkness, so did Crowl, the cunning cobbler, the much-daring, essay to insure his friend's safety. He turned off the gas at the meter.

An Arctic night – unpreceded by twilight – fell, and there dawned the sabbath of the witches. The darkness could be felt – and it left blood and bruises behind it. When the lights were turned on again, Mortlake was gone. But several of the rioters were arrested, triumphantly.

And through all, and over all, the face of the dead man who had sought to bring peace on earth, brooded.

Crowl sat meekly eating his supper of bread and cheese, with his head bandaged, while Denzil Cantercot told him the story of how he had rescued Tom Mortlake. He had been among the first to scale the height, and had never budged from Tom's side or from the forefront of the battle till he had seen him safely outside and into a by-street.

"I am so glad you saw that he got away safely," said Crowl, "I wasn't quite sure he would."

"Yes; but I wish some cowardly fool hadn't turned off the gas. I like men to see that they are beaten."

"But it seemed – easier," faltered Crowl.

"Easier!" echoed Denzil, taking a deep draught of bitter. "Really, Peter, I'm sorry to find you always will take such low views. It may be easier, but it's shabby. It shocks one's sense of the Beautiful."

Crowl ate his bread and cheese shame-facedly.

"But what was the use of breaking your head to save him?" said Mrs. Crowl with an unconscious pun. "He must be caught."

"Ah, I don't see how the Useful does come in, now," said Peter thoughtfully. "But I didn't think of that at the time."

He swallowed his water quickly and it went the wrong way and added to his confusion. It also began to dawn upon him that he might be called to account. Let it be said at once that he wasn't. He had taken too prominent a part.

Meantime, Mrs. Wimp was bathing Mr. Wimp's eye, and rubbing him generally with arnica. Wimp's melodrama had been, indeed, a sight for the gods. Only, virtue was vanquished and vice triumphant. The villain had escaped, and without striking a blow.

Chapter X

THERE WAS MATTER and to spare for the papers the next day. The striking ceremony – Mr. Gladstone's speech – the sensational arrest – these would of themselves have made excellent themes for reports and leaders. But the personality of the man arrested, and the Big Bow Mystery Battle – as it came to be called – gave additional piquancy to the paragraphs and the posters. The behavior of Mortlake put the last touch to the picturesqueness of the position. He left the hall when the lights went out, and walked unnoticed and unmolested through pleiads of policemen to the nearest police station, where the superintendent was almost too excited to take any notice of his demand to be arrested. But to do him justice, the official yielded as soon as he understood the situation. It seems inconceivable that he did not violate some red-tape regulation in so doing. To some this self-surrender was limpid proof of innocence; to others it was the damning token of despairing guilt.

The morning papers were pleasant reading for Grodman, who chuckled as continuously over his morning egg, as if he had laid it. Jane was alarmed for the sanity of her saturnine master. As her husband would have said, Grodman's grins were not Beautiful. But he made no effort to suppress them. Not only had Wimp perpetrated a grotesque blunder, but the journalists to a man were down on his great sensation tableau, though their denunciations did not appear in the dramatic columns. The Liberal papers said that he had endangered Mr. Gladstone's life; the Conservative that he had unloosed the raging elements of Bow blackguardism, and set in motion forces which might have easily swelled to a riot, involving severe destruction of property. But "Tom Mortlake," was, after all, the thought swamping every other. It was, in a sense, a triumph for the man.

But Wimp's turn came when Mortlake, who reserved his defense, was brought up before a magistrate, and, by force of the new evidence, fully committed for trial on the charge of murdering Arthur Constant. Then men's thoughts centered again on the Mystery, and the solution of the inexplicable problem agitated mankind from China to Peru.

In the middle of February, the great trial befell. It was another of the opportunities which the Chancellor of the Exchequer neglects. So stirring a drama might have easily cleared its expenses – despite the length of the cast, the salaries of the stars, and the rent of the house – in mere advance booking. For it was a drama which (by the rights of Magna Charta) could never be repeated; a drama which ladies of fashion would have given their earrings to witness, even with the central figure not a woman. And there was a woman in it anyhow, to judge by the little that had transpired at the magisterial examination, and the fact that the country was placarded with bills offering a reward for information concerning a Miss Jessie Dymond. Mortlake was defended by Sir Charles Brown-Harland, Q. C., retained at the expense of the Mortlake Defense Fund (subscriptions to which came also from Australia and the Continent), and set on his mettle by the fact that he was the accepted labor candidate for an East-end constituency. Their Majesties, Victoria and the Law, were represented by Mr. Robert Spigot, Q. C.

Mr. Spigot, Q. C., in presenting his case, said: "I propose to show that the prisoner murdered his friend and fellow-lodger, Mr. Arthur Constant, in cold blood, and with the most careful premeditation; premeditation so studied, as to leave the circumstances of the death an impenetrable mystery for weeks to all the world, though fortunately without altogether baffling the almost superhuman ingenuity of Mr. Edward Wimp, of the Scotland Yard Detective Department. I propose to show that the motives of the prisoner were jealousy and revenge; jealousy not only of his friend's superior influence over the workingmen he himself aspired to lead, but the more commonplace animosity engendered by the disturbing element of a woman having relations to both. If, before my case is complete, it will be my painful duty to show that the murdered man was not the saint the world has agreed to paint him, I shall not shrink from unveiling the truer picture, in the interests of justice, which cannot say *nil nisi bonum* even of the dead. I propose to show that the murder was committed by the prisoner shortly before half-past six on the morning of December 4th, and that the prisoner having, with the remarkable ingenuity which he has shown throughout, attempted to prepare an alibi by feigning to leave London by the first train to Liverpool, returned home, got in with his latch-key through the street-door, which he had left on the latch, unlocked his victim's bedroom with a key which he possessed, cut the sleeping man's throat, pocketed his razor, locked the door again, and gave it the appearance of being bolted, went downstairs, unslipped the bolt of the big lock, closed the door behind him, and got to Euston in time for the second train to Liverpool. The fog helped his proceedings throughout." Such was in sum the theory of the prosecution. The pale defiant figure in the dock winced perceptibly under parts of it.

Mrs. Drabdump was the first witness called for the prosecution. She was quite used to legal inquisitiveness by this time, but did not appear in good spirits.

"On the night of December 3d, you gave the prisoner a letter?"

"Yes, your ludship."

"How did he behave when he read it?"

"He turned very pale and excited. He went up to the poor gentleman's room, and I'm afraid he quarreled with him. He might have left his last hours peaceful." (Amusement.)

"What happened then?"

"Mr. Mortlake went out in a passion, and came in again in about an hour."

"He told you he was going away to Liverpool very early the next morning."

"No, your ludship, he said he was going to Devonport." (Sensation.)

"What time did you get up the next morning?"

"Half-past six."

"That is not your usual time?"

"No, I always get up at six."

"How do you account for the extra sleepiness?"

"Misfortunes will happen."

"It wasn't the dull, foggy weather?"

"No, my lud, else I should never get up early." (Laughter.)

"You drink something before going to bed?"

"I like my cup o' tea. I take it strong, without sugar. It always steadies my nerves."

"Quite so. Where were you when the prisoner told you he was going to Devonport?"

"Drinkin' my tea in the kitchen."

"What should you say if prisoner dropped something in it to make you sleep late?"

Witness (startled): "He ought to be shot."

"He might have done it without your noticing it, I suppose?"

"If he was clever enough to murder the poor gentleman, he was clever enough to try and poison me."

The Judge: "The witness in her replies must confine herself to the evidence."

Mr. Spigot, Q. C.: "I must submit to your lordship that it is a very logical answer, and exactly illustrates the interdependence of the probabilities. Now, Mrs. Drabdump, let us know what happened when you awoke at half-past six the next morning."

Thereupon Mrs. Drabdump recapitulated the evidence (with new redundancies, but slight variations) given by her at the inquest. How she became alarmed – how she found the street-door locked by the big lock – how she roused Grodman, and got him to burst open the door – how they found the body – all this with which the public was already familiar *ad nauseam* was extorted from her afresh.

"Look at this key" (key passed to the witness). "Do you recognize it?"

"Yes; how did you get it? It's the key of my first-floor front. I am sure I left it sticking in the door."

"Did you know a Miss Dymond?"

"Yes, Mr. Mortlake's sweetheart. But I knew he would never marry her, poor thing."

"Why not?"

"He was getting too grand for her." (Amusement).

"You don't mean anything more than that?"

"I don't know; she only came to my place once or twice. The last time I set eyes on her must have been in October."

"How did she appear?"

"She was very miserable, but she wouldn't let you see it." (Laughter.)

"How has the prisoner behaved since the murder?"

"He always seemed very glum and sorry for it."

Cross-examined: "Did not the prisoner once occupy the bedroom of Mr. Constant, and give it up to him, so that Mr. Constant might have the two rooms on the same floor?"

"Yes, but he didn't pay as much."

"And, while occupying this front bedroom, did not the prisoner once lose his key and have another made?"

"He did; he was very careless."

"Do you know what the prisoner and Mr. Constant spoke about on the night of December 3d?"

"No; I couldn't hear."

"Then how did you know they were quarreling?"

"They were talkin' so loud."

Sir Charles Brown-Harland, Q. C. (sharply): "But I'm talking loudly to you now. Should you say I was quarreling?"

"It takes two to make a quarrel." (Laughter.)

"Was the prisoner the sort of man who, in your opinion, would commit a murder?"

"No, I never should ha' guessed it was him."

"He always struck you as a thorough gentleman?"

"No, my lud. I knew he was only a comp."

"You say the prisoner has seemed depressed since the murder. Might not that have been due to the disappearance of his sweetheart?"

"No, he'd more likely be glad to get rid of her."

"Then he wouldn't be jealous if Mr. Constant took her off his hands?" (Sensation.)

"Men are dog-in-the-mangers."

"Never mind about men, Mrs. Drabdump. Had the prisoner ceased to care for Miss Dymond?"

"He didn't seem to think of her, my lud. When he got a letter in her handwriting among his heap he used to throw it aside till he'd torn open the others."

Brown-Harland, Q. C. (with a triumphant ring in his voice): "Thank you, Mrs. Drabdump. You may sit down."

Spigot, Q. C.: "One moment, Mrs. Drabdump. You say the prisoner had ceased to care for Miss Dymond. Might not this have been in consequence of his suspecting for some time that she had relations with Mr. Constant?"

The Judge: "That is not a fair question."

Spigot, Q. C.: "That will do, thank you, Mrs. Drabdump."

Brown-Harland, Q. C.: "No; one question more, Mrs. Drabdump. Did you ever see anything – say when Miss Dymond came to your house – to make you suspect anything between Mr. Constant and the prisoner's sweetheart?"

"She did meet him once when Mr. Mortlake was out." (Sensation.)

"Where did she meet him?"

"In the passage. He was going out when she knocked and he opened the door." (Amusement.)

"You didn't hear what they said?"

"I ain't a eavesdropper. They spoke friendly and went away together."

Mr. George Grodman was called and repeated his evidence at the inquest. Cross-examined, he testified to the warm friendship between Mr. Constant and the prisoner. He knew very little about Miss Dymond, having scarcely seen her. Prisoner had never spoken to him much about her. He should not think she was much in prisoner's thoughts. Naturally the prisoner had been depressed by the death of his friend. Besides, he was overworked. Witness thought highly of Mortlake's character. It was incredible that Constant had had improper relations of any kind with his friend's promised wife. Grodman's evidence made a very favorable impression on the jury; the prisoner looked his gratitude; and the prosecution felt sorry it had been necessary to call this witness.

Inspector Howlett and Sergeant Runnymede had also to repeat their evidence. Dr. Robinson, police-surgeon, likewise retendered his evidence as to the nature of the wound, and the approximate hour of death. But this time he was much more severely examined. He would not bind himself down to state the time within an hour or two. He thought life had been extinct two or three hours when he arrived, so that the deed had been committed between seven and eight. Under gentle pressure from the prosecuting counsel, he admitted that it might possibly have been between six and seven. Cross-examined, he reiterated his impression in favor of the later hour.

Supplementary evidence from medical experts proved as dubious and uncertain as if the court had confined itself to the original witness. It seemed to be generally agreed that the data for determining the time of death of anybody were too complex and variable to admit of very precise inference; *rigor mortis* and other symptoms setting in within very wide limits and differing largely in different persons. All agreed that death from such a cut must have been practically instantaneous, and the theory of suicide was rejected by all. As a whole the medical evidence tended to fix the time of death, with a high degree of probability, between the hours of six and half-past eight. The efforts of the Prosecution were bent upon throwing back the time of death to as early as possible after about half-past five. The Defense spent all its strength upon pinning the experts to the conclusion that death could not have been earlier than seven. Evidently the Prosecution was going to fight hard for the hypothesis that Mortlake had committed the crime in the interval between the first and second trains for Liverpool; while the Defense was concentrating itself on an alibi, showing that the prisoner had traveled by the second train which left Euston Station at a quarter-past seven, so that there could have been no possible time for the passage between Bow and Euston. It was an exciting struggle. As yet the contending forces seemed equally matched. The evidence had gone as much for as against the prisoner. But everybody knew that worse lay behind.

"Call Edward Wimp."

The story Edward Wimp had to tell began tamely enough with thrice-threshed-out facts. But at last the new facts came.

"In consequence of suspicions that had formed in your mind you took up your quarters, disguised, in the late Mr. Constant's rooms?"

"I did; at the commencement of the year. My suspicions had gradually gathered against the occupants of No. 11, Glover Street, and I resolved to quash or confirm these suspicions once for all."

"Will you tell the jury what followed?"

"Whenever the prisoner was away for the night I searched his room. I found the key of Mr. Constant's bedroom buried deeply in the side of prisoner's leather sofa. I found what I imagine to be the letter he received on December 3d, in the pages of a 'Bradshaw' lying under the same sofa. There were two razors about."

Mr. Spigot, Q. C., said: "The key has already been identified by Mrs. Drabdump. The letter I now propose to read."

It was undated, and ran as follows:

> *Dear Tom – This is to bid you farewell. It is the best for us all. I am going a long way, dearest. Do not seek to find me, for it will be useless. Think of me as one swallowed up by the waters, and be assured that it is only to spare you shame and humiliation in the future that I tear myself from you and all the sweetness of life. Darling, there is no other way. I feel you could never marry me now. I have felt it for months. Dear Tom, you will understand what I mean. We must look facts in the face. I hope you will always be friends with Mr. Constant. Good by, dear. God bless you! May you always be happy, and find a worthier wife than I. Perhaps when you are great, and rich, and famous, as you deserve, you will sometimes think not unkindly of one who, however faulty and unworthy of you, will at least love you till the end. Yours, till death, Jessie.*

By the time this letter was finished numerous old gentlemen, with wigs or without, were observed to be polishing their glasses. Mr. Wimp's examination was resumed.

"After making these discoveries what did you do?"

"I made inquiries about Miss Dymond, and found Mr. Constant had visited her once or twice in the evening. I imagined there would be some traces of a pecuniary connection. I was allowed by the family to inspect Mr. Constant's check-book, and found a paid check made out for £25 in the name of Miss Dymond. By inquiry at the Bank, I found it had been cashed on November 12th of last year. I then applied for a warrant against the prisoner."

Cross-examined: "Do you suggest that the prisoner opened Mr. Constant's bedroom with the key you found?"

"Certainly."

Brown-Harland, Q. C. (sarcastically): "And locked the door from within with it on leaving?"

"Certainly."

"Will you have the goodness to explain how the trick was done?"

"It wasn't done. (Laughter.) The prisoner probably locked the door from the outside. Those who broke it open naturally imagined it had been locked from the inside when they found the key inside. The key would, on this theory, be on the floor as the outside locking could not have been effected if it had been in the lock. The first persons to enter the room would naturally believe it had been thrown down in the bursting of the door. Or it might have been left sticking very loosely inside the lock so as not to interfere with the turning of the outside key in which case it would also probably have been thrown to the ground."

"Indeed. Very ingenious. And can you also explain how the prisoner could have bolted the door within from the outside?"

"I can. (Renewed sensation.) There is only one way in which it was possible – and that was, of course, a mere conjurer's illusion. To cause a locked door to appear bolted in addition, it would only be necessary for the person on the inside of the door to wrest the staple containing the bolt from the woodwork. The bolt in Mr. Constant's bedroom worked perpendicularly. When the staple was torn off, it would simply remain at rest on the pin of the bolt instead of supporting it or keeping it fixed. A person bursting open the door and finding the staple resting on the pin and torn away from the lintel of the door, would, of course, imagine he had torn it away, never dreaming the wresting off had been done beforehand." (Applause in court, which was instantly checked by the ushers.) The counsel for the defense felt he had been entrapped in attempting to be sarcastic with the redoubtable detective. Grodman seemed green with envy. It was the one thing he had not thought of.

Mrs. Drabdump, Grodman, Inspector Howlett, and Sergeant Runnymede were recalled and re-examined by the embarrassed Sir Charles Brown-Harland as to the exact condition of the lock and the bolt and the position of the key. It turned out as Wimp had suggested; so prepossessed were the witnesses with the conviction that the door was locked and bolted from the inside when it was burst open that they were a little hazy about the exact details. The damage had been repaired, so that it was all a question of precise past observation. The inspector and the sergeant testified that the key was in the lock when they saw it, though both the mortise and the bolt were broken. They were not prepared to say that Wimp's theory was impossible; they would even admit it was quite possible that the staple of the bolt had been torn off beforehand. Mrs. Drabdump could give no clear account of such petty facts in view of her immediate engrossing interest in the horrible sight of the corpse. Grodman alone was positive that the key was in the door when he burst it open. No, he did not remember picking it up from the floor and putting it in. And he was certain that the staple of the bolt was not broken, from the resistance he experienced in trying to shake the upper panels of the door.

By the Prosecution: "Don't you think, from the comparative ease with which the door yielded to your onslaught, that it is highly probable that the pin of the bolt was not in a firmly fixed staple, but in one already detached from the woodwork of the lintel?"

"The door did not yield so easily."

"But you must be a Hercules."

"Not quite; the bolt was old, and the woodwork crumbling; the lock was new and shoddy. But I have always been a strong man."

"Very well, Mr. Grodman. I hope you will never appear at the music-halls." (Laughter.)

Jessie Dymond's landlady was the next witness for the prosecution. She corroborated Wimp's statements as to Constant's occasional visits, and narrated how the girl had been enlisted by the dead philanthropist as a collaborator in some of his enterprises. But the most telling portion of her evidence was the story of how, late at night, on December 3d, the prisoner called upon her and inquired wildly about the whereabouts of his sweetheart. He said he had just received a mysterious letter from Miss Dymond saying she was gone. She (the landlady) replied that she could have told him that weeks ago, as her ungrateful lodger was gone now some three weeks without leaving a hint behind her. In answer to his most ungentlemanly raging and raving, she told him it served him right, as he should have looked after her better, and not kept away for so long. She reminded him that there were as good fish in the sea as ever came out, and a girl of Jessie's attractions need not pine away (as she had seemed to be pining away) for lack of appreciation. He then called her a liar and left her, and she hoped never to see his face again, though she was not surprised to see it in the dock.

Mr. Fitzjames Montgomery, a bank clerk, remembered cashing the check produced. He particularly remembered it, because he paid the money to a very pretty girl. She took the entire amount in gold. At this point the case was adjourned.

Denzil Cantercot was the first witness called for the prosecution on the resumption of the trial. Pressed as to whether he had not told Mr. Wimp that he had overheard the prisoner denouncing Mr. Constant, he could not say. He had not actually heard the prisoner's denunciations; he might have given Mr. Wimp a false impression, but then Mr. Wimp was so prosaically literal. (Laughter.) Mr. Crowl had told him something of the kind. Cross-examined, he said Jessie Dymond was a rare spirit and she always reminded him of Joan of Arc.

Mr. Crowl, being called, was extremely agitated. He refused to take the oath, and informed the court that the Bible was a Fad. He could not swear by anything so self-contradictory. He would affirm. He could not deny – though he looked like wishing to – that the prisoner had at first been rather mistrustful of Mr. Constant, but he was certain that the feeling had quickly worn off. Yes, he was a great friend of the prisoner, but he didn't see why that should invalidate his testimony, especially as he had not taken an oath. Certainly the prisoner seemed rather depressed when he saw him on Bank Holiday, but it was overwork on behalf of the people and for the demolition of the Fads.

Several other familiars of the prisoner gave more or less reluctant testimony as to his sometime prejudice against the amateur rival labor leader. His expressions of dislike had been strong and bitter. The Prosecution also produced a poster announcing that the prisoner would preside at a great meeting of clerks on December 4th. He had not turned up at this meeting nor sent any explanation. Finally, there was the evidence of the detectives who originally arrested him at Liverpool Docks in view of his suspicious demeanor. This completed the case for the prosecution.

Sir Charles Brown-Harland, Q. C., rose with a swagger and a rustle of his silk gown, and proceeded to set forth the theory of the defense. He said he did not purpose to call any witnesses. The hypothesis of the prosecution was so inherently childish and inconsequential, and so dependent upon a bundle of interdependent probabilities that it crumbled away at the merest touch. The prisoner's character was of unblemished integrity, his last public appearance had been made on the same platform with Mr. Gladstone, and his honesty and highmindedness had been vouched for by statesmen of the highest standing. His movements could be accounted for from hour to hour – and those with which the prosecution credited him rested on no tangible evidence whatever. He was also credited with superhuman ingenuity and diabolical cunning of which he had shown no previous symptom. Hypothesis was piled on hypothesis, as in the old Oriental legend, where the world rested on the elephant and the elephant on the tortoise. It might be worth while, however, to point out that it was at least quite likely that the death of Mr. Constant had not taken place before seven, and as the prisoner left Euston Station at 7:15 a. m. for Liverpool, he could certainly not have got there from Bow in the time; also that it was hardly possible for the prisoner, who could prove being at Euston Station at 5:25 a. m., to travel backward and forward to Glover Street and commit the crime all within less than two hours. "The real facts," said Sir Charles impressively, "are most simple. The prisoner, partly from pressure of work, partly (he had no wish to conceal) from worldly ambition, had begun to neglect Miss Dymond, to whom he was engaged to be married. The man was but human, and his head was a little turned by his growing importance. Nevertheless, at heart he was still deeply attached to Miss Dymond. She, however, appears to have jumped to the conclusion that he had ceased to love her, that she was unworthy of him, unfitted by education to take her place side by side with him in the new spheres to which he was mounting – that, in short, she was a drag on his career. Being, by all accounts, a girl of remarkable force of character, she resolved to cut the Gordian knot by leaving London, and, fearing lest her affianced husband's conscientiousness should induce him to sacrifice himself to her; dreading also, perhaps, her own weakness, she made the parting absolute, and the place of her refuge a mystery. A theory has been suggested which drags an honored name in the mire – a theory so superfluous that I shall only allude to it. That Arthur Constant could have seduced, or had any improper relations with his friend's betrothed is a hypothesis to which the lives of both give the lie. Before leaving London – or England – Miss Dymond wrote to her aunt in Devonport – her only living relative in this country – asking her as a great favor to forward an addressed letter to the prisoner, a fortnight after receipt. The aunt obeyed implicitly. This was the letter which fell like a thunderbolt on the prisoner on the night of December 3d. All his old love returned – he was full of self-reproach and pity for the poor girl. The letter read ominously. Perhaps she was going to put an end to herself. His first thought was to rush up to his friend, Constant, to seek his advice. Perhaps Constant knew something of the affair. The prisoner knew the two were in not infrequent communication. It is possible – my lord and gentlemen of the jury, I do not wish to follow the methods of the prosecution and confuse theory with fact, so I say it is possible – that Mr. Constant had supplied her with the £25 to leave the country. He was like a brother to her, perhaps even acted imprudently in calling upon her, though neither dreamed of evil. It is possible that he may have encouraged her in her abnegation and in her altruistic aspirations, perhaps even without knowing their exact drift, for does he not speak in his very last letter of the fine female characters he was meeting, and the influence for good he had over individual human souls? Still, this we can now never know, unless the dead speak or the absent return. It is also not impossible that Miss Dymond was entrusted with the £25 for charitable purposes. But to come back to certainties. The prisoner consulted Mr. Constant about the letter. He then ran to Miss Dymond's lodgings in Stepney Green, knowing beforehand his trouble would be futile. The letter bore the postmark of Devonport. He knew the girl had an aunt there; possibly she might have gone to her. He could not telegraph, for he was ignorant of the address. He consulted his 'Bradshaw,' and resolved to leave by the 5:30 a. m. from Paddington, and told his landlady so. He left the letter in the 'Bradshaw,' which ultimately got thrust among a pile of papers under the sofa, so that he had to get another. He was careless and disorderly, and the key found by Mr. Wimp in his sofa must have lain there for some years, having been lost there in the days when he occupied the bedroom afterward rented by Mr. Constant. Afraid to miss his train, he did not undress on that distressful night. Meantime the thought occurred to him that Jessie was too clever a girl to leave so easy a trail, and he jumped to the conclusion that she would be going to her married brother in America, and had gone to Devonport merely to bid her aunt farewell. He determined therefore to get to Liverpool, without wasting time at Devonport, to institute inquiries. Not suspecting the delay in the transit of the letter, he thought he might yet stop her, even at the landing-stage or on the tender. Unfortunately his cab went slowly in the fog, he missed the first train, and wandered about brooding disconsolately in the mist till the second. At Liverpool his suspicious, excited demeanor procured his momentary arrest. Since then the thought of the lost girl has haunted and broken him. That is the whole, the plain, and the sufficing story." The effective witnesses for the defense were, indeed, few. It is so hard to prove a negative. There was Jessie's aunt, who bore out the statement of the counsel for the defense. There were the porters who saw him leave Euston by the 7:15 train for Liverpool, and arrive just too late for the 5:15; there was the cabman (2,138), who drove him to Euston just in time, he (witness) thought, to catch the 5:15 a. m. Under cross-examination, the cabman got a little confused; he was asked whether, if he really picked up the prisoner at Bow Railway Station at about 4:30, he ought not to have caught the first train at Euston. He said the fog made him drive rather slowly, but admitted the mist was transparent enough to warrant full speed. He also admitted being a strong trade unionist, Spigot, Q. C., artfully extorting the admission as if it were of the utmost significance. Finally, there were numerous witnesses – of all sorts and conditions – to the prisoner's high character, as well as to Arthur Constant's blameless and moral life.

In his closing speech on the third day of the trial, Sir Charles pointed out with great exhaustiveness and cogency the flimsiness of the case for the prosecution, the number of hypotheses it involved, and their mutual interdependence. Mrs. Drabdump was a witness whose evidence must be accepted with extreme caution. The jury must remember that she was unable to dissociate her observations from her inferences, and thought that the prisoner and Mr. Constant were quarreling merely because they were agitated. He dissected her evidence, and showed that it entirely bore out the story of the defense. He asked the jury to bear in mind that no positive evidence (whether of cabmen or others) had been given of the various and complicated movements attributed to the prisoner on the morning of December 4th, between the hours of 5:25 and 7:15 a. m., and that the most important witness on the theory of the prosecution – he meant, of course, Miss Dymond – had not been produced. Even if she were dead, and her body were found, no countenance would be given to the theory of the prosecution, for the mere conviction that her lover had deserted her would be a sufficient explanation of her suicide. Beyond the ambiguous letter, no tittle of evidence of her dishonor – on which the bulk of the case against the prisoner rested – had been adduced. As for the motive of political jealousy that had been a mere passing cloud. The two men had become fast friends. As to the circumstances of the alleged crime, the medical evidence was on the whole in favor of the time of death being late; and the prisoner had left London at a quarter past seven. The drugging theory was absurd, and as for the too clever bolt and lock theories, Mr. Grodman, a trained scientific observer, had pooh-poohed them. He would solemnly exhort the jury to remember that if they condemned the prisoner they would not only send an innocent man to an ignominious death on the flimsiest circumstantial evidence, but they would deprive the workingmen of this country of one of their truest friends and their ablest leader.

The conclusion of Sir Charles' vigorous speech was greeted with irrepressible applause.

Mr. Spigot, Q. C., in closing the case for the prosecution, asked the jury to return a verdict against the prisoner for as malicious and premeditated a crime as ever disgraced the annals of any civilized country. His cleverness and education had only been utilized for the devil's ends, while his reputation had been used as a cloak. Everything pointed strongly to the prisoner's guilt. On receiving Miss Dymond's letter announcing her shame, and (probably) her intention to commit suicide, he had hastened upstairs to denounce Constant. He had then rushed to the girl's lodgings, and, finding his worst fears confirmed, planned at once his diabolically ingenious scheme of revenge. He told his landlady he was going to Devonport, so that if he bungled, the police would be put temporarily off his track. His real destination was Liverpool, for he intended to leave the country. Lest, however, his plan should break down here, too, he arranged an ingenious alibi by being driven to Euston for the 5:15 train to Liverpool. The cabman would not know he did not intend to go by it, but meant to return to 11, Glover Street, there to perpetrate this foul crime, interruption to which he had possibly barred by drugging his landlady. His presence at Liverpool (whither he really went by the second train) would corroborate the cabman's story. That night he had not undressed nor gone to bed; he had plotted out his devilish scheme till it was perfect; the fog came as an unexpected ally to cover his movements. Jealousy, outraged affection, the desire for revenge, the lust for political power – these were human. They might pity the criminal, they could not find him innocent of the crime.

Mr. Justice Crogie, summing up, began dead against the prisoner. Reviewing the evidence, he pointed out that plausible hypotheses neatly dove-tailed did not necessarily weaken one another, the fitting so well together of the whole rather making for the truth of the parts. Besides, the case for the prosecution was as far from being all hypothesis as the case for the defense was from excluding hypothesis. The key, the letter, the reluctance to produce the letter, the heated interview with Constant, the misstatement about the prisoner's destination, the flight to Liverpool, the false tale about searching for a "him," the denunciations of Constant, all these were facts. On the other hand, there were various lacunae and hypotheses in the case for the defense. Even conceding the somewhat dubious alibi afforded by the prisoner's presence at Euston at 5:25 a. m., there was no attempt to account for his movements between that and 7:15 a. m. It was as possible that he returned to Bow as that he lingered about Euston. There was nothing in the medical evidence to make his guilt impossible. Nor was there anything inherently impossible in Constant's yielding to the sudden temptation of a beautiful girl, nor in a working-girl deeming herself deserted, temporarily succumbing to the fascinations of a gentleman and regretting it bitterly afterward. What had become of the girl was a mystery. Hers might have been one of those nameless corpses which the tide swirls up on slimy river banks. The jury must remember, too, that the relation might not have actually passed into dishonor, it might have been just grave enough to smite the girl's conscience, and to induce her to behave as she had done. It was enough that her letter should have excited the jealousy of the prisoner. There was one other point which he would like to impress on the jury, and which the counsel for the prosecution had not sufficiently insisted upon. This was that the prisoner's guiltiness was the only plausible solution that had ever been advanced of the Bow Mystery. The medical evidence agreed that Mr. Constant did not die by his own hand. Someone must therefore have murdered him. The number of people who could have had any possible reason or opportunity to murder him was extremely small. The prisoner had both reason and opportunity. By what logicians called the method of exclusion, suspicion would attach to him on even slight evidence. The actual evidence was strong and plausible, and now that Mr. Wimp's ingenious theory had enabled them to understand how the door could have been apparently locked and bolted from within, the last difficulty and the last argument for suicide had been removed. The prisoner's guilt was as clear as circumstantial evidence could make it. If they let him go free, the Bow Mystery might henceforward be placed among the archives of unavenged assassinations. Having thus well-nigh hung the prisoner, the judge wound up by insisting on the high probability of the story for the defense, though that, too, was dependent in important details upon the prisoner's mere private statements to his counsel. The jury, being by this time sufficiently muddled by his impartiality, were dismissed, with the exhortation to allow due weight to every fact and probability in determining their righteous verdict.

The minutes ran into hours, but the jury did not return. The shadows of night fell across the reeking, fevered court before they announced their verdict –

"Guilty."

The judge put on his black cap.

The great reception arranged outside was a fiasco; the evening banquet was indefinitely postponed. Wimp had won; Grodman felt like a whipped cur.

Chapter XI

"SO YOU WERE RIGHT," Denzil could not help saying as he greeted Grodman a week afterward. "I shall not live to tell the story of how you discovered the Bow murderer."

"Sit down," growled Grodman; "perhaps you will after all." There was a dangerous gleam in his eyes. Denzil was sorry he had spoken.

"I sent for you," Grodman said, "to tell you that on the night Wimp arrested Mortlake I had made preparations for your arrest."

Denzil gasped, "What for?"

"My dear Denzil, there is a little law in this country invented for the confusion of the poetic. The greatest exponent of the Beautiful is only allowed the same number of wives as the greengrocer. I do not blame you for not being satisfied with Jane – she is a good servant but a bad mistress – but it was cruel to Kitty not to inform her that Jane had a prior right in you, and unjust to Jane not to let her know of the contract with Kitty."

"They both know it now well enough, curse 'em," said the poet.

"Yes; your secrets are like your situations – you can't keep them long. My poor poet, I pity you – betwixt the devil and the deep sea."

"They're a pair of harpies, each holding over me the Damocles sword of an arrest for bigamy. Neither loves me."

"I should think they would come in very useful to you. You plant onc in my house to tell my secrets to Wimp, and you plant one in Wimp's house to tell Wimp's secrets to me, I suppose. Out with some, then."

"Upon my honor you wrong me. Jane brought me here, not I Jane. As for Kitty, I never had such a shock in my life as at finding her installed in Wimp's house."

"She thought it safer to have the law handy for your arrest. Besides, she probably desired to occupy a parallel position to Jane's. She must do something for a living; you wouldn't do anything for hers. And so you couldn't go anywhere without meeting a wife! Ha! ha! ha! Serve you right, my polygamous poet."

"But why should you arrest me?"

"Revenge, Denzil. I have been the best friend you ever had in this cold, prosaic world. You have eaten my bread, drunk my claret, written my book, smoked my cigars, and pocketed my money. And yet, when you have an important piece of information bearing on a mystery about which I am thinking day and night, you calmly go and sell it to Wimp."

"I did-didn't," stammered Denzil.

"Liar! Do you think Kitty has any secrets from me? As soon as I discovered your two marriages I determined to have you arrested for – your treachery. But when I found you had, as I thought, put Wimp on the wrong scent, when I felt sure that by arresting Mortlake he was going to make a greater ass of himself than even nature had been able to do, then I forgave you. I let you walk about the earth – and drink – freely. Now it is Wimp who crows – everybody pats him on the back – they call him the mystery man of the Scotland-Yard tribe. Poor Tom Mortlake will be hanged, and all through your telling Wimp about Jessie Dymond!"

"It was you yourself," said Denzil sullenly. "Everybody was giving it up. But you said 'Let us find out all that Arthur Constant did in the last few months of his life.' Wimp couldn't miss stumbling on Jessie sooner or later. I'd have throttled Constant, if I had known he'd touched her," he wound up with irrelevant indignation.

Grodman winced at the idea that he himself had worked *ad majorem gloriam* of Wimp. And yet, had not Mrs. Wimp let out as much at the Christmas dinner?

"What's past is past," he said gruffly. "But if Tom Mortlake hangs, you go to Portland."

"How can I help Tom hanging?"

"Help the agitation as much as you can. Write letters under all sorts of names to all the papers. Get everybody you know to sign the great petition. Find out where Jessie Dymond is – the girl who holds the proof of Tom Mortlake's innocence."

"You really believe him innocent?"

"Don't be satirical, Denzil. Haven't I taken the chair at all the meetings? Am I not the most copious correspondent of the Press?"

"I thought it was only to spite Wimp."

"Rubbish. It's to save poor Tom. He no more murdered Arthur Constant than – you did!" He laughed an unpleasant laugh.

Denzil bade him farewell, frigid with fear.

Grodman was up to his ears in letters and telegrams. Somehow he had become the leader of the rescue party – suggestions, subscriptions came from all sides. The suggestions were burnt, the subscriptions acknowledged in the papers and used for hunting up the missing girl. Lucy Brent headed the list with a hundred pounds. It was a fine testimony to her faith in her dead lover's honor.

The release of the Jury had unloosed "The Greater Jury," which always now sits upon the smaller. Every means was taken to nullify the value of the "palladium of British liberty." The foreman and the jurors were interviewed, the judge was judged, and by those who were no judges. The Home Secretary (who had done nothing beyond accepting office under the Crown) was vituperated, and sundry provincial persons wrote confidentially to the Queen. Arthur Constant's backsliding cheered many by convincing them that others were as bad as themselves; and well-to-do tradesmen saw in Mortlake's wickedness the pernicious effects of socialism. A dozen new theories were afloat. Constant had committed suicide by Esoteric Buddhism, as witness his devotion to Mme. Blavatsky, or he had been murdered by his Mahatma, or victimized by Hypnotism, Mesmerism, Somnambulism, and other weird abstractions. Grodman's great point was – Jessie Dymond must be produced, dead or alive. The electric current scoured the civilized world in search of her. What wonder if the shrewder sort divined that the indomitable detective had fixed his last hope on the girl's guilt? If Jessie had wrongs why should she not have avenged them herself? Did she not always remind the poet of Joan of Arc?

Another week passed; the shadow of the gallows crept over the days; on, on, remorselessly drawing nearer, as the last ray of hope sank below the horizon. The Home Secretary remained inflexible; the great petitions discharged their signatures at him in vain. He was a Conservative, sternly conscientious; and the mere insinuation that his obstinacy was due to the politics of the condemned only hardened him against the temptation of a cheap reputation for magnanimity. He would not even grant a respite, to increase the chances of the discovery of Jessie Dymond. In the last of the three weeks there was a final monster meeting of protest. Grodman again took the chair, and several distinguished faddists were present, as well as numerous respectable members of society. The Home Secretary acknowledged the receipt of their resolutions. The Trade Unions were divided in their allegiance; some whispered of faith and hope, others of financial defalcations. The former essayed to organize a procession and an indignation meeting on the Sunday preceding the Tuesday fixed for the execution, but it fell through on a rumor of confession. The Monday papers contained a last masterly letter from Grodman exposing the weakness of the evidence, but they knew nothing of a confession. The prisoner was mute and disdainful, professing little regard for a life empty of love and burdened with self-reproach. He refused to see clergymen. He was accorded an interview with Miss Brent in the presence of a jailer, and solemnly asseverated his respect for her dead lover's memory. Monday buzzed with rumors; the evening papers chronicled them hour by hour. A poignant anxiety was abroad. The girl would be found. Some miracle would happen. A reprieve would arrive. The sentence would be commuted. But the short day darkened into night even as Mortlake's short day was darkening. And the shadow of the gallows crept on and on and seemed to mingle with the twilight.

Crowl stood at the door of his shop, unable to work. His big gray eyes were heavy with unshed tears. The dingy wintry road seemed one vast cemetery; the street lamps twinkled like corpse-lights. The confused sounds of the street-life reached his ear as from another world. He did not see the people who flitted to and fro amid the gathering shadows of the cold, dreary night. One ghastly vision flashed and faded and flashed upon the background of the duskiness.

Denzil stood beside him, smoking in silence. A cold fear was at his heart. That terrible Grodman! As the hangman's cord was tightening round Mortlake, he felt the convict's chains tightening round himself. And yet there was one gleam of hope, feeble as the yellow flicker of the gas-lamp across the way. Grodman had obtained an interview with the condemned late that afternoon, and the parting had been painful, but the evening paper, that in its turn had obtained an interview with the ex-detective, announced on its placard:

GRODMAN STILL CONFIDENT

and the thousands who yet pinned their faith on this extraordinary man refused to extinguish the last sparks of hope. Denzil had bought the paper and scanned it eagerly, but there was nothing save the vague assurance that the indefatigable Grodman was still almost pathetically expectant of the miracle. Denzil did not share the expectation; he meditated flight.

"Peter," he said at last, "I'm afraid it's all over."

Crowl nodded, heart-broken. "All over!" he repeated, "and to think that he dies – and it is – all over!"

He looked despairingly at the blank winter sky, where leaden clouds shut out the stars. "Poor, poor young fellow! To-night alive and thinking. Tomorrow night a clod, with no more sense or motion than a bit of leather! No compensation nowhere for being cut off innocent in the pride of youth and strength! A man who has always preached the Useful day and night, and toiled and suffered for his fellows. Where's the justice of it, where's the justice of it?" he demanded fiercely. Again his wet eyes wandered upward toward heaven, that heaven away from which the soul of a dead saint at the Antipodes was speeding into infinite space.

"Well, where was the justice for Arthur Constant if he, too, was innocent?" said Denzil. "Really, Peter, I don't see why you should take it for granted that Tom is so dreadfully injured. Your horny-handed labor leaders are, after all, men of no aesthetic refinement, with no sense of the Beautiful; you cannot expect them to be exempt from the coarser forms of crime. Humanity must look to for other leaders – to the seers and the poets!"

"Cantercot, if you say Tom's guilty I'll knock you down." The little cobbler turned upon his tall friend like a roused lion. Then he added, "I beg your pardon, Cantercot, I don't mean that. After all, I've no grounds. The judge is an honest man, and with gifts I can't lay claim to. But I believe in Tom with all my heart. And if Tom is guilty I believe in the Cause of the People with all my heart all the same. The Fads are doomed to death, they may be reprieved, but they must die at last."

He drew a deep sigh, and looked along the dreary Road. It was quite dark now, but by the light of the lamps and the gas in the shop windows the dull, monotonous Road lay revealed in all its sordid, familiar outlines; with its long stretches of chill pavement, its unlovely architecture, and its endless stream of prosaic pedestrians.

A sudden consciousness of the futility of his existence pierced the little cobbler like an icy wind. He saw his own life, and a hundred million lives like his, swelling and breaking like bubbles on a dark ocean, unheeded, uncared for.

A newsboy passed along, clamoring "The Bow murderer, preparations for the hexecution!"

A terrible shudder shook the cobbler's frame. His eyes ranged sightlessly after the boy; the merciful tears filled them at last.

"The Cause of the People," he murmured, brokenly, "I believe in the Cause of the People. There is nothing else."

"Peter, come in to tea, you'll catch cold," said Mrs. Crowl.

Denzil went in to tea and Peter followed.

* * *

Meantime, round the house of the Home Secretary, who was in town, an ever-augmenting crowd was gathered, eager to catch the first whisper of a reprieve.

The house was guarded by a cordon of police, for there was no inconsiderable danger of a popular riot. At times a section of the crowd groaned and hooted. Once a volley of stones was discharged at the windows. The news-boys were busy vending their special editions, and the reporters struggled through the crowd, clutching descriptive pencils, and ready to rush off to telegraph offices should anything "extra special" occur. Telegraph boys were coming up every now and again with threats, messages, petitions and exhortations from all parts of the country to the unfortunate Home Secretary, who was striving to keep his aching head cool as he went through the voluminous evidence for the last time and pondered over the more important letters which "The Greater Jury" had contributed to the obscuration of the problem. Grodman's letter in that morning's paper shook him most; under his scientific analysis the circumstantial chain seemed forged of painted cardboard. Then the poor man read the judge's summing up, and the chain became tempered steel. The noise of the crowd outside broke upon his ear in his study like the roar of a distant ocean. The more the rabble hooted him, the more he essayed to hold scrupulously the scales of life and death. And the crowd grew and grew, as men came away from their work. There were many that loved the man who lay in the jaws of death, and a spirit of mad revolt surged in their breasts. And the sky was gray, and the bleak night deepened and the shadow of the gallows crept on.

Suddenly a strange inarticulate murmur spread through the crowd, a vague whisper of no one knew what. Something had happened. Somebody was coming. A second later and one of the outskirts of the throng was agitated, and a convulsive cheer went up from it, and was taken up infectiously all along the street. The crowd parted – a hansom dashed through the center. "Grodman! Grodman!" shouted those who recognized the occupant. "Grodman! Hurrah!" Grodman was outwardly calm and pale, but his eyes glittered; he waved his hand encouragingly as the hansom dashed up to the door, cleaving the turbulent crowd as a canoe cleaves the waters. Grodman sprang out, the constables at the portal made way for him respectfully. He knocked imperatively, the door was opened cautiously; a boy rushed up and delivered a telegram; Grodman forced his way in, gave his name, and insisted on seeing the Home Secretary on a matter of life and death. Those near the door heard his words and cheered, and the crowd divined the good omen, and the air throbbed with cannonades of joyous sound. The cheers rang in Grodman's ears as the door slammed behind him. The reporters struggled to the front. An excited knot of working men pressed round the arrested hansom, they took the horse out. A dozen enthusiasts struggled for the honor of placing themselves between the shafts. And the crowd awaited Grodman.

Chapter XII

GRODMAN was ushered into the conscientious Minister's study. The doughty chief of the agitation was, perhaps, the one man who could not be denied. As he entered, the Home Secretary's face seemed lit up with relief. At a sign from his master, the amanuensis who had brought in the last telegram took it back with him into the outer room where he worked.

Needless to say not a tithe of the Minister's correspondence ever came under his own eyes.

"You have a valid reason for troubling me, I suppose, Mr. Grodman?" said the Home Secretary, almost cheerfully. "Of course it is about Mortlake?"

"It is; and I have the best of all reasons."

"Take a seat. Proceed."

"Pray do not consider me impertinent, but have you ever given any attention to the science of evidence?"

"How do you mean?" asked the Home Secretary, rather puzzled, adding, with a melancholy smile, "I have had to lately. Of course, I've never been a criminal lawyer, like some of my predecessors. But I should hardly speak of it as a science; I look upon it as a question of common-sense."

"Pardon me, sir. It is the most subtle and difficult of all the sciences. It is, indeed, rather the science of the sciences. What is the whole of Inductive Logic, as laid down, say, by Bacon and Mill, but an attempt to appraise the value of evidence, the said evidence being the trails left by the Creator, so to speak? The Creator has – I say it in all reverence – drawn a myriad red herrings across the track, but the true scientist refuses to be baffled by superficial appearances in detecting the secrets of Nature. The vulgar herd catches at the gross apparent fact, but the man of insight knows that what lies on the surface does lie."

"Very interesting, Mr. Grodman, but really—"

"Bear with me, sir. The science of evidence being thus so extremely subtle, and demanding the most acute and trained observation of facts, the most comprehensive understanding of human psychology, is naturally given over to professors who have not the remotest idea that 'things are not what they seem,' and that everything is other than it appears; to professors, most of whom, by their year-long devotion to the shop-counter or the desk, have acquired an intimate acquaintance with all the infinite shades and complexities of things and human nature. When twelve of these professors are put in a box, it is called a jury. When one of these professors is put in a box by himself, he is called a witness. The retailing of evidence – the observation of the facts – is given over to people who go through their lives without eyes; the appreciation of evidence – the judging of these facts – is surrendered to people who may possibly be adepts in weighing out pounds of sugar. Apart from their sheer inability to fulfill either function – to observe, or to judge – their observation and their judgment alike are vitiated by all sorts of irrelevant prejudices."

"You are attacking trial by jury."

"Not necessarily. I am prepared to accept that scientifically, on the ground that, as there are, as a rule, only two alternatives, the balance of probability is slightly in favor of the true decision being come to. Then, in cases where experts like myself have got up the evidence, the jury can be made to see through trained eyes."

The Home Secretary tapped impatiently with his foot.

"I can't listen to abstract theorizing," he said. "Have you any fresh concrete evidence?"

"Sir, everything depends on our getting down to the root of the matter. What percentage of average evidence should you think is thorough, plain, simple, unvarnished fact, 'the truth, the whole truth, and nothing but the truth'?"

"Fifty?" said the Minister, humoring him a little.

"Not five. I say nothing of lapses of memory, of inborn defects of observational power – though the suspiciously precise recollection of dates and events possessed by ordinary witnesses in important trials taking place years after the occurrences involved, is one of the most amazing things in the curiosities of modern jurisprudence. I defy you, sir, to tell me what you had for dinner last Monday, or what exactly you were saying and doing at five o'clock last Tuesday afternoon. Nobody whose life does not run in mechanical grooves can do anything of the sort; unless, of course, the facts have been very impressive. But this by the way. The great obstacle to veracious observation is the element of prepossession in all vision. Has it ever struck you, sir, that we never see anyone more than once, if that? The first time we meet a man we may possibly see him as he is; the second time our vision is colored and modified by the memory of the first. Do our friends appear to us as they appear to strangers? Do our rooms, our furniture, our pipes strike our eye as they would strike the eye of an outsider, looking on them for the first time? Can a mother see her babe's ugliness, or a lover his mistress' shortcomings, though they stare everybody else in the face? Can we see ourselves as others see us? No; habit, prepossession changes all. The mind is a large factor of every so-called external fact. The eye sees, sometimes, what it wishes to see, more often what it expects to see. You follow me, sir?"

The Home Secretary nodded his head less impatiently. He was beginning to be interested. The hubbub from without broke faintly upon their ears.

"To give you a definite example. Mr. Wimp says that when I burst open the door of Mr. Constant's room on the morning of December 4th, and saw that the staple of the bolt had been wrested by the pin from the lintel, I jumped at once to the conclusion that I had broken the bolt. Now I admit that this was so, only in things like this you do not seem to conclude, you jump so fast that you see, or seem to. On the other hand, when you see a standing ring of fire produced by whirling a burning stick, you do not believe in its continuous existence. It is the same when witnessing a legerdemain performance. Seeing is not always believing, despite the proverb; but believing is often seeing. It is not to the point that in that little matter of the door Wimp was as hopelessly and incurably wrong as he has been in everything all along. Though the door was securely bolted, I confess that I should have seen that I had broken the bolt in forcing the door, even if it had been broken beforehand. Never once since December 4th did this possibility occur to me, till Wimp with perverted ingenuity suggested it. If this is the case with a trained observer, one moreover fully conscious of this ineradicable tendency of the human mind, how must it be with an untrained observer?"

"Come to the point, come to the point," said the Home Secretary, putting out his hand as if it itched to touch the bell on the writing-table.

"Such as," went on Grodman imperturbably, "such as – Mrs. Drabdump. That worthy person is unable, by repeated violent knocking, to arouse her lodger who yet desires to be aroused; she becomes alarmed, she rushes across to get my assistance; I burst open the door – what do you think the good lady expected to see?"

"Mr. Constant murdered, I suppose," murmured the Home Secretary, wonderingly.

"Exactly. And so she saw it. And what should you think was the condition of Arthur Constant when the door yielded to my violent exertions and flew open?"

"Why, was he not dead?" gasped the Home Secretary, his heart fluttering violently.

"Dead? A young, healthy fellow like that! When the door flew open Arthur Constant was sleeping the sleep of the just. It was a deep, a very deep sleep, of course, else the blows at his door would long since have awakened him. But all the while Mrs. Drabdump's fancy was picturing her lodger cold and stark the poor young fellow was lying in bed in a nice warm sleep."

"You mean to say you found Arthur Constant alive?"

"As you were last night."

The minister was silent, striving confusedly to take in the situation. Outside the crowd was cheering again. It was probably to pass the time.

"Then, when was he murdered?"

"Immediately afterward."

"By whom?"

"Well, that is, if you will pardon me, not a very intelligent question. Science and common-sense are in accord for once. Try the method of exhaustion. It must have been either by Mrs. Drabdump or by myself."

"You mean to say that Mrs. Drabdump—!"

"Poor dear Mrs. Drabdump, you don't deserve this of your Home Secretary! The idea of that good lady!"

"It was you!"

"Calm yourself, my dear Home Secretary. There is nothing to be alarmed at. It was a solitary experiment, and I intend it to remain so." The noise without grew louder. "Three cheers for Grodman! Hip, hip, hip, hooray," fell faintly on their ears.

But the Minister, pallid and deeply moved, touched the bell. The Home Secretary's home secretary appeared. He looked at the great man's agitated face with suppressed surprise.

"Thank you for calling in your amanuensis," said Grodman. "I intended to ask you to lend me his services. I suppose he can write shorthand."

The minister nodded, speechless.

"That is well. I intend this statement to form the basis of an appendix to the twenty-fifth edition – sort of silver wedding – of my book, 'Criminals I Have Caught,' Mr. Denzil Cantercot, who, by the will I have made today, is appointed my literary executor, will have the task of working it up with literary and dramatic touches after the model of the other chapters of my book. I have every confidence he will be able to do me as much justice, from a literary point of view, as you, sir, no doubt will from a legal. I feel certain he will succeed in catching the style of the other chapters to perfection."

"Templeton," whispered the Home Secretary, "this man may be a lunatic. The effort to solve the Big Bow Mystery may have addled his brain. Still," he added aloud, "it will be as well for you to take down his statement in shorthand."

"Thank you, sir," said Grodman, heartily. "Ready, Mr. Templeton? Here goes. My career till I left the Scotland-Yard Detective Department is known to all the world. Is that too fast for you, Mr. Templeton? A little? Well, I'll go slower; but pull me up if I forget to keep the brake on. When I retired, I discovered that I was a bachelor. But it was too late to marry. Time hung on my hands. The preparation of my book, 'Criminals I Have Caught,' kept me occupied for some months. When it was published I had nothing more to do but think. I had plenty of money, and it was safely invested; there was no call for speculation. The future was meaningless to me; I regretted I had not elected to die in harness. As idle old men must, I lived in the past. I went over and over again my ancient exploits; I re-read my book. And as I thought and thought, away from the excitement of the actual hunt, and seeing the facts in a truer perspective, so it grew daily clearer to me that criminals were more fools than rogues. Every crime I had traced, however cleverly perpetrated, was from the point of view of penetrability a weak failure. Traces and trails were left on all sides – ragged edges, rough-hewn corners; in short, the job was botched, artistic completeness unattained. To the vulgar, my feats might seem marvelous – the average man is mystified to grasp how you detect the letter 'e' in a simple cryptogram – to myself they were as commonplace as the crimes they unveiled. To me now, with my lifelong study of the science of evidence, it seemed possible to commit not merely one, but a thousand crimes that should be absolutely undiscoverable. And yet criminals would go on sinning, and giving themselves away, in the same old grooves – no originality, no dash, no individual insight, no fresh conception! One would imagine there were an Academy of crime with forty thousand armchairs. And gradually, as I pondered and brooded over the thought, there came upon me the desire to commit a crime that should baffle detection. I could invent hundreds of such crimes, and please myself by imagining them done; but would they really work out in practice? Evidently the sole performer of my experiment must be myself; the subject – whom or what? Accident should determine. I itched to commence with murder – to tackle the stiffest problems first, and I burned to startle and baffle the world – especially the world of which I had ceased to be. Outwardly I was calm, and spoke to the people about me as usual. Inwardly I was on fire with a consuming scientific passion. I sported with my pet theories, and fitted them mentally on everyone I met. Every friend or acquaintance I sat and gossiped with, I was plotting how to murder without leaving a clue. There is not one of my friends or acquaintances I have not done away with in thought. There is no public man – have no fear, my dear Home Secretary – I have not planned to assassinate secretly, mysteriously, unintelligibly, undiscoverably. Ah, how I could give the stock criminals points – with their second-hand motives, their conventional conceptions, their commonplace details, their lack of artistic feeling and restraint.

"The late Arthur Constant came to live nearly opposite me. I cultivated his acquaintance – he was a lovable young fellow, an excellent subject for experiment. I do not know when I have ever taken to a man more. From the moment I first set eyes on him, there was a peculiar sympathy between us. We were drawn to each other. I felt instinctively he would be the man. I loved to hear him speak enthusiastically of the Brotherhood of Man – I, who knew the brotherhood of man was to the ape, the serpent, and the tiger – and he seemed to find a pleasure in stealing a moment's chat with me from his engrossing self-appointed duties. It is a pity humanity should have been robbed of so valuable a life. But it had to be. At a quarter to ten on the night of December 3d he came to me. Naturally I said nothing about this visit at the inquest or the trial. His object was to consult me mysteriously about some girl. He said he had privately lent her money – which she was to repay at her convenience. What the money was for he did not know, except that it was somehow connected with an act of abnegation in which he had vaguely encouraged her. The girl had since disappeared, and he was in distress about her. He would not tell me who it was – of course now, sir, you know as well as I it was Jessie Dymond – but asked for advice as to how to set about finding her. He mentioned that Mortlake was leaving for Devonport by the first train on the next day. Of old I should have connected these two facts and sought the thread; now, as he spoke, all my thoughts were dyed red. He was suffering perceptibly from toothache, and in answer to my sympathetic inquiries told me it had been allowing him very little sleep. Everything combined to invite the trial of one of my favorite theories. I spoke to him in a fatherly way, and when I had tendered some vague advice about the girl, and made him promise to secure a night's rest (before he faced the arduous tram-men's meeting in the morning) by taking a sleeping-draught, I gave him some sulfonal in a phial. It is a new drug, which produces protracted sleep without disturbing the digestion, and which I use myself. He promised faithfully to take the draught; and I also exhorted him earnestly to bolt and bar and lock himself in so as to stop up every chink or aperture by which the cold air of the winter's night might creep into the room. I remonstrated with him on the careless manner he treated his body, and he laughed in his good-humored, gentle way, and promised to obey me in all things. And he did. That Mrs. Drabdump, failing to rouse him, would cry 'Murder!' I took for certain. She is built that way. As even Sir Charles Brown-Harland remarked, she habitually takes her prepossessions for facts, her inferences for observations. She forecasts the future in gray. Most women of Mrs.

Drabdump's class would have behaved as she did. She happened to be a peculiarly favorable specimen for working on by 'suggestion,' but I would have undertaken to produce the same effect on almost any woman under similar conditions. The only uncertain link in the chain was: Would Mrs. Drabdump rush across to get me to break open the door? Women always rush for a man. I was well-nigh the nearest, and certainly the most authoritative man in the street, and I took it for granted she would."

"But suppose she hadn't?" the Home Secretary could not help asking.

"Then the murder wouldn't have happened, that's all. In due course Arthur Constant would have awoke, or somebody else breaking open the door would have found him sleeping; no harm done, nobody any the wiser. I could hardly sleep myself that night. The thought of the extraordinary crime I was about to commit – a burning curiosity to know whether Wimp would detect the *modus operandi* – the prospect of sharing the feelings of murderers with whom I had been in contact all my life without being in touch with the terrible joys of their inner life – the fear lest I should be too fast asleep to hear Mrs. Drabdump's knock – these things agitated me and disturbed my rest. I lay tossing on my bed, planning every detail of poor Constant's end. The hours dragged slowly and wretchedly on toward the misty dawn. I was racked with suspense. Was I to be disappointed after all? At last the welcome sound came – the rat-tat-tat of murder. The echoes of that knock are yet in my ear. 'Come over and kill him!' I put my night-capped head out of the window and told her to wait for me. I dressed hurriedly, took my razor, and went across to 11 Glover Street. As I broke open the door of the bedroom in which Arthur Constant lay sleeping, his head resting on his hands, I cried, 'My God!' as if I saw some awful vision. A mist as of blood swam before Mrs. Drabdump's eyes. She cowered back, for an instant (I divined rather than saw the action) she shut off the dreaded sight with her hands. In that instant I had made my cut – precisely, scientifically – made so deep a cut and drew out the weapon so sharply that there was scarce a drop of blood on it; then there came from the throat a jet of blood which Mrs. Drabdump, conscious only of the horrid gash, saw but vaguely. I covered up the face quickly with a handkerchief to hide any convulsive distortion. But as the medical evidence (in this detail accurate) testified, death was instantaneous. I pocketed the razor and the empty sulfonal phial. With a woman like Mrs. Drabdump to watch me, I could do anything I pleased. I got her to draw my attention to the fact that both the windows were fastened. Some fool, by the by, thought there was a discrepancy in the evidence because the police found only one window fastened, forgetting that, in my innocence, I took care not to fasten the window I had opened to call for aid. Naturally I did not call for aid before a considerable time had elapsed. There was Mrs. Drabdump to quiet, and the excuse of making notes – as an old hand. My object was to gain time. I wanted the body to be fairly cold and stiff before being discovered, though there was not much danger here; for, as you saw by the medical evidence, there is no telling the time of death to an hour or two. The frank way in which I said the death was very recent disarmed all suspicion, and even Dr. Robinson was unconsciously worked upon, in adjudging the time of death, by the knowledge (query here, Mr. Templeton) that it had preceded my advent on the scene.

"Before leaving Mrs. Drabdump there is just one point I should like to say a word about. You have listened so patiently, sir, to my lectures on the science of sciences that you will not refuse to hear the last. A good deal of importance has been attached to Mrs. Drabdump's oversleeping herself by half an hour. It happens that this (like the innocent fog which has also been made responsible for much) is a purely accidental and irrelevant circumstance. In all works on inductive logic it is thoroughly recognized that only some of the circumstances of a phenomenon are of its essence and causally interconnected; there is always a certain proportion of heterogeneous accompaniments which have no intimate relation whatever with the phenomenon. Yet so crude is as yet the comprehension of the science of evidence, that every feature of the phenomenon under investigation is made equally important, and sought to be linked with the chain of evidence. To attempt to explain everything is always the mark of the tyro. The fog and Mrs. Drabdump's oversleeping herself were mere accidents. There are always these irrelevant accompaniments, and the true scientist allows for this element of (so to speak) chemically unrelated detail. Even I never counted on the unfortunate series of accidental phenomena which have led to Mortlake's implication in a network of suspicion. On the other hand, the fact that my servant Jane, who usually goes about ten, left a few minutes earlier on the night of December 3d, so that she didn't know of Constant's visit, was a relevant accident. In fact, just as the art of the artist or the editor consists largely in knowing what to leave out, so does the art of the scientific detector of crime consist in knowing what details to ignore. In short, to explain everything is to explain too much. And too much is worse than too little. To return to my experiment. My success exceeded my wildest dreams. None had an inkling of the truth. The insolubility of the Big Bow Mystery teased the acutest minds in Europe and the civilized world. That a man could have been murdered in a thoroughly inaccessible room savored of the ages of magic. The redoubtable Wimp, who had been blazoned as my successor, fell back on the theory of suicide. The mystery would have slept till my death, but – I fear – for my own ingenuity. I tried to stand outside myself, and to look at the crime with the eyes of another, or of my old self. I found the work of art so perfect as to leave only one sublimely simple solution. The very terms of the problem were so inconceivable that, had I not been the murderer, I should have suspected myself, in conjunction of course with Mrs. Drabdump. The first persons to enter the room would have seemed to me guilty. I wrote at once (in a disguised hand and over the signature of 'One Who Looks Through His Own Spectacles') to the 'Pell Mell Press' to suggest this. By associating myself thus with Mrs. Drabdump I made it difficult for people to dissociate the two who entered the room together. To dash a half-truth in the world's eyes is the surest way of blinding it altogether. This letter of mine I contradicted myself (in my own name) the next day, and in the course of the long letter which I was tempted to write I adduced fresh evidence against the theory of suicide. I was disgusted with the open verdict, and wanted men to be up and doing and trying to find me out. I enjoyed the hunt more. Unfortunately, Wimp, set on the chase again by my own letter, by dint of persistent blundering, blundered into a track which – by a devilish tissue of coincidences I had neither foreseen nor dreamt of – seemed to the world the true. Mortlake was arrested and condemned. Wimp had apparently crowned his reputation. This was too much. I had taken all this trouble merely to put a feather in Wimp's cap, whereas I had expected to shake his reputation by it. It was bad enough that an innocent man should suffer; but that Wimp should achieve a reputation he did not deserve, and overshadow all his predecessors by dint of a colossal mistake, this seemed to me intolerable. I have moved heaven and earth to get the verdict set aside and to save the prisoner; I have exposed the weakness of the evidence; I have had the world searched for the missing girl; I have petitioned and agitated. In vain. I have failed. Now I play my last card. As the overweening Wimp could not be allowed to go down to posterity as the solver of this terrible mystery, I decided that the condemned man might just as well profit by his exposure. That is the reason I make the exposure tonight, before it is too late to save Mortlake."

"So that is the reason?" said the Home Secretary with a suspicion of mockery in his tones.

"The sole reason."

Even as he spoke a deeper roar than ever penetrated the study. The crowd had again started cheering. Impatient as the watchers were, they felt that no news was good news. The longer the interview accorded by the Home Secretary to the chairman of the Defense Committee, the greater the hope his obduracy was melting. The idol of the people would be saved, and "Grodman" and "Tom Mortlake" were mingled in the exultant plaudits.

"Templeton," said the Minister, "have you got down every word of Mr. Grodman's confession?"

"Every word, sir."

"Then bring in the cable you received just as Mr. Grodman entered the house."

Templeton went back into the outer room and brought back the cablegram that had been lying on the Minister's writing-table when Grodman came in. The Home Secretary silently handed it to his visitor. It was from the Chief of Police of Melbourne, announcing that Jessie Dymond had just arrived in that city in a sailing vessel, ignorant of all that had occurred, and had been immediately dispatched back to England, having made a statement entirely corroborating the theory of the defense.

"Pending further inquiries into this," said the Home Secretary, not without appreciation of the grim humor of the situation as he glanced at Grodman's ashen cheeks, "I have reprieved the prisoner. Mr. Templeton was about to dispatch the messenger to the governor of Newgate as you entered this room. Mr. Wimp's card-castle would have tumbled to pieces without your assistance. Your still undiscoverable crime would have shaken his reputation as you intended."

A sudden explosion shook the room and blent with the cheers of the populace. Grodman had shot himself – very scientifically – in the heart. He fell at the Home Secretary's feet, stone dead.

Some of the workingmen who had been standing waiting by the shafts of the hansom helped to bear the stretcher.

Biographies & Sources

Stephanie Bedwell-Grime
Honey of a Jam
(First Publication)
Canadian writer Stephanie Bedwell-Grime credits her love of mystery and the macabre to growing up in a house beside a graveyard. Although she never did meet a ghost there, it did get her thinking about things that go bump in the night. She is the author of more than thirty novels and novellas, as well as numerous shorter works. She has been nominated five times for the Aurora – Canada's national award for speculative fiction – and she has also been an EPIC eBook Award finalist.

Arnold Bennett
The Grand Babylon Hotel (chapters VI–XVIII)
(Originally Published by Chatto & Windus in 1902)
Arnold Bennett (1867–1931) worked in theatre, journalism and film but is mainly remembered for his work as a novelist. Bennett was born in Hanley, Staffordshire – one of the towns that joined to form Stoke-on-Trent. Bennett refers to these towns in many of his novels as the 'Five Towns'. Bennett spent some time as editor of *Woman* magazine before moving to Paris in 1903 and dedicating his time to writing. He had a great love for mystery fiction and was particularly well known for *The Grand Babylon Hotel*, a novel about the disappearance of a German prince. In 1931 he published *The Night Visitor and Other Stories*, inspired by real-life experiences.

Joshua Boyce
Longfellow's Private Detection Service
(First Publication)
Joshua Boyce is a PhD student studying philosophy at Western University in London, Ontario, Canada, where he lives with his wife and five children. He has worked as a barista, a teaching assistant, managed a comic book store, and instructed in a martial arts school. Joshua spends his spare time playing far too much Dungeons and Dragons and honing the skills necessary to excel as a detective one hundred years ago. He enjoys writing crime fiction, speculative fiction – both fantasy and science fiction – and horror. 'Longfellow's Private Detection Service' is his first published story.

Ernest Bramah
The Clever Mrs. Straithwaite
(Originally Published in *Max Carrados*, Metheun & Co., 1914)
Owing to his reclusive nature, little is known about Ernest Bramah's (1868–1942) background. The English writer began his adult life as a farmer, but gave it up after three years, pursuing instead a writing career at a London newspaper. 'The Clever Mrs. Straithwaite' features the blind detective Max Carrados, who deftly solves cases using his heightened skills of perception. Like Bramah, Carrados is remarkably precise and witty. The Max Carrados stories existed alongside the Sherlock Holmes tales in *The Strand*, and enjoyed equal success at the time.

Sarah Holly Bryant

Peppermint Tea
(First Publication)
Sarah Holly Bryant lives in New Jersey with her husband Steve and their two misbehaved dogs, Jacques and Kate Woofington. She has a BA in Creative Writing from the University of Wisconsin-Madison and completed graduate work in Business Writing at New York University. Sarah has been published in *The Fly Fish Journal*, *The Drake Magazine* and *Tail Fly Fishing Magazine*. Her flash fiction has appeared on ruescribe.com. Prior to becoming a freelance writer and volunteer with both Casting for Recovery and The Seeing Eye, she spent many years on Wall Street working in Human Resources.

Jeffrey B. Burton
Eykiltimac Stump Acres
(Originally Published in *Potpourri: A Magazine of the Literary Arts*, 2000)
Jeffrey B. Burton was born in Long Beach, California, grew up in St. Paul, Minnesota, and received his BA in Journalism at the University of Minnesota. Novels in Burton's Agent Drew Cady mystery series include *The Chessman*, *The Lynchpin*, and *The Eulogist*. His short stories have appeared in dozens of magazines. Jeff is a member of the Mystery Writers of America, International Thriller Writers, and the Horror Writers Association. Jeff lives in St. Paul with his wife, daughter, and an irate Pomeranian named Lucy.

C.B. Channell
Death in Lively
(First Publication)
Carrie Channell lives and writes in Chicago. Previous credits include the short mystery 'Coffee and Murder' in the anthology *Felonious Felines* and the short fantasy 'The Forge of Creation' in the anthology *Earth, Air, Fire, Water*. She has also contributed book and film reviews for Filmfax magazine. Research is important to her, so she has spent many summer weeks in rural Wisconsin, enjoying cheese, beer, bacon and Kringles, although she has yet to encounter a dead body.

Anton Chekhov
The Safety Match
(Original Published in *Masterpieces of Mystery in Four Volumes* in 1922)
Anton Chekhov (1860–1904) was born in Taganrog, southern Russia. He was a qualified doctor and considered this to be his main profession over writing. Chekhov wrote many short stories and plays. He is considered one of the greatest Russian realist writers and was known for the deceptively simple technique he used to provide an accurate portrayal of Russian life.

G.K. Chesterton
The Secret Garden
(Originally Published in *The Innocence of Father Brown*, 1911)
Gilbert Keith Chesterton (1874–1936) is best known for his creation of the worldly priest detective Father Brown. The Edwardian writer's literary output was immense: around 200 short stories, nearly 100 novels and about 4000 essays, as well as weekly columns for multiple newspapers. Chesterton was a valued literary critic, and his own authoritative

works included biographies of Charles Dickens and Thomas Aquinas, and the theological book *The Everlasting Man*. Chesterton debated with such notable figures as George Bernard Shaw and Bertrand Russell, and even broadcasted radio talks. His detective stories were essentially moral; Father Brown is an empathetic force for good, battling crime while defending the vulnerable.

Gregory Von Dare
The Body in Beaver Woods
(First Publication)
Gregory Von Dare is a writer and dramatist specializing in forward-leaning theatre and fiction, often with a humorous or ironic twist. He attended Chicago City College and the University of Illinois. While living in Los Angeles, he worked for Universal Studios, Disney, Armed Forces Radio and Fox Sports. Recently, his fiction appeared on the *Soft Cartel*, *Out of the Gutter*, *50 Word Stories*, *Rejected Manuscripts*, *Silent Motorist* and *Horror Tree* websites. Greg is an Affiliate Member of Mystery Writers of America. He now lives outside Chicago where certain people will never find him.

Amanda C. Davis
The Glorious Pudge
(Originally Published in *Vitality Magazine*, 2015. Concept by Madison Stuart, 2011; used with permission.)
Amanda C. Davis is an environmental professional living in central Pennsylvania. She's an enthusiastic amateur baker, gardener, and horror-movie-watcher, with side hobbies in book cover design and various kinds of crafting. Her short stories have appeared in Pseudopod, Cemetery Dance, Year's Best Weird Fiction, and others, including *Chilling Ghost Short Stories* and *Swords & Steam* from Flame Tree Publishing. She tweets as @davisac1. You can find out more about her and read more of her work at www.amandacdavis.com.

Arthur Conan Doyle
The Man with the Watches
(Originally Published in *The Strand Magazine*, 1898)
Arthur Conan Doyle (1859–1930) was born in Edinburgh, Scotland. As a medical student he was so impressed by his professor's powers of deduction that he was inspired to create the illustrious and much-loved figure Sherlock Holmes. Holmes is known for his keen power of observation and logical reasoning, which often astounds his companion Dr. Watson. 'The Man with the Watches' is not a Holmes case as it features an unnamed detective (there are however rumours this is Sherlock Holmes). Whatever the subject or character, Doyle's vibrant and remarkable writing has breathed life into all of his stories, engaging readers throughout the decades.

Martin Edwards
Foreword: Cosy Crime Short Stories
Martin Edwards is the author of 18 novels, including the Lake District Mysteries, and the Harry Devlin series. His groundbreaking genre study *The Golden Age of Murder* has won the Edgar, Agatha, and H.R.F. Keating awards. He has edited 28 crime anthologies, has won the CWA Short Story Dagger and the CWA Margery Allingham Prize, and is

series consultant for the British Library's Crime Classics. In 2015, he was elected eighth President of the Detection Club, an office previously held by G.K. Chesterton, Agatha Christie, and Dorothy L. Sayers.

Andrew Forrester
Tenant for Life
(Originally Published in *The Female Detective*, 1864)
Andrew Forrester was a pseudonym used by James Redding Ware (1832–1909). Ware was born in Southwark, south London and wrote stories for newspapers in order to supplement his income. It was not until a pamphlet containing one of Andrew Forrester's stories was discovered printed with J. Redding Ware as the author, that Forrester's true identity became known. Forrester is famous for being the first author to write about a female detective with a collection of seven cases being published under the title of *The Female Detective*. He also wrote a dictionary of Victorian slang, which he became famous for after his death and is still used by researching authors today.

R. Austin Freeman
The Anthropologist at Large
(Originally Published in *John Thorndyke's Cases*, 1909)
London-born R. Austin Freeman (1862–1943) was at the forefront of Edwardian detective fiction, along with his contemporary G.K. Chesterton. Freeman trained a physician, working as a colonial surgeon in West Africa until illness sent him back to England. He continued to practise medicine, producing in his spare time a crime series centred on the character Dr. Thorndyke. An early forensic scientist, Thorndyke uses a precise scientific approach to analyse data in his laboratory. Beginning with *The Singing Bone* (1912), Freeman is credited as being the first to develop the inverted detective story, where the focus rests not on the culprit – who can be known from the start – but on the process of solving the case.

Michael Martin Garrett
Twenty Column Inches
(First Publication)
Michael Martin Garrett is a poet, author, and recovering journalist. He has investigated courthouse corruption scandals, penned a religion column documenting his experience visiting different houses of worship as a non-believer, and worked as the communications director of a US Senate campaign. His fiction has appeared in anthologies from Vagabondage Press and Flame Tree Publishing, and his poetry has been commissioned by the Pennsylvania Center. He lives in Central Pennsylvania, where he works in higher education and spends his free time wondering if his antidepressants are working.

Anna Katherine Green
Missing: Page Thirteen
(Originally Published in *Masterpieces of Mystery In Four Volumes*, 1922)
Mother of detective fiction Anna Katharine Green (1846–1935) was born in Brooklyn, New York. A poet even at a young age, she later turned her hand to detective novels, perhaps partly inspired by stories from her lawyer father. She enjoyed immediate success with *The Leavenworth Case*, the first outing for the amiable but eccentric Inspector

Ebenezer Gryce. Having found a successful formula, but always coming up with original and intriguing plots, Green went on to write around 30 novels as well as several short stories. She created interesting detective heroes and established several conventions of the genre, her name becoming synonymous with popular, original and well-written detective fiction.

Philip Brian Hall
Sir Robert's Gargoyle
(First Publication)
Yorkshireman Philip Brian Hall is a graduate of Oxford University. A former diplomat and teacher, at one time or another he's stood for parliament, sung solos in amateur operettas, rowed at Henley Royal Regatta, completed a 40 mile cross-country walk in under 12 hours and ridden in over one hundred steeplechase horse races. He lives on a very small farm in Scotland. Philip's had short stories published in the USA and Canada as well as the UK. His novel *The Prophets of Baal* is available as an e-book and in paperback. He blogs at sliabhmannan.blogspot.co.uk.

E.E. King
Open House
(First Publication)
E.E. King is an award-winning painter, performer, writer, and biologist – she'll do anything that won't pay the bills. Ray Bradbury calls her stories 'marvelously inventive, wildly funny and deeply thought-provoking. I cannot recommend them highly enough.' Her books include *Dirk Quigby's Guide to the Afterlife*, *Electric Detective*, *Pandora's Card Game*, *The Truth of Fiction* and *Blood Prism*. She's worked with children in Bosnia, crocodiles in Mexico, frogs in Puerto Rico, egrets in Bali, mushrooms in Montana, butterflies in South Central Los Angeles, lectured on island evolution in the South Pacific, painted murals in Los Angeles and Spain and has been published widely.

Maurice Leblanc
The Seven of Hearts
(Originally Published in *The Extraordinary Adventures of Arsène Lupin, Gentleman Burglar*, 1909)
Born in Rouen, France, Maurice Leblanc (1864–1941) dropped his law studies in favour of a literary career, publishing his first novel, *Une Femme*, in 1887. His fame is largely due to his Arsène Lupin series of stories. 'The Arrest of Arsène Lupin' was the first story to feature the roguish gentleman criminal, appearing in 1905 as a commissioned piece for a new journal. The character was an instant success, and the thief-turned-detective went on to appear in over 60 of Leblanc's works. Some of the Lupin tales even feature a parodied Sherlock Holmes, with Lupin invariably outwitting his English rival.

Tom Mead
The Whittaker-Chambers Method; Or, Mulligan's Last mysetry
(First Publication)
Tom Mead is a UK-based author and playwright. He has previously written for *Litro Online*, *Flash: The International Short-Short Story Magazine*, *Glassworks and Open: A Journal of Arts and Letters* (amongst others). He also has work forthcoming from *Lighthouse*,

Crimson Streets, *Millhaven Tales*, *THAT Literary Review*, *Two Hawks Quarterly* and *Alfred Hitchcock Mystery Magazine*. He is a great admirer of golden age authors of the locked-room mystery subgenre (John Dickson Carr, Clayton Rawson, Helen McCloy, Christianna Brand et al), and has written many stories in tribute to these masters.

Arthur Morrison

The Case of the Dixon Torpedo

(Originally Published in *The Strand Magazine*, 1894)

Arthur Morrison (1863–1945) was born in the East End of London. He later became a writer for *The Globe* newspaper and showed a keen interest in relating the real and bleak plight of those living in London slums. When Arthur Conan Doyle killed off Sherlock Holmes in 1893, a vacuum opened up for detective heroes. In the wake Morrison created Martin Hewitt, publishing stories about him in *The Strand Magazine*, which had also first published Sherlock Holmes. Though a man with genius deductive skill, Morrison's Hewitt character was the polar opposite to Holmes: genial and helpful to the police. He was perhaps the most popular and successful of these new investigator fiction heroes.

Trixie Nisbet

Scoop!

(Originally Published under the title 'No News Isn't Good News' in *Take a Break's Fiction Feast*, 2016)

Trixie Nisbet has read every Agatha Christie and seen *The Mousetrap* far too many times, so considers herself well placed to plot a crime story. She has had over forty stories printed, mostly in women's magazines, in the UK, Australia and South Africa, and has won several national short story competitions. 'Scoop!' is set in her home town of Peacehaven on the south coast near Brighton, U.K.; as a haven of peace, it is the last place you might expect a 'cosy crime' to take place. The town may be real, but the story is fiction – so she claims.

Baroness Orczy

A Day's Folly

The Fordwych Castle Mystery

(Originally Published in *Lady Molly of Scotland Yard*, 1912)

Baroness Emma Orczy (1865–1947) was born in Tarnaörs, Heves County, Hungary. She spent her childhood in Budapest, Brussels and Paris before moving to London when she was 14. After her marriage to a young illustrator, she worked as a translator and illustrator to supplement their low income. Baroness Orczy's first novel, The Emperor's Candlesticks, was a failure but her later novels faired better. She is most famous for the play 'The Scarlet Pimpernel', which she wrote with her husband. She went on to write a novelization of it, as well as many sequels and other works of mystery fiction and adventure romances.

Catherine Louisa Pirkis

The Murder at Troyte's Hill

The Black Bag Left on a Door Step

(Originally Published in *The Ludgate Monthly*, London, February–July, 1893)

Catherine Louisa Pirkis (1839–1910) was born in London, England. She wrote numerous short stories and novels between 1877 and 1894, including the works that contain her best-known character the female detective Loveday Brooke. Following her success as an author and journalist, she moved into helping animal charities and was one of the founders of the National Canine Defence League (now known as Dogs Trust) in 1891.

Annette Siketa
The I's Have It
(First Publication)
In 2008, Annette Siketa lost her eyesight after a routine eye operation went terribly wrong. She turned to writing to cope with her blindness, and has now amassed a considerable body of work. Titles include, 'Chameleon – The Death of Sherlock Holmes', 'The Sisterhood – Curse of Abbot Hewitt', and its sequel, 'The Sisterhood – Cathy's Kin', which are all available through Smashwords and its affiliates. The first volume of, 'The Other Conan Doyle', which is a fully edited collection of his lesser known works, including the haunting 'Mystery of Cloomber', will be released in early 2019. Annette lives in Adelaide, Australia, with her cat, Millie.

B. David Spicer
Murder on the Lunar Commute
(First Publication)
B. David Spicer graduated from Ohio University, earning a BA in English. His first name is Brian, but thinks B. David sounds more artsy and pretentious. He's had short stories in more than a dozen anthologies, including *Out of Phase* and *Wicked Deeds: Witches, Warlocks, Demons & Other Evil Doers* from Sirens Call Publications, *Strangely Funny II* and *III* from Mystery and Horror, LLC, *Pernicious Invaders* and *From the Corner of Your Eye* from Great Old Ones Publishing. He lives in Ohio and owns more books than ought to be legal.

Nancy Sweetland
Just the Fax
(Originally Published in *Cosy Detective*, 1998)
Nancy Sweetland has been writing since the age of 13 when she received her first rejection slip and determined to become a published writer. She's the author of seven picture books, novels for middle grade readers, and a chapter book mystery for young readers. Along with many short stories for juveniles and adults, she's written three murder mysteries, *The Spa Murders*, *The Perfect Suspect* and *The Virgin Murders*, and five adult mystery/romances: *The Door to Love*, *Wannabe*, and *The House on the Dunes*, *The Countess of Denwick* and *The Shopkeeper's Secret*. She lives in Green Bay, Wisconsin and loves to hear from readers. She can be contacted on nancysweetland@gmail.com.

Louise Taylor
Raven Nevermore
(First Publication)
Louise Taylor was born in Colwyn Bay, Wales. She lived in Dorset, England, California and New York before settling in Paris, France. A high-school English teacher by day, Louise juggles work, family, housework and homework with fiction writing. She has had short stories published by Six Little Things and Level Best Books (*Noir at the Salad Bar Anthology – Culinary Tales with a Bite*). She is currently working on a novel and two new mystery short stories.

Edgar Wallace
Discovering Rex
(Originally Published in *The Cat Burglar and Other Stories*, 1929)
Edgar Wallace (1875–1932) was born illegitimately to an actress, and adopted by a London fishmonger and his wife. On leaving school at the age of 12, he took up many jobs, including selling newspapers. This foreshadowed his later career as a war correspondent for such periodicals as the *Daily Mail* after he had enrolled in the army. He later turned to writing stories inspired by his time in Africa, and was incredibly prolific over a large number of genres and formats. Wallace is credited as being one of the first writers of detective fiction whose protagonists were policemen as opposed to amateur sleuths.

Elise Warner
A Mouthful of Murder
(First Publication)
Elise Warner's eBook titled *Scene Stealer* was published by Carina Press and a short mystery, 'The Tree House', was included in the *Deadly Ink* anthology. She has also had stories published in *Mystery, Time, Kaleidoscope* and *RTP*, and a piece about Jackie, her theatrical poodle, was part of the anthology *Good Dogs Doing Good*. She has written non-fiction for the Travel Section of *The Washington Post* and magazines such as *American Spirit*, *Recreation News*, *International Living* and *Enchantment*. Her play *Small Time* won Theatre Guinevere's Guinny Award and was part of the Maxwell Anderson Playwright's Series. She is a born and bred New Yorker.

Israel Zangwill
The Big Bow Mystery
(First Published by Rand, McNally & Co. in 1895)
Israel Zangwill (1864–1926) was born in London to a family of Jewish immigrants. He became famous for his political activism, championing the Jewish cause and writing about the Jewish East End of London. Zangwill's play *The Melting Pot* gave rise to the popular term 'melting pot' to describe the American absorption of immigrants. His novel *The Big Bow Mystery* is renowned for being one of the earliest locked room mysteries, which also lays out all the evidence for the reader but uses misdirection to keep it from being easily solved.

FLAME TREE PUBLISHING
Short Story Series

New & Classic Writing

Flame Tree's Gothic Fantasy books offer a carefully curated series of new titles, each with combinations of original and classic writing:

Chilling Horror
Science Fiction
Crime & Mystery
Dystopia Utopia
Lost Worlds
Heroic Fantasy
Agents & Spies
Alien Invasion
Lost Souls
Chilling Ghost
Murder Mayhem
Swords & Steam
Supernatural Horror
Time Travel
Pirates & Ghosts
Endless Apocalypse
Robots & AI
Haunted House

Also, new companion titles offer rich collections of classic fiction, myths and tales in the gothic fantasy tradition:

H.G. Wells • Lovecraft • Sherlock Holmes
Edgar Allan Poe • Bram Stoker • Mary Shelley
Celtic Myths & Tales • *Chinese Myths & Tales*
Norse Myths & Tales • *Greek Myths & Tales*
King Arthur & The Knights of the Round Table • *Irish Fairy Tales*
Alice's Adventures in Wonderland • *The Divine Comedy*

Available from all good bookstores, worldwide, and online at
flametreepublishing.com

See our new fiction imprint
FLAME TREE PRESS | FICTION WITHOUT FRONTIERS
New and original writing in Horror, Crime, SF and Fantasy

And join our monthly newsletter with offers and more stories:
FLAME TREE FICTION NEWSLETTER
flametreepress.com

GOTHIC FANTASY